THE WINTER ROSE

THE
WINTER
ROSE

A Novel

Jennifer Donnelly

HYPERION

New York

First published in Great Britain by HarperCollins Publishers 2006.

DOCTOR MY EYES
Words and Music by JACKSON BROWNE
© 1970 ATLANTIC MUSIC CORP. and OPEN WINDOW MUSIC
All Rights Reserved   Used by Permission of ALFRED PUBLISHING CO., INC.

Library of Congress Cataloging-in-Publication Data is available upon request.

ISBN: 978-1-4013-0103-3
Paperback ISBN: 978-1-4013-0746-2

Hyperion books are available for special promotions,
premiums, or corporate training. For details contact Michael Rentas, Proprietary Markets,
Hyperion, 77 West 66th Street, 12th floor,
New York, New York 10023, or call 212-456-0133.

Design by Fritz Metsch

FIRST PAPERBACK EDITION

1 3 5 7 9 10 8 6 4 2

In memory of

FRED SAGE

and the London he knew

Doctor, my eyes
cannot see the sky.
Is this the prize
for having learned how not to cry?
—Jackson Browne

PART
ONE

May 1900

Lily Walker could smell a copper a mile away.

Cops reeked of beer and bay rum. They walked as though their shoes pinched. In poor neighborhoods filled with hungry people, they looked as plump and glossy as veal calves, fattened up from all the free meals they cadged.

Cops scared Lily. It was a cop who'd taken her kids away from her and put them in the workhouse. It was another cop, a man named Alvin Donaldson, who'd put her in jail after she'd gone on the game to get them back.

And now there was one sitting at the bar right in front of her. Inside the Barkentine, the Firm's own stronghold. Pretending to be a regular bloke. Talking. Drinking. Reading a paper. Ordering food.

The bloody *cheek*.

What did he want? Was he looking to nick Sid? To shut the place down?

The thought of the Bark closing more than scared Lily; it terrified her. She had her kids with her now. They had a room. It was small, but it kept them warm and dry. If she lost her barmaid's job, and the wages it brought, she would lose the room. And her kids. Again.

As she stood behind the bar, nearly paralyzed with worry, a sudden movement caught her eye. It was Frankie Betts, Sid's right-hand man. He'd been sitting down, knocking back glass after glass of whisky, but now he was on his feet. He stubbed out his cigarette and pushed back his sleeves.

He's sussed the cop, Lily thought, he must have. And now he's going to do for him.

But before Frankie could make a move, a fresh drink appeared on the bar. Desi Shaw, the publican, had put it there.

"Not leaving yet, are you, mate?" Desi said. "You only just got here." Desi was smiling, but his eyes flashed a warning.

Frankie nodded. "Ta," he said tightly, sitting back down.

Desi was right to have stopped him. Sid would be angry. He would say he was disappointed. Frankie knew better than to disappoint Sid. They all did.

Desi turned to Lily. "Look lively, darlin'. Bloke down the end needs a refill."

"Sorry, Des. Right away," she said.

Lily served her customer, barely smiling, her nerves taut. It was a tense time. For Sid. For the Firm. For all of them. A dangerous time. The rozzers were all over Sid. He and his lads had robbed a wages van last week and had made off with more than a thousand quid, prompting Freddie Lytton, the local Member of Parliament, to declare war. He'd had Sid arrested. Frankie and Desi, too. But the beak had let them go. Turned out there were no witnesses. Two men and a woman had seen the robbery, but when they'd learned it was Sid Malone they'd be testifying against, they'd suddenly been unable to recall what the robbers looked like.

"A mistake's been made. The police arrested the wrong man," Sid had said to the press on the steps of the Old Bailey after he'd been released. "I'm no villain, me. Just a businessman trying to make an honest living." It was a phrase he'd used many times—whenever the police raided his boatyard or one of his pubs. He said it so often, in fact, that Alvin Donaldson had christened him the Chairman and his gang the Firm. Lytton had been furious. He vowed he'd have Sid's head on a platter. He swore he'd find someone, some honest man, who wasn't afraid to speak the truth, who wasn't afraid of Malone and his pack of thugs, and when he did, he'd lock them away for life.

"He's just blowing smoke," Sid had said. "Wants his picture in the papers. It's almost election time."

Lily had believed him, but now this cop was sitting here, as bold as brass, and she was no longer sure he was right. She picked up a rag and wiped the bar with it, stealing glances at the man.

Is he one of Lytton's? Or someone else's? Why the hell is he here?

Lily well knew that where there was one cop, there were usually more. She scanned the room, looking for more unfamiliar faces.

If ever a pub deserved to be called a den of thieves, she thought, it's the Bark.

Dark and low-ceilinged, it sat squeezed between two wharves in Limehouse, on the north bank of the Thames. Its front touched Narrow Street and its back sagged brokenly over the river. At high tide you could hear the Thames lapping at the rear wall. She recognized almost every face. Three local blokes were standing by the fire, passing bits of jewelry back and forth. In a corner, four more played cards while a fifth threw sharks' teeth at a dartboard. Others sat clustered around rickety tables or at the bar itself. Smoking and drinking. Talking too loudly. Laughing too hard. Bragging and swaggering. Minor villains, all.

The man this cop was after, well . . . he didn't brag and he didn't swagger, and there was nothing minor about him. He was one of the most powerful, most feared criminal bosses in London, and Lily thought that if this barmy rozzer knew what was good for him, he'd get up and leave now. While his legs still worked.

While she continued to watch the man, Desi came bustling out of the kitchen and banged a bowl down in front of him, sloshing broth on his newspaper.

"One Limehouse hotpot," he said.

The man stared at the steaming horror. "It's fish," he said flatly.

"Proper Sherlock Holmes, you. What was you expecting? Rack of lamb?"

"Pork, I guess."

"This is Limehouse, innit? Not the bloody home counties. That'll be tuppence."

The man slid a coin across the bar, then stirred the gray broth with a dirty spoon. Bits of bone and skin whirled through it. A scrap of potato, some celery. A chunk of white flesh.

"Oi, Lily!" Frankie shouted, pointing at his empty glass.

"Right away, luv," Lily said, taking the glass from him. As she put the new pint down, Frankie caught her hand, pulled her toward him, and kissed her cheek. She batted him away. It was an act. They were both laughing, but there was no mirth in their eyes. He kissed her again. "Find out what he's after," he whispered in her ear, then he let her go.

Lily knew what to do. She served a few more customers, then took a handkerchief from her pocket and made a show of mopping her neck with it.

"It's like a bloody furnace in here tonight," she said aloud. "You lot have me run off my feet."

Then she unbuttoned the top of her blouse, fanning herself with her hand. Her soft, freckled bosom was large and firm—so large, in fact, that Sid often joked he could hide his dosh down it. She walked over to the man, placed her hands on the bar, and leaned forward, giving him an eyeful.

"Something wrong with your supper, luv?" she asked, smiling warmly. "You ain't touched it."

The stranger put his spoon down. He hesitated.

This ought to be good, she thought.

"Can't eat a bloody thing no matter how hard I try," he finally said. "Been livin' on porter. Anything else and me stomach just heaves at it."

"What? Nothing at all?" she asked, feigning concern.

"Porridge. Milk. Sometimes an egg. Screws did it. Kicked me guts in. Haven't been right since."

Lily nearly laughed out loud, but she kept her face straight. "Sent down, was you?" she asked.

"Aye. Smash-and-grab. Jewelry shop up Camden way. Had a clasp knife in me pocket so the coppers said I was armed. Beak gave me five."

"You just come out?"

The stranger nodded. He pulled his cap off, revealing what looked like a prison-issue haircut.

"You poor bloke," Lily said. "Think your stomach's bad, you should see your head. What nick was you in? Reading?"

"Pentonville."

"My late husband did a bit of bird there. Warden's a right hard case. Willocks, his name was. He still giving everyone gyp?"

"Oh, aye."

Drummond, you git, Lily thought. Should have asked round. There was no Willocks at Pentonville; there never had been. The bollocks was pretending.

"Well, that's all behind you now," she said brightly. "Like another pint, would you?"

The man said he would. As she moved off to get it, Frankie's eyes caught hers. Take care of this, they said.

Lily nodded. She pulled a pint, then returned to her customer. "Here you are. On the house." As she set the glass down, she purposely sloshed some of its contents onto his newspaper.

"Oh, how clumsy!" she said. "I'm so sorry. Between me and Desi, we've soaked your paper."

"No harm done," the man said, smiling. "Mopping spills is about the only thing this bloody rag's good for."

Lily laughed prettily and the man took her false good humor for an opening—just as she'd known he would.

"Name's Michael Bennett," he said. "Pleased to meet you."

"Lily Walker. Likewise."

"You hear about this?" Bennett asked, pointing to a story on the paper's front page. "It's about that wages robbery. They say Sid Malone done it. That he got away with ten thousand quid."

Doesn't Sid wish, Lily thought. Those flipping papers always exaggerated.

Bennett touched the back of her hand. "I heard Malone stashes some of his dosh on a barge in the Thames," he said. "And some in a sugar warehouse."

"Did you?" Lily asked, leaning in to give him a better look at her breasts.

"Aye. I also heard he keeps some here in the Bark. Why, we might be sitting on it right now," he said, tapping his foot on the floorboards. "Don't happen to have a prybar in your pocket, do you?"

Lily forced another laugh.

"Wherever he stores it, it must be a big place. The Firm don't go in for any tuppenny-ha'penny Fagin rubbish. One bloke told me their bullion thefts alone have brought them thousands. Thousands! Cor, can you imagine having all that money?"

Lily felt anger flash inside of her. Her fingers twitched. She wished she were a man; she would break this bastard's nose. It would teach him to keep it out of other blokes' business.

"I've also heard Malone frequents this pub," Bennett said. "Heard it's his headquarters."

"I wouldn't know about that," Lily replied.

Bennett leaned in close. He took her hand in his. "I need a word with him. Just a word, is all. Know how I can find him?"

Lily shook her head. "I'm sorry, luv, I don't." She leaned over farther and bent her head to his. "What do you want with him anyway? Good-looking man like yourself . . . just out of the nick . . . seems to me it's a woman you'd be wanting, not a bloke."

Bennett mulled over her offer. "How much?" he finally asked.

"I usually get a pound."

The man snorted. "A bloody *pound*?" he said. Too loudly.

Typical rozzer, quibbling over money, she thought. Villains never did. She placed a finger on his lips. "For you, darlin', fifty pence."

Bennett's eyes flickered back to her chest. He licked his lips. "All right, then," he said. "Where do we go? Upstairs?"

Lily shook her head. "Meet me outside. By the river. There's a stairway round the side. It'll be quiet there this time of night. Quiet and dark."

"When?"

"Give me fifteen minutes."

She winked at him, then disappeared into the kitchen. Once there, she swiftly climbed a flight of wooden steps that led from the kitchen to the upper floor. Her fake smile was gone now; her expression grim. She ran down a dingy hallway and knocked twice on a locked door. It was opened by a rangy man in shirtsleeves and a waistcoat who made no effort to hide the cosh he was holding. Behind him, in the middle of the room, another man sat at a table, counting money. He raised his emerald-green eyes to hers.

"Trouble," she said. "One of Lytton's. Must be. Says his name is Bennett. I'll have him out back in a few minutes."

The emerald-eyed man nodded. "Keep him there," he said, resuming his counting.

Lily shot back to the kitchen and made her way down to the basement. She let herself outside through a rickety door and crept behind a cluster of pilings. It was low tide. She could barely see the river in the darkness, but she could hear it—lapping at the hulls of barges moored midstream, hissing about the lines and buoys, gurgling in tiny, whirling eddies. Bennett was already there. Lily watched him as he took a long piss. When he finished, he lit a cigarette.

Good, she thought, that'll take up some time. She didn't want to do this. Not with him. Not with any man. She didn't want to go back to what she'd been.

She bit her lip, remembering what it was like to be on the game. To give herself to any man who asked her. She'd done it so many times she'd lost count. She'd done it for her children.

She'd lost them a few weeks after her husband died. He'd been a tanner, working fourteen-hour days in the yards in all sorts of weather. The coroner had written pneumonia on his death certificate, but Lily knew it was the work that had killed him.

She'd taken what she could find after he'd died—a bit of charring, a few hours behind the counter of a tuckshop. And then a full-time job had come along at a jam factory. It paid, but not enough. She got behind on the rent, and then the factory went under. It was wintertime when the place closed. People were hungry and cold and desperate for work. Every job in East London was taken. When she was two months in arrears, the bailiff evicted her. She slept rough with her children for a few days, but then a pair of cops had caught her begging and they'd taken the children to the workhouse. Sometimes, in her sleep, she still heard them screaming, still saw their little hands knotted in her skirts as the officers pulled them from her.

Desperate, she'd done the only thing left to do—she went on the game. She forced herself to go numb while she was with the men, and she let herself cry afterward—but she made money, for unlike a lot of women on the streets, she still had her looks. She'd managed to earn a few shillings, and was just beginning to have hopes of renting a new room, a place to bring her children, when she'd been arrested.

Alvin Donaldson's men had done it. Word had it Lytton leaned on him to clear the streets. She and a dozen other women had been rounded up and kept overnight. They'd been let go the next day—all of them except for Lily, for Donaldson had taken a liking to her.

He'd had her brought up from the cells to his office. He'd closed the door, and then he told her what he wanted. He said he'd send her down for good if she refused him. He knew she needed money badly. And he knew she couldn't earn it if she was in prison. He'd taken her then and there, and many times afterward. In filthy alleys and lodging houses. Behind pubs. And he'd never given her a penny.

One night, after she'd been on the streets for a few months, Sid had caught sight of her.

"Lily?" he'd called out. He knew her from when she'd worked at the tuckshop. She'd tried to hurry away, but he'd run after her. "Tell me you're not on the game," he'd said.

She hadn't answered. She couldn't; she'd been too ashamed.

"Don't do this, Lily. You're not the type. You'll never survive it."

"I've no choice. I've lost me job. Me kids are in the spike," she'd said, her voice cracking. He'd given her a new job on the spot. Barmaid at the Barkentine. He'd told her a girl had just quit and Desi was shorthanded. It was a lie; she'd known it was. The fact that he'd taken the trouble to tell it had made her cry.

"Here now, none of that," he'd said sharply, for he didn't like tears. Then he'd marched her to the Bark, pointed at pile of dirty glasses, and told her to get busy.

Lily Walker knew who Sid Malone was; she knew what he did, but she didn't care. He'd done more for her than any cop, any priest, any Sallie Army do-gooder ever had. He'd given her her children back, and as long as she lived, she would never forget it.

"Bloody woman! Where the hell are you?" Bennett suddenly yelled, startling her.

He'd finished his smoke. There was no more putting it off. She took a deep breath, then stepped out from behind the pilings.

"What took you?" he asked.

"Had to wait till me guv's back was turned," she answered. "He's not too keen on his help sneaking off."

"Come on, then," Bennett said, reaching for her.

"Not so fast, luv. Business before pleasure," she said, stalling.

Bennett reached into his pocket. He counted out fifty pence and gave it to her. She counted it again, then pocketed it. He pulled her close and kissed her, thrusting his tongue into her mouth. She nearly gagged. His rough hands were everywhere—inside her blouse, between her legs. It was all she could do not to push him away.

Bloody hell, Sid, where are you? she wondered desperately.

She twined her arms around his neck. Bit his ear. Whispered dirty things to him. Did anything and everything she could think of to play for time. But he was getting impatient.

"Lift your skirts, girl," he said. "Quick, or I'll have my money back."

Lily did as he asked. There were only four people she cared for on this earth, only four people she'd do anything for, *anything*—her three children and Sid Malone.

And then, just as Bennett had dropped his trousers, a match flared behind him. He spun around. Lily looked past him and saw Sid and Frankie. They were standing at the bottom of the stone steps. Frankie was lighting a lantern.

"That'll do, Lily," Sid said.

Lily spat the man's taste from her mouth, then ran back into the Bark's basement to fix her clothing. The door was half off its hinges. She peered around it as she buttoned her blouse. If Sid was in trouble, she wanted to know.

"Michael Bennett, is it?" she heard him say.

Bennett, holding his trousers up with both hands, stared, but made no reply.

"My guv asked you a question," Frankie said.

"Are you . . . are you Malone?" he stammered, buttoning his fly.

"What do you want?" Frankie growled. "Who sent you?"

"I'm not looking for any trouble," he said. "I only came to pass on a message, that's all. A woman I know wants to see Sid Malone. She'll meet him anytime, anywhere, but she's got to see him."

"You a cop?" Frankie asked. "Did Lytton send you?"

Bennett shook his head. "It's nothing to do with Lytton. I'm a private detective. That's the truth."

Malone cocked his head, appraising Bennett.

"You've got to give me an answer," Bennett said to him. "You don't know this woman. She won't stop. She'll come herself."

Malone still hadn't said anything, but he was listening. Bennett seemed to take encouragement from this. He grew bolder.

"Never takes no for an answer, that one. Can't tell you her name. She don't want it known. She's a right pushy bitch, though, that's something I *can* tell you," he added, venturing a laugh.

Later, Lily would remember that Sid's mouth had twitched at the word *bitch*. She would remember how he had walked up to Bennett, slowly, easily, as if he were going to shake his hand, grateful for the information. Instead he grabbed the man's forearm, and in one quick, fluid motion, broke it with a cosh. The pain dropped Bennett to his knees, but it was the sight of his bones protruding from his skin that made him shriek.

Sid grabbed a handful of his hair and yanked his head back, choking off his noise. "That's me answer. Loud and clear," he said. "You tell Fiona Finnegan the man she's after is dead. Dead as you'll be if I ever see you again."

Sid released him, and he crumpled into the mud. He turned and walked away. Frankie followed.

"Who is this girl, guv?" Frankie asked. "She up the duff?"

Sid made no response.

"She a relation, then?"

In the darkness, Lily could only hear Sid's voice; she couldn't see his face. If she had, she'd have seen the pain there, deep and abiding, as he said, "She's nobody, Frankie. No relation. She's nothing to me at all."

CHAPTER 1

"Jones!"

India Selwyn Jones turned at the sound of her name. She had to squint to see who'd shouted it. Maud had taken her eyeglasses.

"Professor Fenwick!" she finally shouted back, beaming at the bald and bearded man hurtling toward her through a sea of bobbing mortarboards.

"Jones, you clever little cat! A Walker grant, a Lister, *and* the Dennis Prize! Is there anything you *didn't* win?"

"Hatcher got the Beaton."

"The Beaton's a humbug. Any fool can memorize anatomy. A doctor needs more than knowledge, she needs to be able to apply it. Hatcher can barely apply a tourniquet."

"Shh, Professor! She's right behind you!" India whispered, scandalized. The graduation ceremony was over. The students had exited the auditorium's small stage to the strains of an inspiring march and were now posing for photographs or chatting with well-wishers.

Fenwick flapped a hand at her. Nothing scandalized him. He was a man who spoke freely, pointedly, and usually at the top of his lungs. India had firsthand experience of his scorching invectives. They'd been directed at her often enough. She remembered her first week in his classroom. She'd been assigned to question a patient with pleurisy. Afterward Fenwick had called on her to open her case book and describe her findings. She could still hear him roaring at her for starting with the words "I feel . . ."

"You *what*? You *feel*? You are not in my classroom to *feel,* Jones. This is not Early Romantic Poets. This is *diagnosis,* the taking of cases. You are here only to *observe,* for you are far too ignorant to do anything else. Feelings cloud judgment. What do they do, Jones?"

"They cloud judgment, sir," India had replied, her cheeks blazing.

"Very good. *Feel* for your patient and you harm him with foolish preconceptions. *See* him, Jones . . . see the oedematosis of heart disease and know it from kidney failure . . . see the colic of gallstones and know it from lead poisoning . . . only *see* him, Jones, with clarity and with dispassion, and you will cure him."

"Well, come on, come on, let's have a look," Fenwick said now, motioning impatiently to the leather folder tucked under India's arm.

India opened it, eager herself to look again at what it contained—a buff-colored document with her name written in copperplate, the date—26 May 1900—the seal of the London School of Medicine for Women, and the proclamation there for all the world to see. She had earned her degree in medicine. She was now a doctor.

"*Doctor* India Selwyn Jones. Has a nice ring, doesn't it?" Fenwick said.

"It does, and if I hear it a few more times I might actually start to believe it."

"Nonsense. There are some here who need a piece of paper to tell them that they're doctors, but you're not one of them."

"Professor Fenwick! Professor, over here . . . ," a woman's voice shrilled.

"Ye gads," Fenwick said. "The dean. Looks like she's got the head of Broadmoor with her, the poor devil. Wants me to convince him to hire some of you lot. You're damned lucky you got Gifford's job, you know."

"I do, sir. I'm very eager to start."

Fenwick snorted. "Really? Do you know Whitechapel?"

"I did a bit of clinical work at London Hospital."

"Any house calls?"

"No, sir."

"Hmm, I take it back then. Gifford's the lucky one."

India smiled. "How bad can it be? I've done house calls in other poor areas. Camden, Paddington, Southwark . . ."

"Whitechapel's like nowhere else in London, Jones. Be prepared for that.

You'll learn a lot there, that's for certain, but with your mind, your skills, you should have a nice research fellowship at a teaching hospital. And your own surgery. Like Hatcher. Private practice. That's where you belong."

"I can't afford to open my own surgery, sir."

Fenwick gave her a long look. "Even if you could, I doubt you would. One could hand you the keys to a fully furnished Harley Street office and you'd hand them right back and scuttle off to the slums."

India laughed. "I'd like to think I'd *walk,* sir."

"Still dreaming your pipe dreams, eh?"

"I prefer to think of them as goals, sir."

"A clinic, is it?"

"Yes."

"For women and children."

"That's right."

Fenwick sighed. "I remember you and Hatcher talking about it, but I never thought you were serious."

"Harriet isn't. I am."

"Jones, have you *any* idea what's involved in that sort of thing?"

"Some."

"The raising of monies . . . the hunt for a suitable location . . . why, the administration alone simply boggles the mind. You need time to get a clinic off the ground, oceans of it, and you won't have a spare minute. You'll be worked off your feet at Gifford's practice. How will you manage it all?"

"I'll find a way, sir. One must try to make a difference," India said resolutely.

Fenwick cocked his head. "Do you know you said the same thing to me six years ago? When you first came here. What I've never understood is why."

"Why?"

"Why an aristocratic young woman from one of Britain's wealthiest families feels she needs to make a difference."

India colored. "Sir, I'm not . . . I don't . . ."

"Professor! Professor Fenwick!" It was the dean again.

"I must go," Fenwick said. He was quiet for a few seconds, seeming to study his shoes, then added, "I don't mind telling ——— Jones. You're the best student I've ever had. Rationa A shining example to my current crop of ninnies. I you that the hard part is over, but it's only beginning difference, to change the world, but the world might know that, don't you?"

He sh

"I do, sir."

"Good. Then know this—no matter what happens out there, remember that you are a *doctor*. A very good one. No one can take that from you. And not because it's in here"—he tapped on the diploma—"but because it's in here." He tapped India's forehead. "Never forget that."

It was India's turn to study her shoes. "I won't, sir," she whispered.

She wanted to thank him for all that he'd done, for taking a know-nothing girl of eighteen and making her into a doctor, but she didn't know how. Six years it had taken. Six long years of hardship, struggle, and doubt. She'd made it only because of him. How could she thank him for that? Where would she even begin?

"Professor Fenwick . . ." she said, but when she looked up he was gone.

Feelings of loss and loneliness swept over her. Around her, fellow graduates laughed and chattered, surrounded by friends and family, but she was alone. Except for Maud. Freddie was away on government business. Wish was in America. Her parents were at Blackwood, hundreds of miles away, but even if they'd lived next door to the school they wouldn't have come. She knew that.

For an instant, she thought of the one person who would have come if he could—a boy who would have walked all the way from Wales to be with her today. *Hugh*. She saw him in her mind's eye. He was running up Owen's Hill, laughing. Standing on Dyffyd's Rock, head thrown back, arms outstretched to the wild Welsh skies. She tried to push the images from her mind, but failed. Tears burned behind her eyes. She hastily blinked them away, knowing Maud would be looking for her, to take her to tea. Knowing, too, that Maud had little patience for tangled emotions.

"Stop it, Jones. Right now," she hissed at herself. "Feelings cloud judgment."

"So does champagne, old girl, but that's why we like it!" a male voice boomed, startling her.

India whirled around, astonished. *"Wish?"* she exclaimed, as her cousin kissed her cheek. "What are you doing here? I thought you were in the States!"

"Just got back. Ship docked yesterday. Got the car off it and drove hell for leather all night. Wouldn't have missed this for the world, Indy. Didn't you see me in the back? I was clapping like a lunatic. Bingham, too."

"Bing, is that really you?" India asked, peering around her cousin.

George Lytton, the twelfth Earl of Bingham, was standing behind Wish. He raised a hand in greeting. "Hullo, Indy," he said. "Congrats."

"This is such a lovely surprise! I didn't see either of you. Maud swiped my specs. Oh, look at you, Wish! So suntanned and handsome. Was your trip a success? Are you a billionaire?"

"Not quite yet, old mole, but soon," Wish said, laughing.

"Oh, for God's sake, darling, don't encourage him. His head's fat enough." The voice, her sister's, was heavy with boredom.

"Maud! Give me back my glasses," India said.

"Certainly not. They're beastly. They'll ruin the photographs."

"But I can't *see*."

Maud sighed. "If you insist," she said. "Really, though, India, if your specs get any thicker you'll be wearing binoculars." She wrinkled her nose. "Can we leave now? This place has the stinks."

"Listen to your *much* older sister and get your things, Windy Indy," Wish said.

"Very funny, Wish!" Maud said.

"Don't call me that horrible name, Wish!" India scolded.

Wish grinned. "It *is* horrible, isn't it? I gave it to you, remember? When you were ten and holding forth on the nesting habits of wrens. A proper boffin even then. And such a wordy old thing."

"That nickname doesn't make her sound *wordy*, it makes her sound flatulent," Bing said, blinking owlishly.

Wish and Maud roared. Bing cracked a smile and India tried not to. They'd all grown up together and tended to revert to old ways the minute they were reunited. She watched them—all three were nearly breathless with laughter now—half expecting Wish to thump Bingham with a serving spoon or Maud to pour ink in the teapot. Finally, unable to help herself, she dissolved into giggles, too. Their sudden appearance had made her forget her earlier sadness and she was very happy they'd come. As children they'd all been inseparable, but now they were rarely in the same place at the same time. Maud tended to swan off to exotic destinations on a whim. Wish was forever starting up new ventures. A banker turned speculator, he was known to make a fortune in a matter of days—and lose it again just as quickly. Bingham hardly ever left Longmarsh, preferring its quiet woods and meadows to the noisy streets of London. And Freddie—India's fiancé and Bingham's brother—practically lived at the House of Commons.

"Look, we've got to shake a leg," Wish said impatiently, "so get your things, *Lady* Indy."

"Don't call me *that*, either," India warned.

"How about we call you late for lunch, then? We've a reservation for half one at the Coburg—a little party for you—but we'll never make it unless we get started."

"Wish, you mustn't—" India started to say.

"No worries. I didn't. It's on Lytton."

"Bing, you shouldn't—"

"Not me, Indy," he said. "My brother."

"Freddie's here?" India asked. "How? When? He said he'd been summoned to C-B's for the weekend."

Wish shrugged. "Dunno. S'pose he got himself unsummoned. He was just trotting down the steps when I called at his flat so I gave him a ride."

"Where is he now?"

"Outside. Bringing the car round."

"No, I'm not. I'm right here," a young blond man said. He was tall and slender, beautifully dressed in a cutaway coat and cheviot trousers. A dozen female heads turned to admire him. A few—a doddery aunt, a younger sister—might have asked who he was, but most recognized him. He was a Member of Parliament, a rising star whose bold defection from the Conservatives to the Liberals had his name constantly in the papers. He was Bingham's younger brother—only a second son—yet Bing, shy and retiring, faded beside him.

"Freddie, what took you?" Wish asked. "You had me worried."

"I'm touched, old man. Truly."

"Not about *you*. About the car." Wish's motor car, a Daimler, was brand-new.

"Mmmm. Yes. Had a spot of trouble with the car," Freddie said. "Couldn't get the damned thing in reverse. Or neutral. Couldn't shut it off, either."

"Freddie . . ." Wish began, but Freddie didn't hear him. He was kissing India's cheek.

"Well done, my darling," he said. "Congratulations."

"Freddie, you ass!" Wish shouted. "What do you mean you can't shut it off? What's it doing? Driving itself?"

"Of course not. I told the porter to drive it. Last I saw, he was headed for King's Cross."

Wish swore, then dashed out of the auditorium. Bing followed.

Freddie grinned. "Car's perfectly safe. Parked it out front. Did you see Wish's face?"

"Freddie, that was awful! Poor Wish!" India said.

"Poor Wish, my foot," Maud said, lighting a cigarette. "Serves him right. He's gone absolutely car mad. Now, can we please go, too? I can't bear the smell of this place. Really, Indy, it's awful. What *is* it?" she asked.

India sniffed. "I don't smell a thing."

"Have you got a cold? How can you not?"

She sniffed again. "Oh, *that*. Ca—" She was about to say *cabbages*. A nearby church ran a soup kitchen for the poor and cooking smells were always drifting over, but Freddie cut her off.

"*Cadavers*," he said. "Indy told me about them. The best go to Guy's and Bart's. The women's school gets all the ripe ones."

Maud paled. She pressed a jeweled hand to her chest. "*Dead* people?" she whispered. "You're joking, Freddie, surely. Say you are."

"I'm not this time. I'm being most grave. I swear it."

"Good God. I feel quite ill. I'll be outside."

Maud left and India turned to her fiancé. "Most *grave*?" she said. "Must we *always* become twelve years old again when we're all together?"

"Yes, we must," Freddie said. He gave her a golden smile and India thought then, as she had a million times before, that he was the most gloriously handsome man she had ever seen.

"You are awful, Freddie," she said. "Truly."

"I am. I admit it. But it was the only way I could get five minutes alone with you," he said, squeezing her hand. "Now get your things, old stick. We're off to the Coburg."

"Wish said. But really, Freddie, you mustn't."

"I want to. It's not every day of the week one becomes a doctor, you know."

"This is so lovely. So unexpected. I thought you'd be at C-B's all weekend."

C-B was short for Henry Campbell-Bannerman, leader of the Opposition. There was talk that Lord Salisbury, Britain's prime minister and head of the incumbent Conservative Party, would call a general election in the autumn. Campbell-Bannerman had called his shadow cabinet together to prepare the Liberal Party's platform. A handful of prominent backbenchers, including Freddie, had also been summoned.

"The old boy canceled," Freddie said. "Felt a bit punky."

"When did you find out?"

"Two days ago."

"Why didn't you tell me?" India asked, hurt. She'd been so disappointed when he'd said he couldn't be here today.

"I was going to, darling," Freddie said contritely. "And perhaps I should have. But as soon as I knew I was off the hook, I decided to surprise you with a party. Now stop looking daggers at me, will you, and get your things."

India felt ashamed. How could she have scolded him? He was always so thoughtful. She led the way out of the auditorium down a narrow hallway to a lecture theater where she and her fellow graduates had stowed their belongings. It was quiet in the room when she and Freddie entered it, quieter than she'd ever heard it. Freddie sat down in one of the wooden seats and busied himself with a bottle of champagne he'd swiped from the drinks table. India looked around—not for her things, but at the room itself. She looked at the raked benches and the dissection table, at the bookcases crammed with heavy texts, at Ponsonby the skeleton dangling from his stand—and realized that it was the last time she would do so. The sadness she'd felt earlier overwhelmed her again. She walked over to Ponsonby and took his lifeless hands in hers.

"I can't believe it's over. I can't believe I'll never sit here again," she said.

"Hmm?" Freddie was frowning at the cork.

"This place . . . this school . . . all the years I spent here . . . it's all behind me now . . ."

Her voice trailed off as images came back to her. Bright fragments of time. She saw herself and Harriet Hatcher in anatomy lab bent over a cadaver. They were peeling back the derma, naming and drawing muscles and bones as fast as they could, trying to stay ahead of the rot. Trying not to vomit. Sketch and retch, they'd called it. Professor Fenwick had been there, calling them ham-fisted bumblers one minute, bringing them bicarb and a bucket the next.

He'd been there again, materializing out of thin air like a guardian angel, when a group of drunken first years from Guy's had surrounded herself and Harriet outside the school's entrance. The men had exposed themselves, demanding to have their members examined.

"Unfortunately, gentlemen, my students cannot comply with your request," he'd said, "as they are not permitted to take their microscopes out of the building."

And Dr. Garrett Anderson, the dean. She was a legend, the first woman in England to earn a medical degree and one of the school's founders. Brisk, brilliant, stronger than Sheffield steel, she had been a constant inspiration to India, a living, breathing rebuttal to those who said women were too weak and too stupid to be doctors.

"This foil is a bugger," Freddie muttered, fiddling with the champagne bottle. "Ah! There we are."

She looked at him, wanting so much to tell him what this place meant to her, wanting him to understand. "Freddie . . . ," she began. "Never mind the champagne. . . ."

It was too late. He aimed the bottle at Ponsonby and popped the cork. It glanced off the skeleton's head.

"Poor Ponsonby," India said. "You've hurt his feelings."

"Stuff Ponsonby. He's dead. He has no feelings. Come and have a drink." Freddie patted the chair next to him. When India was seated, he handed her a glass. "To Dr. India Selwyn Jones," he said. "The cleverest little brick in London. I'm so proud of you, darling." He clinked her glass, then emptied his. "Here," he added, handing her a small leather box.

"What is it?"

"Open it and see."

India eased the lid up, then gasped at what was inside—a beautifully worked gold pocket watch with diamond markers. Freddie took it out and turned it over. *Think of me* was engraved on the back.

India shook her head. "Freddie, it's so beautiful. I don't even know what to say."

"Say you'll marry me."

She smiled at him. "I've already said that."

"Then do it. Marry me tomorrow."

"But I start with Dr. Gifford next week."

"Bugger Dr. Gifford!"

"Freddie! Shh!"

"Run away with me. Tonight." He leaned toward her and nuzzled her neck.

"I can't, you silly man. You know I can't. I've work to do. Important work. You know how hard I fought for that job. And then there's the clinic. . . ."

Freddie raised his face to hers. His beautiful amber eyes had darkened. "I can't wait forever, India. I won't. We've been engaged for two bloody years."

"Freddie, please . . . don't spoil the day."

"Is that what I'm doing? Spoiling the day?" he asked, visibly hurt. "Is my telling you that I want you for my wife such a dreadful thing to hear?"

"Of course not, it's just that . . ."

"Your studies have come first for a long time, but you're finished now and a man can only be so patient." He put his glass down. There was a seriousness to him now. "It's just that we could do so much good together. You've always said that you want to make a difference—how can you do that working for Gifford? Or in some ill-funded clinic? Do something bigger, India.

Something huge and important. Work with me on health reform. Counsel me. Advise me. And together we'll make that difference. A *real* difference. Not just for Whitechapel or London, but for England." He took her hands in his and continued talking, giving her no opening to reply. Or to object. "You're a remarkable woman and I need you. At my side." He pulled her close and kissed her. "And in my bed," he whispered.

India closed her eyes and tried to like it. She always tried to like it. He was so good and so kind and he loved her. He was everything any woman could want, and so she tried to warm to his kisses, but his lips were so hard and insistent. He knocked her spectacles askew with his fumblings and when he slid his hand from her waist to her breast, she broke away.

"We ought to go," she said. "The others will be wondering what's become of us."

"Don't be cold to me. I want you so."

"Freddie, darling, this is hardly the place."

"I want us to set a date, India. I want us to be man and wife."

"We will be. Soon. I promise," she said, adjusting her glasses.

"All right, then. Coming?"

"I've got to find my things," she said. "You go. I'll only be a minute."

He told her to hurry, then went to join the others. India watched him go. He's right, of course, she thought.

It had been two years since he'd gotten down on bended knee at Longmarsh and proposed to her. She would have to decide on a wedding date soon, and she knew what would happen when she did—they'd be required to attend an endless round of dinners and parties and to listen to incessant chatter about dresses, rings, and trousseau. And he would press her again to give up her hopes of a clinic and work with him on health reform. It was a noble cause, she knew it was, but healing was her calling, not committee work, and she could no more give it up than she could give up breathing.

India frowned, upset at herself. Freddie was so good to her and she was being unkind to him; she knew she was. She should have decided on a date by now. It should have been so easy for her to simply pick a day. Some lovely summer Saturday.

Should have been. *Would* have been.

If only she loved him.

She sat for a bit longer, simply staring at the empty doorway, then shrugged out of her robe. The others were waiting; she mustn't keep them any longer. She folded the robe and placed it on the chair beside her, then ran her hands over her hair. It was a disaster. Her blond curls, brushed into a neat twist only a few hours ago, were already corkscrewing loose. Try as she might, she could never keep them under control. She started to smooth them, then stopped. Her fingers found the jeweled comb she always wore and pulled it free. She turned it over in her palm. It was a Tiffany dragonfly, one of a pair, and worth a small fortune. Worked in platinum and embellished with dozens of flawless gems, it was completely at odds with her plain, sober clothing: the gray skirt and waistcoat, the crisp white blouse.

She had taken the comb the day she'd left Blackwood—the day she'd turned her back on her home, her parents, and their godforsaken money.

"If you leave, India, I shall cut you off," her mother had said, her beautiful face white with anger.

"I don't want your money," India had said. "I don't want anything from you."

There were three swirling initials engraved on the underside of the comb. She traced them with her finger—*I S J*, not hers, but her mother's—Isabelle Selwyn Jones, Countess of Burnleigh. India knew that if it were not for this comb she would not be here today. If her mother hadn't left it in her carriage. If Hugh hadn't picked it up. If, if, if.

She closed her hand around it, pressing the teeth into her palm, trying to stop herself from remembering. Don't, she told herself, don't think about him. Don't remember him. Don't feel him. Don't feel anything. But she did. Because Hugh had made her feel. More than anyone in her entire life.

She could see him again in her mind's eye, only this time he wasn't laughing. He was running through the trees with his sister Bea in his arms. Bea's face was white. Her skirts were crimson with blood. He'd bundled her into the trap and crooned to her all the way to Cardiff. Never stopping, not once. Never even faltering. She could still hear his beautiful voice, soft and low, *Paid ag ofni, dim ond deilen, Gura, gura ar y ddor; Paid ag ofni, ton fach unig, Sua, sua ar lan y mor*. She'd known enough Welsh to know what he was singing. *Fret you not, 'tis but an oak leaf, Beating, beating at the door. Fret you not, a lonely wavelet's, Murmuring, murmuring on the shore.* "Suo Gan," a lullaby.

India looked at the comb still, but didn't see it. She saw only Hugh, his face riven with grief as the police came to take him away.

"You're thinking of him, aren't you?" said a voice from the doorway now, startling her. She turned. It was Maud. "Poor Indy," she said. "Couldn't save Hugh. So you've decided to save the world instead. Poor world. It doesn't know what it has coming."

India didn't answer. She wished that for once Maud could talk about sad things without mocking them.

"I've been sent back into this charnel house to fetch you, so stop holding seances and get your things," Maud continued. "I can't control the pack any longer. Wish is trying to talk the poor dean into investing in some mad land scheme. Freddie's arguing with a creaky old Tory . . . and, oh, India . . . have you been blubbing?"

"Of course not."

"Your nose is all red. And look at your hair. It's an absolute tangle. Give me that comb." Maud raked her fingers through India's blond mane, twisted it, and secured it. Then she stepped back to assess her work. "Very nice," she said.

India smiled and tried to accept the gesture gracefully. It was the sort of thing that passed for love between them.

Maud's eyes traveled over India's clothing; she frowned. "Is that what you're wearing to the Coburg?"

India smoothed her skirt. "What's wrong with it?"

"I thought you might have brought a change of clothes. These are so . . . *dreary*. You look like you're going to a funeral."

"You sound exactly like Mother."

"I do not!"

"You do."

As Maud continued to deny any similarities with their mother, India put her jacket on and then her hat. She gathered her black robe and her doctor's bag, then followed her sister up the steps. When she reached the doorway, she turned around for one last look at her classroom, at the books and charts and specimens, at Ponsonby, and then she whispered a soft goodbye. Her eyes were clear now, her expression calm. She'd boxed the pain away. She was herself again. Cool and unflappable. Brisk and sensible. Feelings firmly in check.

"Keep them that way, Jones," Ponsonby seemed to whisper. "Never forget: Feelings cloud judgment."

And so much more, old chap, India thought, and so much more.

CHAPTER 2

Joseph Bristow bounded up the steps to 94 Grosvenor Square, his towering Mayfair mansion. His train had arrived at King's Cross early. It was Sunday, and only one o'clock. Cook would have just sent up dinner. He hoped it was a leg of lamb or a roast beef with Yorkshire pudding. He'd been in Brighton for a week scouting a site for a new Montague's shop. He missed his home. And home cooking. Most of all, he missed his family. He couldn't wait to see Fiona and their little daughter, Katie. He raised his hand to ring the doorbell, but before he could, the door was opened for him.

"Welcome home, sir. May I take your things?" It was Foster, the butler.

"Hello, Mr. Foster. How are you?"

"Very well, sir. Thank you for inquiring."

Joe was about to ask Foster where Fiona was when two fox terriers flashed by. "Since when do we have dogs?" he asked.

"They are recent acquisitions, sir. They were abandoned in the park. Mrs. Bristow found them and took them in."

"Why am I not surprised?" Joe said, shaking his head. "Do they have names?"

"Lipton and Twining," Foster replied. "Mrs. Bristow says they are like her competition. Always yapping at her heels."

Joe laughed. He watched the dogs as they circled the foyer, yipping and tussling. One broke away, trotted to an umbrella stand, and was about to lift his leg on it until a swift kick from Foster persuaded him otherwise. The second dog leaped into a large potted fern and began to dig furiously.

"If you'll pardon me, sir . . ."

As Foster advanced on the animal, two blond children came charging into the entry, brandishing walking sticks like spears. They were Susie and Robbie, his sister Ellen's children. They were dragging a small silk rug behind them. Its ends had been knotted to form a pouch. Sitting in it was a pretty blue-eyed toddler—his daughter, Katie. She was nibbling a biscuit. He knelt down and kissed her.

"Hello, my lovelies," he said to the children. "What on earth are you doing?"

"Kidnapping Katie for ransom," Robbie answered. "We're Kikuyu. Katie's not. She's Masai. Those are tribes. From Africa. I read about them in *Boy's Own*."

"Did you now?"

A loud whoop was heard from the drawing room.

"A war party! Head for the Ngong Hills!" Robbie shouted.

Katie waved bye-bye as she was skidded off to the dining room. Two more children—twins belonging to Joe's brother, Jimmy—came todding after them. Jimmy's wife, Meg, was hot on their trail, scolding all the way. She blew her brother-in-law a kiss as she ran by.

Joe shook his head. A quiet afternoon? A peaceful meal? In this house? What had he been thinking? "I wonder what it's like at me neighbors' homes," he said aloud. "I wonder if it's half the madhouse it is here."

"At the Granville Barkers'? The Walsinghams'?" Foster said, reappearing with one of the terriers tucked under his arm. "I shouldn't think so, sir."

"Where's me missus, Mr. Foster?"

"In the garden, sir. Hosting a party."

"A *party*?"

"A fund-raising luncheon for the Toynbee Mission Girls' Vocational School."

"She didn't tell me we were having a party today."

"Mrs. Bristow didn't know herself until three days ago. The Reverend and Mrs. Barnett approached her. It seems a portion of the school's roof fell in. Water damage, I believe."

"Another hard-luck story."

"Those do seem to be her specialty."

"Any chance of getting something to eat round here?"

"Refreshments are being served in the garden, sir."

Joe started toward the back of his house. He walked into his sun-dappled garden, thinking he might see twenty or so people there, and was surprised to find more than a hundred. Strangely, they were all quiet. He soon saw why. At the far end of the garden about forty girls aged ten to sixteen stood together, surrounded by a breathtaking flush of pink roses. They were scrubbed and combed, wearing hand-me-down skirts and blouses. One of them began to sing, sweet and clear, and the rest joined in, serenading their listeners with "Come into the Garden, Maud." Every single person had gone as still as stone and a few were dabbing at their eyes.

"Fiona, lass, you are shameless," Joe whispered. He scanned the sea of people, searching for her. He didn't see her, not immediately, but he spotted many famous faces. Captains of industry, titled ladies, politicians—

Fiona mixed them all. Merchants mingled with viscounts, actresses with cabinet ministers, socialists with socialites. The society pages called Joe and Fiona *'Arry and 'Arriet*—a snide reference to their Cockney roots—and sniffed that 94 Grosvenor Square was the only house in Mayfair where the butler spoke better English than his employers. And yet all of society clamored for invitations to the parties Fiona gave, for they were nothing short of stellar.

People enjoyed themselves at 94. They talked and laughed, gossiped and argued. They ate good food and drank the best wines, but what won even the snootiest critic over was Fiona herself. She was direct and disarming, equally at ease with charladies and duchesses. As head of an international tea empire—and as one of the wealthiest women in the world—she was an object of fascination. People talked about her constantly. How she'd come up from nothing. That her dockworker father had been murdered. Her mother, too. How she'd fled London and caught the eye of a robber baron in New York, but married a viscount instead. He had died, but she still wore his diamond. "There were no children, darling. He was *that* way, don't you know." Eyes grew even wider as her daring takeover of a rival's tea company was recounted. "She did it for revenge, my dear. The man killed her father. He tried to kill her! Can you *imagine*?"

Sargent hounded her to sit for him. Escoffier named a dessert after her. When Worth christened a jacket and skirt ensemble the Fiona Suit, women flocked to their seamstresses to have it copied. It was whispered in drawing rooms over tea and cakes that she wore no corset. It was shouted in gentlemen's clubs over port and Stilton that she had no need of one for she was really a man—she *must* be—she had the biggest balls in London.

Joe finally spotted his wife sitting off to one side of the garden. As the girls finished their song, she stood and addressed her guests.

"Ladies and gentlemen," she began. "The beautiful voices you have just heard belong to the children of the Toynbee Mission Girls' Vocational School. Now I beg you to listen to a far less lovely voice . . . my own." There was laughter and fond heckling, then Fiona continued. "These girls come from families whose incomes are less than one pound a week. Imagine a family of six existing for a week on what some of us spend on magazines or chocolates. Because of their exceptional intelligence, these girls have been chosen to attend a school which will train them into a trade and afford them a way out of poverty. When the Reverend and Mrs. Barnett told me that the children must huddle together to avoid the rain that pours in from a damaged roof, I knew each and every one of you would be as outraged as I am." She paused again, this time for a volley of "Hear! Hear!"s.

"A new roof is needed desperately, but the roof is only the beginning. Once we have it, we will need more desks. And blackboards. And books. We will need more teachers and the money to pay them. Most of all, we will need *you*. We will need your continued help, your kind generosity, in order to expand the number and type of courses we can offer. We have turned out housekeepers, governesses, and cooks. Now we must do more. We must turn out shop owners instead of shop girls, managers instead of secretaries, presidents of companies rather than the pieceworkers they employ. Perhaps even a woman tea merchant or two, eh, Sir Tom?" she said, winking at Thomas Lipton.

"Good God, not another one!" Lipton cried.

"Mathematics, economics, accounting . . . yes, those are unusual courses for girls, but what should we teach them? Why are we educating them? So that they can read Shakespeare in a cold room by candlelight when the sweatshop closes? No, if they are to break the cycle of deprivation, they need better jobs, better wages, better opportunities. . . ."

Joe looked at his wife as she spoke, and thought—as he had a million times before—that he had never seen a more captivating woman. He had known her since they were children, and it seemed to him that her beauty never diminished; it only grew richer. She was wearing a white blouse and a sky-blue silk jacket. Its matching skirt had been cleverly cut to hide her growing belly. She was three months pregnant with their second child, and radiant. Her black hair, thick and lustrous, had been swept up and secured with pearl combs. Her cheeks glowed pink with the warmth of the day and her incomparable sapphire eyes flashed with feeling. No one chatted or fidgeted as she spoke. Every eye was upon her.

Pride surged in him as he watched her, but beneath the feelings of pride, worry gnawed. There were smudges under her blue eyes and her lovely face looked thin. She does too much, he thought. She kept a punishing work schedule, rising at five, working in her study until eight, breakfasting with Katie and himself, then departing for her Mincing Lane offices. She was almost always home in time for the nursery tea, and then it was back to work until nine, when she and Joe met to share supper, a few glasses of wine, and details of their day. And somehow she still found the time to work tirelessly on behalf of her charitable foundation—the East London Aid Society—and the schools, orphanages, and soup kitchens which it funded.

He often told her that the problems of East London were far too huge for one woman to solve, and that she was only sticking her finger in a dike. He told her that real help had to come from above, from government. Programs had to be devised to help the poor and monies allotted by Parliament to fund them. Fiona would smile sweetly and tell him he was right, of course he was, but in the meantime, the such-and-such soup kitchen had a line down the street and around the corner, and if she sent a wagon to Covent Garden would he and his mates donate some fruit and vegetables? He would tell her yes and then he'd tell her to stop working so hard, or at least slow down, but she never listened.

Fiona finished her speech—to a burst of applause—and was engulfed by people eager to contribute. Joe was still clapping loudly himself when he felt a hand on his back. "Old chap!"

It was Freddie Lytton, Member of Parliament for Tower Hamlets, a district which included Whitechapel, where the girls' school was located. Joe wondered what he was doing here. He doubted Freddie was making a contribution. Fiona had met him many times in the hope of getting government funds for her various causes, but all she'd ever received for her trouble were a few vague promises.

"Hello, Freddie," Joe said now. "Glad to see you here."

"Fantastic do," Freddie said, swigging champagne. "Thought I heard someone say Fiona had raised two thousand. Splendid sum."

Joe decided to put him on the spot. "It *is* a nice sum, isn't it?" he said. "Be even nicer if the government was to kick in. Any chance of that?"

"As it happens, the Reverend and Mrs. Barnett came to see me, too. I put forth a request for funds in the Commons—five hundred quid—and made a damned good case for it, if I say so myself," Freddie said smoothly. "Been pushing hard. Should have an answer any day."

Joe was not placated. In his opinion, his wife worked harder on behalf of the children of Whitechapel than Whitechapel's elected representative did, and it angered him.

"The morning papers said Parliament just approved the sum of forty thousand pounds to refurbish the queen's stables," he said. "Surely it can find five hundred quid for a school. Are children less important than horses?"

"Of course not."

Joe gave him a shrewd look. "No, not children per se. *Poor* children, well, that's another matter. Their fathers don't vote, do they? *Can't* vote. They don't make enough money. God help you all when they can. You'll all be out of a job."

"It'll take another Reform Act to extend the vote to the entire working class. And that won't happen. Not on Salisbury's watch," Freddie said dismissively.

"The prime minister's knocking on. He won't be around forever and neither will his old hat policies," Joe said, bristling at Freddie's patronizing tone. "Perhaps one day government will allow all of its citizens to have a voice. Poor as well as rich."

"The policies of government should be determined by those who best understand them," Freddie said.

"The policies of government should be determined by those who have to suffer them, mate."

"So what you're saying is that any man—any shiftless know-nothing—should have a voice in government?"

"Why not? Plenty already do."

"Oh, touché, old man. Touché," Freddie said. There was a smile on his mouth, but there was a sudden flash of something hard and menacing in his eyes. Then, as quickly as it had come, it was gone, and he was his polished, affable self again. "Listen, Joe, we're on the same side, essentially."

Joe snorted.

"No, we are. We're both concerned about East London, its people, and its prospects, are we not?"

"Yes, but . . ."

"I knew we were. That's why I'm here, Joe. I've been wanting to talk to you. There's talk of a general election being called in September, you know . . ."

Ah, that's it, Joe thought. He knew Freddie hadn't turned up to hear "Come into the Garden, Maud."

". . . and the Tories are certain to win it. I need your help. I need your support to keep Tower Hamlets a Liberal seat. We must all of us stand together as a bulwark against the Tories."

Joe raised an eyebrow. "Who's *we*?"

"The upper class."

"Don't count me in that group."

"Don't count you in what group?" said a female voice. Fiona had joined him. She squeezed his hand and smiled at him, her eyes shining.

"Your husband's being very modest, Fiona—lovely do, by the way—I was just telling him that he's a member of the upper class now. One of society's leaders."

"Freddie, I'm not—" Joe began.

"But you are," Freddie said, as if reading his mind. "You're *from* the working class, but no longer *of* it, Joe. You're a self-made man. Owner of the biggest chain store in the country and the biggest produce concern as well. And you've done it all under your own steam. By harnessing the forces of private enterprise."

"Blimey, Freddie, hop off your soap box, will you?" Joe said. "What do you want?"

"I want your endorsement. Yours and Fiona's."

"Mine? But I can't even vote!" Fiona exclaimed.

"But you wield influence," Freddie replied. "You have factories and warehouses in East London, both of you. You employ hundreds of men there, many of whom are eligible to vote. I need those votes. I won the seat as a Conservative then crossed the floor. The Tories want it back. Dickie Lambert's their man and he's damned aggressive. Means to give me a proper fight. He's already canvassing in the pubs on the mere rumor of an election."

"What makes you think the working man won't vote Labour?" Fiona asked.

Freddie laughed. "You must be joking! They're a bunch of potty Marxists! No one takes them seriously."

"I think our workers can sort out the candidates for themselves," Joe said. "They don't need us to tell them how to vote."

"Ah, but they do. You're an example to them. They look up to you. They want to be like you and they'll do as you do."

"And what will you do for them?" Fiona asked.

"Work with private enterprise to bring more capital into East London. More refineries. Breweries. Factories. We'll offer incentives to businessmen—tax relief, for example—to get them to relocate."

"All that's going to do is make the factory owners richer."

"That's beside the point," Freddie said dismissively. "There'll be more factories and more factories mean more jobs."

Joe shook his head, astonished. Freddie's lack of understanding about the lives of his own constituents was astonishing. Even offensive. "Yes, but what *kind* of jobs?" he asked, his voice rising. "The jam factory, the match works, the tannery, the docks—they pay nothing. The poor bastards taking those jobs work from dawn till dark six days a week and still have to decide between coal and food."

Freddie gave Joe a pitying look, as if he were a backward child. "It certainly isn't government's fault if a man can't manage his money," he said.

"But there's no bloody money to manage!" Joe nearly bellowed.

"There's money enough to keep the public houses busy. I know that for a fact," Freddie said. "I've overseen the closure of some of the worst. And that's another thing the Liberals will do for East London—enforce law and order. I'm personally going to oversee a crackdown on crime. I've already started. I've put more officers on the streets and started river patrols as well. I'm pushing for harsher sentences for offenders."

"Every politician says that," Joe said.

"Not every politician means it, though. I'm after Sid Malone, you know. Yes, Malone."

Joe's heart lurched at the sound of that name. He stole a glance at Fiona. She caught his eye, warning him to say nothing. He looked away again quickly, not wanting Freddie to see what had passed between them. If Freddie had noticed, he gave no indication. He kept on talking.

"I haven't got him yet," he said, "but I will. I'm going to make an example of him. He'll slip up. They all do. He'll maim someone in a robbery, or kill someone, and then I'll hang him. You have my word on that."

Fiona was now so pale that Joe was afraid for her. He took her arm and was about to steer her toward a chair when Foster suddenly appeared at her elbow. Joe heard him quietly tell her that she had a visitor.

"Please ask him to join us," she said.

"I think not, madam," Foster replied. He inclined his head toward the glass-walled conservatory.

Joe followed his gaze and saw an unfamiliar man standing there. He was wearing an ill-fitting suit and what looked like a sling on one arm. Joe took an instant dislike to him and was about to ask Fiona who he was, but she was already excusing herself.

"A bit of business to attend to," she said briskly. "Won't be a minute."

An uneasy feeling gripped Joe. He was protective of his wife—overly protective, she always said. Though he had no idea why, he wanted to stop Fiona and almost went after her, but then Freddie said something to him and Joe saw Fiona shake the man's good hand. He told himself he was being silly.

"I'm sorry, Freddie, what was that?" he said.

"I said if Malone were hanged, it would send a strong message to the rest of East London's thieves and cutthroats."

"Law and order's all well and good," Joe said, "but it's not the whole answer. Drunkenness, violence, crime . . . they all come from the same thing—poverty. Fix that and you fix the other problems, too."

Freddie laughed. "You know, old mole, you're sounding increasingly like one of those crackpot socialists. How exactly would you have the government *fix* poverty? Perhaps we should just open the doors to the Royal Mint and hand out guineas?"

Joe's simmering irritation with Freddie flared into anger. He reminded himself that Freddie was a guest in his home, then he said, "How about this, mate? Offer working men and women decent wages for their work. Offer them compensation if they're hurt on the job so their families don't starve. Offer their children a proper education so they have something better to look forward to than a factory or the docks. You really want to win this election, Freddie? It's easy. Offer your voters some hope."

He excused himself, glancing toward the conservatory again. Fiona and her visitor were nowhere to be seen. The uneasiness he'd felt became alarm. He went into the house and collared Foster. "Where's Mrs. Bristow?" he asked tersely.

"In her study with her visitor, sir," Foster replied.

"Who is this bloke? Why's he here?"

"His name is Michael Bennett, sir. He would not state his business."

Joe headed toward the staircase. He didn't like the sound of that. No respectable visitor would hesitate to state his business. He took the steps two at a time, wishing he'd followed his instincts instead of staying to argue with Freddie. The door to Fiona's study was closed. He knocked, then opened it without waiting for an answer. Fiona was at her desk. Her eyes were red; she was clutching a handkerchief. Michael Bennett was seated across from her.

"Fiona, what's going on? Are you all right?" Joe asked. He looked at Bennett. "Who the hell are you?"

"I'm fine, Joe," Fiona said. "This is Michael Bennett. He's a private detective."

"A *detective*? Why do you need a detective?"

Fiona looked away, then said, "To find Charlie."

Joe's face hardened. He turned to Bennett. "How much do we owe you?"

Bennett shifted in his chair. "There's fifty quid outstanding. That's what we agreed to, but that was before me arm and all. There's doctor's bills and . . ."

"Will a hundred do it?" Joe asked.

Bennett's eyes widened. "Aye. Quite nicely," he said.

Joe paid him. He pocketed the money and said, "As I was telling your wife—"

"That's all, Mr. Bennett, thank you," Joe said.

"But I haven't told Mrs. Bristow everything yet. I was just—"

"Thank you, Mr. Bennett," Joe said. The study door had closed. He opened it again.

Bennett shrugged and left. When he was gone, Joe turned back to Fiona. "What happened to his arm?" he asked her.

"It was broken. Charlie did it. He told Mr. Bennett to tell me that that was his answer. Loud and clear."

Joe was furious. "Damn it, Fiona!" he yelled. "I thought we'd talked about this. I thought we agreed that it was much too dangerous to try to contact him. What were you going to do if he did agree to see you? Invite him to Sunday dinner? Have him dandle Katie on his knee? Maybe he could fit in a bedtime story between cracking safes and breaking heads."

"I want to see him, Joe."

"Well, I don't want to see him. I don't want him within ten miles of us. You know what he does. What he *is*. Bloody hell, Fiona! What were you thinking?"

Fiona's beautiful blue eyes had filled with tears. There was a raw and wild sadness in them. "He's my brother, Joe. My *brother*."

"Fiona, Sid Malone is a criminal."

"That's *not* his name!" she said angrily, slapping her hands on the desk. "His name's Charlie. Charlie Finnegan."

"Not anymore it isn't."

"If I could just see him," she said. "If I could just talk to him . . ."

"You could what? Convince him to go on the straight and narrow? Become an upstanding citizen? Not bloody likely. There are some fights you can't win, luv. Even you. You've got to bury the past. He made his choice. He told you so himself."

She looked away. He could see that she was struggling with herself.

"Fiona, I know what you're thinking. Do *not* go after him yourself. It's too dangerous."

"But Joe, you heard Freddie Lytton. You heard what he said. He means to arrest Charlie. To *hang* him!"

"Fiona, promise me you won't—" His words were interrupted by a knock on the door. "What is it?" he yelled.

"Begging your pardon, sir, but the Reverend and Mrs. Barnett are leaving and wish to say their good-byes," came Foster's voice.

"I'm coming, Mr. Foster," Fiona said. She wiped her eyes, avoided Joe's, and hurried out of the study, ending the discussion.

Joe sighed. He sat down on the desk. He didn't want to rejoin the party. Not just yet. The argument with Fiona had rattled him. He looked around the room and his eyes fell on the tall piles of folders on top of her desk. He knew what they were—dozens of applications to the East London Aid Society. Fiona used the same hard-headed approach toward her charitable endeavors that she did to make business decisions. Applicants were required to submit a dossier on their organization and its administrators, and a detailed plan of how funds were to be spent. Visits were then made and interviews conducted. The foundation was well endowed, but its funds were not limitless and Fiona was adamant that every penny be well spent. Joe knew that she spent hours reading the applications. He often found her in here at one or two in the morning.

"Come to bed, luv," he'd say.

"I will. Just one more," she'd reply, knowing that another check written meant fewer hungry children.

There were reasons for her dedication. She had a good heart for starters, and couldn't stand to see a stray dog go hungry. Plus, she was from East London, as was he, and they both wanted to see the place that had made them made better for the ones still there. But Joe knew there was more to it. If only she could change ten . . . a hundred . . . a thousand East London lives, they might begin to make up for the one life she couldn't change— her brother's.

He rose from his chair now, his forehead creased with worry. He of all people knew that when Fiona loved, she loved forever. He worried that she would no more give up on Sid Malone than she would have given up on her quest for revenge against her father's killer. Ten years it had taken her to bring the man down, and she'd risked everything to do it—her fortune, her business, her life. What would she risk to save her brother?

Nothing, he told himself. Fiona might have been heedless of her own life ten years ago, but she had a family now, and she would not take those same chances again. *You've got to bury the past,* he'd told her only moments ago, and he was sure she would. She was no fool. She'd seen Bennett's arm.

As he turned to leave the room, a lone folder caught his eye. It lay open on the floor near the desk. Fiona must have knocked it off when she left, he thought. He picked it up. *Malone* was written on the front in a hand he didn't recognize. Michael Bennett's writing, no doubt. He didn't bother to open it. He didn't want to know. It was over, done. He threw the folder into the rubbish bin.

"Bury the past," he said aloud, as he left Fiona's study, never realizing, never even suspecting, that the past might well bury him.

CHAPTER 3

Sid Malone stepped out of his carriage at 22 Saracen Street. Frankie Betts and Tom Smith, two of his men, were there to meet him. The late hour and a hard rain meant there was little traffic in Limehouse. Sid was glad; he wasn't one for audiences.

Except for the carriage, he looked like he belonged in the neighborhood, like a working man on his way home from the pub. He wore heavy boots, a pair of dungarees, and a sailor's navy wool jacket. A flat cap covered his head. He wore no flash jewelry. Nor did his men. He wouldn't allow it. It made a bloke stand out. His face was smooth. He shaved it himself. His red hair was bound into a ponytail. When it grew too long, he lopped it off with a clasp knife. He never visited a barber. He had too many enemies to allow anyone holding a razor close to his throat.

"Got your message," he said to his men, tossing his fag end into the gutter. "What's this about? Where's Ko?"

"Inside," Frankie replied. "He's got a bit of bother."

Number 22 was a shopfront with Canton Superior Laundry painted on its windows. They were dark now. Sid knocked on the door and a few seconds later it was opened by a young Chinese woman in a red gown. Wordlessly, she led him and his men to a room at the back of the shop, bowed, and disappeared.

Teddy Ko, the Cockney son of Chinese immigrants, was seated with his feet on his desk. His hair was stylishly short. He wore a narrow-cut suit, gold knots in his cuffs, and a large pocket watch. His spit-shined shoes gleamed like jet. He got to his feet when he saw Sid and came around the desk to shake his hand. When he'd settled Sid and his men, he shouted down the hall in Cantonese. Instantly an old man in a cotton jacket and skullcap appeared carrying a tea tray. He served small cups of strong black Keemun tea, then set the pot down. His gnarled hands shook as he did, sloshing tea on Teddy's desk. He tried to mop the spill, but Teddy ripped the cloth from his hands, threw it at him, then shoved him out of his office.

"Fucking coolies," he muttered, slamming the door. He sat back down, looked at Sid, and frowned. "You want the name of a good tailor, mate? Got a bloke in Nankin Street. Cut you a suit looks like it's right off Savile Row."

"He don't want no suit and he ain't your mate," Frankie growled.

"What's up, Teddy?" Sid said. "Frankie says there's been trouble."

"That's a bleedin' understatement. Got a doctor here, one of them SSOTs, and . . ."

"You called us here because someone's *drunk*?" Frankie asked.

"You read anything besides the racing sheet, Frankie? Not *sot*, S-S-O-T," Teddy said. "The Society for the Suppression of the Opium Trade. They're right sneaky bastards. Paid their way in tonight like they was regulars then started going room to room hasslin' the punters and the brasses, too. Lecturin' them all on the evils of drugs. Wreckin' my business, they are."

Sid shook his head, disgusted. He was worried it was Big Billy Madden from the West End or the Italians from Covent Garden meddling where they shouldn't. "I don't have time for this, Teddy," he said, standing. "Throw the wanker out yourself."

"Let me finish, will you? The doctor brought a friend—Freddie Lytton. You know . . . the MP? He's up there right now. With a bloke from a newspaper. And he's threatening to shut me down."

Sid frowned. That *was* troubling. Lytton had been making noise about the Firm's robberies recently, but he'd never made ructions about their opium dealings and Sid didn't want him to start. The Firm made good money out of Ko. He—and others like him—bought opium from them and also paid them to keep any comers off their turf.

"You told Lytton to go?" Sid asked.

"My girls did. And the old man."

"Your *girls*?" Sid said. "Get in there yourself, Teddy. Break some heads."

Ko leaned back in his chair, offended. "I'm a respectable citizen, ain't I? Fuckin' pillar of the community, me. Breakin' heads ain't in my line of work."

Frankie snorted. "What he means is he don't want the Honorable Member to see his face," he said. "Won't get invited for tea at Westminster if Lytton twigs that Ko the Chinese striver is also Ko the opium peddler and Ko the ponce. He's a bit of a climber, our Teddy."

"Hell, Frankie! I pay you protection money, so fucking protect me!" Ko yelled, banging his fist on his desk.

"You want to watch your tone, Edward," Frankie warned.

Sid saw that Frankie was getting restless and he wasn't in the mood for a smash-up tonight. The lad was like a bull terrier that needed regular exercise to keep him from chewing up the furniture.

"Come on," Sid said. "We're here. Let's do this and go."

Frankie led the way out of Teddy's office and up a narrow flight of stairs. He banged on a locked door at the top of the first-floor landing. A glass peephole was opened but the door was not.

"Havin' yourself a gander, are ya?" he asked, smiling into the peephole. Then he drove a cosh into it, shattering it. "Open the bleedin' door or I'll kick it to pieces and you with it!" he shouted.

The door was yanked open. The wizened old man who'd served them tea stood on the other side, rubbing his eye. Sid entered and looked around, disoriented by the opulence. Wooden platforms painted with flowers and dragons and canopied with heavy silks lined the walls. Thick rugs overlapped on the floor. Candles flickered in what seemed like a thousand paper lanterns and a bitter blue smoke hung in the air. These were exotic rooms that belonged in some fabled Chinese city, not London.

Teddy Ko owned a dozen buildings in the area. He called them laundries, and by day people washed and pressed clothing in them, but the laundries were only the respectable façade of a much darker enterprise. At night, long after the wash kettles had been emptied and the irons cooled, men and women, hurried and furtive, knocked and entered, slipped coins into the hands of Ko's hostesses, then slipped into oblivion.

Sid saw them now—lying on the platforms or sprawled on the floor—heavy-lidded, slack-jawed. The young woman who'd let him in moved among them, stooping to refill pipes with chunks of brown paste or to tuck a pillow under a lolling head. Other young women lay entwined with male customers in curtained beds. There were people with money here—Sid could tell by their clothing—and others whose night's high had cost them a week's wages. Frankie bent over one well-heeled woman who was lying dazed in a corner. He patted her cheek and, when he got no response, helped himself to her rings. Sid looked around the room but there was no sign of Lytton.

Teddy came up behind him. "Where's Lytton? And the doctor?" Sid asked him.

"Round here someplace," he said, waving Sid through a doorway.

They entered another room, which was much like the first, only noisy because two women in it were arguing. The first, a brunette, was reclining languidly on a platform next to a handsome boy who couldn't have been more than eighteen. The other woman, a slender blonde, was chafing the first woman's wrists, berating her.

"It's a very powerful drug, Maud," she said, "one that should be used only by doctors. It's addictive and damaging."

The dark-haired woman let out a pained, trailing sigh and looked imploringly around the room. Her eyes came to rest on Teddy. "Ko, darling, can't you throw her out?" she asked, propping herself up on one elbow.

"Who is she?"

"My sister."

"Then you throw her out, Maud!" Teddy shouted. "You get out, too! She's only here after you!"

The blond woman stood up. She was slight and wore spectacles. Sid guessed she stood about five feet six inches in her boots.

"You are wrong, sir," she said. "I am here for every poor, miserable, addicted soul in this room."

Sid groaned. He and Frankie were supposed to be at the Bark talking with the rest of his men about an upcoming job—a very lucrative job—and instead he was larking about doing work Teddy could've paid a boy in short pants to do.

"Teddy, where's the bloody doctor?" he snapped.

"Are you blind? She's right in front of you!" Teddy said.

"Who? *Her*? She's a woman," Sid said.

"How very observant of you," the blond woman said. "I am indeed a medical doctor and I'm also a member of the Society for the Suppression of—"

"Aye, luv. I know all about it," Sid said.

She faltered for a second, then recovered. "Yes. Well. Then you also know that I and my colleague, the Member of Parliament for Tower Hamlets, are determined to close down these dens of misery. These people should be at home with their children, not giving their hard-earned wages to drug lords and prostitutes."

Sid had heard enough. "Frankie, Tom, get her out of here," he ordered.

Just then, a tall, wheaten-haired man emerged from yet another doorway in the rabbit warren of rooms. Sid knew him. He was Freddie Lytton. Another man was with him. Sid knew him, too. His name was Michael McGrath. He was one of Bobby Devlin's reporters from the *Clarion* and he was carrying a camera. They hadn't seen Sid yet.

"Did you get one of me breaking the opium pipe in two?" Lytton asked McGrath. McGrath nodded. "Good man. Make sure you get my name in the headline. 'Lytton Uncovers London Drug Peril' . . . or maybe 'Lytton Teaches Firm That Crime Doesn't Pay' . . ."

"Not as well as politics," Sid said to Frankie. "That's for sure."

"But that might be over-long for a headline, no?" Lytton said. "And don't forget to mention all my good work with the SSOT. When will the story run?"

"Day after tomorrow," McGrath said, folding the legs of the camera's tripod.

Frankie gave a low whistle. "A flipping camera no less, guv. If that ain't taking liberties, I don't know what is." He was on McGrath in an instant. He'd ripped the equipment out of his hands and thrown it out of a window before the man knew what had happened. The sound of shattering glass carrying up from the street told him.

"Jesus Christ!" McGrath cried. "That was a brand-new camera!"

"Get out. Now. Or you're going out the window after it," Sid said.

McGrath, a big lad, rounded on Sid, ready to take a swing. His eyes widened. He took a step back. "Bloody hell." He turned to Freddie Lytton, ashen. "You never said *he'd* be here!" And then he was out the door and gone, feet pounding down the stairs.

"Let's go, missus," Sid said to the doctor.

"Keep your hands off her!" Freddie Lytton ordered. "I should've known *you'd* be behind this, Malone." He turned to the doctor and said, "India, get Maud out of here now. I'm going to fetch the police and have these men arrested and this place closed down."

Frankie burst into laughter. "Not bloody likely, mate. Teddy Ko pays the rozzers more money than he pays us."

"You can repeat that to the magistrate, Mr. Betts," Freddie said angrily. "I want that name . . . Ko, was it?"

"Frankie . . ." Sid said through gritted teeth. His patience was wearing thin.

"Righto, guv." Frankie walked over to Lytton, grabbed him by the back of his mackintosh, and marched him out of the room. Sid heard curses and scuffles, a few thumps, and then a door banging back on its hinges.

"What are you doing to him? Leave him alone!" the doctor shrilled.

Sid smiled at her regretfully. "It's time to go, luv," he said.

"I'm not going anywhere."

"Don't let's have a scene now, miss," Sid said.

"It's *Doctor,* not luv. Not miss. *Dr.* India Selwyn Jones."

"India, dear, be quiet for once and listen," the dark-haired woman said. "Do you have *any* idea who that is? It's Sid Malone. Surely you've heard the name. Even you. Be the clever girl I know you are and walk out of here now while you still can."

India leveled her chin at Sid. "I'm not afraid of you," she said.

"Nor should you be, Miss—*Doctor* Jones. I would never lay a hand on a woman. Frankie and Tommy neither. Men . . . well, they're a different matter. There's no telling what my lads will get up to with Mr. Lytton. They don't call Frankie *Mad Frank* for nothing. He's a bit unpredictable."

The doctor's eyes grew round. She bent down for her bag and jacket, then said to the woman she'd called Maud, "You're destroying yourself."

"Oh, for God's sake, India, stop being such a bore. You never have any fun and you don't want anyone else to, either."

"Is addiction *fun,* Maud? Is syphilis?" She turned to Sid. "Not only are you enslaving addicts, you're exploiting young women for financial gain."

"We don't take prisoners here, Dr. Jones. If a girl's at Ko's, it's because she wants to be."

"*Wants* to be? You're telling me that she wants to be degraded? That she wants to expose herself to disease?"

"No, I'm telling you she wants to earn her rent money. It's warmer in Ko's than it is on the streets. And a damn sight safer."

The doctor shook her head. She looked as if she wanted to say something more, but she didn't. She put her jacket on and left. Sid cast a last glance around the room; Ko was nowhere to be seen. He followed the doctor down the stairs, simmering with anger.

She and her silly society were not a threat, but Lytton was. He complicated things. When he got outside, he saw that Lytton and the doctor were already halfway down the street. The rain had stopped.

"You know where he's going, don't you? And it won't be the local boys he fetches this time. It'll be some big noise from the Yard," Frankie said.

Sid nodded. He couldn't have that. Not yet. Teddy would need time to set the place to rights first.

"Oi! You two!" Sid shouted after them. Lytton turned around. Sid nodded to his carriage. "Get in."

Freddie took the doctor's arm and kept walking.

"Persuade them, lads," Sid said.

Frankie and Tom took off after them. There were words, another scuffle, then Lytton and the doctor were walking back toward Sid. Lytton helped the doctor into the carriage, then Tom climbed in and sat down next to them. Frankie and Sid took facing seats.

"Whatever you're planning, Malone, you won't get away with it," Freddie said. "Dr. Jones comes from an important family and so do I. There will be people looking for us."

"What the hell are you on about?" Frankie asked.

"The bollocks thinks we're kidnapping him," Sid said, rubbing his temples. "Where do you live, Dr. Jones?"

"Don't say a word, India. You don't want this man knowing your address," Freddie warned.

Sid took a deep breath and blew it out again. His head had started to ache. "Either give me an address, in *West* London, or I'll drop you both on the Ratcliff Highway." He didn't know if the doctor would recognize the name, but he was certain Lytton would. The highway was the most dangerous stretch of road in London, teeming with thieves, whores, and cutthroats.

"Sloane Square," Lytton said.

"Chelsea, Ronnie," Sid yelled out of the window to his driver. "Make it quick."

The carriage lurched off. Sid noted with satisfaction that Lytton was nursing a fat lip. He couldn't see the doctor's face; she was looking at the floor. Her leather bag was on her lap; her hands were gripping its handle. He saw that they trembled and he was sorry for it. He would have happily popped Lytton in the gob himself, but he did not make a habit of frightening women. She looked up just then. Her frank gray eyes met his and held them and he saw to his surprise that she wasn't frightened at all. She was angry. Furious, in fact.

"You're despicable," she said, her voice shaking with emotion. "You trade in misery. You batten on people's despair. Do you know what drug addiction can do? What it can drive people to? The people in those rooms, they're spending their rent money on that poison."

"That's not my lookout, is it, Dr. Jones? I'm just a businessman. Certainly isn't up to me to tell people how to spend their brass," Sid said.

"Have you ever seen an opium addict when he can't get the drug?" India continued. "He starts out shaking and sweating. Then the pain starts."

"Being a little dramatic, aren't we, luv? From what I saw, a handful of tossers was smoking themselves silly. Seemed pretty harmless to me."

"Those people were ruining themselves, Mr. Malone, body and soul. Can't you see that? Can't you see that what you're doing is terribly, terribly wrong?"

"India . . . ," Freddie cautioned, his eyes darting nervously to Sid. But the doctor didn't hear him. Or she didn't care if she did.

She has bottle, Sid thought, I'll give her that.

"Come to London Hospital, Mr. Malone," she pressed. "I'll give you a tour of the psychiatric ward. I'll show you what addiction does. I'll show you how harmless it is."

"India, for God's sake, let it go," Freddie hissed. "You're not going to reform Sid Malone."

"And what makes you think that I, or any of Teddy's punters, want to be reformed?" Sid asked. "Those dope fiends looked a damn sight happier than you do, luv."

Frankie and Tom laughed. Freddie shot forward in his seat, a threatening look on his face. Frankie pressed his fingers into Freddie's chest and eased him back. Sid could see that Lytton was seething, and that he probably would have taken a shot at him had it not been for Frankie. That took balls. As he watched him, he saw Freddie cover India's hand with his own and squeeze it. Ah, *that's* it, he thought. Nothing made a man stupider than being shown up in front of his girl. Sid looked at the doctor with new interest, as if he'd somehow forgotten in all the prior commotion that she was, in fact, a woman.

He could see how it might happen—the forgetting. She did little to keep it fresh in a man's mind. Her hair wasn't styled; it was just pulled back into a hasty twist. She might be pretty; it was hard to tell with those awful glasses. Her clothes were awful, too. She wore a dark skirt and waistcoat that completely hid whatever figure she might have, and no jewelry except—he saw now—for a gold chain that ran across the front of her waistcoat.

". . . men will take bread from their children's mouths to get opium. Women will sell their bodies . . ."

Good Christ, he thought. She's still at it. He leaned forward and tugged on the chain. A watch emerged from her waistcoat pocket. She gave a little gasp.

"Very nice," he said, flipping it open.

"You wouldn't dare," Lytton said.

"What's a watch like this go for, Frankie?" Sid asked, ignoring him.

"Gold case, diamond markers . . . I'd say a hundred quid, easy."

"A hundred quid," Sid said thoughtfully. "You know, that would feed and clothe a docker's family for a year. Fine thing, isn't it, Frankie, to tell other people what they should do when you're going home to a fire in the grate and a nice hot meal and the poor bleeders at Ko's are working fourteen-hour days in some hellhole of a factory, living five or six in some shithole of a room, eating bread and marge three times a day because it's all their rotten teeth can handle." India, still glaring, blinked, but Sid did not. "Why, if it was me in their shoes, Frankie," he added, "I'd smoke me fuckin' head off."

Sid returned the doctor's watch to her pocket. It was quiet then and remained so for the rest of the ride. The carriage rolled westward, hugging the river. He was relieved when he finally saw Westminster Bridge and the Houses of Parliament. A few minutes later, Ronnie veered north off the

Grosvenor Road. Sid rapped for him to stop as they neared the Pimlico Road, near Sloane Square. He'd decided to boot his passengers out just shy of their destination in case the good doctor got it in her head to make a farewell speech.

She did not disappoint him. "Mr. Malone, I must once again implore you . . ." she began, as the carriage slowed.

"Dr. Jones, it's been a pleasure," Sid said, opening the door before the carriage had fully stopped. Freddie scrambled out, then took the doctor's hand and helped her down. He was reaching back in for his coat when Sid said, "Mr. Lytton, Dr. Jones, do not let me catch either of you on Saracen Street again."

"You won't be seeing Dr. Jones there, but you'll be seeing me," Lytton warned. "You'll go down, Malone. Sooner or later. You'll make a mistake. And when you do, I'll see that you're put in prison. You have my word on that."

Sid's arm shot forward. His hand closed on Freddie's tie. He jerked him into the carriage, using both hands to twist the fabric tight. No one threatened him with prison. No one.

"Freddie?" he heard the doctor call. She was standing on the pavement and couldn't see inside the carriage.

"Let go!" Freddie wheezed, his fingers scrabbling at Malone's.

"Does the doctor care for you, mate?" Sid asked him.

"Take your filthy hands off me!" Each word was gasped.

"Answer me."

"Let go! Jesus . . ." His eyelids fluttered. He was going blue.

"Does she, Freddie?" Sid asked, tightening his grip.

"Y-yes!"

Sid released him. "Then for her sake, lad, don't come for me alone."

CHAPTER 4

"Liverpool Street!" the conductor barked. India felt the train slow as it neared the station. She hoped the doors would open quickly. It was only 7:30 and already the underground was impossibly crowded. People were mashed together and a horrible man in a bowler hat was making use of every lurch and pitch to rub against her.

"Stop it or I shall call the guard," she hissed. He didn't and she finally thought to put her doctor's bag between them. At last the train stopped, the doors opened, and she was carried along in the surge of people. She made her way up the stairs, bumped by briefcases and poked by umbrellas, vowing to take the omnibus home.

Outside the station, a woman clutching a baby to her chest pressed a dirty palm up at her. "Please, miss, a penny for the baby," she said, her breath reeking of gin.

"There's a mission on the High Street. You can get soup there and milk for the baby," India said, but the woman, hollow-eyed and desperate, had already moved off. She saw her tug on the sleeve of a man in a suit. He gave her a few coppers. India frowned. He'd meant well, she knew, but he was only encouraging drunkenness.

"The *Clarion*! Getcher news 'ere! Read about the Chairman! King of Crime! Only in the *Clarion*!" a newsboy cried on the pavement, waving the morning edition at her. *The Chairman*. That's how Freddie had referred to Sid Malone, India thought, shuddering at the memory of their meeting. She briskly sidestepped the newsboy and his pile of papers, glancing at the headline. "The New Underworld," it said. There was a sketch underneath it. The artist had gotten the shape of the face right, but not the eyes. They don't look like that, shifty and brutal, she thought. His eyes were hard, but piercing and intelligent. They had unsettled her. Far more than his violent reputation had. The memory of them unsettled her now, so she put it out of her mind. She had more pressing things to think about this morning.

She crossed Bishopsgate and headed for Middlesex Street, a busy thoroughfare that would take her to Whitechapel's High Street then to Varden Street and Dr. Gifford's surgery, just south of the London Hospital. She cut a crisp figure in her black straw hat, gray duster, and white shirtwaist, all of which were several seasons out of date, but freshly starched and pressed. Her pace was brisk and her expression eager. It was her first day at Gifford's. She remembered how she'd gotten the job—by agreeing to accept roughly half the salary a male doctor was paid for nearly twice the hours—but even that memory couldn't dampen her spirits. She was truly excited—excited to be a practicing doctor at last, and excited to be practicing *now*, in 1900, at what many said was the dawn of a golden age in medicine. The advances of the last half century were astonishing, and India found their implications for the future nothing short of mind-boggling.

The contributions of Lister, Pasteur, Jenner, and Koch to the understanding of germ theory—combined with advances in anesthesia—had enabled amazing gains to be made in surgery. Wounded or fractured limbs, once certain to become gangrenous, could now be disinfected and repaired instead of amputated. Cancers could be excised. Why, entire organs could be removed without hemorrhage or infection—she'd seen it done. The eminent American gynecologists Simpson and Kelly had made successful hysterectomies and ovariotomies, and there had even been recent reports of a successful Cesarean surgery, in which both mother and baby had actually lived.

In Germany a man named Roentgen had discovered light rays that could pass through human tissue, and already battlefield doctors were using them to locate bullets in soldiers. In France, Becquerel's work with uranium and the Curies' with radium promised that doctors would soon be able to peer all the way inside the body without cutting, blood loss, shock, or infection.

There were new drug discoveries, too—painkillers such as aspirin, heroin, and chloroform, and antitoxins for smallpox and diphtheria. Some felt it was only a short matter of time—a year, maybe two—before one was found for tuberculosis.

There were times when India felt breathless just thinking about these advances and how she would use them to better the lives of the Whitechapel poor. And yet all she had to do was pick up a city newspaper to be reminded of all that medicine had still to accomplish. Scores of public health acts, designed to safeguard citizens from contaminated water, filthy sewers, and overcrowded housing, had finally caused a sharp decline in deaths from cholera, typhus, and smallpox, but scarlet fever, influenza, and typhoid still raged through the slums. Gin and opium destroyed minds, while malnutrition and poverty destroyed bodies. India knew that for every social reformer, every doctor or missionary trying to pull the poor out of the pub, the gin palace, and the opium den, there was a Sid Malone pulling them back in.

The challenges to medicine were still many and daunting, and as excited as she was to be starting her professional life, she was also nervous. Could she meet the demands of a busy surgery? Cope with the case load? Correctly diagnose the staggering array of symptoms she would encounter? There would be no Professor Fenwick to back her up now; she was on her own.

She dodged a group of chattering factory girls and climbed a short flight of steps to 33 Varden Street. It was a sandy-colored Georgian house, two stories high. Dr. Edwin Gifford's surgery was on the first floor; the second was rented out to a family. India paused at the front step for a few seconds to calm herself. It wouldn't do to arrive breathless on her first day.

She had just raised her hand to knock when the door was wrenched open and a woman about India's age, wearing a nurse's uniform, hurtled smack into her.

"*Oy vey!*" she exclaimed, taking India by the arm. "There you are! *Got sei dank!* Was just on me way to look for you. Dr. Selwyn Jones, innit? Where on earth have you been? I was worried you weren't coming at all."

India checked her watch. "It's only a quarter to eight," she said.

The woman snorted. "Are you a doctor or a banker? We start at seven sharp here."

"*Seven?* Dr. Gifford said eight."

"He always tells the new hires that. This is Whitechapel, Doctor. A lot of people here work in factories or down the docks and need to see us before the whistle blows. Come on, let's get you settled."

She tugged on India's sleeve, leading her past a waiting room full of patients, through a narrow hallway to the back of the building and Dr. Gifford's office. She managed to get her hat and duster off along the way and hustle her into a white jacket. The jacket's hem hung down past India's knees and the sleeves covered her hands.

The woman frowned. She rolled up the sleeves. "Too big, this. Fit Dr. Seymour perfectly, but you're not a man, are you? I'll have to order some small ones." She pointed to an open door leading off the office, and said, "Exam room's through there—" Before she could finish, there was a loud metallic crash. She ran into the room and came out again dragging a young boy by his ear. He wore a black skullcap and long side curls. "*Ach, du Pisher! Du fangst shoyn on?*" the young woman scolded. "Go in the waiting room and stay put!"

India was about to ask the woman who she was, but she'd disappeared into the exam room again. India followed and found her on her hands and knees, picking up the tray of instruments the little boy had dumped.

"Where's the autoclave?" she asked, kneeling down to help.

"The what?"

"The water bath. These will have to be sterilized."

"We don't have one."

"But how can you not? The need for an aseptic environment during diagnosis, as well as surgery, has been proven repeatedly. Dr. Lister is very clear on the germicidal properties of—"

"Well, Dr. Lister ain't here today, is he? I am."

India sat back on her heels. "But how do you clean the instruments?"

"I take them home and give them a wash in the kitchen sink. When I can remember," she replied, tossing a scalpel and two clamps back on the tray. "You all set, then?" she asked, getting to her feet. "I'll send the first patient in."

"Wait! I didn't get your name."

"Oh, sorry. Ella Moskowitz," the woman said, extending her hand.

India took it. "Dr. Jones," she said. "You're the receptionist?"

"And the nurse, secretary, clerk, and bookkeeper. Zookeeper, too. I can't stay to chat. We're way behind. Going to have to go at it hammer and tongs to get you through that lot by lunchtime."

"What? *All* of them? By noon?" There were more people in the waiting room than she could see in an entire day, never mind a morning.

"Yes, all of them."

"Is Dr. Gifford here?"

"No. It's just yourself today."

"My word. Is there some kind of epidemic?"

Ella Moskowitz burst into laughter. "Epidemic! That's a good one. Oh, it's an epidemic, all right, it's Whitechapelitis. This is just a normal day. You want to see true pandemonium, wait till there really is an epidemic. *Got zol ophiten!*"

"I beg your pardon?"

"Sorry. *God forbid*. You're not Jewish, are you?" she asked. "Can't imagine you are. Don't recall a lot of Selwyn Joneses at temple. Many of your patients are, though. Any trouble with the Jews, call me. Any trouble with the Irish, you're on your own."

Ella hurried off, leaving India to stare after her. She barely had time to orient herself before Ella was back with a patient—a small, thin woman whom India guessed to be in her mid-forties. "This is Mrs. Adams, and this is her file," Ella said, slapping a folder on the desk.

"Wait one bleedin' minute!" Mrs. Adams cried.

Ella stopped in the doorway. "Yes, Mrs. Adams?"

"I'm payin' good money to see a doctor and I want to see a *doctor,* not a flippin' nurse."

"Dr. Jones *is* a doctor, Mrs. Adams."

Mrs. Adams looked at India. "Pull the other one, it's got bells on," she said.

India looked down at herself, at the too-long jacket, the rolled sleeves, and realized that she looked like a child playing dress-up.

"Now, Mrs. Adams—" Ella began.

"It's all right, Ella," India said, closing her office door. "Good morning, Mrs. Adams. I assure you I am a doctor. I have a diploma. Would you like to see it?" She reached into her bag and took the document out.

She had other things in her bag, too. Colorful illustrations of smiling fruits and vegetables. Booklets on economical and nutritious cookery. Pamphlets on the principles of proper hygiene. She planned to share them with her patients during examinations.

Mrs. Adams gave the diploma a look but remained unconvinced. "You have one of them things Dr. Gifford wears? Round his neck?" she asked.

India pulled her stethoscope out of her bag and held it up.

"All right, then. I reckon you'd have to be a doctor to have one of them." India smiled. "Can you tell me what's troubling you?"

"Baby's paining me something terrible. Dr. Gifford gave me laudanum and it helped for a while, but not no more."

"Do you have the bottle with you? May I see it?"

Mrs. Adams reached into her dress pocket for the bottle and handed it to India.

She read the label. It was laudanum, all right, which was not usually prescribed for pregnant women. "How long have you been taking this, Mrs. Adams?" she asked.

"About three months."

"And how far along are you?"

"Five months. Maybe six."

India nodded. She scanned Mrs. Adams's file, but saw no mention of pregnancy. She did see Dr. Gifford's notations for pain and fatigue, and that he'd started her on a weak laudanum solution and had been increasing the strength of the dosage. She led Mrs. Adams into the exam room and persuaded her to remove her dress and lie down on the table. Mrs. Adams wondered aloud why it was necessary and said Dr. Gifford never made her, but did as she was asked. When India saw her bare arms, she had to work to keep her expression neutral. Mrs. Adams's bones were practically protruding through her skin.

"Are you eating well?" she asked.

"I haven't much of an appetite. Been feeling a bit green, but that's to be expected with babies."

"Nausea is very common," India agreed.

"You don't have to tell me. Nine pregnancies I've had, and five living children. None was easy, but this one's the hardest. I'm that tired, there's days I fall asleep standing up. Once by the stove. Nearly set me pinny on fire."

"How are you sleeping at night?"

"Poorly. Pains me to sleep on me side, and I can't get comfortable on me back."

"How old are you, Mrs. Adams?"

"Forty-six. Never thought I'd quicken again at this age. Thought it was the change because me periods stopped. But then there was quite a bit of bleeding right before, y'see, and there's no bleeding with the change, is there?"

"May I look at your belly?"

Mrs. Adams nodded. India undid the buttons of her camisole and the tie at the waistband of her petticoat to expose her abdomen. She saw immediately that instead of the pleasing, symmetrical swell of pregnancy, there was an uneven, lumpy look to her belly. Starting just under the ribcage, she pressed down into the muscle, feeling for the fundus, the top of an expanding uterus, but could not find it. Her hands moved lower, probing for a bony nub—a skull, heel, or elbow. Nothing. She fished in her bag for her fetal stethoscope, a wooden device that resembled a bicycle horn. She pressed the bulb end to Mrs. Adams's belly and put her ear to the trumpet-shaped cup. Again, nothing. There was something growing inside Mrs. Adams, of this India was certain. But it was not—and had never been—a baby.

"Is everything all right? There's nothing wrong, is there?"

India dodged the question. "Do you know what a speculum is?"

The woman shook her head.

"It's a device that enables doctors to view the reproductive organs. I would like to take a look if I may."

Mrs. Adams opened her mouth and stuck out her tongue.

"Um . . . no, Mrs. Adams. It's the other end I need to examine."

"You *what*?"

"I need to do a vaginal exam. I can't tell what's going on inside you unless I look inside you."

Mrs. Adams sat up. "Why, you filthy little monkey! I've never heard of such a thing in all my born days. Is that what they teach you in medical school? To use dirty words and look up people's privates?" India heard anger in the woman's voice, but in her eyes there was only fear. "Why can't you just give me my prescription like Dr. Gifford does?" she asked, her voice rising.

"Now, now, now. What's all this noise, Mrs. Adams?"

India started and turned around. A compact man with gray hair and a neat goatee stood by the desk. It was Dr. Gifford. He hadn't bothered to knock; he'd simply walked into the exam room, not knowing who was inside it or what was occurring. India found it highly discourteous to both herself and her patient.

"Oh, Dr. Gifford, I *am* glad to see you! This lass of yours has me stripped to me drawers when all I want is me prescription filled."

"Dr. Gifford, there is no gravidity," India said, choosing language she hoped her patient could not follow. "There's a uterine mass. A large one . . ."

"That will be all, Dr. Jones."

"But, sir, Mrs. Adams should be examined internally. She should—"

"That will be *all*."

"What's she on about, Dr. Gifford? Is me baby all right?" Mrs. Adams asked anxiously.

"Everything's fine, Mrs. Adams." He scribbled on a piece of paper and handed it to her.

"Here's a new prescription. Three drops every two hours in your tea."

Mrs. Adams's drawn face shone with relief. She thanked Dr. Gifford, dressed hurriedly, and left.

"Dr. Gifford . . ." India began.

"You are far too slow, Dr. Jones," Gifford said briskly, noting the prescription in Mrs. Adams's file. "Ninety percent of the time you should simply perform a quick exam and prescribe laudanum."

"That woman probably has uterine cancer. She needs surgery, not laudanum."

"I'm afraid surgery is not possible in Mrs. Adams's case."

"You . . . you knew she wasn't pregnant?"

Dr. Gifford looked up. "Yes, I knew. Do you take me for an idiot?"

"Of course not. I didn't mean to imply anything of the sort. But . . . why didn't you tell her?"

"To what end? She's going to die, whether I tell her or I don't. Why make her last months harder than they have to be? Let her think she's pregnant. What harm is there in it? And keep her out of pain. More I cannot do."

India could not believe what she was hearing. Gifford was making an outrageous set of assumptions. He was playing God. Elizabeth Adams was a grown woman, not a child. She deserved to be told the truth and allowed to make her own decisions.

"Dr. Gifford, the tumor may be operable," India said. "Or benign. If I could persuade her to allow a vaginal examination, I could take some cells. Make a slide. See if by some chance it is benign and if her pain is caused by the pressure it's exerting."

Dr. Gifford put his pen down. His expression was thunderous. "Dr. Jones, you are a new doctor, and inexperienced, so I will make allowances for you . . . up to a point. In case it has escaped your notice, this is an exceedingly poor area. The patients who come to this practice barely have money for treatment, never mind surgery. Even if Elizabeth Adams could afford surgery, she would not survive it. She's weak and malnourished. We are overwhelmed here, and must put our resources where they will be rewarded."

India swallowed hard. This particular issue hadn't been covered in her ethics class. "I'm sorry, sir. This is not the medicine I was taught," she said.

"It's the medicine you must learn," Dr. Gifford said. "This is not a textbook, Dr. Jones, this is reality. Elizabeth Adams is a lost cause, but the people waiting downstairs may not be. That is, if you deign to examine them before the turn of the next century." He closed Mrs. Adams's file and stood. "No more than ten minutes a patient, Doctor. Good day."

"You're leaving, sir?"

"Is that a problem?"

"No, sir."

"I have patients to visit at London Hospital. I merely stopped in on my way to see how you're getting on. Not well, from what I've witnessed. I hope I have not made a mistake."

"You have not, sir."

"I would hate to disappoint your dean. Good day, Dr. Jones."

"Good day, sir."

India put her head in her hands. What a terrible beginning. She could not lose her position. The mere thought of explaining to Dean Garrett Anderson that Gifford sacked her because she hadn't been up to the demands of the job was unbearable. As she sat fretting, a snatch of the dean's graduation address came back to her: *The eyes of the world are on you now. Many will applaud your every triumph. Many more, your every failure. . . .*

India had heard the words people used against herself and other medical women—*immoral, indecent, unsexed*. She'd felt the ugliness behind them, and she knew she must never give Dr. Gifford any reason to regret his decision to hire her. She must not fail.

She remembered how every quarter, the same few lines appeared in the school's magazine at the dean's behest: "Medical women are earnestly requested to send notice of any appointments they obtain, or any vacant appointments they know of, to the secretary of the Medical School." There were so few appointments obtained by medical women, so few available to them. India knew that if she lost this one, she wouldn't find another. But what Dr. Gifford had done—lying to a patient about her condition—was unconscionable. She didn't have long to dwell on her dilemma, however, as Ella was already leading another patient into the office—a little boy accompanied by his mother.

"Henry Atkins," she announced. "Worms."

After young Henry there was Ava Briggs, a sixteen-year-old girl with a severely infected jaw. Her mother had had all her teeth pulled two days ago. By a blacksmith. "As a birthday present," she explained. "No man'll marry a girl with her own teeth. Costs him a fortune in dentist bills." After Miss Briggs there was Rachael Eisenberg, married a whole month and still not pregnant. And Anna Maloney, who thought she was seventy but couldn't really remember and had been constipated for two weeks. Fifteen more followed, and then at noon, just when India thought she would surely drop, Ella bustled in with a teapot and hamper.

"Bring anything to eat?" she asked. India shook her head. "Didn't think so. We'll share mine. Lucky for you I keep an extra plate around."

"Oh, I couldn't, Sister Moskowitz."

"It's Ella . . ."

India bristled at her informality.

". . . and you'd better. I don't have time to pick you up off the floor when you faint from hunger."

India forced a smile. Something was gnawing at her, but it wasn't hunger. She'd put aside her misgivings about Dr. Gifford earlier to concentrate on her patients, but could ignore them no longer.

"Roast chicken," Ella said, placing half a bird on the desk, "parsleyed potatoes, and kasha." She frowned, dug deeper, then brightened. "And noodle kugel!" She handed India a plate and fork. "Tuck in."

"There's enough for ten here. Did you cook all this yourself?"

"My mum did. My parents have a caff on Brick Lane. Kosher food."

India speared a potato with her fork. She was still standing up.

"Sit. Eat. Rest. You'll need your strength for this afternoon," Ella advised.

India sat. She picked at her potatoes some more, then put her fork down.

"Is something wrong?" Ella asked.

India told her about her contretemps with Dr. Gifford.

"Yes . . . so?" Ella said, between bites of chicken.

"*So?* So how can I possibly continue to work here? To do so would be to condone the worst sort of medicine."

"Don't you even *think* of leaving," Ella warned.

"But how can I stay? I understand the need for expediency and practicality in a busy surgery—of course I do—but this isn't a question of efficiency. It's a question of ethics. Of morality."

Ella laughed. "Oh dear. Brought your morals with you, did you, Dr. Jones?

To Whitechapel? That was a mistake. Tomorrow, leave those little buggers home."

India did not laugh. She glared. "What Dr. Gifford did is indefensible. He should have informed Elizabeth Adams of her true condition, explained her prognosis, offered her a choice of treatment, including no treatment if that's what she wanted. But the choice should have been hers. Not his."

Ella stopped eating. She stopped joking. "Dr. Jones, why did you take this job?" she asked.

"To help the poor."

"Then help them."

"But Dr. Gifford—"

"Shit on Dr. Gifford."

India sat back in her chair, shocked. "What a thing to say! You work for him."

"No. He pays me, that's all. I work for *them*," she said, hooking her thumb in the direction of the waiting room. "There are two dozen people downstairs. Poor people. Sick people. A lot of them are kids. Put your qualms and quibbles aside and help them. That's all the morality you need. All right, Dr. Jones?"

India didn't reply at first. Then she said, "It's India."

Ella smiled. She put another piece of chicken on her plate before clearing up. "Sneak a few bites between patients if you can. I'll send the next one in."

India never touched the food. She drove herself mercilessly all afternoon and into the evening, seeing children with rattling chests, a docker's wife whose husband had cut off her finger during a fight, laundresses who could barely move because of wrecked backs, girls with scurvy, a prostitute with syphilis, a boy who'd been attacked by a bull terrier, several children with dysentery, two toddlers burned in their hearths, a tubercular baby, and a little boy who'd swallowed a sixpence—and whose mother wanted it back. She was just finishing with her last patient, a factory worker with a swollen liver, when the clock struck the hour—seven p.m.

"I'm giving you a prescription for liver pills," she told the woman. "And I want you to abstain from alcohol."

"How's that?"

"No more drinking. No whisky, porter, ale . . . none of it."

The woman looked at her as if she were mad. "I'd sooner give up breathing."

"You will if your liver gets much worse," India replied.

The woman laughed merrily and took her leave. Not one ounce of self-control, India thought, watching her go. Working-class people astonished her. They had so little, and yet they spent their hard-earned wages on alcohol, sweets, and unnourishing foods they called *relishes*—trotters, bacon, pickles, and such. Like Mrs. Burns, the woman who had the tubercular baby. The little girl had been thin and pale and gumming a brandy snap.

"Your daughter needs wholesome foods like milk and vegetables," India had told her, holding up the colorful illustrations she'd brought.

Mrs. Burns had given her a look. "Aye, missus. I do know what a carrot is."

India colored. She put the pictures away. "Is she getting any milk?" she asked.

"It's not often we've the money for milk," Mrs. Burns said. "And me old man, he's not too fond of greens."

When India pointed out that if there was money for brandy snaps, there must be money for milk, Mrs. Burns said, "Ah, now, missus, the poor little mite likes her sweets, don't she? And as me old gran always said, 'A little of what you fancy does you good.'"

Milk did you better. And spinach and porridge. India tried to tell her patients this, over and over again. She'd watched her professors at the Royal Free Hospital do the same with their patients. Often to no discernible effect.

She sat down now to write up her notes on her last patient, but before she could start, Ella poked her head in to tell her there was one more. "A Miss Emma Milo," she said. "I tried to tell her to come back tomorrow, but she's in a bit of a state."

"What's wrong?"

"She won't say. Said she heard there was a lady doctor here and she has to see her."

"Send her up and then we'll go home."

She returned to her file. A few minutes later, a voice said, "Excuse me, miss?"

India looked up. A red-haired girl, no more than eighteen, stood in the doorway.

"Sit down," she said, gesturing to the chair in front of Gifford's desk. "How can I help you, Miss Milo?"

Miss Milo didn't reply. She was fretting the drawstring on her small silk reticule.

"Miss Milo?"

"I need something . . . something to prevent babies from coming. I've heard there are such things. Devices that doctors have." She looked up at India with eyes that were huge and pleading. "I thought with you being a lady doctor, you might help me." She dropped her eyes. "Please, miss," she whispered. "Please."

"I'm afraid I can't help you," India said regretfully. "This is Dr. Gifford's surgery, and he does not dispense contraceptives. I don't agree with his policy, but my hands are tied. If you are having relations and don't wish to become pregnant, you must stop having them."

The young woman smiled bitterly. "It's that easy, is it?" she said.

"Miss Milo, I—"

"Thank you," she said and then she was out of her chair in a flurry of swirling skirts, and for an instant India saw another young woman hurrying away—not Emma Milo, but Bea Mullins, Hugh's sister. Emma Milo turned back once to look at India, but India didn't see her, she saw only Bea—pale, bloodied, mutely accusing. She willed the vision away. There was nothing she could do. Nothing. Gifford had made his views on contraceptives clear during India's interview. He felt they were immoral devices that encouraged licentious behavior in the lower classes, and he would not prescribe them. India had thought him a dinosaur. She'd wanted to tell him that the greater immorality was the poverty and wretchedness that came from too frequent pregnancies, but she bit her tongue. She'd had to—it was Gifford's job or no job.

It was the first compromise she'd made. She saw now that it would not be the last. She sat back in her chair. Her eyes traveled over the wall opposite the desk, over all of Dr. Gifford's awards and honors. No one at medical school—not Professor Fenwick, not the dean—had warned her of this. How many compromises were too many? Four? Ten? A thousand? Would denying Emma Milo contraceptives make her moral? Was lying to Elizabeth Adams mercy? Or murder?

"Excuse me, Confucius, are you ready to go?" It was Ella.

India blinked, lost in her thoughts. "I am," she said, shuffling her papers together. "I'll finish these at home." She was weary and wanted to get her boots off her swollen feet and eat a bowl of soup. She turned off the lights, made her way downstairs, and was just helping Ella tidy the waiting room when the door opened. It was Dr. Gifford. He was dressed in evening attire.

"How did you fare?" he asked.

"Very well," India said. "We got through the entire roster."

"Well done!" Gifford exclaimed, looking over the patient log. "Fifty-four patients seen. Not bad for a first day, Dr. Jones."

"Thank you, sir."

"I was just checking in. Must dash. Dinner with the bishop. You don't mind locking up?"

India was too tired to turn the key in the lock, but she said she didn't mind a bit. Gifford was bidding herself and Ella good-bye when there was a battering on the door.

"Hold on a mo', will you?" Ella shouted, opening it.

A boy was standing on the step. "Can you come help us? The baby's stuck!" he cried. India groaned. The soup would have to wait. Wondering what kind of bandages she should bring, she asked the boy, "What did the baby get stuck in? A drain? A chimney flue?"

"No, no! It's stuck inside me mum! It won't come out! She's in a bad way, miss, you've got to come!" the boy said.

"You can handle this, can't you?" Gifford said.

"Of course, Dr. Gifford," India said, reaching for her kit bag. She opened it to check her supplies and realized she was low on a few things. "Ella, do we have gauze? And I'm nearly out of chloroform. Have we any?"

Gifford, already on his way out, turned around. "That won't be necessary," he said.

"Beg your pardon, sir?"

"The chloroform won't be necessary," he said. "I do not allow the use of anesthesia on laboring women."

"But Dr. Gifford, there's no threat of danger to the mother. Simpson and Kelly both agree that chloroform does not impede labor, and furthermore—"

Gifford cut her off. "Thank you, Dr. Jones, but I do not require instruction on anesthesia from my junior. I am well aware of chloral's properties. Labor pain is Eve's legacy, and to ameliorate it would be against God's will. Birth pains are good for women. They build character and inhibit indecent feeling."

India looked at the man, aghast. Had she thought him old-fashioned? A bit of a dinosaur? He was downright medieval. A monster from the dark ages.

"Don't let me keep you, Dr. Jones. You have a patient to attend to," he said curtly. "Give her a rag to bite or a piece of cloth to pull. And remind her of our dear Lord's sufferings."

CHAPTER 5

Fiona Bristow sunk her hands into a wooden tea chest, lifted a mound of fragrant leaves to her face, closed her eyes, and inhaled.

All around her, the dockers of Oliver's Wharf stopped what they were doing to watch. Old hands leaned on their tea rakes, well used to this sort of thing from Mrs. Bristow, but the new men stared goggle-eyed, unaccustomed to the sight of a woman in a warehouse. Few women ventured into the docklands. Fewer still made the trip in a silk suit and plumed hat, striding past sailors and stevedores, sidestepping ropes and winches, to inspect a tea ship's cargo. But Mrs. Bristow was no ordinary woman.

"Darjeeling," she finally said, opening her eyes. "A good one."

"No prizes for that," Mel Trumbull, the foreman at Oliver's Wharf, said. "A child could have told me as much."

"Hold on a mo'. I'm not finished yet. It's a single estate . . . ," Fiona said.

"Which one?"

The men nodded and nudged one another; coins changed hands.

Fiona closed her eyes and inhaled again. "Margaret's Hope."

"Harvest?"

She hesitated, then said, "Second flush." She opened her eyes and grinned. "Plucked from a north-facing field on a Wednesday afternoon by a woman in a pink sari."

The men roared laughter.

"All right, all right. Very funny," Mel sputtered.

"Am I right?" Fiona asked.

Mel didn't answer. Instead he grudgingly reached into his trouser pocket, pulled out a sixpence, and tossed it to her. Fiona caught it. A cheer went up.

"Are you lot paid to lark about?" Mel barked. "Back to work!"

"I was right!" Fiona crowed. "I won the wager! I told you I could name any tea in here blind. Any tea at all!"

"Don't be such a gloater, Mrs. B. It's unbecoming." Mel sniffed.

Fiona laughed. "Don't be such a sore loser!" she said, as her workers went back to their tasks. "And do give me two pounds of that Darjeeling. It's wonderful."

"I can't. We can't spare it."

"Why not?"

"The Kensington shop just rang up. They've sold five chests and want four more. Knightsbridge wants three. That leaves me with six. And Buckingham Palace wants eight. Seems the princess is very partial to it."

Fiona frowned, all business now. "I *knew* I should have bought more. Short the Kensington shop and give the palace whatever they want. With our compliments."

"What . . . for *free*?" Mel squawked. "That's four hundred pounds of premium tea! Cost us a small fortune!"

"Yes, but they'll make us a big one, Mel, don't you see? Princess Alexandra hasn't ordered yet. We have a royal warrant from the queen. We've got one from Prince Edward, but not from Alexandra, and we *need* her. She's a fashion plate. She's in every magazine, on all the social pages. Every woman in the country wants to be like her. If she drinks TasTea, they'll drink TasTea, too. Her patronage is the kind of publicity a thousand advertisements can't buy."

Mel looked doubtful. "It's a bit of a gamble, Mrs. B."

"And I'm a bit of a gambler," she said, tossing his sixpence in the air and catching it again. "But you know that."

"All too well," he grumbled.

"Have one of the men take the chests to the palace in the morning. And throw in a chest of our vanilla tea. She might like that, too. Has the Numalighur Assam arrived yet?" she asked, already halfway up the stairs to the second floor. "Have you sampled it? Let's get a chest opened up then. It had better be good. . . ."

Mel ran after her, sweating in the June heat. He was always chasing after her. Everyone was. She was a hard woman to keep up with. At thirty years of age, Fiona Bristow was head of her own company, TasTea—a multimillion-pound tea empire that was begun with a few crates of tea in a small shop in New York and now included TasTea shops and Tea Rose tearooms in all of the world's most fashionable cities.

"This is very good," she said now, examining a handful of rich, dark leaves. "I'm thinking of launching a new label, Mel. Something strong enough and bold enough to appeal to coffee drinkers. This could be the ticket."

The rest of her words were drowned out by a loud and cheery, "Fiona, old trout! There you are!"

She turned and saw a tall blond man striding toward her. "Freddie? Is that you?"

"None other. I looked for you at Mincing Lane. Your girl told me you were here."

"This is a surprise."

"Not at all, just your Member of Parliament at work for you and for East London." He drew an envelope from his breast pocket and handed it to her.

"What is it?" she asked.

"Open it and see."

She did. It contained a bank draft for five hundred pounds made out to the Toynbee Mission Girls' School.

"From the government. House approved my request," Freddie said, smiling. "I'm delivering it to the Reverend Barnett, but I wanted you to see it first."

"Then you weren't just . . ." She paused, unsure how to tactfully say what she wanted to.

"What? Blowing smoke? Talking rubbish? No, I wasn't. I'm very serious about working hard to make things better for my constituents, Fiona. I only hope that my dedication is noted and remembered. . . . I say, what *are* you doing?"

Fiona was turning the paper over and over in her hands. "Looking for strings," she said cheekily.

"You won't find any," Freddie huffed, taking the draft back. "But it *would* be awfully nice of you to put in a good word for me with Joe."

"For five hundred quid, I'll put in two. Thank you, Freddie. I'm very, very grateful to you. Truly."

Freddie nodded. "You might also want to tell him that I'm working on a new Irish Home Rule Bill, with my Irish constituents—and your workers— very much in mind. And I'm working night and day on my anti-crime measures."

"Would you care for a cup of tea?" Fiona asked, hoping to change the subject. "We've plenty here, as you can see. A nice Darjeeling, perhaps?"

"No, thanks. Must dash," Freddie said, barely pausing for breath. "But do tell Joe that I've been meeting officials from Scotland Yard and the Home Office. And we are absolutely getting things done. Funds have been apportioned to pay for extra officers in Tower Hamlets. Five men from the Wapping station nabbed a pair of housebreakers two nights ago and some Whitechapel chaps broke up a counterfeiting ring last week. Sid Malone is next. I'm certain he's a concern both to Joe and yourself, to any merchant who uses the wharves. Malone's gang has struck twice along the river in the past six months alone. But I assure you, I'm getting closer to him every day. I almost had him for the wages robbery, and I nearly got him the other night in Limehouse. Turns out he's got his busy fingers in opium, too. The pressure's on and he knows it. He's a vicious, brutal man and he deserves the harshest punishment. Pity hangings are no longer public. His would be one I'd dearly love to attend."

Terror gripped Fiona. She felt as if she couldn't breathe, but she forced herself to smile. Freddie must not see her emotion.

"Well, I must be off. Do give my regards to Joe," he said.

Fiona said she would and bade him good-bye. Mel, who'd been busying himself with another tea shipment while Fiona and Freddie talked, returned to her side.

"Come have a gander at the Keemun. . . . Mrs. Bristow? Is there something wrong, ma'am? You've gone as white as chalk."

Fiona shook her head. She tried to tell him she was fine, but her knees buckled. She grabbed for the edge of a tea chest, but managed only to slow her fall.

"Bloody hell!" he shouted, catching her just before she hit the floor. He lifted her up and sat her down on the chest.

"Mrs. Bristow? Mrs. Bristow, are you all right?"

Fiona nodded weakly. "Just a little . . . dizzy. Must be the heat . . . and the baby. I'm expecting."

"I'll call for a doctor."

"It's not necessary. I'll be fine. It was just a spell." She mustered a smile, but Mel looked unconvinced.

"Can I fetch you something? A glass of brandy?"

"No brandy, but a cup of tea would be nice."

"Can you walk downstairs?"

"I'd rather sit here for a minute. I don't trust my legs just yet. Would you bring it up?"

"But you shouldn't be alone, Mrs. Bristow. What if you faint again? I'll send a man up to sit with you. . . ."

"No, Mel, really. I want to be alone. Just for a minute or two. To gather myself."

Mel nodded uncertainly, then hurried downstairs to his office where he kept a kettle simmering on top of a small iron stove.

As soon as he was gone, Fiona covered her face with her hands, sick with fear. Freddie Lytton had stood next to her, smiled, and said he was going to kill her brother. He'd said the same things at the garden party for the girls' school. They'd upset her then, too, but after he'd left she'd denied his words, telling herself that he was only grandstanding, as politicians did. She'd pushed the fear from her mind, but it had returned now with a vengeance.

She stood and took a few faltering steps toward the stairs. She had to find Charlie. Right away. She had to warn him before it was too late. "But how?" she whispered, stopping dead. She couldn't send anyone else after him, not after what he'd done to Michael Bennett.

She remembered Bennett's arm, and Freddie's voice echoed in her head. *He's a vicious, brutal man. . . .*

Joe had said the same thing. He'd said Charlie was dangerous, and insisted that she stop looking for him. How could she do that? He was her brother.

Tears suddenly welled in her eyes as she remembered the way Charlie once was. Not brutal, but good and kind. Full of life and laughter. She remembered how he used to play football with their little brother, Seamie, or take him to the riverside to watch the ships. She remembered how he fetched groceries from the corner shop for neighbors too old or ill to get there themselves, refusing to take money from them even though he needed it.

They'd had so little then. Nothing, really. They'd lived in Whitechapel in a draughty two-up, two-down. There was barely enough money to buy food after the rent had been paid. And yet they'd had everything—parents who loved them. Songs and stories by the fire at night. Laughter. Hope. Dreams. Until, almost overnight, it had all been taken away. They'd lost their father. Their mother. Their baby sister. Finally, Charlie disappeared, too. She and Seamie had survived only because of caring people who'd helped them—their uncle Roddy, their uncle Michael in America, her first husband, Nicholas.

But Charlie had had no one to help him then. Only Denny Quinn and his pack of thieves. He had no one now, either. No one to tell him about the danger he faced. If he didn't leave East London, and turn his back on the life he was leading, Freddie Lytton would do for him.

Don't get involved, Joe had told her. Forget him. Bury the past.

She wondered now if Joe had forgotten the lesson they'd both learned—that the past was a restless corpse that never stayed buried. It crawled out of its grave again and again, trailing its bitter stench of sorrow and regret.

Sid Malone was a product of that past—a violent and bloody past—one that had begun in 1888 when a murderer had stalked the streets of Whitechapel. When dockers worked sixteen-hour days for fivepence an hour. When villainous lodging houses spilled forth thieves and prostitutes.

It had all begun when their father died. Paddy Finnegan had had an accident at Burton Tea, where he worked. He'd fallen from a high doorway at the company's wharf. The children had weathered his death, but then their mother was killed—stabbed by a madman called Jack the Ripper—and something had happened to Charlie. He'd come home to find his mother dying in the street and it had unhinged him. He'd run off and no one had been able to find him. A few weeks later a body had been fished from the Thames, so badly decomposed that the authorities had been able to identify it only because of a watch they'd found on it—a family heirloom that Paddy had given to Charlie.

Alone with Seamie, and desperate for money, Fiona had pursued a claim for compensation her mother had made after her father's death. She'd gone to Burton Tea one evening, determined to speak with the owner, William Burton. Instead, she'd overheard him discussing her father's death with a criminal named Bowler Sheehan. Her father hadn't died accidentally, she learned; he'd been murdered by Sheehan at Burton's behest because he'd been trying to convince his fellow workers to join a dockers' union. Discovering this had put Fiona's own life in jeopardy. She'd fled London, vowing that Burton would pay for what he'd done, and she'd kept that vow, returning ten years later to take his tea company from him.

Burton had tried to kill her then, too, but was thwarted. He escaped the police, but they hunted for him. When weeks passed and he wasn't found, it was assumed he'd gone to the Continent, but he hadn't. He'd hidden in his old tea wharf. Eventually, he managed to lure Fiona there and had made a third attempt on her life. The only reason he hadn't succeeded was because of Sid Malone.

Unbeknownst to Fiona, Sid had been watching her ever since her stunning takeover of Burton Tea made the newspapers. His men had followed her to the wharf and had saved her and Joe, spiriting them away to the south bank of the Thames. There they'd learned that Charlie Finnegan had not died back in '88; instead, he'd become Sid Malone.

After Charlie had run away from the sight of his murdered mother, he'd wandered East London half mad, not knowing where or who he was. One night, while digging in a rubbish bin for food, he was attacked by an old enemy, a lad named Sid Malone. Sid beat him viciously, robbed him of his watch, and tried to kill him. Charlie hit back in self-defense, but he hit too hard and fractured Sid's skull. In a panic, he dumped the body into the river, forgetting to take his watch back.

Little by little he'd recovered his mind, eventually remembering who he was and where he lived, but when he went to look for his family, they were gone. Alone, terrified he would be found out for Malone's murder, he went to the only person he could trust—Denny Quinn, a minor underworld figure. Denny had advised him to lay low and to take Sid Malone's name. Malone had been a loner, and with his red hair he'd looked like Charlie. If the police ever grew suspicious and started asking questions, Quinn reasoned, Malone was alive and well and could answer them.

Fiona had been undone by meeting the brother she'd thought was dead. She'd hugged him and wept, overjoyed to see him, but she'd been upset to discover who and what he'd become, and pleaded with him to leave the villain's life behind. Hurt and angered, he'd told her he'd done what he'd needed to do to survive, and had refused to see her again. Her uncle Roddy, a police officer, had looked for him, combing the river's north and south banks, but hadn't been able to find him. "Let him go, Fee," Joe had urged, and she'd reluctantly agreed, deciding never to tell Seamie what had really become of the older brother he'd loved and admired. That he'd become a criminal, vicious and brutal.

"Mrs. Bristow! What are you doing, ma'am? You should be sitting down."

It was Mel. He'd returned with the tea. Fiona hadn't even heard him come up the stairs.

"You still don't look well," he said, placing a steaming mug on top of a tea chest. "I think you should go home. I'm going to fetch your driver now, and I don't want any arguments. Sit there and drink your tea while I get him."

Fiona nodded gratefully. He was right. She should go home. As she sipped her tea, she saw something glinting at her from the floor. It was the sixpence she'd won from Mel. She'd had it in her hand when she came up here, and she must have dropped it when she'd collapsed. She picked it up. Sixpence was nothing to her now, but once it would have meant the difference between eating and starving.

She looked at it, but saw other coins. Pennies, tanners, shillings. Charlie was pulling them from his pocket and putting them on the rickety table in the damp, dingy room where they lived. There was a pound note, too—crumpled and bloodstained—his winnings from a dreadful bare-knuckle brawl he'd fought. "Take it," he'd said. "All of it." She hadn't wanted to, but she did. It had bought milk for the baby. Meat for their supper. Coal for the grate. Boots for Seamie. It had paid their rent.

"Charlie," she whispered brokenly, curling her fingers closed over the coin.

She had needed him then, desperately. They all had. And he had been there for them, giving up his own dreams—dreams of going to America— to take care of them.

Now he needed her.

"And I will be there," she said.

She would search for him herself. He wouldn't listen to strangers—he'd made that clear—but he'd listen to her, she would make him. If only she could get to him.

But how? She had no idea where to even begin searching. She knew he moved about in the East End, but didn't know where he lived. Bennett told her he'd met him at a riverside pub, but he hadn't told her which pub, and Joe had shown him the door before he could. *Joe.* Fiona felt guilt prick her at the thought of her husband. He would be furious if he knew what she was planning to do. She heard his voice in her head, cautioning her. He was only trying to protect her. To keep her safe. He wanted her to let go of the thing she couldn't have, and concentrate on all the things she did have. She was so fortunate, so blessed. She had everything money could buy and everything it couldn't. She was happy, truly happy. And yet, alongside her happiness lived a deep and aching sadness for the one who was missing. The one who never came to Sunday dinners. The uncle whose name the children never shouted. The brother absent from every family photograph.

She *would* do it. She would find him. It was a risk, a gamble, but one she was prepared to take. She would tell no one of her plans, not even Joe. She felt terrible about the deception, but she saw no other choice. Joe was intractable on this issue. He saw her brother as a hard man, a lost cause. But he wasn't, and when she'd found Charlie, when she'd brought him back to them, Joe would see he'd been wrong. He would forgive her for going against his wishes. Charlie didn't belong to the dark underworld of wide boys and villains. He never had. He belonged to her, and she would get him back. Somehow, some way, she would get him back.

"Mrs. Bristow!" Mel bellowed, hurrying back up the stairs. "Carriage is out front! Driver's waiting!"

She got to her feet, still weak, but resolved.

"Are you ready, ma'am?" he asked, huffing and puffing up the stairs to help her.

She nodded. "Yes, Mel," she said. "I am."

Fiona realized she was still clutching the sixpence. She squeezed the coin tightly, then put it in her pocket. She *was* a gambler, and this time she would bet on Charlie.

CHAPTER 6

"Guv!" Frankie Betts yelled. "Guv, we're through!"

Sid Malone motioned for the lantern and shone it on the bricks. There was a hole all right—he could see the pillars that held up the Stronghold's roof through it—but it was only about a foot wide. Nowhere near big enough.

"Ronnie, Oz, take over!" he barked. "Move!"

The sledgehammers changed hands. Ronnie and Oz smashed away while the others, winded and sweating, picked up the shattered brick and loaded it into empty crates. Sid looked at his pocketwatch. Half past twelve. Only one more hour until O'Neill's boat docked. Only two until the tide turned. If they weren't gone by then, they were done for.

"Des, where's the guard?" he asked, his voice on edge.

"Still outside having a gander at the wagons."

"The fat bastard," Sid swore. Earlier that night, he'd had two of his men set fire to an abandoned warehouse a street away. As planned, the blaze had drawn every watchman within a mile to battle it—every one but this one. The man weighed twenty stone if he weighed a pound. It was too much work for him to walk up a street to watch the fire, so he'd settled for watching the fire brigade. He could come back inside any minute, and that would complicate things. At least he couldn't hear the noise they were making. The fire brigades were using the street that ran in front of the wharf for access to the burning warehouse—as Sid had known they would. Their bells and wagons made an unbelievable din.

"Oi! The rozzers!" Desi suddenly shouted.

Sid grabbed Ronnie's shirt and Oz's arm, nearly getting whacked with a sledgehammer.

"What is it?" Oz said, panting.

"Quiet!" Sid hissed. "Desi, what are they doing?"

"Testing the lock."

Sid felt every muscle in his body tighten.

"They've left it. They're talking to our fat little friend. That's it, be good lads now. . . ."

"*Des!*"

"It's all right, guv. They're moving off."

Sid exhaled. With his next breath he grabbed Ozzie's hammer and attacked the wall. Fear drove him. The muscles in his broad, bare chest rippled and flexed with every swing. Sweat ran off his body. The impact of iron against brick sent painful shock waves up his arms, but he barely felt them. It was taking too long. They'd never get out in time. He saw Tom waving wildly at him and stopped swinging.

"Stop, guv, stop! It's enough. We're in."

Sid dropped the hammer. He was through the hole before Tom stopped speaking. Five men followed, with Ozzie dragging the lantern. Desi stayed behind in the London Wharf as sentry. Sid motioned for the lantern now and shone it around the cavernous room. There was nothing but roll upon roll of fabric. Heavy silks and brocades, all wrapped in brown paper. No boxes, no crates.

"Frankie, we didn't come here to make dresses," he said.

"They're in here," Frankie insisted. "I know they are. Me mate said on six. Maybe he got the floor wrong. Let's try five."

The men were as quiet as death on the stairs. When they reached the fifth floor they fanned out, lifting tarpaulins and moving boxes. After a few minutes, Ozzie doubled back. "Nothing, guv," he said.

"Then we'll try four!" Frankie snapped, stalking off to the stairwell.

Sid checked his watch in the lantern's light. Fifteen more minutes gone, and all they'd done was arse about. This was no good. They were cut off from Desi now, too far away to hear if he called for them. He had no idea where the watchman was, or if the police were still near. He would give Frankie another five minutes to find what they were after and then they were out, goods or no.

When he reached the fourth floor Frankie was in the middle of the room, working the lid off a crate with a prybar. The nails screeched as they pulled free, making Sid flinch. Then there was a low laugh and Frankie's voice, "Here, guv! Over here!"

Sid saw the markings, stamped in big block letters, as he approached the boxes: Winchester Repeating Arms Co., Manufactured by Bonehill Gun Works, Birmingham. Frankie took a rifle out of the crate and hefted it admiringly.

"Let's go," Sid said. "Time's running out. We've got to shift the whole lot up two flights of stairs now before we can even begin shifting it down six more. Where are the rest of them?"

Frankie put the gun back and the rest of his men quickly counted fifty-four more crates of rifles and another twenty of revolvers.

"Ronnie, half a dozen Bristols in a sack for us," Sid said, motioning to the revolvers. "The rest go on the boat. Let's move."

Pairing off as planned, each man and his partner hoisted one of the long crates between them and headed for the stairs. Sid heard grunts and curses. The crates contained twenty-five rifles apiece. They were heavy and awkward. He was worried. The weight. The extra stairs. The added time. And where was that fucking watch?

Desi was nearly dancing with agitation when they pushed the first crate through the hole. "Where the hell have you been? I thought you was nicked!" he said. Sid explained. "I don't like it," Desi said. "Too many crates, too many stairs. We'll never make the boat in time."

"We will. Just keep an eye on your man down there."

One by one, the crates were pushed through the hole and into the London Wharf. Sid heard every rattle and bump. The Stronghold's wooden stairs were old and dry, and they creaked with every footfall. The sounds plucked at his nerves like fingers on a harp. Again and again he and his men went back into the Stronghold, Sid glancing at Desi first, Desi giving him a tense thumbs-up. They were on their second-to-last trip, almost done, when Sid heard the voices. Two of them. On the first floor. At the mouth of the staircase. "Freeze!" he hissed. His men stopped dead, the heavy crates suspended between them. Sid was at the bottom of the fifth-floor staircase, completely exposed. If only he had the pistols he'd told Ronnie to put in the sack. They weren't loaded, but the watch wouldn't know that. The sack was now up on the London's sixth floor with Desi. Along with the hammers and prybars. And his shirt and jacket, with his knife in its pocket. He had nothing, not one bloody thing. It was a beginner's mistake. How could he have been so stupid? If the watch came all the way up, if he saw them, he and Frankie would have to drop the crate and run after him. He didn't want that. Didn't want the noise. Or the blood. He hadn't planned it that way.

He'd planned it so that the watch would be distracted. So that no one would find out the guns were missing for days. Maybe weeks. That would give O'Neill time to get to Dublin without interference. He'd be docked on the Liffey, cargo unloaded, drinking Guinness in his favorite pub before the rozzers even twigged.

Involve the watch and things got tricky. You had to knock him out and tie him up. Make sure he didn't see your face. His men would find him the next morning, or his wife would tell the police he hadn't come home. When he was finally untied, he would tell the police what had happened and a hue and cry would go up immediately.

Sid waited and listened, his muscles straining with the effort of keeping the crate aloft. It was all on him, this. It had all been his idea. Desi had tried to talk him out of it.

"Forget it, guv. It's a one-way ticket to the nick," he'd said. "Wharf's got no roof access. Got doors like a fortress. Walls are five feet thick. Why do you think it's called the Stronghold?"

"Same reason the piss-water you serve's called beer—wishful thinking," Sid replied. "The walls *are* five feet, but only at the base. They narrow as you go up. By the time you're on the sixth floor, they're only a foot thick."

"How'd you know that?" Desi asked sulkily, put out by the beer remark.

"Looked at the blueprints," Sid said.

"You never. Where?"

"The Guildhall. Me and Frankie. Wore our Sunday best and told them we was architects. This is how we'll do it. In through the London's riverside doors, up to the sixth floor, then smash through the wall into the Stronghold. Get the goods, cover our tracks, and get out."

"Jesus, guv, you're a bloody genius, you," Oz had said excitedly, as Sid spread out the drawings they'd made. "The Guildhall, architects . . . who'd have thought of it? We pull this off, we'll make ourselves a pile."

And if they didn't, they'd go to prison.

An image flashed into Sid's mind now. A swirl of gray with flecks of black and white. The stone floor at Wormwood Scrubs prison. Granite, he'd thought, in the instant before his head smashed into it. Then nothing, just a blinding white pain as Wiggs kicked his ribs in. Years later, the man's shrill laughter still echoed in Sid's head.

Below him, in the Stronghold, the footsteps kept coming. Up the first flight, across the floor and up the second. He could hear the voices clearly now. One belonged to a woman. They were talking about the fire. The woman wanted to see it from the wharf's windows. Sid could hear her clearly for she was halfway up the stairs to the fourth floor. They would be face-to-face in seconds.

And then the watchman, grunting and groaning, said, "For Christ's sake! How far up do you want to go? You can see it same from here as you can up top."

"You sure? It's part of me price. Like I said, fourpence and a gander."

"Go see for yourself, then. These flippin' stairs are going to be the death of me."

"Are there rats?"

"Aye."

"Oooh, I don't like rats, me."

And then Sid heard boot-heels on the steps as the woman trotted back downstairs.

He heard them move off. He waited, straining to catch a voice, a few words. And then he heard grunts and groans and a few wheezy Oh-oh-oh's. Letting out a quick breath of relief, he turned to give Frankie the nod and saw to his alarm that Frankie was shaking. At first he thought it was the strain of the heavy crate, but then he realized the lad was laughing. He'd sunk his teeth into his bottom lip to keep from making noise. His cheeks were shiny with tears.

"How the hell did she ever find it?" he whispered.

"*Move,* will you?" Sid rasped.

Frankie gave the signal to the men ahead of him, and they were climbing again. He wondered sometimes if Frankie had any nerves anywhere in his body. Guns were not jewelry or silver or paintings. Guns were for killing, and the beaks took a dim view of those who trafficked in them. They'd each get twenty if they were caught, there was a watchman only a floor away, and Frankie was laughing. Sid knew it was because he'd never been inside, never made the acquaintance of men like Wiggs. Most of his men hadn't done heavy bird—only Des. He wanted to keep it that way.

"Jesus Christ, where were you? Takin' a bleedin' holiday?" Desi said when they finally got back inside the London Wharf. "I saw him come in. Tried to get word to you, but you was already down. O'Neill's here. I heard the motor."

"It's all right, Des. We had a bit of bother, but we're here now," Sid said, picking his shirt and jacket up off the floor. "Go down and tell O'Neill we're coming, then come back up for the gear," he added, shrugging into his clothes. As he talked to Desi, two of his men went back into the Stronghold, collected rolls of fabric, and leaned them against the wall in front of the hole they'd made. They squeezed back through and carefully nudged the last few rolls into place from the London's side. Then they shoved the crates they'd filled with broken bricks in front of the hole and piled a few more crates on top of those, to hide the damage.

Sid looked at his watch again and swore. It was nearly two. They should've been out by now. He reckoned they had half an hour at most. Half an hour to get seventy-two crates down six flights of stairs and into the hold of a boat.

"All right, lads, last leg," he said. "Go fast and go quiet. All the way into the hold just like we planned. Don't leave nothing on the dock." The men nodded. Sid saw that Ronnie was drenched in sweat. Oz had taken off his cap to wipe his brow. Pete was bent over, hands on knees, trying to catch his breath. They were played out, and the hard bit was still to come.

The crates were lifted again and the descent began. At least the weight's going down instead of up this time, Sid thought, that's something. As in the Stronghold, the London's wooden steps creaked and popped under their feet. But unlike the Stronghold's watch, the London's wasn't a problem—because there wasn't one.

The London's foreman locked the place up tightly at seven each evening and unlocked it again at six the next morning. He never came by to check the premises during the night. Sid knew that because he'd had Ozzie take a job as a casual hand at the London two months ago. He'd worked there for about six weeks before telling the foreman, Larkin was his name, that he was heading back home to Durham.

During that time, he'd gained the man's trust. By the end of the six weeks, Larkin had Oz locking up. He thought he was safe with only one key. No one could nick the spare when his back was turned and make a copy. He hadn't counted on the bar of soap in Ozzie's pocket. It had taken him only seconds to make an impression. And it had taken a blacksmith friend only a couple of hours to make a duplicate from it. A bargeman had rowed them to the London's dock earlier in the night and Ozzie had let them in. He would let them back out when they were finished. *If* they finished.

When they got down to the first floor, Sid automatically looked for Desi, who was supposed to be stationed by the front door. The fire's glow had illuminated the top floors but it didn't reach the lower ones.

"All right?" he said into the darkness.

"All right," came the reply.

Oz and Ronnie set their crates down and opened the dockside doors. Sid heard the burble of a boat's motor. And then the furious voice of O'Neill, its captain.

"Jaysus, what kept you? I've been waiting here since half one. T'ought you wasn't coming."

"Unforeseen difficulties," Sid said, hurrying by with a crate. "The hold open?"

"No, the feckin' hold's not feckin' open. I was just about to push off."

Sid stopped dead, forcing his men to stop behind him. "You want the guns?"

"Aye, but—"

"Then shut your gob and open the hold. *Now.*"

O'Neill did as he was told. Everyone put his crate down. Oz and Ronnie jumped into the hold. Sid and Frankie handed down the crates. Tom and Dick ran back inside.

"Tide's ebbing. I'll never make open water by daybreak now," O'Neill said. "If I'm caught heading to Ireland with guns . . ."

"That's your problem," Sid said. "Keep the hold open and keep out of me way."

Suddenly they all heard the sound of a second motor.

Sid's guts lurched. "River police. Where the fuck did they come from?" He turned to his men. "Inside. Go!"

O'Neill made a move to follow them.

"Not you," Sid said, planting a hand on his chest. "You're staying here. Tell them you've got engine trouble."

"I'm dead if they see what I've got!" he cried. "What if they search me boat?"

"See that they don't."

The sound of the motor grew louder. Sid sprinted across the dock and through the doors. Frankie closed them and locked them. They all huddled behind them, away from the windows, listening.

They heard the police hail O'Neill and pull up to the dock, lamps blazing. Sid risked a glance out of a small window to the left of the door. O'Neill was rubbing a dirty rag between his hands. "Bit of trouble," he heard him say. "Smoke from the engine. I t'ink I've got her sorted."

"What's your cargo?" one officer asked. A second eyed the vessel. He put his foot on the gunwale. The boat was riding high. Three crates of guns were nowhere near heavy enough to make her draw.

"Sure, she's empty now," O'Neill said. "Had a load of mutton out of Dublin. Turned maggoty on me. Didn't half stink."

The second officer made a face and removed his foot from the gunwale. Good lad, Sid thought.

"Where are you bound?" the first policeman said.

"Butler's. Unloaded yesterday evening. Should've stayed put till daylight, but a lad I was drinking with down the Ramsgate says there's a fellow at Gravesend wants a load of scythe blades taken to Dublin. I'm hoping I can get to him before anyone else."

Without warning, the first constable turned toward the building. Sid ducked down, heart hammering, hoping he hadn't been seen. He pressed his back into the wall. He heard footsteps approach, heard the man test the door handle. Light from a bull's-eye lantern spilled into the window, casting its glow across the floor, over crates and boxes. The light disappeared.

Sid released a breath. A split-second later he jumped as the officer battered on the door.

"Open up!" the man shouted. "Open up in there!"

No one made a move. Sid tried to swallow but had no spit. His heart was thumping in his chest, the blood banging in his ears. The constable pounded again. Sid was just about to give his men the signal to run when they heard the second officer say, "That's the London, isn't it? There's no night watch there."

"You see anything odd while you've been here? Hear anything?" That was the first officer again.

"No, sir," O'Neill said. "I was belowdecks, though, till I heard your boat."

"Finish your business and go. I don't want to see you here on my way back upriver."

Sid closed his eyes and breathed a ragged sigh of relief. He heard the police boat's motor engage, the sound of churning water, and then it was gone.

Frankie opened the doors again, then they all shot back upstairs, fueled by fear. They worked until their lungs were burning and their legs were shaking. It was nearly three o'clock when they got the last crates.

"That's only sixty-nine in all," O'Neill said. He'd been standing on the dock, counting.

"You said there'd be seventy-five. You're six short."

"Three more are coming, that'll make seventy-two," Sid said. "We couldn't get the last three. The Stronghold's watch came in. You want them, get them yourself."

"I'm holding back some of the money, then. Fair's fair."

"You do that. And I'll hold back me men. No guarantees, though. There's six of them and only one of me."

O'Neill spat into the water. He motioned for Sid to follow him and they both disappeared into the pilot house. He unlocked a strong box, took an envelope out of it, and handed it to Sid, who ripped it open and counted the notes. Two thousand quid, as agreed.

"The Irish pay well," he said.

"No price is too high for freedom from English tyranny," O'Neill said. "Ireland will be free. English guns will be used against English despots."

Sid nodded, pocketing the bills, barely hearing him.

"Malone . . . you're Irish, aren't you? With a name like that, you should be giving us the guns, not selling them. You should be working for the cause of freedom."

"The only cause I recognize is me own, mate," Sid said. He told O'Neill it was a pleasure doing business, then left the boat for the dock.

It was then that everything went badly wrong.

As he stepped off the boat, Sid saw Oz and Ronnie running with a crate. Tom and Dick were behind them with another, and behind them was Frankie, carrying the last crate on his shoulder. It was too much for him. He was staggering underneath it. Desi brought up the rear holding the sack of pistols and the tools with one hand, locking the door with the other.

"Go, boss, go! Get on the boat. The watch's coming," Frankie said.

"What? Why—" Sid started to ask. The bloody watch never came during the night. They'd watched the place for three weeks running to make sure.

"The fire. He must've come to check on things. Get on the boat!" he hissed, running past Sid.

"Wait a minute! You lot aren't getting on—" O'Neill began.

Sid dipped a hand into his jacket pocket and suddenly O'Neill was staring at a six-inch blade. "You're taking us to the Bark," he said. All O'Neill could do was nod.

Desi was already on the boat. Oz and Ronnie were stepping over the side.

"Go! Fucking go!" Sid mouthed, motioning at Tom and Dick.

They got on, dragging their crate over the gunwale. Now there was only Frankie. He was only a few feet away. Sid ran to him, hoping to take one end of the crate and hurry him along, but just then Frankie stumbled and pitched forward, slamming the end of the crate into Sid's head. Sid lurched backward, blinded by the impact. He took one step back, then two, windmilling, trying to right himself against the dock. And then there was no dock, only air under his feet. He fell into the water and landed on top of a submerged piling.

The jagged wood ripped him open. He opened his mouth to scream, but it filled with water and no sound came out. He couldn't see, couldn't breathe. He knew he had to surface or drown, but he couldn't move his right arm. Flailing, his lungs bursting, he found the piling with his good hand and used it to pull himself up. As his head broke the surface, he heard his men calling for him as loudly as they dared, panic in their voices. And then he heard something else—the police boat again, distant but approaching. It was on its return trip. They'd taken too long.

"Get a rope! We need a fuckin' rope!" That was Frankie.

Sid could see the edge of the dock and the crate still sitting on it. It couldn't be there when the police arrived or they'd all go down.

"Get him up! Get him up!" Ronnie said.

"Leave me! Get the crate loaded!" Sid ordered.

The engine was getting louder. The boat would break out of the fog any second. Sid had released the piling to motion at Ronnie and was now drifting away from the dock. The water around him was darkening with blood. He went under for a few seconds, then bobbed back up. There wasn't time enough to get him up and he knew it.

"O'Neill, you fucker, where's the fucking rope?" Frankie again. He was too loud. The rozzers would hear him. Sid heard O'Neill push the throttle and was glad of the noise. He motioned at Frankie, who was lying on the dock stretching out his arm toward him, to get on the boat.

"No, guv," Frankie said.

"Go!"

The sound of churning water grew louder. Sid knew he was done for. He was losing too much blood. He'd soon be out of it. And he was glad. Anything, even death, was better than going back to the nick. But his men still had a chance—if only they would take it. He finally saw Oz and Ronnie get on. He saw Frankie look fearfully in the direction of the police boat. He's getting on, thank Christ, Sid thought. But he didn't. Instead he lowered himself off the dock and into the river.

"I told you to get on the boat!" Sid hissed at him.

"Is *that* what you said, guv?" Frankie said. He slung an arm across Sid's chest and dragged him under the dock just as the police boat pulled up to it. He found a length of half-rotted rope hanging from a piling and grabbed it to keep them from drifting.

"Dodgy piston, it was! Just shoving off!" O'Neill yelled, pushing the throttle harder. He was churning the water on purpose.

"Bastard's tryin' to kill us," Frankie growled, bracing against the wake.

Sid knew he wasn't. He was distracting the cops with the noise so they didn't notice that his boat was drawing more water than she had an hour ago.

"'Night, officers!" O'Neill called, and then Sid heard his boat pull away. Finally. His men were safe.

"You hang on, guv," Frankie whispered. "They'll be at the Bark and back before you know it. O'Neill will make that tub fly. Oz'll gut him if he don't."

Sid nodded. His eyes fluttered closed. He heard footsteps on the dock and then Larkin, the watch, asking the police what happened, telling them he'd heard their noise from inside.

"Bloke with a dodgy motor," one of the constables said. "Everything all right?"

"Right as rain," the watch said.

"You sure? No signs of a break-in? Nothing missing?"

"Not a thing. She's locked up tighter than a cat's arsehole," the watch said.

He bade the officers good night and went back inside. The police boat pulled away and Sid and Frankie were left alone floating in the Thames.

Sid's pain was excruciating, so strong that he knew it would drown him before the water ever did. He was lightheaded now and cold. Very cold. It wouldn't be much longer.

"Frankie . . . ," he whispered.

"Aye, guv?"

"I want you to know . . ."

"That you've always loved me?"

Sid laughed. He couldn't help it. There were no more worries now. No more sorrows. Everything seemed funny. He'd always thought it would be good to go out laughing. ". . . the dosh . . . it's in my jacket pocket. Split it even. Give Gem my share."

"Give it to her yourself. Tomorrow when you see her."

Frankie's voice got farther and farther away until Sid could hear it no longer. And then there was no pain, no cold, nothing. Just the black night, the black water, and the black abyss of unconsciousness.

CHAPTER 7

"Condoms?"

"Never."

"Dutch caps?"

"Forget it."

"Sponges, then," India said, stopping dead in the middle of Brick Lane.

"I guess you really do want to get sacked," Ella said. "If Gifford twigs, you will be."

"He doesn't have to find out. We could dispense them quietly."

"Even if we can get the patients to keep shtum, who's going to pay for them?"

India frowned. "I hadn't thought of that."

"And where are you going to get them? The medical suppliers have them, but they know Gifford and he knows them. If his junior places an order for a case of rubber johnnies, you can be sure he'll be told." Ella pulled India out of the way of an oncoming milk wagon. "Come on. The caff's this way."

"I can't believe he's so medieval," India said. "How can he object to chloroform? To deny a laboring woman relief in this day and age . . . it's nothing short of barbaric. Did you hear what he said as we left?"

"I did. I've heard that particular speech a thousand times. I've attended him at the most awful births and I've seen him read—even eat a meal—while his patients were in agony. I've wanted to run away, right out of their homes, but I didn't. I knew I was all they had. I could rub their feet. Let them grip me hands. If I'd have left, they'd have had no one. Just him. Looking at his watch and frowning and telling the poor miserable things to bear up. Spouting Genesis at them: *'In sorrow thou shalt bring forth children'*—the pompous ass. Telling them to think of Jesus. *Jesus?*" She laughed bitterly. "I don't know much about your Jesus, but I do know he was a man and he never had himself a baby."

"Before I took the job, people told me Gifford was a saint. For using money from his Harley Street practice to minister to the poor at Varden Street."

"Oh, please. I do the books for both surgeries. He makes more off his Whitechapel practice than he does at Harley Street. Cramming in fifty or sixty patients a day, and spending all of ten minutes with them . . . well, you add it up."

"I can't continue to work for him. I can't," India said.

"Don't start that again," Ella warned. "You're needed in Whitechapel."

The two women crossed the street in front of a synagogue. India heard prayers coming from within and realized they were in the heart of Jewish Whitechapel, an enclave of streets and courts clustered north and south of Whitechapel High Street, bounded by Aldgate to the west and the Jews' Burial Ground to the east.

It was early, not six a.m. yet, but the streets were already bustling with people. Tailors carried heavy piles of piece goods on their shoulders. Cabinetmakers lugged canvas bags containing planes and chisels. Bakers' boys balanced baskets of black bread on their shoulders. Inside the doorway of a narrow slaughteryard, a *shochet* sharpened his knife.

Wagons with Hebraic writing on their sides stopped to deliver produce or coal. Notices pasted on billboards announced a speech by Prince Kropotkin, the celebrated Russian anarchist, a meeting of Polish socialists, and the services of a matchmaker.

And the languages. India had never heard so many different tongues on one London street. A woman called out to Ella from her stoop. Ella answered her.

"Was that Russian?" India asked.

"Yes, my family's from St. Petersburg." Another woman waved. Ella greeted her in a different-sounding tongue. "That was Polish," she said. "I speak a bit of it. You'll also hear Romanian, Dutch, German, and Litvak here. Some Bessarabian. Ukrainian, too. Everyone comes from somewhere else. Most of the children speak English. Some of the parents. None of the grandparents."

"My goodness! How does anyone understand anyone else?"

"Yiddish."

India was puzzled. "In which countries is Yiddish spoken?"

"All of them."

"How can that be? How can *everyone* understand it? Where does it come from?"

Ella laughed. "Yiddish? It comes from the heart," she said. She stopped in front of a humble brick building. "Here we are at the caff. Let's eat. I'm famished."

India noted the gleaming windows, the freshly painted sign. MOSKOWITZ'S RESTAURANT, it read. WHOLESOME KOSHER FOOD. The tiny establishment was packed. Workmen and factory girls sat elbow to elbow. Housewives lined up three deep at the counter, buying beigels for their family's breakfast. Bearded elders sat around a samovar, sipping cups of strong, sweet tea, gnarled hands curled around walking sticks. Here and there new immigrants sat nibbling rolls, wide-eyed and uncertain, the women as bright as parrots in their flowered shawls.

Ella found two seats at a table, then went off in search of her mother. India sat down, tucking her doctor's bag underneath her. A pot of tea arrived. She poured herself a cup, drank it black, then closed her eyes. She felt she could sleep sitting up.

Neither she nor Ella had slept all night. The birth they'd been called to, in Dolan's Rents, a row of rundown houses on Dorset Street, one of Whitechapel's worst, had been a difficult one. The woman—a Mrs. Stokes—had been in labor for over twenty hours with little progress, and both mother and infant were in distress by the time they'd arrived. They'd found Mrs. Stokes whimpering between contractions and screaming during them. India had quickly taken off her jacket, tied an apron over her clothing, and rolled up her sleeves while Ella unpacked her instruments.

Mrs. Stokes's husband was nowhere to be found. Her three young children were cowering in the corner. "Have you any hot water?" India asked them. The eldest nodded and pointed to a kettle on the hob. "Pour it into a basin, please, and get me some soap," she instructed. When her hands were scrubbed, she began the examination.

"I sent for a doctor," Mrs. Stokes rasped. "No midwife. Midwife almost killed me last time."

"I *am* a doctor, Mrs. Stokes," India said. She began the examination, coaxing the woman to bring her feet together and drop her knees. Speaking to her in low, soothing tones, she placed one hand on her stomach, and pushed the other inside her, feeling for her cervix and the baby. "An inch and a half. Occiput posterior," she told Ella. She listened for the baby's heartbeat, then said, "Random fluctuations. Possible cord compression. Contracted pelvis."

Ella nodded, understanding the verbal shorthand. Mrs. Stokes was nowhere near fully dilated. The baby was trying to come out face up. The back of its skull was pressing against its mother's spine, making an already painful process worse. Its heartbeat was abnormal, possibly because its umbilical cord was constricted. In addition, Mrs. Stokes's pelvis was deformed. India had expected it. Poor women usually suffered from rickets, a disease of malnutrition. Rickets caused malformed bones, which in turn led to horribly obstructed labors.

By the time India finished her exam, Ella had readied a forceps, clamps, scissors, gauze, needles, a spool of suturing silk, carbolic, and chloral. She then reached into India's bag for one last instrument—a cephalotribe.

India looked at it and shook her head. It was a forceps-like instrument, and was used only when there was no hope for the baby and no other way to save the mother. Its wide, powerful blades were designed to collapse an infant's skull so that the dead child could be pulled from its mother's body. India had one in her kit—there was no choice—but she despised the sight of it. Butchers used them. Butchers, drunks, and incompetents.

"Put it back," she said. "I haven't used one yet. I won't tonight."

"Are you sure? Dr. Gifford always wants one prepared."

"Dr. Gifford's not here. I am."

Although Gifford had not allowed them to take any chloroform with them, India had had a little in her own kit. It wasn't much, but it might beat back the pain enough to allow the mother to stop screaming and start breathing, and allow her contractions to pick up, her cervix to stretch and efface, and her ligaments and stunted bones to shift, just slightly, just enough to give India the space she needed to ease the baby out.

Ella dampened a cloth with the chloral sparingly, as if it were liquid gold, and held it over Mrs. Stokes's nose and mouth. The suffering woman clutched at her wrist, weeping with relief, and India silently cursed Gifford.

When the drug had taken effect and Mrs. Stokes was calmer, India and Ella sat her up on the edge of her bed. India had heard good, experienced midwives tell how sitting upright, leaning against a wall, or walking around the room often helped bring a baby faster. India had sought these women out during her student years. They'd taught her about the benefits of massage, the efficacy of herbs, and how important it was not to hush a laboring woman, but to let her howl, for it would open her up.

For hours, all throughout the long night, India and Ella worked in concert. They walked with Mrs. Stokes when she could manage it, and let her lie down and weep when she could not. They rubbed her temples, arms, and legs; applied hot compresses; fed her teas of pennyroyal and ginger; gave her castor oil; and sparingly doled out the chloral.

The hours dragged on. Mrs. Stokes dozed briefly. India and Ella grew tired themselves, and hungry, and Ella remembered she had their leftover dinner with her. She unwrapped it, and India was glad of some sustenance—until she heard a whimper and looked across the room, where the children had been dozing, and saw the youngest staring at the food hungrily. She and Ella looked at each other, and then Ella took the leftovers to them.

"Is my mummy going to die?" the youngest asked when she'd finished. "I'd be afraid if she did. My dad hits us. My mummy tries to stop him. He says we're ugly little bastards and not his. Am I, miss? An ugly little bastard?"

India was speechless for a few seconds, then she said, "No, my sweetheart. You are beautiful. Very beautiful. And do you know what?"

"What?"

"There's a wonderful story about a little creature whom everyone called ugly. They called him names and he was very sad, but then something wonderful happened to him. It was my favorite story when I was your age. Shall I tell it to you?"

"Yes, please!"

India pulled the little girl onto her lap and told her the story of the ugly duckling. And when she got to the part where the duckling learned that he was a swan, and beautiful, the little girl's eyes were shining.

India loved that story, for she had been that duckling. At five, when she had run across the lawn to show her father a robin's nest she'd found, and he called it a dirty thing and slapped it out of her hands. At ten, when she got her first pair of spectacles and Maud called them ghastly. At sixteen, when her mother told her she would never be pretty, so she would have to be charming. There were so few times, so few places, she had ever felt a swan. In the nursery with Hodgie, her nanny, who told her stories by the fire. With Hugh, who'd held her in the dark and told her she was beautiful. And in London. At medical school.

The little girl kissed India's cheek and thanked her. Sleepily, she said, "I wonder what that feels like." India carried her over to the pile of old coats, sacking, and rags that served as the children's bed and laid her down.

"What what feels like?"

"Being a swan."

India didn't know how to answer. She tried to frame a reply, but before she could get any words out, the little girl had fallen asleep. She gazed down at her, her heart aching, wanting to tell her and not knowing how.

"India, she's ready to push," Ella said.

Mrs. Stokes was back on the bed now, panting and straining.

"Good," India said. She left the children, and bunched up an old blanket, a tattered sheet, and her own duster—there were no pillows—and placed them behind their mother's back.

"I want you to curl forward, Mrs. Stokes. Round your back, there you go. Now tuck your chin into your chest and grab your thighs."

Mrs. Stokes shook her head. "I can't do it," she sobbed. "Not again. I just can't. The last one tore me so."

India had seen the scars. "We won't let this one. We'll go slow and you'll be all right." Mrs. Stokes's eyes searched hers and India saw she didn't believe her. "Trust me. And help me. When I say go, give it all you've got. To the count of ten, then rest. All right?"

Mrs. Stokes nodded. "Good. Deep breath, and . . . push!"

For nearly two hours Mrs. Stokes pushed, with India and Ella holding her legs and cheering her on. She panted and cried and heaved, and between each contraction she swore she could not push even one more time, but then Ella would wipe her face and India would coax and the urgency would come on her again and she would.

Finally, at 4:30 in the morning, the baby's head crowned. "Easy now. Take a breath, Mrs. Stokes. That's it. Stop pushing for just a second . . . hold on . . . almost there . . ." India said, carefully easing the baby along. And then its head was out and Mrs. Stokes fell back against the bed and laughed out loud with the relief of it.

But India did not join her. She had seen the cord wrapped around the baby's neck and the bluish tinge of its skin. "Clamp it, Ella," she barked.

Ella swiftly clamped the pulsing cord in two places. India cut between the clamps, then pulled the cord away. She tugged the baby—a boy—all the way out. He was motionless.

"Come on now, old chap," she whispered, laying him on the bed. She swept his mouth clean with her finger and suctioned his nose. When he didn't respond, she picked him up, supporting his back with her left hand, holding his legs with her right, then gently arched his spine, pushing his chest up and out, allowing the abdominal organs to drag the diaphragm downward and suck air in. Then she carefully bent his tiny body the other way, bringing his knees to his face to force the air out. He wanted to go back, but she wouldn't let him. He was hers. All through the long, tortured night she'd coaxed him here, and she wasn't about to let go of him now. Two more flexes and compressions. Nothing. Another three, and then miraculously he twitched and mewled, and the mewl became a cry and India heard his mother let out a great sob and she knew she had them both, mother and baby—breathless, bruised, and battered—but here. In this world. Alive.

This is what it feels like, she thought, smiling, as she wrapped a cloth around the baby and held him close, just for an instant. She glanced over at the children. They were still asleep. She wished the little girl was awake. She would hand her her brother and tell her *this* was what it felt like to be a swan. . . .

"Wakey, wakey."

India opened her eyes. Ella was back with a plate of toast and a pot of jam. She sat down across from her. "What a bleedin' night. And you know we're going to be back there in nine months' time, don't you?"

"If we are, it'll be with a coroner," India said grimly, remembering what she'd told the woman before they'd left: "Mrs. Stokes, you cannot bear another child. You must stop having relations with your husband."

"How am I to do that?" Mrs. Stokes had asked, bewildered.

"You'll have to tell him no," India had replied.

Mrs. Stokes had looked at her in disbelief. "Missus," she said, "have you ever tried to tell a fifteen-stone bricklayer no?"

Ella had cut in then. She'd told Mrs. Stokes to use a hollowed-out lemon half or a small sponge soaked in vinegar. Mrs. Stokes said she'd tried both of those and a fat lot of good they did. She still ended up pregnant. India told her she could get a cap from certain chemists. Mrs. Stokes had shaken her head. "You're not from these parts, are you?" she asked. "I can find the sort of chemists you mean, but I can't pay them. Nobody can. The bloody things cost two shillings and thruppence apiece."

India had looked at the poor woman, half-dead. At the baby hungrily seeking milk its mother could barely produce. She had looked at her wide-eyed kids and she'd known she would have to find a way to help her. But how?

"We have to do something for her, Ella," she said now, pouring herself more tea. "We have to."

"I know, but what?"

India sipped her tea then said, "Dispense birth control."

"I told you earlier, that's a very dangerous idea."

"I got it from you."

"Me?!"

"Yes, you. Remember what you said yesterday . . . regarding morality and helping suffering people?"

Ella shook her head. "Don't pay attention to what I say. I talk too much."

"Your words stayed with me. They made me think."

"Uh-oh."

"About Mrs. Stokes and others like her. About the things I saw in medical school. Infants smothered by broken-down mothers driven mad from their crying. A pregnant, unmarried teenager beaten to death by her father. Women damaged beyond repair by too many pregnancies."

"Blimey, luv. You're a right ray of sunshine this morning, you."

"We have to *do* something, Ella. We have to make a start."

"Can I eat me breakfast before we save the world?"

"I'm very serious."

"Come on, India. What can we do, the two of us? Nothing."

"Something."

"What?"

"Provide free medical care to the women and children of Whitechapel."

Ella, who'd taken a bite of toast, nearly choked on it. "Is that all? And here I thought it might be complicated."

India fixed Ella with her intense gray eyes. She'd known her only twenty-four hours, but already she felt close to her. Maybe it was the kindness she saw in Ella's eyes, so dark and warm, so different from her own. Maybe it was having brought a new life into the world together. Maybe it was sheer exhaustion, but for some reason India felt she could tell her anything.

"I want to open a clinic someday, Ella. For the poor. To minister to the ill, but to do more, so much more. The best medicine is preventive, you know, not curative. If we can get to children while they're very young—before they're born, even—we can break the cycle. We have to start in the womb. Give pregnant women and babies good care, educate new mothers on nutrition and hygiene. Help them limit the size of their families . . ."

India was so busy talking, she hadn't noticed that Ella had stopped eating. She hadn't seen her pull a small book from her bag. She saw it now, though, as Ella pushed it across the table. *Introductory Notes on Lying-in Institutions,* by Florence Nightingale.

"I know this book by heart!" India cried, her eyes lighting up. "I particularly support Miss Nightingale's belief that each woman on the lying-in ward should have two thousand three hundred cubic feet of space, plus a window."

"I lie awake at night dreaming about being matron in a place like she describes—a clean, modern lying-in hospital with brand-new plumbing," Ella said.

"With good sanitation, proper ventilation, and sterile linen," India added.

"Wholesome food, fresh milk."

"A body of health-care visitors. Trained nurses whose job it is to go into the community to check up on mothers and babies after they've been discharged."

"An entire ward just for women's diseases. And another one for children's."

"A modern operating theater employing Lister's rules for aseptic environments."

Ella sat back in her chair. "Crikey, an operating theater. Now, *that's* ambitious."

"Maybe it is," India conceded. "Maybe we'd have to wait a bit on that one. It would have to be a small clinic to start, wouldn't it?"

"Even a small one would cost a pile," Ella said. "Have you got anything?"

"Yes. I've started a fund."

Ella arched an eyebrow. "How much have you got?" she said.

"Fifty pounds in prize money. From my graduation."

Ella's face fell. "That's all? We couldn't open a fruit stall with that."

"I'm going to add to it. I'm saving my wages."

"You haven't earned any yet!"

"I will. I'm going to do it, Ella. I'm going to make a difference."

Ella rolled her eyes, but before she could say anything else her mother came bustling over with two plates of fried eggs, hashed potatoes, and stewed apples. She set them down with a bang, took her daughter's face in her hands, and kissed her forehead.

It was a gesture so full of emotion, one could be forgiven for thinking mother and daughter had been separated for the past ten years. But watching her, India sensed that Mrs. Moskowitz kissed her daughter like this every day. She shyly looked away. She couldn't remember ever being kissed like that by either of her parents, though she did recall being allowed to kiss her mother's cheek when she was tiny—if she promised beforehand not to rumple her gown.

Mrs. Moskowitz sat down. Ella introduced her to India. She looked at her, then back at Ella, then said, "Why such long faces?"

Ella told her about their shared dream of a clinic, but that it was only that—a dream.

Her mother clucked her tongue. "Instead of moping, you must make a start. If only a small one. God helps those—" she said.

"*Oh, Mamaleh!*"

"Who help themselves," she finished, wagging a finger. "And don't *Oh Mamaleh* me, Ella. You know I'm right. Mr. Moskowitz!" she yelled, waving at her husband. "You're going to the cellar? Bring me up some eggs, please!"

Her husband, who was embroiled in a conversation at the samovar with a group of men and most definitely not on his way to the cellar, looked up at her and blinked.

"Three dozen."

Mr. Moskowitz sighed and got to his feet.

Mrs. Moskowitz turned and looked behind her. Her eyes narrowed at the sight of two young men seated at another table. "Yanki, Aaron—why are you here?"

"Do you ask that in the philosophical sense, Mama?"

"Don't be so fresh, Mr. Yeshiva Student Who Still Needs His Mama to Tie His Shoes. Finish and go or you'll be late. Aaron, come here. When did you last wash? You could grow potatoes in those ears."

"Mama!"

"Go and wash!" She turned back to India and Ella. "Small children give you headache; big ones heartache. Do you have any little ones, Dr. Jones?" she asked, eyeing India's left hand.

"It's India, please. And no, Mrs. Moskowitz, I haven't. I'm not married."

"Ach, I don't understand girls these days. Tell me, why do you and my daughter do this awful doctoring work instead of marrying? How will either of you ever find a husband? Look at yourselves! Pale, tired, shadows under the eyes. What man would want to wake to such a face? Would a little jewelry, maybe a little scent, go so wrong?" She reached over and pinched India's cheeks to redden them. "*Eine shayna maidel,*" she said, smiling, then frowned again. "But you should do your hair differently."

"Mama, *genug!*" Ella said.

A delivery boy came in. Mrs. Moskowitz sprang up, berated him for taking so long to return, then took her position by the cash register.

"I'm sorry, India. My mother lives to meddle."

India laughed. "I think she's lovely. And she's right."

"About what? Your hair?"

"That, too. But I meant about making a start. If only a small one."

"What do you have in mind?"

"We can begin by helping Mrs. Stokes. We'll make some inquiries about obtaining reliable, affordable birth control for her and other women like her. There *has* to be a chemist, a doctor, an affordable source *somewhere*. We'll find it and tell her."

"We'll have to be bloody careful."

India nodded. Contraceptives were not illegal, and discreet prescriptions were a matter of course for middle- and upper-class women, but many in the public sphere—clergymen, politicians, members of the press—considered them immoral and angrily denounced those who advocated them. She knew that people had been vilified, sent to prison, even had their children taken from them, merely for publishing pamphlets on birth control.

"We *will* be careful."

"All right, then, Dr. Jones," Ella said gamely. "Today, we fix Mrs. Stokes. Tomorrow, we build a shiny, new, fully equipped clinic for the women of Whitechapel."

"It's a deal," India said.

The two women clinked their teacups and tucked into their food. Ella told India to eat every last bite, for she would need it. Dr. Gifford's appointment book was even more crammed today than it was yesterday. Then she reminded her that she was expected to take rounds at the hospital in the evening, too.

India wondered how she was going to get through the morning, never mind the whole day. She looked at Ella and saw that she was weary, too. They would get through the day together. She smiled, happy in the knowledge that she had made a friend.

Not a difference—not yet—but a friend.

CHAPTER 8

Freddie Lytton turned heads wherever he went. As he loped across Mayfair's stately Berkeley Square in the rain, females from fifteen to fifty stared after him, their eyes drawn by the thick shock of golden hair, the chiseled jaw, the languid amber eyes. Long, lean, and loose-limbed, he epitomized an effortless patrician elegance. And though he affected not to notice, he registered every feminine glance. Glances indicated interest, and interest proved useful. In ballrooms and bedrooms and at the ballot box. Women couldn't vote, thank God; but they often influenced their husbands, who could.

He dodged a carriage, skirted a pram, then bounded up the steps to number 45, an enormous Adam townhouse. He was greeted by a butler and escorted past opulent rooms containing extraordinary antiques. All of them had come from Lady Isabelle's side, he knew, none from her husband's. Lord Burnleigh was a nobody, a Welsh coal baron who just happened to have more money than God. Isabelle was an Audley, and could trace her bloodline back to the de Clares and William the Conqueror.

Freddie could trace his line back almost as far, which earned him high marks in Isabelle's book. Richard Lytton, the first Earl of Bingham, had been ennobled under Edward I at the end of the thirteenth century. He had conquered Wales for his king, then he'd led his armies north to put down William Wallace, attacking at Falkirk with a staggering brutality. Wallace named him the Red Earl, and said there wasn't enough water in all the oceans of the world to wash the blood off his hands. A portrait of him had hung in the gallery at Longmarsh. Blond, amber-eyed, handsome, the Red Earl looked exactly like Freddie's late father. Exactly like Freddie himself. The painting hung in Freddie's own flat now. His mother had insisted he take it. She hated the sight of it.

As he passed Isabelle's dining room, Freddie's eyes swept covetously over a Holbein portrait, a Chippendale table, a pair of Tang Dynasty urns. What a magnificent collection, what a stellar house, and what an incalculable boon both would be to a young MP. His own family boasted few such possessions; most had been sold to pay the bills. As for houses, there was a squat brick monster in Carlton Terrace and there was Longmarsh, the family seat, a decrepit estate in the Cotswolds. Both of them belonged to his brother.

At the thought of Bingham, the benign smile on Freddie's handsome face slipped, and like a base metal showing under thin plating, something darker emerged. He thought, with bitterness, of how tired he was of standing in other men's shadows. By the time he reached Isabelle's drawing room, however, the smile was back in place.

"The Honorable Sir Frederick Lytton, my lady," the butler announced, ushering him inside.

"Freddie, my dear."

His future mother-in-law was sitting by the fireplace, looking formidable in pearls and gray silk faille. The icy color matched her eyes. Other London hostesses had long ago put off formal dresses in the afternoon for more comfortable tea gowns. Not Isabelle. She was born wearing stays, Freddie thought, and would die in them. She sat ramrod straight. Looking at her, he realized that not once in all the years he'd known her had he seen her back touch the upholstery.

"Isabelle," he said, bending to kiss her hand. He straightened and smiled.

"What a pleasure it is to see you, Freddie. How gracious you are to take time from your political duties to visit me."

As if I had a choice, he thought grimly.

Her summons to tea had arrived in the morning post. Although politely worded, it was a command. He guessed she'd heard that India had graduated and was practicing medicine. And if that letter hadn't made his morning ghastly enough, another had arrived with it—sent by the lovely Gemma Dean, telling him they were finished. She was angry at him for standing her up. He'd planned to spend the weekend with her. He'd even plumped for a present—a watch that he'd ended up giving to India. He'd nearly been out the door and on his way to forty-eight hours of bedded bliss when that idiot of a Wish had appeared, ruining everything. He'd had no choice but to go with him to India's graduation, pretending that's where he'd been headed all along. Gemma's letter had been full of recriminations. She wanted to marry him and was angry that he didn't want to marry her. The very idea. A Lytton marrying a girl from East London. It would be like pairing the Darley Arabian with a carthorse. She'd found someone else, she'd written. Someone who *would* marry her.

"How is political life treating you, Freddie? Has Salisbury forgiven you your trespasses?" Isabelle asked.

She was making small talk. She'd sent for refreshments, and Freddie knew the civil tone would last only as long as it took for the maid to bring them.

"He speaks to me again," Freddie said. "I suppose that's something."

"I wouldn't. It was a dreadful thing to do. Downright traitorous."

"It was a bid for survival, Isabelle. Mine. Yours. The entire ruling class's. I had no choice."

Two years ago, shortly after winning the Tower Hamlets seat, Freddie had stunned the political world by deserting the Conservative Party for the Liberals. Publicly he'd ascribed the move to a desire to see government do more for the poor. In truth, his defection had nothing to do with politics, but everything to do with a cause—his own. A shrewd political animal, Freddie had scented the wind and determined which way advantage lay. The Liberals would soon lead England—and he would lead them.

"I fail to see how turning your back on your own party, on the prime minister himself, insures one's survival, my dear."

"Salisbury won't be prime minister for much longer. He's been at the helm since 'eighty-five. Nearly sixteen years. The Liberals challenged him repeatedly during that time, and twice they won."

Isabelle waved her hand dismissively. "They barely managed to hold the premiership when they had it. A year here, two there."

"Yes, in 'eighty-six and 'ninety-two, but Salisbury was stronger then. The old boy's tiring. He's a creature from another age. He was ready to step down a year ago and would have, were it not for the Boer War. As soon as we have a victory, he'll go."

"And his nephew will take his place. Another *Tory,* Freddie."

"Arthur Balfour won't last long. The writing's on the wall. The Tories are finished. Times are changing. The country is changing. New voices are making themselves heard. Radicals, socialists, suffragists . . ."

"Dreadful people, all of them. I wish they would just go away."

"I quite agree, but they won't. And no matter what they call themselves, they all want the same thing—a new order. The Tories are not listening; the Liberals are. They understand that it's time for the ruling class to share some small bit of power."

"And you believe that's right, Freddie?" Isabelle asked waspishly. "You believe that the man who delivers my milk and the man who sweeps my chimneys—men who can barely *speak* proper English, never mind read it or write it—should rule England? These men rather than men who have been born into great political families, who have been educated and groomed for a life in government? Are you going to tell me that is right?"

"I'm afraid it has nothing to do with what is wrong or right, and everything to do with what is necessary," Freddie said. "Look at what's happening on the Continent—the strikes and marches. The anarchists with their bombs and assassinations. They wish to abolish property. To destroy the social order. That cannot happen here. We must prevent it. We must give the workers crumbs, and quickly, before they rise up and take the entire cake."

Isabelle turned her gaze to the window. She was visibly distressed. "The white lilac needs pruning," she said at length. "It's grown far too shaggy."

Discussion over, Freddie thought. Isabelle was typical of her generation. What they didn't see—or didn't wish to see—didn't exist. Ireland's agitation for Home Rule, the war in South Africa, restive trade unions—to Freddie these troubles were all ominously related, all signs of a gathering storm that might well shake the foundations of Empire. To Isabelle, they were mere nuisances to be solved either by the colonial service or the local constabulary.

While she talked on about her gardens, a clap of thunder sounded. Freddie glanced at the window. Rain pattered against the mullioned panes. Summer clouds were passing over. For a moment he saw another window, heard another voice. He was a child again, in his grandmother's bedroom at Longmarsh. She was winding her music box. It was Chopin. The "Raindrop Prelude." She was playing it to drown out the sound of his father, drunk again, and raging. Bing and Daphne were lying on her bed, crying. His mother was sitting on the window seat. Her arm was broken.

Bing had left his bicycle on the lawn again. Their father had found it there, wet from rain. He'd come after Bing, a brass poker in his hand, intending to beat him with it for being careless. Their mother had gotten between them, so he'd gone for her instead.

He stopped when she was insensible, then staggered off to his study to find more drink. Freddie's grandmother had come in from the garden just then. She rushed the family to her bedroom and locked the door behind them.

"You must *act*, Caroline," she'd said, wiping the blood from his mother's face. "You must leave him. Now. He could have killed you."

"I've tried. You know I have. He threatens to divorce me. He says the courts will give him the children and I shall never see them again. Who will protect them if I leave?"

His grandmother had walked to her dressing table to hunt for some salve. On the way her gaze had fallen upon Freddie, who was not crying like his brother and sister, but watching and listening.

"Lie down, boy," she said. "Go to sleep."

"What shall we do, Grandmother?" he asked.

"I don't know. I dearly wish I did. We are two women and three children and quite powerless against him."

Freddie did not wish to be powerless. Though he was only ten at the time, he told her that he would be powerful. "I promise, Grandmother," he'd solemnly said.

He had kept that promise. He would always keep that promise.

"But then again, Freddie," Isabelle said now, calling him back from the past, "what is the point of hiring Gertrude Jekyll to do the herbaceous borders when the house is largely unused?"

She was still talking about her garden. The maid arrived with a tray of finger sandwiches and cakes, and a pot of tea. Freddie knew another discussion was about to begin—on a topic far less appealing than herbaceous borders. He braced himself for the maid's departure. The drawing-room doors clicked shut. They were alone.

"It didn't used to be so. This house used to be full of life. There were parties and dinners and dances. We spent the entire London season here. My daughters made their debuts here. Do you remember?"

"Indeed I do."

"Indeed you do," Isabelle echoed, fixing him with eyes gone glacial. "Tell me, what is India doing these days?"

Freddie decided against any sugar-coating. "She graduated from medical school a week ago, and is working for Dr. Edwin Gifford at his Whitechapel practice."

Isabelle swallowed hard. When she spoke again, her voice shook with anger. "I blame you for this. How *could* you have allowed it? You should have married her by now. As her husband, you could have forbidden it."

Freddie's temper sparked, but he kept it under control. "It isn't my fault," he said. "She refused to even think about setting a date until she'd finished her studies. You know how stubborn she is."

"But Freddie, you must *do* something. You must make her see reason. She cannot keep this up, this . . . this paddling about in filth and gore. Traipsing through the slums. Working side by side with men. You must stop her practicing medicine. It will ruin her."

"I told her at her graduation that I wouldn't wait any longer. She agreed to set a date. Soon."

"Soon is not soon enough," Isabelle snapped. "You are her fiancé. If you of all people cannot bring her to heel, perhaps it is time I found someone who can."

Freddie affected a stricken look. He stood and said, "Perhaps you're right, Isabelle. You know how I feel about India, I love her more than my life, but perhaps she would be happier with someone else. Someone more of her world. She has her school friends and she has Maud. Perhaps this matter would be better left to the knowing heart of a girlfriend or sister."

Isabelle paled. The last thing she would want was for one of India's doctor friends to matchmake for her, never mind Maud. The mere suggestion that one wayward daughter might shepherd the other had its intended effect.

"Freddie, sit down. That is not what I want at all. I want India back. Back in our world. She is our only hope, mine and my husband's. You realize that, don't you? Maud is completely past redemption. India isn't. Not quite." Freddie started to say something soothing, but Isabelle cut him off. "Our two families have known each other for years. There is a trust between us and an understanding. I hope that I may be direct with you."

"Of course," Freddie said. This was going even better than he had hoped. He felt certain that Isabelle was about to make his fondest wish come true. The two of them had been dancing around this topic for ages, but she had never made him any firm guarantees. All she had ever said was that if he were to marry India there would be a dowry.

"As you know, India's father and I have no male heirs, only a nephew, Aloysius, whom we will name as our heir if there are no grandchildren. We need a son-in-law, a right-thinking man who can steward the family fortune. I am, as I have always told you, more than pleased that you will be that man, but the engagement has gone on far too long. Marry India, bring her back within the fold, and do it quickly. We are prepared to be very generous about the marriage settlement . . . *if* there is a wedding—and an end to this doctoring nonsense—before the year is out."

Freddie nodded, struggling to maintain a calm expression. He was close—so tantalizingly close—to getting what he wanted.

"India will receive a sizable dowry—including a lump sum of £100,000 and an additional £20,000 per annum. She will also receive the Berkeley Square house and, upon my death, Blackwood."

Freddie had to fight the urge to whoop with joy. This was beyond his wildest dreams. A fortune in cash, the London house, and the Welsh estate—all *his*.

"Isabelle, that is more than generous, and it is lovely to think that India and I would be starting our lives, our family, in this wonderful house that holds so many happy memories. But all that really matters to me is India's happiness."

"There is no greater happiness for a woman than marriage and society. If you do love my daughter, if you bear any affection toward myself and Lord Burnleigh, please use all haste in making her your wife."

Freddie finished his tea, then took his leave, promising Isabelle that he would invite India to Longmarsh presently to press his suit. She allowed him to kiss her cheek and said she would await the good news.

Outside, the clouds were breaking up and the sun was shining. Freddie was so pleased at his good fortune that he vaulted over the iron railing surrounding Berkeley Square, startling a little boy in a sailor suit. As he strode out of the park toward Piccadilly, he thought about how he'd soon be able to outstrip Bingham, Wish, and Dickie Lambert. With the Selwyn Jones fortune behind him, he'd be unstoppable.

Of course, his well-laid plans all hinged on convincing that awkward bore of an India to actually set a date. Easier said than done. They barely saw each other these days, what with his work at the Commons and her hours at Dr. Gifford's, plus her involvement in the Society for the Suppression of the Opium Trade, the Fabian Society, and the Women's Franchise

League. He sighed, thinking how much easier it would all be if that gorgeous Gemma Dean were titled and rich, but she wasn't. Far from it.

He thought about the time he'd invested in India—years, actually—and marveled at his own fortitude. He'd been playing a long and masterful game of chess, carefully engineering each piece into place, feigning an interest in her medical studies and her tedious do-gooding—and yet the endgame still eluded him. He had to find a way to get her to set a date for their wedding, but how? There was the time-honored way, of course, and he had tried to make love to her on several occasions, but she was cold—frigid, in fact—and it had always ended badly.

There had to be another way. Bingham had invited them all to Longmarsh for the last weekend of June. That gave him a fortnight to come up with a plan. He had planned to use the weekend to draft an important speech in support of the Irish Home Rule Bill, but there would be mornings and evenings. Time for long walks or horse-riding. He would get her alone, appeal to her emotion, accuse her of being unfaithful, threaten to break off the engagement—something, *anything*—to force her hand.

It would be a tricky business. Even if he did get her to commit to a wedding date, the job would still be only half done. Isabelle wanted more than a wedding—she wanted India to stop practicing medicine. Well, one thing at a time. First he would make India his wife, then he would worry about how to end her career.

Freddie reached Piccadilly and, spotting the Ritz Hotel, decided to treat himself to a bottle of Bolly. He was about to come into a fortune, after all, and that deserved a toast. It was such a relief to know that there would be money soon. His financial situation was almost always dire, and he would need a good deal of cash for his campaign. The latest rumors had the PM calling the election in September. Dickie Lambert was continuing to make inroads in East London, visiting businessmen there, buying rounds in pubs and clubs. Freddie knew he would have to work hard to counteract him. He'd already started. He'd invited Joe Bristow and other leading merchants and manufacturers with concerns in East London to join him for dinner at the Reform Club. He planned to wine them, dine them, and convince them that he was their man. It would be hellishly expensive, but votes never came cheap.

Freddie was walking under the Ritz's tall stone colonnade when he heard it—the "Raindrop Prelude." A man was standing under one of the arches playing it on a violin. The case was open at his feet. A sprinkling of coins glinted from it. Freddie stared at them, but didn't see them. Instead, he saw the drawing room at Longmarsh. He was twelve, his sister, Daphne, was six. She was lying on the floor crying. His father was standing over her, his face contorted with anger. He'd been drinking again. Freddie could smell the gin.

There was never any telling what would set him off. An over-salted soup. A book misshelved in the library. Some childish infraction. That night it had been Daphne's skipping rope. She'd left it on the dining room floor and he'd tripped over it. He'd slapped her small face so hard that he'd knocked her down. He was about to hit her again when Freddie, desperate to stop him, picked up the skipping rope and whipped it against his backside as hard as he could.

Robert Lytton turned around. "Come here, boy," he said, stumbling toward him.

But Freddie was too quick. He darted away. "Run, Daff!" he shouted. "Lock yourself in your room. Go!"

Daphne ran in one direction and Freddie in another, the skipping rope still in his hand. He knew where he was going. He'd had to escape his father many times before. He ran up to the first-floor landing, down the long portrait gallery, and crawled behind a skirted chair. A few minutes later his father staggered by, knocking into the paintings on the wall, kicking at the furniture. Then he lumbered up to the second floor, where the children's bedrooms were. Freddie heard him battering on Daphne's door, yelling at her to come out, that he'd teach her to respect him, by God.

Freddie put his hands over his ears, trying to block out the noise. Their mother and grandmother were visiting a neighbor. Bingham was probably hiding in the stables. That's what he usually did. The servants had scattered. There was no one but him to stop his father. But he didn't know how. What if he got into Daff's room? He had to act. He had to *do* something, but what?

A new noise started up. His father was kicking Daphne's door. He heard Daff sobbing. He'll kill her, he thought frantically. This time he'll kill her. There was no one to help him, no one. Not his mother. Nor his grandmother. Not even the God he'd prayed to in church, for He never answered. Freddie was alone, all alone. And terrified.

There was another kick, and then the sound of wood splintering. He heard Daphne shriek with fear.

"No!" he cried. "Stop it! Please stop it!"

He banged his head against the chair in fear and frustration. The chair shifted, scraping across the floor on its wooden feet—and it was then that Freddie discovered that he was wrong. He was *not* alone.

Richard Lytton, the Red Earl, was staring down at him.

The earl's eyes—fierce, shrewd and pitiless—seemed to ask him what the devil he was doing sniveling while his sister was being terrorized.

"I . . . I don't know. I have to stop him. But I don't know how," Freddie whispered. He ran across the hall and touched the portrait. "Help me. Please," he said.

The earl had been painted in full armor astride a fearsome black destrier. He held the horse's reins in his left hand, a sword in his right. Beneath the animal's hooves were the maimed and bloodied bodies of soldiers. In the background, castles and villages smoldered, and women knelt, weeping over the dead.

Freddie knew his ancestor's history. Richard Lytton had been a child-hood friend to Edward, son of Henry III. Henry was a weak ruler, a man who favored compromise over conflict. His rebellious nobles rose against him. Led by Simon de Montfort, Henry's own brother-in-law, they defeated him at the Battle of Lewes, then kept him and his family under house arrest. While de Monfort ruled in Henry's place, Henry's eldest son, Edward, also under arrest, simmered. Richard, who had always attended Edward, remained with him during his imprisonment.

"I will take the crown back, Richard. I will be king one day," Edward told him. "And when I am, I will rip out de Montfort's heart."

Richard thought of the old king, pious and indecisive, soft when he should have been ruthless. "Would'st be king?" he finally said. "First rip out thine own heart."

Edward followed his friend's advice. He escaped imprisonment with Richard's help, assembled an army, and captured de Montfort at Evesham. It was the age of chivalry, when nobles were not killed in battle. Edward ended that age. He beheaded his uncle, gutted him, and scattered his remains to the crows. It was but a foretaste of his reign. When he finally became king he rewarded Richard Lytton, giving him money and lands, putting him in charge of his armies, making him one of the most powerful men in England.

"But you *could* be powerful," Freddie said to the Red Earl now. "You had horses and weapons." He didn't have any of those things. All he had was a blasted skipping rope and you couldn't hurt someone with that unless they were stupid enough to trip over it.

Or drunk enough, said a voice inside his head.

Freddie's breath quickened. He looked down at the rope in his hands. It was as if the Red Earl had heard his plea. And answered it. He lost no time. The stairs were flanked by two newel posts. It took only minutes to tie the rope around one, tuck it just under the edge of the Turkish runner, and hide the other end behind the second post. The portrait gallery, and the staircase leading down to the ground floor from it, were poorly lit. He knew that his father, half blind with gin and rage, would never see it. When he had finished, he took off his shoes. He hid one and placed the other on the stairs.

Then he walked upstairs to the second-floor landing. His father had nearly kicked Daphne's door in. Freddie heard her keening with fear.

"Stop that!" he shouted. "Leave her alone!"

His father turned around. His once-handsome face was bloated. His eyes were heavy and bloodshot, but they could still register surprise.

"You are very bold today, boy," he said, taking a few steps toward him.

Freddie backed away. "And you are very drunk," he said, careful to keep his distance. "I should like to beat *you,* you drunken pig."

And then he ran. For his life. He was down the long staircase, across the landing, and behind the newel post before his father had left the second floor.

Freddie could see his father coming. He looked over the banister as he descended, spotted Freddie's shoe on the stairs, and smiled. He quickened his pace, rounded the landing, and rushed for the main stairs.

Freddie pulled the rope as hard as he could. He felt his father's leg catch against it, saw him pitch forward. He heard an endless crashing tumble, and then the sickening crack of bone against marble, as his father's skull smashed open on the foyer's floor. Freddie stood up then and looked over the banister. His father's eyes were open but unseeing. His limbs were splayed. Blood pooled under his head.

Freddie unknotted the rope. He put one shoe back on, walked down the stairs, and put the second one on. When he reached the bottom, he side-stepped his father's twitching body and placed the skipping rope back in the drawing room. He found the butler in the cellar dusting off the claret and told him that there had been an accident.

"I don't *know* what happened," he told the frantic man. "I was hiding in the portrait gallery. He was angry. He had beaten Daphne and wanted to beat me. I heard a shout and a crash and then I found him at the bottom of the stairs."

He said the same thing to the doctor, and his mother, and his grand-mother, and the vicar, and the police inspector. By the time they'd all left, it was very late. His grandmother had given him a cup of warm milk with a tot of rum in it and put him to bed. Although he was exhausted, he didn't fall asleep, but lay staring at the ceiling, sick to his very soul. Some time af-ter midnight he rose and crept quietly back to the portrait gallery.

"I killed him," he said. "That makes me like him. Like you. It does, doesn't it?"

There was no reply.

Freddie started to weep. "I didn't want to hurt him. I wanted to save Daphne. I'm afraid now. So afraid. What do I do? Please, sir. Please. Tell me. Help me."

The earl's voice seemed to come to him from beyond the centuries. *Would'st be king? First rip out thine own heart* . . .

"How?" he asked, his voice an agonized whisper. *"How?"*

His heart still beat inside him. He could feel it. It remembered the man his father had once been. Long ago. Before the gin and the money troubles. Before the defeats in the Commons. Before the bitterness and rage. It still loved that man.

He was only twelve. He didn't know yet that it wasn't done all at once. It was done over time. In bits and pieces.

He'd returned to his room and climbed back into bed, still afraid. He thought there might be repercussions—a wailing ghost or demons with pitchforks. But there weren't. There was nothing at all. Only quiet, and a deep relief that came from knowing neither his mother nor his siblings would ever be brutalized again. As dawn broke over Longmarsh, he'd closed his eyes and slept.

Some weeks after the funeral, he was alone at breakfast with his mother. She was wearing mourning and gazing out the window. "How sad for you, Freddie, to be a fatherless boy," she'd said.

"No, not very," he'd replied, buttering a piece of toast.

She turned her head and looked at him. Her eyes widened, and although she was as still as stone, he felt her recoil from him. He had touched his palm to his chest, checking. It was getting easier. Already. It didn't hurt as much now. He'd smiled, then dipped his toast in his egg.

Outside the Ritz, the violinist finished. The last notes of the prelude rose and faded and with them Freddie's memories. He threw a handful of coins into the violin case and walked into the hotel. He thought of India, of the sham marriage he would soon dupe her into making, and his hand reflexively went to his chest, palm against his heart. It barely hurt at all.

The pieces were in place. He was poised for checkmate. He would make his final move at Longmarsh in a fortnight's time, and he would win.

For £20,000 a year, he'd damn well better.

CHAPTER 9

Fiona stood in her nightgown in front of her mirrored armoire, flushed and flustered. Her stockings and petticoat were in a heap on the floor nearby. She looked at the silver clock on her vanity table anxiously. She was late. Again. It was only seven in the morning, but already she was late.

"Which one, Joe? The rose silk or the plaid sateen?" she said to her husband, holding two suit jackets up for his inspection.

"Neither," he replied, coming up behind her and kissing her neck.

"Joe, luv. I'm just about to have a bath. I'm sweaty as a navvy. Leave off."

"I love you all sweaty," he said, fumbling with her nightgown's buttons. "All warm and salty and tasty . . ."

"You make me sound like a chipped potato."

"You're almost as delicious."

"*Almost!*"

"I love you, Fee, I do, but chips are chips." He opened her nightgown and cupped her ripening breasts. "Blimey, lass, just look at them!" he said, ogling her reflection.

"Will you *stop*? I've a train to catch."

"They're twice as big as usual," he said appreciatively.

"Will you let go of me?"

Joe didn't reply. Instead, he pushed the gown off her shoulders and let it fall to the floor. He kissed her neck again, moving his hands down to her swollen belly. "Let me have you, Fee. I'm hard as a rock for you."

"I don't have time!"

"Won't take long, luv, believe you me." He moved one hand down lower, between her legs.

"Stop, Joe. I can't. I really can't."

But she didn't want him to stop. She craved his touch. More than ever. It had been like this when she was carrying Katie, too. She had wanted him all the time then. Couldn't get enough of him. His fingers found her and stroked her, making her breathless and wet. She closed her eyes and leaned her head back on his shoulder.

"Still want me to stop?" he whispered.

"Don't you dare."

He led her to their bed and sat her on the edge of it. Then he knelt down and pushed her legs apart. His tongue on her, then in her, made her groan with desire.

"God, you feel good," she whispered. He always knew just how to touch her, and where. He had always known. Now he was making her impossibly hot, teasing her, bringing her to the verge of pleasure again and again, then pulling away, making her need of him build until it was almost unbearable. "Oh, yes," she moaned, burying her hands in his hair. "Oh, Joe . . . now, please now . . . oh—"

"Mummy!"

Fiona froze. There was the sound of little feet pounding down the hallway outside her room. Then little fists against the bedroom door.

"Mummy! Mummy! Mummy! Mummy!"

Fiona bolted to the armoire and grabbed her dressing gown. She got it on just as the doorknob turned, a split second before Katie burst into the room.

"Hello, Mummy!" she crowed.

"Hello, my darling!" Fiona bent to scoop her daughter into her arms. She kissed Katie's cheek, then buried her face in her neck, inhaling her little-girl smell.

"Play, Mummy!"

"I can't right now, my love. Mummy has to get ready for a trip."

Anna, Katie's nurse, appeared in the doorway. "I'm terribly sorry, Mrs. Bristow," she said breathlessly. "The little minx darted out of the nursery while I was drawing her bath."

"It's all right, Anna. Leave her here for a bit. I want to see her before I go."

"Yes, ma'am. Good morning, Mr. Bristow."

"Morning, Anna," Joe said.

He was sitting in a chair near the bed, holding a pillow in his lap to hide the bulge in his pajama trousers. Poor lad, she thought. She was rather hot and bothered herself.

Fiona walked over to Joe, still carrying Katie. "Go to Daddy for a bit, duck. Mummy has to . . ."

"No!" Katie yelled, clasping her mother in a death grip. "Mummy, play!"

"Katie, darling, I can't right now."

"Please, Mummy," Katie said.

Fiona swallowed hard. Katie's words were like a knife to her heart. She had just returned from a business trip to Edinburgh yesterday and was leaving for Paris this morning. She'd barely seen her little daughter all week.

"We *will* play, Katie," she said. "On Saturday. As soon as I'm home. I promise."

"No! No! No!" Katie howled, kicking her legs. Fiona deftly shifted the wailing toddler so that her flailing feet would not catch her belly.

"Oi, you!" Joe scolded. "That's enough!"

"Katie, behave yourself," Fiona said.

"Play, Mummy!"

"All right then, look . . . we'll play dress up. Mummy will have a bath, then put her nice plaid suit on, and you can sit on the bed and put her jewels on. Would you like to play that game?"

Katie nodded vigorously. Fiona sat her down, handing her bracelets and a rope of pearls to keep her occupied. She was just about to pick her plaid suit up off the floor when a growling, snapping bundle of white fur came hurtling into the room, sending her clothes flying. It was Lipton and Twining, the fox terriers.

Katie laughed and clapped her hands at the sight of them.

"Are those mongrels *still* around?" Joe grumbled. "How'd they get in here?"

"Anna must not have closed the door all the way," Fiona said. "They've got something. Someone's tie, I think."

The dogs were playing tug of war with a blue silk necktie. Each had sunk his teeth into an end, and from the sound of their growls, neither had any intention of letting go.

"Is it yours, luv?" Fiona asked Joe, lunging for the tie.

"My what?"

The dogs scooted out of her reach, still snarling and tugging.

"Come on, Lipton . . . there's a good dog. The tie, Joe, the one that these filthy beasts are destroying. Is it yours?"

"I have no idea. Katie, luv, don't eat those," Joe said, jumping out of his chair to pull the pearls out of Katie's mouth.

There was another knock at the door.

"Yes?" Fiona called, an edge of desperation in her voice.

A young woman stuck her head into the room. "Beg pardon, ma'am, but Mr. Foster says to tell you that the carriage has been brought round and if you don't leave smartish you'll miss the eight oh five train and the next one's not till eleven fifteen and that one won't get you to the coast in time to board the ferry for Calais and . . ."

"Thank you, Sarah," Fiona said. "Tell Mr. Foster I'll be right along."

"Yes, ma'am," Sarah said, closing the door.

Fiona glanced at her clock again. There was no time left to take a bath. Not if she wanted to make the earlier train. She would have to go to France sweaty. What a lovely way to start an important business trip. Skirting around the dogs, who were still whirling about with the tie, she found fresh underclothes and quickly put them on. She kicked her dirty things into a heap, then stepped into her skirt.

"Joe, luv, Cathy rang yesterday. She said to tell you not to forget supper tonight. She wants to go over the plans for the Brighton site," Fiona said, reaching for her blouse.

"Good thing you mentioned it. I had forgotten."

"Look, Mummy! Pretty?" Katie asked, showing Fiona the bracelets she'd put on.

"Very pretty, my love," Fiona said, pulling her jacket on.

"Did the newspapers come yet, Fee?"

"Um . . . yes."

"Do you have them?"

"I do."

Joe rolled his eyes. "Can *I* have them?"

"Um, well, they're in my carpetbag. All packed away with sales reports and Seamie's appalling school report," she said, hoping to change the subject. "It came yesterday. He failed French again and English Literature. Barely passed History."

Joe stood up. "I won't disturb things. It's only the *Times* I'm after. There's talk of an apple blight in Normandy. I'm hoping there'll be something in there on it."

"I'll get it," Fiona said quickly. There was one paper she did not want him to see.

Joe waved her away. "Don't be silly. I can find it."

He dug in Fiona's bag and pulled out a pile of newspapers. Fiona held her breath, hoping the *Times* was on top.

"The *Clarion*? What are you doing with this rag, Fee?" he asked, laughing. He looked at the tabloid's front page, jokingly reading off headlines about mayhem, murder, and the music halls. And then he stopped laughing. "'The New Underworld,'" he read aloud. "'Crime Pays Handsomely for East London Firm.'"

It was quiet in the room while he read the article. All Fiona could hear was Katie singing as she slipped a rope of pearls over her head. She didn't have to ask Joe what the article said. She knew. She'd read it earlier.

Robert Devlin, the *Clarion*'s editor, had done a series of stories on a powerful East London crime lord. Calling him a new breed of villain, Devlin said that he ran crime like a business. There were no smash-and-grabs, no pickpocketing, no unnecessary violence. The Firm, as he called them, did nothing to attract any unwanted attention. Instead, they ran a series of legitimate operations, pubs and clubs among them, but these were only fronts for far more lucrative concerns—prostitution, gambling, extortion, and opium. In addition, the Firm was widely believed to have been behind a recent spate of shockingly bold robberies.

"These are not the random and impulsive acts of the petty street thief," Detective Inspector Alvin Donaldson had been quoted as saying, "but the well-planned campaigns of a group of bold, ruthless, and highly organized criminals."

Freddie Lytton had been quoted, too. He'd recalled how he had confronted the gang's leader man-to-man in a Limehouse opium den and had been assaulted, but felt it was a small price to pay for the safety of his constituents. The article explained that Lytton had returned to the scene the following morning with the police in tow, but the evidence had been entirely cleared away. There was not even one opium pipe left with which to make a case.

"The enemy is cunning and slippery," Lytton had said, "but we know who he is and how he works and he *will* be brought to justice. It is only a matter of time."

Devlin hadn't identified the man by his name—he wasn't stupid—only by a nickname, the Chairman. But he had run a photograph. It was a profile shot. The man's cap was pulled down over his eyes and his face was blurred, but even so Fiona had recognized him. It was Charlie.

Joe finished reading. He lowered the paper and looked at her. "Is that why you have the *Clarion*?" he asked. "Because of Sid?"

Fiona looked away, dreading his next question.

"Fiona, are you still looking for him?"

"I am."

"You've hired someone new. After I asked you not to."

"I've hired no one."

Joe looked at her, disbelief on his face. "You've gone after him *yourself*?"

She nodded.

"When? Where?"

"I just . . . I made some inquiries. In Limehouse."

"*Where* in Limehouse?"

"Ko's laundry."

"Jesus Christ, Fiona! That's a bloody hop den!" Joe thundered.

Katie, startled by the raised voices, stopped playing and looked from her mother to her father, wide-eyed.

"Please stop shouting," Fiona said.

"No, I bloody well won't stop shouting! You *know* what happened to

Michael Bennett. You saw his arm. Do you want to end up the same way? We talked about this, Fiona. You said you would stop!"

"No, *you* said I would stop. I never agreed," Fiona retorted. "He's my brother, Joe."

"I don't give a damn who he is. I won't have you mixing with the likes of Sid Malone!"

"Charlie! His name is Charlie Finnegan. *Not* Sid Malone."

Katie burst into tears.

"That's just bloody great," Joe said disgustedly.

"Don't cry, my love," Fiona said, picking her up. "It's all right. Please don't cry."

Katie wailed piteously. Fiona, trying to shush her, noticed that she had two more teeth. When had that happened? she wondered. How did I miss it?

There was another knock on the door.

"What is it?" Joe barked.

"Beg your pardon, sir, but Mr. James is here to see you. And Mrs. Bristow is certain to miss the eight oh five. Will you want the carriage for the eleven fifteen, ma'am?"

"No, Sarah, I'm coming," Fiona shouted. "I've got to go now, Katie love," she said to her daughter.

"No, Mummy, no!" Katie pleaded, tightening her hold.

Fiona looked helplessly at Joe.

"Come on, Kate the Great," he said, pulling her away. "Let's go and see if Cook's got your porridge ready."

But Katie wasn't to be placated with porridge. She began to cry harder, reaching her arms out to her mother. Fiona faltered. She was torn in two. She quickly kissed her sobbing daughter, then her husband.

Joe caught her arm. "Sid Malone is *not* Charlie Finnegan. Not by a long shot. Charlie is dead. Remember that."

"Don't say that. Ever!" Fiona shouted, suddenly blindly furious at him. "He's *not* dead. He's not!"

She grabbed her jacket and valise and ran out of the bedroom, near tears herself now. Sarah had packed her trunks earlier, and they were already in the carriage. She flew down the stairs and out the front door. Katie's wails followed her.

"Hurry, Myles," she shouted at her driver as he closed the carriage door behind her. "I have to make that train!"

Myles climbed into his seat and cracked his whip. Fiona fell back against her own seat as the carriage rolled forward.

"Damn it!" she said out loud, as if Joe were with her, as if he could hear her. "Why can't you understand? You don't even try!"

She was so upset. This fight, and the one they'd had during her party for the girls' school, was the first real discord of their married life. They almost never disagreed, and they certainly never shouted at each other—not unless they were talking about Charlie.

Since they had reunited three years ago, Fiona and Joe had been blissfully happy. They'd lost each other once. They'd known a sad and second-best life without each other, and both had been careful never to take one second of their new happiness for granted. In all the years she'd known Joe, Fiona had only once ever been truly angry with him—the day he'd left her for someone else. Years ago, when they were both teenagers and engaged to be married, Joe had made a girl named Millie Peterson pregnant. He'd had to marry her. The day he told Fiona what he'd done, he had shattered her. The anger she'd felt then had been mixed with grief and despair for everything he'd destroyed—their love, their life together.

He'd betrayed her then, and a part of her felt like he was betraying her now by forcing her to ignore her heart, to turn her back on her brother. He had never lost family, but she had. She knew the searing pain of burying her own blood. She had buried her father, her mother, her infant sister, and she was determined that she would not do the same for Charlie.

She sighed heavily, knowing it had to stop—the harsh words, the arguments. This was the second time they'd fought over Charlie. It wasn't good. Not for them, not for Katie. She knew there was only one way to make that happen. She had to stop searching for Charlie—and bloody well *find* him.

When she returned from Paris, she would redouble her efforts. She would try Wapping's riverside pubs, Whitechapel's gambling dens. She would go on foot, dressed in shabby clothes. She would be careful, of course she would. She wasn't a fool. She knew as well as anyone how dangerous the dark streets of London could be, but like her brother, she also knew how to survive them.

"It'll be all right," she said, still talking to Joe. "You'll see. I'll find him. I will. Nothing will happen to me. Charlie wouldn't let it."

But Joe wasn't there to answer. He wasn't there to tell her that she was headstrong and blinded by love, and that her words were at best foolish, at worst dangerous.

And so Fiona made a bad mistake.

She believed them.

CHAPTER 10

"Home Rule is defeatist politics, that's what it is! It's capitulation!" bellowed Sir Stuart Walton, a sugar baron with a refinery in Whitechapel, as he ripped a leg off his truffled roast quail.

A round of "Hear! Hear!"s rose from the assembled company of merchants and manufacturers. Freddie held his hands up for silence. He was standing, not sitting. He'd left the table to pace the room. He could never sit still when talking politics.

"I understand your views completely, Sir Stuart," he said, "but if I may beg your indulgence . . . if I may ask you to think not only as a loyal subject, but also as the brilliant businessman we all know that you are . . ."

There were more cheers at that, the sound of crystal glasses clinking. Sir Stuart flapped a hand. Freddie continued, "Ireland demands much in terms of money and manpower, and unlike India or South Africa, it gives a poor return on the investment. There is no cotton to be had from it. No tea or coffee. No diamonds, gold, or sugar. Home Rule will give the truculent Irish self-government—*limited* self-government—but still allow Britain to collect taxes. We don't feed the cow, we don't shelter the cow, but we take the cow's milk. It's good business, Sir Stuart, you can't deny it. And today— at the dawn of a new century—an international century which finds Britain competing like never before against Germany, Russia, France, and the colossus that is America, good business *is* good government."

"Absolutely right, my boy!" shouted John Phillips, a paper manufacturer.

There were shouts of approval, words of encouragement, applause. Even Sir Stuart nodded, seemingly mollified. John Phillips stood, wiped his mouth, and proposed a toast.

"To Freddie Lytton," he said. "He understands us, he speaks for us, and I, for one, want him to represent us. Freddie, my boy, you have my full support."

Another chorus of "Hear! Hear!"s went up. Glasses were raised. Nearly all of them. Freddie smiled warmly, but his sharp eyes were busy. He noted that Edwin Walters, a button manufacturer, hadn't raised his, but only because he was motioning for a refill. Donald Lamb, who owned a silver-plating works, hadn't either, because he'd dropped a roll in his lap and was busy retrieving it. Joe Bristow had not raised his glass either, but he seemed to have no reason for not doing so. He was sitting back in his chair, an unreadable expression on his face.

"What does Home Rule do for East London, Freddie?" he finally asked when the cheering died down. "What does it do for dockers and matchgirls and charladies in Whitechapel and Wapping and Limehouse?"

Freddie's smile tightened. He should have expected as much from Bristow. He was a merchant, but he didn't act like one. He didn't complain about taxes. He didn't demand that the government control unions and jail striking workers. Instead, he championed labor's causes. It was bloody irritating. Bloody perverse.

"Well, Joe, as you know, quite a few of my constituents, and your workers, are Irish. By speaking for Home Rule, I speak for them. Ireland's concerns are their concerns. Surely you see that?"

"No, Freddie, I don't," Joe said. "If an Irishman's in East London, then he's no longer in Ireland, is he? Why has he left? To find work. To earn higher wages. So he can feed and clothe his kids. Keep them in school instead of sending them into the factories. He doesn't give a damn if Westminster's rowing with Dublin. He wants to know he can join a union without getting sacked. What are you going to do for him?"

"I'm very glad you asked that," Freddie said, practiced and smooth. "The answer is this: as much as I *possibly* can. I've already embarked on an ambitious agenda of social reform in the East End. I've recently secured a donation to the Toynbee Mission Girls' School, as I'm sure you know, and I'm working closely with a young doctor in Whitechapel on an idea of mine to open free clinics for expectant mothers and babies. I'm looking into milk allowances for infants, a program of health and hygiene instruction for primary-school children, and I'm chairing a committee on how to promote better school attendance among poor children of all ages. There's more to my plan, so much more, but I see that the waiters are trying to bring out the Beef Wellington, and I fear I shall have an insurrection on my hands if I delay them a minute longer."

Joe looked as if he wished to say more, but laughter from the other guests curtailed further questions—as Freddie had known it would. Phillips, Walton, and all the rest were more concerned about their beef growing cold than they were about transplanted Paddies who couldn't even vote.

Freddie took his seat again and smiled, pleased. It was shaping up to be a successful evening—despite Joe Bristow. Freddie calculated that he'd bought himself the support of nearly every man here—about forty in all—and by extension the votes of their enfranchised East London workers, which would total in the thousands. His guests were certainly enjoying themselves—eating and drinking, laughing and talking.

He'd certainly given them plenty to talk about. Earlier in the evening, he'd spoken at length on his anti-crime measures and his strong support for the Employers' Parliamentary Council—an organization that existed to curb the advances made by workers and their unions. He'd made sure that when answering Joe's questions, he kept his concessions to workers focused on children. Even the most grasping employers realized that today's slum children were tomorrow's dockworkers, and that ignorance and hunger would leave them too stupid to read the label on a tea chest and too weak to lift it. The hardest sell of the evening had been Home Rule, but he'd even managed to make that palatable.

Freddie commended himself on his decision to host the dinner at his club. There was something about the Reform Club, something that immediately put a man at ease, made him feel genial and expansive. No matter how terrible a day he'd had, Freddie always felt better when he walked through its doors. Perhaps it was the smell—leather mixed with wine, wood, and tobacco. Perhaps it was the calming presence of the waiters—polite, unobtrusive souls who always knew what he wished to eat and drink, and brought it, before he himself did. Perhaps it was the company—all fellow Whigs with whom he could talk politics endlessly. Or perhaps it was the refreshing lack of women.

The Reform was a club for members of the Liberal Party. Built of Portland stone in the style of an Italian palazzo, its exterior was solid and commanding, its interior spare and masculine, totally devoid of feminine clutter. It was an oasis, a place where men could escape their wives and mistresses. Where they could sit in comfortable chairs by a blazing fire and read the papers with a glass of port and a plate of Stilton, undisturbed. A place where they could speak freely and colorfully, without worrying about offending feminine sensibilities.

Freddie had reserved a private room for his guests. He had told the chef to spare no expense on the food, the wine, or the cigars. And it had paid off. He was just beginning to relax, to enjoy the meal, when a waiter bent to his ear and quietly informed him that a visitor, a detective, wished to see him.

Freddie followed the waiter downstairs to a small reception room. Alvin Donaldson was waiting for him. He was Freddie's man. He paid some villains for information, knocked it out of others, and generally kept Freddie apprised of laws bent or broken by both sides—the villains and the police.

"I'm sorry to disturb you," Donaldson said, skipping a greeting, "but there's been a robbery on the river and I thought you'd want to know."

"Where?" Freddie asked tersely.

"The Stronghold Wharf."

"Damn it!" That was in Limehouse. His constituency.

"It's a big one. A large shipment of guns was taken. No one knows exactly how or exactly when, but they were stolen. No doubt about it. And the papers are all over it."

"Bloody hell! It's Malone!" Freddie said, furious. "You know it is! Arrest him! I want his head!"

"We can't arrest him. We have suspicions, that's all. Nothing concrete."

"Find something!"

"We don't even have a witness."

"Get one! Pay somebody, can't you? How much do you need?" he asked, reaching for his wallet.

Donaldson laughed. "There isn't enough money in all of London to pay a man to finger Sid Malone. You know that, Mr. Lytton."

Freddie swore again. He ran a hand through his hair. This was a disaster. He'd just spent the evening, and a small fortune, trying to convince forty important businessmen—all of whom owned premises on or near the river—that he was tough on crime, that he had the criminal element under control. What would they think when they saw the morning papers?

"I want him in jail by tomorrow morning."

"But—"

"I said *I want him in jail.* Since you can't seem to nab him for any robberies, find something else. Does he beat his horse? Kick his dog? Are his bloody library books overdue? Get something on him, Donaldson. Don't disappoint me or I'll make some other crooked detective rich," he said, slapping two ten-pound notes into the man's hand.

Then he left Donaldson to pocket his cash and rejoined his guests.

"Everything all right?" the man on his left asked him. He owned two breweries in Whitechapel and a wharf in Wapping.

"Right as rain," Freddie said, smiling. "A bit of government business to attend to, that's all." He took a deep breath, cut into his beef, and pretended to enjoy it. His nerves were humming, but he couldn't show it. Hopefully his twenty-pound bribe would motivate Donaldson. If he found a reason to arrest Malone, if the man was already in jail when the story broke, then he—Freddie—might just come out of this a hero.

And if not? he asked himself. Well then, old mole, he thought, you've just guaranteed a win come election time . . . for Dickie Lambert.

CHAPTER 11

"You still here, Dr. Jones?" asked Bridget Malloy, matron of the London Hospital's casual ward, where the poorest patients were tended. "I thought you'd finished your rounds."

"I have, but I want to stay for a bit to check up on the little girl who came in an hour ago. Mary Ellerton. Admitted as an emergency. Couldn't catch her breath. She's stable now, but I'm still worried," India replied, flipping back pages on her clipboard to get to the notes she'd taken.

"TB?"

"I think so."

"Has she had any treatment? Have the parents done anything at all for her?"

"As a matter of fact, yes. They gave her a fried mouse to eat."

Sister Malloy laughed. "I can't believe that one's still around. It was old when I was a girl."

India did not laugh. "I wouldn't believe it either if I hadn't seen it once myself. As a student. I also saw a child fed live maggots to cure her of tuberculosis. Another was made to walk seven times around a donkey to ease her whooping cough."

"Well, at least little Mary Ellerton got a bite of meat," Sister Malloy said.

"What could her mother have been thinking? Frying vermin . . ."

"You've children yourself, have you, Dr. Jones?"

"No, I haven't." People were always asking that. It drove her mad.

"Ah, well," Sister Malloy said. As if that explained everything.

It didn't. Not to India. "'Ah, well' what?" she pressed.

"Mrs. Ellerton's a very poor woman, isn't she? The poor don't have money, but they have mice."

"Sister Malloy, I deplore such willful ignorance. Surely you don't defend it?"

Sister Malloy's pale blue eyes regarded India. The look in them suggested that she indeed deplored willful ignorance, but not in Mrs. Ellerton.

"Dr. Jones," she said, "it's a terrible thing to love a child and see her suffer and not be able to do anything for her. Frying a mouse is doing something. Not the best thing, I'll admit, but something. It's only an old wives' tale to you and me, but to a poor desperate mother whose child is failing . . . well, it's hope, isn't it?"

India was just about to lecture her on the diseases mice carried when a junior sister came flying down the corridor. "Dr. Jones!" she yelled. "You're needed on the emergency ward, ma'am."

"Stop shouting, Evans," Sister Malloy ordered.

"Yes, ma'am. Sorry, ma'am."

"Is it Mary Ellerton?" India said, starting down the corridor.

"It's a new patient. Just came in. Off his head with fever."

"Where's the house surgeon?" Sister Malloy asked.

"There was a crash on the High Street. Two carriages and an omnibus. Dr. Merrill's up to his neck. He asked me to fetch whomever's available."

India could hear the screams coming from the emergency ward well before she got there. As she burst through the swinging doors that closed the cavernous, whitewashed room off from the rest of the hospital, she saw three nurses and a medical student struggling to hold down a man whose legs were mangled. Next to him, two more nurses were cutting the clothes off an unconscious woman.

Dr. Merrill rushed past India with a keening child in his arms. "Bed One. By the sink," he shouted. "Fever, hallucinations. Might be infectious. . . . Evans! Chloral! Now!"

India ran to the far end of the ward, skidded on a slick of blood, and righted herself. She saw Bed One and she saw a man stretched out on it. At least, she thought he was a man, she could see his shoes and the top of his head, but the rest of him was covered with jackets. Two men stood near him in their shirtsleeves.

"What's going on here?" she asked, peeling the jackets away. "Why have you covered him like this? He can barely breathe!"

"He's freezin' to death, ain't he?" one of the men said. He had the mashed nose of a brawler. "Where the hell you been, missus? Where's the bloody doctor?"

"I am the bloody doctor," India replied. "What's his name?" As she uncovered his face she realized with a start that she knew it already. It was Sid Malone.

"I never heard of a lady doctor," the man blustered.

"Hold on, Tommy, she *is* a doctor. She's the doxie from Ko's. Remember?" the second man said. He was young and wiry.

India didn't hear them; she was too busy taking her patient's vital signs. His pulse was frighteningly weak, his breathing was shallow, and his pupils constricted. He was barely conscious. The heat of his skin told her that his fever was dangerously high, but when she tried to insert a thermometer into his mouth, he struggled so violently that she thought he would bite through the glass.

"How long has he been like this?" she asked, trying the thermometer once more. "Come on now, Mr. Malone."

"Since this morning," the wiry man replied.

India timed the thermometer, then pulled it out. "Good God. One hundred and six. Has he vomited? Had any head pain? Rashes? Has he been around ships or sailors?"

The man hesitated, then said, "He has a cut."

"A cut? Where?" India took Sid's hands in her own and turned them over, thinking she might have missed a puncture.

"Not there. On his side. His right side."

India opened Sid's jacket. Yellow and brown stains bloomed like rotted flowers across his shirt. A dark, low odor hit her. She opened his shirt, peeled away a makeshift dressing, then gasped. A yawning, jagged wound ran from his armpit to his hip. Its edges were black and weeping pus. She could see his ribs showing whitely through the ripped flesh. India knew she didn't have a second to lose. She scanned the ward; it was bedlam. All the staff were busy with accident victims.

"You," she barked at the second man. "What's your name?"

He hesitated.

"Your *name*!"

"Frankie. Frankie Betts."

"Get his clothes off, Mr. Betts."

"What, all of them?"

"Yes! Now! Move! You"—she beckoned to Tommy—"come with me." She rushed to the sink, plugged it, and turned on the cold tap. Then she snatched half a dozen sheets from a shelf and tossed them in. "Wet them, wring them, lay them on Mr. Malone."

"But how—"

"Just do it."

She raced to a glass cabinet and grabbed vials of quinine, chloral, and carbolic acid. She veered off to the supply room and threw a basin, needles, suturing silk, scissors, a scalpel, dressings, a cautery iron, and a syringe onto a tray. She grabbed a second basin on her way out, mindful that most people were not used to the smell of burning flesh.

As she headed back to Bed One, she could hear Tommy insisting to Frankie that Sid have a private room. They were barmy to have Sid in an open ward, he said. He was off his nut. There was no telling what he'd say, or who he'd say it to. What if someone heard him? What if Billy Madden found out he was in the hospital? The sneaky sod would be sniffing around their manor in no time.

"The doctor said he's to stay here for now. And here's where he's staying. It's your fault he's in this condition, Tommy. I said we should have brung him two days ago."

"You was wrong, Frankie! He said himself he wasn't goin' to no bleedin' hospital."

"Move!" India shouted.

Frankie stepped aside and India slammed her tray down on the table next to Sid's bed. The two men had managed to get Sid undressed and were swathing him with wet sheets.

"Make sure you wrap one around his head," she ordered, racing off one last time to scrub her hands and fill one of the basins with hot water.

When she returned, she pulled a stool over to the bed with her foot. Sid was completely encased in cold wet sheets and shivering convulsively.

"How did this happen?" she asked, lifting his head and coaxing him to swallow a dose of quinine to fight the fever. Neither man answered. "Mr. Betts," she said, "I am a doctor, not a police constable. I don't care what Mr. Malone was doing when he got this injury, but I need to know how and when he was injured."

"Can you help him, missus?"

"That is precisely what I am trying to do."

"He fell into the river and hit a piling. Opened him right up."

India shook her head. Not the Thames. There was no place dirtier in all of London. "How long was he in the water?" she asked.

"About two hours."

"When?"

"Saturday night."

Today was Tuesday. The infection had been raging for three days. "Why on earth didn't you bring him in earlier?"

There was no reply. "Can you fix him?" Frankie asked.

"I can try. He's very ill. The wound is gangrenous."

"He's to have the best of care. We can pay. He's to have a private room, not no poxy bed in a common ward," Tommy said.

"I need him here right now. We can transfer him later."

"But he should be somewhere else, all quiet like."

"Keep delaying me and he'll only get worse," she said, dripping chloroform onto a piece of gauze.

"Get out of it, Tommy. Let her work," Frankie said.

She held the gauze over Sid's nose and mouth. She gave him only enough to dull the pain, not enough to knock him out. He was too weak. He turned his head away from it, but she held the pad firm.

After a few more seconds she removed the pad and turned to Frankie Betts. "You," she said, "hold up his right arm. Up over his head. Like this. Put your other hand on his left shoulder. You," she motioned to Tommy, "hold his ankles."

"Why? What for? What are you doing?" Tommy asked nervously.

"Debriding. I'd advise you not to watch."

India grabbed another piece of gauze, rolled it, and inserted it between Sid's teeth. Then she sat down and swabbed carbolic onto his wound. Sid stiffened, then struggled against his men's hands.

"I can't do this, missus," Tommy said.

"Hold him now. You must hold him steady."

Tommy did not heed India's advice not to look, and within seconds he was retching. "The basin," she said, without looking up. He had ceased to exist for her. She'd become unconscious of everything, even herself. There was nothing, no one, except for her adversary—the infection. It was terrible. Draining and cleaning the wound alone wouldn't stop the gangrene. The outer layer of muscle had begun to blacken; she had to cut it away. She worked for more than an hour, carefully making her way down the length of the wound, her nimble fingers deftly cutting and swabbing, chasing the deadly rot, thwarting its progress. She felt Sid's ribs expand and contract with each breath, and listened closely for hitches or gurgles. She pressed her fingers inside his wrist every few minutes, feeling for his pulse, leaving bloody prints on his pale skin. Sid's blood flowed under her nails, over her knuckles, down the backs of her hands, and into her sleeves.

She was vaguely aware that his men shifted position now and again, when one of them needed the basin. She heard their groans, the sounds of them being sick. When she held the tip of the cautery iron to the end of a vein, she heard Frankie say that she wasn't a woman, she couldn't be. She realized that the only one who made no noise was Sid. He bit down on the gauze, he shook and strained, but he did not cry out. Not once. India knew the pain had to be excruciating, and was astonished by his toughness.

When she was satisfied that she had done all she could to arrest the infection, she sliced the ragged edges of the wound, then stitched them together. It was slow going. Sid had a good deal of puckered, thickened skin on his back and sides. She'd seen scar tissue like it before—on men who'd been in prison. Her eyes swept up from his side to his face, checking his color. She was surprised to see him looking back at her, clear-eyed and cognizant. It's the pain, she thought, it's dragged him back into consciousness.

He spat out the gauze. "Should never have tossed you out of Teddy Ko's," he rasped. "Found a way to get your own back, didn't you?"

"I'm very sorry for the pain, Mr. Malone," she said. "I don't dare risk narcotics on top of the chloral. You're too weak."

Sid's head fell back on his pillow. She took his temperature again. The mercury hadn't budged. She told Frankie and Tommy to remove the sheets. She was going to soak them again and try once more to break his fever.

"Is he going to be all right?" Frankie asked.

"I don't know," India said. "He has a tremendous fight ahead of him."

There was a hair-raising wail from a nearby bed. India saw Sid's eyes flicker open, saw him try to rise. "Lie back, Mr. Malone. It's all right." She turned to Frankie, who was busy bundling the wet sheets together. "I'm going to see about a private room. He needs quiet and rest. Sleep will help him fight the infection."

In the time since India had begun to treat Sid, some progress had been made with victims from the omnibus crash. She was able to find the matron and explain what she needed. When India returned to Malone's bedside, she found Sid shivering under freshly soaked sheets. Frankie Betts stood over him, stroking his forehead.

"Come on, guv," he said. "You've got to get up out of this. You've got to try." He told Sid how all the girls were languishing without him and that someone named Desi had a huge steak and a bottle of whisky waiting for him and all the dosh, too.

"We'll all buy ourselves the flashest togs in London when you're better and sovereign rings the size of dinner plates. You'd like that, wouldn't you, guv?" Tommy chimed in.

India listened, surprised at such a show of tenderness from these two hard men, then told them they must leave now and let their friend rest. She explained that he would be moving off the emergency ward shortly.

"Who'll be looking after him then?" Frankie asked.

"I will," India replied.

"He's to have the best of everything, missus," Tommy said. "We don't want no expense spared."

India was about to usher them to the door when three men suddenly approached them. One wore a suit, the other two were constables in uniform.

"Is there a Dr. Jones here?" the one in the suit asked.

India just had time to say, "That's me," before Frankie started shouting.

"What are you doing here, Donaldson? What's your business here?"

"Mr. Betts, please do not—" India began.

"Well, well. Sid Malone, Mad Frank Betts, *and* Tommy Smith all in the same place. Must be my lucky day," Donaldson said. "You're all under arrest, lads."

India saw Sid swallow, saw his eyes flicker open. The noise had woken him. "Excuse me, but you can't—" she tried to say.

"I need to talk to your patient for a few minutes, Dr. Jones," Donaldson said, walking around India. "Here now . . . get up, you!" he barked, prodding Sid.

"Now see here!" India said. "This is a *hospital,* not a police station. Mr. Malone is *my* patient, and *I* will do the talking!" Both Donaldson and Betts turned to look at her. "Mr. Malone is in no condition to answer any questions," she continued. "He's gravely ill."

"*Mr.* Malone, is it? That's rich," Donaldson said, smirking. He took a step back from the bed and looked at Frankie. "Well, if I can't question Sid, then you'll have to do."

"I've nothing to say to the filth," Frankie said.

"No? Nothing about a little job down the Stronghold Wharf?"

Frankie shrugged. "I have no idea what you're on about."

India tried again. "Mr. Betts, Mr. Donaldson, I must ask that you—"

"Gun running is a serious business, Frankie. If you know what's good for you, you'll pull out of it."

"Like your father should have."

"Why you . . ."

Sid's eyes flickered open again, just in time for him to see an enraged Donaldson punch Frankie in the face. Sid tried to sit up, but couldn't. "You bastard," he rasped. And then India's tray of medical instruments went sailing through the air, followed by the basin Frankie and Tommy had used.

"Son of a bitch!" Donaldson shouted, as vomit splashed over his shoes. "I'll *kill* you, Malone."

Sid was sitting up now. He'd pulled the wet sheets off himself and was trying to swing his legs down.

India could not believe what she was seeing. "Stop it! Stop it!" she shouted. "Get out of here now! All of you! Evans, call the orderlies!"

She ran to Sid, who was glassy eyed and raving and, using moves she'd learned on the Royal Free's psychiatric ward, knocked his arms out from underneath him and pinned him to the bed with her body.

"Lie down!" she shouted. "You'll rip the sutures!" He was much larger than she was and was thrashing wildly.

"Frankie! Tommy!" she yelled. The two men came to her aid, and together they were able to subdue Sid. Three orderlies appeared. They grabbed one of the wet sheets Sid had thrown off, ran it over his chest and under the bed, and tied it fast. They did the same with his legs. As soon as he'd been bound, India called for a syringe and sedative. She didn't want to use it, but she had no choice. He was out of control. His fresh white dressing was rapidly turning red. As she readied the dosage, she could hear Donaldson still talking.

"Officers, arrest these men," he said.

"*Arrest* us?!" Frankie spluttered. "What for? We haven't done nothing!"

"You stayed open past closing time."

"We *what*?"

"The Barkentine was open until four in the morning today. I had plain-clothes officers in there. That's a violation of licensing laws."

"You must be joking!"

"Cuffs, please."

"It's a fucking *fine* for that, Donaldson, not jail! You know that!" Frankie shouted.

"That's for the magistrate to decide."

There was a second of silence, then India heard Tommy's anxious voice. "Don't, Frankie!" he said. "That's just what he wants. He wants you to hit him. He wants us all sent down. It's all right. Bowesie will come. He'll have us out in no time. Keep your head, lad."

Donaldson walked over to Sid's bedside. India had just pulled the needle out of his arm. "He'll have to come with us, I'm afraid, Dr. Jones," he said. "He's under arrest."

"That's quite impossible," India said, pressing gauze to Sid's vein. "If you move him, you'll kill him. Do that, and I will see *you* arrested, sir."

Donaldson angrily drew a pair of handcuffs from his belt and secured one of Sid's wrists to the bedframe. "Reed," he barked at one of the officers. "Stay here and guard Malone." India raised her head. Her eyes, glacially cold, held Donaldson's. "You will take those off my patient. Now," she said.

"I'm afraid I can't do that. He might run."

"Does he look like he's in any condition to *run*?" she snapped.

"It's your choice, Doctor. He can stay here cuffed or he can sit in a jail cell uncuffed."

India, fuming, turned to the officer. "See that you stay out of my way," she said.

As soon as the sedative began to take effect, India had Sid moved to a private room. She refused to let the constable into the room and made him sit in the hallway. His presence upset Sid. He was still muttering and thrashing his head and saying, "They're after me, they're after me."

India, desperate to quiet him, told him over and over again that he was all right, that no one was after him. She unwound the sheets that had held him, took off his dressing, and shook her head, furious. "Are you trying to kill yourself?" she asked. "Look what you've done!" She cut out the loose sutures and redid her work. Sid tried to get up once, straining so hard against the handcuffs that she could see the cords standing out in his neck. "Stop it, will you? For God's sake, lie still!"

He turned his head toward her, and in that instant she saw such a look of despair in his eyes that she caught her breath. Despite her hatred of what he was, and what he did, she felt compassion for him.

"Is this what your life is?" she asked. "This violence? This constant wariness?"

"What's that to you?" he said, before collapsing against his pillow.

When India finished suturing, she took Sid's temperature again. Still no change. As she was going to get more quinine, Dr. Gifford poked his head in the door. Ella Moskowitz was right behind him, jotting down notes as he dictated them.

"Dr. Gifford, Sister Moskowitz," India said by way of a greeting.

"I'm leaving for the night, Dr. Jones," Gifford said. "Thought I'd check in first." He gave Sid a cursory glance. "Heard about this one. Looks like he's on his way out."

Anger boiled up inside India. Sid was in and out of consciousness. He might have heard that. "He's strong. He's fighting it. I can bring him through," she said, a bit louder than she needed to, hoping that if Sid had heard Gifford he would hear her, too.

"Mmm. Well. Wouldn't waste my time on the likes of him if I were you. Most annoying if he does die, though. That will be two in one night and a damned lot of paperwork tomorrow."

"Two?" India echoed.

"Yes," Gifford said. "We lost Elizabeth Adams. An hour ago."

India remembered her. Elizabeth was the woman Gifford had told was pregnant and whom she had wanted to examine for a uterine mass.

"What did she die of?" India asked.

"Uterine cancer."

"Ah."

"It was completely inoperable, of course."

India nodded, knowing that though most cancers became inoperable, they didn't start out that way. Knowing, too, that Mrs. Adams might possibly be alive tonight, at home putting her children to bed, if an attempt had been made to arrest the tumor months ago.

"You'll learn that you can't always go by the book, Dr. Jones. In time, as you gain more experience, you'll get a better feel for these things. Sometimes it's more merciful to give patients hope instead of truth. Sister Moskowitz, I'll want those notes on my desk first thing in the morning."

"Yes, Dr. Gifford," Ella said.

India waited until she heard his footsteps fade, then angrily turned to Ella. "I remember Mrs. Adams. I remember her telling me about the pain she was feeling and the terrible exhaustion. Where, exactly, is the hope in that?"

"Now, India—"

"This is *impossible*. He makes a mockery out of the Hippocratic Oath. I swear to God, Ella . . . the things that he says, his archaic views . . . I don't feel like a doctor in his employ. I . . . I feel like a *prostitute*." She whispered the last word.

"Wish you were. You'd make us a lot more money. What's in the fund, anyway?"

India sighed. "Fifty-eight pounds, five shillings."

"Quit and we won't even have that. You'll need it to pay your rent."

"You're quite right. I'm sorry. I just get so *angry*. 'Sometimes, it's more merciful to give patients hope instead of truth,'" she said, mimicking Dr. Gifford's pompous delivery. "What about both, Ella? Why can't we give them both?"

"We can. We will. Just not quite yet."

India nodded unhappily. "Do you know that when I was first interviewing with him, people told me he was a godly man. Can you imagine?"

Ella's dark eyes shone with mischief. "He *is* a godly man, India. Only problem is, he thinks *he's* God."

India laughed despite herself. Ella could do that—get her to laugh no matter how angry she was. It calmed her, enabling her to get her mind off whatever was bothering her and back onto her work.

"Who's this, then?" Ella asked, nodding at her patient..

"Sid Malone."

"You're joking!"

India said she wasn't and explained what had happened to him.

Ella immediately went to his bedside, took Sid's hand in hers, and squeezed it. *"Gott in Himmel,"* she said. "What's the world coming to when grown men lark about in bed all day?"

"Ella? Is that you?" Sid rasped.

"Shh. Don't talk."

"No chance with you, luv."

"You rest up now. You're in good hands. The best. Just say your prayers that me mum don't catch wind of this. She'll be over here right quick pouring so much chicken soup down you, you'll grow feathers. Sleep now, all right?"

Sid nodded and Ella walked to the door. "He's as hot as a steampipe. I hope he pulls through. He's a good bloke."

"Sid Malone? A good bloke?" India said.

"Better than many."

"Ella, how on earth do you know Sid Malone?"

"He eats at the caff. Him and his lads. Once, a bunch of yobs came in, looking to start trouble. Four good-sized lads. They pushed Yanki, made him drop the tray he was carrying. Then they cursed at me dad and mum, called my sister Posy over and told her she was a dirty Yid. Said that to a little tiny girl, India." Ella shook her head and India could see the fury in her eyes. "Sid was there that day. Eating dinner. Him and Frankie. He told me mum to take Posy upstairs and then him and Frankie took those lads out on the pavement and beat them silly."

"Just the two of them?"

Ella smiled. "Ever see Sid in a fight? Never had any trouble from that crew again. Nor anyone else. You're looking at me like I'm the biggest fibber in Whitechapel. It's true, I swear it."

"I believe you. I'm just surprised."

Ella shrugged. "He's not a bad man. He's a good man who happens to do some bad things. Listen, you all right? You need any help?"

"I'm fine," India said. It was after seven p.m. and she knew that Ella had started at six that morning. She could see the weariness in her face.

"All right, then. See you tomorrow."

"Good night, Ella."

India returned to Sid's bedside to take his vital signs once more. There was no improvement. She crossed her arms over her chest and looked at him, debating between a cold bath, another course of quinine, or both. As she watched him, he began to toss and mutter again.

"Fee," he said. "Where are you, Fiona?"

Out of his mind, India thought. Completely delirious. "Come on, Mr. Malone," she said, readying the quinine. "You're going to have to do better than this. After all, we can't give poor Dr. Gifford any more paperwork."

CHAPTER 12

Short Susie Donovan, the Taj Mahal's colorful madam, put her hands on her broad hips and frowned. "What's wrong with Addie, then?"

Frankie Betts shrugged.

"For Christ's sake, Frankie, she's brand new! Young. Clean. Tits pointing up at you like two horns on a bull. And here you sit cryin' in your beer. Take her upstairs, will you? You're getting up my nose with all your moaning."

"I can't. Me heart's not in it."

"It's not your heart what's needed, lad. Look at Bowesie there," Susie said, pointing to a fat man who was halfway up the stairs with a girl on each arm. "He didn't waste no time, did he? You should be celebrating, not moping. You got out, didn't you?"

"Aye, we did," Frankie said.

In fact they'd barely spent any time in jail at all. Harry Bowes, the Firm's legal counsel, had rushed down to Whitechapel police station only an hour or so after Frankie and Tommy had been arrested. He bustled down to the cells and asked them what had happened. Frankie told him.

Bowes listened, frowning. He paced a bit, then pointed at Frankie's blackened eye, and said, "How'd you get that?"

"Donaldson hit me," Frankie said.

Bowesie smiled.

"Where?"

"In the hospital."

"Anyone see it?"

"Tommy did."

Bowesie rolled his eyes. "Anyone a magistrate might believe?"

Frankie thought hard. "The doctor saw. She was right there."

"Beautiful!" Bowesie crowed. "I'll be right back. You wait there," he chuckled, patting the bars. "Don't go anywhere."

"Very fucking funny," Frankie grumbled.

Half an hour later Harry Bowes was back with a disgruntled constable in tow. "You're out," he said, as the officer unlocked the cell. "You'll have to pay a fine for the pub violation, is all. No arraignment. Donaldson's sending one of his men to take the cuffs off Sid straightaway."

"You're the cream, Bowesie! How'd you do it?" Frankie asked.

"Told him I'd have him up on assault charges if he kept you in here one minute longer. Told him I knew he'd walloped you, that there were witnesses, and that we'd call Dr. Jones to testify."

They passed Donaldson in the station's entryway on their way out. Frankie was ready to open his mouth, but Bowesie grabbed his sleeve. "None of that," he said, leading him straight out through the doors.

"C'mon, Bowesie, he deserves to be told what an arsehole he is," Frankie complained.

"Frankie, lad," Bowes said, "you and the boys will want to watch your step for a bit."

"How do you mean?"

"Rumor has it that the Honorable Mr. Lytton is out to collar Sid. He wants him for the Stronghold, but he can't get him, so he'll use anything at all to put him away. Be careful. No wrong moves. We were lucky this time. Might not be next time."

Susie snapped her fingers in front of Frankie's face now. "Go on," she said. "Get yourself upstairs."

But Frankie still wasn't in the mood. He was relieved to be out of the nick, but there was something worrying him far more than his arrest had.

"For Christ's sake, Susie, how do you expect me to go and have it off with me guv dying in the hospital?" he asked.

Susie sighed. "Will you stop? Sid's *not* dying."

"You didn't see him! He was bad off. You can't imagine how bad. I never should have listened to him. Nor Tommy neither. Should have taken him to a doctor days ago."

"He's going to be all right. Sid's made from tough stuff. You don't survive life on the streets of London, a spell with Denny Quinn's crew, hard time in the nick, fights with the peelers, and Bowler Sheehan and Billy Madden and God knows how many other villains, just to call it a day in a hospital bed."

Frankie looked down at his pint. "He's all I've got, Susie. Something ever happened to him, I don't know what I'd do."

Susie nodded sympathetically. She knew Frankie's story. Everyone around Sid did. Sid had saved Frankie's life. He'd been orphaned at ten and put in a workhouse. He'd run away from the place after a month. He'd been on the street for two years, barely surviving, when he'd met Sid. He was a pickpocket. A good one. But one day he picked the wrong pocket— Sid's. He didn't know it was Malone, or he never would have done it. He'd made it halfway down the street and thought he was in the clear when Sid nabbed him. Lifted him clear off the ground and practically threw him into the Bark. Frankie prayed then like he never had before. Not for his life, he knew that was a lost cause, but that Malone would make the end come quick.

Instead, Malone sat down and talked to him. He told him that if he hadn't reached for his wallet just then, he'd never have known it was gone. He asked him to do it again. Frankie did and Sid, impressed, said he hadn't felt a thing. "You've talent, lad," he said. "You're good." Frankie remembered those words to this day. He treasured them.

Then Sid asked his story. After Frankie told it, Sid sent Desi for a plate of food. An hour later, instead of finding himself dead, Frankie had found himself quite alive—with a full stomach and a bed in the Bark's attic.

That was six years ago. He was eighteen now and no longer a street kid, cold and hungry. People stepped out of his way these days. Publicans hurried to serve him. Tailors to fit him. Barbers to shave him. He was Mad Frank to his friends, but Mr. Betts to everyone else.

Sid had given him a whole new life. A good one. He'd given him a job, plenty of dosh, and a family of sorts. Made him one of his crew, a villain who was feared and respected. Most important to Frankie, though, was the interest Sid had taken in him. He'd taught him things. Small things at first—how to crack a safe. Pick a lock. Case a building. And then he'd taught him bigger things. How to gain power and how to wield it. Who to trust. He made him understand that being tough was only part of the equation—being smart was the rest of it.

It had taken him time to learn, though. For a while it seemed like he was getting into a fight every day. Desi had fixed a broken nose for him. A cracked jaw. An ear that nearly had been torn off. He remembered sitting at the bar one night, barely able to see out of his swollen eyes, with Desi pouring him whisky to kill the pain. Sid had sat down next to him and asked him what the fight was about this time. Frankie told him one of Billy Madden's boys had looked at him the wrong way and the next thing he knew it was tables going over and fists flying.

Madden controlled London's West End, running whorehouses and gaming dens there, knocking off mansions. He made a tidy sum, but he was greedy. He wanted East London, too, with its docks and wharves and immense river wealth. He was always sending his boys over to nose around. It drove Frankie wild.

Sid had listened, then he'd said, "It's not about Madden's boys, though, is it? What they say and what they do don't really matter. It's about you, Frankie. You're angry. Furious, in fact. It smashes at you from the inside, don't it? Makes you half mad."

When he heard that, Frankie felt as if Sid had seen right inside of him. Seen his drunken mother stumble in front of the carriage. Seen the workhouse matron beat him senseless. Seen the other boys steal his food, his blanket, his shoes. He couldn't answer Sid. Couldn't speak at all.

Sid didn't make him. He'd just stood up, patted his shoulder, and said, "You want your own back? Then use your rage. Don't let it use you."

Frankie tried. He could control his anger better now. Not always, but most of the time. He'd started to see things the way Sid saw them—that it was better to keep shtum, to let the other bloke swagger and boast about a five-quid blag, and get himself nicked into the bargain, while you walked out of Stronghold Wharf with two thousand in your pocket and the rozzers scratching their heads.

Frankie listened and learned. And in return for all the things that Sid had given him, Frankie gave Sid his loyalty, and—though he would never have used the word—his love. Sid became everything to him—father, brother, boss, friend. And Frankie was never happier than when he was in Sid's company, picking a lock, cracking a safe, plotting a job, living the life.

And then he'd gone and nearly wrecked everything. He'd got into another fight with some of Madden's boys and had so thoroughly destroyed a pub that the police were called. He'd been arrested, held in the Deptford nick, and was about to be sent down for half a dozen different charges. Word was, Sid was furious and refused to do anything for him. And then the day before he was supposed to go before the magistrate, the door to his cell had suddenly been opened and he was free to go. Sid had been waiting outside. He'd taken him straight back to the Bark. It was deserted. Even Desi was gone. Frankie had thought that odd. The Bark was never empty.

"Cost me a thousand bleedin' pounds to get you out, you tosser," Sid had said to him.

"I'm sorry, guv. I didn't mean—"

Sid hadn't let him finish. "I saw you smirking when the screws marched you out. You think the nick's funny? What if I wasn't around to pay off the beak? Think you'd be sitting here now? You wouldn't. You'd be looking at five in Wandsworth. *Prison,* Frankie."

Sid took off his jacket and put it on the table. Then he started to unbutton his shirt. Frankie wondered why he was doing that. And then it hit him—he didn't want to get blood on his clothes.

"Please, guv. Don't. I'm sorry. I'll never do it again. I swear," he pleaded.

Sid said nothing. He finished unbuttoning his shirt and took it off. His chest was broad. Muscles rippled under the smooth, pale skin. He looked

Frankie hard in the eye, then turned around. It was all Frankie could do not to gasp.

Sid's back was an obscene crosshatch of welted red flesh. The scar tissue was thick and knotted in some places, and so thin in others that Frankie could see his ribs moving underneath it.

"Jesus Christ," he whispered.

"Cat-o'-nine-tails. Tore me to ribbons. Sentence was ten lashes. Screw gave me thirty."

"*Why?*"

"Because he felt like it and there was no one to stop him. When he finished, he slung me into a punishment cell. No mattress. Damp dripping down the walls. No one thought I'd make it. Bastard told me he'd ordered my coffin." He put his shirt back on. "Remember that, Frankie. And remember this: the scars the screws put on the outside of you are nothing compared to the ones they put on the inside."

Frankie had wanted to ask Sid about those scars, the ones on the inside. He'd wanted to ask if they were why he never slept, why he walked the streets at night to the point of exhaustion. Why Desi sometimes found him asleep sitting up in a chair by the fire, but rarely in his bed. He wanted to know if the scars had anything to do with the money he gave away to any sorry sod who asked. And how he'd look at the dosh they'd made from a job—the notes stacked up on the bar—as if he hated it. He'd wanted to ask about all of these things, but something in Sid's eyes had forbidden it. So instead he promised to try harder to stay out of the nick, and he'd mostly succeeded.

Frankie felt Susie's hand on his back now. "Sid'll be out in no time, mark my words. And you lot will be right back at it. Wearin' my girls out and the coppers, too."

"You think so?"

"I know so. Meantime, get out and about and do some work. Go back and see if you missed anything at the Stronghold. Go hassle Teddy Ko. Work takes your mind off your troubles."

Frankie nodded. "Think I will, Susie. Ta, luv," he said.

"Don't come back until you're smiling," she warned. "Long faces are bad for business. I don't want to have to tell Sid I'm short this week."

"You're short every week, darlin'," Frankie said, kissing the top of her head.

"Go on with you!" she scolded.

Frankie left the Taj with a spring in his step. Susie was right on both counts. Sid was tough, and a bit of work was just the thing. Sid would come out of the hospital, and when he did Frankie wanted to be able to show him that he'd been busy in his absence. He wanted him to know that he was good for more than picking locks and cracking safes. He wanted to show him that he was not just a fighting man, but a thinking man.

He'd show Alvin Donaldson, too. And that pillock of a Lytton. Throw him in the nick because they hadn't closed the Bark on time? He'd give them a bleeding crime. Just watch.

Out on the street, Frankie headed south. Toward the river. He wouldn't be mucking about at the Stronghold again any time soon, and Teddy Ko was in the good books this week. No, tonight would be all about new prospects.

After a half hour's walk, Frankie arrived at his destination—the Morocco Wharf on Wapping's High Street. It loomed up at him, immense and impenetrable. Well, that was all right. He wasn't looking to break into it. He was only looking for a chat with the watch. Bloke by the name of Alf Stevens.

Sid had always shied away from Morocco Wharf. He'd never given a reason for doing so, and as far as Frankie could see, there was none. It housed goods for a firm called Montague's—a very profitable business owned by a bloke named Joe Bristow. He had shops on every corner in London. Frankie had heard that Bristow was an East End lad. All the better. He would understand that there were costs of doing business . . . and that it was high time he started paying them.

CHAPTER 13

There had to be a way to let go. A way to die.

There had to be something inside a man that held body and soul together. Some handle or clasp or lock that could be turned or slid, releasing one from the other.

If only I can find it, Sid thought.

He was drowning in a sea of pain. Red waters washed over him, dragging him under, tumbling him along in their currents.

He felt a hand upon him. Pulling him out of the sea. Fingers at his wrist. He heard a voice, a woman's voice. It sounded distant. *Concerned,* she said. *Threat. Sepsis.*

"Release it," he whispered to her. "Release *me*. Please . . ."

"Shh . . ." And then the hand again, small and strong, pressed against his heart.

It was later, much later. Days later. Weeks. Or maybe it was only minutes. He didn't know. He heard water still. Not the sea this time, but rain lashing against a window. He couldn't tell if it was real or in his head.

He opened his eyes. It was her. The doctor. She was looking at his face. She had gray eyes. As pale and soft as a gull's wing.

"Where am I?" he asked.

"In the hospital. You have a bad wound. You're very ill."

In the hospital. That was bad news. Hospitals grassed you up. Someone had taken the cuffs off him, but Donaldson might come back any minute. Or Lytton. He didn't trust this place. He didn't trust her.

"Give me my clothes. I'm leaving," he said.

He tried to sit up, but the pain broke over him like a tidal wave, slamming him back against the bed.

"Don't do that," the doctor said.

He felt a thermometer slide between his lips.

She timed it, pulled it out, and said, "A hundred and five. Better. Maybe we've got it on the run."

"Why are you doing this?" he asked brusquely.

"To see if the fever's breaking."

He shook his head. "No. Why are you helping me?"

"Because I'm a doctor, Mr. Malone. This is what I do. Now, hold still. This will prick a bit."

Something bit his arm. His skin went all warm. His pain receded slightly. He was so grateful he nearly wept. "More. Please," he said.

"I can't. Not for another few hours."

"What time is it?"

"Just after nine. You can have another dose at midnight." She stood to go.

"Three hours? I'll never make it. Where are you going? Talk to me."

"Talk to you? I can't. I have to—"

He grabbed her wrist, startling her. He hadn't wanted to do that, to frighten her. But he was afraid himself. He was terrified.

"Please," he said, trying to sit up again.

"Mr. Malone, lie down!"

"Will you stay?"

"Yes, all right, but only if you lie down."

He did. "Tell me something," he said. "Anything. Just talk. Tell me how you became a doctor."

She laughed wearily. "You'd weep with boredom," she said.

"I won't. I want to know."

"Dr. Jones?" A young nurse was standing in the doorway.

"Yes?"

"Here's the beef tea you sent for. And Sister Abel thought you might like a cup of plain tea yourself."

"Thank her for me, will you? And thank you, too."

The girl put her tray down by Sid's bedside and left. Sid saw that she could barely keep from curtseying. Her eyes were shining with admiration as she looked at the doctor, but the doctor didn't even notice.

"Could you get a bit of beef tea down?"

"I couldn't. I'd only heave at it. Just talk . . . please."

"Mr. Malone, are you *quite* certain you want to hear about medical school?" she asked. "I want to keep you out of a coma, not put you into one."

Sid nodded. "The talking . . . your voice . . . it takes me mind off the pain," he said.

Her forehead creased with worry. "Is it bad?"

"Bleedin' horrible."

"All right, then. But quid pro quo. After I tell my story, I want to hear yours."

Sid nodded. He would have agreed to anything. The doctor sat down by his bedside and started to talk. She was self-conscious and halting. She stopped once, embarrassed, and said, "I can't believe I'm nattering on like this. I've never told anyone these things before."

"Why not?"

She thought for a few seconds, then said, "No one ever asked."

And then a few minutes later she was telling him what it felt like to be eighteen years old, standing on Hunter Street, on the steps to the London School of Medicine for Women, all alone. The frown that was often present, clouding her eyes and creasing her forehead, disappeared. She told him about her first F—in Chemistry. And her first A—in Diagnosis. She told him about the endless nights in the library, her house appointment at the Royal Free. And how she'd been pelted with mud by other medical students—male students—who thought women had no business studying medicine. Sid had asked her to talk to take his mind off the pain, but to his surprise he found himself interested in what she was telling him. Interested in her. He didn't want to be.

She described how it felt to examine another human being—to talk with someone who was ill, sometimes in terrible pain, to gain her trust, to touch her. She told him how important it was to her to always be worthy of that trust. She told him about the indescribable joy of healing, of making a person well, of battling for someone's life. He watched her face as she spoke. Usually contained, it became animated and radiant.

He asked her how she could cut someone open, and she told him about the terror she experienced the first time she did it because she saw a person then. But over the years she'd trained herself not to. Now she saw only a tumor, a hernia, a ruptured appendix.

"How did you train for that? The cutting," he asked.

"We practiced on cadavers. People. Dogs. Pigs. Whatever we could get."

"You never."

"What else would we practice on? Live people? They might object to being sat down and cut open, don't you think? The only problem is the decay. We always got the ripe cadavers at the women's school. It's not the same, cutting through decayed flesh. It's slippery. The scalpel skids instead of catching. And sutures? They rip right through. Living flesh is tougher, more resilient."

"Bloody hell, *stop*. Please."

"Sorry," she said. "That's why I don't talk about my work much. I get carried away. Can't help myself."

"Bet you're a popular dinner guest."

She laughed. "Not very."

"What's it like when your patient pops off?" Sid asked, desperate to keep her talking. The red wall of water was building. He knew if it caught him again it would take him out, and this time he would not be able to make his way back.

"I don't know. I've never lost one."

"I think I'm going to be your first."

"You will *not*."

She almost sounded arrogant. "Don't see how you know that," he said.

"It's a fight, Mr. Malone. A human being—the most beautiful, complex, miraculous machine ever created—against a single-celled parasite. A bacterium. An organism that lacks a mind, a soul, consciousness, purpose, and reason. Would you like to be bested by such an opponent? I would not. And will not."

Her gray eyes sparked with passion as she spoke. Sid looked into them and for a second he glimpsed her soul. He saw what she was—fierce and brave. Difficult. Upright. Impatient. And good. So good that she would sit covered in gore, shout at dangerous men, and keep a long, lonely vigil—all to save the likes of him. He realized that she was a rare creature, as rare as a rose in winter.

He wanted to tell her what he saw. Wanted to tell her that he had known good people once. A lifetime ago. But he couldn't. She would think him mad. So instead he said, "Tell me why."

"Why what?"

"Why you became a doctor."

"I . . ." she began, then stopped speaking and shook her head no.

"Give me more dope, then," he said. "One or the other. You've got to."

"It's getting worse?"

He nodded unwillingly. He felt helpless, totally dependent on this woman, and he hated it. He didn't allow himself to be dependent on anyone. For anything. Ever.

She took his pulse again and frowned.

"No dope?"

"Not yet."

"All right, then. Once upon a time . . ." he prompted.

She looked away, at the rain on the window, and he knew she was seeing another window, another place.

"Once upon a time," she began, "there was a little girl who lived at Blackwood, a beautiful castle in Wales."

"I was joking about the once upon a time. I want a true story."

"Keep quiet and you'll get one."

"Go on, then."

"The castle was an unhappy place, but around it were woods and streams and the black hills towering, and the girl had wonderful friends to play with. A sister named Maud. A cousin named Wish. Their friends Freddie and Bing. Bea, the gamekeeper's daughter. And Hugh, Bea's brother. Hugh and Bea lived in a cottage in the woods, where there were always fairy stories by the fire told by a lovely, smiling mum. And tea and biscuits. They grew up together and were inseparable, the girl and her friends."

"Was there a witch? A wolf?"

"No, Mr. Malone, there were not. Who needs make-believe monsters when there are so many real ones?"

That was aimed at him, he knew it was. His anger flared. Who was she to judge him? And why did he care what she thought? For God's sake, *why*? He wanted to tell her to leave, but he couldn't. Her voice was the only thing keeping the pain at bay.

"But then the children grew older and had to leave the forest. Hugh became a groom at the castle. And Bea became a maid."

"And the girl?"

"A sad and useless prisoner in a corset and gown."

"That's not a very happy story."

"I quite agree, and I'm afraid it gets worse. When Bea turned sixteen, she fell in love. She wouldn't tell me, or any of us, who he was. We thought she was only telling stories, playing games."

Sid noticed that the little girl had become "me" and that India's voice had grown wistful, her eyes faraway. He stared at those eyes. As long as he could see them he could stay above the pain, tread its dark waters.

"One day I went to look for Hugh in the stables. Bea was there. She'd been crying. She told us that she was going to have a baby. The father was a boy from the village. He'd run off when she told him about the baby. I wanted to help her. I told her to wait. We would figure something out. But she was frightened of her parents' finding out. And mine. My father was her employer. Had he known, he would have sacked her immediately."

India took a sip of her tea, then continued. "A few days later, a pair of very valuable hair combs that belonged to my mother went missing. One of them reappeared at the local pawnbroker's. The pawnbroker got scared, I think. He recognized the comb's worth—and the initials on it—and turned it over to the police. He described the young man who'd sold it to him: it was Hugh. The police went looking for him, but they couldn't find him. I did, though. I found him in our meeting place, the ruins of an old cottage on my father's estate. Bea was there, too. Lying on the ground. Hugh had made her a bed out of horse blankets. They were soaked with blood. She'd had an abortion and whoever did it had butchered her. Hugh had taken the combs to pay for it.

"When he saw me, he told me to leave, but I wouldn't abandon Bea. She needed a doctor. I told him to bring her to the gates in half an hour. I went to the stables and waited for the head groom to leave for his dinner. Then I rigged one of our traps. I met Hugh and Bea at the gates as planned and hid them in the back under blankets. I drove all the way to Cardiff, to the hospital there. Freddie came with us." She stopped and shook her head. "I was so stupid. I had brought no money. My mother believed that well-bred young ladies don't carry cash, you see. I had to find a pawnbroker and sell my earrings. By the time I got back to the hospital Bea was dead. The police were summoned. I was frightened for Hugh. We tried to get out of the place, all three of us, but we went the wrong way." She stopped talking again and gave a bitter laugh.

"What? Why are you laughing?"

"We ended up on the pulmonary ward. *The pulmonary ward!* Everywhere I looked there were miners dying of black lung."

"I don't follow you."

"Forgive me, I thought you knew. Many people do. My father is Lord Burnleigh. He owns half the coal mines in Wales. Most, if not all, of the men dying on the ward worked for him. We saw men of thirty who looked like they were a hundred. Miners' children wasted by consumption. A little girl—no more than six—coughed blood into her sheets as we passed. A woman saw me and recognized me. I had a peacock-blue coat on that day. Mother had bought it for me in London. The woman spat at me. She told me she hoped I liked my coat because it came dear. Her husband's life had paid for it." She stopped then, unable to continue.

Sid was quiet for a few seconds, then he said, "So that's why you're a doctor. Because of Hugh, the gamekeeper's lad." There was something harsh in his voice, something mocking. *Don't,* he told himself, but it was too late.

India heard the harshness and flinched, suddenly vulnerable. "I have no idea why I told you all this, Mr. Malone. I must have bored you dreadfully. Please forgive me." She stood.

"Wait. What happened to him?"

"The police arrested him," she said, gathering the tea things.

Sid snorted. "Of course they did. Your father pressed charges, didn't he? Even though he got the combs back."

"He got only one back. Hugh said he hadn't taken the second one, but neither my father nor the police believed him."

"And you?"

"I did believe him. I still do."

"He loved you, didn't he?"

The teacup she held slipped from her hands, clattering noisily onto the tray.

"That's rather too personal a question."

"And you loved him."

She did not answer.

"But you're not with him now."

"No, Mr. Malone, I am not," she finally said, picking up the tray.

"Poor bollocks. Probably back in some coal mine eating his heart out for you. But I can't quite see Dr. Jones, Lady India, hitched to a jailbird."

"Hugh died, Mr. Malone. In prison. Of typhus."

You stupid arsehole, Sid said to himself. "Bloody hell," he said to India. "I . . . I'm sorry. I didn't know. Didn't think . . ."

"No, of course you didn't. I can't imagine you ever do."

The curtain had come down. The radiant face, so open, was closed off again. Because of him. He'd said those things to hurt her. Because she'd hurt him. Calling him a monster. Or had she? Had he just imagined that? He was furious with himself. He wanted to apologize again. He wanted her to stay, to tell him more about herself, but he couldn't ask her to. Not after what he'd said.

"I'll be back in a little while to check your temperature," she said, moving toward the door.

"Wait . . . please." The pain was growing stronger. And there was something more . . . something underneath the pain. Hiding. Waiting. He began to shake. "I need another blanket," he said, through chattering teeth.

"You've two already. Are you cold again?"

"Freezing."

She put the tray down and opened another blanket. He shivered convulsively as she put it over him. His heart started hammering, so fast and so loud, he was certain it would smash through his ribs.

"Dr. Jones . . . I . . ." He tried to tell her about the pain, and the dark thing lurking beneath it, but he couldn't. He was suddenly gasping for breath.

"Sister Abel!" he heard her shout. There were the sounds of running feet. Someone was shouting. He heard the words *septic shock*.

It was rising fast, the red tide of pain. He reached for the doctor's hand and clasped it. He mustn't let go. No matter what. He was safe with her. She would hold him here, keep him from drowning, no matter how high the waters surged.

But then her voice faded, and then he heard nothing, only the sound of the sea as the red waves crashed over him, pulling him out and dragging him under.

CHAPTER 14

"Do you love her?"

Freddie ran a hand over Gemma Dean's bare breast, her hip, the soft skin of her thigh. "No, Gem, I don't," he said. "I love you. I know you don't believe me, but I do."

"I do believe you, Freddie. At least, I believe you love me as much as a man like you can love. In other words, not very much at all."

"Gem . . ."

"If you don't love her, why are you marrying her?"

"Because she's rich. Very rich. And I, unfortunately, am not."

Gemma snorted.

"It's true. My bloody brother controls all the family money. What there is of it. He gives me an allowance. A pittance, really. I need real money to get where I want to go in life."

"And where's that, Freddie?"

"Downing Street."

Freddie rolled over onto one elbow. He lay tangled in the sheets in Gemma's large bed. They had just made love. For the last time, she'd said.

"Wait until I'm married," he said. "Things will be better between us, I promise. I'll be so bloody rich, I'll have money coming out of my ears. I can take care of you then. I'll pay for your flat. A carriage and horses. Whatever you like."

"Why should I wait for you?" Gemma sniffed. "I'll be married myself by then. My new man's rich. He buys me everything I need. Dresses. Furs. He's already paying for this flat."

Jealousy, hot and lethal, gripped Freddie. "Who is he?" he asked.

"None of your business," she said, getting out of bed.

"What's his name?" He grabbed her wrist and pulled her back.

"Leave off!" she said. "I've said enough. I never should have done this. I should have pitched you out on your arse. Would have, too, if you weren't so bloody good-looking."

Freddie smiled. "But I am. And a good lover, too."

"Don't flatter yourself."

"I'm not," he whispered, pulling her back, pulling her close, nuzzling her ear.

"Stop, Freddie. It's time for you to go now. Really."

"No, it isn't," he whispered. He sat up and straddled her, then grabbed her hands with one of his and pinned them to the bed.

"Get off me!"

He kissed her, savoring the taste of her, all champagne and chocolate. "Tell me you don't want me," he said. "Go ahead."

"I don't want you," she said.

He snaked a hand between her legs, pushed his fingers inside of her, making her gasp. "Liar," he said. "You're dripping wet." He stroked her there, softly at first, then harder.

He stopped to kiss her neck, the place behind her ear, then felt her shiver as he bent his head to her breasts. He knew she wouldn't stop him now. Gemma was made for love. She had the most beautiful body he'd ever seen, all rosy silken curves. She drove him wild with desire. Sex with her was explosive, combative, noisy—the best he'd ever had. He couldn't imagine losing that, losing her.

"Tell me, Gem . . ." he whispered, thrusting into her. "Say you want me."

"Fuck you, Freddie."

He laughed. "Exactly."

He ground into her. Slowly at first, then faster, until he felt her move with him, heard her moan and swear. And then he suddenly stopped. Her eyes, pleasure-dazed, half-closed, opened wide.

"Tell me," he said, an edge of menace to his voice. When she would not, he bit her shoulder, breaking the skin.

"Ouch! You little shit!" she cried.

She struggled, got one hand loose, and slapped him. He grabbed her by the throat and squeezed, just slightly. He kissed her again, but she bit his lip, drawing blood.

"Bitch," he whispered, squeezing harder. Tears leaked out of the corners of her eyes. He kissed them away, savoring their bitterness, then he moved inside her again, slowly, deeply.

"Tell me . . ."

He felt a shudder go through her. And then another. "Yes," she finally gasped. "I do. I do want you, Freddie . . . now. Oh, God . . . *now* . . ."

She drowsed in his arms afterward. He stroked her hair, twining his fingers in the long brown tresses. He felt sated, exhausted, relieved.

He'd come to her flat to plead with her to take him back. They'd argued a few weeks ago. She'd found out about India, that he was engaged. She was furious and said she never wanted to see him again.

He'd brought flowers and chocolates, a bottle of champagne, and a little present.

"I miss you, Gem," he'd told her, standing in her doorway. "Don't you miss me, too? Just a bit?"

"Not at all," she'd said, trying to shut the door on him. "Leave, please."

But he hadn't. He'd handed her the roses instead. Yellow for forgiveness. And then he'd sweet-talked her into letting him come inside, just for a minute, to share some champagne. For old times' sake. He'd poured her a glass and then another, and then he'd moved close to her on the settee where they were sitting and slipped a gold ring on her pinkie. It was a twining serpent with an emerald eye.

"A snake," she said. "How appropriate."

It didn't take much after that to get her into bed. Jewelry always soft-ened her. He was glad she hadn't refused him. He wanted her back. He would have her, too. Soon. He would find her a nicer flat than this one and fill it with pretty things—furniture and flowers, paintings, a Victrola. He would buy her jewels, one bigger than the next, and she would fuck him silly. As soon as he was married.

He thought of India, his future wife. He hadn't seen her for days, but would in a week's time at Longmarsh. And he would get a wedding date out of her there, too. One way or another.

Gemma stirred in his arms, nestling in closer to him. He kissed the top of her head. He was happy here, in her rumpled bed. Drinking champagne in the twilight.

He would never be like this with India. He would never show her his heart. He knew that. He could only ever show that to Gemma. For hers was even darker.

Do you love her, Freddie? Gemma had asked.

He had told her no, but long ago, had he been asked the same question, he would have answered yes. He *had* loved India. Once upon a time. When they were children and innocent. Before they had changed. Before every-thing had changed.

She was beautiful as a child. And good, so good. He remembered now how she was forever rescuing injured animals. Birds with broken wings. Or-phaned squirrels. Tiny, blind moles. Keeping them in a makeshift animal hospital in the stables. She'd had an enormous heart. He knew she did. She'd shown it to him one summer at Blackwood. The summer before he killed his father.

He was twelve then, and India ten. They'd all been catching frogs by the edge of the pond with their butterfly nets, all of them except Daphne, who was in the nursery because she was little, and India, who refused to catch anything because she thought it was mean. Wish, tiring of frogs, suggested they go in the water and catch minnows instead. He, Bingham, and Hugh quickly rolled up their trouser legs and chucked their shirts. Maud and Bea knotted their skirts and waded in holding hands. The pond was shallow and they were all soon far from the bank.

Freddie sat down to roll up his trousers, too. He started to unbutton his shirt, forgetting for a minute that he mustn't. By the time he remembered, it was too late. India, who'd decided to sit on the bank in protest, was look-ing at him. He looked away, unable to meet her eyes. He tried to button his shirt up again, but she wouldn't let him. She opened it and peered at his body, at the ugly bruises staining his chest. She touched her fingers to

Jennifer Donnelly

them—with infinite gentleness—but he still winced. It was the shame of it that hurt most.

"Freddie, how did this happen?"

"My father," he said tersely.

"He . . . he beats you?" she whispered.

"Why do you think we always come here for the summer? And you never come to Longmarsh? Our mother sends us to keep us out of his way. If we're not there, he can't beat us. Only his horses. And her."

He had looked at her then. Her eyes were full of tears. For him.

"Don't, India, please," he said. "I can't bear it, your pity."

"It's not pity, Freddie," she said in a broken voice. "It's grief."

She'd wiped her tears away and said no more, but she'd taken his hand in hers and held it and they'd sat that way for quite some time. Together on the river bank in the quiet of a summer evening. It was the only time in his entire life he had not felt alone.

He had loved her then as a child loves, but as he grew older his love had changed. During the summer of his nineteenth year, and her seventeenth, he had loved her as a man loves, and had come to Blackwood in the hopes of making her his wife.

Things had changed by then, of course. Their group no longer played as children do. They'd grown, and this was to be their last summer together. Maud and India had made their debuts into society, and Maud was being courted by half a dozen titled men. Bea was working in the house as a parlor maid. Hugh was a groom. Wish would start at Barings in the autumn. Bingham was doing his best to manage Longmarsh.

Maud and India had greeted them all with warmth, and had been eager to spend time with them, but Freddie had sensed a distance in India right from the start. She seemed distracted, her thoughts forever somewhere else.

He was in his room one night, sitting by the window and brooding over her strangeness, when he suddenly saw a slender figure, a woman, dart across the lawn below. The moon was full and it shone on her, illuminating her pale face, her blond hair. It was India. She was heading in the direction of the stables.

Surprised and worried—for it was past midnight—he left the house and followed her. By the time he reached the stables, she was already on her way into the wood, and she had company—Hugh Mullins, one of the grooms.

Freddie could not believe what he was seeing. Determined to find out what was between them, he followed them in the darkness, careful to hang back and walk quietly. India and Hugh walked hand-in-hand through the woods to Dyffyd's Rock, India's favorite place. Hugh climbed up the huge boulder and pulled India up after him. When they were both seated, he kissed her. He pulled her close and kissed her, and Freddie felt his world fall apart. He crept closer, desperate to hear what they were saying.

"I'm so glad you were able to come. I wasn't sure if you would. I have competition now, don't I?" Hugh said.

"Competition? *Who?*"

"Freddie. I've seen how he looks at you. He's in love with you."

India had laughed at that. "Don't be ridiculous!" she'd said. "Freddie's not in love with me. If he feels anything for me at all, it's the love one feels for a sister."

"He's the one you should marry, India."

India shook her head. "Freddie will marry someone as golden and dazzling as he is. Not me. I'm far too plain for him. And anyway, I've set my heart on someone else."

She had taken his face in her hands then and kissed him, tenderly, passionately. "Make love to me, Hugh. Here. Now," she said.

"On this bloody hard rock? Are you barmy?"

"In the woods then, under the trees."

"Not until we're married. It's not right."

"Prude!" she teased, giggling.

"Hussy."

Watching her, Freddie had realized that he no longer recognized her. She had never been like this with him, with any of them. She wasn't the quiet, stifled girl that she was inside the house. She was laughing and happy. She was free. Hugh made her this way.

She leaned against Hugh, lifting her face to the stars. "Oh, I can't wait until we're married! We'll live in a cottage like your mother and father. With a fire in the grate. And a kettle on the hob. And stories and songs in the evenings. And our lovely children all around us."

"India," Hugh said, his voice solemn, "you know that if we do marry, we'll never be allowed to come back here. To Blackwood. Your father will probably disown you."

"Do you think for a second that I'd want to come back here? To this unhappy house? I want to leave. I want us to go far away. I would go anywhere with you."

"You don't know what you're saying. You're too young to see the consequences."

"I'll be eighteen soon. Old enough to decide for myself what I want. In two months' time. We'll go then. On my birthday. Promise me, Hugh."

"No, I won't. Because if I do, you'll hate me someday. When you're missing your home and wishing for things I can't give you. Wishing you'd never met me, much less married me."

"Don't talk that way. I'll never hate you, Hugh. *Never*. Now promise me we'll go away together. Promise me, Hugh Mullins."

"India, you have everything to lose."

She touched a finger to his lips. "I have everything to gain," she said. "I have you."

Hugh had taken her in his arms then. "I love you, India," he said.

"Promise me."

"I promise, you stupid, stupid girl. . . . I promise."

Freddie had turned away then. He'd heard enough, seen enough. The Red Earl's words came back to him. *Would'st be king? First, rip out thine own heart. . . .* He thought he had, the day he'd walked down the stairs at Longmarsh to view his father's broken body. But he was wrong. A small piece of it was still there, still alive. He knew because he'd just felt it shatter.

He walked back through the woods, to Blackwood, the love he'd felt for India turning into something else now. Something black and hateful. Rage and jealousy whirled about madly inside of him. The pain was staggering. He thought that night that he would not survive it, but he had. And only a week later, the pain had served him well. It had made it easy to do what he'd done. Easy to hand Hugh Mullins the hair comb. Easy to hurt India as badly as she had hurt him.

Gemma stirred again now. "What time is it?" she asked.

Freddie squinted at the clock on her bureau. "Half seven," he said. He would have to get moving. He was due at a dinner at half eight. Another political dinner. This time with the local leadership of the dockers' union where he would have to practice the politician's art of offering much, but promising nothing. They were a tedious lot, union types, with all their damned questions on strikes and wages and shortened working days, and he was not looking forward to it.

Thank God the Stronghold debacle had been contained. That, at least, would be one less thing they could grill him over. The robbery had made all the papers, but happily, so had the arrests of Sid Malone and two of his men. Donaldson had taken them in. True, they'd hardly spent any time in jail at all, and Malone, ill in the hospital under India's care—India, of all people!—didn't spend any time in a cell, but Freddie had glossed over that unfortunate fact by saying that the investigations were continuing, evidence was being gathered, and justice would shortly be done. Not a perfect outcome, but at least he'd limited the damage. All things considered, he thought he'd come out of it looking rather good—swift, tough, in control.

He extricated himself from Gemma's embrace now. "Must be off, old girl. I've a dreary dinner to attend," he said, getting out of bed. He ducked into the loo to wash his face and comb his hair, then he gathered his clothes off the floor and quickly dressed. Before he left, he bent over the bed and kissed Gemma, still drowsing, good-bye.

"I'm awfully glad we're back together," he said.

Gemma opened her languid cat's eyes. "Who said we were? We're not, Freddie. I'm with someone else now. I told you that."

Freddie sat down. He took her hand in his. "As soon as I'm married, things will be different. I promise you."

"I need something more than promises, Freddie. Promises don't pay my dressmaker's bills."

"Gemma—"

"Good-bye, Freddie. Come back after your wedding . . . or not at all." She closed her eyes and rolled over, her back to him.

Freddie wanted to argue with her, but he had no time. If he didn't leave, he'd be late. He hurried out of her flat and trotted down the stairs to the street. She lived on a quiet street in Stepney. He knew he would never find a cab on it, so he hurried south toward the Commercial Road.

A week's time till we're all at Longmarsh, he thought. Only seven days. No matter what it took, he would pin India down to a date then. He would pull out all the stops—declare his undying love, say he couldn't go on living without her, tell her how much he longed for children, and all that rubbish—and if that didn't work . . . well, there was always another way. A way that would all but guarantee a wedding.

As Freddie turned the corner onto the Commercial Road, his hand raised to flag a hackney, he smiled grimly, more determined than ever to marry as quickly as he could, for he desperately needed to gain a wife—and keep a mistress.

CHAPTER 15

"Jesus Christ!" Joe shouted. "Jesus bloody Christ!"

"The whole damn thing's going up!" his driver cried.

But Joe barely heard him. He was out of his carriage and running down Wapping High Street before Myles had even stopped the horses.

Morocco Wharf was burning. Angry, roiling flames were shooting out of loopholes and windows. Thick, black smoke was billowing into the midnight sky. A police constable had come to 94 Grosvenor Square an hour ago to tell Joe his wharf was on fire. He'd woken the entire household. Foster had called for the carriage. Joe had thrown some clothes on and run out the door.

He was trying to get into the burning wharf now, but was being held back by a burly fireman.

"Let go of me!" he shouted, shaking the man off. "Where is he? Where the hell is he?"

"Who?" the fireman yelled.

"The foreman. Alf Stevens. Have you seen him?"

Another fireman took Joe's elbow. "Sir, if you'd just—"

"Touch me again, mate, and I'll break your fucking head. *Where's Alf?*"

A scream rose on the night air. A jagged, tearing sound of a human being in agony. It came from up the street. From the neighboring Eagle Wharf.

"Oh, God. Oh, no . . ." Joe said.

"Don't go over there," the first man said. "It is nothing you want to see."

But Joe was already gone, running as fast as he could. A group of men was clustered in front of the wharf, looking at something on the ground.

"Can't anyone do anything?" one of them said.

"Where's the bloody doctor?" another shouted.

Joe pushed his way through them. Alf Stevens, his foreman and his friend, was writhing on the ground. He'd been horribly burned. The left side of his face looked as if it had melted. The skin on his arms and chest was charred black. It had split in places, revealing streaks of raw, red flesh. The eyes were the same, though. Wild, frantic, they were still Alf's eyes. He saw Joe and reached his hand out to him. Joe knelt beside him, afraid to take his hand, afraid to hurt him.

"Bets bets bets," Alf rasped. "No chance bets I says I hit him he swung lamp fell bets bets did for me bets . . ."

Alf was making no sense. He was delirious.

"Hang on, Alf," Joe said. "Don't talk. Help's coming. Just hang on. . . ."

Another man pushed through the crowd as Joe was speaking. His frock coat and leather bag told Joe that he was a doctor. He looked down at Alf and shook his head. "How did this happen?" he asked.

"I don't know. He must have been inside the wharf when the fire started. Knowing him, he tried to put it out."

The doctor took a deep breath. He dug into his bag and pulled out a syringe and a small brown bottle. "Morphine. For his pain," he said quietly.

Joe watched him fill the syringe. He'd had morphine once for a broken leg. His doctor had given him a fraction of what this man was giving Alf. He knew it was a lethal dose. The doctor looked up; his eyes met Joe's.

"It's all I can do," he said.

"Then do it," Joe said.

The doctor searched for a vein in Alf's leg. His arms were too far gone. Alf began to convulse. It took the doctor three tries before he could get the needle in. He emptied the syringe and the spasms subsided.

"Bertie . . . my wife . . ." Alf said, suddenly lucid.

"I'll take care of her, Alf. She won't want for anything. I promise you."

Alf nodded. And then his eyes lost their focus. And dulled. A few minutes later, the doctor listened for his heartbeat and said, "He's gone."

Joe sat back on his heels. His face was wet with tears. The men standing around him stared. He didn't care. He felt a hand on his shoulder. It was Myles.

"The coroner's here, sir," he said. "They have to take Alf. There's going to be an inquest. There's a detective inspector here, too. He would like a word with you."

Joe stood up. He looked back down the street at the Morocco. It was still burning. The fire was consuming the roof now. By morning it would take the entire wharf. And everything in it. Thousands and thousands of pounds' worth of stock. It would be a huge blow to his business. But worse than all that, much worse, the fire had taken a man's life. A good man. A man whom Joe had trusted and loved.

"Mr. Bristow?"

Joe turned around.

"I'm Detective Inspector Alvin Donaldson. I understand you were the last person Alfred Stevens spoke to. Might I ask you a few questions?"

Joe nodded. Donaldson asked how long Stevens had worked for Joe and in what capacity. He asked if there had been any trouble at the wharf lately.

"What kind of trouble?" Joe asked.

"Yobs trying to get you to pay protection money."

"No," Joe said. "Alf would have told me."

"Did Mr. Stevens say anything to you before he died?"

"Yes, he did, but it was gibberish," Joe said.

"Would you mind repeating it for me?" Donaldson asked. Joe did. Donaldson listened attentively, then nodded. "Well, that explains it," he said.

"Not to me," Joe said. "Alf kept talking about bets but he wasn't a gambling man. None of what he said made any sense at all."

"It wasn't wagers he was talking about. It was a name—B-e-t-t-s. Frankie Betts."

"Still doesn't make any sense to me."

"You're quite certain you don't pay anyone off, Mr. Bristow? I'm not looking to land you in any trouble, I just—"

"I told you, I don't pay a sodding soul."

"Then Frankie Betts probably decided it was time you started. Betts is a criminal, Mr. Bristow. I'd wager that this is what happened here tonight— Frankie paid Alf Stevens a call and attempted to extort money. Stevens told Frankie to bugger off. A fight broke out. A lamp was knocked over and it started a fire. Frankie legged it. Alf tried to put the fire out and was trapped."

Joe digested this, then said, "I want you to get Frank Betts. I want you to hang him."

"There's nothing I'd like better but it's not going to happen. I've been talking to people, the watch at the Eagle Wharf and the Baltic, and from what I can gather, there were no eyewitnesses to what happened here tonight. All I have is Alf Stevens's dying words. You yourself said they were gibberish. And that's what Betts's solicitor will say, too. We won't be able to make any charges stick. We haven't yet, and believe you me, we've tried."

"Since when do East End yobs get themselves solicitors?" Joe asked.

Donaldson laughed. "This is not your average yob, Mr. Bristow. This one's rather well connected. Maybe you've heard of his boss. He's the head of a group of thieves known as the Firm."

Joe knew what Donaldson was going to say. He braced himself against the words, hoping that he was wrong. But he wasn't, and his heart sank like a stone in the river when Donaldson spoke them.

"He's called the Chairman, but his name is Sid Malone."

CHAPTER 16

India heard birds. Sparrows, she thought. Nasty things. They were always congregating on the windowsill of her flat, shrilling and fighting. She wished they would go away. She was exhausted and wanted to go back to sleep. She'd been having such a lovely dream. She'd dreamed she was a child again at Blackwood. Wrens and bramblings were chirping in the trees, welcoming the dawn. It was summer and she had the entire day ahead of her. Hodgie, her nanny, would give her breakfast—boiled eggs and toast soldiers—and then she and the others would find Bea and Hugh, and they would have adventures in the woods. Her father and mother were at Ascot for race week, so there was no one to say they shouldn't.

She sighed and opened her eyes, expecting to see the dreary wallpaper of her Bedford Square bedroom. Instead she saw a pair of eyes staring back at her. They were kind eyes, beautiful eyes, smiling with amusement. And they were green, as deeply green as the dales of Blackwood.

I'm still dreaming, she thought. She closed her eyes again and buried her face in her pillow. She wrapped her arms around it, squeezing it tightly.

"Ouch," the pillow said. "That's me sore spot, luv."

India yelped and sat bolt upright. It took her a few seconds to realize that she wasn't at her flat in her bed. She was at the hospital. With a patient. With Sid Malone. And it appeared she had fallen asleep on him.

"Oh, God . . . sorry," she babbled. "I fell asleep. I slept. Here. With you—"

"Just a minute, missus," Sid cut in. "That's how rumors get started. I've me reputation to consider. You were not sleeping *with* me, all right? You were sleeping *on* me. It's a different thing entirely."

India reached for Sid's wrist, her cheeks flaming. It all came back to her. It was Monday morning now. The infection had overwhelmed his system on Saturday night, and he'd gone into septic shock. She'd fought for his life for the last thirty-six hours, and thought for certain several times that she'd lost him, but he'd held on. His pulse was regular now. Not strong, not yet, but regular.

She stood up to get a thermometer and caught sight of her reflection in a mirror on the wall. Her once-crisp blouse was sweat-soaked and rumpled. Her curls were springing up like coils out of a mattress. She was bleary-eyed and mortified to discover that she had drool on her cheek.

"You look terrible, Doctor. I think you need a doctor," Sid said.

India did not react. She was not going to give him the satisfaction. She wiped the drool off, popped the thermometer in his mouth, and regarded the second hand on her pocketwatch. Three minutes later, she took it out.

"Ha! One hundred point seven!" she shouted. And then she smiled. It was a broad, beautiful, utterly unself-conscious smile that lit up her entire face. Her embarrassment was forgotten, as was the sorry state of her appearance. Only one thing mattered to her: She'd saved a life. Sid Malone was not in the morgue. He was here, in this room, living and breathing and being difficult. She'd fought hard and she'd won.

"You're doing much better, Mr. Malone. Much better. I have every confidence that you'll live to rob another bank," she said triumphantly.

"It's Sid, I insist. May I call you India? I mean, after last night and all . . ."

"You may not." She was still smiling as she put the thermometer down. "Feel like eating?"

"No."

"Well, you're going to. I'm going to get some beef tea into you, if I have to strap you down to do it."

"Promise?"

India rolled her eyes. She sat down again and removed Sid's dressing. Her movements were brisk and energetic. Her exhaustion was gone, swept away by her victory. She inspected the wound. The swelling had diminished.

"You're remarkably strong," she said. "What you've been through would have killed a weaker man."

"It's nothing to do with me. It's you," he said. "I heard your guv saying I wasn't worth the effort. Most wouldn't have taken the trouble. I owe you one, Dr. Jones."

Her eyes met his. She didn't know what to think. Had he meant what he said, or was he mocking her again? She thought of his first night here. Of the things she'd told him about herself. She didn't know why she'd done it, and wished she hadn't.

"It's my job, Mr. Malone," she quickly said, brushing his gratitude off.

"Ah. Your job. Of course."

"Bleedin' hell! Are you *still* here?" said a voice at the door.

"Overstay me welcome, did I?" Sid asked.

"Not *you*, Malone," Ella Moskowitz said. "Dr. Jones."

"I guess I am," India said.

"You didn't go home?"

"No."

"But India, you've been here since Saturday night. Yesterday was your day off. You're due at Gifford's in an hour!"

"It's all right, Ella. I've got a change of clothing there."

"It's not how you look that I'm worried about. You've had no rest. You're going to drop down dead."

Sid looked at India, who looked away. "Why, Dr. Jones, I do believe you care," he said.

"You may believe whatever you like."

Ella looked from India to Sid and back again. "Did I miss something?"

"I have to go," India said. "Will you tell the matron that he's to have beef tea and ten milligrams of morphine subcutaneously every three hours? I want the dressing changed at noon. I'll be back this evening to check on him. I'll see you at Gifford's. Good day, Mr. Malone."

"Wait a minute! When can I get out of here?" Sid asked.

"Not for a week at least," India said, collecting her things.

"A week? You're joking!" Sid bellowed. "I can't stay here for a whole bloody week. I'm checking meself out."

"Do that, and you'll be back by evening. Only this time you won't be in a private room. You'll be in the morgue."

"Oh, bollocks. I'm fine. As right as rain."

"Go on, luv. I'll sort him," Ella said to India. "You get to work. Get yourself some breakfast first."

India dashed out of the room. She could hear Ella's voice carrying all the way down the hall. "Now look, you. If you don't quiet down I'll call the orderlies. They'll come with a big long needle and stick you straight in the arse with it. That'll shut you up."

As she hurried out of the hospital, anxious to get to work on time, India felt that she'd forgotten something. She mentally reviewed her instructions to Ella and found that she'd left nothing out. She'd also taken and recorded Sid's vital signs. She would write up his notes later. What was it? What had she forgotten?

As she turned off the Whitechapel High Street onto Varden Street, it hit her—it was Sid's story. She'd never heard his story. They'd agreed on a quid pro quo. She'd tell her story, and he'd tell his. But he never had. And she realized, to her discomforted surprise, that she wanted to hear his story. She wanted it very much.

CHAPTER 17

"Let me get this straight," Joe's brother Jimmy said. "Alf is dead. The Morocco's burned to the ground. You know who did it. And the police can't do anything about it?"

"So they say. There are no eyewitnesses. Just one man's word against another's," Joe replied.

He and Jimmy were in his study drinking Scotch. It was nine o'clock in the morning. Joe's clothes stank of smoke. His face was streaked with soot. He'd returned home two hours ago and had rung up Jimmy. Jimmy had come right over.

"Aren't they going to even try to get the bloke?" he asked now, devastated by Alf's death.

"Oh, aye. They said they'd try, but they won't be able to make any charges stick."

Joe swallowed another mouthful of Scotch. He hadn't slept for more than twenty-four hours, but he wasn't tired. In fact he couldn't recall ever having felt more awake. A storm of emotion had engulfed him over the course of the night—fury, outrage, grief. But now the storm had subsided and something quite different was emerging in the calm—a fierce, implacable resolve.

"Nothing ever changes there, Jimmy, do you know that?" he suddenly said. "The crime. The poverty. The sheer fucking brutality. I was looking out the carriage window on the way home. At the houses. The bleak streets. Wapping, Whitechapel . . . the whole bloody East End. None of it ever bloody changes."

"It's grim, all right," Jimmy said.

As he was speaking, they both heard footsteps in the hallway, light and quick.

"We're in here, Fee," Joe called. "Don't run, luv. You'll jostle the baby."

Two seconds later Fiona was in the study, flushed and breathless, still in her coat and gloves, just home from her trip to Paris.

"Mr. Foster told me what happened," she said. "Are you all right, Joe? You look terrible! And Alf! My God, is it true? Is he really dead?"

"Aye, luv, he is."

She sat down, stricken. Her eyes filled with tears. Jimmy stood. He said he was going to the kitchen to get something to eat. Joe appreciated his tactful departure. There were things he had to discuss with Fiona alone. When she could speak again, Fiona asked him how the fire had started. He told her about Frankie Betts. When he finished, she stood up and began to pace the room.

"What about your deliveries? I'm sure the river pilots have heard about the fire, and they'll hold off any new ships, but some may have already headed upriver. Can you reroute them to Oliver's?" she asked. "I've room enough there."

"We stopped there on our way home. Mel said the second floor's empty. Jimmy's going to the Morocco shortly. He's going to get two of the lads who worked there to stay on-site and redirect any incoming barges."

"What about the insurers? Shouldn't we contact them?" Fiona said. She continued to pace, her hands on her hips, her gaze directed at the floor.

"Trudy's done it. She's going to meet them at the Morocco later this morning."

Fiona nodded. "And the Customs House . . . we'll have to tell—"

Joe cut her off. "Fiona, there's something I have to tell *you*."

She stopped pacing and raised her eyes to his. He could see the fear in them.

"You don't have to," she said softly. "It's him, isn't it?"

Joe nodded. "There was a detective inspector there. He said Frankie Betts works for Sid Malone. He also said that without eyewitnesses we'll never be able to touch him."

"I can't believe it, Joe. I just can't," she whispered.

"I'm sorry, Fee. I know it's a hard thing to hear. Part of me didn't want to tell you, but part of me did. To make you see what Sid Malone really is. To make you stop trying to find him."

Fiona said nothing.

"We never finished our discussion about Sid. The one we were having when you left for Paris. I want to finish it now. I want you to stop looking for him. He burned my warehouse to the ground. He killed Alf Stevens."

"Don't say that, Joe. It's not true. He didn't do those things. Frankie Betts did."

"On Sid's orders."

"You don't *know* that."

"Fiona, how can you *be* so bloody blind?"

"I'm not being blind. He's my brother, Joe, and I can't give up on him. He *needs* me. I know he does. More than ever now. I can't tell you how I know. I just . . . *feel* it."

Joe shook his head. "Fiona, *I* need you," he said.

There was an ottoman by Joe's chair. Fiona sat down on it. She took his hands in hers. "I know you do. I know how sad you are, how much Alf meant to you," she said.

"Aye, he did. But it's not just about Alf," Joe said.

"What *is* it about, then? Tell me," she said.

Joe looked at his beloved wife. In her beautiful sapphire eyes, he saw everything that he was. His past, present, and future. They had known each other since they were children. She was his heart and soul, and he shared every dream and hope he had with her. She supported the decisions he made, the risks he took in order to expand his business, and, more important, she supported *him*. But what was brewing inside him now had nothing to do with shops and business. What he wanted to tell her now might well change their lives forever, and he wondered if she would still support him when she heard it.

"I'm *angry,* Fee. I'm so bloody angry I could burst. That's why I'm sitting here with a drink in me hand. Why I haven't gone to work. I'm afraid I'll punch a hole in a wall or kick over a table."

"There's a lot to be angry about," Fiona said. "A good man was killed. Your wharf was burned to the ground."

"But that's only a part of it. I'm angry at what led to all that. I'm angry that things never change in East London. Twelve whole years have gone by since the Ripper murders. Eleven years since the dock strike. Every newspaper in the country was writing stories about East London then. About the terrible conditions people endured. Every politician was calling for change. And what's happened, Fee? Bloody nothing. Do you remember it? From when we were kids? Your mother and mine struggling to keep us fed. My father out selling seven days a week. Yours trying to bring a union into Wapping. And getting himself killed for it."

"I remember," Fiona said. "I remember my father practicing a speech he was going to give about the union, striding back and forth in front of the fireplace. We were his audience. Charlie, Seamie, our mam, and the baby." She smiled at the memory, then said, "He'd probably still be giving speeches if he'd lived. Organizing his fellow dockers. Calling for a strike."

Joe sat forward in his chair. There was an intensity to his voice now. "No, Fiona," he said, "I'm not sure he would. Your father was a sharp man. He started organizing the dockers' union in 1888. A dozen years on he would have seen the futility of strikes. He would have seen the writing on the wall."

"What do you mean?"

"Strikes are only battles, and this is a war. If things are to change for the working class, to *really* change, they have to learn that it's no use fighting on the factory floor or on the waterfront. They have to learn to fight where it matters—at Westminster."

"Joe . . . how did we get from the Morocco Wharf to Westminster?" Fiona asked, puzzled.

"Freddie Lytton came by this morning. Just as the fire brigade put the blaze out."

"Offering his condolences, was he?"

Joe laughed bitterly. "Oh, aye. For all of two seconds. Then he launched into a campaign speech. Told me for the tenth bloody time that a general election will be called this autumn, and that if he gets reelected, his first priority will be a crackdown on crime. Asked me for my endorsement . . ." His words trailed off.

"And you said?" Fiona prompted.

Joe didn't answer her. Instead he reached for the locket Fiona was wearing, opened it, and gazed at the photograph of their daughter inside. "Look at our Katie," he said. "She's the picture of health. Her little arms and legs are straight and strong because she eats good food. She's never known what it's like to cry in her bed at night from hunger. Or to shiver because she's got no coat."

"Luv, where is all this coming from?" Fiona asked.

"From everywhere. From everything. From watching Alf die. From riding home this morning and seeing kids with no shoes playing in a dirty gutter and thanking my lucky stars it's not our Katie."

Fiona shook her head. "I don't follow you," she said. "You're all over the place." She paused, then said, "Joe, luv . . . are you drunk?"

"A little, maybe. But I swear, I've never been more clear-headed in me life. Can't you see, Fee? It was the same when we were coming up. And when our parents were. And their parents, too. It's *still* going on. It doesn't change. You've got villains on the streets and villains in the counting houses and villains in Parliament—and in the last few hours, after everything that's happened, I can see something I've never seen before. That I'm as big a villain as any of them. For standing back and letting it happen and not doing a bloody thing to stop it."

"Joseph Bristow, that is not true!" Fiona said hotly. "We give a great deal of money to East London causes."

"I know we do," he said impatiently. "And it's good, it's something, but it's not enough. Nowhere near enough. It's too big for us, Fiona. We could throw every penny we have at it and never change a thing."

Fiona sighed with frustration. "What *exactly* are you trying to tell me?"

Joe looked at her. He took a deep breath then said, "I want to run, Fee."

"To *run*? Where?" she asked, completely confused now.

"Not where. *For*. I want to run for Parliament. For the Tower Hamlets seat."

Fiona blinked at him.

"Against Freddie Lytton."

Her mouth dropped open.

"On the new Labour ticket."

CHAPTER 18

"India! For God's sake stop!" Freddie shouted.

India didn't hear him. She dug her heels into her cantering mount. The mare, a dappled gray named Long's Lady, broke into a gallop, heading directly for an impossibly tall hedge that Wish had dared her to jump.

"Indy, I was joking!" Wish yelled. "Don't do it! It's too high!"

"Bloody hell! *India!*" Freddie bellowed.

His breath caught as Lady's front legs came off the ground. Wish, Bingham, and Maud gave a collective gasp as the animal sailed over the hedge and disappeared from sight. A whoop on the other side told them that both horse and rider had landed well.

"God, but she's brave," Bingham said. "I'd never have dared it."

"She's a damned fool, that's what she is!" Freddie said.

"I say, Lytton, is that your heart showing? Didn't know you had one!"

"Shut up, Wish!"

"Why, old man, how positively touching."

Freddie did not answer. He dug his heels into Boy, his own horse, and cantered toward the stables, fuming.

Wish was right—he *did* care. Deeply. He cared about the Selwyn Jones fortune. In his mind's eye he'd just seen Lady's foreleg catch on the too high hedge. He'd seen India disappear under the animal's flailing hooves, and with her, all his cherished hopes.

In the stable yard a groom came out to take the reins of Freddie's horse. A second came for India's.

"Freddie? Why didn't you wait for me?" she asked, trotting up behind him.

"That was a stupid stunt," he said angrily, swinging down out of his saddle. "Damned stupid." For once his emotion was genuine.

"You're not angry with me, are you?"

"I certainly am!" he snapped. "For God's sake, India, you're a doctor! You've seen enough broken necks and crushed bodies to know better."

"I'm sorry I worried you, but I knew Lady could take the hedge."

She was contrite. Good. He would use that. Maybe he could make her sorry enough to give him a wedding date. He'd been trying for the last twenty-four hours to get one out of her and had gotten nowhere. She was still putting him off, just as she'd done at her graduation, just as she'd done for the past two years.

Freddie threw his crop at the groom and headed into the house. He strode through the enormous foyer up the main staircase to his bedroom on the second floor. Still angry, he tossed his jacket onto his desk, knocking to the floor a few pages of the speech he'd been writing. They'd all arrived at Longmarsh yesterday afternoon—himself, Wish, Maud, and India. It was now Saturday evening. Tomorrow they would return to London. Isabelle would be expecting good news. He'd promised her he'd have a date.

He grabbed a decanter of gin, poured himself a drink, and banged the decanter back down. The force jarred an ebony box that was also on the desk. A few notes of music floated out of it: The "Raindrop Prelude." Freddie picked the box up. It was inlaid with malachite and silver. His grandmother had given it to him before she died. He never went anywhere without it. Instinctively, his fingers felt for the indentation, nearly invisible to the eye, that was on the box's underside. He pressed it, and pressed one of the malachite panels on the back of the box at the same time. There was a soft click and a drawer slid out. In it was a woman's hair comb. A Tiffany dragonfly. One of a pair.

As he stared at it, he heard footsteps in the hallway. A knock at his door. India had followed him—as he'd known she would. He slid the drawer back into the music box and placed the box on his desk. Then he downed his drink, fortifying himself for what was to come.

"Freddie? Darling, are you in there?" India opened the door and came in. "Don't be angry," she said. "Come and walk outside with me. It's such a beautiful summer evening. And we're having the loveliest time, all of us."

Freddie put his glass down and looked at her. "You don't care, do you?" he said.

"I beg your pardon?"

"It's perfectly plain, India. You don't care for me."

"Freddie, how can you—"

"You know full well that if anything ever happened to you it would absolutely destroy me, yet you take risks with your life with utter disregard for my feelings."

India rushed to his side, explaining, trying to make him understand that her jump was only an impulsive bit of fun, and that far from disregarding his feelings, she held them in the highest possible esteem.

Chatter, chatter, chatter, Freddie thought. He broke away and sat down on the ancient Chesterfield at the foot of his bed, brooding. The smell of roses and newly mown grass wafted in through his open windows. June was nearly over. Parliament would rise next month. The Liberal whip had told him it was all but certain that when they returned in September, Salisbury would call an election. He needed to be married by then. His funds were frighteningly low. Longmarsh's ancient roof required repairs, and Bingham had told him there would be little to give him until the winter. That wouldn't do. He needed money *now*. But he couldn't get it, because he couldn't get his bloody fiancée to give him a bloody wedding date.

India was sitting next to him now, fixing him with that deadly earnest stare of hers, still assuring him of her feelings.

"Tell me something, India," he said abruptly. "Are we *ever* going to marry? I have waited patiently for you for a long time. Your studies are over, yet still you refuse to decide upon a wedding date. There can be only one reason for this," he said, doing his best to look like a broken man. "If you don't want me anymore, if there's someone else, you must tell me and I shall step aside."

"Freddie, what are you saying?" she asked, shocked. "Of course there's no one else! How can you even think such a thing? I am completely faithful to you."

"What else *can* I think? What would *you* think? Why else would you possibly continue to put me off?"

"Freddie, there is only you. You have my word. How can I prove it to you? Will marrying you convince you?"

"You know it would. You know that is my fondest wish."

"Very well, then. Will October do? I think it best to wait until after the election. You'll be so preoccupied until then."

Freddie blinked at her, nearly speechless. "October would be wonderful," he said.

"It would be the most practical choice," India said. "I could ask Dr. Gifford for a week's holiday, but I fear that with being so new to the job, that would be all I could ask for. Did you have your heart set on a long honeymoon?"

"A trip of any length would be difficult right after the election."

"Perhaps we could go to the west country for a few days," she said. "To Cornwall."

"That would be so lovely. Just the two of us." He took her hand. "India, are you certain?"

"I am," she said, leaning over to kiss his cheek.

Freddie turned and caught the kiss on his mouth. His fingers stroked her cheek, her neck. "You have made me so happy. You are my life. My entire life. I would be lost without you."

"And I without you. I'm so sorry I've caused you such pain, Freddie. I had no idea. I've been terribly selfish. Far too preoccupied with my work. Do forgive me."

"Of course, my darling," he said, putting his arm around her. "And you must forgive my dreadful fit of temper," he said. "I know you didn't mean any harm. I'm overtired, I think. Long days at the House. I'm to give my speech on Home Rule next week and I still haven't finished it. It's jolly important. Could make or break me."

"Poor dear. I'm so sorry I worried you. It's the last thing you need. You've so much on your plate. You work far too hard."

"I do it for my constituents. And my country."

His pompous words almost made him laugh out loud, but they had the desired effect on India. She nestled closer to him and said, "You're a good man, Freddie Lytton."

"You make me good." He lifted her face to his, then said, "Kiss me again, India. I ache for you."

India shyly kissed his lips. He held her close, going slowly, being careful not to spook her. It might well end in tears this time just like all the other times, but if he succeeded, it would hardly matter. She had given him a date, finally, but he was taking no chances. He would make sure she could not change her mind as she'd done before. He would make love to her, and with a bit of luck he would make her pregnant.

He kissed her again, softly and gently. When he felt her soften in his arms, he moved his hands to her riding jacket and quickly undid the buttons. He pushed it off her shoulders and started on her blouse, all the time murmuring endearments to her.

"Freddie, I don't think—"

"Shh, darling, I only want to look at you. You're lovely . . . so lovely. . . ."

There was a corset underneath the blouse, boned and stiff, hard enough to stop a bullet. He would leave it alone. Too much work. He opened the top of her camisole and fondled her small breasts. They barely filled his hands. He bent his head to them so she could not see his disappointment.

"Freddie, don't . . ." she said, pulling away from him.

"Please don't tell me no again, India. Don't be cold to me. You're always so cold to me, and I want you so."

"But Freddie, this is how babies are made."

"I have something. I'll use it." He grimaced, making a show of adjusting himself. "My God, the pain . . . you've no idea what it's like."

She bit her lip. "Freddie, are you . . . are you a . . ."

"Of course I am. I saved myself for you."

"Do you know what to do?"

He smiled. "Silly girl, don't you? Didn't they cover this in medical school?"

"I guess I do . . . in theory. However, this is actual, not theoretical," India said, pulling her blouse together and looking around the room anxiously.

"Darling, we're quite alone, I assure you," Freddie said. He stood up, locked the door, then returned to her. "There's no one here but us. Let me make love to you. Here. Now. I want us to belong to each other. Don't you want that, too?"

India's eyes searched his. "Yes," she whispered. "Of course I do."

Freddie took her hand, stood her up, and undressed her. He got her riding habit off, her awful corset, stockings, and boots, and even her bloomers, but when he tried to get her chemise off, she protested.

"Wait," she said. "I'm sorry . . . too modest, I guess." She climbed into his bed, got underneath the covers, and took it off herself. Then she closed her eyes and leaned back against the pillows.

Good God, Freddie thought. This is going to be work. He grabbed his glass of gin and offered her a swallow. She took one, grimacing as the alcohol went down. Then he peeled off his own clothes and got into bed beside her.

He took her in his arms, murmuring endearments, telling her how much he loved her. He pulled the comb from her hair; kissed her face, her neck, her breasts; slipped his hand between her legs. He heard her breath catch as he pushed one finger inside her, then another. She was as dry as salt. He'd never known such a cold woman. There wasn't a spark of passion in her entire body, not an ounce of desire. He wondered how on earth he was ever going to perform. Then he thought of Gemma Dean, with her magnificent bosom and her round bottom, and he was hard in seconds. Relieved, he tried to slip inside India, but couldn't.

"Darling, this is impossible. You've got to open your legs," he whispered.

She opened them a little. Freddie pushed himself against her again. Her knees came up, her heels dug into the bed. He looked at her face. She was staring up at the ceiling, biting her lip. Patience, old boy, he told himself, patience. Men have worked much harder than this for twenty thousand a year.

"Shh, my darling. It's all right," he said. "Everything's all right."

He kissed her lips again. He tugged at her breasts and told her that he loved her. Then he pushed himself against her again, impatient to have done with it. He felt her arch against him, heard her gasp. Not with pleasure, he was sure of that, but with pain.

He knew he had to finish this. Quickly.

"I want you, India," he said. "So much . . ."

And then he wrenched her knees apart and shoved himself inside her. Something inside her gave way and she cried out. "Shh, my love, it hurts for only a second," he whispered. "That's what the chaps all say." He thrust into her again and again, covering her mouth with his own, stopping her cries. He gave one final thrust, shuddered, and then lay still, panting, his head on her chest. After a minute or so he sat up. India sat up, too. Her limbs were stiff and shaky. Her face was pale.

He took her hand and frowned with feigned concern. "Did I hurt you awfully?"

"A bit."

"My beautiful girl. Please don't be upset with me. I'm an oaf. Truly. I was mad with desire. I never meant to hurt you. Please say you're not angry with me." He took her face in his hands and kissed her. "Please?"

"Of course I'm not," India said quietly, trying to smile.

"The first time is hard. It gets better." He took her in his arms again. "You've made me so happy, darling," he said.

"I'm glad, Freddie."

He smiled at her, then slowly let his smile fade. "Oh, no. Oh, blast," he said, panic in his voice.

"What is it?"

"I forgot."

"Forgot what?"

"The rubber johnnie."

"Freddie, you didn't!"

"Don't worry. I'm sure it's all right. I'm sure nothing happened. And . . . and if it did, well, we'll be married soon, won't we? We'll just tell everyone the baby came a bit early."

He was gratified to see her already pale face turn white. He was about to say more when his mantel clock sounded. It was six. "Blast, is it that late? We're going to have to get bathed and ready for dinner."

"Yes, I suppose we are," she said. She pulled her chemise over her head, got out of bed, and put her clothes on.

"I love you, India. So much. You know that, don't you? I can't wait to be married. To have a home, a family, a life with you."

She twisted her hair up, secured it with her comb, then turned to him and smiled. "I can't wait for those things, either."

"I'll hardly be able to live without you until dinner. Wear something lovely. Pick out something just for me."

India said she would, then unlocked his door. As soon as she closed it behind her, Freddie collapsed back into his bed, heaving a long, ragged sigh. He raised his glass to his lips and drank deeply. He'd done it. Secured a wedding date and bedded that cold bitch at last. And with any amount of luck, she was up the duff. How he'd relished the look on her face when he'd told her he hadn't used anything. India fancied herself an emancipated woman, but even she wasn't insane enough to bear a child out of wedlock. The stigma, for both her and the child, would be crushing. Gifford would sack her immediately, and the British Medical Association would strip her of her license.

Freddie got up, shrugged into a dressing gown, and turned his gaze to the open windows. Longmarsh's lands loomed in the distance, wild and untended. There wasn't money enough for gardeners. His drunken father had seen to that. Freddie remembered how it had been before the accident—creditors at the door. Things being sold. Small things at first, rings and pillboxes. Then larger things such as paintings and furniture. Daphne in worn dresses, their collars and cuffs turned and mended. Bingham called home from Eton because their mother couldn't pay the school fees.

His gaze drifted to the music box again. He opened it, listening to the sad, halting strains of Chopin, then opened the drawer and lifted the dragonfly comb out again. It was beautiful, the exact match to the one he'd pulled from India's hair only moments ago. It had lived in the secret drawer of his music box for a long time. Years, in fact. Ever since the day he'd slipped it into his pocket as he handed its mate to Hugh Mullins.

Take it, Hugh. No one will ever know. . . .

Freddie saw Hugh again. Pale, frightened. Standing in the stables. He hadn't slept in days. Bea, his sister, was in serious trouble. She was pregnant. It was a boy from the village, and he'd done a runner as soon as she'd told him. She needed help. Needed money to pay a woman in the village who could take care of it. Otherwise it would mean disaster for her family. She'd lose her position; so would Hugh, and their father. They'd be forced to leave their home, a cottage that belonged to Lord Burnleigh.

Freddie had found all this out only days after he'd seen India and Hugh together and learned of their plans to elope. Maud had told him. She said India knew, and was trying to figure out how to get the money from her parents without explaining what it was for. He hadn't thought much more about it—he was too mired in his own misery over losing India—until a distraught Isabelle asked him to help her find a pair of missing hair combs.

"They've disappeared, Freddie," she said. "I can't think where I left them. My husband will be furious with me if I've lost them. He had them made especially for me."

"When did you last see them?" Freddie had asked, glad of a distraction from his own sorrows.

"I wore them to Cardiff yesterday, when I went to do some shopping. I remember taking them out before I arrived home—they were hurting me— and putting them into my reticule. I haven't seen them since."

Freddie had asked to see the reticule and discovered that it had split along a seam. Isabelle had been very upset when she'd seen it, convinced that the combs were gone forever, but he told her to remain calm. Perhaps they'd fallen out as she walked from the stables to the house and were lying in the grass. He himself would go look for them. He looked everywhere— in the grass, on the path, in the drive, and in the stables themselves. Finally he thought to look in Isabelle's carriage.

There, he spotted them. One was on the seat, the other on the carriage floor. As they glinted up at him, he had an idea. He would take one. He would say he'd found only a single comb and then he would sell the other. Quietly. To some London pawnbroker. He was desperate for money. As always. He'd put the first in his pocket and was just reaching for the second when he heard a voice behind him.

"Freddie? Is that you? Does Lady Burnleigh need her carriage brought round?"

It was Hugh.

The sound of Hugh's voice infuriated him. Jealousy over India boiled up in him again. He wanted to take a swing at Hugh. To flatten him. But he didn't. Because as his fingers closed around the second comb he suddenly had another, better idea. A wonderful idea.

He closed the door to the carriage and put the comb in Hugh's hand. "Take it, Hugh," he said. "No one will ever know."

Hugh looked at the comb, puzzled. "Take it? Why?"

"To help Bea."

Hugh drew in a sharp breath. "You know?"

Freddie nodded. "Maud told me. She tried to get ten quid from her mother, but Isabelle refused when she wouldn't say what it was for. Maud's upset. We all are. She said you'll be tossed out if her father finds out what's happening. Your whole family. Take it. Don't be stupid."

Hugh looked at the comb. "It's Lady Burnleigh's, isn't it?"

"She lost it. I said I'd look for it. When I go back in, I'll say I couldn't find it. She won't question me. She already thinks it's gone."

Hugh shook his head. He tried to hand it back, but Freddie wouldn't take it.

"It's only silver. The stones aren't real. It's not very valuable at all, but it'll bring you a few pounds at the pawnbroker's. Enough to help Bea. Think of her, Hugh. Think of Bea."

Hugh was struggling with himself. Freddie could see the anguish in his face. Finally he nodded, and without a word, put the comb in his pocket.

A week later, Bea was dead and Hugh was in jail. The pawnbroker had turned in the comb, and Hugh, to the police. Hugh hadn't peached on Freddie. He hadn't said a word. He was an honorable man. Freddie knew that.

Lord Burnleigh was outraged when he'd learned what had happened. India begged him to drop the charges against Hugh, and moved by her pleading he agreed to—*if* Hugh returned the second comb. But Hugh didn't. Because he couldn't. Because he didn't have it. Freddie did.

So Hugh went to prison, all the time insisting he didn't have the second comb, that he'd never had it. The place he was sent was a hell hole, full of vermin. He caught typhus from the lice in his mattress and was dead within a month. Mrs. Mullins, Hugh's mother, unable to bear the loss of her children, hanged herself. Hugh's father, homeless and alone, had wandered the countryside, sometimes sane, sometimes mad. His body had been found later that year in a nearby valley. He'd died of exposure.

Wouldst be king? First rip out thine own heart. . . .

That summer, he'd stilled the feeling in his heart almost completely.

By the time September came, and he was back at Oxford, everything and everyone had changed. Hugh and Bea were dead. India had fallen out with her parents and left Wales for London. Maud was about to make what would turn out to be a disastrous marriage. Their days spent together at Blackwood were gone forever. Their childhood was over.

The Red Earl was right. It was so much easier to function in the world without a heart. Easy to despise India, whom he'd once loved. Easy to watch her heartbreak unmoved, to offer only feigned sympathy, when the man she loved died. Easy to contemplate a loveless marriage to her when a distraught Isabelle visited him during his third year at university and begged him to marry India and put an end to her medical studies. He would never have India's heart, never have anything more than affection from her, so he would take her money instead. It was far more useful.

There was another knock on his door. Freddie put the comb back into the drawer. He'd never sold it; he never would. It was too dangerous. With the Tiffany mark and Isabelle's initials, it was too identifiable to show to even the most discreet of pawnbrokers.

"Enter," he said.

"Beg pardon, sir, but I've come to draw your bath." It was his man.

"Thank you, Armstrong," he said, putting the box down. "Armstrong . . ."

"Yes, sir?"

"When you've finished, will you please tell the butler to bring out some champagne before dinner? I wish to celebrate this evening. I will be announcing my wedding date."

"Very good, sir. And if I may offer them, my sincere congratulations."

Freddie accepted the man's good wishes. He felt as if a huge burden had been lifted from his shoulders. And indeed, one had—penury. He'd fixed that particular problem quite nicely. As he'd fixed other things. Because no one else would. And someone had to. Soon he would fix himself a starring role in the Liberal Party—something a damn sight better than backbencher—chief whip perhaps, or shadow foreign secretary. He would do it with his Home Rule speech and with his anti-crime efforts. Donaldson would continue to harass Malone. He would turn up something eventually, Freddie was certain. India had told him that Malone had nearly died in the hospital. He'd told her to make certain to keep him alive, for he wanted the pleasure of sending him down. By October, he'd be returned as MP for Tower Hamlets, married, and happily ensconced at Berkeley Square. Perhaps in November he'd take a journey to Blackwood, too, to inspect his future estate.

Blackwood didn't have Longmarsh's pedigree—it hadn't been designed by Wren—but it was much bigger, and it had all the modern conveniences. Today even this shit-heap of a Longmarsh was out of his reach, but soon nothing would be. Not even the one thing he wanted more than anything in the world—the sound of people calling him not Sir Frederick or Honorable Member, but Prime Minister.

He would do it. With brains and boldness and India's money. He had ripped out his heart, just as the Red Earl had advised, and one day he would be king.

CHAPTER 19

Maud Selwyn Jones sat at the vanity table in her room at Longmarsh, trimming her jet-black bangs. She snipped and shaped, then sat back in her chair, assessing the result. She shook her head, loving the way the bobbed ends felt against her neck. Freddie's and Bing's mother had blanched when she'd seen the cut. Maud smiled at the memory. She enjoyed shocking the wrinklies.

She picked up a coral earring. As she fastened it to her earlobe, her arm started to itch. "Have you gone and got yourself fleas, you dirty imp?" she asked Jerome, the tan pug who was lying at her feet. The dog looked up at her, blinking his coal black eyes. "No? Hmmm. Must be the beastly wallpaper then. Toile always brings me out in hives."

But Maud knew it wasn't the wallpaper. And she knew the itching would engulf her entire body, making her feel as if there were thousands of ants crawling on her. Unless she did something about it. Immediately.

She rose, opened the wardrobe, and dug in the pockets of her duster. To no avail. She opened her hat boxes and dragged her suitcases out, cursing the maid all the while.

"Where did that damned girl put it, Jerry?" she said, raking her nails over her forearm. She bit her lip, turning around in the center of her room. Her eyes, frantic now, came to rest on the night table. She ran to it and pulled open the drawer.

"There you are!" she said, lifting out a slim enameled case. She drew a cigarette from it, lit it, and took a deep drag. She held the blue smoke in her lungs, then slowly exhaled, eyes closed. When she opened them again, they were soft and liquid.

"God bless Teddy Ko," she murmured, smiling. He'd rolled a bit of pow-dered opium with tobacco for her to make what looked like proper ciga-rettes. She had just settled herself down at her vanity again when the door to her room was abruptly opened. It was India, still in her riding habit.

"Good ride?" Maud asked.

India said nothing. She closed the door, pulled off her jacket, and tossed it on the bed. Then she tossed herself on the bed, flopping into the soft cushions.

Maud turned around. She saw from her sister's face that she was upset. "Indy? What's wrong? What happened?"

India didn't answer. She just lay on the bed looking up at the ceiling. "Maud, am I cold?" she finally asked.

Maud walked to the bed. She felt India's forehead. "You feel quite warm, actually. Are you ill?"

India sat up. "Oh, Maud. Not that kind of cold. I mean . . . you know . . . *cold*."

"Ah," she said. "Trouble with Freddie?"

"Yes," India said. She twisted her engagement ring as she spoke. It was an old-fashioned emerald that had belonged to Freddie's mother. India wore it only around him to please him. She didn't care for jewelry; it harbored bacteria. "We settled on a wedding date."

"Did you? That's splendid news!"

"Yes, I suppose it is. Afterward, he kissed me, you see. And . . . and more. It didn't go very well. Does that mean I'm cold?"

"You and Freddie just made love?"

"Yes."

"But you've been engaged for two years! Do you mean to tell me you haven't slept with him in all this time?"

"Yes."

"India, you *are* hopeless," Maud said, sitting down at the vanity again.

"I suppose I am," she said miserably.

Maud softened. "Look, don't despair. There's nothing wrong with you that a little practice won't put right. Men are like bicycles. Not much fun till you learn how to ride them," she said, taking another drag of her cigarette.

"How . . . how do you learn?" India asked.

Maud coughed up a lungful of smoke. "*How*?! Didn't they teach you anatomy in medical school?"

India looked at the floor, pink with embarrassment, and Maud saw that this was painful for her. She regretted her flippant remark. "Look, darling, next time have a nice bottle of wine first," she said. "Then just let your feelings take over."

India nodded uncertainly.

"India, you do know what I'm talking about, don't you? You do have those feelings?"

"For Freddie?"

"Yes, of course for Freddie!"

India frowned as if concentrating on some thorny medical problem, then said, "Yes. Yes, I do. He'll make a wonderful husband." She continued talking, telling Maud what a brilliant leader Freddie was and how much he cared about the poor. "Why, just last week he accompanied me to a lecture by Benjamin Seebohm Rowntree, the Quaker reformer, on his ground-breaking study of poverty in the city of York. We'll be so effective as a couple, Maud. We'll do such important work together."

Maud sighed, exasperated. "Yes, Indy, I know all that. The question is: Do you want to fuck him?"

India blushed crimson. "Maud!"

"Oh, stop being such a prude. It sounds to me like you love Freddie the way I love Jerome. Or Wish."

"You love Wish? Well, of course you do! Who wouldn't love Wish?" Wish boomed, striding into the room.

"Does *anyone* believe in knocking?" Maud asked.

"Never! Gives a girl too much warning. How am I to catch a glimpse of ankle that way? Or something even better?" He hooked his finger in the V of Maud's silk robe and peered down the gap. She slapped his hand away.

"You didn't used to mind showing me your bosoms," he said.

"When I was ten and had none. And besides, you used to pay me for a look then."

"I'll pay you now. As much as you like. I'm about to have pots of money. Pots and pots and pots," Wish said. He plunked himself down at Maud's feet and scooped Jerome into his lap. Maud picked up a hairbrush and attempted to make order out of Wish's unruly brown mop. He smiled, enjoying the petting. "Don't you want to know how?"

"No," Maud and India said in unison.

"I knew you would. I'll tell you all about it." And with that, he launched into a pitch for his latest investment scheme—a land development project in California. "The place is called Point Reyes, and it's paradise," he said. "It's about fifty miles north of San Francisco. You've never seen anything so beautiful. You've never even *dreamed* anything so beautiful. It's an outcropping of land on the California sea coast. And twelve hundred acres of it are for sale. I'm going to buy the entire parcel and put a hotel at the water's edge. Not just *any* hotel, mind you, a luxury hotel. There's more money than you can possibly imagine in San Francisco, and I'm going to lure it north. The venture can't fail. You've got to get in on it. Both of you. I'll make you a bloody fortune."

"That would make a change," Maud said. "You lost me a bloody fortune on that South African diamond mine."

"How did I know they'd start a war over there? I made you money on U.S. Steel, didn't I? Quite a bit, actually."

"I suppose you did," Maud admitted.

"And you, Indy? Are you still living off that Bank of England account?"

"What? Oh, yes. Yes, I am."

"Well, it's time you got rid of that. The return is far too low. It's too safe, that account. It's for vicars and little old ladies and . . . I say, old hound, is something wrong?"

"How very observant you are, Wish," Maud said archly.

"What is it, Indy?" he asked.

"Nothing, really. I'm fine."

Wish gave her a look.

"India just met the Honorable Member's member. And didn't particularly like him."

"Maud!" India screeched, mortified.

Maud flapped a hand at her, then told Wish what had happened.

He nodded sagely, then said, "Not to worry. I know exactly what the problem is."

"Oh, do you?" Maud asked.

"Yes. Absolutely. Let me ask you something, Indy—do you love Freddie?"

"Of course I love Freddie."

He clapped his hands together. "Well, stop it. Love buggers everything. Love be damned, I say. You should *never* be in love with your spouse. You should only be in love with your lover. And he should be someone entirely unsuitable. An actor, perhaps. Or a painter. That sort."

"That's some fabulous advice," Maud said.

"It's excellent advice!" he protested. "One should only marry for heirs and spares, houses and horses. Why else would one do it? It's like volunteering to go to prison. I'll never do it. Prefer to make my money honestly."

"Go wash, Wish," Maud said. "They'll be calling us for supper soon."

Wish looked from Maud to India. "Wasn't I helpful?"

"Not in the least," India said.

"Hmmm. Guess I'm better at money than love." He stood to leave. "See you at dinner, my darlings."

He left, and Maud turned back to her sister. She still looked unhappy.

"India?"

"Hmm?"

"You didn't answer my question earlier. About your feelings. What I meant was—"

"I know what you meant," India said peevishly.

"So you do love Freddie?"

"I just told Wish I did. Didn't you hear me?"

"I heard you perfectly well. I just didn't believe you."

"All right then, no," she said angrily. "I don't love Freddie. And that is *exactly* why I intend to marry him. I had those feelings once. A long time ago. I never want them again."

"Hugh?" Maud asked.

India said nothing.

"You don't *have* to marry Freddie."

"I *want* to marry Freddie. We belong together. He's perfect."

"You mean he's safe."

India was silent for a few seconds, then she said, "Hugh Mullins was a fantasy, Maud. We both know that. A fantasy cooked up by a silly young girl."

"I don't remember you dismissing Hugh as a fantasy at the time. I remember you being heartbroken."

India shook her head. "It was all romance novel nonsense. Marriages—the good ones—are built on mutual interests, similar backgrounds, affection, respect, regard, not necessarily love."

"Where'd you get that insight? From one of your textbooks?"

"Go ahead, Maud, make remarks. What about Duff? That was all about love and attraction and . . . and *sex*. We all tried to talk you out of *that*, but you had to have him."

When she was nineteen, Maud married Duff Haddon, a duke's son. He was rakishly handsome, smart, funny, exciting to be around. Unfortunately—as she found out shortly after they were married—he was also a drunk. He was killed while they were holidaying in Cairo. He'd had too much wine at a restaurant and insulted the proprietor. His body was found the next morning in a filthy alley. He'd been stabbed to death. Maud was not quite twenty-one when she was widowed. Desperate to put the pain of losing Duff behind her, she'd taken back her maiden name and tried to forget him.

"Yes, Indy, I made a disastrous marriage," Maud said. "We all know that. And it's very useful to your argument to hold it up as an example and say that you don't want to make the same mistake, but it is also dishonest. The truth is that you are going to marry a man you don't love because losing the man you did love nearly destroyed you, and you won't open yourself up to that kind of pain again."

India glared at her, about to make a retort, then suddenly she surrendered instead. In typical India fashion, Maud noted. Not by admitting defeat, but by changing the subject.

"Let me have that," she said, motioning for her cigarette.

"Oh, you don't want this," Maud said hastily. "It's . . . um . . . unhealthy."

"I do. Just a puff," India said.

"Really, India, I don't think . . ."

India got off the bed, walked over to Maud, and snatched the cigarette. She took a couple of quick drags, then coughed violently.

"Good God, what's in this? Gunpowder?" she asked, handing it back.

Close, Maud thought.

India coughed again, said she felt lightheaded, and lay back down on the bed.

Wonderful, Maud thought. All we need tonight is India higher than a kite at dinner with her future in-laws. Good God, what'll I do? I'll ring for tea. No, coffee, extra strong. She did so.

"Coffee. What a good idea," India said. "I feel ever so sleepy suddenly. Must be the country air." She closed her eyes, and after a minute or so quietly said, "He was beautiful, wasn't he, Maud? He was so very beautiful. I still dream about him."

Maud barely recognized this soft, languid voice. It was such a change from India's usual brisk tones. She knew it was the opium talking.

"He was indeed," Maud said. "What is it the poets say? *'Tis better to have loved and lost, than never to have loved at all*."

"Tennyson. What a prat," India said. "I bet he never loved anyone. He wouldn't spout such tripe if he had."

Maud remembered that awful day—the day Bea died and Hugh was arrested. The house had been in an uproar. They had disappeared, Hugh and Bea. Neither had come to work for two days and no one could find them. India was beside herself with worry. Maud, too. They knew Bea was pregnant.

It was India who'd finally found them, huddled in the ruins of an old cottage on their father's estate. Bea had had an abortion. Hugh'd paid for it, but he wouldn't say how.

Something had gone wrong. The bleeding wouldn't stop. Bea had a fever, she was terribly ill, but she wouldn't let Hugh take her home or to the village doctor. She was afraid of anyone finding out what she'd done.

India had fetched them and they'd all gone to the cottage together—herself, India, Freddie, Bing, and Wish—to try to work out what to do. Bea was wrapped in old horse blankets. Maud could see the blood seeping through them. Bingham was standing in a corner of the ruined cottage, pale and silent. Freddie was pacing. Wish was holding Bea's hand, telling her stupid jokes, trying to jolly her out of it.

"We have to get her to the hospital," India said. "We have to take her *now*."

"India, slow down. Let me think for a minute," Freddie had said.

"We don't have a minute!"

Freddie had taken her by the elbow then and marched her away from Bea and Hugh, so they couldn't hear him. But Maud had.

"What she's done is against the law," he whispered. "If we're not careful, we'll all catch it."

"For God's sake, Freddie, she's ill! She needs help. Don't you see that? Don't you care for her at all?"

"I do care for her!" he'd hissed. "Of course I do, but I care for you more. What if you're arrested? Just wait, can't you? Wait until I can think of a proper solution. Until I can sort this out."

"I can't wait. She can't wait," India said flatly.

Then she'd told Hugh to carry Bea down to Blackwood's gates and stay behind the trees there. The gates weren't far from the cottage. She would come for them. In one of the traps. She would take them to Cardiff. To the hospital there. Where they weren't known. She'd stalked off alone, leaving the rest of them to worry and whisper. When she'd shown up by the gates, a furious Freddie got into the trap with her. He made Maud stay with Bingham, who looked like he might faint any second, and had Wish go up to the house to explain to Lord Burnleigh what had happened, and to assure him that he, Freddie, would safeguard India.

It was because of Freddie, Maud thought now, that the family had avoided an enormous scandal. He had intimidated the hospital staff, and two members of the press, telling them that the Earl of Burnleigh would have their jobs if any of them dared to mention his daughter's name in connection with Hugh and Bea Mullins. When they arrived home, the earl had raged at India and told her to get out of his sight. After she'd gone to her room, he thanked Freddie and commended him on his quick thinking, then he'd sacked Hugh's grieving father and mother and threw them out of their cottage.

Everything changed after that. They were none of them ever the same people again. The memories of what had happened at the cottage—of what each had done, or failed to do—haunted them. Maud knew that Hugh's death was the reason behind Wish's inability to settle and Bingham's withdrawal from the world. She blamed Freddie's drivenness on it, and her own constant need to divert herself with unsuitable men and equally unsuitable substances. Losing Hugh and his family had traumatized them all, but it had damaged India the most. It was why she'd become a doctor. Why she'd turned her back on their parents. And why she now wished to marry a man she did not love.

Maud looked at her sister now. She was breathing softly. Her eyes were closed. She saw her, for a moment, as she was when she was seventeen—shy and smart, always blinking behind her spectacles. Flinching at their mother's voice. Awkward inside the house. Brave outside of it. Riding horses no one else dared even mount. Getting cats out of tall trees. Taking Christmas boxes to the poor. Going right up to their cottage doors and handing them to the thin mothers and their dirty, wide-eyed children.

Most of all, she remembered India's face aglow in the darkness of their bedroom as she told her what Hugh's lips and hands felt like, and how much she loved him. Her voice had been so full of feeling, so full of passion when she talked about him. And his death had broken her heart. She'd been inconsolable. Eventually, she had picked up the jagged pieces, put them into a box, and put the box on a high shelf, never to be opened again. All the passion in her life went into her studies after Hugh. Not to a man. And certainly not to Freddie.

It was no way to enter into a marriage, Maud thought.

Or was it?

Maybe it was better to put your heart up on a nice high shelf, rather than risk its getting broken. Perhaps India has the right idea after all, she thought. Maybe it's best to marry a good, sensible partner and have companionship and affection, rather than love.

Maybe.

India had fallen asleep. Maud placed a woollen throw over her. She touched the back of her hand to her sister's cheek, smoothed her furrowed brow. She thought of the years India had spent studying the human body, how hard she had worked to unlock its mysteries. She knew the names of muscles and bones. Knew how organs worked. Knew everything there was to know, except the most important thing.

"Poor little Indy," she whispered. "You know so much, so bloody much, but you don't even know your own heart."

CHAPTER 20

"Mel, what'll I do?" Fiona asked the foreman at Oliver's Wharf. Her heart was racing. She was trembling with excitement. "We were going to have lunch. A quiet lunch on the Old Stairs. Just the two of us. Can you imagine? I couldn't get near the Old Stairs now if I tried."

A roar went up, rolling over her like thunder. She laughed, then shook her head in disbelief.

"I've never seen anything like it," Mel Trumbull said. "Not in all me born days. You shouldn't venture down there, Mrs. B. Too many blokes shouting and carrying on. Stay up here out of harm's way."

Fiona and Mel were standing at an open loophole in Oliver's tea wharf. Below them, in Wapping High Street, about a thousand men stood shoulder to shoulder, shouting, whistling, and clapping. Some stood in the backs of delivery wagons or hung off lampposts. Scores more crowded the doorways of neighboring wharves. All of them were craning their necks to get a better view of a blond man who was pacing back and forth on top of a lumber wagon, thundering at them with passion and conviction.

"How did he get up there?" Fiona asked.

"Word got out that he was in the pub with Tillet and Burns. Some blokes collared him on his way out and hoisted him up on their shoulders. They stuck him on top of the wagon and asked for a speech," Mel replied.

"Looks like they're getting one," Fiona said.

Her heart swelled with pride as she watched the man. A smile as broad as the Thames broke over her face. She knew him. So well. And yet watching him now, watching him command the attention of thousands, she felt she was seeing him anew.

It was Joe. Her Joe.

He'd gone to the Town of Ramsgate, a riverside pub next to Oliver's, for an exploratory meeting with Ben Tillet and John Burns—two influential labor leaders and architects of the 1889 dockers' strike. He'd meant only to feel them out, to seek their advice, possibly their support, for his bid for the Tower Hamlets seat. He'd known that Fiona planned to be at Oliver's that morning inspecting a tea shipment, and had asked her to join him for fish and chips on the Old Stairs, to tell her what, if anything, had resulted from the meeting. Their meal would have to wait, however, for the voters clearly would not. Fiona gripped the edge of the loophole as another roar went up from the crowd.

"Does he do this often?" Mel asked.

"He's never done it in his life," she replied.

"Blimey, Mrs. B. Has he been taking elocution lessons?"

Fiona laughed. "Yes, in fact he has. For the last thirty years!"

Some would have been overwhelmed by the demand for an impromptu speech in front of such a huge, boisterous crowd. Not Joe. He might be head of a retail empire now and more used to plush boardrooms than street corners, but he'd been born and bred a costermonger—and costers were *never* short of words. He'd grown up in the streets of Whitechapel, spending more of his life on the cobbles than in his house. His first words were "Buy my fine parsley-o!" yelled from his cradle—an old vegetable basket—tucked behind his parents' barrow.

He knew East London, knew the people who lived there, and he knew how to speak to them. He had a way of making his speech into a dialogue. He joked with his spectators one minute, challenged them the next. As a lad, Joe had used costers' tricks to catch people's eyes. Now he was using his words to capture their hearts and minds.

She saw that he'd flung off his suit jacket. His sleeves were rolled up; his tie was gone. She knew he'd done it only because he hated suits and always said he couldn't think straight in a jacket and tie, but the gesture had the effect of uniting him with his audience. In his shirtsleeves and open collar, he was no longer a guv'nor, he was one of them.

A thickset man made a bullhorn of his hands. "The Stronghold's robbed of guns and the guv what owned them takes his business to Southwark," he shouted at Joe. "The Morocco burns and it's fifteen more blokes out of work. We need more coppers. Will you get them for us?"

Joe shook his head. "No," he said. "No, I won't."

There were sounds of astonishment, boos, and guffaws. Joe waited them out, then said, "Why would I waste ratepayers' money like that? There are enough constables here already. Enough station houses."

The booing died down; the crowd quieted.

"Lytton promises you more constables," Joe said, "because it makes for good headlines. Sometimes he even gives them to you, but it doesn't matter. He could send in a thousand more constables and it wouldn't matter. You want to get rid of crime? Get rid of its causes—poverty, ignorance, hunger, disease. No, I won't get you more police officers or jails, I'll get you more schools and more hospitals. I'll get you better wages for your work and compensation for your injuries. You want more rozzers, vote for Freddie Lytton. You want a living wage, a better life, a future . . . vote for me."

A cheer went up. There were whistles and applause.

Fiona watched Joe, amazed. "It's as if he were born to this," she said to Mel.

Mel nodded. "I think he was, Mrs. B. He's a coster like you said. Selling's in their blood, and what's politics if it ain't selling? Only difference is, it ain't apples he's selling now, it's himself."

"And it looks like the crowd is buying," she said.

Fiona had been shocked the morning Joe told her he wanted to run for the Tower Hamlets seat, but she'd soon recovered herself and said it was a wonderful idea, that he must do it, and that she would support him every step of the way. She knew he would need her support, and the support of many others besides, for he had a tremendous battle ahead of him.

During the last general election, in '95, the Independent Labour Party had failed to get even one of its candidates elected. A new Labour Party had come into being just this year, when the ILP combined with another political group, the Social Democratic Federation, and a handful of trade unions to form the Labour Representation Committee. Joe would be an untried candidate running under the banner of an untried party. The odds were totally against him, but he was determined to run anyway. He planned to make his status as a political outsider an asset instead of a liability. He would make it very clear that were he to be elected, it would *not* be business as usual. His would be a new voice in Parliament, one not bound by tradition or title, one who spoke solely for East London and its people.

"Why should we trust you?" a man in a flat cap yelled out. "You're not a working man. You're running on the Labour ticket, but you're not Labour, you're Capital!"

Joe smiled. "Too right I am!" he said. "I'm one of the richest men in the whole flipping country!" There was surprise at his answer, then delighted laughter at the honesty of it. "I'm rich enough that no one owns me and no one ever will," he continued. "But make no mistake, I didn't start out that way. I was selling apples on the streets in the wind and the rain when I was five years old. Costers had no union when I was coming up. We still don't. If I was ill or injured and couldn't work, I went hungry. I never forgot that. Never forgot what it's like to be on the outside looking in. I know what you're up against, the others don't. Do you think Lytton or Lambert ever went without a meal? Ever shivered because they hadn't the money for coal? I'm Capital, all right, but I'm Capital with a conscience."

"That's a good one, that. He should put that on a banner," Mel said approvingly.

Fiona shushed him. Another man was speaking.

"Why should we vote Labour?" he asked. "Why should we vote at all? What's Parliament to us? The toffs in government don't give a toss about the working man. They never have. Any power we've won for ourselves, we've won through the unions."

A cheer went up. Joe waited until it died down, then he said, "Yes, you've won power—through a great deal of courage and sacrifice, I might add—but how long can you keep it?"

No one answered.

"Capital wants it back, and they've formed a group called the Employers' Parliamentary Council to get it. You read the papers same as me, you've heard of it. And you know what they're doing. They're not going to fight you on the picket line anymore; they're going to fight you in Parliament. They've got blokes lobbying the government day and night to stop any bills favorable to the working man. And they're succeeding. They're breaking strikes with lockouts and blacklegs, and they won't stop there. Rumor has it they're trying to get a law on the books that will allow them to sue unions for damages, and even take away the right to strike."

"What'll you do about it?" someone shouted.

"I'll meet them on their own battlefield," Joe shouted back. "I'll take the fight from the factory floor and the sweatshop and the waterfront all the way to Westminster. You live in the wealthiest city in the wealthiest country in the entire world. That's wealth you—each and every one of you—helped to create. With your graft, your sweat, your blood."

He paused here, paced back and forth, then suddenly rounded on his audience and shouted, "So why are your kids hungry? Why do your wives go without? Why do you work twelve, fourteen, sixteen hour days and *still* have to choose between shoes for your son and a coat for your daughter?"

There were more cheers, urgent and impassioned. Joe held up his hands for silence. Fiona could see his sides heaving. He was panting, nearly played out.

"We can't hope to win playing by their rules. It's time we made a few of our own. Marches and strikes were the first step, legislation is the next. Let's go to Westminster together. Let's change the old laws and write some new ones. Laws that protect your wages, your jobs, your families. What do you say? Will you take that step with me?"

Another enormous roar went up. It gathered and rose like a tidal wave, rolling over the brick canyon that was Wapping High Street, engulfing everything in its path. Hats were flung into the air. Hands reached up, straining to touch Joe.

John Burns stepped up onto one of the wagon's wheels. "What do you say, lads?" he shouted. "Shall we give him a crack at it?"

The roar grew louder. The reaching hands grasped Joe and pulled him down. The crowd closed over him like turbulent water. Fiona's heart skipped a beat, her hands came to her mouth, and then he suddenly bobbed up like a cork, seated on the shoulders of two burly workmen. The crowd parted for him and he was paraded down the High Street, past wharves and warehouses, where he was cheered from loopholes and gangways. Fiona saw him waving as he was carried around a bend and out of sight.

"That clinches it. You're on your own for dinner, Mrs. B," Mel said.

"I think you're right. I wonder if they'll bring him back in time for supper." She squinted after her husband. "I wonder where they're taking him?"

"*Where?*" Mel echoed, laughing. "Why, Mrs. B, he's on his way to Westminster!"

CHAPTER 21

"Mary Ellerton, the little girl with TB, had a bad night. You'll want to see her first," the matron said. "And there's a Mr. Randall, a builder, came in an hour ago with a broken arm. Dr. Gifford set it, but wanted you to check on him."

"Dr. Gifford's here?" India asked, surprised.

"Yes. He had emergency surgery this morning. Gallstones. Sister Moskowitz assisted. Here's the entire roster."

India took the clipboard and thanked the woman. She paged through the names. Twenty at least. It was already eight a.m., and she was supposed to see patients at Varden Street at ten. She finished reading the roster, drained her cup of tea, and prepared to start her day. She had just pulled her stethoscope out of her bag when she heard a knock at the door. It opened before India could say "Come in" and a beaming Ella appeared, followed by what seemed to be two enormous fruit baskets on legs. The baskets were breathtaking—lined with moss and decorated with ribbons and fresh flowers—and were piled so high with fruits, nuts, biscuits, and sweets that India could not see the faces of the men carrying them.

"Gorgeous, aren't they?" Ella said.

"Oi! Ella! These ain't light. Tell us where to put them."

"I'll tell you where to put them, all right."

"Come on, will you? Me back's breaking!"

"Ella? What's going on?" India asked.

"Put them on the floor, right there," Ella said.

The men did as she said. When they'd put down the baskets, India saw who they were—Sid Malone's men.

"Mr. Betts, Mr. Smith, why have you brought these?" she asked.

"They're a thank-you, missus. From the guv. And from us. For fixin' him up."

"Mr. Betts, I can't—"

"*Believe* how generous this is," Ella said. "It's much too kind of you. Isn't it, Dr. Jones?" She turned so that only India could see her face and gave her a warning look.

"Why . . . yes. It certainly is."

"Thanks, El," Frankie said. He leaned over and kissed her cheek.

"Wasn't me. It's Dr. Jones you want to be thanking," Ella said.

Frankie looked as alarmed as India felt at the prospect of a kiss. He doffed his hat instead. "Yeah, well . . . thanks, missus," he said.

"Your thanks are not required, Mr. Betts. I was only doing my job."

Frankie looked as if he'd been gobsmacked. Ella shook her head and India felt she'd said something terribly wrong. A wave of irritation washed over her. Why was it always so hard for her to talk to these people?

"Well, we're off now. Ta-ra, El. See you at the caff."

"Ta-ra, lads. Thanks again."

As soon as the door closed behind them, India said, "Ella, throw the baskets out."

"*What?*"

"I don't want them here. We both know how they were paid for. From theft and drugs and God knows what else. I don't want any part of Sid Malone's ill-gotten gains. Get rid of them."

Ella snorted. "The hell I will."

India blinked at her, taken aback.

"Your eyes all right? You see in color? Blue, red, green, yellow?" Ella asked.

"Of course I do."

"Then why is *everything* so bleedin' black and white to you? There's a whole ward of sick kids downstairs. The poor little blighters would love a biscuit or an orange."

"So it's all right to corrupt children, is it?" India asked, stung by Ella's criticism. "Feed them on the profits of others' misery?"

"I don't care if Sid Malone has hooves and a pointy tail. Those kiddies are getting that fruit."

"Fine, Ella. Do what you like," India said stiffly, returning to her roster.

"For God's sake, let your hair down a bit, will you? Let a bad man do a good deed. Even if it's us doing it for him."

India wanted to ask Ella how she, an upstanding woman who dutifully observed the Sabbath, could banter and joke with criminals, but she couldn't. Ella had left.

A sudden knock on the door startled her. A junior sister, Alison Fitch, poked her head in.

"You're needed, Dr. Jones. A Miss Milo just came into the emergency ward. Won't tell us what's wrong. Says she's your patient."

India was out the door before the girl had stopped talking. "Milo . . . Milo . . ." she murmured. The name sounded familiar. It came to her. The young woman who'd asked for contraceptives.

Emma Milo was leaning against the wall in the admitting area. Even from yards away, India could see there was something terribly wrong. Her eyes were half closed. Her face was drained of all color.

"Miss Milo?" she said. "Miss Milo, what is it?"

With effort, Emma Milo opened her eyes. "Please help me," she said.

"Can you walk? There's a bed right over here."

Miss Milo pushed herself off the wall. She took one slow step, then another, keeping her eyes fixed on India.

"Good Lord," Fitch said. She was looking at the floor where Miss Milo had been standing. India followed her gaze. There was blood on the tiles. Far too much of it.

India rushed to the woman, catching her just as she slumped. "Get me a trolley!" she barked.

Fitch raced off and returned with one. Together they lifted Miss Milo onto it. She cried out as they did, then drew her knees up to her chest. The back of her dress was soaked with blood.

India collared another nurse. "Take her to Surgery One," she ordered.

"Dr. Gifford used it this morning. It's still being cleaned," the woman said.

"Two, then. Go!" The nurses rolled the trolley away. India ran ahead of it and burst through the surgery doors. She knew she should scrub, get a clean apron, but there was no time. She raced to the sink, fumbled for a bottle of carbolic and poured it over her hands, then rushed to Miss Milo's side. Fitch was assembling a tray of instruments. The other sister—Arnold—had cut the waistbands of her skirt and undergarments and pulled them off. They lay in a bloodstained heap on the floor.

"Miscarriage?" she asked.

"I don't think so," India said. She'd seen this kind of bleeding before. A long time ago. In a hospital in Wales. Images of Bea and Hugh came flooding back to her, and with them feelings of panic and grief. She clamped down on them.

"Miss Milo, can you hear me? Miss Milo? Salts, Fitch." Her voice was low, confident, and full of authority. It did not betray the fear she felt. She would not allow it to. Fitch waved smelling salts. Miss Milo coughed and tried to turn away.

"Good girl. Stay with me now," India said. "Fitch, get the stirrups up. We'll lift her onto the table."

"This table doesn't have them, Doctor. Only Surgery One," Fitch said.

Fury flared inside India. Gifford had used One for his patient. A male patient. He should have left it open. "Take her left leg, Fitch. Arnold, take the right." The two nurses lifted Miss Milo's legs and bent them at the knee. Her bottom and thighs were covered with blood. More was pouring out of her. India tried to get a speculum in. Miss Milo arched and screamed; the instrument slipped out and clattered to the floor. A piece of Fenwick's advice came back to her: *Screaming is good. Encourage it. It means your patient is still alive.* Once, she'd been horrified by his flip statements. Now she understood why he used them: they were the only armor a doctor had in the face of such suffering.

She tried again. She placed one hand on the woman's abdomen, the other disappeared inside her. Her hands became her eyes. They told her what she had suspected. "Her uterus is punctured. In several places. I'm going to have to operate. Arnold, carbolic. Fitch, chloral and a mask."

"Dr. Jones, please . . ." It was Miss Milo. Her eyes were open and lucid. "When my parents come for me, don't tell them what happened. There was a baby. It was my employer's. He's married."

"Who did this to you? Where did you go?"

"I don't know. Thomas took me. It was in someone's kitchen. A woman did it. It was dirty there and it hurt so."

Miss Milo swallowed, her eyes fluttered closed. Her hands scrabbled at the air. India caught them in her own bloodied ones.

"I'm afraid," Miss Milo whispered. "Oh, God, I'm so afraid . . ."

"The chloral, Fitch!" India shouted.

"Right here."

India watched as the nurse pressed a mask over Miss Milo's face. She took three deep breaths then stopped breathing altogether. Her chest sank.

India ripped the mask off. She started chest compressions. Behind her, the two nurses traded worried glances.

"One . . . two . . . three . . ." she counted, pistoning her palms into the woman's chest. "Fitch, roll a sheet and put it under her back. Arnold, pull her arms above her head. Come on! Where are you? Move!"

"Dr. Jones . . . ma'am, she's gone," Arnold said quietly.

India stepped back, shaking her head. "She's not. She can't be. I've never lost a patient. She *can't* be." She looked at the woman, at the blood between her legs, at her lifeless eyes. "Oh, God," she said, pounding the heels of her hands against her forehead.

"Don't blame yourself, Dr. Jones. She did it to herself and it served her right. What she done was wrong. Dead wrong," Fitch said.

India closed her eyes. She took a deep breath, but it didn't help. "Get out," she said.

"Beg your pardon?"

"Get out of here."

"But I have to take her to the mortuary."

"Don't touch her. Get out. Go."

"Yes, Dr. Jones," Fitch said, looking sullen but stepping smartly.

India straightened Miss Milo's splayed legs, then covered them with a sheet. She wiped her own bloody hands on the hem of her even bloodier jacket, then gently closed the woman's eyes.

"I should be doing that, Dr. Jones," Sister Arnold said.

"I can manage."

India and her nurse picked the dead woman's underthings off the floor in silence, folded them, and placed them next to her body. Arnold snapped open another sheet and draped it over Miss Milo.

"I should have helped her," India said hollowly.

"You *did* help her," Sister Arnold said. "There was nothing more anyone could have done. She'd lost too much blood."

"I meant earlier. When she first came to see me. I should have helped her. I'm a coward. A damned coward." She turned and walked out of the surgery and back to her office. She'd left her roster there in her haste to get to Miss Milo.

She'd meant to get the roster and leave. She had rounds to do. Instead, she sat down in her chair and put her head in her hands. Hot tears welled behind her eyes. She squeezed them back.

She heard Fenwick's voice again. *You what, Jones? You feel . . . You are not in my class to feel.*

Don't feel, she told herself. Don't feel this. Don't feel anything.

There was a knock on the door. India didn't hear it. The knob turned and the door opened.

"Dr. Jones?" a masculine voice said.

She lifted her head. It was Sid Malone. She quickly stood, embarrassed. "Mr. Malone," she said. "What can I do for you?"

Sid said nothing. He was staring at her coat, wide-eyed. She looked down at it. It was covered in blood.

"Sorry. I didn't realize . . ." India started to say. She stopped, then started again. "A girl. No more than seventeen. Botched abortion. I lost her. Just now."

"She's the first, isn't she? The first one you lost."

"Yes, she is," India said. "How did you know that?"

"You told me," he said.

He held her gaze, and she wondered how such a hard man could have such gentle eyes.

"It was bad. She suffered," he said.

India broke his gaze, unnerved.

"No one dies smiling, Mr. Malone. Did you know that? The very idea is a fairy tale. Utter tripe. People die in pain and afraid. Screaming, crying, cursing, begging, but never, ever smiling. So yes. To answer your question . . . yes, she suffered." India angrily ripped her coat off, wadded it up, and threw it in a corner.

"And now you are."

"I don't take your meaning."

"Suffering. Because she did."

"I'm angry, that's all," she said quickly. "I had a useless nurse assisting me and I had to work on a decrepit operating table with no stirrups because Dr. Gifford, my employer, took the best table for a gallstone surgery." She threw her hands up in frustration. "Gallstones! They're a doddle. A monkey could take them out. On a fruit crate. With a corkscrew. And he's got to take the best table without even a thought for what anyone else is going to do if we get a miscarriage or an obstructed labor, never mind a botched abortion."

India talked on, telling Sid about the appalling state of medical care for women and the lethal hypocrisy of a medical establishment that provided birth control to the moneyed classes and forbade it to the poor, the very ones who needed it the most. And Sid said nothing. He did not make faces, spout platitudes, or advise her to calm down. He let her talk. He listened until she ran out of steam and stopped pacing, and then he said, "Your guv's no good."

"My *guv?*"

"Gifford. He's no good. You should be out on your own. You could do things your way then. The right way. Why aren't you?"

"I can't afford to. And I don't want to. At least, I don't want to be in private practice. I have hopes . . . well, only dreams, really . . . of opening a clinic one day. For poor women and children. Here in Whitechapel. I've started saving for it. Patients would pay only what they could afford, even if it was nothing."

She stopped talking. He must think I'm mad, she thought. Maybe I am. Because I've done it again. Poured out my heart to him. First about my studies, then about Hugh, now this. I've never told Freddie some of these things. What on earth is wrong with me? Why do I tell him these things? Him of all people?

"Can't you ask your father for the money? You said he was loaded."

"I don't want his money. I haven't asked him for a penny since the day I left Blackwood. I won't start now."

"I'll give you the money, then."

"I beg your pardon?"

"I'll give you the money for your clinic. How much do you need?"

India stared at him. She couldn't believe that he would make such a wildly generous offer—or that he would think for a second that she would accept it.

"Thank you. Very much. But I couldn't possibly take it," she said.

"Why not?"

She did not reply.

"My money's dirty. Is that it?"

"Mr. Malone, I am a *doctor*. I took an oath to heal people. How can I accept money made by destroying them?"

It was Sid's turn to go quiet. He took a handkerchief from his pocket and touched it to her forehead. "Blood," he said.

India stood stiffly as he wiped it away. He was standing so close to her and his touch was so gentle. She had the sudden overwhelming urge to lean her head on his chest and cry for Miss Milo. To cry out all her sadness and anger.

"I'm sorry, Mr. Malone," she said briskly, taking a step back. "I'm certain you did not come here to listen to a diatribe on the state of medicine in Britain or to a junior doctor's career goals. Why did you come? What can I do for you?"

Sid held his hands up. "No, it's me who's sorry. I only wanted to stop in before I left, that's all. Tell you thanks for what you did."

"Really, Mr. Malone, I was just—"

"Doing your job. I know. All in a day's work, right?" he said, with a touch of bitterness. "I still want to say thank you. And to tell you that if there's ever anything I can do for you—anything you need . . ."

"Yes, well, should I ever find myself in need of a stolen painting or a pound of opium, I shall know upon whom to call," India said tartly.

"Aye, well . . . ta-ra, Dr. Jones," Sid said. The depths of his eyes were hidden to her now. The gentleness was gone. He doffed his cap and then he was gone, too.

India closed her eyes and groaned. *Why* had she said that? He had only tried to thank her, to offer his help, and in return she had all but pushed him out the door. *Why?*

She knew the answer. She knew that if she had cried for Miss Milo, if she had leaned her head upon his chest, he would have let her. There would have been no words, just his strong arms around her, his cheek pressed against her own. And she knew that she'd wanted his warmth just then, his touch, more than she'd ever wanted Freddie's.

She knew it, and it terrified her.

CHAPTER 22 ❧

"Good afternoon, Mr. Lytton."

"Prime Minister."

"I'm ready to hear a brilliant speech. Are you ready to make one?"

"I am, sir," Freddie said, smiling. "And history."

Lord Salisbury's bushy eyebrows shot up. His shrewd eyes sparkled. "Not lacking for confidence, are we? That's the spirit, my boy."

The prime minister, flanked by several of his senior ministers, had just entered St. Stephen's Hall in Westminster, where Freddie had been standing, silently gathering his thoughts for the ordeal ahead of him. In a few short minutes, he would deliver his speech in support of the Irish Home Rule Bill. Salisbury stood with him for a few minutes, complaining about the rush of tedious governmental business that had to be completed before Parliament rose for the summer.

"What was it yesterday? Oh, yes! Wine tariffs, an outbreak of hoof-and-mouth in the Fens, and a petition for funds to establish traffic lights at Basingstoke. Damned dull stuff, I tell you. It's all one can do to stay awake." He paused, then archly added, "I don't mind telling you that I don't think you've the chance of a snowflake in hell today, but I *am* looking forward to watching you melt. Should provide a good hour's entertainment."

"I wasn't aware that you found Liberal victories entertaining, Prime Minister."

Salisbury laughed. "Someone ought to warn Campbell-Bannerman that this young pup's after his job," he said.

"No sir, not his. Yours," Freddie said.

There was laughter from Salisbury's ministers. The prime minister himself was smiling, but the look in his eyes was deadly. He had never forgiven Freddie for crossing the floor. And he would not forgive him for supporting the Home Rule Bill either. To him the bill, and all that it stood for—self-imposed limits on England's reach and its power—was nothing short of traitorous.

"Good luck, Mr. Lytton," he said, still smiling. "You will need it."

The lion in winter, Freddie thought, watching him go. He was the last of his breed. He was a Cecil, a member of one of England's greatest families, born and bred for politics. His ancestors had served as chief ministers to Elizabeth Tudor and James Stuart. And though he might be an old lion now, stooped and gray, he was still a lion and, as Freddie was well aware, perfectly capable of tearing young comers to shreds.

The clock in the hall struck ten.

"Blast!" Freddie said. He would have to hurry to the Chamber now. He was already rattled. Very likely the old boy's intention, he thought, trotting down the hall.

"Freddie! Freddie, have you seen the *Times*?" a voice suddenly called from behind him.

Freddie turned around. "Bingham! You're here," he said.

"I am. Yes. Obviously."

"Come to hear my speech?"

"Yes, but—"

"Good man!"

"Freddie, have you—"

"No time," Freddie said, heading for the Members' Lobby. "I'm bloody late. Must go. See you afterward."

"Freddie, *wait!*" Bingham shouted, waving a newspaper.

"Afterward, Bing, afterward! Meet me at the Reform Club!" Freddie yelled, disappearing into the Members' Lobby. He zoomed into the Chamber and took his seat on one of the tufted leather benches.

Glancing around the Chamber, with its somber Gothic architecture, he saw that attendance was excellent. MPs milled about in their frock coats and silk hats, except for the one and only Labour member, James Keir Hardie, who wore tweeds and a cap. Whips from both parties had made certain a majority of their members had shown up to vote. Freddie looked up and saw various members of the press seated in the Strangers' Gallery, and recognized more than a few faces from the House of Lords.

Today was the most important day of his political career; it was the day the Home Rule Bill went before the Commons for its Second Reading, a period of discussion and debate during which the House would consider the content and principles of the bill, and then decide whether to approve it or kill it. Freddie had been working diligently behind the scenes to garner bipartisan support for the bill. It had been an uphill battle, and he had only just attained the majority required to push it through. Some of those might still change their minds at voting time. He needed to convince a few more doubters and bring them to his side, and to do that he would have to deliver a speech that was nothing short of stupendous.

He'd been writing and rewriting the speech for months, furiously ripping up old drafts and starting from scratch until his words were perfect and polished. Then he practiced. He delivered the speech in his flat again and again until he was hoarse, until he had every word committed to memory. Prepared speeches were not allowed in the Chamber. Notes were, but Freddie, seeing them as a sign of mental weakness, never used them. A riveting orator, he always spoke solely from memory, commanding a stunning array of facts and figures, and he would do so today.

He was keenly aware that his performance would be watched carefully by politicians and the press at home and abroad. If he succeeded, his triumph would virtually guarantee his ascendancy within the party and ensure a win come election time—for many of his Tower Hamlets constituents were Irish, and he had shamelessly played up to their patriotic feelings.

And if he failed . . . well, he wouldn't fail. He couldn't fail. Too much was at stake.

Irish Home Rule had a history of defeat. Under Gladstone, the Liberals had pushed Home Rule Bills through the Commons in '86 and again in '93, only to see them killed in the House of Lords. Hand over power to one part of the Empire, the Lords argued, and you'd soon be forced to do so everywhere else. Home Rule's history of defeat might have intimidated some, but not Freddie. He was confident in his arguments and in his ability to deliver them persuasively. When the bill won today, as it surely would, its former defeats would make his own victory shine all the more brightly.

The Chamber was nearly full now. Freddie felt a current of excitement run through his body. Politics was his life. It was his highest ambition, his one true love, and he was never happier than at times like these—when the game was afoot. His nerves were crackling, but he felt good. Confident. Everything was going his way now. Absolutely everything. India had finally been brought to heel. His finances would soon improve. And Gemma would shortly be back in his life. He would succeed with his speech, too.

The House was called into session. The Speaker's chaplain read the prayers and the day's business began. The Home Rule Bill was first on the Order Paper. As the Speaker finished his opening remarks, Freddie rose from his seat, signaling his wish to be called. "The Honorable Member for Tower Hamlets," the Speaker said.

"Thank you, Mr. Speaker," Freddie replied. "Prime Minister, Right Honorable Gentlemen, fellow Members, I come before you today to address the future of Ireland, and in so doing, to secure nothing less than the future of Britain—" a loud and lusty volley of "Hear! Hear!"s, bellowed from the Liberal benches, filled the Chamber—"Britain today is an empire the like of which has not been seen since the Caesars' Rome. An empire vast and magnificent, one upon which the sun never sets. We, her citizens, rightly bask in the brightness of our country's strength, of her unparalleled achievements . . ." Another round of cheers went up. "And yet I fear that too much time spent basking in the bright sun has blinded Members seated on the right of this esteemed House to the storm that now approaches." Grumbles were heard. Freddie quickly cut them off. "A distant thunder rumbles at our shores," he said, "a thunder that grows louder as these self-same Members continue to make an enemy of our neighbor Ireland by denying her the same political self-determination that we, the heirs of Magna Carta, enjoy . . . by denying her the privileges and rights of Home Rule."

A roof-raising howl went up from the Tories. It was met by a roar of approval from the Liberals. Freddie smiled, pleased that his words had nearly incited a riot, for it meant his colleagues were paying attention. He waited for the noise to die down, then continued, artfully juxtaposing ideological arguments with hard examples, facts, and figures with stirring rhetoric. His supporters frequently broke into cheers. His detractors booed him. But all Members, from both sides of the floor, listened raptly. No one fidgeted. No one yawned. Every man sat forward in his seat.

Half an hour into his speech, Edward Berridge, a Tory backbencher, ran into the Chamber clutching a pile of newspapers. Freddie saw him out of the corner of his eye and assumed he was late. He turned away from him slightly, so as not to be distracted by his movements. He didn't see Berridge hand the papers to the Tory chief whip. He didn't see the whip read the front page and smile. He saw only his own victory, his forthcoming glory.

He spoke masterfully for more than an hour, laying out for the House what it cost to maintain the British Empire in terms of men, money, and the military, arguing impressively for the judicious use of Britain's resources in commodity-rich lands that rewarded investment—Africa, Arabia, India—and a more limited role in Ireland, which did not.

"We are still fighting a war in the Transvaal, and facing unrest in India," he said, concluding his impressive performance. "Let us not turn Republicans into revolutionaries. Home Rule must carry the day. Ireland must govern Irish affairs," he said. "This is not devolutionary politics, gentlemen. This is not defeatism. It is political pragmatism, and it is the future."

When Freddie finally sat, there was thunderous applause from the Liberal benches for what had been a powerful and affecting speech. He smiled, certain he'd gained the majority needed to pass the bill, certain he would shortly be celebrating his success at the Reform Club. He leaned back in his chair, waiting for the Speaker to call for a vote on the bill, but instead Edward Berridge stood.

What the hell is he doing? Freddie wondered, his nerves suddenly taut.

Berridge was a great friend of Dickie Lambert's—Freddie's rival for the Tower Hamlets seat. Not currently a Member of Parliament, Lambert could not be present on the floor, but Berridge could.

"The Honorable Member for Banbury," the Speaker called out.

Berridge cleared his throat, then gravely said, "I wonder if the Honorable Member for Tower Hamlets has seen today's edition of the *Times*?"

The hairs on Freddie's neck prickled. Hadn't Bingham asked him the same thing just as he was hurrying to the Chamber? Why?

"I'm afraid I have not. Perhaps the honorable gentleman's countryside constituency affords him more time for leisurely pursuits than mine affords me," he said.

Freddie's supporters laughed. The Tories sat stony-faced.

"Mr. Speaker, I wish to make a reasoned amendment," Berridge said.

A chorus of "Hear! Hear!"s rang out from across the floor. Freddie felt blindsided. He knew, as did everyone else in the Chamber, that Berridge was following protocol not to have the Home Rule Bill amended, as his words suggested, but to have it killed.

"Your reasons, sir?" the Speaker asked.

Berridge held up a copy of the *Times*. At least two dozen other Tories did the same. "Five Killed in Dublin Shooting," the front page blared. "Republicans Ambush Police with Guns from London Wharf Robbery."

The House erupted in outrage. Catcalls and boos rained down. Freddie felt as if someone had punched him. He could barely breathe.

Berridge waited for the uproar to die down, then continued. "The men killed in Dublin were Englishmen," he said. "They leave behind English wives and English children. Republicans, revolutionaries, rebels . . . call these Irishmen what you will, it does not change what they are—*murderers*. Every one of them. Are *these* men—these criminals, these killers—are *these* the men the Honorable Member wishes England to empower? Are *these* the men who should control the fate of our nearest neighbor, and by extension our own? Are *these* the men who should be granted Home Rule?"

Freddie tried to respond, but he was shouted down by rabid Tory backbenchers. The Speaker called for order, and eventually got it, but as Freddie was about to speak, Berridge attacked again.

"The guns used in the slaughter were stolen from the Stronghold, a wharf in East London, in Tower Hamlets," he said. He paused for a second, then delivered the killing blow. "Apparently the Honorable Member wishes to turn Ireland into a place as lawless and renegade as his own constituency."

Laughter erupted now—harsh, derisive, shattering. Berridge and his pack had attacked, and the Tories—sensing an advantage for one of their own—had let him. Meanwhile, Freddie's own party—realizing that the cause was lost—had abandoned him to them. The Speaker called for order once more. The House quieted. Berridge motioned that the bill be put to a vote. It was, and the nays carried it. Home Rule was finished.

And very possibly so am I, Freddie thought.

Recess was called. Members stood, milled around, left the Chamber for a smoke or a drink. He felt a hand on his shoulder, a pat on his back. There was noise from above him—whispers, gasps, and murmured exclamations. Freddie gazed up at the Strangers' Gallery. He saw a grim-faced Bingham with Wish beside him. He saw his opponent Richard Lambert smiling and members of the press scribbling furiously.

He remained where he was. He was in no hurry to leave his seat and resume the day's business, for he knew that when he did, he would no longer be fighting for Home Rule, but for his very survival. He watched Berridge leave the Chamber, accompanied by the smiling prime minister, and felt curiously free of animosity toward him. He'd only been fighting for his party. Berridge had engineered his defeat, but Freddie knew he would have done the same thing in the same circumstances.

No, there was only one man to blame for what had happened. Not Berridge. Not Lambert. And most definitely not himself.

It was Sid Malone who had done this to him. Had he not robbed the Stronghold, those guns would never have made it to Ireland. There would have been no shooting. Home Rule would have carried the day, and its success would have guaranteed his own.

It was Malone who had ruined him, and it was Malone who would pay. Quite soon. And dearly.

CHAPTER 23

Sid lay splayed out on his bed in his flat above the Barkentine. A naked Gemma Dean lay sprawled on top of him.

"Christ, Gem, me side," he wheezed.

"Hurts, does it?"

"Like a bastard."

"Poor thing," she said, rolling off him. "Any better?"

"Much."

"Like a drink?"

"I would."

Gemma got out of Sid's bed, wrapped herself in a robe, and padded to his bureau to pour two whiskies, singing some music-hall song as she did. Sid touched his fingers gingerly to his wound, making sure the dressing was still in place. It had been three days since he'd come out of the hospital, two weeks since he'd had his accident. His side was healing nicely, but even so it would be some time before he could withstand Gem's sexual acrobatics. What that girl could do with her hands, her mouth . . .

She handed him a whisky and climbed back into bed, sloshing some of her own drink on his chest as she did. She bent over, licked it off, then smiled at him. "Missed you," she said, kissing his mouth.

"Missed you too, luv," he said, downing his drink and placing the glass on his night table.

He reached under his pillow slowly, carefully, so she couldn't see what he was doing. When he had what he wanted, he sat up.

"You'll never believe what Frankie did while you were gone," Gemma said.

"I probably would."

"He nicked one of them listening things from the doctor. You know, the thing they use to hear your heart?"

"From what doctor?"

"The lady doctor. The one who fixed you up."

"Fucking Frankie! She needs that thing," Sid said angrily.

Gemma looked at him as if he were mad. "It's only a wotsit, Sid. Doctors make plenty of brass. Bet she's already bought a new one. Anyway, he's been using it to listen to locks. Been putting it on Desi's safe. Says he can hear the tumblers falling. Des caught him at it and Frankie told him the safe was poorly and he was doctoring it. He almost had him. Funny, isn't it?"

Sid forced a smile. "Aye. Funny," he said. But it wasn't. How could Dr. Jones work without that thing? What if she did have to buy a new one? The price would have to come out of her clinic savings. He would tell that sod of a Frankie to give it back.

"What's up? Something wrong?" Gemma asked.

"Just a bit tired," he said. He remembered what he had in his hand. "That Frankie's a piece of work, ain't he?"

"Aye, and he's not the only one." Sid hooked a finger in the V of her gown. He pulled it open and nuzzled her breasts. "Why, you could bury treasure in here," he said.

Gemma giggled as he reached in and stuck his fingers into the deep cleft between her breasts and let the object he'd hidden in his palm fall into it. "I'm serious, Gem, there's no telling what a bloke might find in here. Why, just look at this!"

He pulled out a dazzling necklace and dangled it before her eyes. It was made of flawless white diamonds. It had a medallion in the center with the initials GD worked in more diamonds. She turned the necklace over. There was an inscription on the back.

"For Gemma. Break a leg. Love Sid," she read. "Blimey!" she gasped. "Is it for me?"

"It is," he said, fastening it around her neck. "Pity there aren't any earrings to go with it."

"Sid, you didn't . . ."

"I didn't check? You're right, I didn't. Very careless of me." He played with her bosom again, pretending to hunt for additional treasure, then frowned. "That's it, I guess."

Gemma pouted.

"Wait a mo'," he said, opening the robe the rest of the way. "There's one more place I could look." He slid his hand between her legs.

"You dirty bugger!" she said, giggling.

"Here we are!" He handed her a pair of chandelier earrings, a match to the necklace.

"Oh, Sid!" she squealed. "They're lovely! Really they are! And huuuuuge!"

She kissed him hard on the lips, then bounced out of bed and ran to the mirror to put them on.

"A little something for your debut," he said. "I'm glad you like them." And he was. The stones were from a job he and the lads had done up in Greenwich some months ago. They'd cracked a mansion there and stolen a good deal of jewelry. He'd had the pieces broken up and the diamonds reset. He'd been sleeping with her for a few months now, and felt that he should show his appreciation. The diamonds were a nice bit of flash. They'd look good on her now, and when she was a bit older and hard up for cash, she could sell them. Sid had known many girls like Gem. They always ended up older and hard up for cash.

Gemma admired herself in the mirror, turning this way and that, twisting her thick brown hair up and letting it fall again. Sid noted the luscious curve of her bottom, the way her breasts swayed as she moved, and found himself wanting her again.

"You look smashing," he said.

She smiled, bounded back to the bed, and straddled him.

"Ooof! Crikey, luv, go easy," he said.

She thanked him again, kissed him, then sat up and took him inside herself, rocking back and forth, slowly, tantalizingly. Her hair was loose and wild about her shoulders, and the diamonds sparkled against her skin in the dim lamplight. He tried to reach for her, but his wound made him wince.

Gemma shook her head. "Lie back," she said. "Be still." She cupped her breasts and squeezed them, sliding her thumbs back and forth over her stiff, dusky nipples.

"Aw, Jesus, Gem . . ." he groaned. It was too much. She was so gorgeous, so wild. He came almost instantly.

When he'd caught his breath, she leaned over him and kissed him. "There's not a third piece, is there?" she asked coyly.

"A third? You want a bracelet, too, you greedy girl?"

"I want a ring, Malone. A diamond ring."

Sid sighed. "Ah, Gemma. You're not going to start that again, are you? I told you what was what from the start. I'm not the marrying type."

"I know what you said, but I thought maybe things had changed, that maybe . . ."

"I take care of you, don't I?" he said brusquely. There had been other jewels. A flat of her own. A dozen dresses. A fur or two. Even her solo in the Gaiety's upcoming revue was due to him, though she didn't know it.

"Of course you do," Gemma said. "You give me so many things, but not the thing that I want most—your heart."

"It's not on offer," Sid said. It never would be. He didn't want to love anyone. Ever. He had loved once, a long time ago. In another lifetime. And the loss of what he had loved—his father and mother, his entire family—had nearly destroyed him.

Gemma was angry. He could see it in her face. "You're walled off. You know that?" she said. "You've been sleeping with me for two months now, and I still don't know the first thing about you. I don't know if you have a mother or where she lives. I don't know where you come from. Who your father is."

"And you never will," he said. "Either get used to it, luv, or get out."

Gemma's eyes flashed. "Good enough to bed, not good enough to wed, is that it?"

"No, that's *not* it. It's because I do care for you that I'd never marry you. You know who I am, what I do. What kind of man would I be to drag you into that life?"

"I'd take the bad with the good," she said.

Sid laughed bitterly. "What good? It's all bad. You should find someone else if marriage is what you're after. I won't stand in your way."

"It's not what I'm after. I don't want to marry for marrying's sake. I want you. I want to be with you proper like. It's all I dream about."

Sid wondered what it was like to have a dream. He was sure he'd never know. Not everyone got to have dreams; some got only nightmares.

He got out of bed, pulled on his trousers, then crossed the room to pour himself another glass of whisky. This row was giving him a headache. Gemma Dean was an East London girl, a girl with few illusions. Sid figured she could probably deal with the darkness of his past better than most. But he doubted even she could deal with the worst of it. He could barely do that.

The memories were always there, lurking. He could keep them down during the day, but at night they tortured him. He barely slept anymore. When he closed his eyes, images came rushing at him—his dockworker father dying in the hospital. His mother lying in the street, her blood seeping into the cracks between the cobbles. His early days with Denny Quinn. Prison.

It had all started with Quinn. Things could have gone so differently for him after his mam's death, if only he'd known it. He might have gone to his uncle Roddy, not a blood uncle but a family friend, and told him what had happened—that he'd run at the sight of his murdered mother. Lost his mind for a bit on the Isle of Dogs. Then got into a fight with the real Sid Malone and killed him. But he'd been afraid. Roddy was a police constable, and Sid thought he might turn him in. So he'd gone to Quinn instead, and that had been the end for him. The sale of his soul hadn't happened all at once, but in bits and pieces. Den had started him out on the softer stuff—collecting debts, strong-arming unruly punters, guarding his whorehouses. He'd done well with those duties, and progressed to more challenging tasks—knocking off wharves, finding buyers for high-end swag, selling smuggled opium.

And then he got caught. He'd broken into a jeweler's, stolen some rings, and had been stupid enough to be seen wearing two of them the very next day. He'd swaggered and boasted, telling anyone who'd listen what a doddle the job had been, and the next thing he knew, he was standing before a magistrate, listening to the man sentence him to three years at Wormwood Scrubs.

He'd turned eighteen two weeks before he was sent down, and he'd felt his life had ended. When he first saw his cell—cold, damp, and dirty—he vowed to put distance between himself and Denny Quinn. He would serve his time, get out, and follow the straight and narrow. The days were horrible. The back-breaking, mind-destroying tasks: smashing rocks, walking a treadmill, turning a crank on a revolving drum—sometimes for eight hours at a time, and all for no reason. The pointlessness. The loneliness. The beatings for the smallest things, talking maybe, or just making eye contact.

The days were bad, but the nights . . . If Sid could have taken a knife and cut out the part of himself where those memories were kept, he would have. The lockdown, then lights out. He would sit on his bunk, barely moving, barely breathing, just leaning over every now and again to vomit into the tin chamberpot. The sick feeling always started early, when daylight began to wane. He would sit there in the darkness of his cell, forsaking sleep, and listen, every muscle in his body tensed, for the footsteps. Hoping that they wouldn't come. Knowing there was nothing he could do if they did. He'd wanted to kill himself in those early days. And he would have, too, if he'd been able to get hold of something to do the job.

Quinn had twigged. He'd come for a visit, taken one look at him, and said, "I want a name."

Sid had shaken his head. There would be another death on his head if he gave it, and he'd be bound to Denny forever.

"Don't be so fucking stupid!" Den had hissed. "You've been in for four months. Your sentence is three years. Can you survive three years of this? Three fucking *years*?"

Sid had finally choked out the name of a guard. "Wiggs. Ian Wiggs."

Two days later, Ian Wiggs was dead. Throat cut. Body dumped in front of the prison. The screws left Sid alone after that. So did the other prisoners. It was the beginning of things. Of a reputation. Of power and respect. When he got out, he was twenty-one years old.

"You have served your time, Mr. Malone. Your debt is paid," the warden said, upon his discharge. "We hope that you have learned from your mistakes and that the justice meted out to you has had a reforming effect upon your character. I trust you will now follow the straight and narrow path."

"Yes, sir," he'd said. The hell I will, he'd thought.

The nick had changed him all right, but not in the way the warden intended. It had made him hard, bitter, determined never to be at anyone's mercy again. Because there was no such thing as mercy. Not for him.

As soon as he returned to the East End, he went straight to the Taj, sat down with Denny, and announced that he was going to take over East London. North and south of the river.

"Bit ambitious, don't you think?" Denny had said. "Bowler Sheehan might have something to say about it." Sheehan, one of the East End's most vicious men, controlled Whitechapel, Wapping, and much else on the north bank.

"I didn't say I'd do it next week," Sid said. "It'll take time." And it had. He'd gathered men around him. Lads he'd known and others he'd met in prison. Lads who understood, as he did, that it was better to be smart and quiet about what you did than dumb and loud. Lads who'd figured out, as he had, that power—real power—was found in a man's head, not his fists.

They had started on the south side of the river. Like a general mounting a campaign, Sid positioned his men in a loop on the outskirts of Rotherhithe and Southwark, then tightened that loop bit by bit, driving out the lesser gangs by reason when possible and by force when not. Letting it be known there was one guv'nor now, one manor. Making his way slowly but surely toward the wharves and the riches they contained.

After two years, he'd gotten the south bank locked up. There was almost nothing going on there—fights, prostitution, gambling, fencing, protection, drugs—that he and his men didn't get a piece of. He'd just started to make inroads on the north bank when Denny Quinn had been murdered. He'd had his throat cut by Bowler Sheehan, who'd objected to Denny's fraternizing with Sid. And then Sheehan himself had wound up dead, his own throat cut in Newgate jail. Sid hadn't done it, but many believed he had. He let them. With Sheehan out of the way, the north bank had been his for the taking, and take it he had.

Sid had never wanted the life, and he didn't want it now, but he was in too deep to ever get out. He'd made too many enemies. And too many friends. Like Billy Madden, who'd murdered dozens on his way up the West End ladder, and the Sicilians—Angie Vazzano and Nicky Barrecca—who ruled Covent Garden and the Haymarket. They all shook hands when they met, bought each other dinners, drinks, and women, but Sid knew they all coveted his patch and would go for him in an instant if they ever scented weakness.

And for Sid Malone, the greatest weakness of all was love.

"Won't you come back to bed?" Gemma asked now, in a conciliatory voice.

Sid was about to answer when there was a knock at the door. He tensed. "What is it?" he barked.

"There's someone here to see you, guv." It was Lily, the barmaid.

Sid yanked the door open. "Who is it? Donaldson? I told him we had nothing to do with the Morocco."

Donaldson had accused Frankie of burning down the wharf and killing its watchman. Frankie had sworn he'd had nothing to do with it, and Sid believed him. He wouldn't have dared do such a thing, not after Sid had told him, and all his men, to steer clear of the place.

"It's not Donaldson," Lily said. "It's a woman."

Bloody hell, Sid thought. Fiona.

"It's the doctor. Ozzie said so. The one that saw to you in the hospital. Missus Jones."

Sid felt a split-second's relief that the visitor wasn't his sister, but the relief was replaced by anger upon learning that it was the doctor. "What?" he said. "*Here?* In the pub?"

"Yes."

"Anyone with her?"

"No. She's on her own."

"Jesus Christ. I'll be right down. Lily, keep an eye on her, will you?"

Sid grabbed his shirt. He stuffed his feet in his boots and reached for his jacket.

"What's she doing here?" Gemma asked.

"I'm wondering the same thing," he said. "Trying to commit suicide, maybe?"

He bolted down the steps two at a time and scanned the bar, but didn't see her. Fear rose in him. She had no idea what sorts frequented the Bark, and what they were capable of. Finally, he spotted her. She was sitting at a table on the far side of the room—hat straight, knees together, hands in her lap. She might have been waiting for a bus on the Brompton Road. He was at her side in a few strides. She smiled when she saw him and started to speak, but he cut her off.

"Have you gone completely mad? What are you doing here?"

"I came to see you. You said if I needed anything to come to see you. Well, I need something. So I came."

"You bloody stupid woman. Do you know where you are?"

"The Barkentine?"

"Don't play the smart arse."

"I beg your pardon!"

"How'd you get here?"

"Hackney, mostly. I had to walk part of the way."

"You're lucky you weren't killed. Or worse."

"I can't imagine there's anything worse than being killed."

"There is. Trust me. Come on," he said, motioning for her to get up.

"Where are we going?" she asked, standing.

"*You* are going home."

She sat back down. "I am not."

"Dr. Jones . . ." Sid said, through gritted teeth.

"I need your help, Mr. Malone. It is truly a matter of life and death."

Sid sat down. He leaned across the table. "Do you know that the rozzers are afraid of this place? Big strong men with big heavy truncheons are scared to walk in here, but you sail in without so much as a by-your-leave."

"I have you to protect me. They do not," she said.

Sid saw he was getting nowhere. "What is it you want?" he finally asked.

"I need devices. For my patients. French letters, Dutch caps, sponges. They're contraceptive devices."

The men on either side of her turned and stared. India didn't notice, or didn't care if she did.

"Aye, I know what they are. Keep your voice down, will you?" Sid passed a hand over his face, mortified. With all that he'd seen, all that he'd done in his life, he didn't think *anything* could mortify him, but he was wrong.

"I need quality goods. No off-the-back-of-a-cart rubbish. Can you get them?"

Sid considered her question. "I don't mind telling you, this is the oddest request for a job I've ever had," he said.

"I'm not asking for a favor. I'd pay you, of course."

He winced at that. It didn't even occur to her that he might not want to be paid. That he might want to help her. Because she wanted to do some good and there were so few in this world who did. *Let a bad man do a good deed,* Ella had said the day he'd left the hospital. He'd overheard her arguing with India in Gifford's office, but India wouldn't let him. Fine. Sod her, then. If she wanted to pay, she'd pay.

"I think I can do it," finally said. "Thing is . . . if I do, they'll be stolen goods. You know that, right? Most likely smuggled in from the Continent. Last I checked, smuggling was still illegal. You'll be breaking the law, too. Not just me. Can you live with that, Dr. Jones? Can your spotless conscience endure the stain?" he added, mocking her.

"Yes, I can live with that. I have to, because I can't live with what happened to Emma Milo. That's not going to happen to any patient of mine ever again. You're a businessman, aren't you, Mr. Malone?" she said, mocking him back. "This is business. Will you do it, or do I have to find someone else?"

"I will. Won't be cheap, though."

"How much?"

"A hundred quid."

India's face fell. "I haven't got that much," she said. "Forgive me for wasting your time."

She looked down at her hands. She must have spotted her watch chain dangling from her waistcoat, because she suddenly dug the watch out of her pocket and handed it to him. "I have this, though," she said. "It's twenty-four carat. Diamond markers. Worth a hundred pounds. That's what Mr. Betts said. On the way from Teddy Ko's, remember? Will it do?"

Sid turned it over in his hand. *Think of me,* the inscription read. "From Lytton, is it?"

"Yes."

"Wonder what he would say about your trading it for a box of rubber johnnies."

"He would understand."

"Somehow I don't think he would."

"Then perhaps you will refrain from mentioning it the next time you see him."

Sid pocketed the watch. "Your secret's safe with me."

He offered her his hand. She took it.

"Honor among thieves, is it?" she asked archly.

"You tell me."

She gave him an acid look. "We have a deal?"

"Give me a few weeks," he said, holding her hand for a beat longer than he should have. It was not like a woman's hand. Not like Gemma's, soft and dainty. It was strong, and the fingers were stained yellow from iodine. It was not a pretty hand at all, but holding it, he wanted—more than anything, more than he'd just wanted Gemma's entire lovely body—to simply press it to his face and feel the cool palm against his cheek.

He felt a slight tug as she withdrew her hand. There was something in her eyes: alarm. She was frightened of him. Bleeding *frightened*. Didn't she know he wouldn't hurt her? That he would never hurt her? That all he wanted to do was help her? Her expression made him angry. What the hell was he doing? Sitting here gassing with this skinny four-eyed harridan when Gemma Dean with her eager mouth and her gorgeous tits was waiting upstairs in his bed? He stood abruptly and looked around for one of his men.

"Oz!" he yelled.

Ozzie, standing at the bar, turned around. "Aye, guv?"

"Mr. Malone . . . ," India started to say.

"Yes, Dr. Jones?"

"I thought perhaps I could buy you supper. To say thank you."

"Won't be necessary."

"But I—"

"OZZIE!"

Oz was at Sid's side in a flash. "What is it, guv?"

"See the good doctor home."

"Good night then, Mr. Malone."

"Ta-ra, Dr. Jones."

He watched Ozzie and the doctor leave, then decided he would leave as well. He threaded his way through the taproom toward the door, passing the stairwell as he did.

Gemma was waiting there, standing in her wrapper.

"I'm sorry for rowing, Sid. Come back to bed, will you?"

"Not now, Gem."

"But why?"

He walked up the steps and gave her a quick kiss on the cheek. "Got business. Stay over if you like, or Ronnie'll take you home."

"When will I see you?"

"When you see me."

Sid walked out of the Bark in time to see Ozzie hand Dr. Jones into the carriage. They would be heading west. He turned east.

He was restless. He knew he wouldn't sleep. So he would walk. Eastward along the river. For hours, maybe for days. Maybe all the way to the sea. And he would think as he walked. Of some new plan. Some new job. Something that would bring more money, more power. Something that would have the villains and the rozzers both saying, *It was a daring job. Bloody dangerous and all. Bloody brilliant! And well nigh fucking impossible. It was Malone, no one else. Had to be.*

He buttoned his jacket, then pulled his collar up against the damp night air. He was alone. And that was fine. He didn't need anyone. Not Gemma Dean. Not his pushy sister. And certainly not India Selwyn Jones.

He was Sid Malone. The guv'nor. And he didn't need a soul.

CHAPTER 24

"What do you mean he walked out, Des? We was supposed to go to Limehouse tonight. Where the hell did he go? It's nearly midnight."

"I don't know, Frankie. Out."

"He left Gemma here?"

Desi shrugged as if to say that he didn't understand it either. "Ronnie took her home."

"When's he coming back?"

"Jesus, what's with all the bleeding questions? I don't know! You know how it is when he goes walkabout. We might see him tomorrow or five days from now. Who knows?" He stuck his head into the kitchen. "Lily, luv," he shouted, "bring out some glasses, will you?" As he returned to his polishing, the pub door opened, squeaking on its rusty hinges.

"That's likely him now," Desi said.

"Sid! That you?" Frankie shouted. He couldn't see the door from where he was sitting.

"I'm afraid not, Frankie," came the reply. A man walked into the taproom. He wore a suit and a tan mackintosh. It was Alvin Donaldson. Behind him, in the pub's large entry hall, what looked like an army of police officers stood waiting.

"Evening, all," he said. "Sid Malone about?"

Frankie was on his feet instantly. "No, he bloody well isn't. What the hell do you want? Here to arrest us for nothing again? Too afraid to come on your own? Need the whole of Scotland Yard to hold your hand?"

"Had a report," Donaldson said, picking up an old porcelain stein and examining it. He dropped it on the floor. It smashed. "Contraband goods were spotted here."

"What kind of contraband?"

"Guns. Stolen from the Stronghold Wharf."

Frankie snorted. "Oh, aye? Who reported it?"

"I did," he said.

"*What?*"

Donaldson nudged a barometer up the wall with his index finger until it came off its hook and crashed to the floor. "I was in here an hour ago," he said. "Didn't you see me? I spotted a rifle and two pistols sitting out on the bar," he said, smirking. "They're not there anymore, though. You must've hidden them."

Frankie realized what was coming next. "Where's your fucking warrant?" he shouted.

"Right here." Donaldson drew a document out of his pocket and handed it over. "Gentlemen," he said, motioning his officers forward. Like a great blue wave they came crashing into the taproom. Lily had just come out of the kitchen carrying a tray of clean glasses. Frankie heard her cry out as one of the constables knocked the tray out of her hands.

"This is harassment!" he yelled, watching a table go over, a clock come down off the mantel.

Donaldson shook his head. "No, but *this* is," he said as he turned and swept everything behind the bar—the bottles of booze, the till, glasses, and plates—to the floor.

"What are you going to do, Frankie? Call the cops?" he asked. One of his officers laughed.

"You'll be laughing out of your arse when I knock your teeth down your throat," Frankie growled, advancing on the man.

"Now, now, careful, Frankie," Donaldson cautioned. "Assaulting an officer'll get you sent down no matter how good your lawyer is. You know that. There are witnesses here. Twenty of them."

Why's he warning me? Frankie wondered, drawing up short. If anything, he'd want me to hit him. Because he doesn't want to arrest you, a voice inside his head said. He wants you here, in the pub, to witness this and tell Sid about it.

"I'm to be the messenger, is that it? Is that what you want?" Frankie shouted over the din.

Donaldson nodded. "Tell him it's time to pack up, Frankie. Tell him this is just the beginning. And while you're at it, tell him Freddie Lytton says hello."

CHAPTER 25

Outside the Varden Street surgery, India buttoned her jacket against the cool evening breeze as Ella locked the door.

"We lost two more women today," she said grimly as she watched Dr. Gifford climb into his carriage. "He told me just now. Did you know?"

Ella dropped the key into her purse. "No, I didn't," she said. "From what?"

"Childbed fever."

Ella sighed. "Mrs. Gibbs?" she asked.

"And Mrs. Holloway. He should be reported to the British Medical Association. He doesn't wash his hands, Ella. He's a murderer."

"Steady on, matey. That's a hard thing to prove. And the bloke has lots of friends in the BMA. Don't forget that. Report him and they'll turn it on you somehow, see if they don't. They'll make out that you were negligent somehow. Or that the nurses were."

"They wash. I know they do. Even when they think I'm not looking. I've drilled it into them."

"That's beside the point. If you report him, *you'll* be finished here. And no one else will take you, either. They'll think you're trouble."

India sighed.

"How'd you make out with the rubber johnnies?" Ella asked.

"Changing the subject, are you?"

"Trying."

"We'll have them soon."

Ella brightened. "Really? How'd you get them?"

"Sid Malone is getting them for me. I went to the Barkentine."

"Crikey, that was brave."

"I didn't have much choice. Soon we'll have supplies, and then all we'll need—"

"Is a clinic," Ella said. "But until we get it, you make sure to hide the johnnies well. We can't have Gifford finding them."

"I'll put them on top of the sink," India said. "Next to the soap. He's sure to miss them there."

Ella laughed out loud. "Why, Dr. Jones, I do believe that's the first time I ever heard you make a joke," she said.

"Did I? I didn't mean to."

"I'm sure you didn't. Come on, let's get going," Ella said, taking India's arm.

The two women were just about to step off the pavement into Varden Street when they were badly startled by a loud and horrible noise. It sounded like a goose being strangled. Ella jumped out of her skin. India spun around—and saw the cause of the racket. It was her cousin Wish. He was sitting in his car, goggles pushed up on his forehead.

"Indy! Over here! Did you forget about me?" he shouted.

Supper! She'd forgotten that they were supposed to have supper tonight after she finished work.

"I'm afraid I did," she said, leaning in through the driver's side window to kiss his cheek, happy—as always—to see him.

"What a dunderhead you are. Hungry?"

"Famished. Ella, meet my cousin Aloysius. Wish, meet Sister Ella Moskowitz."

"A pleasure! Will you join us?"

"Do, Ella," India said.

"I'd love to."

"Any suggestions? I'm not awfully familiar with this part of town."

India bit her lip. "Well, there's the Great Eastern. It's a railway hotel . . ."

"Why don't we go to the caff?" Ella said. "Give your cousin a real taste of East London."

"What a good idea! It's the Moskowitzes' café, Wish. On Brick Lane. It belongs to Ella's mum. The food's wonderful."

"Sounds splendid. Jump in."

India climbed into the passenger seat, Ella into the back. Wish pulled away from the curb and nearly caused an accident before they'd even closed the car doors.

"Wish! Look out!" India screeched.

He veered to the right sharply, sending both women flying across their seats. India struggled to an upright position in time to see the driver of an enormous hay wagon shake his fist at them.

"Sorry. Handles beautifully, don't you think? Far better than the competition. That's a huge selling point."

"Drive, don't talk," India ordered.

She was exhausted after a full day at the surgery, but she soon discovered that it was impossible to be tired when you were terrified. Wish took both straight roads and corners at breakneck speed, passing carriages and buses with no concern whatsoever for oncoming traffic. He pulled up outside the restaurant and nearly hit an elderly gentleman reversing to the curb. India was relieved when he finally switched off the engine.

"It's a marvel, that car," he said. "Daimler cut his teeth on boat engines, then progressed to automobiles. There's none more reliable. Or faster. And the chassis is gorgeous. I'm into the company for ten thousand. They're going to make me stinking rich." He grinned. "Or a complete bloody pauper."

"Aloysius, your language!" India scolded.

She was quite familiar with her cousin's penchant for making risky investments. Sometimes they paid off handsomely, and sometimes they didn't. The car and his invitation to supper told her that things were currently going well. In a month's time, however, he might be sleeping on her floor or living with Maud. It had happened before.

Wish had had a steady and respectable job once. He'd been a director at Barings Bank, but he'd quit, saying the work was endangering his health.

"How?" India had asked, concerned.

"It's boring me to death," he'd replied.

Ella shepherded them inside. As soon as they were seated, Wish closed his eyes and breathed deeply. "Roast chicken, parsley, garlic!" he exclaimed. "Real food! I didn't think it existed anymore. Let's order everything plus a bottle of wine. My treat."

Ella went to tell her mother what they wanted and returned with the wine and a tray of glasses. "Watch out, Wish," she warned. "My mother spotted you, and she's in a matchmaking mood. Said you were a handsome young man and wants to know if you're Jewish."

"Anglican, I'm afraid," he said. His eyes lit up as bowls of ruby-red borscht were brought to the table along with thick slices of black bread. "My word! Did your mother make this?" Ella said that she did. "Tell her I'll convert, but only if I can marry her!"

More plates came out—tasty samplings of vinegary mushrooms, gherkins, salted cucumbers, pickled cabbage, and paper-thin slices of tongue with horseradish.

"Feeling flush tonight, are we?" India asked her cousin.

"Very."

"Because of your Daimler investment?"

"No, something even better. California."

India groaned. "Not that land scheme you've been nattering about."

"The very same. And it's not a *scheme*, it's a sound investment and quite possibly the opportunity of a lifetime."

"Heard that before."

"Oh, come on. Aren't you even the least bit curious?"

"I am," Ella said.

India smiled. She could see he was positively bursting at the seams to talk about it. "All right, then," she said. "Tell us."

"It all started when I was in San Francisco. I was having dinner with a solicitor there and he gave me the most marvelous tip. He told me all about this incredible place north of the city. On the coast. Point Reyes, it's called." He sat forward in his chair, eyes sparkling with excitement. "It's quite simply paradise found. You've never seen anything like it. You take the train north to Point Reyes station and then a trap to the coast. You drive past hills so green, and cattle ranches, and sheer cliffs, and the bluest bays you've ever seen. And then you arrive at Drakes Bay, and you stand there, at the very edge of America itself, only sea and sky before you, and you feel like you're at the end of the world." He corrected himself. "No, I'm wrong . . . you feel like you're at the *beginning* of the world. As if it's the very first day and you're the very first person and there's no ugliness or evil in the world. Not yet. There's nothing but beauty all around you."

India sat back in her chair. "My word! I've never heard you talk like this. You seem quite transported," she said. "Have you bought the land yet?"

"Well . . . um . . . no. Not exactly."

"Why not? What are you waiting for?"

"I need to raise a bit of cash. Rather skint at the moment. Put everything I had into U.S. Steel and Daimler and then this came along."

"Don't even think about it, Wish."

"Did I say anything?" he asked innocently.

"Ask Maud. Or Bing."

"I did. They said no."

"What are you going to do there?" Ella asked.

"I'm going to create the most beautiful resort hotel the world has ever seen," he said. "I'm going to call it the Bluff. It'll rival anything anywhere—Newport, Bath, even the Riviera. First I'm going to buy the land, then I'm going to incorporate, and when the company is properly set up I'm going to sell shares to raise the capital I need to build. I've already chosen my builder. Three years from now—four at the most—the Bluff will be open and I'll be a millionaire."

"It sounds so exciting!" Ella said, carried away by his enthusiasm.

"Are you certain you're not Jewish? Maybe a great-grandfather from the old country? An uncle?" It was Mrs. Moskowitz. She'd just delivered a plate of brisket to a neighboring table.

Ella groaned. "Aloysius Selwyn Jones, meet my mother, Sarah Moskowitz. She has ears like a rabbit."

"Such a good head for business you have. You're going to make some girl a wonderful husband," she said, looking pointedly at Ella.

"*Genug shoyn,* Mama!" Ella scolded.

Mrs. Moskowitz turned on her heel and returned to the kitchen.

"Tell us more about California, Wish," Ella said.

"I can't. It defies description. If you really want to know what it's like, you have to see it. Both of you. I'm going back in a few weeks. Come with me."

"We can't, you silly man. We have work, remember? And I'm too poor. I couldn't come up with the boat fare, never mind the funds needed to cavort across America."

Wish frowned. "Are you still living off that one fund?"

India nodded. She covered her cousin's hand with her own and turned to Ella. "Wish is the one who got me through medical school," she said. "He helped me when no one else would. I'm a doctor only because of him."

"Rubbish," Wish said, flustered for once. "You did it all yourself."

India explained to Ella that she and her parents were estranged and that she'd had to pay for her education herself. To do so she'd sold jewelry left to her by her grandmother and a Gainsborough given to her by an aunt. They'd brought her just over five thousand pounds, some of which she'd used to travel to London, rent a flat, and pay her first year's tuition before Wish found out what she was doing and stopped her.

"Never touch the principal!" he'd barked. And then he'd taken her remaining funds and put them in a conservative investment account at Barings. It didn't make a huge return—she'd had to be frugal—but it generated enough money to cover her expenses.

"How's that account doing anyway?" Wish asked now. "What's it bringing?"

"Five percent."

"Good God! You're living on two hundred and fifty quid a year?" he said. Far too loudly.

"Shh!" India hissed, embarrassed. The people around them were living on far less.

"Sorry," he whispered. "But are you?"

"Barely. Though things should get a little easier now that I don't have to pay tuition."

"What about your wages?" he asked.

"I don't touch them. I'm putting them aside, you see. For a clinic. Ella and I want to open a clinic in Whitechapel."

Wish looked from India to Ella, then burst into laughter. "You're going to open a clinic on your *wages*? And when did you plan on doing this? When you're ninety? It'll take that long to raise the money. You've got to get investors behind you to raise that kind of capital, ladies. You'll need to incorporate. Charge fees for treatment and services and pay your shareholders dividends. Medicine's a business. You have to treat it like one."

"That is exactly the *opposite* of what we want to do," India said, glowering. "We want to provide free services to the poor. We want no mother to watch her child suffer because she doesn't have the shilling needed to see a doctor."

"Mmm," Wish said, biting into a gherkin. "You'll need some angels, then."

"You don't have to mock."

"I'm not. I meant patrons. Donors."

"Machers," Mrs. Moskowitz said, setting down toothsome golden chicken and potatoes fried with onions.

"Precisely," Wish said. "Won't you sit down, Mrs. Moskowitz? Have a drink with us."

"Thank you, my dear, but I must get back to cooking."

"And earwigging," Ella added.

"How do we get them? The donors?" India asked.

"Go begging," Mrs. Moskowitz said, veering off again.

"She's right," Wish said. "Put a proposal together outlining where the clinic will be, how big it will be, what services it will offer, what kind of staff it will have—and then start knocking on all the doors of your wealthy friends. Royal friends are helpful, too, should you happen to have any. Promise them recognition and if they give you something, give them something in return."

"But we have nothing!"

"You will. Give them a bronze plaque in the foyer. Name a ward after them. Use your imagination."

"Benches in the garden," India said.

"Nameplates on the beds," Ella said.

"You can solicit other sorts of donations, too," Wish said. "You could ask a biscuit factory to donate broken rusks. Or a tea merchant to give you the damaged tins he can't sell. You could ask a linen mill for faulty sheets."

"How do you know all this?" Ella asked.

"I used to work for a bank. Some of our clients were orphanages. Or museums. Schools, hospitals, and so on. They came to us for guidance and advice on these matters. We helped them."

"Could you help us?" India asked. "We could pay you . . . eventually."

Wish raised an eyebrow. "You can't afford me," he said.

India's face fell.

"So I'll do it for free. I'll become your . . . um . . . your . . . director of development." He smiled, pleased. "How does that sound?"

"Wonderful!" Ella said.

"Wish, we couldn't ask that of you," India said.

"You didn't. I offered."

"But why? It will be so much work, and you're so busy as it is."

Wish's gaze softened. He laughed. "Oh, dear serious little Indy. You don't even know, do you?"

India shook her head.

"Because you are *good,* old mole," he said. "And I would like to be." Then he grinned devilishly and said, "But I'm not. It's impossible when there are so many pretty women in the world and so much good wine. So you will have to do it for me. You and Ella both. I'll ride to heaven on your coattails."

"That ride might be bumpier than you think," Mrs. Moskowitz said, thumping down another plate of bread.

Wish ate a slice, then said, "The competition for funds is fierce, I can tell you that. It won't be easy. In fact, it'll be quite hard."

India sat back in her chair, feeling overwhelmed. "Can we do this, Ella? Where will we find the time?" she wondered aloud.

"If you want to make your dreams come true, don't sleep," Mrs. Moskowitz chided, bustling by.

"How on earth did she hear me? She was halfway across the room!"

"I've spent my entire life wondering the very same thing," Ella said.

India turned back to her cousin. "How long would this take?"

"It's hard to tell. Five years . . . six . . . it all depends on how much money you can shake out of people and how fast."

India's face fell. "Five years," she echoed, imagining all the lives poverty and disease would claim in that time. She racked her brains, trying to think

of another way, then said, "What about California? You said you were looking for partners."

"If you're serious, India, I'll make you a bundle."

India considered this. "Could you really?"

"It's almost guaranteed."

"More than five percent?"

"Much more."

"What do I have to do?" she asked.

"Become my business partner. Give me the money in your Barings account to help me purchase the land. When I take the company public, and
the cash floods in, I'll buy you out. At triple your initial investment."

"*Triple?* That's . . ."

"Fifteen thousand pounds."

India blinked at him, astonished. Then she frowned. "But I have to give
you *all* of my money?"

"All of it. You'll have to live on your wages."

"But Wish, that money's all I have."

"She who dares, wins. Do you want five percent? Or do you want that
clinic?"

India thought about the jam jar on her desk and about the paltry
amount she was able to put into it each week. She thought about Sid
Malone's repellent offer of blood money, and of how long it would take to
solicit donations. She thought about Dr. Gifford and his callous, mercenary treatment of the poor. And then she said, "All right. I'll do it. I'll get it
for you tomorrow."

"Good girl," Wish said. "I'll have my solicitor draw up a contract naming
you as my partner. And in the meantime we crack on with other avenues.
We need to raise donations and add them to the Point Reyes money. I'll
start a separate account for those. At Barings. I'll need a name. So we can
have people make bank drafts directly to the clinic. What's it called?"

India looked at Ella and Ella looked at India.

"The Whitechapel Clinic?" Ella ventured.

"For Women and Children," India added.

"But it's free, isn't it? You have to say free," Wish said.

"The Whitechapel Free Clinic . . . ," India began.

"For Women and Children," Ella finished.

"Done!" Wish said. "Now, who can we pester for money? Let's make a list."

"How about Nathan Rothschild?" Mrs. Moskowitz said.

"Nathan? Do you mean *Lord* Rothschild? Do you know him, Mrs.

Moskowitz?" Wish asked, astonished. Lord Rothschild, head of a banking dynasty, was one of the wealthiest men in England.

Mrs. Moskowitz shrugged. "I know where he lives. Which is just as good."

Ella rolled her eyes. "And I know where the queen lives," she said.

A waiter arrived with a fresh bottle of wine. Wish refilled their glasses and poured a fourth one. He gave it to Mrs. Moskowitz.

"To the chef," he said.

"To meddling mothers," Ella said, lifting her glass.

"To the clinic," India said, lifting her own.

"*L'Chaim*," Mrs. Moskowitz said, smiling. "To life."

CHAPTER 26

Freddie Lytton was backstage at the Gaiety Theatre, sitting on a chair in Gemma Dean's dressing room. A dress rehearsal for the Gaiety's upcoming musical revue had just finished, and Gemma was wiping off her makeup with cold cream and a flannel.

"Please, Gem. For old times' sake," he said.

"Bugger that, Freddie. Nostalgia doesn't pay my rent."

"But I really need your help. I need someone to break up the Labour rally on Saturday."

Freddie was desperate. His career had suffered badly from the Home Rule defeat, and he was doing everything in his power to shore up his standing with his constituents.

"It's a big event," he continued. "The lefties are all speaking—Tillet, Burns. Keir Hardie, too. Mrs. Pankhurst is going to be there calling for votes for women. And that bloody Joe Bristow. This is his big debut. His first real public appearance. He wants to run against me in the autumn. The election's not even been called yet, and already he's attacking me. The bloody papers are eating it up. They're printing every word he says. I want him disgraced. I want his name blackened."

"And how do you propose I do that?" Gemma asked, working at a stubborn patch of blue shadow above one eye.

"It's easy. All you have to do is get some actress friends together, go to the rally, and pretend to be drunken whores. Heckle the speakers—especially

Bristow—create a disturbance, and then slip away. The police will move in and shut the rally down—I'll make sure they do—and then the papers will tell the public exactly what sort of person attends Labour rallies. Bristow and his bloody party will be discredited. Come on, Gem. Be a brick, will you? I'll give you twenty quid."

"No thanks, Freddie. I don't need your crumbs anymore. I'm quite well looked after these days." She turned and shook her head, making a pair of sparkling diamond earrings dance. "A gift from my fiancé. They're real," she said.

"They aren't," Freddie said. They couldn't be. They were enormous.

"Certainly are. Ten carats apiece. I had them appraised."

"Well, stone me. Who is he? Prince Edward?"

"The prince is nowhere near as rich as this bloke," she said, laughing. She bit her lip, then, unable to keep her secret any longer, said, "It's Sid Malone."

Freddie sat back in his chair. A jealous rage, white-hot and choking, surged through him. Malone. *Again.*

He had shown him up in front of India, he'd made a laughingstock out of him in the Commons, and now he was fucking Gemma Dean—whom Freddie sorely wished he was still fucking.

What did it take to put the man away? He'd lit into Donaldson just the other day, asking him why he still hadn't arrested the bastard, but Donaldson said he had to have something on him first, something that would stick. Malone was too clever, too cautious, to get himself caught. Donaldson had said that he was putting on the pressure, though. He'd destroyed one of Malone's pubs, the Bark, with a trumped-up warrant, and had arrested two of his associates—Nicky Lee and Charlie Zhao—for peddling smuggled opium. They would both do time.

"Patience," Donaldson had said. "We'll get him yet. You'll see."

"Gemma, you can't be serious," Freddie said now, working to keep his voice even. "Malone's a bloody criminal!"

"You want to watch your mouth. Sid Malone's a gentleman. He treats me a lot better than you ever did. And I'll tell you something else. I'm not your only woman friend who keeps company with him."

"What are you talking about?"

"Your intended was with him the other night."

"Who?"

Gemma rolled her eyes. "Blimey, Freddie, the woman you're marrying? Remember her? The doctor?"

"*India?* With Sid Malone?" Freddie laughed out loud. "Maybe you ought to pawn those earrings for a pair of specs, Gem."

"I *know* it was her. She came to the Bark. I saw her leave."

"I'm sure you did."

"I can prove it. She wanted him to do something for her. I'm not sure what. Sid wouldn't tell me. All he'd say was that they had a business deal. I know one of the blokes who was sitting near them, though. He overheard their conversation and said it had to do with rubber johnnies. Hardly sounds right, though, does it? Her coming all the way to the Bark to ask the likes of Sid Malone for rubber johnnies?"

Freddie stopped smirking. It sounded *exactly* right—exactly like the sort of women's welfare bollixy do-gooding rubbish India would get involved with.

"I guess he must've told her a high price for whatever it was she wanted," Gemma continued. "And she must not have had the dosh because she gave him her watch. I saw it on his night table. It had *Think of me* on the back. Now, am I right or not?"

"Yes, Gem, you are," he said slowly, turning this piece of news over in his mind.

Gemma lifted her chin. "He's going to marry me, Freddie. Sid Malone is going to make me his wife."

"Congrats, old girl," he said, forcing a smile. "Let's see the ring."

Gemma hesitated. "I don't have it quite yet. I haven't picked it out," she said.

Gemma was a good actress, not a great one, and Freddie could see that she was lying. Sid Malone had no intention of marrying her, but she wanted to hurt him. She wanted to make him jealous. He would let her. It might get him what he wanted.

He leaned forward, elbows on his knees, and took her hand. "I'm happy for you, Gem," he said, smiling ruefully. "Sad for myself, though. If only my life were my own, things would have been different. So very different."

"What are you on about?"

"You and I. We could have made a go of it."

"That's not what you said a few weeks ago, Freddie. You told me you were getting married—and not to me."

"I don't love her, Gemma, you know that. I love you, but it's impossible," Freddie lied.

"Why?"

"Because I need India's money. MPs don't make much. The job is about public service, not private gain, but it's hard to fight the good fight, to try to make England, and indeed the world, a better place when you can't even pay the rent on your own flat."

"Oh, Freddie, how absolutely full of shit you are. You can't fool me. I *know* you, remember? You're a competitive, power-mad man who needs money to finance his ambitions. You don't want to make the world a better place, you just want to rule it." She leaned forward and kissed him. "And you will one day. So I'd better get into your good books now. I'll do what you ask. I'll get some girls together on Saturday. Cause a few ructions."

"Really, Gem? You'd do that for me?"

"No, but I'd do it for fifty quid."

He wanted to slap her. It was an outrageous sum. Instead he said, "Thanks, Gemma, truly. I'll have the money for you next time I see you."

"You'd better."

He kissed her good-bye and left the Gaiety. Out on Commercial Street he searched for a hackney. Where was he going to get fifty quid for Gemma? The dinner he'd hosted at the Reform Club a few weeks ago had all but bankrupted him. The thought of his debts weighed heavily on him, as did Joe Bristow's campaign, but more troubling than any of those was Gemma's news about India. She was trying to get her hands on contraceptives. She must be forging ahead with her mad scheme for a clinic—which could mean only one thing: that she wasn't pregnant, for she obviously didn't intend to stop working any time soon.

"Damn it!" he swore. Everything had been going so well, and now it was all wrong again. The Home Rule debacle had nearly destroyed him. He was broke. And Isabelle was being troublesome. She was pleased that a wedding date had been set, but was adamant that no monies would be paid, or property transferred, until India had given up medicine.

"What the hell am I going to do?" Freddie asked himself, pacing in the street, his arm outstretched for a cab.

He tried to think of an answer, but all that came to mind was rubber johnnies. What a thing to be thinking about at a time like this. But he couldn't get them out of his head. There was something in all this, something he was missing, but what?

A cabbie driving in the opposite direction noticed him and signaled that he would turn around. Freddie nodded at him. "Calm down, old boy. Calm down and think," he told himself.

He reviewed it all again. He still couldn't believe that India had enlisted Sid Malone's help. Malone of all people. She despised him. So why had she gone to him? He would ask her. In fact, he would take her to task for this. Tell her that someone had seen them together and had told him. It was completely unacceptable, her consorting with the likes of Malone. It was utter madness.

There *must* be a reason, a damn good one, for her to have taken such a measure. But what was it? The more Freddie thought about it, the more he saw that his assumption that India would use the devices in her clinic was wrong, because there was no clinic. Not yet. He knew she was putting aside money from her wages to fund the clinic, and he knew that those savings did not amount to much. Why would she spend the precious little money she had on supplies when the clinic wasn't even open?

Was she going to use the devices at Gifford's surgery? That was a more likely explanation. But if she was, why hadn't she just ordered them from a medical supplier?

And then it hit him. *She doesn't want Gifford to know.*

Gifford must be against it, he thought. It would make sense that he was. He was terribly upright. A bit of a relic, actually. India must be planning to prescribe them without his knowledge.

Freddie watched the hackney carefully turn around in the middle of the street, and decided to do a bit of an about-face himself. He wouldn't confront India about this. Not yet. He would bide his time. Something inside him told him to stow this information away for now. It would serve him better later.

The cab finally pulled up beside him. As he climbed in, he felt a bit calmer. He thought of Gemma and her promise to help him. At least he'd come up with a solution to Joe Bristow. What cheek Bristow had, waltzing into his constituency, denouncing him to all and sundry. Freddie had tried fair means of stalling Joe's progress—arguing the issues, pointing up Bristow's lack of experience—and foul. He'd also paid Donaldson to get some of his lads to smash up Joe's headquarters and rip down his flyers. They'd be at the Labour rally, too. Some in street clothes ready to stir things up; others in uniform waiting to arrest law breakers. With any amount of luck, Donaldson's lads and Gemma and her friends would turn the event into a free-for-all.

As the cab rolled west down busy Commercial Street, Freddie glimpsed a pub called the Red Earl. There were more than a few of them in England. They were named in honor of his ancestor, Richard Lytton. The sign outside this pub showed Lytton in armor, holding a sword. His expression was heartless, fearless, remorseless. He looked like a man who could do whatever it took to get what he wanted. A man who would win no matter the cost.

It comes in handy to be a Lytton at times like these, Freddie thought. He had no conscience whatsoever about scheming to break up the Labour rally and disgrace Joe Bristow. All was fair in love and war. And the contest for the Tower Hamlets seat was indeed turning into a war.

As he passed by his ancestor, he smiled at him. "Buck up, old boy," he said to himself. "A Lytton brought the Scots to heel, and the Welsh. And a Lytton will bring East London to heel, too. No matter the cost."

CHAPTER 27

"Ah, Whitechapel in the summer," Ella said, sidestepping a heap of freshly deposited horse manure. "There's no place lovelier."

India, following her, waved her hat in front of her face as she walked, trying to cool herself. "Why am I doing this?" she wondered aloud. "I'm only fanning the stinks."

Privies and drains, the odd dead dog, market refuse, and the July heat had combined to create an unholy stench. During summer's first hot days, India had felt like retching as she'd walked through the narrow streets and alleys. She'd gotten used to it, however. She'd had to. Whitechapel was not about to accommodate her, so she'd learned to accommodate it.

She walked without her jacket now, and with her sleeves rolled up. She hadn't bothered to roll them down after seeing her last patient, and didn't intend to do so now. It was cooler this way. Her cheeks were pink with the heat, her hair was springing loose from its twist. Her blouse was sodden. She was sweaty and exhausted. She and Ella looked less like doctor and nurse and more like two charladies.

"I could murder a lemon squash. I hope my mother's made some," Ella said.

"I hope she's made a tubful. I could bathe in it," India said.

It was late afternoon. She and Ella were in Stepney, walking back to Whitechapel after seeing their last patient of the day, a child with dysentery. They were seeing many such cases these days as the heat, combined with the unsanitary conditions in so many shops and homes, meant that children were eating tainted food. India knew from several studies, and now from her own experience, that the mortality rate among Whitechapel's children would skyrocket before leveling off again in the autumn.

"Ella, look at this," India said, tugging on her arm. She pulled her over to an old brick building. It was enormous. Five stories tall. At least forty feet wide. "It's for sale. See the sign?"

They both read it. The building was a former bakery and the owner was asking £4,000.

"We don't even have four hundred pounds," Ella said. "And even if we did have four thousand, Wish wouldn't let us buy it. It's too dear. He told us we have to stick to the plan. Weren't you listening?"

"Yes, I was," India sighed. "But it's such a nice, big place."

"We'll find another nice, big place. First we need to raise twenty-five thousand pounds."

India and Ella had met Wish again two nights ago at the café. He had a banker's draft for £100 with him, donated by an old school friend of his, and a rudimentary business plan. He would triple the £5,000 India had invested in his Point Reyes project and put it into an account. Meanwhile they would all work like demons to solicit another £10,000 in donations. Once they had that, Wish would require them to add £5,000 of it to India's £15,000—giving them a total endowment of £20,000. That money he would never allow them to touch. It would go into an aggressive investment account which would return ten percent annually. They would use that return, roughly £2,000, to run the clinic—to pay staff salaries, utilities, and rates, and to buy supplies.

He would allow them to spend the remaining £5,000 of donation money thus: £2,000 on a building, £2,000 on repairs, and £1,000 on furnishings and supplies. He made no bones about the fact that for the first few years of its life the clinic would be run on a shoestring, but he also said that once it was open they would continue to seek donations. These would be added to the endowment. The original £20,000 would grow, the returns on it would grow, and so would the clinic's operating budget. He saw no reason that the endowment wouldn't one day reach £200,000, giving them £20,000 a year to spend on their patients.

"Twenty thousand a year to spend," India said now, peering into one of the building's windows. "Can you imagine? Think we'll ever get there?"

"Not if we don't get busy and get ourselves more money," Ella said. "Come on, let's go."

They crossed Shandy Street, with its Saturday market, planning to head to Ella's house. The restaurant would be closed today for the Sabbath, when cooking, and work of any nature, was forbidden, but they were hoping there might be some leftover brisket from the Moskowitzes' Friday night supper.

Ella warned India that there would be a lecture to endure. Her mother was *frum*, observant of the rules of her faith, and was unhappy whenever Ella went to work on the Sabbath.

"What am I supposed to do?" she said now. "Tell a woman with a baby coming to wait until Sunday? If a woman labors, I labor. If God doesn't want me out on the Sabbath, He should stop sending babies to be born on the Sabbath." She sighed. "You'll stick up for me, won't you, Indy?"

"Not a chance. While you're being scolded, I'm going to sneak into the kitchen and make a start on that brisket."

Ella cocked her head. "Why, Dr. Jones, I do believe you're joking again! That's twice in a week. Better be careful or people will think you've a sense of humor."

India made a face at her. They got to the end of Shandy Street, turned left onto Horse Lane, and headed toward Stepney Green. They'd planned to take a shortcut through the green, then walk west to Brick Lane, but as they approached it they found that the green was jam-packed with people.

"I wonder what's going on?"

"I think it's a rally for the Labour Party. I remember my father saying something about it."

"Oh yes, you're right. Freddie mentioned it. He said that Joe Bristow was going to be speaking. The man who's challenging him for the Tower Hamlets seat. One of them. He said that—"

"Jones! Windy Indy Jones! Over here!"

India whirled around. She knew that voice. She turned, eyes searching, and spotted a young woman in a fashionable straw hat making her way toward her through the crowd.

"Why, Dr. Hatcher, what an unexpected pleasure," she said, as the woman joined them. She hadn't seen Harriet, a fellow alumna, since their graduation day.

"*Windy Indy?*" Ella echoed.

"A childhood nickname that followed me to medical school," India explained. "Good old Harriet heard Wish use it once and made sure it stuck. Dreadful, isn't it? And completely undeserved."

"I don't know, India, I rather think it suits you," Ella said mischievously.

India introduced Ella and Harriet, then commented on the size of the crowd that had assembled on the green.

"I came to hear Mrs. Pankhurst," Harriet said. "Have you heard her speak?"

India said she had.

"She's brilliant, isn't she?" Harriet said passionately. "She'll do it, you know. She'll get us the vote. Mark my words." She squinted up at the podium. "Is the Honorable Member here?"

"Hardly," India said. "It's a Labour rally, Harriet."

"But he should have Mrs. Pankhurst on his side. I thought Freddie was an enlightened politician. A new breed of leader. The future of the Liberal Party. That's what *The Times* says. Doesn't he believe in woman suffrage?"

India looked uncomfortable. "Of course he does. In theory, if not in practice."

"What the hell does that mean?"

"He wants women to have the vote, just . . . not yet. He believes that the Liberals are too vulnerable to fight on too many fronts at one time. He thinks they must first consolidate power and win back the premiership. And once that is accomplished, then they can fight for woman suffrage."

"Sounds like bollocks to me."

"I'll make sure to tell him that."

"I cannot imagine why you're marrying him, Indy. The two of you are like chalk and cheese. No, that's not true. I *can* imagine why. Have you met him, Ella?"

"No, I haven't."

"He's absolutely glorious. Charming, handsome . . . the most golden of golden boys. Every woman in our class got hot and bothered whenever he came to call on India."

"Harriet!" India exclaimed, blushing.

Harriet smiled devilishly. "Oh, right! Sorry, I forgot. We women don't have those sorts of feelings, do we? Not if we're moral and decent and up-standing. That's what old Brearly says."

"Oh, here we go," India said.

Harriet affected the stern, sonorous voice of Dr. Anthony Brearly, their anatomy professor. "Vagina, a narrow conduit between the vulva and the cervix, composed largely of muscle, devoid of nerve tissue. Clitoris, an extraneous appendage, useless to the process of reproduction. A locus of mental instability in women, its removal is often recommended in the treatment of hysteria, psychosis, and persistent nymphomania . . ." She burst into laughter, then said, "Extraneous to him, maybe. Couldn't bloody live without mine."

Ella giggled.

"Good Lord, Harriet," India said. "We're in a public place. Do keep your voice down before we're arrested on obscenity charges."

"Oh, no one even knows what I'm talking about. Clitoris. Sounds like a brand of tooth polish. Can't you just see the advertisement on the side of a bus?"

Ella snorted laughter.

"Stop encouraging her!" India scolded.

Harriet winked at Ella, then took a silver cigarette case from her jacket pocket. She lit one and took a deep drag, eliciting stares. India removed the cigarette from her lips, threw it on the ground, and crushed it with her boot.

"First, do no harm, Dr. Hatcher," she said.

"Hippocrates meant to our patients, Dr. Jones."

"And to ourselves. Still smoking twenty a day?"

"Nowhere near."

"They cause cancer of the lung, you know."

"It's never been proven."

"It will be."

Harriet rolled her eyes. "Still a barrel of fun, I see."

India winced at that. She had been a better student, a better technician, but Harriet had been more popular. She had an easy way and a wicked tongue and made everyone laugh. India had seen her humor work wonders with patients. She could put even the most anxious at ease. India envied her that. Harriet jollied patients, whereas she lectured them. *Windy Indy*. Ella was right. The nickname fit her.

"Well, ladies, I'm off," Harriet said. "I want a better view of Mrs. Pankhurst. Oh, I almost forgot to ask you, Indy . . . how are you getting on at Dr. Gifford's?"

"Fine."

"Liar. Look at yourself. You look like a fishwife."

"All right, then. I'm coping. Barely. How's Harley Street?"

Harriet came from wealth. Her surgery was in a prestigious neighborhood where the city's most eminent doctors practiced.

"Harley's hellish. I'm bored out of my skin. If I have to listen to one more pampered little madam tell me how exhausted she is from the season, or how vexing it is managing the servants, or that her neuralgia flares every time her sons come home from Eton, I'll scream." She let out a long, trailing sigh. "Indy, remember when we used to talk about your clinic? In the wee hours when we should've been studying?"

"Of course I do."

"I still think about it."

"So do I. In fact, Ella and I are trying to make a go of it. We even have a director of development—Wish. We're currently seeking donations—both money and goods—and when we have enough collected we're going to look for a building. In Whitechapel."

"You're really serious, Indy!"

"I am always serious, Harriet."

"How much have you got so far?"

India and Ella traded sheepish glances.

"Um, well, a hundred seventy-eight pounds . . ." India began.

"And five boxes of rusks," Ella finished.

Harriet laughed. "I don't think I'll be closing my office anytime soon."

"Don't scoff," India said, bristling. "We'll get it opened eventually. It's just going to take us a bit of time to get the money together."

"I know you will, India. I wasn't scoffing. Truly. I'm not happy in Harley Street. Not at all. If you get the clinic up and running, I'll work there. For free."

"Really?" India asked, astonished.

"Yes. I don't need money. What I do need is a challenge, and it sounds like your clinic would provide it."

India gave Harriet a long look. "I'm going to hold you to this, Hatch," she said.

"I'm sure you will. Get it going, old girl, and I'll be there. And I'll drag Fenwick with me, too. He's fed up with teaching. Told me that his current class is an even bigger bunch of blockheads than we were."

"Coming from Fenwick, that's quite a compliment," India said.

"Oh, look! There's one of my patients. The only one I actually like. Mrs. Bristow!"

A beautiful woman in a pink suit and rose-trimmed hat was standing on her tiptoes a few yards away. She smiled at Harriet, then walked over. India could see immediately that she was about five months pregnant. Her well-cut suit probably fooled most eyes, but not hers.

"Are you well?" Harriet asked.

"Very well, thank you," Fiona said.

Harriet made introductions all around, then asked Fiona if she'd come to hear Mrs. Pankhurst.

"Actually I'm supposed to be introducing my husband," Fiona replied. "I was supposed to have been here an hour ago. I have to get to the stage, but I'm not sure how I'm going to get through this crowd."

"I'm going to try skirting around the edge of the square," Harriet said. "Do you want to come with me?"

"I've already tried that. There are so many police constables over there, no one can get by. I think I'll try the direct route. Lovely to meet you, Dr. Jones . . . Sister Moskowitz."

"Be careful, please, Mrs. Bristow," Harriet cautioned.

Fiona smiled. "Doctor's orders?"

"Indeed."

When Fiona Bristow was out of earshot, Harriet said, "Now there's a woman for you to approach. Richer than Midas, and very charitably minded."

India made a mental note to ask Wish about her, and Harriet said her good-byes. As she moved off, India said, "Well, Ella, it now looks like we have a hundred seventy-eight pounds, five boxes of rusks, and the head of our children's ward."

"Is she good?" Ella asked.

"Very. An absolute marvel with little ones."

Ella looked at her watch. "It's quarter past four," she said. "I think they were supposed to start fifteen minutes ago. Shall we stay and listen to Mrs. Pankhurst?"

"Yes, let's. They'll probably start soon. Probably just waiting for Fiona Bristow," India said, squinting at the stage. She could see a handful of people sitting behind a podium. And one empty chair. "I wonder if she made it up there? Do you see her?"

India's voice was drowned out by excited cheers and whistles as a woman rose from her seat on the stage.

"Let's get a bit closer," Ella said. They tried, but made little progress. People were standing shoulder to shoulder.

Mrs. Pankhurst took the podium. The cheers increased. India knew that she was a firebrand. She hardly looks the part, she thought. Diminutive, with delicate features, she seemed more fragile than feisty. Until she started to speak. Then she seemed about as fragile as a bricklayer.

"Welcome. Welcome to you women. And you men. Welcome to the officers of the law I see stationed three deep! You may ask why we are here today. We are here not because we are law breakers; we are here in our efforts to become law makers."

Cheers went up again, only this time they were challenged by loud booing. India looked to its source—a group of men, pints in hand, standing outside a pub.

"Go home to yer washin', ya meddlin' bitches!" one shouted.

Mrs. Pankhurst ignored him and kept speaking.

More cheers went up, and then a fight broke out near the pub. Several constables quashed it. It was orderly for a few minutes, then a man's voice bellowed, "Votes for women when hell freezes over!"

Catcalls were heard, this time from women. India looked behind herself uneasily. Not far from where she and Ella stood, a blowsy group, the cut and color of their dresses advertising their profession, hooted and laughed. One screeched an obscenity. India squinted at them, her doctor's eyes automatically searching for any visible signs of venereal disease, but saw none.

"Ella . . ."

"Aye?"

"There's something odd about those women over there. They don't look like . . ."

"Whores," Ella finished flatly.

"They're too healthy."

"Too well fed."

"They look like they're onstage. Like they're only playing prostitutes."

"That's exactly what they're doing."

"I think something bad is about to happen," India said.

"We should go. Now."

India nodded. She turned around and started to head for one of the square's outlets, then stopped suddenly and said, "Ella, wait! Fiona Bristow . . . did she ever make it to the stage?"

Ella looked around, scanning faces. "No. She's there. Halfway to the podium. See her hat?"

India nodded. "Mrs. Bristow!" she shouted. "Mrs. Bristow! Over here!"

Her voice was drowned out as Mrs. Pankhurst was booed again. A tomato sailed through the air and hit the floor near her feet. She flinched, but kept speaking. The tension was growing. It was a tangible thing now. India could feel it moving invisibly through the crowd like a tiger in the tall grass. She knew what was coming. She'd treated victims of riots and she knew how quickly a crowd could turn into a mob. And Fiona Bristow, five months pregnant, was right in the middle of it.

"We've got to get her," she said.

"We'd better hurry," Ella said grimly. She clasped India's hand and together they fought their way through the crush of people.

When they finally reached her, they were sweating and out of breath. India placed a hand on her back and Fiona turned toward them. India wasn't pleased to see that Fiona's face was flushed.

"We're leaving," she told her. "You must come with us. You can't stay here. Not in your condition."

"I've been trying to leave. I can't get through the crowd. There's nowhere to go."

"We just fought our way up here, we'll fight our way back. I'll lead. Stay between us and mind your belly—" Her words were cut off by shouts and the harsh blast of a police whistle.

A brawl had broken out between one of the prostitutes and two constables. A man, drunk and shouting, joined in, harassing the officers. As India watched, a second man swung at the first. A cry went up; she was pushed forward as the crowd surged toward the combatants. Suddenly there was the sound of horses. Riot police had entered the square on its west side and were fording the crowd, truncheons swinging.

India just had time to wonder how they'd gotten there so quickly before one horse spooked, reared, and clipped a woman with its hooves. She screamed. Blood poured from a gash on her cheek. .

"This assembly is hereby declared unlawful!" a man's voice blared over a bullhorn. "Emmeline Pankhurst, I order you to cease speaking!"

A cheer went up, and then an enormous roar of protest drowned it out. Mrs. Pankhurst kept on speaking. A command was shouted and the horses began moving in unison toward the podium. The women standing close to it screamed with terror and surged forward, frantically trying to get away from the podium. But there were so many of them, they could barely move. India glanced back at Fiona. Her hat was gone. Her hair was falling down around her pale face. India feared she would faint in the crush. She looked all around the square. It was lined by shops and pubs, but there was no way they could reach those places before the horses reached them. She looked back at the podium and had an idea. She grabbed Fiona's hand and changed direction.

"Come on! Back the other way! Quickly!" she shouted.

"Where are we going?" Ella yelled.

"The podium! It's our only chance!"

India battered her way through the crowd, fending off flailing hands and elbows, never relinquishing her grip on Fiona. She couldn't see the horses anymore, but she could hear them and knew they were closing in. The front of the podium was draped with an enormous banner emblazoned with the words, VOTES FOR WOMEN NOW! India knew it had been constructed just for the rally. She hoped it was a jerry-built job.

The push to flee the podium had opened up space around it. India finally broke through the crowd and ran the last few yards to the structure, pulling Fiona along with her. She grabbed the bottom of the banner, lifted it, and found what she was hoping for—no wooden sheathing, just a cross-hatched maze of posts and beams.

"Crawl inside!" she shouted. As Fiona did so, India reached back for

Ella—but Ella wasn't there. She searched the crowd frantically, then spot-ted her struggling in the arms of a constable several feet away.

"Behind you, Indy! Behind you!" she screamed.

India turned and saw the horse, black and looming; she saw its huge, frightened eyes far too close to her own. It reared. She raised her arms, try-ing to shield herself, stumbled backward, and fell to the ground. The horse whinnied; its metal shoes crashed down against the cobbles. They seemed to be everywhere at once, a thousand slashing hooves all around her. India curled into a tight ball. A hoof came down on her thigh; she screamed. She rolled to her right, trying to get out from under the animal, trying to get to the podium, but it was too late. There was a blinding explosion of white in-side her skull. And then there was nothing. Nothing at all.

CHAPTER 28

"Jesus, Frankie, what the hell happened?" Sid Malone asked, looking at the scores of women in the receiving area of the Whitechapel police sta-tion. "The Harrods white sale get out of hand?"

"Some suffering women's something or other," Frankie said, gingerly touching his fingers to his swollen eye.

"Make sense, will you?"

"I don't know, guv. Something to do with suffering. They had a rally about it and it turned into a Donnybrook."

"*Suffrage,* you git. The beak's sending all these women down? Where's he going to put them?"

"He's only keeping the ringleader. Mrs. Pankhurst, she's called. He's let-ting the rest go. Just giving them their clobber back now. Held 'em overnight. One of the screws down the men's cells said they didn't even take names. Beak just wanted to give them a scare. A wee taste of the nick."

"Wonder if it'll work. Never seems to have any effect on you," Sid said. He'd gotten word a few hours earlier that Frankie was arrested the night be-fore for brawling. Again. None of his men had been around to go after him, so Sid had had to go himself, and trips to the nick did not make him happy.

"Sorry, guv."

"Who was it this time? Donaldson inventing things again?"

"Madden's crew."

Sid's ears pricked up at this. "Where?"

"Wapping. In the Prospect of Whitby. Two of them sitting there bold as brass, drinking and having a laugh and ordering everyone about. I saw red, guv. Couldn't help meself. They ain't laughing now."

"Big Billy with them?" he asked.

"No."

Sid nodded. Maybe it had just been two wild lads on a spree. Maybe. That's what Billy would say when he asked him about it. And he *would* ask him. There'd be apologies, promises never to let it happen again. And it would be bollocks, every last word of it. Sid knew that Billy Madden wanted the East End. He'd probably gotten wind that Freddie Lytton was after the Firm, probably thought their days were numbered. Sid would have to keep his ear to the ground. Send the lads out to the pubs. See if anyone else had been nosing around where they shouldn't be.

"They charging me?" Frankie asked.

Sid shook his head.

"Who'd you put the frighteners on?"

"No one. A few quid in the right hands and suddenly nobody saw nothing. Money talks, Frankie. Remember that."

"I will. Thanks, guv," Frankie said. He looked relieved and a little disappointed. Negotiations based on words and money held little allure for him. He liked the drama of intimidation, the crack of knuckles against bone. He was still young, though. He'd learn.

There was a sudden commotion in one corner of the room. Sid turned to see what was going on, then frowned.

"It's that flippin' Devlin," he said. "Let's leg it before he takes a picture of us and we have to smash his camera again."

"He already saw me and couldn't have cared less. Word has it a couple members of the quality got nicked at the rally along with all the tarts. Wants to do a story on fine ladies slumming with the riffraff. Dodgy morals of the upper class . . . something like that." Frankie shrugged into his torn, bloodstained jacket, then took a comb from his pocket and raked it through his hair. "I like the sound of dodgy morals, me. Can you imagine stuffin' it to some randy duchess? Makes me hard just thinking about it."

"Spare me, Frankie, will you?" Sid said, heading for the door.

"Heard your friend's mixed up in it."

"What friend?"

"The lady doctor."

"Dr. Jones? She's here?"

"That's what I heard."

"Bloody hell, Frankie. If Devlin finds her, she's done for."

"How do you mean?"

"He'll make her part of his story. Make her look bad. Land her right in the shit."

"So what, guv? What's it to us?"

"A lot. To me, at least. Come on."

"Fuck's sake, Sid, I'm starved! And there's a nice pub right round the corner."

Sid didn't even hear him. He had to find India. He made his way through the crowd of women, some standing, some sitting. Some looked bored, as if the inside of a police station was nothing new to them. Others looked dazed. He saw torn blouses, crumpled hats, bruised faces.

And then he saw India. He didn't recognize her at first. Her face was bloodied. The neck of her blouse was open. Its collar was stained with more blood. She was with Ella Moskowitz. The two of them were bent over a third woman. Sid saw India lift her skirt, tear a strip of fabric from her petticoat and use it to bind up a jagged cut on the woman's hand. That figured. The two of them helping hard-luck cases when they should have had sense enough to get out of there while they could. Sid saw Devlin. He was only a yard away, sniffing, circling, closing in. It was too late. He was nearly on her.

Sid backed away. "Forget it," he said to Frankie. And then India turned toward him and he saw her face, saw her resoluteness and determination, her heart-breaking innocence. She was tired and dirty, he could see that, yet he knew she would stay in this grim, stinking place, tearing up her clothing, until every last wound was bound.

"Oi!" he suddenly boomed. "Annie! Mary! I've been looking all over for you two. Get yourselves up out of this and get back to work!"

India blinked. Ella looked at him as if he'd gone mad. Sid gave a sharp nod toward Devlin. Ella's eyes widened.

"Keep your hair on, guv, we was just leavin'," she said. "Wanted a bit of a holiday, we did. Hard work being on your back all day, ain't it?" she added, elbowing the woman next to her. They laughed bawdily.

"Two of yours, Malone?" a male voice said. It was Devlin. "Thought you were a businessman."

"I am. These are me business partners. Two waitresses from the Taj." Sid looked at India as he spoke. Her mouth was open. He chucked her under the chin and closed it.

"Waitresses, eh?" Devlin said, smirking.

"Aye, and always happy to serve. Aren't you, girls? Mr. Devlin here's got himself a brand-new camera and he's awfully fond of it. Be a shame if it got broken like his last one did."

"Relax, Malone. It's not you I'm after. Got some bigger fish to fry. Word has it the MP's fiancée got picked up. Spent the night in here with all the drunks and brasses. Would make a good story, that, what with election rumors hotting up and all. 'MP Doxie's Liberal Ways' . . . something like that."

"You're a right wordsmith, Dev," Sid said. He turned India's face away from Devlin's toward his own, making a show of examining the ugly gash on her temple. He saw that she'd gone pale. "Get this cleaned up, Mary. It's bad for business," he said, warning her with his eyes to keep quiet. "You sure the bird's here, Dev? What's her name?"

"Jones, I think," Devlin said. "She's a doctor. Works for Edwin Gifford on Varden Street. A somber old Puritan, him. Bet he'd sack her if the story ran. Might make a good follow-up. That or an interview with Lytton. After his lady friend costs him the election."

"You're all heart."

Devlin shrugged. "Not my look-out. I have papers to sell. You know her, Malone? Know what she looks like?"

"I'm afraid not. We don't run in the same social circles, me and the MP."

"No, I don't suppose you do." Devlin frowned. He watched Sid lick his thumb and rub at the dried blood under India's eye. His own eyes narrowed. He studied her face.

Sid smiled at him. "Interested, Dev? You'd never know it from looking at her, but this one's a right goer. Ain't you, luv?" he said to India. He took her chin, lifted it, and kissed her mouth. He licked his lips when he finished, as if savouring a bite of beefsteak. "You want a bit of that, you come round the Taj," he said, winking.

"I'm a married man," Devlin said priggishly.

"All the more reason," Sid replied. Then he clapped his hands. "All right, no more skiving. There's work to be done. Ta-ra, Dev," he called over his shoulder.

Devlin grumbled a reply and moved off. Sid quickly escorted India and Ella out of the station. As soon as they were in the street, Ella kissed Sid's cheek and thanked him. "I've got to run," she said. "Me mum'll be worried to death. 'Bye, India. See you tomorrow."

India didn't reply. She was looking at the ground.

"You all right?" Sid asked her. "That's a bad cut."

She raised her head. Her eyes were blazing. "How *dare* you?" she said, her voice shaking with rage.

Sid was taken aback. He'd expected her gratitude. "How dare I?" he echoed.

"Yes. How dare you?"

"How dare I *what*? How dare I save you from having your picture splashed all over Devlin's rag? How dare I save your bloody job? And likely your bloody engagement, too? Wonder what Freddie would make of his fiancée mixing with whores. Brawling like a common criminal. Wonder what his voters would make of it."

"I *wasn't* mixing with prostitutes, I was—"

"Doesn't matter. That's how the papers will tell it."

"You went too far, Mr. Malone. You shouldn't have said what you did. You shouldn't have kissed me. It was highly improper. I imagine you enjoyed yourself immensely, but—"

Sid snorted. "Don't flatter yourself."

India looked so hurt that he immediately regretted the remark. He was about to say so, when he heard laughter. It was Frankie. He'd forgotten all about him.

"Frankie, see Ella home, will you?"

Frankie looked at Sid, then at India. His eyes darkened. He hesitated, looking as if he wanted to say something.

"*Now,*" Sid said.

Frankie nodded curtly and trotted off in the direction Ella had taken. Sid looked at India again. At her torn clothing. At the jagged cut on the side of her face.

"How'd that happen anyway?" he asked.

"Horse," she said tightly.

"You're lucky it wasn't worse."

"Very."

Christ, why were they at each other again? Sid wondered. They could never talk without rowing. Not at Ko's. Or in the hospital. Not at the Bark. And not here, either. All he'd wanted to do was help her. To make things right for her. Couldn't she see that?

"Sorry for interfering Dr. Jones," he finally said. "My mistake." He touched the brim of his cap and made his way through the milling crowd.

"Mr. Malone, I . . . wait . . . please wait . . ." India said, but he didn't hear her.

"Malone!"

Sid looked around at the sound of his name and spotted Devlin hurrying down the stairs with his camera. "Malone, you tosser, you!"

He turned back to India. Her eyes were fearful. She looked like a trapped animal. "Can you run in your boots?" he shouted.

"Yes!"

"Then for fuck's sake, woman, do so!"

"Come on, it's not far now," Sid urged India.

They'd been running flat out for ten minutes, but they still hadn't managed to shake Devlin.

"Malone, wait! I just want to ask a few questions!" they heard him yelling, only a street away.

India stopped. "Mr. Malone," she wheezed. "It's all right. I'll talk to him. I can't go any farther. I can't. I just won't let him take a picture."

"He'll pop that bleedin' thing while you're walking toward him. That's what he did to me. Told me he just wanted to talk, tucked the bloody thing under his arm, and then _whoosh!_ The flash goes off and he got me. Let him get a picture and you're done for. Right now he's got no proof of anything. The beaks didn't take any names. But if he gets your photograph he's at least got proof you were standing on Dean Street, roughed up and bloodied. It won't look good for Lytton. Not one bit."

"Why do you suddenly care so about Freddie, Mr. Malone? He doesn't care about you. He's trying to put you in jail with all possible haste."

"I don't care," he said, looking away from her searching gray eyes. "Not about Freddie."

"Malone! Just give me a minute!"

"If you can go another few yards, I can get us out of here."

"All right."

They ran to the end of Dean Street, where Sid suddenly pulled India into the doorway of a squat brick house. The door to the ground-floor flat opened as they pounded down the hallway. An old woman stuck her head out. Her milky eyes focused on Sid, then lit up.

"Hello, luv!" she said. "Looking a bit breathless, you are. Needin' me cellar?"

"I am, Sally."

"Come on, then."

She led them to the small, dingy kitchen at the back of the house and opened a door. A flight of steps led down from it into darkness.

"I owe you, Sal," Sid said, kissing her wrinkled cheek.

"You owe me nothing. Raysie sends his regards. Lamp's on the shelf."

Sid grabbed a small miner's lamp and fumbled with a box of matches. They all heard a loud battering from the front of the house.

The old woman sighed. She reached past Sid and took down a heavy iron frying pan from a shelf. "Who's it this time?" she asked.

"Newspapers."

"Diabolical, they are. Worse than the rozzers." She patted his cheek. "You take care of yourself."

"And you, Sally," Sid said. The lamp was glowing now. Sally waited until they were down the stairs then shut the door behind them.

"Mind yourself," Sid said, leading India across the dank, low-ceilinged room. He stopped in front of a battered armoire.

India hesitated. "We're not hiding in there, are we?" she asked. "It's just that it's rather small, and . . ."

"And what? Our elbows might touch?"

"No, that's not it. That's not it at all. I just . . . I . . ."

"Let's go. We've no time for chatting," Sid said. He pushed aside some moldering dresses and an ancient mackintosh. India gasped when she saw what they'd hidden—a narrow passageway.

"Bend low," Sid told her, climbing into the wardrobe. When he was in the passageway, he reached back for her. When she'd climbed through, he pulled the wardrobe's door shut from the inside and put the clothes back as they were.

"It's a bit of a slog—maybe ten or twelve streets from where we are now—but at least we won't have to run it," he said.

India looked wide-eyed at the passageway. Sid followed her gaze, taking in the sodden walls, dripping with rainwater and, worse, the low earth ceiling with its shroud of cobwebs, and the rutted, puddled ground. Denny Quinn had told him about this tunnel. No one knew who'd built it or why.

"Take hold of me jacket and stick close. Ground's a bit treacherous."

"Where are we going?"

"East."

"What about Devlin? What if he follows us?"

"No worries. He won't get past Sally. She's dead accurate with that frying pan."

"How do you know her?"

Sid didn't reply. He was fiddling with the lamp as he walked. There was plenty of kerosene in the base, but the wick was dodgy. It was flickering. They had a long walk ahead of them and he wanted the light to last. There were things in the tunnel that didn't like light.

India tried another question. "Who's Raysie?"

"Sal's old man," he said.

"Where is he?"

"Dying."

"Dying? In the flat? Let's go back. Perhaps I could help him."

"In the hospital. Stomach cancer."

"Which hospital?"

"Bart's."

"That's one of the best."

"So I've heard."

Another pause, then, "You're paying his bills, aren't you?"

"What's that to you?"

She was about to reply when she stumbled. At the same time there was a terrible, high-pitched squeaking. Sid heard her gasp, felt her hands clutch at his back.

"You didn't say there were rats!" she cried.

"I thought it best not to. Are you afraid of them?"

"No." He heard her swallow—hard. Then, "Yes. Yes, I am. And tunnels. I'm claustrophobic."

Sid sighed. "Now you tell me."

"I tried earlier, but you wouldn't let me!"

"Look, just forget you're in a tunnel, all right? Pretend you're walking on the street. Don't think about it."

"What about the rats?"

"They're more frightened of you than you are of them."

"I don't think so."

He was surprised by her admission of fear, by her sudden vulnerability. It softened his angry feelings toward her. He reached for her hand and squeezed it, and was surprised to feel her squeeze back. He tried to get her talking again, thinking it might distract her. He told her he thought he would have the supplies she wanted soon. He asked about her clinic and if she was any closer to opening it.

"You're trying to keep my mind off the rats, aren't you?"

"You've seen right through me." He hurried his pace, pulling her after him. The bloody wick was playing up and they weren't even halfway through the tunnel.

"Tell me something about yourself. It's only fair," India said. "I told you about my family, my studies, everything, when you were in the hospital. Now it's your turn. Quid pro quo, remember? I'll start you off. Where were you born?"

Sid said nothing.

"East London by the sound of your voice. What were your parents like? One of them must have had red hair. According to Mendel's laws, at least.

Mendel was the first geneticist, you know. He studied the inherited traits of peas."

"I'm not a pea, missus."

"I realize that, but all living things contain genetic material and share it when they reproduce. Was it your mother? Did she have red hair?"

Sid said nothing. But he was pleased to see the tunnel snake to the left—the turning was the halfway point.

"Do you have any brothers? Sisters? No?" India pressed. "Did you have a dog when you were a child? Cats? A budgerigar?" She sighed, then said, "This isn't fair! I talked to you when you were in the hospital, now you should talk to me."

When he still didn't reply, she said, "You're angry with me, aren't you? Look, I'm sorry. I really am. Please don't be."

"I'm not. I just don't like talking about meself."

"No, I meant that I'm sorry for earlier. At the jail. You tried to help me. You *did* help me, and I behaved badly in return. I can't imagine how angry Freddie would have been if I'd gotten myself into the papers. I owe you my gratitude, Mr. Malone."

"It's Sid. And you don't owe me anything. We're even."

"I don't understand."

"You saved me. Now I've saved you. We're quits."

"Yes. All right. Quits."

Was it his imagination, or was there a shade of regret in her voice? He didn't have time to dwell on it because he'd seen movement up ahead. On the ground. It seemed, in fact, as if the ground itself were moving, but he knew it wasn't. He was just trying to figure out how to hide what was coming from India when his problem was abruptly solved. The wick guttered wildly, then went out. They were standing in total darkness.

"Please tell me that you know your way out of here," she said. "Please."

"I do. There's a bit of bother up ahead, though. A big puddle. Deep one. I'll have to carry you over it."

India was quiet for a few seconds, then she said, "There's not really a puddle, is there?"

Sid didn't answer. "You hold the lamp and I'll hold you. Ready?"

"We can't go back?"

"I'd wager any amount of money that Devlin's waiting right outside Sal's door."

"All right, then. I'm ready."

There was a bit of fumbling. Sid accidentally brushed India's bottom. "Sorry," he quickly said.

"It's all right," she replied.

Finally he got his arms under her and lifted her off the ground. She was light. As light as a child. She put her arms around his neck and he could smell the scent of her—lavender, starch, and sweat.

"It's not much farther," he said. "Once we get past the puddle."

"Talk to me, Sid. *Please*. Tell me something. Anything. You were a boy once, weren't you? Tell me what you did. What games you played. Hoops? Mumblety-peg? Croquet?"

"Aye, croquet. We played a lot of that in the East End. The cobbles make for a nice level playing field."

"You must have done *something*."

"I sat by the river," he finally said. "With me da. And me sister. Me da would name all the boats. Tell us who built them. Where they'd been. What they were carrying. He brought us things off them. Things he'd nicked when the foreman wasn't looking. A bit of tea. A nutmeg. Cinnamon sticks."

He kept talking, hoping his voice would cover the squeaking and scrabbling. They were underfoot now. He was trying not to step directly on any of them, but it was impossible. There were so many. He thought that he must be walking directly through the largest rat colony in all of London and was glad of his heavy boots.

"Oh, God, I can smell them," India said. "There must be dozens. Hundreds."

Her arms tightened around his neck. He could feel her trembling. She leaned her head into his chest. He rested his cheek against it. "Almost there. Almost out," he said.

And they were, though he didn't want to be. He wanted to stay like this, with the sweet weight of her in his arms, with her needing him. He wanted to keep walking with her, out of this unforgiving city, out of his unforgiving life. He wanted to walk all through the night, then sit with her somewhere radiant and beautiful in the morning. By the coast. At the water's edge. Where the stiff salt breeze would blow away the stench of his sins and the sea would wash him clean.

It was a mad notion and he quickly shook it off, though he didn't put her down, not even when they were past the rats. He carried her all the way to the end of the passage, placed her back on her feet, then said, "Should be a door 'ere somewhere."

He started to feel the walls, his hands searching for the way out. He'd had to find it blind before, when there had been no time for a lantern. He remembered that it was narrow and low. His fingers finally found a hollow, an opening dug into the dense London clay. He crouched down and crawled forward. His head knocked into something hard and curved—a wooden keg. He pushed it out of the way and light spilled into the passage. He felt for India and pulled her through.

"Where are we?" she asked, blinking in the gaslight.

"Cellar of the Blind Beggar. A pub on the Whitechapel Road," he answered, rolling the keg back into place. He turned back around, saw her forehead, and grimaced.

"What is it?"

He took out a handkerchief and touched it to her wound. It had opened up again and the cloth came away bloody. "Who doctors the doctor?" he asked quietly.

"It's nothing," she said, taking the cloth and pressing it against her head.

"You didn't answer my question."

"The doctor doctors the doctor," she said wearily.

"When's the last time you ate?" Sid asked. Her hands were still trembling. There were dark smudges under her eyes.

"I don't know. Saturday morning, I think."

It was now Sunday evening. "Come on upstairs. I'm buying you supper."

"I couldn't. I've caused you enough trouble. I'll just find a cab—"

"And pass out on the way home, making it a doddle for the driver to rob you blind. I think you should eat something before you go."

She surrendered. "All right then, Dr. Malone. I will."

They went upstairs. While India cleaned herself up as best she could, Sid found a table in the pub's snug and ordered a pint of porter and a Cumberland mash, twice. India tried to decline the ale and order tea instead, but Sid wouldn't let her.

"There's no goodness in it," he said. "Drink the porter."

She was looking worse by the minute. He feared she might collapse if she didn't get some food. He'd chosen the table closest to the pub's hearth. A fire burned in it. It was twilight now and the evening had turned cool. He hoped the heat would do her good. Their drinks arrived. India sipped hers, then took several deep, hungry gulps. She put the glass down and looked around awkwardly. The intimacy they had shared in the darkness, the feeling of the words coming so easily, was gone and an uncomfortable silence had taken its place. She was the first to break it.

"Thank you for the drink. And for bringing me here. It's good to sit."

"Rough night?"

"Very."

"What happened?"

India told him everything. When she finished, she said, "It was very odd. The four or five women who started it all, they didn't look like prostitutes. And I didn't see them again afterward. In jail, I mean. They weren't arrested."

"Sounds like a staged job. Somebody wanted to break up the rally, maybe make the speakers look bad, so he paid someone to start trouble. Maybe the rozzers as well. Donaldson and his pack are as bent as a hairpin."

"Who would *do* such a thing?"

Sid gave her a look. He wondered how anyone so smart could be so stupid. "Who was the big draw, luv?" he asked.

"Joseph Bristow. He's supposed to be running for the Tower Hamlets seat."

"And who stands to gain if Bristow's made to look bad?"

"I don't know."

Sid rolled his eyes.

"Who?" India asked.

"Lord Freddie, maybe?"

India recoiled. She shook her head vehemently. "Never! How can you even suggest it? Freddie is a gentleman. He would *never* stoop to such tactics."

Sid held up his hands. "Sorry. My mistake. Must have been someone else."

The barmaid delivered two plates. Each held a mountain of mashed potatoes doused in brown gravy and three fat sausages. India tucked in. Sid watched her, pleased. Just as he'd picked up his own fork, a woman came up to the table, dragging a child by the hand. The child was thin, her expression vacant. The woman's face was bloated. Her breath reeked of gin.

"Spare something for the girl, please, Mr. Malone?" she begged.

India was about to give the child her meal when Sid reached into his pocket and handed the woman some coins. When she realized he'd given her a whole pound, she grabbed his hand and kissed it.

"Oi, Kitty! On your bike!" the barmaid shouted, rushing out from behind the bar. "Sorry, Mr. Malone."

"No harm done," he said.

India stabbed at her potatoes with her fork, then looked at Sid. "Why did you do that?" she asked. "You should have let me give them my meal. You're only encouraging drunkenness. She's going to run straight to the next pub and spend it on gin."

"So what?"

"*So what?* She shouldn't be drinking!"

"Why not? What else has she got?"

"A child, for starters."

Sid shook his head. "Girl's a half-wit. Neither of them's going to last long, are they? Maybe the gin will give them a bit of warmth, a bit of comfort."

"They'd be better off with milk. And porridge. And green vegetables."

"Not a lot of comfort in broccoli."

"No, but there's a lot of nourishment."

There it was—the lecturing tone again. India, the woman he'd held in the tunnel, the soft, vulnerable, feeling woman, was gone. Dr. Jones was back.

"Can you not understand the desire for comfort?" he asked her. "Have you never needed any yourself?"

"If I have, I haven't sought it in a gin bottle. Or an opium pipe," she replied tartly.

Sid shook his head. He regretted inviting her for supper now. It was already going badly and they'd only just been served.

"Don't you shake your head at me," she said hotly. "Look around yourself! At the men drinking their wages. Pint after pint after pint. They starve themselves to drink. And their wives and children, too. They'll go home from here—all of them—with only pennies in their pockets—"

"For Christ's sake, leave it be," he said angrily. "You don't know what you're talking about! Have you ever put in a sixteen-hour day at the docks? Heaving coal or sides of beef in the cold and the rain till you'd thought you'd drop dead? Then gone home to the wife and five kids, all stuffed into one drafty room? Some of them sick, all of them hungry. You have *any* idea of the desperation in those rooms? Of the anger? Can you blame a man for wanting to forget it all for an hour with a pint or two in a nice warm pub?"

India sat back in her chair. "Have you always been this way, Sid? So willfully blind to what's right and what's wrong?"

"Have *you* always been this way, India? Such a righteous bitch?"

India looked as if he'd struck her. Her fork clattered to her plate. Sid stared at it—at the pile of mash, at the half-eaten sausages in a slick of gravy—then he picked it up and heaved it into the fire.

"Have you gone utterly mad?" she hissed.

"Still hungry?" he asked her.

"Yes. As a matter of fact, I am. And you've just wasted—"

"Tired?"

"Yes, but I don't see . . ."

"Sore?"

"Quite."

"Good. Welcome to the working class. Now get up."

"*What?* Why? Where are we going?"

"To meet your patients."

Sid threw some money down, then hustled India up from the table. "Come on," he said, taking her arm.

Out in the street, she shook him off violently. "I'm not going anywhere with you. I've met my patients, thank you. At Gifford's surgery. In the hospital."

"Ever been in their homes?"

"Of course I have! Where do you think I deliver their babies?"

Sid gave a dismissive snort. "Bet they cleaned before you came. Bet the women got down on their hands and knees and scrubbed the floor, pains and all, knowing you were coming. Me mam did that. All the mams did. Didn't want the doctors and the midwives thinking they didn't keep a clean house. And here's another thing—"

"I do *not* need to be told how to do my job. Not by you." India turned toward the street and held her hand up to hail a cab.

"You're wrong about the porridge. Dead wrong," Sid said, trailing after her.

"Good night, Mr. Malone."

"You said your patients should eat porridge. You're wrong about that."

India turned and stalked back to him, her eyes sparking anger. "No, actually I'm *right* about that. I could empty half the hospitals in London if I could convince my patients to eat porridge and milk for breakfast instead of bread and tea."

Sid was only inches away from India now, meeting her anger with his own. "Poor women can't cook porridge, don't you know that? Of course you don't. Because you don't know shit about the poor. Oh, you talk about them plenty. And you probably talk *at* them, too. But have you ever talked *with* them? I don't think so, because if you had you'd know that porridge has to be boiled. That takes coal, and coal costs money. And even if they could afford the expense, they *still* wouldn't eat porridge. Put it on any table in Whitechapel and it'll be thrown straight out the window. It's too much like skilly, the shit that's served in the spike. Ever been taken to a workhouse, India? Ever had your kids taken from you? Every last scrap of dignity stripped away? Think you'd ever want to eat what you'd been forced to eat there?"

India didn't reply. She just waved her hand furiously at an approaching cab.

"Ah, sod it. Why am I wasting my breath?" Sid reached into his pocket, then took her free hand and slapped some coins into it. "For the cab. Ta-ra." He strode off, then he stopped suddenly and spun around. "Do you want to be great?" he shouted at her back. There was no response. "India, do you?" Still no response. "You're a good doctor. Do you want to be a great one?"

Slowly her hand came down. She turned to him. "You tell me why first."

"Why what?"

"Why you're trying to take me on some mad house call instead of robbing banks or cracking safes or whatever it is that you do with your evenings."

"Because a bad man wants to do a good deed," he said, repeating what he'd overheard Ella say some weeks back in India's office.

India looked embarrassed, but quickly recovered. "You shouldn't eavesdrop and you shouldn't be flippant."

"I've never been more serious. They need you."

"*Who?*"

Sid spread his arms wide. "*Them*. All of them. All of the poor fucking blighters trying to stay alive in this poor fucking place."

"You have a colossally foul mouth. Do you know that?" Her eyes narrowed. "I think you're drunk."

"I wish. Are you coming?"

"Not until you tell me why it matters to you."

Sid didn't answer for a few seconds. When he did, his voice was low. "Because I had a family once. Here in Whitechapel. A mum. A brother. Two sisters. Me baby sister was ill. Consumption. We spent all we had trying to cure her. She had a bad turn one night and me mam went out to fetch a doctor. It was dark and late. She was killed, me mam. Murdered. On the street outside our door."

"My God," India said.

"They took our money—the so-called doctors—and did nothing. Nothing except shame me mam, telling her she wasn't taking proper care of the baby. Not feeding her right. Not keeping her away from the damp. Can you believe that? Keep her out of the damp? In fucking *London*?" He shook his head. "If we'd had a place we could have taken her, a good place, things might've been different. For her. For me mam . . ."

"For you," India said softly.

Sid looked away. She stared at him searchingly, then said, "Who *are* you, Sid?"

"No one you want to know."

"Missus! I've got better things to do than stop here all night. Do you want a cab or not?" the driver yelled.

India looked at the driver. She bit her lip. "No, I don't. Sorry," she told him. She handed Sid back his money. "Come on, then," she said. "Let's go."

India sat on the stone steps of Christ Church on Whitechapel's Commercial Street, staring into the darkness, clutching a half-empty bottle of porter. The church bells had just rung the hour—midnight. Sid sat next to her, holding a greasy paper containing two uneaten pork pies.

"You all right?"

"I will be."

"It was too much. I shouldn't have done it."

"I just need a minute."

Four hours ago she had stepped out of the London she'd known and into another city entirely. She'd read Dante's *Inferno* once when she was a girl, and she'd felt this evening, as she had then, as if she'd descended into an abyss. As if each step she took along the narrow streets of Whitechapel brought her deeper into hell itself.

Their first stop had been a lighterman's home—John Harris, a man Sid said he sometimes worked with. India had sat teetering on a three-legged chair in Maggie Harris's kitchen. She was careful to keep her feet together, to avoid stepping on the children sleeping under the table.

"So how much is that total, Mags—between the piecework and John's wages?" Sid asked. He was leaning against a wall, arms crossed over his chest.

"Round about a pound a week," Maggie answered, never taking her eyes from her work. She was gluing the outsides of matchboxes together. A boy and three girls sat with her at the table—they ranged in age from seven to twelve—gluing the insides.

"For how many?"

"There are ten of us. Me, the mister, five girls and three boys."

"What do you get for the matchboxes alone, Mrs. Harris?" India asked.

"Tuppence a gross."

Two pennies for 144 matchboxes, she thought, blinking. Mrs. Harris and her children had to make one thousand four hundred and forty boxes to earn one shilling. She sneezed. The fumes from the glue were eye-watering. They made her dizzy. Or maybe it was the wobbly chair making her feel that way. Or maybe it was Sid. Being with him made her feel totally off balance, as if the ground were shifting under her.

"Mam," the littlest girl whispered. "Mam, I'm tired." Her small, pinched face had no color in it except for the purplish circles under her eyes.

"Just a few more, luv," Mrs. Harris said. "Here," she added, sliding a cracked cup across the table. It contained cold tea.

India glanced at the battered clock on the kitchen mantel. It was ten thirty. The children should have been asleep hours ago.

"What's the rent here?"

"Twelve and six," Mrs. Harris said. Then she dutifully answered Sid's questions about the price of food and coal, and what she spent a week on both. Sid and India had knocked on Maggie Harris's door ten minutes ago. Sid had introduced India and said she was going to open a clinic in Whitechapel and was conducting a health survey.

"Crikey, not another one," Maggie Harris had sighed, ushering them in. "Had one of them do-gooders in just last week telling me to feed this lot bean soup. Bleedin' bean soup! They'd never be out of the jakes."

"You ever feed them porridge or broccoli?" Sid asked, throwing India a look.

She threw him one back. Why did he always make her feel that she was in the wrong? She wasn't the criminal, he was.

Mrs. Harris snorted laughter. "Porridge? Oh, aye. The butler brings it on a silver tray. As for broccoli, it stinks up the house something terrible and the kiddies just heave at it. Bread and marge is what we eat. Cabbage and potatoes for tea. With a relish—trotters or a bit of bacon, maybe—for me husband. Tripe sometimes. Or slink . . ."

"Slink?" India repeated.

"Calves what have been born too early."

"Ah."

"Sometimes saveloys for the nippers when me husband's got something extra." Her eyes flicked up to Sid, worried and hopeful at once. "Any chance of that?"

"In a day or two," Sid said. "Removals job. We'll need John's boat."

The woman's relief was palpable. "God bless you."

"There's a bit of dosh attached to the doctor's survey, too," Sid said, reaching into his pocket. "Five quid."

It was an outrageous amount, and Maggie knew it. "We don't need no hand-outs," she said fiercely.

"It's not a hand-out," Sid said. He looked at India. "It's payment for services rendered."

"Why isn't she carrying the money then?" Maggie asked. "Why've you got it?"

"Because she asked me to. I'm her escort. No one's going to rob me, are they? There's toffs behind this clinic, Mags. Just shovellin' money at it. It's proper wages for proper work. Tell her, Dr. Jones."

"Mr. Malone is correct, Mrs. Harris," India said, quickly stepping in. "We are conducting a survey of the Whitechapel population to ascertain the best way to apportion our resources and to help us draw up a comprehensive and effective plan of treatment that encompasses both preventive and palliative medicine. We have funds to pay those who take part in the survey."

Maggie looked down at the matchbox she was holding. India could see she was struggling with herself. Maggie's children looked at their mother. Without hope. Without expectation. Without anything at all.

She's not going to take the money, India thought. Five pounds, a small fortune, and she's not going to take it. India was about to remonstrate with Maggie when the woman finally lifted her head and said, "You've any more questions need answering, Dr. Jones, you come back and see me."

The woman's words were an attempt at pride. She wanted her children to think she'd earned the money. Pride, of all things! Here in two tiny, dingy, airless rooms. With eight hungry mouths to feed. The stupidity of it made India want to scream. Or cry. She didn't know which. And then the littlest girl, tired as she was, looked at her mother and smiled. And India suddenly understood that this tiny scrap of pride was all that Maggie Harris had to give her children.

"Thank you, Mrs. Harris, I will," she said. "You've been incredibly helpful. A very valuable source of information."

They'd left the Harrises' soon after and walked two streets south. Sid stopped her at the mouth of an alley that snaked between two shops, then motioned at her to go inside.

"More tunnels?" she'd asked worriedly.

"No tunnels. Promise."

The alley was damp. Water trickled down the center of it. Barrels were stacked haphazardly against the sides, along with empty crates and rubbish bins. At the alley's end, however, there was a strangely neat configuration of wooden pallets and crates, topped off by what looked to be a remnant of a ship's sail. Sid held a finger to his lips, then carefully lifted up the sail's edge.

India peered inside. At first she saw only a pile of rags, but then as she continued to stare down at it she realized it was a woman she was looking at. And a child. India recognized her; she was the woman from the pub. The one who'd come begging. She was sleeping, her body curled around her daughter's. They had covered themselves with old clothes, flour sacks, a scrap of carpet. There was a half-empty gin bottle near the woman's head and grease-stained newspaper from what must have been a meal of fish and chips. Just as Sid motioned for them to leave, the woman's eyes flew open. In a heartbeat she was on her feet, a knife in her hand.

"Easy now, Kitty," Sid said, backing away. "We meant no harm. Just wanted to see that you and the nipper were all right."

Kitty blinked woozily. "Sorry, Mr. Malone. Give me a start, you did."

"No, I'm sorry. Go back to sleep now." Kitty's girl whimpered and stirred. Her filthy hands scrabbled at the scraps of fabric. "Here, have this," Sid said. He took off his jacket and placed it over the sleeping girl. "Good night, luv," he said, tipping his hat. Kitty nodded wearily and lay down with her child.

There were more stops. She met Ed Archer, a widower, taking care of his backward son by himself. They were living under a train trestle because no landlord would have the boy. He set things alight when his father went out to work. The authorities tried to put him in a home, but Ed wouldn't have it. He'd been in one once, when he was little. The orderlies said Willie was troublesome. So they'd tied him to his bed. For three months. Ed said he'd kill his son, and then himself, before he ever let anyone take the lad again.

There was Alvin Binns, a dockworker. He lived in a windowless cellar room with his wife and two young children. The wife was consumptive. The children, too. She knew she was dying and had told India that all she wanted now was for her children to go first so that she could look after them until the end and keep them from the workhouse.

There were Ada and Annie Armstrong, sisters. Ada was a cripple who did piecework. Annie worked at the sugar factory by day and helped her sister make paper flowers by night. And still, all they had to eat was bread and marge, sometimes with jam, and boiled potatoes for their tea. Most of their money went to pay for Ada's visits to the doctor and the medicine she needed to dull the pain in her twisted legs, Annie explained. India saw Ada's eyes grow worried at this, saw her thin fingers twist the kerchief she held. Annie saw it, too, and quickly added how fast Ada was with her flower-making, and how she sang while they worked, and that her songs were so pretty it didn't feel as if they were working at all. She said it was the nicest thing in the world to come home from a hard day and find a hot cup of tea waiting. India saw how neatly Ada's hair was plaited. How white her blouse was. Many would have resented Ada. Annie adored her.

Outside the sisters' house, Sid lit a cigarette and said, "Still preaching the gospel of porridge?"

India did not reply to his question. Instead she asked one of her own. "How do they all know you?"

"Who?"

"Don't play games. All the people we've visited, how do they know you? I can't quite see Annie and Ada knocking up a wharf."

"Knocking *off* a wharf."

"Sid . . ."

"I have businesses here, don't I? Some of these people work for me. Others I see coming and going, that's all."

"No, that's not all," India said. "You know their names. You talk to them. Ask after them." She hesitated, then said, "You give them money, don't you?"

Sid picked up his pace. India nearly had to trot to keep up with him. She grabbed his arm, stopping him. "Freddie says you have pots of money. And no one knows what you do with it. You don't have houses. Or horses. You don't wear expensive clothes. You don't have a wife or children." She paused, then said, "Earlier I asked you who you were. I know now."

"Oh, you do?"

"You're a modern-day Robin Hood."

Sid laughed out loud. "You've read too many fairy stories, Doctor. I've told you, I'm a businessman, that's all."

"Then why are you doing this? Why do you care?"

"It's good for business, ain't it? People can't come to me pubs and gaming establishments if they're dead, can they?"

After the Armstrongs, Sid took her through alleys and closes where women sold themselves for fourpence. To basement steps where orphan boys huddled together against the night. To rubbish heaps where old men fought with starving dogs for scraps. And then they'd come to Christ Church. To sit and eat something before she made the trip back to Bedford Square.

India took another swallow of her porter now. And then another. She'd emptied most of the bottle. She wasn't used to alcohol. It made her feel light-headed. She wondered if she was drunk. She suddenly heard a baby's cry. A woman was carrying a basket. She put it down against the wall of the Ten Bells, a pub across the street from the church. She started to sing, importuning the Ten Bells' patrons with pretty ballads, but they ignored her. Each time she finished a song she rushed back to the basket, bending low over it. The cries were coming from the basket, and were punctuated by fits of coughing.

"Pneumonia," India said dully. "Hear the wheezing?"

The woman kissed the baby, then resumed her singing. She switched to a music-hall song, trying hard to make her voice merry, but India could hear the desperation lying just beneath the forced cheer.

The baby's cries, the raucous laughter of the drunken pub-goers, the poor mother singing brokenly—they swirled around in India's aching head until she couldn't bear it any longer. She grabbed the bag of pork pies and dashed down the steps. "Here, take these," she said, thrusting them at the woman. "And here . . ." She reached into her pocket where she had about a pound's worth of coins. "Here's money . . . here's more . . . there . . . for a room. Get a warm room. Keep the baby close to a fire. If there's a kettle, let her breathe steam."

"Thank you, missus!" the woman said. "Oh, thank you!" She kissed India's cheek, then picked up her baby and headed toward Wentworth Street, where there were lodging houses.

"Bring her to Varden Street tomorrow," India shouted after her. "To the surgery there. Ask for Dr. Jones. Do you hear me? Dr. Jones!" She was loud. Too loud. People were looking at her. She didn't care.

"Come on, India." It was Sid. He was suddenly by her side. "It's late. I should get you home." He flagged a hackney, helped her in, then took the seat opposite her.

India, still looking down the street after the woman and her baby, said, "She'll be dead by morning. Her lungs are full of fluid. Did you hear it? Did you see how blue she was?"

She wanted to cry. For the young mother singing for her baby. For Maggie Harris and her children. And Ed Archer and his damaged son. For all the people she'd seen tonight and the thousands more she hadn't. She wanted to cry for them and for herself. For the woman she'd been only hours ago, the confident know-it-all, the doctor who thought she could solve all her patients' problems with porridge and broccoli. She wanted to cry until her throat was raw and her sides ached and there were no more tears left in her. But she did not.

"You've gone quiet. What is it?" Sid asked.

"It's such a hard world. Such an ugly world. Sometimes it seems like a fool's errand to try to change it for the better."

"Don't talk that way."

India looked at him. "After what we've just seen? Why not?"

"Just don't. It's not you."

After half an hour's ride the hackney stopped at Bedford Square. Sid got out, helped India down, then saw her safely inside.

"Thank you for bringing me home. And for what you did at the jail. And for supper. And everything else. It's been quite an adventure." There were a few seconds of silence, then she said, "Would you . . . did you want to come upstairs for a cup of tea?"

Sid shook his head. "You need your rest. And I've got business."

He leaned close, meaning to reach past her and open the inner door for her. And then his eyes caught hers.

"Who *are* you, Sid?" she asked for the second time that night, desperate to know, but he gave her no answer.

She took his face in her hands. She wanted to see him, to look into his eyes, but they were closed now. "Look at me. Look at me, Sid," she whispered. He did. His eyes were dark and beautiful, full of sadness and grief.

He pulled her to him and kissed her, hard and fierce. And she kissed him back, arms around his neck, clinging to him as if she would never let go. He smelled of coal smoke and the river. He tasted of beer and cigarettes. His arms around her felt like nothing she'd ever known and everything she'd ever wanted.

He broke the kiss and looked at her, asking her wordlessly. She knew what he wanted; she wanted the same thing. She wanted to feel his skin next to hers, to press her body, her heart, her very soul, against his.

"I'll tell the cab to go," he said, and his words broke the spell.

What on earth was she doing? She was engaged, for God's sake. To Freddie. Freddie, who was kind and upstanding and good and who loved her. She stepped back, terrified of her own feelings, and shook her head.

"No. No, don't. I can't do this. I'm sorry. . . . I'm engaged. . . . I should never have done this," she said.

Sid nodded. His eyes were wounded, but his voice was biting. "Still scared of me, are you? Too right, Dr. Jones. Never trust us criminal types, we'll kill you soon as look at you." And with that he was gone.

"Sid, wait!" she cried, but he was already down the steps and on the sidewalk.

India watched him climb back into the hackney, watched it pull away.

"You're wrong. So wrong," she whispered. "It's not you I'm scared of. Can't you see that? It's me."

CHAPTER 29

Freddie, seated by the fire in the large sitting room of his Chelsea flat, one leg dangling over the arm of his chair, wondered if Chopin had ever visited England.

He must have, he thought, watching the rain pound against his windows, his music box playing. What other country could have inspired the man to write the "Raindrop Prelude"?

The filthy gray evening matched his filthy gray mood perfectly. Things were still not going well for him. Gemma, as good as her word, had broken up the Labour rally, and the press had run highly unflattering accounts of the event, but it didn't seem to matter. Bristow's popularity had been unaffected. In fact, it was only growing. In direct contrast to his own.

He sighed, took a swallow of port, and wished he could visit Gemma tonight. A good roll in bed with her would do him a world of good, but he was supposed to go to some beastly awful do-gooding thing with India. He couldn't remember where it was, or what it was about. Temperance? Public health reform? Whatever it was, he was certain to find himself forced to make conversation with bluestockings and Quakers all bent on meddling in the lives of the poor. He wanted to shoot himself at the very thought.

A knock on the door to his flat startled him. He rose to answer it. The maid had gone home. He could no longer afford to keep her past noon. He opened the door, expecting the postman perhaps, or a delivery boy, but it was India. She was drenched.

"You're early, darling," he said, surprised to see her. She'd said she would come at seven and it was only five.

"Yes. Yes, I suppose I am. Sorry."

"No, no! That's not what I meant at all. I'm delighted to see you. Take your wet things off and sit down."

She hung her mackintosh in the foyer and took Freddie's vacant chair.

"Cup of tea? Warm you up a bit?"

"I would prefer a brandy, I think."

"Really?" he said.

"Yes, please."

That's unusual, he thought, walking to the sideboard where he kept his liquor. She rarely drinks.

"Freddie, I've something to ask of you," she said.

He put the heavy brandy decanter down with a thump. Oh, Christ. Oh no, he thought, his heart sinking. She's come to tell me she wants to postpone the wedding. Yet again. Bloody hell.

"Could we possibly make the date of our wedding earlier? August perhaps, instead of October?"

He turned, struggling to hide his shock. "Of course we can, darling. Whatever you wish. Why the sudden change?"

"I just . . . I just think that October's too long to wait. You have a difficult election coming up and I thought that it might be helpful to you to have a wife by then. By your side. Helping you."

Freddie smiled. He didn't believe a word of it. There could be only one reason for this and he knew what it was. The signs were all there. She looked thinner. Pale. Agitated. He put her brandy down on a nearby table and knelt by her chair.

"Darling, have you anything *else* to tell me?" he asked, taking her hands in his.

Her eyes widened. She looked alarmed. "Anything else? Of course not! Not at all. Like what?" she asked, a note of panic in her voice.

"Is it possible that you are pregnant? I did forget the rubber johnnie, you know. Please don't worry if you are, my love. I would be delighted by the news."

"I am not," she said briskly.

"You're sure?"

"Quite."

"Ah," he said, disappointed. But then he asked himself, What did it matter? It was July. He would be married in August. If she wasn't pregnant now, he would soon make her so, and once she was with child he would insist she give up doctoring. It was too strenuous for an expectant mother, and all those filthy poor people with their disgusting diseases were too dangerous for an unborn child. He would not allow it.

"Well then," he said, clapping his hands together. "How about a spot of supper before tonight's event?"

"What event is that?"

"Um . . . I'm sorry, old girl, but I can't quite remember. I've misplaced the invite," he said, digging through a pile of calling cards and invitations on the mantel.

"Oh, yes. I'd forgotten myself. It's a talk, isn't it? Henry Mayhew on his study of the London poor. At the Fabian Society."

Freddie frowned. It was unlike India to forget something like that. It was the sort of thing she lived for. He eyed her closely and he noticed, for the first time, a livid red line on her temple.

"Darling, what happened to you?" he said, peering at it.

India's fingers hovered over the gash, blocking it from his sight. "It's nothing," she said. "Flailing patient."

"Are you all right?" he asked. "It looks quite nasty."

"I will be," she said. "I mean, I am. I've been a bit . . . under the weather."

"Simpson's will be just the place, then," he said cheerily. "We'll have a big slab of beef and some roast potatoes. Just the thing to build you back up."

His credit was still good there, thank God. Unlike his club and his tailor, they hadn't started hounding him about his balance. Not yet.

"That sounds lovely, Freddie. We can talk about the ceremony while we're there. It might be hard to book a church at such short notice. Perhaps we could marry at Longmarsh? Get the local vicar to come to the chapel and have a wedding supper at the house. Would it be all right with Bingham and your mother?"

Freddie felt that urge to pinch himself. Was he dreaming? Was this really India talking? Would he really be married to her, and to her lovely money, in only a few weeks' time? Something nagged at him, some small voice inside him told him that this sudden turn of events was too good to be true. He promptly silenced it. Things had been too bad to be true for yonks. He was ready for a change, ready for his fortunes to turn.

"Come, Lady Lytton," he said, standing and pulling her up with him. "Let us go to dine."

"Shh, Freddie. Not Lady Lytton. Not yet. It's bad luck," she said. Too quickly. And was it his imagination, or had she a strange look in her eyes? A sorrowful look. As if she'd lost something. Or someone. He looked again and it was gone. She was smiling.

He smiled, too. "No, not yet. But soon, darling. Very, very soon."

CHAPTER 30

"What a week," Ella said, stuffing folders into her filing cabinet. "We started it in a jail house . . ."

"And ended it in a workhouse," India said, sighing. "*Has* it ended?" she asked. "Is it really Friday?" She was lying down on a wooden bench in Dr. Gifford's waiting room, eyes closed, exhausted.

She'd seen sixty-one patients today. By noon she'd felt as if she were a butcher instead of a doctor, grinding through people as if they were sausages. Lumbago, ringworm, rheumatism, catarrh . . . the list of ailments was endless. Nine women asked her for contraceptives—begged her, actually—but she hadn't been able to help them because she didn't have any yet. And the children—six had come in with rickets; five more had shown signs of scurvy. These diseases upset her almost more than killers such as tuberculosis and typhus because they were so sinfully easy to prevent.

"Is the baby drinking milk?" she would ask, examining a toddler's bandy legs.

"I daren't feed it him, missus. Makes him sick. Shopkeepers near us are dirty," the child's mother would reply.

"Can you give your girl oranges? Say, three a week?" she would ask, noting an eight-year-old's lethargy, her bleeding gums.

"I'd be lucky to get her one a month. We can't afford it," was the answer.

"Supplementary nutrition, Ella," she said aloud now.

"Speak in full sentences, please. I'm not a flippin' mind reader."

India opened her eyes and propped herself up on one elbow. "We need a way to supplement children's diets. If we could do that, we'd keep half of them out of the clinic in the first place. We need to establish a soup kitchen as part of the clinic. Only we'll dispense milk, too. And fresh fruit. I wonder how much extra space we'd need for that."

"Plenty. At the rate you're going, we'll have to buy Victoria Station. How much have we got anyway?"

"Two hundred and thirty pounds," India said. "And Wish says Colman's Mustard gave him fifty damaged tins."

"Wonderful. We can put it on nonexistent sausages and feed them to our nonexistent patients," Ella said.

"I told him about Fiona Bristow," India said hopefully. "He knows who she is and said that he'll approach her."

"Well, that and tuppence will buy me a cup of coffee. Good thing you got her to safety at the rally. It could have gone very badly for her otherwise."

"Yes, it could have," India said, relieved that Fiona Bristow had been spared any harm.

"Could have gone badly for you, too. You're lucky that horse only cut your head and didn't crush it," Ella said, slamming a file drawer shut. "Well, that's me done. I'm ready to get out of here. What are you doing to-night?"

"Collapsing."

"No romantic suppers with the dashing MP?"

"I'm afraid not. I barely see Freddie these days. His party is fashioning its war cabinet in preparation for September. Though we're both invited to a house party in a fortnight's time," she said, forcing herself to sound excited.

Ella smiled wickedly. "No outings with Sid Malone, either?"

"I beg your pardon?" India said, sitting up.

"I heard about your midnight tour, Dr. Jones."

"How?"

"Word travels fast in Whitechapel."

"It was a fact-finding trip, Ella. Purely professional."

Ella snorted. "Oh, aye," she said. "Find a lot of facts, did you?"

"Ella!" India said indignantly. "You can't possibly think that Sid Malone and I . . . that we . . ."

"Oh, I'm just winding you up. Don't get so shirty. Since you've no plans tonight, why don't you come home with me?"

"Thank you, but I couldn't. I really must get to my own home."

"What for? A bowl of soup and *The Lancet*? Come have a proper supper."

"But Ella, it's your Sabbath."

"Which will be made even more blessed by the company of a friend." She laughed. "God, I sound just like my mother. Come on, India. You need some feeding up."

India *was* awfully hungry, and Mrs. Moskowitz's food was so good, and company would take her mind off Sid. "All right," she said, "I will."

The two women turned out the lights, locked up the surgery, and headed for Brick Lane. When they arrived, India was surprised to see that the café windows were dark. "The restaurant is closed?" she asked.

"We close early every Friday," Ella replied. "Mama needs ample time to cook and clean and drive everyone mad."

The Moskowitzes lived above their restaurant. As India and Ella climbed the stairs to the flat, mouth-watering smells of saffron and cinnamon welcomed them.

"I'm home, Mama!" Ella called out, heading to the kitchen.

"Ella! I'm so glad you're here! I'm behind with everything. Your father will be home from *shul* soon and just look at this place!" Mrs. Moskowitz said. She was stirring a pot with one hand, lifting a beautiful braided loaf out of the oven with the other.

"Don't worry, everything will get done," Ella soothed.

"Hello, India dear. Have you come to share our Sabbath meal?"

"I have, Mrs. Moskowitz."

"Good. Take the challah, please, and put it on the sideboard. In the dining room."

"The what?"

"The bread. Cover it with napkins. On the table . . . you'll see. Rebecca! Come here and let me do your hair! Ella, catch your sister, please."

"Rebecca? Do you have another sister?" India asked Ella on her way to the dining room.

"That's Posy's real name," Ella explained, bending over to grab her little sister. "A customer once told her she was pretty as a posy, and ever since she won't answer to Rebecca. Be still, Posy!" she scolded. She sat down, held the squirming girl between her knees, and began to plait her hair.

Mrs. Moskowitz, still stirring, opened the kitchen window. "Miriam! Solomon! The carpet!" she bellowed out of it.

India found the dining room. Its curtains had been washed and starched. The furniture had been pushed to the walls. She walked carefully across the freshly waxed floor to get to the sideboard. On her way back to the kitchen she was nearly run down by two children staggering under the weight of a heavy wool rug.

"Did you get it clean?" Mrs. Moskowitz yelled from the kitchen.

"Yes, Mama! Yes, Mama! Yes, Mama, yes!" Miriam and Solly yelled back.

When India reached the kitchen, she was sent straight back to the dining room with orders to make sure the carpet was indeed clean. Ella joined her and together they moved the furniture back and set the table for supper, using a snowy linen cloth and the best dishes and glasses. When a place had been made for everyone, Ella put two gleaming silver candlesticks and a silver chalice on the table. While they did this, Posy blessed the challah repeatedly, waving a knife over it like a wand.

"Are you doing a blessing or a magic trick? Enough already!" Ella scolded.

India had never seen a Sabbath observance quite like this one. She remembered her own church-going days. The long walk to Blackwood's chapel. The tepid sermons and tedious Sunday dinners at which her family barely spoke, never mind bellowed.

"Ella?" she said.

"Mmm?"

"Is this typical?"

"Of what?"

"Of your Sabbath. I expected yours to be rather like mine—quiet and somber."

Ella burst into laughter. "Quiet? Somber? In this house? Not likely!"

"Can India be our *Shabbas goy*?" Posy asked.

"Your *what*?" India asked.

"Jewish law forbids work after sundown on Fridays," Ella explained. "We can't even light our candles or stoves. So we must find a Christian to light them for us. Will you do the honors?"

"Gladly," India said.

She was happy she'd accepted Ella's invitation. There was a spirit of bustling anticipation in the Moskowitz household, a sense of something wonderful coming, and it was impossible not to be caught up in it. When she and Ella finished in the dining room, they found Mrs. Moskowitz inspecting the ears, necks, and hands of her younger children. When she'd made sure her entire brood was respectably turned out, she turned her attention to India.

"That hair," she said, frowning. "Come."

India followed her, feeling like an errant child. Mrs. Moskowitz led her to her bedroom, sat her on the bed, and pulled the dragonfly comb out of her knot. She brushed India's blond mane with sure, firm strokes. India sat stiffly at first, waiting for a reproving remark—her mother had always taken her to task over her hair—but none came.

"Such beautiful hair you have. Like spun gold," Mrs. Moskowitz said.

India thanked her, then closed her eyes, enjoying her motherly touch. Her own mother had never brushed her hair, only her nanny.

"You are too quiet this evening. You must be in love."

India caught her breath. My God, how does she know? she thought wildly. Can she see? Then she realized Mrs. Moskowitz was only teasing her.

"Yes, I am in love," she replied, trying to keep her voice even.

"*Mazel tov*, my darling! Did this just happen?"

"Oh, no," she quickly said. "My fiancé and I have been engaged for two years."

Mrs. Moskowitz looked puzzled. "Two years? That's a long time, no?"

"I suppose it is. We've chosen to make a life together, but we've had to wait a bit to marry. There was my work, you see. And his . . ."

Mrs. Moskowitz frowned. "*Chosen,* you say?"

"Did I say something wrong?"

"You do not choose love, my India. Love chooses you," Mrs. Moskowitz said, in a voice that implied India must be simple not to know such a thing.

She finished brushing India's hair, made a soft twist, and secured it. "There!" she said. "Much better." Then she rummaged in her jewelry box and found a pretty brooch for her collar. "A woman must look her best for the Sabbath," she said. "After all, God is a man, is He not?"

They returned to the others. Mrs. Moskowitz asked India to light the candles in the dining room and the gas lamps in the rest of the flat. When she had finished, she rejoined the family in the parlor.

"Now we wait for Mr. Moskowitz," Mrs. Moskowitz said. "Yanki, the *Shir HaShirim*. In English, please, so that our guest may follow."

As the sun set, and the darkness came down, the Moskowitz children gathered around their mother and listened to their elder brother read the "Song of Songs."

"Such a voice. A cantor's voice," Mrs. Moskowitz sighed as Yanki began.

Aaron rolled his eyes. Miriam and Solly made faces whenever kissing was mentioned. Posy nestled in Ella's lap. And India listened, transported by the beautiful voice of the serious young man, by the passion of his words: "By night on my bed I sought him whom my soul loveth; I sought him, but I found him not. I will rise now, and go about the city in the streets, and in the broad ways I will seek him whom my soul loveth; I sought him, but I found him not . . ."

She knew the poem was an allegory about mankind's love for God—at least that's what the vicar at Blackwood had said—but it wasn't God whom the poem made her think of, it was Sid. She closed her eyes, trying desperately to hear only Yanki's words, trying to push every memory of their night together out of her mind, but she failed. She could hear him, feel him. She could see him as he'd looked when she'd taken his face in her hands, and when he'd kissed her. She'd kissed him back passionately . . . and then, feeling a terrible guilt over betraying Freddie, she'd driven him away.

The next day, frightened by herself, by how easily she'd allowed her emotions to overcome her judgment, she'd finished early at Gifford's, gone directly to Freddie's flat, and asked him to move up their wedding date. He'd been pleased, and she'd been grateful to him for acquiescing to her wishes. She vowed to herself that she would never betray him again, never give him a moment's worry. She would be a good wife. Helpful. Supportive. Concerned. He deserved that, for he was a good man.

They'd talked about the ceremony during their supper at Simpson's and decided to have it at Longmarsh, on the third Saturday in August. It was only five weeks away. She wished it were sooner, but Freddie had work or social obligations almost every weekend until then. She wanted it to be behind her. Done. Irrevocable. She hoped that when she was married, she would stop thinking about Sid. Stop longing for him.

She had thought of him constantly since that night. Worse yet, she often found herself talking to him in her head. Arguing with him sometimes, but more often telling him about her work at Gifford's and her hopes for her clinic. And at day's end, when she was alone and quiet, curled up by her fire with some thick, daunting text, she found herself picturing his face—his green eyes, the depths as hidden as the deepest Welsh valleys, his generous smile. She would hear his voice, mocking sometimes or tinged with sadness. She would remember what it felt like to be held by him.

And then she would be overwhelmed by guilt and fear and anger and she would tell herself that Sid was the Janus face of Freddie, that he was a man as dedicated to dark and selfish pursuits as Freddie was to the common good—but even she didn't quite believe it.

Could a man who gave money to Kitty the beggar, who watched over Ada and Annie Armstrong, and who found work for Maggie Harris's husband be a bad man? Ella had once told her that she saw only in black and white, and Sid was a study in gray. There was good in him as well as bad; she knew there was. She had seen him at Teddy Ko's. She had seen his blowsy women at the Bark. Had heard about the Stronghold Wharf. Yet she had also seen him tenderly cover a poor, damaged child with his own jacket and give money to orphan boys. He had a kind heart, but a wounded one. Something had happened to him. Something terrible. He had told her about losing his mother, his family—but she sensed there was more. She had glimpsed his heart, ever so briefly, before he'd closed it off again. And now, even though she knew it was impossible and insane and wrong, she still wanted to touch that wounded heart, to heal it.

"Papa! Papa!" Posy suddenly squealed. She jumped out of Ella's lap and ran to the door. India heard the tramp of feet up the stairs, and then Mr. Moskowitz was in the parlor.

"*Shabbat shalom, Zeeskyte!*" he said, swinging Posy off the ground and into his arms.

"*Shabbat shalom*, Papa!" Posy said, kissing his cheek.

He greeted the rest of his family, then India, then he turned to his wife and with a sheepish expression said, "I've brought guests. Two brothers. I met them at *shul*. And a sister. From St. Petersburg. They arrived just yesterday."

India looked past Mr. Moskowitz to the people standing in the entrance. Their faces were haggard; the young woman's was tear-stained.

"He *always* does this," Solly grumbled.

Mr. Moskowitz lowered his voice. "She cries, the girl. They have no food, Mama. Nowhere to go."

"Of course she cries," Mrs. Moskowitz said briskly. "With an empty stomach, nothing can be tolerated." She bustled past her husband, greeting their guests loudly and warmly in Russian. Smiles came to their weary faces at the sound of their own tongue.

"They're not sleeping with me. Not this time. Last bunch gave me fleas," Solly muttered. A swat from Ella silenced him.

Mrs. Moskowitz got the newcomers' coats and hats off. She got them washed and brushed, then she ushered everyone into the dining room. India sat down, but Ella shook her head and she sheepishly stood again.

"Aaron, the kiddush cup," Mrs. Moskowitz said.

Aaron took the silver goblet from the table, filled it with wine, and handed it to his father, who sang a prayer over it, then drank it. His voice was deeper than Yanki's, but every bit as beautiful. Next he uncovered the challah and blessed it. He tore off a small piece, dipped it in salt, and ate it. He did the same with more pieces, handing them to his wife, his children, and his guests. Then he bade everyone sit down to supper.

Yanki and Aaron brought extra chairs from the kitchen; Ella hurriedly set three more places. Mrs. Moskowitz and Miriam brought the food. The meal began with thick mushroom soup, sopped up with challah. It was followed by apricot chicken, sweet and meltingly tender; carrot *tsimmes*, rich with honey and cinnamon; and a golden rice pilaf. India noticed how hard the newcomers tried not to bolt down their helpings.

And with the food came talk. The immigrants spoke to Mrs. Moskowitz in Russian, telling her of their journey, and of St. Petersburg. Ella translated. Mrs. Moskowitz questioned them animatedly, eager for news of her hometown.

"Mama grew up in St. Petersburg," Ella explained. "Papa came from the country. He was a farmer's son selling chickens at the market when they met."

"She was going to marry a rich merchant's son!" Miriam piped up. "But Papa smiled at her and she went with him instead."

"You make me sound like a stray dog, Miriam! That's not how it was at all!" Mrs. Moskowitz protested.

The children giggled. Like all children, they loved their parents' love story, and vied with one another to tell it.

"Mama's father was very angry," Miriam said.

"He called Papa a turnip. He didn't know Papa was to study law at university," Solly added. "The rabbi from his shtetl helped him prepare."

"They said if Mama married him, she was no longer their child."

"But she married him anyway!"

"They were poor and sometimes had nothing but potatoes to eat."

"Then Papa became an important barrister and they had lots to eat. And a nice house, too."

"And Mama's parents were sorry, and said Papa wasn't a turnip after all."

"Enough already!" Mrs. Moskowitz said, laughing. She turned to India. "You see? *Beshert*. That's Yiddish. It means *fated to be together*. It's as I told you—love chooses you." She looked at her husband, and the tenderness in her eyes told India how very happy she was with love's choice.

"But then they had to leave, Mama and Papa did. Bad men burned their home," Miriam said solemnly.

"They had to walk all the way to the border with Ella and Yanki," Solly added.

"Ah, well," Mr. Moskowitz said. "All that is behind us now. He who cannot endure the bad will not live to see the good. And here in Whitechapel, there is much good."

Ella, who'd been translating the children's words all along for the immigrants, translated her father's and the newcomers smiled, bolstered by them. As the others continued to talk, Mrs. Moskowitz sat back in her chair, a faraway look in her eyes. India thought that she must be remembering St. Petersburg and all that she had lost.

"You must miss your home," she said to her.

Mrs. Moskowitz shook her head. "No, my dear," she said, smiling. "I never left it." She nodded at her husband, her children. "My home is where they are."

India smiled, deeply touched by her words, and then suddenly she thought of Sid again and wished that he were here. Not for her sake, but for his. She wished that he was not at the Bark, or on the harsh London streets, or alone, as he so often seemed to be, but seated at this table, encircled by the warmth and light of this night and these people, moved, as she was, by their love for one another and for three poor strangers. He had that same light in him; she knew he did. She'd seen it.

Guilt gnawed at her conscience. Here she was thinking of Sid *again*, when she was engaged to Freddie. Freddie, who was moral and principled.

Freddie, who was facing a terrible political struggle and who needed her love and loyalty like never before. How could she be so disloyal? What in God's name was wrong with her?

Mrs. Moskowitz's words came back to her. "You do not choose love. Love chooses you." And as they did, India realized she had her answer: Love *had* chosen for her. And love had chosen Sid.

CHAPTER **31**

"And then I sez to Old Bill, I sez . . . Oi! Malone! C'mere for a mo'. Listen to this one."

Big Billy Madden, guv'nor of West London, was drunk. He waved Sid over, put his arm around his neck, and proceeded to tell him how he'd coshed a constable with his mam's rolling pin when he was only ten years old.

"Cracked his skull, I did. Put him straight into the hospital. And me only a nipper!" Madden brayed laughter. Sid could see his teeth, black with decay. The smell of Madden's breath, mingling with his cheap cologne, made Sid's stomach lurch.

"You ever done a rozzer, Sid?" Madden asked.

"Of course not. I'm a businessman, me. What truck have I got with Old Bill?"

"Businessman, eh? What line you in? Monkey business?" Billy brayed again. He dropped his voice, suddenly conspiratorial. "You might want to make a start with the rozzers, eh? From what I hear, Alvin Donaldson's become a right pain in your arse. Quick way to fix that." He drew an imaginary knife across his throat.

"What? And take away all me fun?" Sid said. "I live to put the wind up that bloke. Baiting rozzers is me favorite sport. Oi!" He barked at a passing waiter, eager to extricate himself. "More champagne for Mr. Madden and his lads."

Madden tightened his arm around Sid's neck. His knuckles, crusted with rings, grazed Sid's cheek. "I love this bloke. He's the cream!" he proclaimed. "Smartest fucking one of us." His smile faded, just slightly, and his predator's eyes narrowed as he said, "Richest one, too."

"Not after tonight, Billy lad. You lot'll drink me dry. Won't have a farthing to me name come morning."

"Where's the guest of honor?" Madden asked, releasing him. "I'd like to congratulate her."

"Buggered if I know. Hasn't made her grand entrance yet. Tell you what, I'm going to find her," he said, grateful for an out. "Soon as I do, I'll send her round."

Sid walked over to Desi and Frankie. "You see Gem?" he asked.

"Fucking toe-rag," Frankie growled, staring at Madden.

"Easy, Frankie. He's our guest."

"Why'd you invite him?"

"Good relations. Keep your friends close and your enemies closer. You learn things that way." He himself had just learned plenty.

"I'd keep him close, all right. I'd put *him* in a headlock. He shouldn't take liberties like that. It doesn't look right."

Sid heard the accusing note in Frankie's voice. He let it go. He wasn't up to an argument. He hadn't slept for days and his head ached. It hurt more after learning that Madden knew Donaldson was after them. He'd be rubbing his hands together, hoping Donaldson succeeded. With the Firm in jail, he could move into East London.

"He's up to no good, Madden. You know that, don't you? You talk to Joe Griz yet?" Frankie said.

"No. Why?"

"He says a bloke came to his home a week ago looking to move a stolen painting. Griz didn't know him, so he started asking questions. 'Where you from? Who do you know? Who've you worked with?' When he couldn't get any proper answers, he chucked him out. I don't like it, guv. Madden's behind it, I just know it. Looking to land Griz in the shit with the rozzers. Get him sent down. He wants his business. Wants the swag. He always has."

"Could be the rozzers themselves."

Frankie shook his head. "They ain't that enterprising."

"They are now. Donaldson hasn't been able to get us directly. So he's likely taking another route. If he can get Griz for a stolen painting, he can pressure him. Promise to go hard on him unless he grasses on us."

Frankie's eyes widened. "Didn't think of that."

"That's the trouble with you, Frankie. You never think."

He walked away to yell at a waiter. He'd been harsh and he didn't care. He was tired of Frankie. Tired of Madden. Tired of all of them. He was restless, unsettled. He wanted out of this place. Out of the darkness and the smoke. He was gripped by an urge to simply leave. If it weren't for Gemma, he would have.

Ronnie walked by deep in conversation with Tom.

"You two see Gem?" he called.

"What's wrong with your head, guv?" Ronnie asked.

"What?"

"Your head. You're rubbing at it like to take the skin off."

Sid realized he was digging his fingers into his temple. "It's nothing. Where's Gemma?"

"Don't think she's here yet."

It was Gemma Dean's big night. She'd made her debut in the Gaiety's new revue with a solo and was absolutely smashing. As he'd promised, Sid was throwing a huge party to celebrate her success. He'd closed the Alhambra, a flashy gin palace he owned on the Commercial Road, and had invited all of East London's theatrical world, and a great deal of its criminal one, to a fancy catered do there.

Sid ordered a whisky, neat. He downed it, then leaned against the bar and looked around. Joe Grizzard, the city's most notorious fence, was sitting in a corner with half a dozen bent cops. Sid could see the diamonds flash on his fingers as he cut his steak. Across the room, Bertha Weiner from Shadwell was sitting at a table with her pack of house-breakers, tearing the legs off a roast duck. Vesta Tilley, the show's lead, was singing at a piano. Max Moses and Joe Weinstein, who fronted the Bessarabians, a brutal Whitechapel street gang, were drinking at the bar with a couple of big-time bookmakers. Three men from a rival gang, the Odessians, sat at the other end, seeing who could hold his finger in a candle flame the longest. One-eyed Charlie Walker and his Blind Beggars, a group of pickpockets, lifted plates of caviar from a waiter's tray without the man knowing. Teddy Ko strutted by with two more Limehouse drug lords, all blindingly flash in their new suits and shoes. A gaggle of chorus girls eyed them hungrily.

Sid closed his eyes, fingers rubbing his throbbing head again, and for an instant it wasn't night and he wasn't here with Madden and Griz and every other thief and cutthroat in London. He was by the sea. With India. And it was morning. He quickly pushed the image out of his mind. He'd been thinking of her constantly since the night he'd kissed her in Whitechapel. And he didn't want to. She'd hurt him, made him feel like a fool. But worse than that, she'd made him love her. He could forgive a woman a lot of things, but he couldn't forgive that.

Shouts suddenly went up; a burst of applause was heard. Sid opened his eyes. Gemma had arrived, looking spectacular in a turquoise satin gown, its every fold and tuck designed to showcase her splendid figure. She was wearing the dazzling diamond necklace and earrings he'd given her, plus an armful of bracelets and a knuckle-duster of a ring. She turned every head in the place. Madden's eyes crawled over her.

Gemma was stunning, and Sid knew he should feel proud of her. Possessive. Lustful. *Something*. But he didn't. He felt nothing. He also knew he should go to her, so he did.

"Well if it isn't the Gaiety's brightest new star," he said, coming up behind her.

Gemma whirled around. "Why, Mr. Malone, you dressed up for me!" she exclaimed, looking him up and down.

Sid smiled. He'd changed his uniform of dungarees and shirtsleeves for a suit. "You were wonderful, Gem," he said. "Everyone's saying so." He kissed her cheek.

"Who's saying so? Who's here?" she asked, glancing around the room.

Her quick eyes darted everywhere at once, and Sid knew she was sizing up her guests, calculating who could do what for her. She was on the make. As was everyone else in the room. It was their way. Her way. His. It was the East London way.

The urge to walk out came over him again. He wanted to leave the Alhambra, the party, the whole bleeding East End. He took her arm.

"Come for a stroll with me, Gem," he said. He needed to walk with her, talk with her. He needed her to hold him. Hold him here. Hold him down. To this place. This life.

"A *stroll*? Now? Are you mad? I just got here."

Maybe that's it, he thought. Maybe I *am* mad.

"I know what you're after and you're not having it," she added, with a sly smile. "You'll ruin my dress. There'll be time for that later. Now, Sid luv, who said I was great?"

Sid forced a smile. "Billy Madden did. Go say hello to him. He wants to congratulate you."

"You don't mind?"

"Not a bit. Go on, pet. It's your night. Have fun."

Go, Gem. Go to him, he thought, watching her walk away. He'll treat you better than I ever did. He'll give you everything you need. Everything you want.

He'd just ordered another whisky when Frankie, Ronnie, and Tom all walked up to him. He could tell something was wrong. "What's up?" he asked tightly.

"Trouble at the Taj," Ronnie said.

"What kind of trouble?"

"Brass tried to off herself. Made a bit of a mess. Susie's in a right state."

Sid told Tom to tell Gemma he'd been called away and to stay and look after her; then he, Ronnie, and Frankie left for the Taj.

"Flippin' hell, Sid, what took you?" Susie shrilled when they arrived. "What'll I do with the body? How will I get rid of it? What if the rozzers come sniffing?"

"Calm down, Susie. Tell me what happened," Sid said.

Susie explained that one of her girls had become distraught because her best customer had thrown her over for someone younger. "There was a fight. That's something I never tolerate. The men who come here don't want to listen to rowing. They get plenty of that at home."

"The girl?"

"I sacked her for fighting, didn't I? And then the silly bitch goes and swallows a bottle of arsenic I'd got for the mice. Bloody cheek!"

"She's dead now?"

"If she ain't yet, she soon will be."

"Where is she?"

"Upstairs. Room Eight."

When they reached the landing—a large, open room where the girls sat waiting for punters—Susie shook her head. "Just look at this bleeding mess, will you?" she grumbled. "Knocked the whole flippin' room apart, she did. Smashed a good mirror. Me favorite vase, too. I'm taking it from her wages. Dead or not."

She opened the door of Room Eight. A woman lay on the narrow bed, eyes closed, clutching her stomach. White froth flecked her lips. As they stood there, she lunged forward and vomited onto the floor.

"Bloody hell!" Frankie yelled, backing out of the room.

"Still here then, Molly?" Susie asked.

The woman moaned.

"What do we do?" Ronnie asked.

"Let nature take its course," Susie said. "If she lives, she lives. If not, it's into the river with her. I don't want the rozzers involved. They've given me enough trouble lately as it is. That wanker of a Donaldson paid us a visit yesterday, you know. Luckily one of his lads is a customer and gave me advance notice. I had time to get the punters out the back door and the girls downstairs before he showed up. I've had to put two lads on at the door, though, with orders not to let any strangers in. Only regulars. In case it's coppers pretending to be punters. Costing me a bomb, it is."

"April, April!" Molly sobbed.

"What's she saying?" Sid asked.

"April's her baby," said a new voice.

Sid looked up. A group of girls had gathered in the doorway. The one who'd spoken gazed back at him with dark, dead eyes. Another, naked from the waist up, leaned on the jamb. She had the pallor of an opium addict.

"For April, please . . ." Molly said, her eyes wild with fear. She pushed something toward him. He saw that it was a pound note.

"I'll have that," Susie said, reaching for the money. "I've got the whole parlor to refurbish thanks to you."

"Leave it," Sid said.

He looked at the prostitute's face. He saw bruises and scars. Some fresh, some old. He saw her thin, wasted limbs and the threadbare gown covering them. He looked into her eyes and saw something else—a harrowing fear. Not for herself, but for her child. She was hanging on, fighting the poison, fighting the pain, trying to find someone to care for her child.

Sid looked, and saw another woman dying, long ago. Not in a room, but in the street. His mother. He saw her white face, her bloodstained clothes. And he wondered if she had felt this woman's terror at leaving *her* children behind, alone and unprotected in a place like Whitechapel. He remembered holding her lifeless body, trying to stop the constables from taking her away. The despair he'd felt then, the rage and the guilt, flooded back.

"Number eighteen Wentworth Street . . . Mrs. Edwards . . . she has her. . . . Please . . . oh, God!" Molly clutched her stomach again, curling into herself, keening with the pain.

"Listen. Listen to me," Sid said, kneeling by the bed. "The baby'll be all right. I'll see that she's looked after. I promise."

Molly closed her eyes. Tears ran down her cheeks. She gave a wrenching cry, then started to convulse.

"Christ, somebody help her," Sid said wildly. "Call for a doctor. Ronnie, get Dr. Jones. Go!" Some of the girls gasped; others started to cry. "Susie! Frankie! Get her up!" Sid yelled.

The woman's tortured body shuddered through another convulsion and then she was still.

"Jesus Christ," he whispered.

"Guv, it's all right," Frankie said. "It's just a dead brass, is all."

"Shut up, Frankie," Sid said. His hand came up to his head again. The pain inside it was so great, it was nearly blinding. He looked around. At the dingy flocked wallpaper, the stained bed, and the dead woman upon it. At the vomit on the floor and the human wreckage in the doorway. And he felt sick to his very soul.

"Get her out of here. Get her buried," Sid said.

"We can't bury her. There'll be too many questions," Frankie said. "We'll take her to the river. Like Susie said to."

Sid thought of the little girl. How she'd never know her mother. A grave would be something. Somewhere to go. Years from now. Somewhere to mourn.

"Take her to Christ Church. To the digger there. Do it now."

"He'll talk."

"Pay him not to!" Sid shouted, turning on Frankie.

"Sid, she's a fucking whore!" Frankie yelled back. "She's not worth the risk! Not now, when Donaldson's on top of us."

Their noise drew attention. All down the long hallway, doors opened. Disheveled girls and their punters peered out from them.

"Go back inside. This doesn't concern you," Sid said.

Some did, some didn't.

"What's the matter? Are you bleedin' deaf?" he yelled.

A man who was standing in a nearby doorway, puffing on a cigar said, "Who the hell are you?"

His voice was like a match to a fuse. Sid was on him in an instant. He punched him in the face, shattering his nose. The man dropped to his knees, screaming. Sid picked him up, dragged him into the sitting room, and threw him against a table. It collapsed under his weight. The bottles of whisky and gin on top of it smashed. Girls flattened themselves against the walls of the room, or hid behind furniture, squeaking with fright. The man tried to get up. Sid stood over him.

"You know who I am now?" he asked.

The man moaned.

"Good. Get your things and get out."

Susie crawled out from behind the settee where she'd hidden. "That's bloody great, Sid! Look what you've done!" she shrilled. "Smashed up me table and all me booze! Who's going to pay for *that*? Me, I suppose?"

Sid turned to her. He took a wad of notes from his pocket, peeled off one after another, and tossed them into the air. They fluttered to the carpet. He threw the whole wad up. It contained hundreds of pounds. Far more than the cost of the broken furniture. The girls scrambled for the notes. Susie, still on her hands and knees, snatching up as many as she could, screeched at them to leave off.

"What are you doing, guv?" Frankie shouted. "You lost your mind?"

"Get the woman buried. Then find her baby," he said. "Find someone to look after it. Give whoever it is fifty quid and tell her to come to me for more. Tell her if anything happens to the baby, it's me she'll answer to."

"But, Sid . . ."

Sid closed his eyes, trying to control his anger. He didn't want to hit Frankie. He really didn't. "Don't say another word. Do what I told you to."

Frankie shook his head. He stalked off to the dead woman's room and began wrapping her body in the dirty bedsheets. Ronnie helped him. Susie, standing now and stuffing money down the front of her dress, looked daggers at him, but said nothing. The Taj was emptying. Some men stayed, but most hurried down the stairs and out the door. Sid watched them go, then he walked through the parlor, down another hallway, to a room he used as an office. It had been Denny Quinn's office once. Denny had been murdered in it. The stains were still on the floor.

He sat down at the desk and lowered his head into his hands. He had wanted to fetch India to try to save Molly. Now he was glad there had been no time. He remembered how angry she'd been about the whores at Ko's. What would she have thought of this place? And of him for keeping it?

She would have blamed me for Molly's death, he thought. And she would have been right.

"Damn you, woman. *Damn you!*" he shouted.

He picked up an inkwell and hurled it at the wall. He threw books, ledgers, a lamp. He kicked the desk until it splintered. And then, played out and panting, he leaned over, hands on his knees, to catch his breath, and saw a box under the desk tied up with brown paper and string. It had arrived yesterday from Amsterdam, hidden in the hold of a ship. He swore at it, then picked it up.

"This is it. One last visit and then I'm done with you. Done," he said.

He left the Taj, got into his carriage, and gave his driver an address. Inside, he sat back and looked at his hands. They were shaking. He never shook. Never. He felt like he was going to bits. He looked out the window, trying to focus on something else. He saw London's night people go by. Waiters closing down restaurants. Drunks staggering. Toffs hopping into cabs. Beggars. Streetwalkers. Sailors on a binge. He pressed his hands to his eyes, took a deep breath, then studied them again. They were still shaking. He cursed, lit a cigarette, took a few drags, then threw it out the window. Finally the driver pulled up to his destination—Bedford Square, Bloomsbury.

He didn't get out for some time. He just sat in the carriage, looking up at the building. In one of its windows he could see a woman sitting at a desk. She was illuminated by the glow of a lamp.

I'm done with you, he'd said back at the Taj. But he didn't want to be. He wanted to be up there, with her. He wanted to rest his head in her lap, put his arms around her waist, and feel her strong, soothing hands stroke his brow. He thought how happy he would be just to sit in the same room with her. Just to talk and to listen. To ask about her work and see the light come into her eyes as she told him about her day. To watch the expressions play across her face, to make her laugh. Christ, he'd even be happy to argue with her. About porridge or broccoli or any bloody thing.

She was reading. He looked at his watch. It was nearly midnight, but she was still up working. He was about to tell his driver to take him back east, to the Alhambra, when his eyes fell on the box he'd brought with him. He grabbed it and got out of the carriage. JONES, NUMBER 2, the nameplate read. He rang the bell.

A few minutes later India was at the door in a white nightgown and wrapper. Her blond curls hung loosely about her shoulders.

"Sid? My goodness, this is a surprise."

"The things you ordered came in," he said. "Sorry about the hour."

"The things?"

He cleared his throat. "Aye, luv. The things."

The penny finally dropped. "Oh, right! Yes. The *things*. Thank you. It's awfully good of you to come all this way." She reached for the box.

"It's heavy. I'll carry it up for you. No worries, I'll behave myself."

She colored slightly. "Thank you."

"For behaving myself?"

"That, too."

Sid followed India up the stairs and into her flat. Besides the bedroom, there was a tiny galley kitchen and a sitting room. Books dominated the place. They covered the desktop, the mantel, and the kitchen counter. They stood stacked on top of chairs and lay in heaps on the floor. Thick medical periodicals were piled near her desk. A teapot rested on top of them, along with the remains of a sandwich. On top of the desk, balanced precariously on yet more books, was a tarnished silver vase containing the room's only luxury—a dozen flawless winter-white roses just beginning to open.

"Where should I put these?" Sid asked.

"Oh, anywhere."

He put the box by the hearth, then looked around. "Is this how you spend your Saturday nights?"

India looked at the mess as if seeing it for the first time. "I've a sailor for a patient," she said. "It's malaria. At least, I think it's malaria. Could be dengue fever. I haven't seen enough cases of either to be positive so I have to read instead. A poor substitute for clinical experience, but better than nothing."

There was a short silence, then Sid said, "Aye, well . . . I'll be off, then."

"Won't you stay for a minute? Let me get you a cup of tea. It's the least I can do after you came all this way."

He hesitated, then said, "All right."

She fetched her teapot off a pile of books and took it to the kitchen, glancing at him on the way. "Won't you sit?" she asked.

"I'm trying to," he said, looking around for an empty place.

She laughed. "Sorry. Push the books off the settee."

He did so, settling himself while she heated some water. He held his hands up while her back was turned. They were still shaking. He balled them into fists to make them stop.

"I can't thank you enough for those devices," she called over her shoulder.

"It was nothing. Come to think of it, I should have brought them by Varden Street. Save you lugging them."

"Good God, no! I'm going to sneak them in bit by bit. If Gifford saw the box, if he ever found out what I'm doing, I'd be finished."

India brought the teapot, cups and saucers, and a plate of ginger biscuits and set them down on a low-legged table that Sid cleared for her. She poured him a cup, added milk at his request, and handed it to him.

"You never told me what *you* are doing up and about at this hour," she said. "Surely not swotting up on malaria."

"No."

"Don't you *ever* sleep?"

"Not if I can help it."

She was looking at him closely now, with a worried expression. He looked away.

"Sid, is something wrong?"

He laughed. "Aye. Everything," he said, passing a shaky hand over his face.

"Is it your side again?" she asked, alarmed. "Do you have any pain? Are you feverish?"

"It's not me bloody side, India," he said. "It's you. I wish I'd never met you. You've wrecked everything. Wrecked me whole fucking life."

She put her cup down, stricken.

"You make me hate what I do. What I am," he said. "Who are you to do that to me? Everything I had—my family, my home, my future—was taken from me. The only way I could survive was by taking something back."

She didn't answer, just looked at him, her gray eyes huge and wounded.

"When I'm with you, I think of things and remember things and want things I long ago stopped wanting."

"What things?" she asked, her voice barely a whisper.

"Mad things. I want to wake up in a room by the sea. With sunlight streaming in the windows. The smell of salt on the wind. I don't even know where that place is. But I want to wake up there. With you."

"Please, Sid. Please don't."

"Why?" he nearly shouted. "Because I'm no good? Because I don't—"

India cut him off angrily. "Because I'm engaged to be married!"

Sid nodded. He stood, as if to go, then instead he bent to her, took her face in his hands, parted her lips with his tongue, and kissed her deeply. "A wedding gift," he said, when he'd finished. "Give me best to the groom."

"You are very cruel," she said softly.

He walked to the door.

"Please, I don't want to lose . . . to lose your friendship. It means a great deal to me," India said.

"*Friendship?* Is that what you call it?"

India looked down at her hands. "Perhaps we can talk again when you're not so angry."

"No, India, we can't. Because I don't want to see you again. Ever. You'll be the end of me, do you know that? Do you know what I did tonight? I left my girl all alone at a big do I'd thrown for her. Left every villain in the East End there, too. Men I shouldn't turn my back on for a second, never mind the whole night. I wrecked a whorehouse that earns me a lot of money. Scared the punters away. Doubt some of them will ever come back. I've made a right fucking mess of things, and it's all because of you."

He reached into his pocket and pulled out her watch—the one she'd given him to pay for the rubber johnnies. He tossed it across the room to her. She caught it.

India looked at it, then at him. "Why?" she asked. "Why are you giving this back? It was part of our deal. Payment."

He didn't reply, just opened the door to leave.

"Sid, *why?*" she pressed.

He stopped and looked back at her. "Christ knows, India," he said. "I bloody well don't. I don't know anything anymore."

CHAPTER 32

Fiona Bristow stood quietly inside a squat brick warehouse on Whitechapel's Cheshire Street. She thought perhaps she should make her presence known, but the two women she'd come to see were in the midst of such a heated discussion with a third person, a man, that she was hesitant to interrupt.

Dr. Jones was sketching a crude blueprint on the plank floor with a piece of chalk. She was kneeling, oblivious to dust and dirt. Her nurse, Ella Moskowitz, was kneeling beside her.

"We'd need *two* plumbing stacks," Fiona heard the doctor say, "one on the north side of the building and one on the south in order to provide sufficient hot water to all floors—"

"Wait. Stop," Ella said, scribbling furiously in a notebook. "Do you have any idea what that's going to cost?"

"No."

"A bloody fortune. In materials alone, never mind the labor."

"Why *now*? Why *this* building, Indy?" the man cut in, looking at the rusted pipes snaking along the walls and the broken lights dangling from the ceiling. "It's in bad shape and it's small."

"It's also cheap," the doctor replied. "Only five hundred pounds. We've enough money for a down payment, haven't we?"

"Yes, but a down payment is only part of the equation," the man said. "You *know* that. You also need to make the mortgage payments every month, refurbish the building, and fit it out with all sorts of medical clobber."

"But we could make a *start*. At least we'd have a building. We could refurbish it as we got more donations."

"Yes, you *could*, but it's a totally muddled way of doing things," he said.

"But Wish—"

"India, what is going on with you? You drag me out of my flat and hurry me down here, and all to see some totally unsuitable building. Why are you suddenly in such a mad rush?"

India sat back on her heels. "I can't stay at Dr. Gifford's anymore. I just can't."

"But you're going to have to. You can't afford to leave. Not yet. What's going on there? What happened that has you so upset?"

"We lost another patient today," Ella said quietly. "A new mother. Susan Brindle was her name. She was only nineteen years old."

"I'm sorry to hear it, but I imagine that happens frequently in your line of work."

"This woman died from puerperal fever," India said.

"I don't know what that is," the man said.

"Childbed fever. She shouldn't have. Contamination is almost entirely preventable—*if* the examining doctor washes his hands. She's the fifth mother we've lost in a fortnight to the disease. We lost two of their babies as well. It's a struggle for children without their mums. The fathers don't know what to do," Ella said.

"Damn him," India suddenly said. "*Damn him*. Why can't he wash his bloody hands? It's such a simple thing. Its effectiveness has been proven again and again. By Semmelweiss. Pasteur. Lister. A few steps to a sink, a few seconds to scrub his hands. That's all it takes. All it takes to save a woman's life."

Fiona noticed that even in her anger, the doctor kept her voice steady, her emotion controlled. She was intrigued by this woman, who seemed to be boiling with passion, and yet contained it.

Ella smiled bitterly. "Well, Dr. Gifford *did* take the time to see that I got Mrs. Brindle's bill made out. He handed it to her husband—right after I'd handed him his daughter—then told him good day. *Good day*. To a man newly widowed with a poorly baby in his arms. Can you imagine?"

"He must be stopped," India said.

"Why can't you report him?" Wish asked.

"It would be professional suicide," Ella said. "His word against India's. A doctor—a *male* doctor—with forty years' practice under his belt, or a woman who graduated from medical school a little over a month ago. Whose side will the BMA take?"

"The BMA?" Wish echoed.

"It's short for Boys, Men, and Arseholes," Ella said.

Fiona bit her lip to keep from laughing.

"It stands for the British Medical Association," India said.

"Doesn't matter what it stands for," Ella retorted. "There's nothing we can do. We can't stop Gifford."

"No, Ella, we *can* stop him," India said quietly.

"Oh, aye? How?"

"If we open the clinic, we can take his patients. You said his business was up since I joined the surgery, didn't you? And that most of the new patients are mine? If I go, they'll follow me."

"Doesn't sound entirely sporting, old girl," Wish said.

"What choice do I have? I can say nothing and watch more women die. Or I can report him and probably have my own license revoked for my trouble. What would you do, Wish?"

The doctor's voice shook now, ever so slightly. She rose to her feet and Fiona saw the emotion in her face. Her courage touched Fiona deeply. She was brave, this woman, brave in a way no man would ever understand. But Fiona understood, for she well knew the price a woman paid for admittance to a man's world.

"That's why you want this building," the man said. "To make a start. Anything is better than nothing."

India nodded. "It *is* cheap, Wish."

Stop her, a voice inside Fiona said. *And help her.*

"No, it isn't cheap, actually," she said, stepping forward. "The back wall's buckling. Over there, can you see it? The roof's not sound. And that's water damage, the white stain on the brick. It's highway robbery at half the price. If your estate agent's been telling you otherwise, sack him."

India turned around. She looked puzzled for a few seconds, then she smiled. "Mrs. Bristow! You're alive and well!"

"Only thanks to the both of you. And it's Fiona, please. I've been searching all over for you ever since the rally. I wanted to tell you how grateful I am for your help. You saved us." Her hand slid to her belly. "Both of us."

Fiona told them that she'd stayed under the platform until the worst was over, then crawled out and called up to her frantic husband, who promptly took her home. "How did you fare?" she asked them. "Did you make it out of the square?"

"Kicking and screaming," Ella said. "Well, that was me. India was out cold thanks to a police horse. We both spent the night in the nick."

"You *what*?" Wish said, flabbergasted.

"Thank you, Ella. Thank you very much," India said.

"You spent a night in the *nick* . . . you!" Wish laughed out loud. "You were at the Labour rally? India Selwyn Jones, what a checkered life you lead. Does Freddie know all this?" Wish asked.

"No! And don't you tell him either. He has enough to worry about with the campaign."

"Freddie? Campaign?" Fiona echoed. "You don't mean Freddie Lytton?"

"I do. I'm his fiancée," India said.

Fiona smiled. "The incumbent's fiancée and the challenger's wife. Together clandestinely in a tumbledown warehouse in the Whitechapel slums. Oh, if only Mr. Devlin were here. I'm sure he'd find a story in this."

India blanched. "I'm sure he would," she said nervously. "How did you know to look for us here?" she asked, changing the subject.

"I finally thought to ask Dr. Hatcher, who told me to go to Varden Street. I was just there, but the surgery was closed. A neighbor told me to try the Moskowitzes' restaurant on Brick Lane, and a woman there told me where you were. She also told me about your clinic and suggested that I give you twenty pounds for it," Fiona said, laughing.

Ella groaned. "*Gott in Himmel!* I'm sorry. That was my mother."

"No, don't be sorry. Please. What she told me sounded interesting. I'd like to hear more."

India and Ella told her of their plans. Fiona listened intently, nodding and frowning. When they finished, she peppered them with questions.

"You shouldn't buy outright," she said. "Even if you have the money. Take out a mortgage. Claim interest payments and depreciation against income. You do plan to incorporate, don't you? You could also rent the building. There might be greater tax benefits that way. Have you worked up balance sheets both ways? What does your accountant advise?"

India and Ella traded glances. "We don't . . . we don't have one," India said.

"Why not?" Fiona asked.

"They can't afford one. They don't have much to account for as yet," Wish said. "Only about four hundred pounds, I'm afraid."

"I'm so sorry! I haven't even introduced you," India said. "Fiona Bristow, this is my cousin, Aloysius Selwyn Jones, our director of development. He's been working very hard on our behalf soliciting donations. When he can spare the time, that is. We don't pay him anything, you see. We can't afford to." There was an awkward silence as India looked at her boots, then she turned her eyes up to Fiona's and said, "I can't imagine how backward we must appear. Our strength—mine and Ella's—is medicine, not money. We want to build a place where no mother, no child, is ever turned away. Most people cannot understand that." She smiled at Wish. "Even my dear cousin has difficulty with it. Can *you* understand?"

"More than you might think," Fiona said, remembering another night in Whitechapel, twelve years ago, when her frantic mother had gone out into the darkness to fetch a doctor for her baby. "I lived here once. Only a few streets over. We were very poor. We had nothing, in fact. My baby sister became gravely ill and my mother had to go out very late one night to fetch a doctor . . ." Her voice trailed off.

How like Sid's story, India thought. "Did she find one?" she asked.

Fiona shook her head. "No," she said. "No, she didn't. It was too late. Too late for all of us. We lost them both."

"I'm sorry," India said.

"I am, too," Fiona said. She felt embarrassed and a little angry with herself for telling such a personal story to three people whom she barely knew. And yet she had wanted India to know that she understood her. "Make sure medicine remains your strength, Dr. Jones," she said, "and perhaps your cousin and I can work on the money." She looked at Wish. "Would you visit me at my office tomorrow? I'll have a check ready for you."

"Can I put you down for twenty pounds, then?" Wish asked, eagerly pressing his advantage.

Fiona smiled, but her eyes never left India. She was gazing at her, taking her measure. There was something about her. She was so contained, so controlled, and yet Fiona sensed there was fire inside of her, and fearlessness, and a quiet defiance. She sensed, too, that India Selwyn Jones would have her clinic. With or without anyone else's help. She'd have it if she had to earn every penny of its price herself, and if it took her fifty years to do so.

"No, Mr. Selwyn Jones," she said. "You can put me down for a thousand."

CHAPTER 33

"Did you know Sunny's uncle shot a dachshund once?" Bingham said, squinting in the sunshine.

"Whatever for? Was it attacking him?" India asked, distractedly.

"He thought it was a partridge. It was in the fields, you see. It belonged to a friend. The lady was terribly upset. His uncle thought he ought to put it right. So he had the dog stuffed and gave it to the woman as a present."

"Oh, Bing, he didn't!"

"He did, the dreadful man. That was his idea of thoughtfulness. Can you imagine? Sunny said the poor woman cried for a week."

India laughed out loud. She couldn't help it; it was too horrible.

Bing smiled. "It's good to hear you laugh, old mole. You've been mighty glum. Anything wrong?"

Yes, she thought, I'm marrying your brother in a few weeks' time, but I am in love with someone else.

"No, Bing. Nothing. Nothing at all," she said brightly.

"Are you quite certain?"

India gave him a smile. "I'm positive," she lied, keeping her feelings as tightly reined in as the horse she was riding.

She and Bingham were at Blenheim Palace, the country estate of Sunny Churchill, the Duke of Marlborough and Bingham's good friend. He'd invited Bing, Freddie, Maud, Wish, and India for the weekend. It was now Saturday afternoon and Sunny had declared that they must spend it chasing a fox. Freddie and Wish—who'd not been able to come up yesterday because of a dinner party he had to attend in London and who'd only arrived at the house that morning—had been in the lead. India and Bingham had fallen behind. They'd ridden to the crest of a hill to see if they could spot them, but had had no luck. They could see the tawny limestone of Blenheim behind them, and the estate's fields and woods in front of them, but no flash of a red riding jacket, no horses or hounds.

India was desperate to rejoin the chase. She was anxious and restless, and she wanted to ride. Fast. So fast that she couldn't think about anything but the next hill or hedgerow. Her mount seemed to sense this; he shook his head unhappily at having to stand still and stamped his feet.

"Indy, do you know what I love best about Blenheim? And Longmarsh, too?" Bingham asked.

"No, what?" India said, feigning interest.

"The furniture polish."

"*What?*"

"It's a mad thing, I know. Proust had his madeleine and I have Goddard's. I love to stand in the dining room right after the maids have polished and breathe it in. It lingers. Have you noticed that? It's always there, mingling with kippers and bacon in the morning, with pheasant and mushrooms in the evening. I love that smell. It's the smell of my school holidays. My Christmases and New Years. Why, if a woman had a mind to catch me, all she'd have to do is dab a bit of Goddard's behind her ears. I'd be her slave." He went silent for a minute, then said, "I wish it could last forever, Indy. This day. This moment. I wish time would just stop. Right here and now. With all of us together. I want to never move forward and never go back."

"Wouldn't that be lovely? Strawberries and cream on Blenheim's lawns for all eternity," she said.

But that was a lie. She didn't want strawberries and cream. Or Blenheim or this damned stupid fox hunt. She wanted a pint of porter. In Whitechapel. With Sid. She wanted to talk about things that mattered in a place she'd grown to love, with a man she didn't dare to love.

"Croquet on the lawn. Long walks at dusk. And all the females in white walking about so fetchingly with roses in their hair. Heaven's got nothing on England in August." His smile faded. "Won't, though, will it?"

"Won't what?" she asked. She'd barely heard what he'd said.

"Last."

"The summer?"

Bingham shrugged. "The summer. Us. This life."

India turned to him, struck by his wistful tone. "Goodness, Bing, now who's glum?"

"Times are changing, Indy. A few years ago—just last year, in fact— Freddie would have romped home with the Tower Hamlets seat. The very *idea* of Labour mounting an effective opposition would have been laughable."

India's attention was suddenly riveted. "Bing, you don't think Freddie's going to lose, do you?"

Bingham hesitated, then said, "I think he might. The Tories are making hay out of the Stronghold disaster. And he's underestimated Joe Bristow. The press adores the man. He's in the papers nearly every day, and the election isn't even official yet. It's going to be a three-way race and damned hard to call, but if I had to put money on it, I'd go with Bristow. He speaks to workingmen in their language. And that's something neither Freddie nor Dickie Lambert does." He nodded at Blenheim, golden in the afternoon sun. "This can't last. Too few have had too much for too long."

"Is that what you argued about last night?" India asked.

The men had had a terrible fight in the billiard room after supper.

"That, too," Bingham said. "Freddie was cross and in his cups. A terrible combination. He told Sunny he was a silly man who wanted only to chase foxes. And he said Wish was a vulgar man who wanted only to chase money."

India winced. "How dreadful of him. Glad Wish wasn't here last night to hear that. I hope he left you out of it."

Bingham shook his head. "He accused me of cowering in my study with Byron and Longfellow while socialists and radicals overrun the country."

"Oh, dear. I'm sure he didn't mean it, Bing. He's under so much pressure."

"He did mean it. And he's right. Freddie's the best man out of all of us. He's the only one with courage enough to enter the fray."

Freddie had been very upset last night; India knew he had. She tried to cheer him by telling him about her clinic, and Wish's new role as its fundraiser, but it only seemed to make things worse. He'd been quite drunk, too. Drunk enough to whisper, "Leave your door unlocked, darling," as they were all going up to bed.

But she hadn't; she'd locked it. Then she'd sat up in her bed, in the dark, unable to sleep. She'd heard him trying the knob, then rapping softly. He hadn't dared to make any real noise. Someone might have heard him. He'd been cross with her this morning over it. They'd had words after breakfast. She'd told him it was an accident. A habit developed from living alone in London. She'd turned the key in the lock automatically, she'd said, then she'd fallen asleep and hadn't heard him.

It was a plausible explanation and it had mollified him, but it wouldn't work twice. She didn't know what she would do tonight. He wanted to make love to her. Of course he did. He was her fiancé. She should want to make love to him, too. But she didn't. There was a man whose touch she craved, though, a man whose body she longed to feel against her own. And a week ago, he'd told her he never wanted to see her again.

"Halloooo! Indy! Bing! Where are the others?"

India turned in her saddle, grateful for the distraction from her tortured thoughts, and saw Maud riding up behind them.

"My word! What happened to you?" India asked her.

Maud was splattered with mud—her riding costume, her hands, her face. Her hat was gone; there were twigs and leaves in her hair. "I was following the others. We jumped a high wall. The mud on the other side was a foot deep. They made it through. I didn't."

"Are you all right?"

"Mostly."

"Where are they now?"

"Buggered if I know. They disappeared into the woods, Freddie yelling that the fox was his and Wish yelling it was his, and Sunny blowing on his blasted bugle, and the damned dogs baying like hellhounds."

"What's going to happen if those two do actually catch the fox?" Bingham asked. "Does Wish have his pistol on him?"

"Yes, he was brandishing it earlier," Maud said. "Frightened a parlormaid."

Wish loved the chase, but he couldn't abide the savagery of its conclusion. He was an excellent shot and always put the animal out of its misery immediately.

Freddie had teased Wish about this over breakfast, telling him he'd never make a politician, for the savagery in the Commons was far worse.

Bingham sat up in his saddle. "Look! There they are!"

Wish and Freddie were galloping through a clearing toward them, clearly racing each other. Wish flashed by, followed by Freddie, then they slowed to a trot and doubled back.

"You owe me twenty quid, old boy," Wish said to Freddie, as they approached. He looked at Maud, still muddied, and laughed. "Not sure that rouge suits you. A bit dark if you ask me."

"Haw, haw, haw, Wish," Maud said. "Freddie, you did that on purpose."

"Did what?"

"Took us over that hedge."

"Certainly did. But I was hoping to dump Wish in the mud, not you. Sorry, old girl."

"Where's Sunny?" India asked.

"Dunno," Wish said. "He was ahead of us, but we lost him. But listen, India, speaking of Sunny, I've a bit of good news for you. I was talking to him about Point Reyes—trying to get him to invest when I take the whole thing public—and I mentioned your clinic to him, too. I think he's interested. He's talking about making a contribution."

"Is he really?" India asked excitedly. "That is good news. Thank you, Wish!"

"How much did you get? Two pounds?" Maud asked archly.

"More like two hundred, thank you. I like this fund-raising stuff. I'm getting quite good at it. I'll have you all know that I got two hundred from Lady Elcho last night. Collared her at a dinner party. One hundred from Jennie Churchill. And"—he paused for dramatic effect—"five hundred pounds from Lord Rothschild."

"Well done!" India exclaimed. She hadn't seen her cousin for a few days, and this was all news to her. She couldn't wait to tell Ella.

"With four hundred–odd pounds already donated, and a thousand from Fiona Bristow, that'll bring the fund up to around twenty-four hundred pounds. And that's not all, Indy," Wish said. "Your friend Harriet Hatcher was at the dinner last night, too. She said her parents will make a donation. Three hundred pounds, she thinks. And—you won't *believe* this—Princess Beatrice, who's a friend of Harriet's mother, might—*might,* I say—be interested in becoming a royal patron."

India was saucer-eyed. Princess Beatrice was the queen's youngest daughter. Her interest and support would give an immense boost to the clinic. Even Maud and Bing were impressed. Freddie was leaning forward in his saddle, fiddling with his horse's bridle and scowling.

"Apparently Mrs. Hatcher and Harriet are invited to tea with the princess later this month, and the old girl is interested in meeting you. Harriet told me to tell you that you have to go. Could you?"

"Yes, of course!" India said. "Nothing could stop me. Where? When?"

"It's in London. On the eighteenth."

"It's impossible," Freddie said brusquely. "That's our wedding date."

"Oh, damn, that's right!" Wish said. "I completely forgot. You couldn't move it up a week or two, could you?"

"No, we cannot," Freddie said, before India could answer. "Plans are already under way."

India leaned over to him, reaching for his hand. "Darling, could we? We could push it to the twenty-fifth. I'm sure the vicar wouldn't mind. We could ring him from the house. And the caterers and florist, too. I wouldn't ask, but it's for the clinic and you know how important that is to me."

"What if they can't do the twenty-fifth?" Freddie asked.

"Then perhaps we could move the wedding to September. I can't say no to someone like Princess Beatrice. Not when it would mean so much to the clinic's success. Please, darling?"

"Of course, old girl," Freddie said, relenting. "We'll put a call through to the vicar right after the hunt."

"Good man!" Wish said. "You know, I have to admit I thought Indy was mad when she first told me about the clinic, but now I think it's going to happen. I really do. The donations are mounting up. We may have a royal donor, and things are going so well with Point Reyes that I may be able to take the thing public sooner than I thought. Half a year at most. When that happens, Indy, you'll be swimming in cash."

"That means we could be under way with a building by early next year!" India said excitedly.

She was about to thank him for all his hard work when Freddie's horse suddenly reared. He kept his seat, but barely. "He's restless," Freddie said. "He needs to run. First one to the clearing, Wish. Double or nothing."

Wish's eyes flashed. Before anyone could dissuade them, they were off. India spurred her mount. Maud and Bingham followed. The course Freddie had chosen took the riders through a hillocky meadow. Ruts and humps and swampy patches made a treacherous obstacle course. Freddie was riding at a breakneck pace and Wish was right behind him, hooting and laughing. They soon outdistanced the others.

"What are they playing at?" Maud shouted. "Are they trying to kill us?"

India saw the two men streak down a hill. Wish had taken the lead. He disappeared into the woods, hotly pursued by Freddie. Maud and Bingham reached the woods then drew up, waiting for her.

"I hear the dogs," Bingham said. "Sunny must have treed the fox. I bet Wish and Freddie are with him."

India suddenly decided she would ride back to the house. She wanted no part of the finale. She could imagine the trapped animal's terror.

"Ready, ladies?" Bingham asked, taking up his reins.

"I'm not going. I—" India began to say. Her words were cut off by the sound of a gunshot. It came from the woods.

"Well, that's it for poor Mr. Fox," Maud said, sighing. "And that's it for me as well. I'm going back to the house for a hot bath and a cold gin."

They heard a bugle. "Sunny's found them," Bingham said.

Sunny, as master of the hunt, carried the bugle with him. But as they all listened, they realized that Sunny wasn't playing the call used to announce that the fox had been caught, he was sounding an alarm. Instantly, they all spurred their mounts and headed into the woods, navigating by the sound of the trumpet. Bingham led, ducking brush and branches, and it was he who found the others, dismounted in the clearing. The horses had been tied to a tree and were wild-eyed and whinnying. The dogs were howling. It was all that the kennel masters could do to control them. From her place behind Bingham, India could just see Sunny, bent double and heaving.

He raised his head at their approach. "Bingham, keep the women back!" he shouted.

"No, bring them through!" Freddie shouted. "India's a doctor!"

There's been an accident, she thought. Someone's injured. She found an opening in the trees to the left of Bingham and urged her horse through it and into the clearing.

"What happened?" she shouted, drawing up with the others.

And then she saw.

Wish lay sprawled on his back. The left side of his face was gone. His legs were twisted underneath him, his arms splayed. His pistol lay in his right hand.

India jumped down from her horse and ran to him. It was hopeless, she knew it was, but still she pressed her ear to his chest, listening for a heartbeat. There was nothing. She wanted to scream with grief, to throw herself across his body. But she didn't. She did what she was trained to do. She felt for any signs of life—a breath, a pulse. She glanced at her watch. For the coroner. In case he wanted to know the time of death. Around her, Freddie paced, Maud tried to light a cigarette with shaking hands, and Bingham stammered.

"Good God . . . this can't . . . he can't . . ." he said. "Freddie, what the hell *happened*?"

"I don't know. Wish saw a hole and said the fox had gone to ground there. I told him he couldn't have. The dogs were up ahead of us and they were baying. I rode on after them. And that's when I heard it—a gunshot from behind me. I turned back, thinking he must've been right. And then I found him here. Like this." He was silent for a few seconds, then vehemently said, "It was an *accident*. Are we all agreed on this? A terrible, terrible accident."

"What else would it be?" Maud asked, upset. "What are you saying?"

"It's what others may say that worries me," he replied.

"Freddie, what do you mean?" Bingham asked.

"He was anxious. There were difficulties. Money troubles. He'd sold things. A painting. His ring. He confided in me when he arrived this morning. Before the hunt."

India looked down at Wish's right hand. His diamond ring was gone. He was never without it. It was a treasured heirloom. "He had it on earlier," she said.

"What difficulties?" Maud asked. "He just said things were going well."

"I'm sure he had it on at breakfast. I'm sure he did."

"India, it doesn't matter!" Maud snapped. "Freddie, *what* difficulties? He said nothing about difficulties to me."

"He didn't want to worry you. Or India."

"Freddie, you don't think . . . you're not saying that he . . ."

"I'm not saying anything. I'm only telling you what he said to me: that an investment had gone bad. And that he was worried."

"My God, the scandal," Maud said. "Which investment?"

"The California thing. He was just talking about it. I can't remember . . ."

"Point Reyes," India said dully. She sat back on her heels and tenderly stroked Wish's cheek.

Freddie looked at her. "Yes, that's it. You invested in it, didn't you?"

"Yes."

"How much?"

"Everything I had."

"I had no idea. Bloody hell, I'm sorry."

"But he said it was doing well," Maud said shrilly. "He said it was going public. We heard him. All of us. Just a few minutes ago. This just can't *be*!"

"He was putting a good face on it," Freddie said. "He told me this morning that he couldn't interest people."

Money and scandals and saving face. Wish's body was still warm. His blood was seeping into the ground, and this was what they were talking about. She hated them for it. And she didn't, for she was one of them, and she understood. They would talk about Point Reyes, the weather, or last night's supper—if that's what it took not to think about Wish. Not to weep. Not to howl. Not to fall apart in front of family, friends, and the servants.

She stood up and sought Sunny. He was still bent over, still heaving. She would leave him to it. It was the proper thing. He was the host; she was the guest. She must let him heave his noble guts out and pretend not to notice. Funny how etiquette always took over. Especially *in extremis*. Good manners show good breeding, her mother always said. Wouldn't she be proud? India thought bitterly, walking back to her horse.

"India, stop! Where are you going?" Freddie asked.

She turned to him, her fiancé. The man in whose arms she should be weeping now. "To fetch a coroner," she said woodenly. "Excuse me, won't you? My cousin is dead."

CHAPTER 34

"No!" the man wailed, stumbling away from the bed. "Not my Allie! Please God, not my pretty Allie!"

"For God's sake, hold the lamp still!" India yelled. "I can't bloody see!"

"She's dying! Help her, please help her!"

"I'm trying! I need the lamp!"

The man, Fred Coburn, choked back a sob. He tightened his grip on the kerosene lamp he was clutching and lumbered back to the bed.

"Lower. Hold it lower," India barked. He did and the lamp cast its weak glow over the bed and the laboring woman in it.

Blood was gushing from her. It was pooling in the sheets, soaking into the mattress, dripping over the metal bed frame and onto the floor. It covered India's hands and forearms. Her clothing was sodden with it.

"Oh, Jesus, oh God, look at it all."

The lamp swayed wildly again. India lost sight of her forceps.

"Bring the table. Put the lamp on it. Right now," she ordered.

He did so, then sat down, his head in his hands, and wept. The light was still poor. India hooked her foot around one of the table's legs and pulled it closer.

They'd waited too long to send for her. By the time she'd arrived, the mother had been in labor for two days and the baby had barely descended. Its heartbeat had dropped perilously and the mother was exhausted. And then, only minutes ago, just as India was starting to examine her, the placenta ruptured. Mrs. Coburn was hemorrhaging badly. India knew that if she didn't get the bleeding stanched immediately, she would lose her. But she had to get the baby out first, and the mother's pelvis was contracted. She was using a Tarnier, a long, curved forceps with a traction bar—and every bit of strength she possessed—to ease the skull past the mother's misshapen bones.

She took a deep breath now, braced one foot against the bed frame, and pulled. Mrs. Coburn screamed, writhing against the unforgiving blades. The baby moved, barely.

"Hang on, Mrs. Coburn, almost there . . ." India said through gritted teeth. She took another breath, and pulled again with everything she had, until the muscles in her arms and shoulders shook with the strain.

"Please, please don't let my baby die," Mrs. Coburn begged.

India, panting now, pulled again. She felt the head move. Encouraged, she gave another mighty pull, and the baby—a boy—was out.

India laid him on the bed. His skin was blue. He was not breathing. She knew she had only seconds in which to save—or lose—two lives.

"My baby . . ." Mrs. Coburn moaned. The moan turned into a scream of pain as India inserted her left hand into the birth canal, made a fist, and pressed it up into the uterus. She used her right hand, which was on the woman's belly, to press down, trying to force the organ to compress itself, and in so doing choke off the blood supply to its own hemorrhaging vessels.

"He's all right, ain't he?" Fred Coburn cried. He was a big man and half-mad with fear, and India was alone with him. Ella was assisting Dr. Gifford.

"A boy, Fred! Oh, where is he? Why doesn't he cry?" Mrs. Coburn sobbed.

"Mr. Coburn, take the baby. Clean out his mouth with your fingers," India instructed. But Mr. Coburn would not. He backed away from the bed, from his thrashing wife and lifeless baby. "Mr. Coburn, listen to me. I need your help."

Fred Coburn shook his head violently. India needed to soothe him, to coax him. She needed time to do those things, but she didn't have any.

Moving like lightning, she tore the bloodied topsheet off the bed and looped it around Alison Coburn's belly. She grabbed a candlestick off the table and twisted it into the ends of the sheet, tightening the fabric. It was called a Spanish windlass, a kind of tourniquet. She'd seen it done a few times during her training, and once it had actually worked. She hoped now that it would at least buy her a few seconds.

"Why's she so white?" Fred Coburn asked. His voice was higher than it had been.

India picked up the baby. "I need fresh linen. Find me some," she said sharply, hoping to distract him with a task.

"Why's she so still? Why ain't she moving?"

"The *linen*, Mr. Coburn," India said, working feverishly to revive the baby. She swept her finger around the inside of his mouth, dislodging a glob of mucus, then began to compress his chest, trying to prime his tiny lungs. Henry Michael Coburn. That's what they were going to call him. Harry for short, his mother had said. "You come on now, Harry Coburn," she urged him. "You breathe for me. Breathe, little Harry. Breathe."

"Allie? Wake up, Allie luv."

Fred Coburn staggered over to the bed and patted his wife's face. India could hear the edge of hysteria in his voice. She bent over the baby, pinched his nostrils, and breathed gently into his mouth. She was still trying to make the baby breathe when Fred Coburn, kneeling at his wife's side, reared up off the floor.

"She's dead!" he yelled. "Oh, God, my Allie, she's dead!"

He stumbled across the room and into the mantel. A teapot, plates, and picture frames fell to the floor and smashed. He turned and lumbered back toward the bed.

"The lamp!" India shouted at him. "Mind the lamp!"

Her voice startled him out of his rampage. He looked at her, his face contorted by grief and rage, and then he lunged at her. "You bitch! You murderer!" he shouted, punching her again and again. "You killed her, you killed my Allie!"

India could not defend herself; her arms were braced protectively over the baby. But when Fred Coburn's hands were suddenly around her neck, she had no choice. She kicked him. Her hands slapped at him, her fingers scrabbled at his, desperately trying to break his grasp. She was gasping for air, eyes closing, nearly limp, when two men—neighbors alerted by the sound of the smashing crockery—burst into the room and pulled him off her. She fell to the floor, heaving for breath.

"Get him out of here," she rasped.

As they took Coburn out of the room, she pulled herself back onto the bed and bent over the baby. She felt his body for signs of life—a fluttering breath, a weak pulse—but there was nothing. She felt for Alison Coburn's pulse. Again, nothing.

Another man came into the room, followed by two women. They stood, shocked into stillness at the scene before them. "What on earth's happened? Are you all right?" one of them finally asked.

"Mrs. Coburn is dead," India said. "The baby, too. Would you please fetch the coroner?"

She stood up, steadied herself, and walked to the kitchen. A kettle had been set on the stove. She had asked Fred to heat water when she'd first arrived. She poured some into a basin, added cold from the sink's lone tap, and washed her hands. As she was drying them she heard one of the women whisper, "Put the little one in her arms. Never got to hold him, poor thing. It's only right."

"What a bloody shame. Them not even married a year."

"Wouldn't have happened if they'd had a doctor."

"She *is* a doctor."

"I meant a *proper* doctor. Someone who knows what he's doing."

India stood quietly out of their view and covered her face with her dripping hands. Her head was throbbing from the beating she'd just received. Her throat felt like someone had poured acid down it. And yet the livid bruises on her neck, her bleeding mouth, and swollen eyes were nothing compared to the pain of the women's words.

She knew she should attend to her injuries. She also needed to collect her instruments and wash them. She did neither. Instead, she hunted for something with which to cover Alison Coburn and her baby. There was a clothes horse in the kitchen hung with laundry, but there were no sheets on it. She opened the doors to the small cupboard, but found only a few dishes, tea, and sugar.

She returned to the front room and spotted a chest of drawers. She opened the top drawer, but there was only clothing inside it. She was just closing it again when something on top of the chest caught her eye. It was a cup. A small porcelain cup with yellow ducklings and the word *Baby* painted on it. The rim was chipped. Next to it was a rattle. Most of its plating was gone but someone had polished it with care. There was a homemade muslin bonnet and two tiny gowns, each beautifully embroidered. India picked up one of the gowns. *Tate and Lyle*, it said near the hem, in faded blue writing. It had been made from a sugar sack.

It was a layette—a small, meager layette that a poor mother had assembled for her baby. It spoke of careful economies, of doing without, of trips to second-hand markets with only pennies to spend. It spoke of happiness. Of hope.

She traced a line of stitches on the gown and wondered what Alison Coburn had done without in order buy the thread. Coal? Food? She thought of how harshly she would have lectured her for spending money that could have bought milk or greens on a second-hand cup and rattle.

It was all her fault. She had lost them. Both of them. She prided herself on her skill, on her knowledge and technique, and they had failed her. If only she'd been faster, more skillful with her forceps, they might both still be here.

Her legs began to shake so hard that she had to sit down. When the coroner arrived, some thirty minutes later, he found her holding the dead woman's hand and whispering, "They were right, Allie. They were right, little Harry. You should have had a proper doctor."

"My goodness, Dr. Jones, what on earth happened to you?"

It was Dr. Gifford. India had gone back to the surgery to return the Tarnier forceps in case they were needed.

"I lost a laboring mother. Baby, too. The father became violent."

"Were the police notified? Did you press charges?"

"It hadn't occurred to me."

"But the man beat you quite badly."

"He'd just lost his wife and baby," India said.

"You'll have to have tomorrow off, I suppose. I don't know how we'll manage."

India didn't either, but she didn't care. Nausea was gripping her gut. She had to get out of Gifford's office before the sandwich she'd had for lunch landed on his floor.

"Are you quite all right, Dr. Jones?" Dr. Gifford asked, eyeing her closely.

"Fine. Yes. Pardon me, please." She managed to walk out of Gifford's office but broke into a run as soon as she was in the hallway. She'd just made it to the loo when she was violently ill. She fell to her knees in front of the toilet, retching until her eyes watered.

Wonderful, she thought, when she could finally stand again. I could use a nice bout of gastroenteritis right now.

She hobbled to the sink to rinse her mouth and caught sight of herself in the small mirror hanging over it. She jumped, startled into thinking that an injured patient had come into the loo behind her, then realized that she was looking at herself. Her fingers went to her right eye, which was as black and swollen as a leech. They traveled over her mottled cheeks to her split lip. Her legs started to shake violently, just as they had at the Coburns'. A few seconds later she was sick again.

When she finished, she left the bathroom, grabbed her coat and bag, and left without saying good night to Dr. Gifford. She hurried down Varden Street toward the underground, trying to avoid the curious stares of passersby. Before she reached the station, however, she was seized by another fit of shaking and had to sit down. She stumbled to a bench. What is wrong with me? she wondered. The shaking continued, and was joined by a feeling of fatigue so deep, so oppressive, that she had no idea how she would even stand up, much less continue to the underground.

She dug in her coat pocket for loose coins and counted them. One pound, twelve pence. More than enough for cab fare. As she looked at the coins, droplets of water splashed onto them. Tears? She stared up at the darkening night sky and saw clouds. It was raindrops, not tears. She had no tears.

Don't feel, Fenwick had said. And India found, finally, that she didn't. She didn't feel anything. She tried to cry, to force her tears. But she couldn't. Nothing came. Her beloved Wish was gone. He'd died three days ago. A suicide, most likely. And with him, her hopes for a clinic. A brand-new baby had just died. And his mother. She should be weeping, keening, prostrate with grief. But she wasn't. Because she couldn't feel a thing. She was totally numb.

Fenwick's voice echoed in her ears. *Don't feel, don't feel.* His words had always sounded imperious to her. Like a command. But now she heard them differently, she heard them as he'd intended her to—not as an order, but as a warning. Feel for all the men who worked in mills and factories, dockyards and coal mines until they dropped, yet never saw their children warm and well fed; feel for the women whose worn and stunted bodies brought forth life in an agony of pain and blood, only to see it snatched away for want of a bit of meat or milk; feel for all the hungry, hollow-eyed children who made matchboxes and paper flowers and learned to weep silently. Feel for them, and you were lost.

"Here now, what's wrong, lassie?" a male voice said. "Who gave you such a hiding? Your husband? Shame on him!"

India looked up into a pair of kind brown eyes and laughed mirthlessly.

"No, it wasn't my husband. It was somebody else's husband. Thing is, he's not a husband anymore. He's a widower. Because of me. His wife died tonight. His baby, too. I could have saved them if I'd been a better doctor." She remembered tiny Harry Coburn, how he'd looked nestled in the crook of his dead mother's arm. "I wanted to help," she said. "I wanted to change things. That's why I became a doctor. To make a difference. But I haven't.

I wanted to open a clinic, but I haven't. I wanted to try to stop the suffering in this Godforsaken place, but I haven't."

The man, elderly and ragged, frowned. "Well, missus, that does sound terrible. But it can't be *all* bad. There must be something good. That's the thing to do when you're down, think about something good in your life. Maybe you've got a nice home. Or a nice husband. What about childer? They're always a bright spot. Have you any childer?"

"No, I haven't. I live alone."

"Friends, then? People you work with?"

"I can't bear the man I work with. Work *for*. He's careless, negligent, a mercenary," she said, the words pouring out of her in a flood. "He should be in jail, not treating patients. My oldest, dearest friend just died. Killed himself. He was my cousin. I *do* have a fiancé. A wonderful man. A good man. But I don't love him. I love someone else, you see, but he's the wrong man entirely."

"Bloody hell, missus, that *is* all bad," the dosser said. He sat silently for a bit, sucking his teeth. Then he reached into his jacket pocket and pulled out a flask. "Don't know what to tell yer," he said. "It's a right cock-up." He handed the flask to her. "Here, help yourself. It's a bit of comfort."

Comfort from a flask. If only Sid were here to see her. How he would laugh at her. *Have you never needed comfort?* he'd asked her. Her words came back to her now. She cringed at them. *If I have, Mr. Malone, I haven't sought it in a gin bottle.* She took the flask and drank deeply. She coughed as the alcohol burned her throat, then drank again. Let him laugh, she thought. He deserved to, for he was right. About her. About porridge. About everything. He was right and she was wrong.

India drank again and again. "Here," she finally said to the man, giving him the coins in her pocket. "For more. I've nearly drunk you dry."

The man brightened. "Why, thank you, missus." He clapped her on the back. "It'll look better in the morning. You'll see."

"Actually, it won't. Because it's hopeless. Bloody hopeless. It's one bloody big bloody circle of bloody hopelessness. How can it ever get better? Tell me, how?" She took one final pull, a sloppy one. Gin dribbled down her chin. She wiped it off with the back of her hand. "You've no answer, have you? Well, not to worry. I haven't either. Doesn't matter, though."

"Why's that, missus?"

"Because I bloody well quit. That's why."

She rose on unsteady legs, picked up her doctor's bag, and heaved it into the street. It opened as it landed, spilling instruments and dressings everywhere.

She smiled at the mess.

"Good night," she told the man.

"Good night, missus," he said.

And then she turned her back on Whitechapel and headed home to Bedford Square.

CHAPTER 35

Ella, basket in hand, jumped off the omnibus as it slowed to a stop at Bedford Square. It had taken her more than two hours to get there. The evening traffic had been heavy to begin with and a milk wagon had overturned on Gower Street. Ella's pace was brisk as she headed to India's building. India had not come to work for two days, and she was worried. Dr. Gifford told her what had happened at the Coburns'. He also said that India would be taking one day off but would be back the following morning— yesterday. But she hadn't come back.

Ella had wanted to go to her flat right away, but it wasn't possible. The surgery had been diabolically busy. Dr. Gifford had had to cancel his afternoon hours in Harley Street to cope with the backlog. Because of India, the demand for appointments at Varden Street had quadrupled.

When Mrs. Moskowitz had heard what had happened to India, and that Ella was going to see her, she made sure her daughter had food to bring. Ella reached the third-floor landing huffing and puffing under the weight of her basket. She knocked on the door. There was no answer. She tried again, saw that it was ajar, and let herself in. She heard the voices immediately. They were coming from India's bedroom.

"How can you still have the slightest doubt, India? My God, just look at yourself! This is madness—sheer, bloody madness!"

Ella recognized that voice. She had met Freddie Lytton a week ago.

"Freddie's right, darling. You could have been killed."

The second voice, a woman's, was unfamiliar.

Ella hesitated, unsure whether or not she should intrude on what was obviously a private conversation.

"This is not what you should be doing. I've always said as much. You should be spending your time on public health policy. You should put your skills and knowledge where they will benefit the greatest number of people. A cow doctor can pull a baby out. You're better than that."

"I thought I could do more good in Whitechapel than in Westminster."

"Well, you were wrong. You're no good to anyone if you get yourself killed."

"India, for once in your life, listen to reason. Please." That was the woman again.

There was silence for several seconds, and then in a flat, weak voice—a voice Ella barely recognized as her friend's—India said, "All right. I'll resign."

"Chas v'cholileh! Bist meshuganah?" Ella whispered.

"It's the right decision, my darling. Truly. You're completely wrecked. You need a rest. And you'll have one. We'll marry quietly and then I'll take you somewhere marvelous on honeymoon. What would you say to—"

Freddie didn't get to share his travel plans, for Ella came bustling through the doorway and cut him off. "Here you are, Dr. Jones! Havin' yourself a right skive, are you?" she asked brightly.

"Hello, Ella," India said dully.

She looked terrible. Ella had to stop herself from flinching at the sight of her.

"We didn't hear you knock," Freddie said tightly.

"Didn't you? Probably because you were too busy gassing."

Freddie's eyes narrowed. Ella affected not to notice and introduced herself to Maud. Then she bustled Freddie out of his place at India's bedside and sat down herself. She took India's chin in her hand and peered closely at her injuries. "Gave you a right gobsmacking, the bastard. You should have had stitches in that lip. Gifford let you go home without any?" she asked, without waiting for an answer. "You shouldn't have gone alone. I should have been with you. He couldn't have bashed the both of us."

"She shouldn't have gone at all," Freddie said.

Ella turned to him. With a grave smile she said, "Mr. Lytton, Miss Selwyn Jones, would you excuse us for a few minutes? I'm a bit concerned about lividity and tumescence in the orbicularis oris and I'd like to do an examination. Make sure the good doctor is healing properly."

"Of course," Maud said.

Freddie followed her unwillingly. When they'd left, India looked at Ella and said, "My lip is fat? You need to examine me because my lip is fat?"

"Never mind that," Ella said, taking India's wrist. "What's this rubbish I heard about resigning?"

"Heard? Do you mean *over*heard?"

"Sixty-five. Your pulse is fine." She felt India's head. "You don't feel warm. What was your last reading?"

"I haven't taken one."

"Why not? You should have. Where's your bag?"

"I threw it away."

Ella banged her fist on India's night table. *"Nar ainer!"*

"No, I'm not a fool. For once I'm trying to be wise."

"Are you eating?"

"I'm not hungry."

"Vomiting?"

"No."

"So then. Besides a few bruises and an ugly lip, there's nothing wrong with you."

"Ella," India said quietly. "I've made up my mind."

"S'teitsh! Nisht do gedacht!" Ella said, so distraught that she was unaware she was speaking Yiddish.

"Yes, it *is* possible! Two people died because of me. Three, if you count Miss Milo. Four, if you count Mrs. Adams. A lot more if you count the childbed fever cases that I should have reported Gifford for weeks ago. I'm finished. Done. I'm not up to the job. I'd do more good—and far less harm—in Westminster than I've done in Whitechapel."

"Lokshen!"

"No, it's not nonsense. It's—"

"Hert zich ein . . ."

"I *am* listening, Ella."

"No, you're not. That mother and son did not die because of you. They died because they never had proper care. Because they didn't call a doctor until the last minute. Because they couldn't bloody afford to. I thought you wanted to change that. I thought you wanted to build a clinic where poor women could come for care. I thought you wanted to make a difference. You've already started to, India. Don't stop now."

India turned her face toward the wall.

"You look at me!"

"Please, Ella. I'm tired. I want to sleep."

Ella sat back and bit her lip. She wasn't sure what to do. She wasn't sure what to say. Because she wasn't sure what was wrong. Then she heard her mother's voice, *If God wants people to suffer, He gives them too much understanding.* As always, her mother was right. India was in the midst of a breakdown, Ella realized. It wasn't the bruises on her face and body that had caused it, it was the bruises on her heart. India cared. Deeply. Too deeply. And this was the price she paid for it.

"India, listen. Please listen to me. This isn't you. Don't you see that? You're exhausted and hurting and at the end of your rope. You've been through a lot recently. You just need some rest. Give yourself a few days to recover and you'll want to work again, I know you will."

"Sister Moskowitz? How is our patient?" It was Freddie. He was peering around the door.

Out of her mind, Ella wanted to say. "Fine," she did say. "There's nothing wrong that rest and chicken soup won't cure. I left a basket in the other room. It's from my mother. There's plenty if you're feeling hungry."

"That's very kind of her. Please give her our thanks." He turned to India and frowned. "All right, darling?"

"Yes, quite."

There it was again. That dead, flat voice. It scared Ella. More than India's wounds, more than her pallid face and gaunt body. She tried so hard to hide her emotion. It was so important to her to be in control, but her voice always betrayed her real feelings. There was always fire in that voice. Always passion. And Ella would have given anything to hear it now. Why, she would have suffered one of India's endless rants on Dr. Gifford, or the fecklessness of the working class, or the immorality of Sid Malone . . .

Sid Malone.

There was something between them. She wasn't sure what, exactly, but she knew they had spent an entire night touring Whitechapel and that India had been different afterward. Oh, she'd still been India, but she'd softened a bit. She'd stopped going on about porridge quite so much and no longer told everyone who came to Varden Street to stop drinking. Sid had gotten to her that night. Pierced her armor somehow.

Suddenly, Ella knew exactly what to do. "Well, I'm off. Must get back," she said, picking up her carpetbag. "Ta-ra!"

"Miss Moskowitz?" Freddie said smoothly. "Could you possibly do Dr. Jones an enormous favor?"

"Of course. Anything at all."

"Would you please tell Dr. Gifford that she won't be resuming her duties? She'll submit a formal letter in a day or two. When she has a bit of strength back."

"I'll give him the message," she said.

Anyone who knew Ella would have known it was not in her nature to give up so easily. Luckily, Freddie and Maud didn't know her or they would have seen in her too bright smile, in her purposeful expression and hasty departure, that she hadn't given up at all. Like a good general, she'd only conceded a hopeless battle. A war was being waged for India's soul, and she was about to send for reinforcements.

CHAPTER 36

"How long has she been this way?" Sid asked.

"A week now," Ella said.

"You should have come to me sooner."

"Chance would be a fine thing, wouldn't it? I couldn't bloody find you! Ever try to get information out of Frankie Betts? Desi Shaw? It's like trying to pry open a clamshell with a feather."

"She won't get out of bed?"

"No. Barely eats, either. She's had some kind of breakdown. Over the mother and baby she lost. At least that's what I think happened, but maybe there's more to it."

Sid ignored her probing look. "Did you give Gifford Lytton's message?"

"Forgot. Sorry, luv."

Sid smiled. "That's my girl."

A volley of coughing stopped his smile. He turned to the little girl sitting next to him. She was about eight years old. Her cough was loud and harsh, and once it started, she could not breathe. It took several seconds, which felt to Sid like hours, until she caught her breath again.

"Not much farther, luv," he said. She nodded listlessly, too sick to care how far it was.

When the carriage stopped, Sid got out, handed Ella down, and then her basket. Then he lifted the little girl out. She leaned her head against his chest and closed her eyes. Together he and Ella made their way up the steps to India's flat.

Ella knocked. There was no answer. She knocked again. Nothing.

"I told you. She won't even come to the door now. The only one who goes in and out is Lytton. And her sister. They have keys."

Sid handed the girl to Ella. He knew she could carry the weight, for the girl was frighteningly light. He reached into his pocket and pulled out a hairpin and a dentist's pick.

"I'm not seeing this," Ella said.

"Good."

Within seconds he had the door open. He carried the large basket of food they'd brought inside. There was brisket in it. Barley soup. Fresh bread. Half a dozen side dishes. He'd cleaned out the Moskowitzes' café.

Ella carried the girl inside and put her down on India's settee. She rewrapped her blanket to make sure she was warm.

"Freddie," a weak voice called from the bedroom. "Is that you?"

"No, luv. It's me, Ella."

"Ella? Who let you in?"

"The . . . uh . . . landlady did. I'm not here to stay . . . I . . . um . . . just brought your things from . . . um . . . Dr. Gifford's."

Sid rolled his eyes. "Criminal mastermind, you," he said quietly.

"Thank you, Ella. Put them anywhere. You can let yourself out?" India asked.

"Oh, aye," Ella shouted. "Will you be all right?" she whispered to Sid.

He nodded and bade her good-bye. Then he took a deep breath and walked into India's bedroom. She was in her bed, her back toward him. Evening light from the single window washed over her. She did not turn at the sound of his steps.

"What is it, Ella?"

"I'm not Ella."

India gasped, then sat up. "What are you doing here?"

"Jesus Christ," Sid said softly, shocked by the sight of her face. He sat down on her bed.

"Sid, I must ask that you leave," she protested, gathering the bedclothes around her.

"Be quiet." He leaned forward and gently felt the bone beneath her right eye. "You're lucky he didn't smash the socket." He parted the collar of her nightgown and inspected the bruises on her neck. "Actually, you're lucky you aren't dead."

"It's nothing, really," she said bitterly. "He came out the loser, believe you me. I killed his wife and child."

Her collarbones were sharp beneath her skin. She had lost a good deal of weight. Sid was no doctor, but he knew why. It was a condition he was all too familiar with. She was being eaten alive by guilt. He released the fabric of her gown and she quickly buttoned her collar.

"Why are you here?"

"I have a little girl with me," he said. "She's in the other room. She's very ill. I know her mother. She can't afford a doctor."

"Maybe she can't, but you can. There are doctors in East London. You didn't have to bring the child all the way to Bloomsbury."

"I wanted someone good."

"I'm sorry, I'm not practicing any more. I can't help you."

"It's not me who's asking for help. It's the little one in the next room."

"Didn't you hear me?" she snapped. "I said I've stopped practicing. I've left Gifford's. I'm finished."

Sid stood and in one swift motion ripped the bedclothes off her. "Get up out of there. Right now."

India refused; she scrabbled for the sheets. Sid took hold of her arms and lifted her out of bed.

"What are you doing?" she screeched. "Stop it!"

He marched her into her sitting room. The child sat motionless on the settee. Her face was white. Her breathing was labored. Her eyes sought India's, pleading.

"Tell her," Sid said, pushing India forward. "Tell *her* that you quit."

"This is blackmail," she hissed.

"Whatever it takes."

"I need my instruments. My bag. I don't have it anymore."

Sid went to the door and picked up the black leather bag Ella had placed on the floor. "I got it back," he said, handing it to her.

"How?"

"Put the word about. Found out Shakes had pawned it."

"Who?"

"The old toe-rag whose gin you were swilling. On a bench outside the underground station. Or so I heard."

India colored. She snatched the bag. "Do you think I might have my wrapper? For decency's sake?" she asked.

Sid went to get her robe, but when he came back into the sitting room she impatiently waved it aside. She'd begun her examination and was barely aware of him. The little girl—Jessie was her name—didn't even react as she took her temperature, her pulse, and then peered into her eyes, nose, and throat. Then, as India was listening to her chest, Jessie began to cough and could not stop. Her face reddened; her eyes grew large with fear as she struggled for air, and then came a harsh, sucking gasp.

"It's whooping cough," India said.

She dug in her bag, pulled out a pad of paper and a pen, and started scribbling. Sid looked at the little girl. The paroxysm of coughing had stopped. The child was slumped over onto the arm of the settee. Her eyes were closed and her skin was slick with sweat. He felt frightened for her. India tore off two sheets from her pad and handed them to him.

"Take these to Dixon's the chemist's on Tottenham Court Road. While he's filling them, walk three or four shops west to Worth's Hardware and buy me four bamboo poles. Each four feet high. Hurry."

Ronnie was waiting outside in the carriage and Sid was able to get what India needed and get back to her flat quickly. When he returned, a tea kettle was steaming in the kitchen and India had taken Jessie into her bedroom. She was lying well bundled in India's bed. A small table with a porcelain basin had been positioned at her feet.

"I need you," she said when she saw Sid. He gave her the bottles from Dixon's and she handed him a ball of twine and told him to lash the bamboo poles to the four sides of the bed. While he was doing so, she gave the child a dose from one of the bottles. It was quinine; Sid had seen the label. As soon as he had the poles secured, she draped two sheets over them to make a tent. Then she poured some oil from the second bottle into a basin. Immediately the room smelled of eucalyptus. She disappeared and returned with the kettle. Ducking into the tent, she poured the steaming water into the basin, then quickly came back out.

"You all right in there, Jessie?" she said.

"It's awfully foggy, miss," came the weak reply.

India smiled. "It's good for you. Close your eyes and breathe it in."

"I'm afraid. What if it starts me coughing?"

"It's all right to cough, Jessie. It's scary, I know, but it's all right. Try to stay as calm as you can when it's happening."

There was a silence, then a disbelieving "All right, miss."

"You're going to get better. I promise. The medicine and the steam will help you. It may take a day or two, but you'll be well and back home before you know it."

There was no answer.

"Do you believe me, Jessie?"

"Yes, miss." The child's voice was stronger this time, and hopeful.

"Good. Try to rest. I'll be back in shortly to add more hot water. We'll try a bit of hot soup later if you can manage it."

"Thank you, miss."

India waved Sid out of the bedroom. He walked to the sitting room with his hands in his pockets and sat down. India followed and took a seat across from him.

"She'll have to stay here," she said. "She's too delicate to move."

"I'll pay whatever it costs. Buy whatever she needs."

"I'll help her, Sid," India said. "But this doesn't change anything. I'm not going to practice anymore. I can do more good on a parliamentary committee. Working on public health reform."

"Who told you that? Freddie?"

"Nobody told me anything. I arrived at the decision myself."

Sid was silent for a few seconds, then he said, "India, it's not your fault."

She was on her feet immediately, her hands balled into fists. "How the *hell* would you know that?" she cried angrily. "Are you an expert in obstetrics now, Sid? Read your Simpson and Kelly, have you? Know your Blundell?"

"No," he said, calm and unblinking in the face of her fury, "but I know you."

She stared at him, her face a mixture of anger and anguish, then slumped down into her seat again, her shoulders bent, her hands knotted. "Have you ever seen the light go out of a newborn baby's eyes?" she asked. "All that beauty, that hope . . . gone . . ."

Sid leaned forward in his chair and took her hands in his. *"It's not your fault."*

She made as if to pull away, then instead she gripped his hands. Hard. He was surprised again by the strength in those small hands. A droplet of water fell onto his hands and then another. She looked up at him and he saw that her cheeks were wet. Her gray eyes were large and luminous with tears.

"I'm sorry. I don't . . . I don't do this. I don't cry. I don't . . ." And then she leaned her head against him and wept. He felt her shoulders shudder as a torrent of emotion gripped her, heard the sobs wrench themselves out of her. He said nothing, just held her close, giving her his strength until she found her own again.

"It hurts. Oh God, how it hurts," she said, lifting her head. "Elizabeth Adams and Emma Milo and Alison Coburn and her baby . . . I'm sorry. For all of them. I'm so sorry."

"Then don't give up. For their sake, India, don't give up. If you do, you leave those women to the Dr. Giffords of the world."

"But I'm no good."

"You *are* good. You're just not perfect, that's all. You want to be. Perfect and right. But you're not. No one is. Except me."

India gave a weak laugh. Sid smiled.

"Ella brought food," Sid said. "Would you like some? You're very thin."

"No. Later, perhaps. Not now."

"A cup of tea? I could make you one."

"No."

"Your wrapper? You must be cold."

"Sid?"

"Aye?"

"Can I have this? Just this?" she asked, squeezing his hands.

He nodded wordlessly. And squeezed back.

CHAPTER 37

Freddie lifted his whisky glass to his lips and drained it. He waited for the alcohol to make him feel warm and relaxed, pleased with himself and the world, but it did nothing. He put the glass down, then looked at the girl's head between his legs, bobbing up and down. His fingers twined themselves in her hair, pulling her closer.

"Harder," he said.

The girl—she was no more than seventeen—gagged. Her small hand knotted itself in the bedsheets. Freddie leaned back, trying to give himself over to her tongue, her lips, but it was no good. He picked up his whisky glass and took another slug. He heard the hecklers at the speech he'd given in Stepney yesterday. Heard the harsh questions fired at him by reporters.

"Harder, I said. Didn't you hear me?" He tightened his fingers in her hair. The girl whimpered.

He barely heard her. Instead, he heard Isabelle thundering at him. He'd been summoned to Berkeley Square again. Just that morning.

"You said she'd given up her position, Freddie. You told me she'd resigned. But I saw Maud yesterday and she told me that India had been beaten by some drunken lunatic. My daughter—your fiancée—*beaten*! Maud told me she's back at Dr. Gifford's surgery and forging ahead with plans to open a clinic for paupers. This is absolutely intolerable!"

"Isabelle, please," he'd said, trying to soothe her. "It's only a temporary situation."

"I see I've made a terrible mistake. I see that my confidence has been entirely misplaced."

"That's not fair. And it's not true. India was going to resign, but—"

"I'm not interested in excuses. Either get the job done *now* or I will approach someone else. I hear young Winston Churchill's quite ambitious. And quite poor thanks to his spendthrift mother. Ambition and poverty are powerful motivators, but I don't have to tell you that, do I, Freddie? I wonder what Winston would say to a Mayfair townhouse and twenty thousand a year?"

He'd left Berkeley Square in a towering rage and had gone straight to the Reform Club to cool off with a drink or two. But there he'd been taken aside by the manager and informed that if his bill was not settled by the end of the month, his membership would be terminated. He owed them nearly three hundred pounds. He'd called the man a few choice names then headed to a Cleveland Street brothel, run by a discreet woman named Nora. He'd gone there a few times before when Gemma was unavailable. He went a lot more often now. He'd thought to spend the afternoon with Winnie, his favorite, but she wasn't available. So he'd chosen a new girl— Alice—hoping that with her help he could shut out his failing campaign, Isabelle, India . . . and Wish. Most of all Wish.

But it wasn't working.

"For God's sake, get off," he said now, pushing her away. "Where in blazes is Winnie?"

"Off to the country. It's her holidays," Alice said. "Would you . . . would you like some more to drink?" she asked timidly, gathering a silk kimono about her.

Freddie nodded. She hurried to a table in the corner of the room where glasses and bottles stood. She was anxious, upset. He couldn't have cared less. What were a whore's feelings to him now? What was anything, or anyone, to him now? He had killed his best friend. A man he'd grown up with. One he had loved like a brother.

His heart, the tiny piece that was left of it, clenched in pain.

There had been others, of course. He'd killed his father, but he had not grieved long over it, for there had been no other way. If he hadn't, the man might have killed Daphne. And there was Hugh Mullins. That wasn't his fault. Not really. He hadn't meant for Hugh to die. He never thought he would. He'd only wanted him to go to prison for a bit, long enough for India to forget about him.

Now there was Wish, and there was no rationalizing his death. He'd done it out of anger and purely for advantage—his own. Wish had made him furious with his meddling. He'd listened to him talk about raising money for India's clinic, and he'd listened to him encourage her to postpone their wedding date yet again. And then he couldn't listen anymore. He'd challenged Wish to a race, simply to break up his and India's conversation. But once they were in the woods, Wish spotted the fox. He got his pistol out to shoot the animal, then found he couldn't and asked Freddie to do it. And Freddie, seeing his chance, just as he had with Hugh, took the gun and shot him instead. He'd watched Wish's head explode in a shower of blood, watched him fall out of his saddle to the ground. And then, weeping real tears, he'd leaped down, pulled the ring off Wish's twitching hand, and curled his fingers around the pistol.

When the others arrived, he was genuinely in shock. He blurted out that Wish had been having financial difficulties, that he'd pawned his ring. It was partly true. There *were* some financial difficulties. Wish had confided as much to him earlier that morning, but he'd also said they were typical of new businesses and would resolve themselves.

Freddie knew he should've felt grief, horror, and shock over what he'd done. And he had, at first. But they'd faded, and relief had taken their place. Wish was dead, and without him, without his financial know-how and his connections, India's clinic would die, too. He wasn't fearful about being discovered. No one even suspected he'd had a hand in Wish's death—why would they? The only evidence—Wish's ring—was safely hidden inside his music box.

The Red Earl's words echoed inside his mind: *rip out thine own heart* . . .

"I've almost succeeded, old boy," he whispered. "Nearly there."

"What's that?" the girl said.

"Nothing," Freddie replied tightly. "Where's that whisky?"

"Here it is," she said, handing him a glass.

As she climbed back into bed, Freddie's thoughts returned to Isabelle and India. He could not understand what had happened. Only a fortnight ago India had agreed to resign from Gifford's.

He'd been *positive* he'd convinced her to give up practicing. So sure, in fact, that when Bingham said he'd be short again this month on Freddie's allowance, Freddie, in a fit of pique, had told him to stuff his money. He'd told him that he'd soon have twenty thousand a year and the Selwyn Jones townhouse, thanks to Isabelle. And then, only a few days later, he'd gone to visit India and had found a sick child in her bedroom. She wouldn't go into detail about how the girl had gotten there, saying only that a friend had brought her. This same friend, it appeared, had also convinced her not to resign. It was that interfering Ella Moskowitz, damn her. Who else could it be?

And not only was she back at Gifford's, but she was sounding more zealous than ever about her clinic. She and Ella were talking about taking over the fund-raising themselves. She still wanted to take tea with Princess Beatrice. They'd even found a reliable and discreet supplier of birth control, she'd said. She wouldn't tell him who it was, but he knew, thanks to Gemma. It was Sid Malone. India and Ella were using the goods he'd supplied at Varden Street. Very quietly, of course. If Gifford ever found out, there'd be hell to pay.

Freddie rubbed his temples. He'd been so close—so very close—to getting all that he wanted, but despite his best efforts India still hadn't been brought to heel. Emotion rose in him, a combustible mixture of anger and panic, at the thought of losing her dowry. He couldn't let that happen. He'd be finished if he did. There had to be *something* he wasn't thinking of, something he wasn't seeing, some way to derail her plans once and for all.

He thought of the Red Earl again. Richard Lytton would have found a way out of this, he thought. But then again, the Red Earl would never have let things get into so dire a state in the first place. Freddie could picture the cruel face, the mocking eyes, and for an instant he imagined the derision there was aimed at him and him alone. The thought shamed him. And infuriated him.

"I saw a show the other day, me. A musical revue," Alice suddenly said, interrupting his thoughts.

He turned to her. "I couldn't possibly care less," he said, handing her his empty glass.

"I'm sorry. You seem bothered. And me mum always said that talking about your problems helps. She said—"

"Do me a favor, will you?" Freddie said acidly. "Keep your mouth shut and your legs open."

Alice swallowed. She opened her wrapper and lay down on the bed. "Don't lie there like a dead fish," he said. "I've one of those in my life already. Make me hard, Alice. Make me forget. For Christ's sake, make me come. Touch me. Touch yourself. Do *something*."

Alice spread her legs. Her fingers disappeared inside herself. She gave a moan. A stage moan.

Freddie looked at himself, soft and limp. "It's not working, Alice. Nothing's happening. What are we going to do about that, eh?"

"I'm sorry," she said, sitting up. "You won't tell Nora, will you?" She reached for him, tugging at him so hard it hurt.

"Ow!" he shouted. "You useless bitch!" He slapped her. Hard. He didn't mean to, it was a reflex, but Alice burst into tears. The sound of her sobs didn't soften him, though; they made him angrier. He grabbed her by the neck and shook her. "Stop it!" he ordered. "Stop it right now!"

She struggled against him. "Please, don't hurt me," she rasped. Her eyes were large and frightened and Freddie finally felt himself stiffen.

He *wanted* to hurt someone. Badly. He needed somewhere for the anger to go. He wanted to hurt India. And Isabelle. And Gemma. He wanted to smash Joe Bristow and Sid Malone. But he couldn't. All he had was Alice. So she would have to do.

A few minutes later, when he had finished, he lay back on the bed, sipping his whisky and smoking. He felt calm, almost peaceful. Alice had gone behind a screen. He heard her washing and sniffling.

"You done there?" he called. "Get some fresh water, will you? I'd like a wash up myself."

There was another sniffle. More splashing. "I'm sure you're clean enough by now. How about that water?"

As he said it, he suddenly wondered if she *was* clean. He realized, with horror, that he hadn't used a johnny. He always used one with Winnie, but he'd been so distracted this time, he'd forgotten. Christ, what if he'd caught something? He'd never had the clap and he didn't want it now.

How would he explain *that* to India?

He swore. Thinking about rubber johnnies reminded him of his money troubles again. He got his from Payne's, a chemists, and they wanted him to settle his account, too. Their boy had actually been round to his flat the other day asking for payment. He didn't have it. He was short. Again. He'd have to find another source.

Who else has rubber johnnies? he wondered, and then he laughed aloud as he remembered India did. I'll ask her, he thought, chuckling. And then he stopped chuckling and sat straight up in bed. He'd had an idea. A brilliant, flawless, foolproof idea.

"Alice!" he shouted.

There was no reply, then a small, broken, "What?"

"Stop blubbing, will you, and come here. I've a job for you. A good one. I'll pay you five quid and you can keep your knickers on."

CHAPTER 38

"Where are they?"

India, surprised by the angry voice, looked up from her casebook. Dr. Gifford was standing in the doorway to the Varden Street examination room.

"I beg your pardon, sir?" she said.

"The contraceptives. I know they're here. Where have you hidden them?"

India's heart lurched. How on earth had he found out? She had sworn every patient who'd asked for devices to secrecy.

"I was visited in my Harley Street office this morning by a Mrs. Elizabeth Little. She is the mother of Alice Little, one of your patients. Mrs. Little was furious. She informed me that her daughter came to you here requesting a contraceptive device and that you supplied it. Is this true, Dr. Jones?"

India remembered Alice Little. She'd said that she was married, that she had three children and couldn't afford anymore.

"It is, sir," she said. She did not like Dr. Gifford, but she had never lied to him and would not start now. "If you'll allow me to explain . . ."

"There is nothing to explain. Miss Little is nineteen years old, unmarried, and mentally unsound. Her mother says she is promiscuous. A nymphomaniac, Dr. Jones. And you have encouraged her in her illness. I will ask you once more, where are they?"

"Alice Little *has* had children, Dr. Gifford. I performed an exam."

"You may clear out your desk. I will not be requiring your services any longer."

India felt as if she'd been slapped. She was being dismissed. She would have no job, no income. For a few seconds she couldn't speak. "But Dr. Gifford, why?" she said, finally finding her voice.

"You know perfectly well why. You know that I do not sanction the use of contraceptives. Sexual congress is solely for the creation of children. That is God's plan."

"Then why do so many of those children die? Is *that* part of God's plan?" she said. The words were out of her, sudden and sharp, before she could stop them. That was happening more frequently now, since her breakdown, but their vehemence still startled her. It startled Dr. Gifford, too.

"They die because of the slovenliness, drunkenness, and idleness of their parents," he retorted.

India laughed. Two months ago she might have said the same thing. Before Whitechapel. Before Miss Milo and tiny Harry Coburn. Before Sid.

"Dr. Gifford, have you ever seen a mother of six try to raise her children in two small rooms?" she asked, rising from her chair. "How is she to keep them clean with no money to buy coal to heat water? How is she to feed them on a pound a week?"

"Do not change the subject. The use of contraceptives is immoral. It's unconscionable to dispense these devices to any woman, never mind to one who is unmarried and unstable."

India came around the desk. "What is unconscionable, sir, is your refusal to acknowledge the suffering caused to women by constant childbearing and to their children by chronic poverty."

"That will be all, Dr. Jones. You will be hearing from the authorities at the British Medical Association. I intend to have your license revoked. Leave my premises immediately."

"You . . . you wouldn't do that. You can't!" India whispered, stunned.

"What's going on here? What's happened? Dr. Gifford? Dr. Jones?"

It was Ella, wide-eyed. She was standing in the doorway clutching a pile of folders. India knew what they were—the records of recently deceased patients. Once a month Ella brought them to her or to Dr. Gifford to review and sign before packing them off to storage.

India couldn't reply to Ella and Gifford didn't deign to.

"I should never have hired you, Dr. Jones," he said acidly. "Your judgment is deplorable. I did so only because your dean begged me to."

Anger surged inside India—anger at the injustice of his remarks, at his archaic morality, at his careless treatment of his patients—and again the words came tumbling out of her before she could bite them back. "You did it only because you could pay me less than my male colleagues and work me harder," India said. "We're seeing four times as many patients here now as when I started. They come because of me. Not you . . . *me.*"

Ella's jaw dropped.

Gifford shook his head in disgust. "This is what comes of allowing women to study medicine. This insolence . . ."

India's anger at Gifford exploded into rage. "And this"—she said, striding over to Ella—"*this* is what comes of allowing men to practice it."

She snatched a folder from the top of the pile and opened it.

"James, Suzannah. Thirty-one years of age," she read, her voice shaking with anger. "Five children. Tears suffered at her last delivery—performed by *you,* with forceps—resulting fistula rendered her incontinent and incapable of intercourse. Abandoned by her husband, committed suicide.

"Rosen, Rachael. Twenty-five. Admitted to the lying-in ward of London Hospital July twenty-fourth. Delivered of twin boys same day. Contracted puerperal fever July twenty-sixth. Died three days later. Weinstein, Tovuh. Admitted July nineteenth, died July twenty-seventh. Puerperal fever. Biggs, Amanda. Died August first. Puerperal fever. Three in a week, and all your patients. Tell me, Dr. Gifford, did you wash your hands after Rachael? After Tovuh? And Amanda? Who else did you infect? I guess we'll find that out next week."

"See here, Dr. Jones . . ." Gifford spluttered.

India opened another folder. "Johnson, Elsa. Protracted labor. Ergot administered. Twice. Fetus stillborn. Symptoms consistent with overdose."

"Dr. Jones—"

"Randall, Laura. Twenty-two. Delivered of a girl. Incomplete delivery of placenta. Septicemia resulting. Died July sixth. Infant malnourished. Died July fourteenth."

"Dr. Jones, that is enough!" Gifford roared.

India stopped reading. She looked him in the eye and said, "Take my license and I promise you that I will do everything I can—*everything*—to see that you lose yours."

"Give me those folders."

"You'll have to knock me down first."

Ella gasped.

"You forget that you are very much a *junior* doctor. The BMA won't listen to you. They'd never revoke my license based on your accusations."

"Maybe not, but at the very least I'll cost you patients. Here and at Harley Street. Lost patients means lost fees, and that's what really matters to you, isn't it, Dr. Gifford? I'll take these files to the *Clarion, The Times,* the *Gazette.* I'll make certain your wealthy patients find out how carelessly you treat their poorer sisters. Worse yet, I'll make them wonder if you wash your hands before you come to see *them.*"

Gifford blanched. "Get out!" he hissed. "Now!"

India grabbed her coat from the hook behind the door, picked up her bag, and left—with the files tucked firmly under her arm. As she headed down the staircase she heard Gifford call, "Sister Moskowitz, where are you going?"

"Out the bloody door!" Ella shouted. "If she goes, I go." She came flying out the front door as India was standing on the pavement, fumbling the files into her bag.

"Ella, what are you doing?" she asked her.

"Quitting."

"You can't!"

"Too late." She started toward the High Street, pulling India after her. "Come on. This way," she said.

"Where are we going? To the restaurant?"

"No. To a pub. It's not soup we need now, it's alcohol." She led India across Varden Street. After five minutes' walk they were at the Blind Beggar.

"Sit there," Ella told her, pointing to the corner. She went to the bar and India settled herself at a table. Her heart was hammering in her chest and her body had gone cold. She wondered if she was in shock.

Ella returned and set two pints of porter down on the table.

"Good God, what have I done?" India said. "I've lost my position. And I've lost you yours. How will we live? Pay our bills? What are we going to do?"

"We'll just have to find ourselves new positions," Ella said, pulling up a stool.

India laughed mirthlessly. "That shouldn't be a problem. I'm sure Dr. Gifford will give us glowing references."

Ella sat down heavily and picked up her drink. "Well, Doctor. I've really got to hand it to you. Blackmail, intimidation, theft—I think you broke more laws in ten minutes than Sid Malone has all year."

India covered her face with her hands. "You're right. What have I done? Yelling. Threatening. Stealing files. My God, Ella, what have I become?"

"A human being. At last!" Ella said, laughing. She touched her glass to India's. "Cheers!"

CHAPTER 39

"Well, well, well. If it ain't young Francis Betts."

Frankie whirled around. It was dark. There was a gas lamp on the street, but it was ten yards away. Usually the Taj's own lamps were lit, but not tonight. Donaldson's men had raided the place yesterday. They'd broken everything they could, arrested Susie and the girls.

"Who is it?" he growled, squinting into the darkness. "Who's there?"

Three figures stepped out of the gloom. Big Billy Madden and two of his men—Delroy Lawson and Mickey McGregor.

"What are you doing, Frankie? You a charlady now?" Del asked, nodding at the mop and bucket he was carrying. The bucket was full of kitchen garbage that had been forgotten and left to rot. Frankie had been taking it to the curb for the nightmen to collect. "Uh, oh. Looks like someone dropped the soap," Mickey said, giggling.

"Bend over and pick it up, will you, Bettsie?" That was Del again.

A split second later the bucket went over Del's head, and then Del and the bucket went flying into the Taj's brick wall. Del fell to the ground, trying to claw the bucket off. He quickly pulled it back down, however, when Frankie started to kick it.

"Still laughing, Ding Dong? Stand up, you cunt. Stand up and laugh some more. Come on!" Frankie shouted.

"Don't call me Ding Dong!" Del shouted, his words muffled by the bucket.

Frankie would have stomped the bucket—and Del's head—to splinters, if Mickey hadn't come up behind him and pulled him off. Frankie struggled, but Mickey held him fast, arms pinned behind his back.

"All right, boys. That's enough," Billy said. "Calm yourself down, Frankie. We meant no harm. If Mickey lets you go, you promise to behave yourself? Have a think before you answer. There's one of you and three of us."

Frankie made one last effort to heave Mickey off. When he saw he couldn't budge him, he nodded curtly.

"All right, Mick," Billy said.

Frankie straightened his jacket. "What do you want?" he snarled.

"You, Francis."

"I'm flattered, Billy, truly. But I'm not that kind of bloke."

Billy ignored the remark. "Rumor has it Malone's losing his grip," he said. "First the Bark gets raided. Then the Taj."

Frankie shrugged. "It happens," he said. "Susie took a beating, but she kept shtum. Said she ran a lodging house, not a whorehouse. Coppers can't get anyone else to say different."

Billy looked up at the Taj. "Then why isn't the Taj open?"

"We're redecorating. Fancy a new color scheme."

"I heard Sid took a thousand quid out of this place a week. Maybe that's nothing to him. He's got more money than God, right? But what about your cut? What about you, Frankie?"

"I'm fine, thanks. Just rolling in it, me."

"But what of your talent, lad? Your skill? Likely lad like yourself oughtn't to be taking out rubbish, should he?"

Frankie bristled with embarrassment. He'd been thinking the very same thing. "I just came to check on the place is all," he said.

"So you're a watchman now? That ain't right. And from what I hear, it's not just you. Tommy, Ronnie, Oz, Desi—Del says they're in the Bark every evening. Just sitting on their arses. Sid's a businessman, right? Or so he likes to say. But as far as I can see, he ain't taking care of business. So what do you say?"

Frankie smiled. "I say go to hell, Billy."

Madden shook his head. He looked pained. "That was stupid, Frankie. Very stupid. Mickey, Del, teach our young friend here some manners."

But Mickey and Del never got the chance to teach Frankie anything.

There were villains who had to work up their anger in order to become violent. Men who went about the darkest side of their business reluctantly and clumsily. For Frankie, it was just the opposite. Violence was his calling, his art—and there was nothing he liked more than a chance to express himself.

Before Billy had even finished speaking, Frankie had turned, and smoothly, swiftly, even gracefully, thrown a punch to Mickey's windpipe. As the man staggered backward, he leaped at Del, grabbed his lapels, and kneed him in the balls. Del fell to his knees screaming, then vomited his supper onto the cobbles.

"School's closed, Billy," Frankie said. "Sod off back to Hammersmith. Don't come round here no more."

Billy shook his head. "Malone's not worth it, lad. No one is. I'm coming. You know that, don't you?"

"I'm happy for you, Billy. Want me handkerchief?"

For a few seconds Madden was silent, then he said, "Teddy Ko buy any hop off you lately?" He waited for an answer, but Frankie didn't give him one. "Didn't think so. Know why? Because he's buying from Georgie Fook now. Georgie's got his own connections in Canton. Bringing in loads of the stuff in the bottom of tea chests. Got himself quite a gang these days, too, and they're making a play for Limehouse. Better keep an eye on Whitechapel, too, mate. Max Moses and his madmen beat the publican down the Beggar silly last night. Told him he was to pay *them* now, not Sid. Why, Frankie, you look surprised!"

Frankie, never good at hiding his emotion, tried for a neutral expression, but Madden's words had unnerved him. He'd heard about the beating at the Beggar and he'd told Sid just last week that Ko was too quiet. But Sid had done nothing, just buggered off west with some sick kiddie in his carriage. He should've put paid to Ko and Moses. And he should put paid to Billy Madden, too, for standing here bold as brass in his manor. But he wouldn't. Because Madden was right. He'd become weak. Or barmy. Or both.

"It's coming apart, Frankie. Can't you see that? Malone's played out and everyone knows it."

"Shut up, Billy," Frankie warned, but Billy didn't.

"The Chinese, the Italians, the Jews, they're all circling. They all want a piece. Not me. I want the whole thing. And I want you. I'll need a man like you and I'll make it worth your while. Think on it, Frankie. Malone's a sinking ship. Don't let him take you down with him." He turned to his men and barked, "You two! Get up! You're a disgrace, the both of you."

As Del and Mickey gathered themselves, rain began to patter on the cobbles. There was a dull rumble of thunder.

Madden held his palm up. "Storm's coming, Francis," he said. He fixed Frankie with his soulless gaze, then smiled. "See that you don't get caught in it."

CHAPTER 40

India set her teacup into its saucer. She gave a small, bitter laugh, then said, "My God, it never rains but it pours."

"Are you all right, Dr. Jones?" Andrew Spence asked.

"No, I am not."

"Can I get you something to drink? Something a bit stronger, perhaps?"

"Yes, please. After all, it's not every day you find yourself ruined."

India was sitting in the offices of Haddon & Spence, Solicitors, with Maud, Bingham, and Robert Selwyn Jones, Wish's father. They had been summoned to hear the reading of Wish's will. Freddie was to have been with them, but work had prevented him from coming.

Andrew Spence, Wish's solicitor, had informed the assembly that they would be inheriting no monies or personal effects, as the estate would be auctioned to satisfy the claims of Wish's creditors. Then he'd told them that India would be receiving the title to 1,200 acres of ranch-land and an abandoned farmhouse on Point Reyes in Marin County, California.

"Lovely land, I'm told. Bordering a place called Drakes Bay. Quite close to the headlands, as the ordnance survey shows. Stunning view of the water," Spence had said, pushing the map across the desk.

India had glanced at it. It was all wavy lines and numbers and meant nothing to her. "But what about the money?" she'd asked.

"Money?"

"The money I gave to my cousin to invest in the land. Might I have that back, please? Instead of the land?"

"I'm afraid that's impossible."

"But why?"

"Because the money's been *spent*," Spence said slowly, as if speaking to a simpleton. "Your cousin used it to purchase the land. That is the bad news. The good news is that the deed to the land is now yours. You are— *were*—business partners in the Bluffs, a resort hotel that was to be built on the Point Reyes property. Your cousin has since passed away. You survived him. Therefore, as his partner, the land goes to you."

"So there is no money. None at all," India said, still unable to comprehend what the man was telling her: that her money—all of it—was gone.

"There's a little bit of cash, or rather there will be after Mr. Jones's various investments are liquidated, his automobile is sold, his furniture, etcetera—but I'm afraid it will go to settle his debts. His creditors have a claim on the proceeds of his estate. He owes a particularly large amount to a builder whom he engaged to begin work on the hotel. That payment"—he consulted the papers in front of him—"was for ten thousand dollars, and unfortunately it is not refundable. The builder informed us that he used the bulk of it to hire teams and laborers for foundation work. The hole is dug, I'm afraid. In more ways than one. His claim is only the first of a dozen or so that must be satisfied from the proceeds of your cousin's estate."

"And I don't have a claim on the estate?"

"No, you're not a creditor, Dr. Jones," Spence said patiently. "You're a business partner. You *gave* him your money to invest on your behalf. He doesn't owe you goods or services as a result. According to the contract between the two of you, the idea was that once he'd taken his company public, he would buy you out. But sadly that has not happened." He smiled patronizingly. "Those are the risks we must accept when we invest."

Spence rose and bustled about his office offering everyone more brandy. They all accepted except for Wish's father. He kissed his nieces and left. India watched him go and her heart ached for him. He was a broken man after the death of his only child, and rarely left his home now.

The coroner had ruled Wish's death accidental, but India knew her uncle worried that his son had taken his own life. She worried about that possibility, too. Freddie had taken her out to supper a few nights ago, to cheer her up after Gifford dismissed her, and they'd talked about it. She'd tried to tell herself—and him—that suicide was unthinkable. Wish would never do such a thing. It wasn't in his nature. He'd had money troubles before, plenty of times, and he'd always weathered them, but then Freddie had reminded her about Wish's ring. It was given to an ancestor of Wish's mother's, a naval captain, by Lord Nelson himself, and had the Nelson family crest on it surrounded by a ring of diamonds. Wish had valued the ring highly, and often said he would never part with it.

"His troubles must have been very bad indeed—or at least he believed them to be. He would never have given the ring up otherwise," Freddie had said, and India had found herself reluctantly agreeing. Wish had adored that ring. Her uncle Robert had asked for it after his death and had been shocked, and heartsick, to learn it had been pawned.

Spence sat down behind his desk again, then said, "At least your cousin had no other business partners, Dr. Jones. Only yourself. Therefore the land need not be subdivided. There will be no protracted legal wrangles over who gets how many acres. You're quite lucky, you know."

India shook her head. *Lucky* was not the first word she would have used. Destitute was a better choice. I can sell the land, she thought. But how? And to whom? It was terribly remote, accessible only by a long carriage ride down a bad road from a train station in the middle of nowhere. Wish said the owner had been trying to sell it for years before he'd bought it. It would probably take her years to resell it.

"India, did you give him everything?" Maud asked.

"Yes."

"My God, how could you be so foolish?"

"I thought I could make money for my clinic."

"You and this damned clinic!" Maud said angrily, her voice raised. "It's not enough that you poke around in guts and muck . . ."

India did not want a lecture now. She felt as if she were holding on by only a thread, and the thread might snap any second. She had just gotten back on her feet after Wish's death, and after her beating at the hands of Fred Coburn. She'd lost her position with Dr. Gifford, and now she'd lost all her money, too. What would she tell Ella? She tried to calm herself. At least they still had the donors' money. It was in an account in Barings Bank, in the clinic's name, and was not affected by Wish's death.

"It's not enough that you expose yourself to every disgusting disease, or that you were nearly beaten to death . . ."

"Maud, please," India said, irritated. She was trying to think of what she was going to do for money, how she was going to keep the clinic going, and all Maud wanted to do was scold.

"Don't *Maud, please* me, India! I saw you! Your eyes were swollen shut. Your face was fifty shades of purple. Freddie said it was insanity, and he was right." There was a brief silence, then she added, "You're totally ruined. You'll have to give up your flat. You'll live with me, of course."

"Thank you, Maud, truly. But you *know* that won't work. We'd be at each other in ten minutes."

"I don't know why you would say that."

"Teddy Ko. Limehouse."

Maud glared. "Oh, *you're* a fine one to talk about self-destructive habits."

"You know how I feel about it," India began.

Maud cut her off. "What if I were to give you some money?"

"There would be strings attached, I'm sure."

"India, how very rude you are! I'm trying to help you!"

"You were raised by the same mother as I was, and you know as well as I do that where money is concerned there are always strings."

"What strings? I would simply give it to you!"

India gave her a look. "And this money could be used to open a clinic?"

"I was rather thinking you might use it to establish a private practice. In Harley Street."

"You see? Strings."

"You're impossible! I don't know why you won't let me help you," Maud said.

"Is Harley Street your idea of help, Maud? It's the last place I would go!"

India was on her feet now. Maud's expression was thunderous.

Bingham, distressed, looked anxiously between the two angry women.

"Here, Maud old mole, have another," he said, grabbing Spence's brandy. "Indy, you too. Sit down. Calm down. You're upset. Neither of you is thinking straight." He poured, then sat on the edge of Spence's desk. He stayed that way for a few minutes, biting his thumb. Then he said, "You've blown this all out of proportion. You're *not* ruined, India. Of course you're not."

India raised an eyebrow. "I'm not?" she said.

"No, aren't you forgetting something?"

"Am I?"

"Yes! You'll be married soon. And when you are, you'll have the dowry. A very generous one, I might add. That will keep you and Freddie very comfortably, won't it? And then there's the Berkeley Street house."

"Bingham—" Maud began.

"What on *earth* are you talking about?" India finished.

"The London house. *Your* house. Well, yours and Freddie's," he said, smiling, as if that explained everything. He soon saw that it didn't, so he continued. "You know . . . Lady Isabelle's wedding gift."

"*What?*" Maud said, shocked. She turned to her sister. "India, Mama's giving you the London house? Why didn't you tell me?" she asked indignantly.

"Because I didn't know!" India retorted. She sat back in her chair and

tried to take a deep breath, but couldn't. Her corset suddenly felt excru-
ciatingly tight. Had her mother been talking to Freddie about a dowry?
When? Why hadn't he told her? She didn't want anything to do with her
parents' money or their possessions. He knew that. Why had he gone
behind her back?

"You didn't know?" Bingham echoed, confused. And then he went
pale. "Oh, blast. Oh, damn. I've let the cat out of the bag. It must've been
a secret. Freddie probably wanted it kept a surprise. He'll gut me. You
won't tell him I blabbed, will you, Indy? You'll pretend to be surprised,
won't you?"

"I won't have to pretend, Bing. When did he tell you this?"

"A few weeks ago. But I'm sure it's true. He mentioned it again just the
other night. When he told me what had happened to you at Dr. Gifford's.
The mad girl—Alice Little—and her mother. The rubber johnnies and all
that."

Bingham continued talking but India barely heard him. She now felt as
if she couldn't breathe at all. "Bing," she said quietly, "how do you know my
patient's name?"

"What? Oh, um . . . Freddie told me."

"But I never told *him*."

"India, you're making no sense. You *did* tell him. He took you out to
supper to cheer you up—remember? Look, it's been a shocker of a day.
Wish's will. The money. Maybe we should get a spot of lunch."

"No, I never told him my patient's name," she said again, more to herself
than to Bingham. "To do so would violate her privacy. I would never tell
anyone her name."

Maud groaned. "Oh, for God's sake, what does it matter? I saw a Lyons
tea room on the way in. Let's go there."

But tea was the last thing on India's mind. She rose. "I have to go," she
said abruptly. "Now."

"To Lyons? Good. We're coming with you," Maud said.

"No, to see someone. A patient." She rushed to the door and pulled it
open.

"Indy, wait! What's going on? What's wrong?" Bingham called after her.

She turned. Her eyes were huge in her face. Her expression was anguished. "Oh, Bing," she said. "Absolutely everything."

CHAPTER 41

India stood on the steps of 40 Myrtle Walk, a shabby two-up two-down in Hoxton.

"I'm looking for a woman by the name of Little, Alice Little," she said to the man who'd answered the door. "Does she live here?"

The man shook his head. "No one here by that name. You try next door?"

"I've tried every house on the street," India said wearily.

"Sorry, luv," the man said, closing the door.

India walked down the steps, bitterly disappointed. That was that. There was no Alice Little. At least not in Myrtle Walk. Maybe there never had been. For all she knew the woman could have given a false address or name. She stared down the narrow street, wondering what to do next. She wanted to find Alice Little. *Had* to find her. There were things she needed to ask her.

Right after she'd left Maud and Bingham, she'd taken a hackney to Brick Lane. She had no idea where Alice Little lived, but she knew Ella might. The woman had an incredible memory. She knew nearly every patient at Varden Street by face and by name, and often by address, as she was constantly sending them reminders to pay their bills. Alice Little had given Ella no trouble, though. She'd come to Varden Street only once and had paid her bill the same day.

"I remember filing her information," Ella had said, standing outside the café. She'd closed her eyes and pressed her fingers to her forehead.

"Is this a conjuring trick?" India asked.

"Shh! Little, Little, Alice Little. It was Hoxton, I know it was. And flowers, something to do with flowers, I'd teased her about it . . . about the name being wishful thinking." Her eyes snapped open. "Myrtle! Myrtle Walk. That's it. I'm sure of it."

"You're a marvel, Ella, thank you!" India had said, already starting down the street.

"Hold on a mo'! Why are you looking for her?"

"I'll explain later!"

She'd been so certain she'd find Alice in Myrtle Walk. What would she do now? As she stood on the pavement a gas lamp flickered to life above her. Night was coming. She would go home and work out her next step there. She had just begun walking when the door to Number 40 opened again.

"Oi!" the man called. India turned. "You sure she's on Myrtle Walk? The missus says there's also a Myrtle Close."

"Where?"

A scrawny woman, arms folded over her chest, popped out from behind her husband. "Go to the end of this street, straight up Hoxton Street, and turn right on Nuttall Street. It'll be on your left."

"Thank you," India said, heading off.

Fifteen minutes later she arrived—breathless and panting—at Myrtle Close. The streets had grown dingier as she'd walked north and the people on them poorer-looking. The close was tiny and had only nine houses on it—four facing four across a narrow patch of muddy cobbles and one at the end. India started at number 1. She told herself she was only prolonging her fool's errand, but when the blowsy woman at Number 3 who answered her knock said, "Wotcher want with Alice?" she couldn't believe her luck.

"To speak with her. I'm her doctor," India said.

"That right?" the woman asked, eyeing her suspiciously. "Since when have they got lady doctors?"

"Since 1849 when Elizabeth Blackwell graduated from the Geneva Medical School in New York," India said. "May I see Mrs. Little, please?"

The woman snorted. "She ain't no missus. Never will be, neither. Won't find no man to marry her. Men want only one thing from the likes of her."

India smiled tightly, nearly beside herself with impatience. "Might I see her?"

The woman turned and bellowed up the stairs. "Oi! Allie! Someone here for you!"

India heard the sound of a door opening, a baby crying, and then footsteps. A wan young woman whom India immediately recognized came down the stairs. She stopped midway; her eyes widened when she saw India. She was about to flee back up the stairs, when the landlady—glaring at India—said, "Am I a bleedin' doorman? Come in or go out!"

In a flash India was up the steps. She grabbed Alice's arm just as she was about to disappear into her flat.

"Please, miss. I don't want no trouble," Alice said, flinching.

"Nor do I. I just want to talk to you." A baby wailed again from inside the flat. "May I come in?"

The woman nodded.

The flat was one small, dingy room. A choking stink of mutton, onions, and soiled nappies hit India as she entered it. A single kerosene lamp lit the room, throwing its weak light over a table and two chairs, a narrow iron bed and a crib pushed up against the wall. A sad-eyed toddler stood in it on bowed legs, blinking in the gloom. Next to her lay a wailing infant. Alice lifted the baby out of the crib and rocked her. The infant's cries became whimpers. Alice fed her a spoonful of goody—a sop made from bread, water, and sugar—from a bowl on the table. A fly crawled over its rim.

"You're not nursing her?" India asked.

Alice gave India a sullen look. "That wouldn't go over well in my line of work."

"What is your line of work?"

Alice looked at the floor and did not answer.

India sighed. This was not going well. She had so many questions. She needed answers—and she dreaded them. She tried another tack. "Your mother said you live with her. You don't, do you?"

"No. As you can see."

"Alice, your mother came to see Dr. Gifford—my superior—three days after you came to see me. She told him that you are mentally unstable. Is that true?"

Alice laughed bitterly. "Between the punters and the sprogs, I'm sure I am."

"She also reported me for dispensing a contraceptive to you. Dr. Gifford forbids it. I took a huge risk helping you. When your mother told him what I'd done, he dismissed me."

Alice looked at India, stricken. "I'm so sorry, miss! I didn't mean you no harm. I never thought . . . He told us what to do and say, but he didn't tell us *why*. Not me, not Nora neither. I should've figured it was something evil. He's evil."

"Wait, slow down. I don't understand. Who's Nora? Is she your mother? Why did she go to Dr. Gifford?"

Alice shook her head. "She ain't me mum. She's me employer. Me real mum don't speak to me. Lad put me up the spout two years ago. That's how I got Mary, me eldest. Said he was going to marry me, but he buggered off. Me dad threw me out. Nora found me. Put me to work." She paused, then said, "She's a madam, is Nora. So you know what that makes me."

India suddenly felt light-headed. "May I sit?" she asked.

Alice hurriedly pulled out a chair for her. "I'll get you some tea."

"No, thank you," India said woodenly.

Alice bit her lip. She sat down across the table from India. "I'm sorry, miss. Truly I am. I needed the money. He paid us well. Five quid each. But I never would have done it if I'd known you'd get the sack. I swear it."

"Alice . . ." India began, then—losing her nerve—she stopped.

"Yes, miss?"

"You mentioned a *he*. Who is that?"

"A punter."

"Does he have a name?"

"Freddie something. They never tell us their full names."

India felt nauseous. She closed her eyes.

"You all right?"

"Far from it."

When the roiling inside her subsided, India opened her eyes again. "Is he blond? Tall?" she asked.

"Aye."

"Do you see him regularly?"

"Me? No. He only chose me once. When Winnie, his usual girl, wasn't working. That's fine by me. I don't like him. He's a mean bloke. And rough. It hurts with him."

Yes, it does, India thought. "And he *paid* you to do this?" she asked. "He paid you to visit me at Varden Street and for Nora to go to Dr. Gifford posing as your mother?"

"Yes."

India nodded. She felt hollow. It all made sense now—Freddie knowing her patient's name. Bingham's talk of a dowry. The Berkeley Square house. Her mother's involvement. It all made sickening sense.

"Thank you for your help, Alice," India said, rising to leave.

"You won't tell him, will you?" Alice asked. "Freddie, I mean."

"Alice, I have to tell him. I'm engaged to him."

"But you can't, miss! If you do, he'll twig that I'm the one who told you. He'll tell Nora and she'll throw me out. I need me job."

"I needed mine, too," India said.

Alice looked away, shamefaced. Her baby had started to whimper again.

India reached into her purse and took out ten pounds. It was the last of her money. She had a pound note or two inside a tea canister in her flat, and some coins in a bowl, but that was it. She put the money on the table. "Don't go back, Alice. Find something else. Anything else. Syphilis is a long and horrible death. Your children need you."

"Blimey, miss, thank you!" Alice said, quickly pocketing the note. "What will *you* do now? For work, I mean?"

"I don't know."

"You can always go on the game," Alice said, trying for a laugh. "Pretty woman like yourself, you'd make enough to see you through."

India thought of her months at Gifford's. She thought about how she'd set her ideals and convictions aside again and again to keep her job and how dearly it had cost her to do so. She thought of Freddie and how he'd pressured her all these weeks to set a wedding date. How he'd told her he loved her and needed her. How he'd said they would do good things together. For London. For England.

And then she stood and said, "Thank you, Alice, but that won't be necessary. I've been whoring long enough."

CHAPTER 42

"Lytton, get the door, will you?"

Freddie stopped winding his gramophone. He could see his old school friend Dougie Mawkins—who was sprawled out on the sofa, his head resting in the lap of a fetching brunette—pointing at something, but he couldn't hear a word he was saying.

"What is it, old man?" he yelled. "This sodding thing's made me deaf!"

"The door! There's someone at the door!"

"Right-o." Freddie gave the machine one last crank. Ragtime tinkled out of it, as light and bubbly as the champagne he'd poured, as giddy as the women drinking it.

"Who is it, Freddie?" Bertie Gardner, another friend, asked. He swayed as he spoke.

"Dunno. Elliot maybe? That plonker's always late."

Freddie looked at his watch. It was after eleven. He hoped Elliot hadn't brought too many chaps with him. The ratio was rather thin as it was. Any more fellows and there wouldn't be enough girls to go round. Champagne, either.

He grabbed an open bottle and refilled glasses on his way to the door. He'd invited some of the chaps from his club home with him. A few of the fellows had automobiles, and they'd gone round to the Theatre Royal in Haymarket and found some girls. Freddie knew one of the actresses in a show playing there. He'd paid the back-door man a pound to let him in and surprised her in her dressing room. She'd brought some friends with her—girls who were eager to ride in automobiles and meet posh chaps.

Freddie had felt like a party tonight. He'd been working damned hard. The word had come down that Parliament would be dissolved by the end of September and the General Election would officially be called. The Commons had a mountain of unfinished business to plow through before then, and Freddie had been working day and night. He was eager for the campaigning to begin. He was ready for the fight, and would shortly—finally—have the money he needed to finance it.

India had been sacked a few days ago. They'd had dinner and she'd told him all about it. He'd had to appear shocked, then sympathetic, but he'd managed.

"Where's more Bolly, Lytton?" George Manners shouted across the room.

"In the bathtub," Freddie shouted back.

He smiled as he thought about how India was practically penniless now. Wish's will had been read today, Freddie knew. She had no income, and thanks to Wish, her savings were gone, too. She still had donor money, but it was a trifling amount—only a couple thousand pounds or so, nowhere near enough to fund a clinic. Perhaps now—without Wish and without funds—she would see how futile the idea of a clinic was and give up on it altogether. It was a good plan, he thought, using Alice and Nora to get India sacked, a good investment. It had cost him only ten quid, but it would bring him thousands.

But it was all damned tiring, too, and tonight he wanted a break from all his worries. He wanted some fun. He would have it, too, with a luscious redheaded dancer with whom he'd been necking before the blasted grammo ran out of steam. She was staring at him now from across the room. Staring and smiling. She blew him a kiss and he pretended to catch it—and then a fresh volley of knocking was heard.

Freddie rolled his eyes. He pretended a big hook was dragging him toward the door. Laughing, his collar open, his shirt undone, he was still looking at the redhead as he opened the door. "Steady on, Elliot, you tosser, you—"

He didn't get to finish his sentence. As he turned to face his guest, he felt a stinging blow across his cheek. He took a step back, shocked and furious. India was standing in the doorway.

"Good God!" he said, his hand coming up to his cheek. "*India?* What the devil are you . . . why did you hit me?"

"I *know*, Freddie," she said, her eyes blazing, her hands clenched into fists.

"Know what?" he said, slipping into the hallway and pulling the door closed behind him. "Darling, I don't understand."

"I spoke to Alice Little today. She told me what you did. You are despicable. A fraud."

Freddie felt his heart lurch. "India," he said smoothly, "I have no idea what you're talking about."

"I also found out that you and my mother have been talking. About dowries. And town houses. How much did I cost, Freddie? How much did she have to pay to get me married off? I can't imagine *any* price would have been too high for her."

"India, darling, I never—"

"When you asked me to marry you, I told you that my parents had cut me out of their will. You said it didn't matter. You said you loved me for myself alone. And that we would live modestly and make our own way in the world. But that was a lie, wasn't it? Why else would you negotiate with my mother? And scheme for my dismissal? It wasn't me you wanted, was it? It was my family's money."

"Who have you been talking to? Who's been telling you these lies?"

"Freddie, don't you understand? It's over. I know *everything*." She laughed bitterly. "Well, almost everything. I still don't know how I never saw what sort of man you are." She reached into her jacket pocket, pulled out the engagement ring and the gold pocketwatch he'd given her, and put them into his hand. "Or rather, what sort of man you've become."

She looked into his face and he saw anger in her gray eyes, and sorrow, and bewilderment. "When did you change, Freddie?" she asked softly.

"I didn't . . . I haven't . . ." he stammered, reaching for her.

"Freddie, I know you. *Knew* you. We grew up together, remember?" She backed away, looking at him as if she no longer recognized him. "You didn't used to be like this. You used to be good. Kind. Is there *anything* left of the Freddie I once knew?"

"India, please."

She shook her head. There were tears in her eyes. "I never want to see you again. Never." With those words, she turned and ran down the stairs.

"India! Wait!" he shouted. But she didn't. He heard her boot heels on the steps, and then a door slamming below.

Freddie pressed the heels of his hands to his eyes. "Fuck," he said. "Fuck. Fuck. Fuck. Fuck. Fuck." He'd just watched his entire future, everything he'd worked so long and so hard for, turn on its heel and walk away.

No, he told himself. He would get her back. Somehow. He would convince her it had all been a misunderstanding, a terrible mistake. But he knew she would not listen to him. She never wanted to see him again. Never. It was gone, all gone. The money, the house. The life he'd been carefully constructing for years, bloody *years,* had disappeared in a heartbeat. The game was over. He had lost.

He walked back into his flat, through his sitting room, past his guests, and into his bedroom. George Darlington had a girl on the bed. Her skirts were up around her knees.

"Get out," he said to them.

"In a minute, old man. Rather busy just now," George said testily.

"I said get out."

"Bugger off, Freddie, will you?"

Freddie was across the room in a few quick strides. He hauled George off the bed and threw him through the doorway. The girl followed, clutching the sides of her blouse together. Freddie locked the door behind them, then sat down on his bed and stared at the wall. The Red Earl stared back.

There was a knock on the door, then pounding. His friends called his name, one after another. The redheaded dancer wheedled prettily, but he did not respond. He just sat motionless, staring at the painting. The clock struck midnight. Then one. The music stopped playing. The voices faded. And still Freddie sat.

In the dim, flickering lamplight, he had never looked more like his ancestor. There had been humor in his face, a readiness to smile, some small shred of humanity. Now there was only a ruthless resolve.

When did you change, Freddie? India had asked, tears in her eyes.

When did I? he wondered. After my father? After Hugh?

He had deceived her cruelly. *India.* One of his oldest friends. The girl who had cried for him one summer's day on the banks of a pond at Blackwood. The only person who had ever cried for him. He had lied to her, manipulated her, bartered for her. He had cost her her livelihood, her dreams of a clinic. He had killed two men whom she had loved dearly. All in the hope of obtaining her money.

With Wish, Hugh, even with his father, Freddie had felt grief and remorse over what he had done. Now he felt nothing. Nothing except a curious freedom. Once things like love, compassion, and conscience had limited him. Now he knew that nothing would. Nothing *could.* Ever again.

He heard the earl's voice again: *Would'st be king? First rip out thine own heart . . .*

No, he thought. You were wrong. First rip out someone else's heart. Someone innocent and good. After that, everything else will be easy.

He pressed his palm to his chest.

He looked at the man in the painting.

"Done, old boy," he said. "At last."

CHAPTER 43

The ancient hackney cab Fiona Bristow was riding in slowed to a halt. "No, not here," she told the driver, leaning forward in her seat. "Further up."

"Aye, missus, I know where the Bark is, but this is as far as I go."

"But we're still a good half mile away!"

The driver shrugged. "I'm happy to take you back west, but if you want to go down the Bark, you're walking from here."

"I'll pay you double the fare. Triple."

The cabbie snorted. "You don't have money enough to get me down there. Now, are we turning 'round or are you getting out?"

Fiona angrily slapped coins into the man's hand, opened the cab's door, and stepped down onto the Ratcliff Highway, a dangerous stretch of road lined with tumbledown pubs, cheap lodging houses, and chandlers' shops. A lone gas lamp sputtered a few feet away, illuminating a wan child scurrying out of a pub with a jar of gin, and a man carrying a basket of rats. The cabbie cracked his whip. He urged his horse on, rounded a corner, and was gone. Fiona stood where he'd left her, biting her lip, until a man approached her, hands behind his back, asking the time.

"Sorry, I've no watch," she said, setting off before he got too close. "Stupid!" she hissed at herself.

She'd purposely dressed down, choosing an old skirt and mismatched cotton jacket. She'd worn her hair as she had when she was a girl, coiled and pinned. And yet she'd still managed to call attention to herself, and that was a bad idea in Limehouse.

Go back, a voice inside urged as she hurried down the street. *Now. While you still have a choice.*

Fiona ignored it. There was no choice. Not for her. There never had been. She'd known this day would come ever since she discovered her brother was alive.

Charlie was hers. *Hers.* He belongs with me, with us, she said to herself. He doesn't belong here, to these streets, these people, this life. He belongs in our home. At our table. At every Sunday dinner. She thought of all the things Charlie had never known. The years in New York that she and Seamie had had with Michael and Mary Finnegan. Reuniting with Uncle Roddy. Watching Seamie grow up. Standing beside her on the day she married Joe. Welcoming Katie. They had been taken from him, these things, because he had been taken from them. But she was going to get him back. Somehow, she was going to get him back.

Fiona followed the highway until it turned into Narrow Street. She could feel the river's damp breath on her skin, hear the mournful clanging of the buoys. The walk down unfamiliar streets that were pitted and pocked would have challenged anyone, never mind a woman who was five months' pregnant, but Fiona persisted. Charlie was in danger—grave danger.

Freddie Lytton was on the warpath. He was suddenly everywhere, doing everything, all at once. Determined to hold on to the Tower Hamlets seat, he had been visiting soup kitchens, the docks, and Whitechapel pubs, shaking hands and kissing babies. He'd renewed his call for a crackdown on crime north and south of the river. Police sweeps were picking up beggars, vagrants, even truant children, and herding them into jail cells already overflowing with thieves, ponces, and murderers. Police officers had already ransacked both the Taj and the Barkentine. Fiona knew this because it was in all the papers.

She had paid a discreet visit to Michael Bennett earlier in the day to find out what he knew. He'd told her that two days ago Lytton had personally walked into every police station in his constituency—and a few that were not—promising advancement to the man who helped him nab Sid Malone. Every newly minted constable looking to make rank, and every sergeant looking for a desk job at the Home Office, was beating the streets, leaning on informers, trying to get something—anything—on Malone.

Fiona had left Bennett's office distraught. She'd decided then and there that she must find Charlie immediately. Tonight. Joe was in Leeds on business and wasn't due back until tomorrow. She knew his feelings about her brother, and felt tremendous guilt over what she was about to do, but Joe didn't understand: Charlie was family. As much a part of her as he himself was, and Katie, and the new baby sleeping under her heart.

As Fiona continued east, the gas lamps grew sparser and the ruts and potholes more plentiful. She picked her way carefully down the street, frightened of stumbling or wrenching her ankle, protective of her unborn child. She had tried to find her brother at the Taj, but had had no success. She'd also tried Ko's—Bennett had told her Charlie often put in an appearance there—but had had no luck there, either. Bennett had warned her away from the Bark, saying that unfamiliar faces were not welcome there, but Fiona had assumed he'd meant male faces. She couldn't imagine any of Charlie's crew, hard men all, would find a woman threatening. She planned to find the publican and ask him to tell Charlie that she was there. She was certain he'd see her. She wouldn't leave until he did.

She was only about twenty yards from the Bark when she heard the footsteps. Someone was following her; she was sure of it. She could see the pub and knew that she'd be all right if she could only make it there. She picked up her pace.

"Oi! Oi, missus," came a voice. "Wait!"

She didn't wait. She broke into a run, but it was too late. A hand closed on her arm, jerking her to a stop.

"Where's your manners, missus?" a rough voice said, spinning her around. "Didn't you hear us calling? We was trying to make your acquaintance."

"Let go of me!" Fiona said, trying to pry the fingers off her arm. They belonged to a heavyset man. A lad of no more than sixteen was with him.

"I'll have that," the man said, catching her left hand and pulling her wedding ring off her finger. He thrust his filthy hand into her skirt pocket, searching for money. Then he moved his hand inside the pocket, groping between her legs.

"Stop it!" she cried.

The man leered. "You're a pretty one, ain't you?" He pushed her against the wall of a dark, crumbling wharf and kissed her. His hands traveled over her breasts.

Fiona wrenched her face away, sickened and terrified.

The man turned to his companion. "Billy, go on in without me," he said. "Me and me new friend here are going to take a little stroll."

"Please!" Fiona screamed after the boy. "I'm pregnant. For God's sake, help me!"

Billy hesitated.

"Get out of here!" the other man shouted. Billy did as he was told, slinking off, head down.

Fiona screamed as loudly as she could, desperately hoping someone would hear her. The man slapped her. He grabbed her arm, twisting it behind her back until she cried out. "Any more noise and you'll get worse. Understand?"

"Please, *please* let me go," she sobbed. "For decency's sake."

"Never heard of her," the man said. "Move," he ordered, pushing Fiona toward a flight of wooden steps that hugged the Bark and led down to the water.

Fiona walked, her legs trembling. Don't anger him, she told herself. Don't provoke him. He'd hit her once; he'd do it again.

Halfway down the rickety wooden steps, she stumbled. The man jerked her upright by her twisted arm, sending another jolt of pain through her body. She cried out again. The man fumbled in his pocket. He took out a filthy handkerchief and gagged her.

Fiona's mind was racing, searching for a way out. Nobody knew where she was. He could do anything to her and no one would know. Her free hand slipped down protectively to her belly. No matter what, she had to survive. She had to make sure her baby survived.

She reached the end of the stairs, stepped down into the mud, and stopped. Still holding her arm, the man pushed her toward an old stone building that seemed to be sinking into the mud. She realized it was the Barkentine. He walked her to a narrow door at the far end of the building, opened it, and dragged her in after him. It was dark inside. He fumbled in his pocket. She heard him strike a match and then a lantern hanging on the wall over her head was glowing.

With one swift, brutal motion, he tore open her jacket and blouse and then his hands were on her, all over her. Fiona wanted to scream with revulsion. She looked around as quickly as she could. She saw old, moldering barrels, coils of rope, a shovel, and in the far corner a flight of stairs. They led to the upper floors of the Bark, she was sure of it. If only she could get to them.

The man turned her around roughly and bent her over a beer barrel. She could feel the barrel's rim pressing into her belly. She tried to beg for her baby, but her words were muffled by the gag. The man held her wrists with one hand and lifted her skirts with the other. He tore off her knickers, then kicked her legs apart. Hot tears scalded her cheeks.

I'm sorry . . . I'm sorry . . . she sobbed wildly, thinking of her baby, of Katie, of Joe, but it was too late now.

The man unbuttoned his fly and pulled at himself, grunting. Fiona felt him against her. There was a sudden stamp of feet above them and the braying of an accordion. A mighty thump rattled the door at the top of the stairs. The man raised his head and glared at the ceiling, his small eyes narrowing. He grabbed Fiona's wrist and dragged her to the middle of the room. With her free hand she tugged at the gag, trying to pull it off, but he had knotted it tightly. Her fingers went to the knot, scrabbling at it.

The man bent down, grabbed an iron ring in the floor, and pulled. A trap-door opened. The lantern's flame cast just enough light for Fiona to see the top of a set of iron steps leading down into a deep black tunnel.

"Go on. Get down there," he said, motioning to the steps.

Fiona knew if she went into that tunnel she would never come back out. He would rape her and when he was finished he would kill her. She thought of her daughter, and her husband, of never seeing them again, and then she lunged at the man, clawing at his eyes.

He fell backward and hit the floor hard, surprised by the suddenness of her attack. Fiona fell with him, but his body broke her fall. She quickly scrambled away, stood up, and used both hands to tear at the gag. She got it loose, tossed it away, and ran for the staircase. The man saw her and sprang to his feet, blocking her.

He nearly caught hold of her again but she was too quick for him. She backed away, opened her mouth, and screamed, "Help! Help me! Please, somebody!"

She stopped, waiting for the sound of footsteps, of voices. But there was nothing, only more raucous laughter, music, feet pounding out a hornpipe on the floorboards. No one was coming, no one would help her.

The man eyed her menacingly. "I'm not playing games. Get down those steps."

She screamed again and again, in fear, in an agony of remorse, in sorrow. And then, wondrously, the door at the top of the stairs opened.

"Help me! Please!" she shouted.

There were heavy footsteps on the stairway, and then a male voice, deeply Cockney, bellowed, "What's going on down here?"

A young man emerged from the stairwell into the dim light. He was thin and rangy-looking and Fiona was immediately afraid of him. She tried to run past him and up the stairs, but he grabbed her wrist.

"Hold on a mo', missus," he said. "What happened?"

"Please let me go," she sobbed, terrified and hurting.

"In good time. I asked you what happened."

"He . . . he grabbed me in the street. He robbed me and then he . . . he forced me to—"

"Is that you, Frankie?" the man quickly cut in. "We was just havin' a bit of fun, that's all."

Frankie squinted at him, then said, "Well, if it ain't Ollie the nonce. Out of prison already?" His eyes went back to Fiona, taking in her ripped clothing, the marks on her face. "What's the matter, Olls? Can't find any kiddies to diddle?"

The man laughed nervously. "You take her first, Frankie. Go on. I'll have her afterward."

"Shut up, you filthy sod."

"Please," Fiona said. "I came here to see Sid. Sid Malone. I'm a friend of his. I have to see him. Can you take me to him?"

Frankie's face darkened. "You're with the doctor, ain't you?" he said. It sounded more like an accusation than a question.

"The doctor," Fiona repeated. She was frightened and confused. She hadn't understood the question.

"I thought so," Frankie said angrily. "You meddling bitches can't leave well enough alone, can you? Causing trouble wherever you go. But you don't care, do you? It's all a game to you. You enjoy slumming. Gives you a thrill, rubbing elbows with villains. Gives you something to talk about at your tea parties. Want to live the life, do you? Well, here you go, then."

Frankie released her wrist and picked up a barrel stave.

"No, please no," Fiona begged, raising her hands.

But it wasn't meant for her. Instead, Frankie swung the stave straight into her attacker's face. There was a wet, sickening crunch as his mouth exploded in a spray of blood, spit, and teeth.

Fiona screamed. She closed her eyes and pressed her hands over her ears, but she couldn't block out the man's cries. It went on and on and on, until she thought it would never stop. And then it became moaning, and then there was nothing, no sound at all. She lowered her hands and opened her eyes. The man, Ollie, was on the ground, motionless.

"No," she moaned. "Oh, God, no."

Frankie was standing over him, sides heaving. He dropped the stave, turned to her, and grinned. She was backed against the wall, crouched down. Frankie walked to her and crouched, too, until his face was only inches from her own.

"Enjoy that?" he asked. "Still want to mix in our world?"

"Please let me go," she sobbed, hysterical now. "Please."

"You've messed him right up, you lot," he said. "He's turning his back on his friends, his business. All because of you. He belongs here. With us. Not with you. So here's a message for you: Leave Sid Malone the fuck alone." He grabbed her chin. "Do you hear me?" he shouted.

Fiona tried to pull away from him, but he tightened his grip. "I said, *Do you hear me?*"

"Yes," she cried.

Frankie stood. "Go on. Get out of here," he said. Then he disappeared back up the stairs.

Fiona thought she would choke on the stench of death. Her head swam, her vision blurred. *Faint and you're done for,* a voice inside her said. *Get up. For Katie's sake, for the baby's, get up!*

She forced herself to stand. She was too afraid to climb the stairs, too afraid she would see him again if she did—Frankie. She hurried to the riverside door, past the motionless body and the blood puddled under it. She trudged through the river mud, pulled herself up the wooden steps that hugged the Barkentine, and found herself once again standing on the cobblestones outside of the pub.

I'm alive, she thought. Thank God, I'm alive.

The realization, sudden and bracing, got her moving. She stumbled, started walking, then, hands holding her torn jacket together, she ran. As fast and as far as she could. Away from the Barkentine and what lay in its basement. Away from the man called Frankie. Away from her brother. Down Narrow Street and into the dark London night.

CHAPTER 44 ❧

India sat on an overturned tea chest in the Moskowitzes' yard. Her face was flushed. Her sleeves were rolled up. She had a howling child in a half nelson.

"Martin! Stop your bloody squirming!" the child's mother yelled.

"Hold still now, Martin, that's it. I've got a sweetie for you if you do," India wheedled.

She aimed a pair of tweezers at Martin's right ear, willing her hand to be steady. Insert them just far enough and she could grasp the dark mass deep inside. Too far and she might puncture his eardrum.

Two chickens ran past, clucking loudly. Mrs. Moskowitz leaned out of the kitchen window and shouted for potatoes. A dog barked in the alley at the bottom of the yard. A cat screeched. Then a rubbish bin went over, clanging loudly against the cobblestones. India took a breath and shut it all out, her attention focused completely on the boy's tender ear.

"Do you like chocolate buttons, Martin?" she asked him, turning his head slightly to take better advantage of the light. "Or allsorts? I've lemon drops, too. And mint humbugs."

Martin stopped squirming at the mention of humbugs and India saw her chance. Two seconds later he was in his mother's arms, howling again, and India was examining the mass pinched between the prongs of her tweezers.

"A collar button," she said. "That explains the pain, Mrs. Meecher. We'll give the ear a wash with carbolic and you do the same at home for a week with salt water, and he'll soon be right as rain."

Martin sniffed loudly. "Humbugs," he said, eyeing India reproachfully. "I like humbugs."

"And you will have one, brave lad," she said, pulling a fat green sweet from her pocket.

"Thank you, miss," Martin's mother said. "Poor mite was sufferin' something terrible." She paused then sheepishly added, "Haven't got much this week. Me old man's gone to the call-on every single morning and not got picked. I brung you this. Will it do?" She drew a square of butcher's paper from her pocket and handed it to India. India opened it. Inside was a hand-tatted doily.

"It's lovely, Mrs. Meecher," India said warmly. "I know we'll find a good use for it. Thank you very much."

Mrs. Meecher smiled.

India stood. Ella was hurrying past, heading toward the shed with a basin of warm, soapy water. "Your next is a six-year-old girl. Eczema, I think. A bit hard to tell under all the dirt."

"Is the rash—" India started to say. She felt a sudden bump on her backside and turned around. It was Posy. She was scraping her fingers around the inside of an empty honey jar and licking them.

"Watch where you're going, Posy!" Ella scolded.

"Mmmmmm . . ." Posy murmured, lurching off in a sugar trance.

"The rash, it's—" India began again.

"I'll be home by nine o'clock, Mama. Maybe ten. Don't wait!" shouted a voice at the kitchen door. Yanki came bounding into the yard. He was washed and brushed, neatly dressed, and eating an apple. He handed his sister a pair of cuff links.

"Where are you skiving off to, Yeshiva Boy?" she asked, putting the basin down.

"I'm not *skiving*. I'm going to Rabbi Abramovitz's. For intensive study," Yanki said, holding out one wrist then the other, between bites of apple.

"Of what?"

"Torah, of course. What else?" he replied, sauntering off.

"Hmm. I don't know. Maybe young Mimi Abramovitz?"

Yanki didn't reply. Instead he turned and lobbed the remains of his apple into Ella's basin, dousing her.

"*Ach, du Pisher!*" she cried, blinking water from her eyes.

Yanki grinned. "*Kush in toches arein, El.*"

"Yanki!" a voice screeched, but it wasn't Ella's. India looked toward the back door and saw Mrs. Moskowitz advancing, wooden spoon in hand. "I heard that! You go to read the Torah with such a mouth? At the rabbi's house no less? With such a mouth you kiss your mother?"

"And Mimi Abramovitz," Ella said, smirking.

Mrs. Moskowitz stopped short. She put one hand to her chest. "The *rabbi's* daughter? Yanki, is this true?"

"*No*, Mama!" Yankie said, blushing furiously. "And don't go telling the world that it is." He glared at his sister. "Just you wait," he growled, then hurried through the yard and let himself out the back gate.

Mrs. Moskowitz stood looking after him, smiling. "Imagine that! The Abramovitzes for in-laws . . . *halevei!* That awful Alma Rosenstein tells anyone who listens that the rabbi has chosen *her* son for his Mimi. Won't she be pissing vinegar?" She turned and walked back toward the café, waving her wooden spoon like a conductor's baton, her anger at her son's fresh mouth forgotten. Then she turned suddenly at the door, and shouted, "Aaron! Miriam! Solomon! My chicken! Sometime this year, yes?"

"Yes, Mama!" Aaron shouted back from where he and his siblings were plucking chickens.

Ella shook her head. "If Florence Nightingale could only see this," she said.

"Twenty-three hundred cubic feet of space per lying-in patient."

"Impervious glazed tiles."

"Unlimited hot water."

"We've really got to do something about the chickens."

"And the cat."

India and Ella were silent for a few seconds, looking at the tattered awning, the tumbledown shed. It was everything the textbooks said a clinic should not be. And it was full of patients. Of poor mothers and their children. Of pregnant women. Of the elderly. All sitting silently and stoically. Never complaining. Prepared to wait all today and tomorrow, too, if that's what it took to have a child's tonsils seen or a baby's cough cured.

"I believe you asked about the rash, Dr. Jones. It's red, cracked, and weeping."

"Thank you, Sister Moskowitz."

"I'll be right in to assist. As soon as I get a fresh basin of water," Ella said. She started for the kitchen, then turned around again. "Indy?"

"Yes?"

"Still happy you moved into this madhouse?"

India smiled. She looked at the yard—at Posy toddling about with the honey jar, at Miriam and Aaron and Solomon sitting in a swirling cloud of feathers. At the old patched awning that Mr. Moskowitz and Yanki had stretched from the shed to the privy to make a waiting room. At the women sitting under it on an assortment of fruit crates and tea chests, children on their laps. She looked at the old garden shed, all six by eight of it, made spotless by soap and buckets of water. At the underwear flapping on the clothesline. And then she laughed. It was a real laugh—loud and genuine. It made her cheeks flush and crinkled her eyes. It made her beautiful.

"I couldn't be happier, Ella," she said. "Truly."

She had her clinic. Despite the loss of her savings, and everything else that had happened to her, she was seeing patients and practicing medicine the way she wanted to—with compassion and integrity.

As she headed toward the shed to see her next patient she thought about the transformation her life had undergone. Only a fortnight ago she was living at genteel Bedford Square, earning a living at the eminent Edwin Gifford's surgery, and engaged to the Liberal Party's rising star. Now she was penniless, living with the Moskowitzes above their café, running a clinic in their yard. Her life was a shambles, yet she was happier than she had ever been.

She remembered how it had all come about. She'd been so upset after finishing with Freddie that she couldn't bear to be alone. After a sleepless night she'd traveled to Brick Lane to see Ella. Ella had known immediately that something was wrong. She'd hustled India to an empty table, sat down with her, and demanded to be told everything.

So India told her. About Wish's will. And the fact that the money for the clinic was gone. About Freddie and his scheming, and how he'd used Alice Little to get her dismissed. She meant to have a quiet conversation with her friend, but there was no such thing to be had at the Moskowitzes'. Posy soon spotted her and climbed into her lap. Then Miriam came with a comb and brush to pester Ella to braid her hair. Yanki was next, looking for help with his tie. And then Mrs. Moskowitz, sensing all was not well, came with a pot of tea. Where Mrs. Moskowitz was, the rest of her family had to be, so in no time Mr. Moskowitz was seated with them, along with Aaron, Solomon, and Solomon's friend Reuben, who lived next door.

India spoke haltingly, expecting every minute to be told that her tears made her ugly, that emotional displays were for actresses and lapdogs. Those were the things her mother had always said. Instead there were ex-clamations of sympathy and outrage from the older Moskowitzes. Kisses from little Posy. A hug from Miriam. A grubby handkerchief from Sol. And then there was talking. A great deal of it. Arguing, really—as the family tried to decide upon India's best course of action.

"She should get the jewelry back. It's hers," Yanki said.

"No, she shouldn't. It has bad feelings attached to it," Ella countered.

"Feelings, shmeelings! She can pawn it," Mrs. Moskowitz said.

"She doesn't need to pawn his *dreck*. She can make her own way, she's a doctor."

"How? She can't find work anywhere! You neither, Ella!" That was Yanki again.

"That's not true! We've only started looking!"

India tried to get a word in, but she was only talked down. It soon became clear to her that she was to sit silently and drink her tea. She didn't understand why she was not to speak. She felt as if she were entirely incidental to her own predicament.

She looked from one of them to another. At Mr. Moskowitz frowning intently at his steepled fingers. At his wife refreshing everyone's teacup. At Ella yelling at Yanki. At Posy, still in her lap, the fingers of one tiny hand curled tightly around India's thumb.

And then tears welled behind her eyes, sharp and sudden, as she understood: this is what a family is. She was weary and frightened and heartsick. And they knew it. So they had taken her troubles away from her, if only for a little while, and made them their own. She wiped her eyes, hoping no one would see. No one did. They were all listening to Ella, still yelling at her brother about her and India's job prospects.

"We've only tried three hospitals. There are plenty more. We'll find something," she said.

Yanki laughed. "It'll be the same story wherever you look. You'll be lucky to get a cleaner's job. I'll bet Gifford blacklisted you."

"You don't know that."

"Wait, wait, wait!" Mrs. Moskowitz said. "I don't understand something. Why are you both begging for work at these hospitals? All I've heard for weeks is the clinic, the clinic, the clinic. You both still want it, no?" she asked, looking from India to Ella.

"Of course we do," Ella said.

"So make a clinic already. Right here."

Ella looked around uncertainly. "In the restaurant, Mama?"

"*Bist du meshuganah?* In the backyard! There's room. We'll move the washpot to the far end. We have the old shed. You can make an office from that."

India found her voice again. "In the backyard? But Mrs. Moskowitz, it's . . . it's a _yard_," she said, aghast.

"So?"

"There's no examination table. No hot water. No instruments. No autoclave. Those are hardly ideal conditions for a surgery."

Mrs. Moskowitz flapped a hand at her. "You want ideal? Or you want your clinic? In St. Petersburg we would see healers in the marketplace. Have our teeth pulled in the butcher's stall next to the pigs' heads. The more we screamed, the less the butcher charged us. It helped his business. People watched his patients and bought his sausages."

"But where will we find patients? How will they know about us?" Ella asked.

"_Oy vey_, how you two make problems." She turned in her chair and barked, "Herschel! Herschel Fein!"

A burly young man on his way to the kitchen with a basket of onions on his shoulder turned around. "Yes, Mrs. Moskowitz?"

"Your Eva, when is her baby due?"

"Next month."

"Does she have a doctor yet?"

Herschel Fein laughed. "A doctor? On a coster's wages? We'll be lucky to get a vet."

"What if I tell you she can have both a doctor and a nurse—the best in London!—in exchange for one week's worth of fruit and vegetables for the restaurant."

Herschel Fein looked at Mrs. Moskowitz. He frowned. He sucked his teeth. Then he said, "Minus the raisins. They're pricey just now and you go through five pounds at least. One week's worth, minus the raisins."

Mrs. Moskowitz sighed. "You're a hard man, Herschel Fein, a very hard man. But yes, yes, we will leave out the raisins. A deal, then?"

"A deal."

"Tell Eva to come here tomorrow and they will see her."

"But the baby's not due for another month."

"The price includes an examination before the delivery. To make notes and observations."

Herschel Fein nodded, impressed. "I'll tell her," he said, and continued on his way to the kitchen.

"There, girls!" Mrs. Moskowitz said, smiling triumphantly. "Your first patient. Your clinic is now officially open. Better get the shed cleaned out. Mr. Moskowitz will help you, won't you, Mr. Moskowitz?"

Before Mr. Moskowitz could say whether he would or he wouldn't,

India said, "But Mrs. Moskowitz, it just won't work. I still have to find a proper, salaried position. I have to cover my expenses. Pay my rent."

"You will stay with us."

"Thank you. Truly. But it would be impossible."

Mrs. Moskowitz reached across the table. She covered India's hand with her own. "With all respect, my dear India," she said, "I look to God to tell me what is possible. Not to you."

"But I don't want to be a burden to you."

"*Zeeskyte*, you don't know from burdens. *I* know from burdens. Cossacks, they are a burden. Watching your father, your husband, beaten in the streets—*that* is a burden. A slip of a girl who eats nothing and takes up no room is not a burden." Then, as if remembering herself, she added, "But of course this is all up to Mr. Moskowitz. If Mr. Moskowitz says you stay, then you stay." She banged her palm on the table. "Mr. Moskowitz?"

Mendel Moskowitz blinked thoughtfully at his wife. He tugged at his beard. He sipped from his teacup, put it down again, and said, "She stays."

A cheer went up from the younger children.

"It's settled, then," Mrs. Moskowitz said.

And it had been. India had sold everything but her bed, her clothing, and her books, all of which Yanki and Aaron had moved to Brick Lane with a donkey cart. The bed had been shoved into the attic, where Ella and her sisters slept, and was now shared by Posy. There was barely room to swing a cat up there. It was stuffy in the summer heat, and Posy kept her up half the night giggling and telling stories. Yet India thought it was the finest accommodation she had ever had. Every night she crawled into bed exhausted and happy. Every morning she woke eager and excited to meet the day and its challenges.

And there were many. She and Ella worked from dawn to sunset, with an hour off for dinner, typically seeing upward of seventy patients a day.

And even when they had finished with their appointments, as they had now, they still had to scrub down the examination room, sweep the dirt floor of the waiting room, and boil their instruments in Mrs. Moskowitz's kitchen.

India was just carrying a bucket and mop to the shed when the door to the kitchen opened again. She expected to see Mrs. Moskowitz, hands on hips, bellowing about something, but it was Sid Malone. She hadn't seen him for several weeks, since the day he'd brought the sick little girl, Jessie, to her flat. He was handsome in dungarees, shirtsleeves, and a waistcoat. His eyes found hers and he smiled his cheeky smile. India felt torn in two at the mere sight of him. She wanted to run to him and hide from him at the same time. A maddening mix of emotion gripped her, and it was all she could do to simply smile back and wave.

"Malone!" Ella cried cheerily. "What's troubling you, lad? Catarrh? Rheumatism? Lumbago? Have a seat, we'll check you out."

"No, thank you. I remember how it went the last time you two got hold of me." He walked over to them and looked all around—at the patched awning, the old shed, and the chickens roosting under it. "I just finished me supper. Your mother told me you were out back. What are you doing?"

"Isn't it obvious?" India asked. "Ella and I have opened our clinic. We're seeing patients."

She nudged a chicken out of the way with her foot. "In fact, you're standing in the waiting room."

Sid looked surprised. "Why aren't you at Gifford's? What happened?" he asked India, as Ella bustled off to sweep the waiting area.

India told him. About Dr. Gifford. And the Moskowitzes. And Freddie.

He whistled. "Lytton did all that? Bloke's a damn sight trickier than he looks. You tell him if the MP thing don't work out he can always work for me."

"I doubt I'll have the opportunity."

"Not on speaking terms?"

"Not exactly."

He grinned. "Inconsolable, is he? Can't live without you?"

"It's not me he can't live without, it's the money," she replied. "Had we married, my parents would have given us a town house and twenty thousand a year."

Sid blinked. "Twenty *thousand*?! Blimey, luv, I'd be inconsolable, too. Is that what you're worth?"

"Not anymore, I'm afraid. It was a limited-time offer."

"Guess the honorable gentleman isn't so honorable after all, is he? I guess some of us aren't what we seem."

India gave him a penetrating look. "I'd say none of us is."

Sid looked away. He toed the ground. "Aye. Well," he said.

"Aye. Well," she echoed.

"So you're a free woman now? Available?"

India blushed. She looked at the ground, feeling awkward and embarrassed.

"I guess that would be a bad idea," Sid said.

India looked up at him, wondering if he meant it, almost hoping he didn't, but he was smiling. He was teasing her. He didn't mean a word of it. She quickly recovered herself and smiled, too. "The worst," she said, teasing him back.

But it wasn't what she wanted to say. Not at all. She wanted to tell him that she didn't care if it was a bad idea, she loved him. She wanted to put her arms around his neck, to pull his face to hers and kiss him, but she didn't. She loved him, fiercely, but it would never work between them. Even if she was no longer engaged to Freddie. They were too different. She knew that; she'd always known it.

The day Sid had brought Jessie to see her, they had established a fragile détente—one governed by an unspoken rule: talk about anything and everything but what mattered most—their feelings for each other. It allowed them to be cordial. To be friends. Their conversation was good-natured and careful now, and India hated it. She preferred their old habit of yelling at each other on the streets of Whitechapel.

"Well, I guess I'm off, then," Sid said.

"To where?"

"To nick the crown jewels. Feel like a challenge tonight, me."

"Sid, that's not funny. You have to stop. You have to leave the life. You know what Freddie means to do."

"And speaking of jewelry . . ." Sid cut in.

"But we weren't speaking of jewelry. Not anymore."

"Where's your watch? You're not wearing it. What did you do? Barter with it again?"

"In a manner of speaking," she said. "But that's not—"

His eyes darkened. "Bloody hell, India! Why'd you do that?" he asked angrily, the forced civility gone.

"Because I—"

"You should have come to me if you needed something. Why are you always so bloody stubborn?"

India tried again to reply, but he wouldn't let her, he kept railing at her.

"May I speak?" she asked huffily.

"No. Because I know what you're going to say. *I can't accept that, Sid. It's blood money, Sid.* Well, fuck that."

She whistled at the profanity, but he continued, unheeding.

"You *need* that watch. How are you going to take a . . . a bleeding pulse and all that? What did you buy with the money? Whatever it was, I'd have gotten it for you."

"You couldn't have."

Sid snorted. "Of course I could. What was it?"

India grinned, enjoying the sparks, the flash of real feeling, and said, "My bloody freedom!"

CHAPTER 45

Joe Bristow, tired, haggard, and sick with worry, ran up the steps to the door of Guy's Hospital. He'd arrived home from a trip to Leeds an hour ago to find a police constable sitting in his foyer, his butler white as a sheet, and his cook crying. Apparently Fiona had gone missing for nearly twenty-four hours and had only just been located. According to the constable, she'd been found by police officers in Limehouse and had been taken to Guy's, where she was currently in the care of a Dr. Taylor.

He barged through the door into the foyer, then breathlessly asked the nurse at the front desk where he could find Dr. Taylor. The woman pointed him toward a short, barrel-chested man berating a young nurse whose shoes were merely shining, not gleaming.

"Dr. Taylor?" Joe asked. "I'm Joe Bristow."

In an instant the nurse was forgotten and the doctor was leading Joe down a hallway to his office.

"What's happened? Is my wife all right? Is the baby all right?"

"The baby's fine. And your wife will be, too."

"*Will* be? She's not now? What happened to her?"

"I'm glad you came, Mr. Bristow," the doctor said evasively. "Mrs. Bristow told me that she wanted to make her own way home, but I wouldn't allow it. I wanted her released into a family member's custody. I thought it better for her to be accompanied home."

"Where was she?"

"In Limehouse. At a place called the Barkentine."

"Bloody hell."

"You know it?"

"I know *of* it."

"She was attacked there, Mr. Bristow. She was very nearly raped."

The doctor took Joe into his office, then told him everything that had happened. How the police had brought Fiona in, how worried she'd been for her baby, how he'd examined her and treated her wounds. When he'd answered all of Joe's questions, he asked one of his own. "Mr. Bristow, do you know what she was doing in Limehouse?"

Joe did know, but he didn't reply.

"I only ask, sir, because I don't understand what a woman of her position—and in her condition—would be doing in such an area alone at night." The doctor paused, then said, "Mr. Bristow, has your wife been behaving at all erratically? Wandering in her thoughts, perhaps?"

"Why are you asking me these questions?"

"Because I'm worried that she may be delusional."

"*What?* Why?"

"There's one thing I didn't tell you, and that's that Mrs. Bristow says she saw a man killed at the Barkentine. Right in front of her eyes. Sergeant Hicks, one of the officers who found her, sent half a dozen constables to check the pub, but there was no dead body. No report of a dead body. No witnesses. Nothing. They did find blood on the cellar floor, but the publican claims it came from some chickens he killed to make a stew."

Joe nodded. He said nothing. It did indeed sound crazy—if you didn't know who frequented the Bark. Dr. Taylor knew it was a bad place, but Joe was quite certain he had no idea how bad.

"Sergeant Hicks came back here and told Mrs. Bristow what his men had found, but she wouldn't accept his explanation. She still insists a murder was committed. You can see why I'm concerned. She's had a dreadful shock and she must now have rest and quiet both for her sake and for the baby's. Keep all newspapers away from her. She's to have no upsets. No excitement or agitation. I have tried to impress this upon her. I hope that you will do the same."

"I will, Dr. Taylor."

"Very good. If this fails to effect a change in her behavior, please do inform me. I can recommend a very good doctor at the Bethlehem Hospital who works wonders with female hysteria."

Bedlam. Joe shuddered at the very thought. He quickly thanked the doctor, then asked to see his wife.

Dr. Taylor led him upstairs to a room on a private ward. "I'm sure you would like a bit of time to yourselves. Please send for me if you need me."

Joe entered the room. Fiona was sitting on her bed dressed in torn and dirtied clothing. Her hands were in her lap, her head was down. There were newspapers on the bed next to her.

"The doctor said you weren't supposed to have those," he said. "Where did you get them?"

"From the other patients," she said quietly.

"He thinks you've lost your mind. Thinks you're one step away from the loony bin."

Fiona made no reply.

"Is it true? Was a bloke really murdered?"

"Yes," she whispered. "It was the man who attacked me. Another man, a man named Frankie, did it."

"Jesus Christ, that's Betts. The same sod who killed Alf. Who burned me warehouse to the ground. And you *saw* it? You were there when it happened?"

"Yes."

Joe felt sick. There were men who went to pieces over witnessing something like that, never mind a pregnant woman. She should never have seen it. She should never have been anywhere near Sid Malone and his pack.

"Still think he's some poor stray dog, your brother?" he asked her. "Still think all he needs is a pat on the head and a biscuit or two and he'll come round?"

"He didn't do it."

"He may as well have! You know who Frankie Betts is, don't you? Don't you, Fiona? No? Well then, I'll tell you. He's your brother's right-hand man. The heir apparent. Not just a hard man, a bloody lunatic. And you were in the same room with him! It could have been *you* he killed!"

"Charlie wants to go, Joe. He wants to leave the life. Frankie Betts said so. He told me to stop meddling. To leave Charlie alone. But if I could just see him, just speak with him, he *would* leave. I know he would."

Joe made no reply. He turned away from Fiona. His rage was so great that he wanted to upend the bedside table, throw the water jug across the room. It took all his self-control not to.

"Do you have any idea how angry I am?" he asked, turning back to her. "How could you do it, Fiona? How could you put yourself and our baby in such danger? After I told you ten times not to?"

Fiona still made no reply.

"Did you ever think, for even one bleeding second, what it would be like for Katie to grow up without a mother? For me to become a widower? Answer me!"

She lifted her face then and the sight of it broke his heart. It was horribly bruised. Her lip was cut. One of her eyes had been blackened. There were livid finger marks on her neck.

She picked up one of the newspapers on the bed. He saw that it was the *Clarion*. A shrill headline quoted Freddie Lytton's latest diatribe against Sid Malone. Staring at it, she started to speak.

"Once, when I was ten years old and Charlie nine, we were coming back from the corner shop when we saw a group of boys—there were five of them—tormenting a cat. They'd tied its front legs together and were kicking it, trying to make it run, then laughing when it fell over. They were older than us. Bigger, too. Charlie handed me the tea and sugar we'd bought, walked up to the ringleader, and punched him in the face. He didn't break his nose, but he bloodied it. The boy started crying. Charlie punched a second boy in the stomach and they all ran off.

"When they'd gone, he picked up the cat. It was in a bad way. One of its legs was broken. He took it home and made a bed for it out of rags and an old egg basket. When our Mam saw the poor thing, she didn't have the heart to make him put it out again. He sat up with that animal the entire night, keeping it close to the fire, feeding it milk with a spoon. He even made a splint for its leg. He was so kind, my brother. Even as a little boy." She gestured at the paper. "And now this . . . this is what that little boy has come to. How, Joe? How?" Her voice broke.

Joe sat down next to her. He put an arm around her. They sat that way for several minutes, then she said, "Can we go home now?"

He shook his head. "No, luv, we can't."

She looked up at him, confused.

"Not until you promise me you'll never do this again. Never."

"I can't do that. You know I can't. Please don't ask me to."

"I *am* asking. Choose. Right now. Me or Sid Malone."

Fiona looked at him with huge, wounded eyes. "But Joe . . ."

Joe's heart sank. "I guess I have me answer, don't I?" he said. "You'd do it again, wouldn't you? You'd tear the world apart with your two bare hands if it would bring him back. Nothing I could say would change that. I'm only wasting my breath."

He tried not to show the grief he was feeling. He tried to summon the courage he needed to do what he had to do. She was everything to him; he didn't know how to even breathe without her, but he didn't know what else to do. He didn't know how else to make her stop, and he refused to simply stand aside and allow her to destroy herself and their family in this mad, doomed pursuit of her brother.

"Our carriage is downstairs," he said. "I'll tell Dr. Taylor that you're traveling alone and I'll have the driver wait for you. I'll make me own way back in a cab."

"Joe, *please*. Don't do this."

"I'll be at the Coburg until I find something more permanent. I'll have Trudy fetch my things from the house. I love you, Fiona, and I love Katie. More than my own life. I hope you change your mind."

"You're leaving me? You're leaving me again?"

"First time was my fault," he said. "This time it's yours."

Fiona's face crumpled. She dissolved into tears. He nearly faltered at the sound of her weeping, but he forced himself to stand up and leave.

"I hope you do choose, Fee," he whispered, on his way out of the door. "And I hope to God you choose me."

CHAPTER 46

"You know, I think old Florrie Nightingale was sniffing the ether when she wrote this book," Ella said, holding up her copy of *Introductory Notes on Lying-in Institutions*. "Twenty-three hundred cubic feet for every patient? Plus a window?"

India nodded, frowning. "We're going to have to make do with less, aren't we? A lot less. Less space, fewer windows. Less water, fewer sinks and privies."

"The only thing we'll have more of is patients."

"But it's not a bad building, is it?"

"No, it's in rather good shape, I think. Roof seems sound. No water damage. Lights work. Plumbing works. Sinks on every floor. It's bare bones, but it has what we need."

"We'd have to put in toilets. A kitchen. Or at least a stove."

"I'm sure we could do that for under a thousand. But then how do we pay for sheets and towels? Syringes and bedpans and scalpels and . . ."

India sighed. "I know. I know. We need twenty-four thousand, not twenty-four hundred."

India and Ella were standing inside an old paint factory on Gunthorpe Street that Mrs. Moskowitz had heard was for sale. Cheap. Twelve hundred pounds reduced from fifteen hundred. The owner was bankrupt and needed to sell it quickly. She had told Ella and India to go look at it, and they'd laughed.

"Mama, it may as well be a million pounds!" Ella had said. "We don't have the money. We have only the twenty-four hundred our donors gave us. It's nowhere near enough to buy the building, renovate it, and furnish it."

"Is there so much harm in looking? God gives the nuts; He doesn't crack them," Mrs. Moskowitz had said.

And so they'd gone. The estate agent had escorted them through the building, then told them that in his opinion they could offer a thousand. He'd gone for a cup of tea and left them to wander the premises.

"*Only* a thousand," India said now.

"A bargain," Ella said.

"You know what your mother would say."

"I do, but I think God will have to rob a bank if He wants to help us with this one."

"Hullo!" a voice shouted from the doorway. "India, Ella . . . are you in there?"

India turned in time to see Harriet Hatcher take a long drag on a cigarette, then flick the fag end into the street.

"Harriet!" she exclaimed. "What are you doing here?"

"I stopped by the caff for a visit. Wanted to see if you two had made any progress with the clinic. Ella's mum told me where you were. Look who I brought with me," she said, smiling impishly.

A bulky figure hurtled in through the open door. "Jones!" a familiar voice boomed. "Still dreaming those pipe dreams, are we?"

"Professor Fenwick!" India cried, delighted to see her teacher. "What brings you here?" But Fenwick had already veered off to inspect the gas lighting.

"Word's out about what you two are doing in the Moskowitzes' backyard," Harriet said. "It's all anyone talks about. At the school. At the hospitals. Fenwick wanted to come and see for himself. Says he's giving up teaching. Says he can't bear this year's graduating class."

"Dunces, every one of them!" Fenwick bellowed, striding past them toward the staircase. "They spend more time at estate agents asking about the prices of fancy premises on Harley Street than they do with their casebooks!" He disappeared up the steps.

"We were thinking of putting the children's ward on the first floor, Professor," India called up after him.

"No, no, no, no, no! This is an old building. Who knows how good the water is? Put the maternity ward up here. It requires the most hot water. Pressure's bound to be better on the first floor than the second or third. 'Gads, Jones, you *have* been inside a hospital, haven't you?"

Harriet gave India a quick thumbs-up. "He's in!" she whispered, grinning.

"You'll need an administrator, you know. Someone to run the place. Balance the books. Hire and fire," Fenwick said, walking back downstairs. "Arthur Fenwick. How do you do?" he added, extending his hand to Ella.

"Do you know of anyone who might be interested, Professor?"

"Don't be cheeky, Jones. When you get this place up and running, give me a call."

"*If*, Professor, *if*," India sighed. She explained what had happened to her cousin and the clinic's funds they'd raised.

Fenwick frowned. "How much is the owner asking?"

"Twelve, but the agent thinks we could offer a thousand."

"Offer them eight, settle at nine, and I'll give you the down payment. Twenty percent should do it. And you may use me as a guarantor on the mortgage."

India was nearly speechless. "Seriously, Professor? You'd do that?"

"Consider it done."

"But *why*?" India asked, amazed by his generosity.

He looked at her over the top of his glasses. "Student I once had—absolute ninny of a girl—told me she wanted to become a doctor to make a difference. I think I'd like to see what that's all about."

India flung her arms around her teacher and hugged him tightly.

"Oof! That'll do, Jones," he said.

She released him, beaming, then embraced him again, despite his protests, then the four of them took another look around the building, noting its strong points and its weaknesses. Fenwick said that the Royal Free Hospital was getting rid of some old beds, and if they could get a carter to pick them up, he was sure they could have them for free. And he'd heard Dean Garrett Anderson talking about modernizing the library. He would be sure to have her save any unwanted furniture for them.

"It wouldn't be ideal, of course," Fenwick said. "The tables from the library are old. The beds from the Royal Free are wooden, not the new metal ones with the sanitary finishes, I'm afraid."

"The poor can't wait for ideal, Professor Fenwick," India said briskly. "They need care, even if it's rudimentary care, and they need it now. Old beds are better than no beds. We'll give them a good scrub with carbolic and hot water."

Harriet raised an eyebrow. "That makes a change. Aren't you the girl who set off for Varden Street armed with a bag of porridge and pictures of smiling fruits and vegetables? What happened?"

"Whitechapel happened," India said, laughing. "Now I think myself lucky if the chickens stay out of our examination room."

The agent returned. India took him aside and made an offer of £800. He shook his head, told her it was far too low, but said he was duty-bound to convey it to the building's owner. Then he hurried them out, saying he had another appointment to keep.

Fenwick watched him scuttle off, and said, "He doesn't have another appointment. He's going straight to the owner. You'll get it for nine. Mark my words."

As India and Ella half-walked, half-ran back to Brick Lane, they tried to figure out how they would come up with the money for the monthly mortgage payments and the renovations. The £2,400 they had wouldn't cover it all. "We'll just have to take up where Wish left off and start knocking on doors," Ella said.

"And try to get that Point Reyes land sold," India added.

"But then there's the problem of staff," Ella said, frowning. "How will we pay them?"

"I think I might have an answer to that," India said. "The London School of Medicine for Women. The students there are desperate for clinical training. If I talk to the dean, once we're up and running, maybe she'll send some of the students to us."

"That's a wonderful idea!" Ella said.

India stopped. She took Ella's hand, and squeezed it. "We can *do* this, Ella. We can! Maybe not the way Wish planned. Maybe not the right way . . ."

"But our way," Ella said, grinning.

They walked into the Moskowitzes' flat, excitedly calling for Ella's mother, eager to tell her the good news. As Mrs. Moskowitz joined them in the hallway, wiping her hands on her apron, Solomon informed them that India had received a package.

"From whom, Solly?" India asked.

The little boy shrugged. "Doesn't say."

"It must," Ella said. "There's bound to be a return address."

"There isn't. I looked. It came in a carriage. The driver handed it to me."

"Maybe Freddie had second thoughts. Maybe he's returned your jewelry," Ella said.

"Maybe you're the one sniffing the ether," India replied.

Posy skipped into the hallway. "It's a present for India!" she sang. "Open it! Open it!"

"I bet it's another doily," Miriam grumbled. "We only have five hundred of them."

The door opened and Mr. Moskowitz came inside, followed by Yanki and Aaron. "What is the reason we are all standing in the hallway?" he asked.

Mrs. Moskowitz told him as India looked at the package in her hands. Its plain brown wrapping gave no clue as to who'd sent it. She undid the twine and pulled off the paper.

"What's *Macanudo* mean?" Solly asked.

"It's a kind of cigar," Yanki answered, worldly wise.

"India smokes cigars?" That was Posy.

"No, you wally. It's just a box."

"Solomon! Do not call your sister a willie!" Mrs. Moskowitz scolded.

The children screeched laughter. "*Wally*, Mama! Not willie!" Solly said. "Don't say willie!"

"But I didn't, Mama! *You* said willie."

"Solomon Moskowitz! This is how you talk? Yanki, I blame you."

"*Me?* What did I do?"

Mrs. Moskowitz was about to tell him, but just then India lifted the cover of the cigar box and gasped so loudly that she couldn't.

"*Gott in Himmel!*" Mrs. Moskowitz cried, peering into the box.

It contained thick stacks of bank notes.

"Count it!" Ella said.

India shook her head. She put the box down on the hall table. She knew who had sent it and she didn't want it. Not from him.

"*I* will, then," Ella said. She lifted the notes out and counted them three times with her family counting along. When she finished, she had to lean against one of the walls. "It's ten thousand pounds, India. Ten thousand bloody pounds."

Mrs. Moskowitz, still in shock, didn't even scold her for the *bloody*. "Tonight in Whitechapel, it is raining money," she said.

"Look! There's a letter inside," Solly said, pointing at the box.

Ella pulled it out. There was no salutation, no signature, just three words: *For your clinic.* "India, we can buy the building outright," she said. "And renovate it, too. And buy sheets and pay doctors . . ."

"No, we can't," India said flatly.

Ella looked at her. "Why not?"

"I know who sent this. Sid Malone. This is blood money and I want no part of it. I'm going to give it back."

"India, are you *mad?*"

"It's not a fruit basket this time, Ella! It's ten thousand pounds."

"Too bloody right it is!"

"Each one made from opium. Or smuggling. Or prostitution. Or robbery. How can we start a clinic that's supposed to ameliorate human suffering with money made by augmenting it?"

"Watch me."

India gathered the money together, put it back in the box, and closed the lid.

Ella closed her eyes. She shook her head. "You can't be this stubborn. Even you."

"I'm right, Ella. You know I am."

"No, not right. *Righteous*. There's a difference."

India flinched, but did not back down. "I'm sorry you feel that way," she said. Then she took the money and left the Moskowitzes' flat.

CHAPTER 47

Sid was lying on his bed, eyes closed, waiting for sleep to come. Insomnia had kept him up for three days straight. He was hollowed out by exhaustion and wanted to sleep now, but the voices wouldn't let him. He heard them—coming up through the floorboards—one stubborn, one shrill, both loud. Finally, unable to tolerate them a minute longer, he got out of bed, stuffed his feet into his boots, and stomped downstairs. It was early evening. The Bark was nearly empty, and he was able to spot the cause of the commotion almost immediately. It was India. She was standing at the bar arguing with Lily.

"I know he's here. I need to see him. Will you at least give him my name?"

"Sorry, miss. Never heard of him."

"Never *heard* of him? You work for him!"

"Sorry, miss. Will you be ordering a drink?"

"Now see here, I insist that you stop this charade."

"It's all right, Lily," Sid finally said.

India turned.

"To what do I owe the pleasure, Dr. Jones?" he asked blearily.

India held up the cigar box. "I think you know."

"Ah. Why don't we go to my office?"

He led her up the stairs and into his room. When he'd closed the door behind them, he said, "You came here again. After I told you not to. And this time with ten thousand pounds in a cigar box. Are you out of your bloody mind?"

"I took a cab. Almost all the way."

"I don't care if you flew. Don't do it again."

India didn't reply. Instead, she looked around. At the iron bed with its rumpled sheet. At the clothes on the floor. The whisky bottle on the nightstand.

"See here," she said awkwardly, thrusting the box at him, "I can't accept this. You have to take it back. You shouldn't have sent it. You know how I feel about . . . about . . ."

"Blood money?"

"Yes. Blood money."

"Don't be so damned stubborn, India."

"It's nothing to do with stubbornness. For God's sake, Sid, we both know where this money came from!"

"Not another lecture. Please. I'm too tired to hear about people sunk deep in misery because they can't eat porridge."

India glared at him. "It's not their misery I'm thinking of. It's yours, Sid. *Yours.*"

He turned away. Suddenly, he couldn't meet her eyes.

"You want to give me this money so you can feel better about what you do. So you can stay in the life and ease your conscience at the same time. I won't let you."

He spun around, furious. "I want to give you this money to help you! To help your patients!" he yelled.

They were shouting at each other again. And he wanted . . . he wanted to ask her to lie down with him. To put her arms around him and tell him stories. About her childhood. About her patients. About anything at all. Her touch, her voice . . . they would soothe him. He could sleep, he knew he could, if only she would lie down with him.

"Do what you like, India," he finally said. "Leave the money here. I'll just send it again tomorrow. I'll address it to Ella. I've a feeling she'll take it. She's nowhere near as pigheaded as you are."

India angrily tossed the box onto his bed.

Sid stared at it. "Great. You gave it back. What did that accomplish? You want to teach me a lesson? Hurt my feelings? Well, here's a bit of news for you. It doesn't hurt me. It only hurts the people who would use the clinic. Refuse the money, and you can stay warm and dry on your moral high ground. That's where you like to be, isn't it? Or take a chance. Step down into the mud with the rest of us and save a few lives."

India looked near tears. His exhaustion had made him brutal.

"I'm sorry. I didn't mean to . . ." he began.

"There is one life," she began brokenly. "One life I would like very much to save. If I take this money I will be damning that life, not saving it. You have to get out, Sid. You have to get away from all this."

"Christ, you never give up, do you? The bloody clinic's not even open yet and you're already trying to rehabilitate the hard cases." His eyes met hers and held them. "Don't you know that some are past saving?"

"That's not true!" India said. He was surprised by the sudden ferocity in her voice. And then, before he knew what was happening, she had crossed the room, pulled his face to hers, and kissed him. Hard and hungrily. He closed his eyes, as wave after wave of emotion washed over him—shock, desire, love, sadness, and fear. Fear of her and of all she would ask of him. Fear for her.

He wrapped his arms around her and crushed her to him. And then he pulled away. She looked up at him, her eyes questioning. He shook his head.

"Why?" she asked.

"Because you are *good,* India," he whispered fiercely. "So bloody good that you make me believe in better things, even when I know damn well there are none."

"You don't want me."

"I *do* want you. More than I've ever wanted any woman in me whole life. But I can't do this. I won't. It would be a mistake. A bad one. You know it would. You said as much yourself. You should go," Sid said gently. "I'll have Oz take you. He'll get you back to Brick Lane safely and—"

"I don't want to go."

"India . . ."

"I . . . I love you, Sid."

It was quiet in the room. Sid heard a coal tumble in the grate, a dog barking in the night, and his own heart thumping.

"What did you say?" he finally asked.

"I said that I love you."

"You don't."

"Actually, I do." She looked down at her hands, overcome by emotion.

Sid tried to speak, but found he couldn't. No woman had ever meant anything to him. This one did. She meant the world. Her love was everything he wanted and everything he feared.

"It would be a disaster," he said at last. "You know that, don't you?"

She looked at him and he saw the pain in her eyes. "I can understand if you don't love me and I will accept it," she said. "But if you do, please don't make me beg you."

He pulled her to him again and held her tightly. "I *do* love you, India," he said. "God, how I love you."

They stayed that way for some time, and then he felt her lips on his cheek, his mouth. Her kisses were passionate and fierce. His own were bruising. He wanted her. He wanted her naked in his arms, so he could feel her body next to his, feel the crashing of her heart. Here. Now. Without preliminaries. It was darkness, this love, he knew it was. It was sorrow and damnation, and it would crush them both. There was no road back from it, but that was all right now. He no longer wanted one.

His hands went to her blouse. He pulled it off her, and then her camisole. The firelight flickered and danced over her skin, casting shadows. He kissed the graceful curve of her shoulder, the delicate hollow below her throat. Her breasts were small and delicate, and barely filled his hands.

"I'm not very good at this," she said. "Not without a drink, I'm afraid. I'm . . . I'm cold."

"I'll warm you."

"Not that kind of cold. I mean . . ."

"I know what you mean. You're wrong."

He fumbled at the waistband of her skirt, pushed it down, and then her petticoats. He unlaced her boots and pulled her stockings off. When she was naked, he gazed at her, drinking her in. She colored under his gaze and tried to cover herself with her skirt.

"Don't," he said, taking it from her. "I want to see you, India. You're beautiful. So beautiful. Don't you know that?"

He pulled her down to him on the bed. He kissed her lips, wanting the sweet softness of her. Wanting only this night. This room. Her. He moved his mouth to her breasts. He kissed her smooth, flat belly. He bit the curve of her hipbone, found she was ticklish there, and did it again until she laughed out loud and begged him to stop. He wanted that so much, the sound of her laughter. The sound of her pleasure, her happiness. He bit her again and again, and when she was helpless with laughter he parted her legs and kissed the soft place between them, lapping at her until she was breathless and wet.

"Make love to me, Sid," she whispered. "I want you."

He pushed himself inside her gently, caressing her until she opened herself to him. Then he gripped her bottom and rocked into her, aching with his need of her. Her eyes met his, searching. And then she closed them and moved with him. Slowly at first.

"Oh, that's lovely," she murmured. "So lovely . . ." She sought his mouth, tangled her fingers in his hair. He felt her movements grow stronger, more urgent, felt her body grow warm and slick with sweat. Just as he thought he couldn't hold himself back another second, he felt her shudder and cry his name. He closed his eyes and let himself come, lost in the feel and sound and smell of her. When it was over, he did not let go of her, but held her close.

"I love you, Sid. I love you so," she murmured, blinking up at him.

She closed her eyes and nestled against him, her head upon his arm. He smoothed a damp curl off her cheek. After a few minutes, her breathing slowed and evened, and she drifted off to sleep. Sid stared into the firelight for some time. He would stay with her here through the night and when morning broke, he would love her again and then take her somewhere. Somewhere bright and beautiful. To the coast. To the sea.

India stirred in his arms, sighing softly. Sid looked down at her, at her beautiful face, and wondered if he hadn't just committed the worst crime of his entire sorry life.

PART
TWO

London, September 1900

"Gentlemen, gentlemen! Is this Utopia? Or is this Whitechapel?" Freddie Lytton shouted, addressing the men—dockers, factory workers, builders—packed thickly into the smoky Ten Bells pub. "We may wish for an ideal world, but we certainly don't live in one. We live in the real world, where we must face real facts, make real choices. Vote for Labour and you've thrown your vote away. The Labour Party does not stand a chance. Any sane man can see this. We must all of us stand together and defeat the real enemy—Salisbury's Tories!"

Men nodded gravely from their chairs or stood stroking their chins. Scattered cheers went up. Before they had died down, Joe Bristow attacked.

"They said the same to the matchgirls in eighty-eight," he called out from across the room. "The politicians, the press, the factory owners—all the powers that be: *Labour doesn't stand a chance.* They said it right before the girls struck for safer working conditions—and *won.* They said it to the dockers in eighty-nine. Right before *they* struck for the docker's tanner—and won. Don't hope, they told them. Don't dare. Don't dream. I'm telling you not to listen to them. I'm telling you that you *can* make a change. I'm telling you to send a message to Westminster and to the world. I'm telling you to hope. To dare. To believe. Believe in the Labour Party. Believe in me. But, more important, believe in *yourselves.*"

There were more cheers. Whistles. Shouts. Joe barely heard them. He was still talking, still haranguing Freddie.

Parliament had been dissolved a week ago and a general election had been called for the twenty-fourth of October. Throughout the country, candidates for Parliament were canvassing in the month allotted them, making speeches, debating with rivals, jousting with hecklers. All of Britain was in the grip of election fever, but no contest had captured the public's interest quite like that for the Tower Hamlets seat.

It was nearly ten o'clock at night now. Joe had been campaigning at a nearby union hall when word came in that Freddie Lytton was in the pub across the street with reporters in tow. Joe's supporters, eager for a debate, had practically picked him up and carried him into the Bells. His voice was hoarse, he'd had no rest, and yet he did not hesitate. Anger was fueling him, and there was so much of it inside of him, he felt like he would never run dry.

He was angry all the time now. Angrier than he'd ever been in his life. The rage drove him. It kept him knocking on doors, talking to voters, giving interviews, making speeches, long after other men would have dropped from exhaustion.

He was angry at East London. Angry at the deprivation and crime, the despair, the bleak, unending poverty. It had been years since he'd shivered in a patched jacket. Years since he'd seen his father skip his breakfast so that he and his brother and sisters could have a bit more to eat for theirs. He and Fiona were wealthy. They'd left poverty behind, but he saw now that it would never leave them.

Poverty tore families apart. It didn't matter how far you got from it, it would still catch up with you. He knew this for a fact now. It had torn his apart. He and Fiona were no longer together. He had left her three weeks ago and was now living in the Coburg. She was at 94 Grosvenor Square with Katie. And it was all because of Sid Malone, her brother. Because once—long ago—poverty and despair had worked on him, changed him, pulled him into a dark underworld, and Fiona could not accept it.

Joe wanted to stamp it out, that poverty. He wanted to crush it as fiercely as its brutal legacy was now crushing him, forcing him to spend day after day apart from those he loved best in this world, his wife and daughter.

"Those are fine, high-flown words!" Freddie mocked now, as Joe finished speaking. "But words are cheap. It's experience that counts in government. The ability to work within the system, to get things done."

"Experience?" Joe shot back. "I'll tell you what my experience is, mate. Being hungry. Being cold. Working sixteen-hour days in all kinds of weather. What's *your* experience? You know what it's like to work hungry, Freddie? You know what it's like to be cold? Of course you don't!"

"Let's speak to the issues, Joe, shall we?" Freddie blustered.

"I thought I was!" Joe said, provoking laughter.

"I think you should tell these good people your plans for controlling Whitechapel's terrible crime. *Have* you any plans?"

"Yes, I do. I plan to build more schools."

Freddie burst into laughter. "Schools? We don't need schools, if anything we need—"

"What? More prisons?"

"I didn't say—" Freddie began, but Joe didn't give him the chance to finish.

Joe was goading him, leading him, but he didn't have him quite where he wanted him. Not yet.

"Can I tell you why Mr. Lytton thinks prisons are more important than schools?" he asked. "It's because he'd rather jail you than educate you! Educated people ask too many questions. You might start asking why you're working fourteen-hour days for only a pound a week. Why your kids have to go into factories and mines and sculleries, while other people's children go to Oxford and Cambridge."

"Why, that's nothing but a load of Marxist claptrap!" Freddie shouted, outraged. "If government determines more schools are needed, then more schools will be provided. Of course they will. I promise you that . . ."

Freddie railed on, and for the first time that evening Joe smiled. He turned to a man sitting close by, a reporter who was scribbling in a notepad.

"You getting all this?" he asked him.

"Every word," the man said, still writing.

The newspapers were all covering the Tower Hamlets contest, and they put into print every barb and insult the candidates tossed at each other and every promise they made. In his heart of hearts, Joe doubted he'd ever see the inside of Westminster, but when the election was over, he would make it his business to see that every promise made by the winner and documented by the press was a promise kept. And maybe come the new year, with a new government, there'd be a few more schools in Whitechapel, a few more health visitors, a few less broken homes, a few less desperate men.

Joe took a swallow of the pint someone had brought him. The porter was soothing to his raspy throat. He licked foam from his lips and waited for his chance, waited to jump in and challenge his rival to fund more clinics, build another soup kitchen, another orphanage, another widows' home.

Unlike Freddie, Joe was fighting for more than the Tower Hamlets seat, for more than the honor of sitting in Parliament. For more than a career in politics.

He was fighting for justice for the people of East London. For opportunities and rights. He was fighting for an end to poverty and ignorance. An end to hopelessness.

And he was fighting—in the only way left to him—to get his family back.

CHAPTER 49

Sid could see her—India. His India now. She was hurrying up Richmond Hill ahead of him in the cool, darkening evening. One hand was pressed to her head, holding her hat in place. The other held a carpetbag. A wine bottle poked out from under its flap.

She was trying to walk, but kept breaking into a run. She turned the corner onto Arden Street and let herself into a small, three-story house. He had insisted on this—on a flat far away from their own homes. It was the only way he would see her. The only way to keep people from finding out—his people. The only way to keep her safe.

He found his key and let himself into the building's narrow foyer. She was already pounding up the stairs to the second floor. He heard her greet an elderly neighbor on the first floor. "Hello, Mrs. Ainsley. How are you keeping?"

"Very well, dear, thank you. How's Mr. Baxter?"

Mr. Baxter. He smiled at that. It was how he had introduced them to the landlady the day they'd inquired about the flat: "I'm Sidney Baxter and this is me wife, Theodora." He'd gotten the name from an advertisement for Baxter's cocoa on the side of a bus. He said he was a traveling salesman and that his wife spent most of her time with her mother in the country because she didn't like being alone. They wouldn't be there much and they'd pay in advance. Would a year's rent do? The landlady, astonished at her good luck, had let them the flat immediately, no questions asked.

He heard India bid Mrs. Ainsley good day, run up the last flight of stairs, and unlock their door. He followed her, letting himself in. She'd dropped her bag and coat in the entryway and was moving through the rooms, calling for him. He closed his eyes and listened, loving the sound of his name on her lips. Loving the eagerness in her voice. The happiness.

He knew it wouldn't take her long to find out he wasn't in any of the rooms. The flat was modest, just a large, open sitting room with a huge, sunny window, a bedroom, scullery, and loo. It had come with a few pieces of furniture and she'd bought rugs and curtains. He closed the door behind him. She came running out of the bedroom and stopped short when she saw him.

"Hello, Mrs. Baxter," he said, smiling as he held out a bunch of white roses. "Went out to get these. Planned to be back before you, but I—"

He didn't get to finish because she ran to him, threw her arms around his neck, and kissed him wildly.

"I was so worried," she said. "When I saw you weren't here, I was so worried you weren't coming."

He kissed her back, then turned away from her—just for a second—to talk about something else. It was too much, this love. It would drown him.

"You hungry?" he asked. "Must be, after working all day. I brought food." He went to the scullery and came back with a basket and two glasses. He set the basket on the table under the window and began to take things out of it.

India shook her head no. "I want only you," she said, kissing him again.

"How about a drink? A glass of wine?" He fished the wine bottle out of her carpetbag. As he did, the bag toppled over and a folder slid out, spilling hand-tinted photographs of rolling green meadows, a cobalt bay, and soaring sea cliffs. He picked them up and looked at them and for a few seconds he was stunned into silence.

"What is this place?" he asked, still staring at the pictures.

"It's the land my cousin left me in California. Point Reyes. The land I can't sell, at least according to the American estate agent. Sid? What's wrong? You look so strange."

Sid shook his head and laughed. "I . . . I don't know. Just had the oddest feeling. As if I'd seen this place before. In my dreams, maybe. Daft."

And then he remembered. It was when he first held her. In the tunnels. That's when he'd first seen this place—Point Reyes. It was when he'd wanted to keep walking with her. Out of London. To someplace beautiful and new. To the sea. It was *this* place he'd envisioned. This place exactly. He wanted to tell her that, but she was too busy kissing him.

He put the pictures down and kissed her back. Then he uncorked the wine and poured two glasses. India took hers from him. She drank half of it, wiped her mouth with the back of her hand, then pulled him into the bedroom.

"Blimey! If I'd known I was going to be molested, I would've brought my men to protect me," he said, trying not to slosh his wine.

"They wouldn't have stood a chance. Not against me," she said, unbuttoning his waistcoat. She opened his shirt and kissed his chest, his throat, his mouth. She undid his trousers. They dropped to the floor. She pushed his drawers down.

"Hold on, missus!" he protested. "How about a little sweet talk first? You know: *'How are you, Sid? How was your day?'*"

"Later. When I've had my way."

She took his wine away from him, then pushed him back onto the bed—a wide, ornately carved thing she'd found in a second-hand shop. He sank into the plump feather duvet. She had her own things—or most of them—off in a flash, throwing her jacket, blouse, and skirt onto the floor as if they were rags, tossing her eyeglasses onto a night table. She straddled him, still in her camisole and stockings, took his face into her hands, and kissed him long and hard. He closed his eyes, remembering their first time, the time she'd told him she was cold. *Cold?* She was the most passionate lover he'd ever had.

She reached for his hands and pinned them against his pillow. She kissed his cheek, his eyes, his lips. She buried her face in his neck, breathing him in. Then she stretched her slender body against him and he was suddenly inside of her. She was soft, so soft. And so wet. After only a few seconds, she shuddered and cried his name.

Sid blinked at the ceiling. He'd barely had time to get hard. When she opened her eyes again, he looked at her, laughing, and said, "That's it? That's *all*? I feel so cheap." He sat up and kissed her. "I'm just an object to you. That's all I am," he said, pulling a jeweled comb out of her hair. Her blond curls fell down over her shoulders. He unbuttoned her camisole, pushed it off her arms, and kissed her breasts, his hands trailing over the silken skin of her back.

She moaned softly, buried her hands in his hair.

"I think you should say you're sorry," he said.

"Do you? For what?"

"For treating me like a plaything. Like a kept man."

She laughed out loud and he smiled, loving her laughter. He grabbed her hips and thrust into her. And then again. Her smell made him achingly hard.

"Oh, Sid," she whispered. "I'm . . . I'm . . ."

"Yes?"

"Not sorry in the least!" She giggled.

"Ah. Well, then. We'll just have to make you sorry."

He buried his face in her breasts, teasing her with his tongue and teeth until he felt her grow wet again and breathless. He rocked into her, back and forth, back and forth, until he felt her arch into him, then he stopped.

"No, don't . . . oh, don't! Please . . ."

"Sorry yet?"

"No!" she cried, twining her slender arms around him, biting his ear. He brought her to the edge of pleasure over and over, always stopping just short, until she was mad with her need of him.

"How about now? Are you—"

"No," she said, stopping his mouth with a kiss. And then another. She pulled away and looked at him, her gray eyes large and dark and suddenly serious in the twilight of their bedroom.

"I'm not sorry, Sid," she said fiercely. "Do you hear me? Not for making love to you. Not for loving you. I'm not now and I never will be. Never."

He gathered her into his arms, overcome with emotion, and made love to her as he had their first night together, passionately, desperately, wanting only to lose himself in her. Afterward, as the night came down, he pulled her to him and held her curled within the safety of his arms. When he heard her breathing deepen, he rose, careful not to wake her. He pulled the covers up over her shoulders, kissing the damp curls on her neck, then frowned. She looked so pale in the darkness, so slight and fragile.

He pulled on his trousers, then padded off to cobble together a meal. She worried him. She was too thin. She worked too hard and ate too little. The clinic was due to open in a month's time, and she and Ella were working around the clock soliciting donations to keep the repair work going, barking at builders and deliverymen, making sure every tile, spout, lamp, and doorknob was just so. He had stopped by a few days ago to see how things were going and found her sitting on the floor of the lying-in ward, a chisel, screwdriver, and bucket of grout nearby, resetting a drain cover by herself. The chisel had slipped and sliced her finger open. She'd bandaged it and kept right on working.

"It has to be perfectly flush," she'd explained. "And the seams have to be sealed. Otherwise matter will build up in the cracks and breed disease."

"Why didn't you have the builder's men do this?" he asked, kneeling down to do it himself.

"I did. Twice. They didn't get it right. They don't care."

She did, though. Deeply. He saw that in her. She cared enough to devote herself to the poor women and children of Whitechapel. To make a change for the better. To make a difference.

She was so unlike any woman he'd ever been with. Most of them had wanted jewels and furs and dresses. Not India. She didn't give two seconds' thought to her wardrobe. If her clothing was clean and presentable, if her sleeves could be unbuttoned and rolled up, she was happy. Jewelry held no interest for her; she thought it a nuisance. Her eyes lit up over the most god-awful things, things that made him feel light-headed just from glancing at them—sharp, shiny metal things, mostly. Scalpels, clamps, and syringes. Chloroform masks. Bottles of this and vials of that. Needles and tubes, beakers and flasks.

The day a thing called an incubator—a contraption of metal and glass with a gas boiler attached—arrived from New York, she'd been so excited she couldn't sleep. "It will save babies, Sid," she said. "The early ones. The ones we've never been able to help."

His money had paid for these things. The money she'd tried to give back. He'd finally convinced her to take it. "Take it for them," he said, meaning her patients. "And for me." Giving her the money was the second-best thing he'd ever done; loving her was the first.

Pottering about in the kitchen now, Sid made a nice tray of foods he thought might tempt her. He'd stopped at Harrods before he'd come here. He'd heard that that was where toffs shopped for food, and since India had come from a wealthy home, he thought there might be things there that she'd like more than fish and chips or pork pies. He was just placing the opened bottle of wine on the tray when he heard her cry his name. She sounded upset, frightened.

"Sid!" she cried again.

"What is it? What's wrong? I'm right here," he said, rushing into the bedroom with the tray.

She was sitting up in bed, blinking in the darkness. "I thought you'd gone," she said plaintively. "I thought you'd left. I thought it was morning."

Sid put the tray down on the bedside table. "Shh. I'm right here. I just went to get us some supper."

India rubbed her eyes. She looked confused. Sid sat down on the bed and kissed her furrowed forehead. It was so hard to steal time together. So bloody hard. They'd had the flat for a month, and had been together in it only twice. India had to be back at the clinic tomorrow before dinnertime to supervise the installation of an operating table. And he had visits to pay. To Teddy Ko. And to the Blind Beggar. Visits he dreaded. But he wouldn't think of that now. That belonged to tomorrow, not tonight.

"You've been asleep, luv. Only for a few minutes. It's just gone eight. We've got the whole night ahead of us. Hours and hours."

India looked at him, disconsolate. "I don't want hours. I want days. Months. Years."

"Don't start. You know that's impossible."

"Why?"

"Because of who I am. And who you are. We've talked about this, India. Here," he said. "I brought you some food. You should eat."

He topped up her wineglass and handed it to her. As she sipped from it, he picked up the tray and set it on the bed. "I couldn't find any broccoli. Or porridge. I hope this will do," he said.

"Very funny."

There were all sorts of delicious things: a roast Cornish hen, fragrant with lemon and thyme. Slivers of salty glazed ham. Asparagus in vinaigrette. Blush-pink new potatoes. Brussels sprouts flecked with bacon. And for afters, a wedge of sharp crumbly Cheddar. Blue-veined Stilton. Plump apricots. A punnet of cherries. And chocolates.

"My goodness, this is a feast! Where did you get it all?" she asked.

"Harrods," he replied, pleased with himself.

India looked at him in disbelief and giggled.

"What?"

"The thought of *you* in Harrods. Rubbing shoulders with all the dowager ladies and sniffy shop clerks."

"Taking the piss, are we? Right, then. Next time it's pickled whelks and jellied eels for you." He picked up a bit of ham and popped it into her mouth.

She caught his hand in hers, kissed the palm, and held it to her cheek. "Marry me, Sid," she said.

"Finish your ham."

India swallowed, then said, "I mean it."

"Give us that wine glass back. You've had enough."

"I'm not drunk, I swear it. Marry me."

"The woman isn't supposed to ask the man."

"Stop joking. I'm serious, and I want you to be."

He gave her a long look, but said nothing.

"You could make a new beginning."

He laughed bitterly. "You don't know my world. Or the people in it. There are no new beginnings."

"*Make* one. Walk away. Tell them that you quit."

"Just pick up me bat and ball and go home, is that it?"

"Yes."

"It's a little late for that, luv."

"But *why*? Don't you want to leave it behind? The violence? The fear?"

"Fear is all I've got. Keeping people afraid is the only thing that keeps me alive."

"But, you could—"

"Christ, India, I don't want to talk about this!" he exploded. "For a few hours I get to forget who I am and what I do, and I get to have something beautiful and good in my life. For just a few bright hours. Just one night every now and again. It's little enough. Please don't take it from me."

He felt anguished. He would have given anything to be able to do what she asked of him—to turn his back on his life and start again. With her. But he knew it was impossible. Although he didn't say it out loud, because he didn't want to upset her, he knew that once you were in his world, you never got out. Unless it was in a pine box.

India kissed him. She shushed him. She put her arms around his neck and pulled him to her. "I'm sorry, I'm sorry. I won't say another word about it, I promise. I love you, Sid. I love you so," she whispered.

Sid buried his face in her neck. "I love you, too, India. I wish to God I didn't."

CHAPTER 50

"Mummy?"

"Yes, Katie?" Fiona said, balancing her daughter on her knees. There was hardly room for them all in the chair—Katie, Fiona, and Fiona's enormous belly.

"Can I have a story?"

"Of course you may."

"Ten stories?"

"Two stories."

"Five stories?"

"You'll make a wonderful merchant someday," Fiona said, laughing. "I'll have to start bringing you to the tea auctions."

"Five, Mummy. Five."

"Five stories it is. Sold," Fiona said. "Now run along and have your bath, and when you're finished, we'll read."

Katie clambered down and ran to her nurse, Anna, who was waiting for her in the doorway of Fiona's study. She turned back to Fiona on her way out. "Mummy?" she said.

"Yes, duck?"

"I want Daddy."

Fiona winced. "I know you do, Katie, but Daddy's not here right now."

"I want him."

"He'll come to see you soon, my love."

"But . . ."

Anna, awkward but gentle, said, "Come on, little Katie. We'll have a treat. We'll put some pretty pink bath salts in your water. Would you like that?"

Katie nodded and followed Anna out of the room. Fiona watched them go, heartsore. The damage her attacker had left on her face and body had faded. The damage Joe had inflicted was still raw. She was missing him horribly. Katie was missing her father. Everyone was unhappy and it was all her fault.

Or so Joe said.

He blamed her for this. All she had to do was go to him and tell him she would no longer search for Charlie. He would come home, they would be a family again and happy. Except for me, she thought.

She had lost so much. Her parents. Her sister. Nick. She would lose Charlie, too, if she couldn't find him, couldn't make him see reason. To prison or the gallows. Was it so wrong not to want to lose the brother she loved? Was it wrong to want them both—husband and brother? Joe wanted her to choose. She would if she could, but she didn't know how. She didn't know how to turn her back on someone she loved.

She thought of her parents and wished they were here. She missed them so much right now that it hurt. They would know what to do. Her mother would tell her the right things. She'd always known what the right things were. Her da would have upended every pub in East London until he'd found his son, then dragged him out by the scruff of his neck.

"Tell me, Mum. Tell me, Da," she whispered, eyes closed. "Tell me what to do."

She waited for the sound of her mother's voice, whispering in her heart. For her father's words, echoing in her mind. For some kind of sign, some direction, but her only answer was a knock on the door.

"Come in," Fiona said, grateful for the distraction from her sad thoughts.

It was Foster. "Mr. Finnegan is here to see you, madam," he said.

"Mr. Finnegan? My *brother*?" Fiona whispered, unable to believe what she was hearing.

"Yes, madam. Shall I send him in?"

"Yes!" Fiona cried, rising from her chair.

Charlie was here. He had finally come. *Charlie*. Oh, how she had longed for this! They could talk at last. She would tell him of the danger he was in. She would convince him to leave London. And when he was safely away, she could go to Joe and tell him the good news, tell him to come home.

She heard footsteps in the hallway and was suddenly gripped by nerves. Would he be friendly to her? Angry? What would he say to her? What would she say to him? She didn't have long to worry, for the door suddenly opened and a red-haired man stepped into the room.

"Hey, Fee."

Fiona blinked at the tall, wiry teenager standing before her. *"Seamie?"* she said, completely surprised to see my younger brother instead of Charlie. "What on earth are you doing here?"

"Um . . . nice to see you, too," he said, kissing her cheek. She kissed him back, tried to embrace him. "Wow, I can hardly get around this," he said, patting her belly. "You having one baby or half a dozen?"

His teasing didn't even register. She knew why he was here. Something bad had happened. Why else would he come all the way from America without wiring first? Someone was ill. Or hurt. Or dead.

"Seamie, what's wrong?" she said. "Uncle Michael, Aunt Mary, the children . . ."

"Nothing's wrong. Everyone's fine. They all send their love."

"But why are you here, then? It's only October. You're not on your holidays yet."

Seamie took off his jacket and sat down on the settee. "I've finished with school, Fiona," he said.

"Finished? How?" she asked, sitting down herself. "The school year's only just begun. Did you graduate early?"

"Not exactly."

"Oh, no," she said. "Seamie, you weren't expelled, were you?"

"Um . . . well . . . yes."

"Why?"

"The head said I was spending too much time climbing and sailing and not enough time in class."

"He said that and then he expelled you? Without letting you make amends? Doesn't he believe in warning his students before he chucks them out?"

"Yeah, he does, actually," Seamie said, looking uncomfortable. "He gave me four warnings, *then* he chucked me out. Can't blame him. My grades were pretty bad. But the way I saw it, there was nothing left to learn. Nothing more they could teach me."

Fiona blinked at him, unable to believe what she was hearing. Seamie was—or had been—in his final year at Groton, an exclusive private school in Massachusetts. He was to have graduated in June and then gone on to university.

"Nothing more they could teach you, Seamie?" she sputtered. "What about science and maths and history and Latin? What about—"

"It doesn't matter, Fee. None of it matters. The head was right. I *was* spending all my time climbing and sailing. I became the youngest person to climb all forty-six high peaks of the Adirondacks. The youngest person to sail from Nova Scotia to the Keys alone."

Fiona listened, incredulous, as he went on about peaks and ridges, sextants and stars. When he finished, she said, "You've thrown it away. Your education. Your future. What are you going to do?"

"I'm going to go exploring. It's the only thing I want to do."

She shook her head. This conversation was becoming more unreal, more outlandish, by the second.

"That's why I'm here, Fee. In London. The Royal Geographical Society is financing an expedition to Antarctica. Captain Robert Scott's leading it. I'm going to approach him. Ask him to take me on as a crew member. Beg him, if I have to."

"*Antarctica?* You can't go to Antarctica! You can't go anywhere! You're only seventeen!" Fiona shouted. She had recovered from Seamie's sudden appearance and his news. The shock she'd felt upon seeing him had been replaced by anger at his rash, foolish move.

"Fiona, I know this is hard on you, I know it was unexpected—"

"To say the bloody least!"

"But you have to try to understand something: The world is getting smaller every day. If I wait until I'm through university—nearly five years from now—it'll be too late. Everything will be found and climbed and crossed and mapped."

"Seamie, I'm not interested in a bloody geography lesson!"

"Listen, Fiona, *listen*—the source of the Nile's been found and just about every other river, too. There have been attempts at the North Pole, and many of the major mountains have been taken. *Everyone's* talking about Everest now. It's the third pole. All the good climbers want a shot at it, but the Tibetans won't let anyone in. Francis Younghusband, the explorer, spoke at the Royal Geographical Society last month. I got a copy of his paper. Word is that the viceroy's going to send him in. To Lhasa. To open talks. He's been everywhere. Manchuria. The Gobi Desert. Mongolia. Nepal. And now he wants Everest. *Everest!* Can you imagine?"

"What I *can't* imagine," Fiona said, "is how you've taken the opportunity I've given you, and all the money I've spent, and chucked them into the rubbish bin. Do you have *any* idea how lucky you are? There were boys who would have given their eyeteeth to have the education you were getting. I want you to finish and graduate, Seamie. I want you to go to university."

"What you want and what I want are two different things."

"Apparently so! *I* want what's best for you."

"But you don't know what's best for me, Fee. Only I know that."

"Oh, you do? At seventeen years of age, *you* know what's best?"

"Look, you didn't stay in school. You left when you were fourteen, but you want *me* to stay."

"Left? *Left?* I was taken out of school. I had no choice. I had to go work at Burton Tea to help feed the family."

"It doesn't change the facts," he said. "You were on your own at seventeen. In charge of your own life. You had more adventures before you were eighteen than most people have in a lifetime."

"Is that what you call them, adventures? I've news for you, they weren't adventures, Seamie, they were tragedies," she said, beyond furious now.

She saw that he at least had the good grace to look shamefaced.

They were both silent for a few seconds, then Fiona said, "I'm going to telegraph the headmaster. I'll beg him to take you back. If I succeed in fixing this disaster, you are getting on the first ship back to New York."

"No, I'm not. I'm not going back."

"And what if you don't get on this expedition? What are you going to do for money? There would have been a place for you at TasTea or Montague's—a good place—after you'd graduated from university."

"I was hoping—"

"Well, don't! Don't hope for a handout, Seamie. Or for any special treatment. You can work in the bloody warehouse if you want a job. I've an opening at Oliver's. You can go see the foreman in the morning."

"I was hoping you'd let me have the money Nick left me."

Nicholas Soames, Fiona's first husband, had married Fiona when Seamie was a child. Nick had adored Seamie and regarded him as his son. When he died, he left Seamie a legacy. The money—two hundred thousand dollars—had been placed in a trust for him until he turned twenty-one. Fiona was its executor.

"You must be joking," she said.

"I'm not."

"Do you really think I'm going to hand over that kind of money to a seventeen-year-old truant?"

Seamie stood up. He picked up his jacket.

"Where are you going?"

"To stay with friends," he said, wounded. "With the Aldens. It's clear I'm not welcome here."

"Seamie, don't be ridiculous. Of course you're welcome here," Fiona said.

"As long as I agree to what you say and do what you want. Well, I'm not going to. I'm not a boy anymore. I'm a grown man. And I'm going to Antarctica. I'll see you around."

"Seamie . . ." Fiona said, trying to get up out of her chair. Her belly slowed her, though, and by the time she had gotten up he was already downstairs. She hurried to the window and watched him walk out of the house and down the street, a duffel bag in his hand.

She closed her eyes, trying to hold back her tears. My God, how had this happened? How had she managed to chase Seamie from the house? He'd arrived only a few minutes ago and now he was gone again.

Her elder brother wouldn't see her. She'd driven her husband from the house. And now she'd driven her younger brother away, too. All the men she loved had left. A tear rolled down her cheek, then another. Her family was fracturing. Right before her eyes. They were coming apart when all she wanted was to hold them together. To keep them near her. To keep them safe.

She heard the door open. Foster was there again, a tea tray in one hand, a handkerchief in the other. He cleared his throat. "I'm sorry, Mrs. Bristow, I don't mean to intrude, but I thought you might be in need of a cup of tea."

Fiona realized he'd probably heard the row between herself and Seamie. She watched him as he set the tea tray down on her desk, and the handkerchief discreetly beside it, then made his way back to the door.

"Thank you, Mr. Foster," she said, grateful for his thoughtfulness and his tact.

"Is there anything else you need, Mrs. Bristow? May I be of any help to you at all?"

"Can you tell me how to make men stay put in one place?"

"Yes, madam, I can. It's quite simple."

"Really, Mr. Foster? How?"

"Turn them into women."

CHAPTER 51

Frankie heard the voices from the street. He was surprised anyone was in the Bark. It was half four, and Des closed the pub punctually now from three to five to avoid trouble with the rozzers. He listened for a bit before going inside and realized he knew the voices—one was Gemma's, angry and shrill. The other was Sid's. His was low and contained. Barely.

Frankie grasped the door handle, then thought better of it. He went around the side of the Bark instead, down the steps to the river, and then up into the kitchen by way of the basement stairs. Desi was there, washing glasses and stirring a pot of swill he called soup.

"All right, Des?"

"Aye, Frankie. Yourself?"

"Fine, thanks. What's up?"

"The guv's in the shit with Gem."

Frankie knew that Sid had finished with Gemma. He should've been surprised, but he wasn't. Nothing Sid did surprised him now.

He walked over to the door that separated the kitchen from the taproom and looked through its small, grimy window. Sid was seated by the windows, looking out at the river. Gemma was pacing back and forth. Sid might have finished with her, but she hadn't finished with him. She held a handkerchief. Her eyes were red.

"Why, Sid? Just tell me why."

"Gemma, please. We've been through all this."

"There's someone else, isn't there? Who is she?"

"There's no one else."

"You're a liar!" Gemma shouted. There was a loud crash.

"Bloody hell," Desi muttered. "Tell me that wasn't me gran's blue platter."

"I won't," Frankie said.

"Does she kiss you like I did, Sid? Does she fuck you like I did?"

"I think it's time we got you home, Gem."

"I'm not going anywhere. Not till you tell me the truth. You said you'd never fallen in love. You said you never would. But you have, haven't you?"

Sid made no reply.

"I thought so." It was quiet for a few seconds, then Gemma spoke again. "Hard thing of it is, it's not with me."

Desi shook his head. "Can't understand for the life of me why he broke it off with her," he said, salting his soup. "I'd never kick a woman like that out of my bed. Something's not right."

"Nothing's right, Des. Not anymore."

"You can say that again. What are you doing here anyway, Frankie? Come to eat, have you?"

Not bloody likely, Frankie thought, glancing at the soup pot. "Came to talk to the guv," he said.

"About what?"

"Fucking Madden. Fucking Ko. And the fucking Italians."

Des nodded. "Good. Madden's taking some diabolical liberties."

"Too right, he is."

Big Billy Madden was doing things he wouldn't have dared to do even a month ago. Throwing his weight around in Whitechapel pubs and making his presence felt along the waterfront. Someone had knocked off Butler's Wharf, done a ship in St. Katherine's Dock, and robbed a chandler's on Wapping High Street. It was Madden, Frankie's gut told him so. The man was like a shark scenting blood in the water. Sid needed to deal with him. Now.

Madden had sent a message to Frankie through Ding Dong just last week that his offer was still open. Frankie had sent Del packing with a few choice words and a toe up his arse. Billy Madden didn't understand. It wasn't a *job* he wanted. If that was all he was after, he could work for any bleeder who paid him. It wasn't about the money. Well, not entirely. It was about the Stronghold. Planning it, doing it, and getting away with it. It was about owning East London. Being a prince of the city. It was about the life. The brotherhood. Love of a kind. And loyalty. It was about Sid.

There was another loud outburst from Gemma.

Frankie saw Sid stand and put on his jacket. Gemma tried to stop him leaving. Next thing, Frankie heard the front door open and close.

"Bloody great," he said. "The guv's legged it and stuck us with Gem."

"Poor lass. Go get her a drink, will you? I have to put the finishing touches on me soup."

Frankie wondered what those touches might be—a sprinkling of black beetle? A handful of rat feet? Desi's soup looked like it belonged in a cauldron. Frankie pushed open the kitchen door and walked into the taproom. He found Gemma standing by the bar.

"Here, Gem, what's all this, then?" he said. "Trouble with the guv?"

"You heard us?"

"Hard not to."

"I'd hoped we could talk. Hoped I could get him back . . ." Her words trailed away.

"How about a drink? Help take the pain away."

"Gin."

"I'm sure it'll blow over, whatever it is."

Gemma gave a bitter laugh. "It won't. He's found someone else."

"Aw, Gem. He's a bloke, ain't he? He'll come back. We always do." Frankie reached under the bar and pulled out a bottle. He uncorked it, filled a short glass, and pushed it toward her.

"Better pour yourself one, too, mate," she said, throwing hers back.

"*Me?* What for?"

She looked at him pityingly. "Crikey, Frankie, you aren't half stupid."

"Steady on! I know you're upset and all, but—"

"Can't you see what's happening? He's leaving."

"Looks like he's already left, luv."

"Not just me. *Us.* You. The lads. This place. East London. The life."

"Bollocks," Frankie said, but a sliver of fear needled at his heart.

Gemma picked up the bottle and poured herself another drink. She swallowed a mouthful, then said, "You love him, too, don't you? More than I ever did. Doesn't matter, though. He'll leave you as well."

"Shut it, Gem," Frankie growled.

Gemma laughed. "Actually, I'm wrong. He won't leave. He can't. He's already gone."

"I said, *Shut it!*" Frankie yelled, banging the gin bottle on the bar.

Gemma finished her drink, lifting the glass to her lips with a shaking hand. Frankie was glad she'd stopped talking. He didn't want to hear it, couldn't bear to hear it, because deep down he knew she was right. Sid had always been a bit of a Robin Hood, giving the dosh in his pocket to every sorry tosser who asked, but lately he'd become worse. Ever since he'd met the lady doctor. First, he'd helped her get a box of rubber johnnies and didn't even take any money off her for them. Then he'd gone all soft over the old tart at the Taj who'd topped herself. And then he'd given the doctor money to open some kind of poxy clinic—a lot of money.

And who knew what he was doing now? Even if he'd found himself a new doxie, as Gemma seemed to think, Frankie knew he'd never let any woman interfere with business. But *something* was. Something was keeping him away. He was letting the Firm go straight to hell. And letting all of them go with it.

Frankie knew he had to do something, but what? He watched Gemma throw her third glass of gin back, eyes closed, and had a vision of himself sitting here doing the same after Sid walked out and left him to the tender mercies of Big Billy Madden, Nicky Barrecca, and whoever else wanted a piece of the East End.

Without warning, he snatched her glass away. "Come on," he said.

"Christ, Frankie, I was drinking that!"

"Get your things. We're leaving."

"Why? Where are we going?"

Frankie grabbed Gemma's coat, her bag, and her arm. "To find out where Sid Malone spends all his time."

CHAPTER 52

"The boxes are here, Joe! Get up!"

Joe Bristow opened his bleary eyes. It was dark. And noisy. It smelled odd. Of wood and books. For a moment he didn't know where he was. Then he remembered—the schoolhouse on Brick Lane. It was being used as a polling station. Today was polling day. He lifted his weary head off a hard wooden desktop.

"Wake up, will you?"

His brother was standing in the doorway of the empty classroom where Joe had gone to collapse.

"What time is it, Jimmy?" he rasped.

"Half nine. The first ballot boxes have arrived! Get up, you lazy bollocks! They're counting!"

Joe put his head back down and closed his eyes. He'd never known such deep exhaustion. He'd been out canvassing for the last two days—not stopping to sleep, barely eating. He felt as if he'd been in every public house, every union building, every wharf and factory in East London. His throat was so raw, he could barely speak.

His supporters felt he was leading over his Liberal and Tory rivals and they'd urged him to press his advantage. Joe had, but he felt far from confident about his chances. Lambert and Lytton were experienced politicians; he was not. In addition, Lytton was an incumbent and those were notoriously hard to beat.

Freddie was downstairs in the schoolhouse's small assembly room right now together with Dickie Lambert, the ballot counters, the Returning Officer, supporters, and various members of the press. Joe knew he should be downstairs, too.

Just a few more hours, he told himself. All he had to do was watch and wait while the ballots were counted and then congratulate Freddie. After that, he could go home and sleep.

No, not home, he thought, with a sudden ache. Home was 94 Grosvenor Square, where Fiona and Katie lived. Where he didn't live. Not anymore. It had been more than a month since he'd left Fiona but he still forgot. Every morning he woke up in his bed at the Coburg thinking he was in his real bed, his and Fiona's. And then he would open his eyes and see the hotel's flocked wallpaper, the strange crimson curtains, his clothes on the floor— and he would remember that he had given her a choice between himself and her brother, a choice she had refused to make.

And so they were in limbo. They barely spoke. She made sure she was out of the house when he came to see Katie. He made sure he left before she returned. Last week, though, he'd lost track of the time and had stayed too long. She'd come into the hall just as he was leaving. She'd nodded at him wordlessly and moved off toward the stairs, but he'd caught her wrist and stopped her.

"I miss you," he'd said. "And I love you."

"Then why did you leave me?"

"You know why. There are some fights you can't win, Fiona. Even you."

"I can try, damn it!" she said, wrenching free of his grip.

"What will it take, Fee? What does Sid Malone have to do to make you give up on him? Me warehouse is gone. Alf's dead. You were almost killed. Your attacker *was* killed. What will satisfy you? Seeing him kill someone himself?"

She had stalked off then, furious. Her anger, combined with her stubbornness, would not let her back down. Not yet, at any rate. But soon, he hoped, for he hated living apart from her, hated being at odds with her. She needed him, he knew she did. And he certainly needed her. Everything he did felt pointless without her by his side. He was weary in his body and weary in his heart. It had been a hard few weeks, a hard campaign, a hard fight.

And now he wondered if it had all been for nothing. Would anything change because of what he'd done? If Lytton won, would he follow through on his promises? Joe didn't know. He didn't know anything anymore, other than that he wanted to go home. To be welcomed by his wife.

To crawl into bed beside her. To tell her everything that had happened. Just the two of them talking in the dark. He wanted to make love to her and fall asleep in her arms. Instead, he fell asleep on the hard desk again. It was dark in the room and very late when he felt a hand on his shoulder, shaking him violently.

"Joe, you tosser, get up!" a voice bellowed.

"Jesus Christ, Jimmy, give me a minute, will you? I'm shagged," he said groggily.

"No! You have to come downstairs. Right now! It's finished, Joe. It's over."

Joe raised his head. He fumbled in his jacket pocket. "Hold on a mo'. I've got me concession speech here somewhere. Lytton won, did he?"

"No, he didn't."

"You're joking! It's Lambert? Lambert's the new MP?"

Jimmy beamed at him. "No, you silly bugger. *You* are!"

Joe stared at him, stunned and speechless.

John Burns, a Labour leader and an adviser to Joe throughout his campaign, burst into the room. "I've just had a telegram!" he shouted. "Keir Hardie's taken Merthyr Tydfil and Richard Bell's won Derby. That's three victories for the new Labour Party!" he crowed.

"Three?" Joe said. How could Burns be excited about three bloody seats? The Tories and Liberals had undoubtedly won hundreds between them.

"Three's a start, lad. In the last government we had only one seat. We've tripled our presence! Pebbles can start avalanches, you know. Labour's out of the gate and on its way! Today, three. Next time, thirty, and the time after that, three hundred!"

"Crikey, Joe, get up, will you?" Jimmy said.

Joe struggled to his feet.

"We've got reporters downstairs," Burns said. "They want a speech. Make it a good one. Photographs, too. Smarten yourself up, lad. I'll tell them you'll be down in a few minutes."

As Jimmy and John trotted back downstairs, Joe straightened his tie and raked his fingers through his hair. He tucked his shirt into his trousers and buttoned his jacket. A bath and a change of clothes would have been ideal, but this would have to do.

He took a deep breath and closed his eyes, preparing himself for what was ahead. Excitement and emotion began to replace the weariness he'd felt. He realized that he'd won. He'd actually *won*. He was an MP now, part of something much bigger than himself, and he knew that after tonight he would never be the same man again. But it was more than that. He sensed that his city, his entire country, would never be the same again. There would be celebrations tonight—here, in East London. In a valley in South Wales. In a mill town in the Midlands. Burns was right. This *was* the start of something. The Tories, the Liberals . . . they'd all courted the working man, they'd taken his vote, and they'd given him nothing in return. Now workers would have a voice—a small voice, yes, but a voice. Someone would speak for them, tell their story. Someone would fight for them in Westminster.

It was a victory, at once small and monumental, and for Joe it was bittersweet. He was proud, excited, beyond happy, but he wished Fiona were here. He wanted to share this with her, just as they had always shared everything else. He wanted to feel her arms around him, her hand in his. He wanted to see her eyes shining . . . for him.

This had to stop. They had to get back together.

He knew what to do. He would go to see Sid Malone himself. He would go, not as Sid's brother-in-law, but as the new MP. He would go alone—no police—and he would call a truce. They would talk. And he would warn Sid what lay ahead if he did not shut up shop. He had no idea if he'd succeed or not, but he knew that the gesture alone would show Fiona that he understood her, that he cared. He would try—for her.

Joe opened his eyes and headed downstairs. There was a feeling of excitement in the polling room. Election workers were chattering madly. Members of the press scribbled and smoked and looked at their watches. Freddie Lytton, haggard and gaunt, was talking to them, trying to put a brave face on defeat. Dickie Lambert had already left.

Joe was spotted immediately.

"Mr. Bristow! Can you give us a statement, sir? Mr. Bristow, over here! Mr. Bristow, can you hold it right there? I need a photo."

Joe first went to Freddie and shook his hand. Freddie gave him a tired smile and congratulated him.

"Mr. Bristow, have you a speech?" a reporter shouted. "Any words?"

Joe turned to them. As he did, he caught a glimpse out of the school's open doors to the street beyond. Men stood in it. His supporters. Now his constituents. Working men who'd been standing there in the cold for hours, who faced an early start in the morning.

"Aye, gentlemen," he said. "I've some words. But they're for *them*." He hooked his thumb in the direction of the door. "For the people who just made me their MP. You're welcome to join me outside if you want to hear what I have to say."

John Burns heard him. He smiled, then hurried out ahead of him.

"Gentlemen, allow me to introduce to you the Honorable Member for Tower Hamlets—Mr. Joseph Bristow!"

For a split second there was a shocked silence and then a deafening cheer went up. It grew, rolling down Brick Lane, not stopping. Hats went up in the air. Grown men hugged one another like children. Some of them danced. Lights went on in houses, doors and windows opened, people came out and stood on their steps in their night clothes, and still it didn't stop. Little kids rubbed their bleary eyes and bawled. Men opened bottles of beer and toasted one another. Housewives banged pots together. And still it didn't stop.

Joe finally held up his hands, trying to quiet them, trying to speak, but they paid him no attention. He turned to Burns. The man was grinning from ear to ear.

"See that, lad?" he shouted, clapping him on the back. "Know what it's called? *Hope*."

CHAPTER 53

"Holy cow, Albie, that's Norman Collie!" Seamie said.

"Where?" Albert Alden asked.

"There! Halfway up the steps, hands in his pockets. See him?"

"He was with Mummery on Nanga Parbat, wasn't he?" Albie said.

"Yes, he was."

Seamie and Albie and everyone who knew anything about mountains knew that five years ago Collie, Albert Mummery, and another British mountaineer, Geoffrey Hastings, had made the first attempt at the Himalayan peak. Mummery and two of his Sherpas were buried in an avalanche and never seen again. Collie and Hastings survived.

"Do you think we could talk to him?" Seamie said.

"I bet he only talks to the other mountain gods," Albie said. "Crikey, Seamie, *look*! There's Nansen!"

Seamie spun around. He saw the man walking across the street. A tall Norwegian, with white-blond hair and a walrus mustache, he was hard to miss. "Fridtjof Nansen," he whispered, awestruck. He took off his cap.

Albie laughed. "You're not going to genuflect, are you?"

"I might."

Nansen had been the first to cross the Arctic Ocean in an attempt to reach the North Pole. When his ship, the *Fram,* had become hopelessly icebound, he'd continued the journey on foot. He hadn't made the Pole, but he had succeeded in pushing north to 86° 14′ N—the highest latitude ever attained.

"I wonder who else is here?" Albie said.

"I don't know, but let's go in before all the good seats are taken," Seamie said.

The two men were fishing in their pockets for their membership cards when a voice behind them called out, "Albie! Albie Alden, wait for me!"

Albie grimaced. "Oh, no," he groaned. "It's Willa."

"Where?" Seamie asked. He looked around. There was a wiry boy in plus fours with a rucksack over his shoulder running toward them, but no Willa.

"Hi, Albs!" the boy said, then he noticed Seamie. "Seamie? Seamie Finnegan! Is that you?" He kissed him on the cheek.

"Steady on, mate," Seamie warned, taking a step back.

The boy burst into laughter. "Seamie, you great bloody fool, it's me! Willa!"

"*Willa?* What happened to your hair?" The last time he'd seen her, at a garden party at the Aldens' house more than a year ago, her long brown curls had been neatly plaited and pinned. Now they barely grazed her chin.

"I cut it off. It was always getting in my way. Mum had fits. Took to her bed for a week. How are you, Seamie? It's been an age. What are you doing here? Aren't you supposed to be in school?"

Seamie explained that he'd left school—and why—and how his sister had reacted to the news. Then he told her that he was staying at hers and Albie's house until Fiona cooled down. Or until he got himself on the Discovery Expedition. Whichever happened first.

Willa's eyes sparkled with excitement as he talked and Seamie noticed that she had changed since he'd last seen her. She had only ever been Albie's pesty sister, but now she'd become something more—beautiful. When had that happened? Even her cropped hair and her brother's old tweed jacket couldn't diminish her beauty.

"Do you think you can do it? Do you think you can get a place on the expedition?" she asked, when he'd finished talking.

"I mean to try. I've got a strategy. I've decided not to approach Captain Scott. He won't give me the time of day. That's why I'm here tonight. I'm going to approach Ernest Shackleton. He's a third lieutenant in charge of holds, stores, and provisions. I know the best I can hope for is a dogsbody job and he'll be the one handing them out. If he turns me down, I'll keep trying. I won't take no for an answer. I've got to go. I've got no choice. It's either that or move crates of kumquats around my brother-in-law's warehouse."

Willa laughed. "I wish I were you, Seamie. How lucky you are. Imagine if you *do* get to go. You'll go places no human being has ever gone before. See things no one's ever seen."

Her large moss-green eyes held his and for a few seconds he could not look away. Embarrassed, he finally broke her gaze and said, "What about you, Willa? What have you been up to? Albie told me you were in Scotland. On holiday with some friends."

Willa grinned. "I was. Sort of. I was in Scotland and my friends were there, too. But they stayed in the hotel. I went to Ben Nevis. Cracker of a mountain." Seamie raised an eyebrow. Ben Nevis, in the Scottish Highlands, was the highest peak in Britain. Those who climbed it had to be good navigators as well as good climbers for its weather was rough and unpredictable and the routes were often obscured.

"Take the Ben Path, did you?" he asked.

Willa smirked. "The granny climb? No. I climbed the Carn Mor Dearg Arête."

"Really?" Seamie said, trying his best not to sound too impressed. He'd tried that route twice, and both times he'd had to give up because of sheeting rain. "You must have had good weather."

Willa shook her head. "Sleet and rain and the wind blew a gale."

"Turn back, did you?"

"No. Took a bit of doing, but I got up." She laughed. "And got down again. It's the getting down part that counts, isn't it?"

"Look, you two, you can stay out here talking about climbs all night if you like, but I'm going inside. I want a seat. See you later, Wills," Albie said.

"Wait, Albie!" she said. "I want to go with you. I rushed back just so I wouldn't miss Shackleton's talk, but the train was late and I don't have my card and I couldn't get home in time to get it. Let me come in with you, will you? As your guest."

"Looking like that?" Albie said.

Men greatly outnumbered women at the RGS lectures but a few women were in attendance this evening—all properly attired in dresses or suits, overcoats and hats.

"Come on, Albie, be a brick!"

"You can't come in like that, Willa! What will people say? You're a girl, not a boy. It's not proper. You'll get us all thrown out, and I don't want to miss this."

Willa gave him a dirty look. She snatched Seamie's cap and put it on her head, tucking her curly brown hair up under it. "Now I'm a boy, all right?"

"Go home, Wills," Albie said through gritted teeth. "If Mum finds out you were out and about in London dressed up like a bloke, she'll gut us both."

"She won't find out. How will she?"

"She always finds out and I'm always the one who catches it."

"I *won't* go home," Willa said. "I'll wait outside. Right here on these steps. In the dark. Prey to every robber and murderer in London. Alone and defenseless."

Albie snorted. "Defenseless? *You?*"

"It's not *fair!* I want to hear Shackleton. I know more about Antarctica than the two of you put together!" Willa said. She didn't stomp her foot or cry or use any feminine tricks to get her way. She just looked from her brother to Seamie and back again, pinning them like frogs to a dissecting tray with her intense gaze. "Just let me come in with you. Please? I'll sit in the back. No one will ever know. If you don't, I'll just sneak in. You know I will. *Please*, Albie?"

Albert sighed, defeated. "All right. Fine," he said, pulling the cap down over her ears.

"I can come?" she asked hopefully.

"On one condition."

"*Anything.*"

"If Mum catches wind, I knew nothing about it."

"You're a peach!" Willa said, giving him a quick kiss on the cheek.

"Stop that, Wills. You're supposed to be a bloke."

"Sorry."

Albie buttoned his sister's tweed jacket and straightened her shirt collar. Not satisfied, he took off his spectacles and put them on her. She was a slender, angular girl, and the disguise succeeded; to the casual eye she looked like Albie's younger brother. Seamie was glad Albie had relented. He wanted Willa to come with them. He wanted to sit beside her. To talk to her.

The three teenagers loped up a flight of steps and through the doorway of a shabby, tumbledown lecture theater in Burlington Gardens. It belonged to the Civil Service Commission, which allowed the Royal Geographical Society to use it for talks. Shackleton's lecture had been announced a week ago, and Seamie had barely been able to sleep or eat ever since.

Albert Alden was Seamie's best friend. They were both seventeen, and had met several years ago at the RGS and, bound by their common enthusiasm for mountaineering, had taken an immediate shine to each other. Willa was Albert's twin sister. Seamie had learned early on in his and Albert's friendship that you didn't get one Alden without the other. He didn't mind, though. Most of the time he quite forgot that Willa was a girl. She rarely behaved like one. She knew more about climbing than most men did. More than he did, in fact, though he'd never admit it.

She often told them—in a hushed voice so that her mother couldn't hear—that she was going to be the first to climb Everest. When they told her she couldn't—that even men hadn't done that—she would smile and say, "Watch me."

Seamie had holidayed with the Aldens in the Lake District. Willa would tell her mother that she was just going to watch the lads climb, and then, as soon as she was out of her parents' sight, she would change into a pair of Albie's old trousers and beat them both up a rock face.

"One member," Albie said now, showing his RGS membership card to the man in the ticket booth. "And one guest." The clerk barely glanced at Willa, he simply pushed two tickets at him. Seamie showed his own card next, thinking that most people were too preoccupied to see past their own noses. The three of them went into the hall, then Seamie led the way to the front. He was taking no chances.

He wanted to be near the podium so that he could get to Shackleton afterward, talk to him, and hopefully convince him that he was expedition material. He spotted four empty seats in the middle of the third row. As they settled into three of them, a young man who looked about their age came in from the other end of the row and sat down in the fourth. He looked familiar. Seamie was certain he'd seen him at other lectures.

"Supposed to be a ripping good speaker," the lad said.

Willa was about to reply when Albie talked over her. "One of the best," he said.

"They say he strong-armed his way onto Scott's expedition," Seamie said.

Within seconds all four were buzzing excitedly about the expedition. They all knew its background, and Shackleton's, too. He was a hero to them. He'd defied his father's wishes to enter medicine and had left school for the sea when he was sixteen—a year younger than they were. His first ship was the *Hoghton Tower* out of Liverpool, bound for Valparaiso via Cape Horn. The ship made the cape in the dead of winter and battled blizzards for two months before rounding it. Shackleton spent the next five years sailing to and from the Far East and America before making first mate and then master. He'd worked on merchant ships until just last summer, when he'd wangled himself an introduction to Llewellyn Longstaff, the principal financier of the Antarctic expedition. He'd persuaded Longstaff to put him forth as a member of the expedition and the man had done so, together with Sir Clements Markham, the RGS's president. With their influence, he'd been accepted. Shackleton had basically talked his way onto the expedition and Seamie was convinced that he could do the same.

While the four were talking, the lights suddenly dimmed, signaling everyone to quiet down.

"Here we go!" Willa said. "Antarctica!"

"I'd give anything to be on board that ship," the newcomer said, his eyes lingering on her.

Seamie was curiously quiet.

"I'm Albert Alden, by the way," Albie said, reaching across to shake the newcomer's hand. "And this is my . . . uh . . . my . . ."

"Twin," said Willa, her color suddenly high, her eyes sparking mischief.

"George Mallory," the lad said, shaking hands all around. "Pleased to meet you."

Seamie wondered if George Mallory knew that Willa was a girl. It bothered him to think he might. To think that might be why she was suddenly full of smiles. He sat back in his seat, irritated and perplexed, as George and Willa made plans for all of them to visit a pub afterward. What was any of that to him? So Willa was pretty. So what? He didn't give a monkey's bum who she smiled at. Or who smiled back. He was here to see Shackleton.

The lights went down. An austere figure took the stage—the society's president.

"It's Barkers," Albie groaned. "He can't half drone."

Willa snorted. George smiled. Seamie glowered. After an interminable introduction by Sir Clements Markham, Ernest Shackleton took the stage.

Ten seconds into his speech, Seamie had forgotten all about Willa Alden and George Mallory and everything and everyone in the entire world except for Ernest Shackleton. The man was mesmerizing. He strode about the stage, a compact, manic bundle of energy, talking about the call of uncharted lands, of endless seas and stalwart ships and the brave brotherhood of sailor scientists, of the honor that would accrue to the society, to all of Britain, should Scott and the crew of the *Discovery* be the first to claim the South Pole. He warned all present that their rivals for the glory and conquest of the Pole were relentless—hadn't Nansen almost taken the North

Pole? Hadn't another Norwegian, Carsten Borchgrevink, just returned from Antarctica, having trekked farther south than any man had before? Wasn't it a question not of *if*, but *when*?

Seamie sat on the edge of his seat, listening and watching, barely breathing—and felt every fiber of his being strain toward the man, toward his boldness and courage and vision. Ernest Shackleton was doing everything Seamie wanted to do, he was being everything he wanted to be. And he had started out, as Seamie felt *he* must, by leaving school and taking to the seas. An hour later, Shackleton finished his lecture to a roar of applause, then stepped back from the podium to down a glass of water. He bowed, held up his hands, then took the podium again to answer questions.

Seamie watched the questioners stand one after another, some older, some younger, and knew as he listened to them that questioning the likes of Shackleton was the closest most of them would ever come to exploration. To adventure. And he knew, too, that he would rather die than remain one of them.

He was going to collar Shackleton. Tonight. Even if he had to follow him home and sleep on his steps. Shackleton would hear him; he would understand. They were the same inside. All he needed was a minute, maybe two, to convince him. Let Albie and Willa and George bloody Mallory go to the pub. Ernest Shackleton was going to Antarctica. And Seamie Finnegan was going with him.

CHAPTER 54

"Damned shame about the election, Lytton," Dougie Mawkins said. "Labour victory, was it?"

"Yes, it was," Freddie said.

"Thin end of the wedge, old man. Next thing you know, there'll be barrow boys in the Lords and a docker in Downing Street."

Freddie smiled tightly. He wanted to break Dougie's nose. If the man offered any more condolences, spouted any more inanities, he would. He'd come here tonight to forget about his disastrous loss, not to be reminded of it.

"Ripping good party, though, don't you think?" Dougie asked.

"Just got here," Freddie replied. He'd heard about the party as he was leaving his club. It was in a Chelsea atelier, all done up in the Moorish style, and it was being thrown by a duke's son for his mistress, a painter, to celebrate the first exhibition of her work.

"Have you seen Gemma Dean?" Dougie asked.

"No. Is she here?"

"Over by the windows. Looks a bit drawn, if you ask me. Or maybe it's just that I haven't seen her in a while. Out of circulation for a bit, I understand. Back now, though. Guess the rent's due." Dougie recognized another friend and chased off after him.

Freddie watched him go. Had he wanted to break his nose? Now he wanted to break his skull for the crack about Gemma's bill. Dougie didn't have to worry about bills. His family owned ten thousand acres in Cornwall and scores of buildings in London. That an idiot such as Mawkins had fallen into a life of such ease and splendor, while he had to worry about every pound—well, just thinking about it made him sick with envy.

He craned his neck, looking for Gemma. He finally spotted her, or rather her diamonds. She was wearing only the earrings, but they sparkled like stars in the gaslight. He remembered her saying that Sid Malone had given them to her, and that they were worth a fortune.

He could use a fortune now himself. Just last week Bingham had paid his bill at the Reform Club—just as they were going to post his name. His tailor had cut him off completely. Things were getting rather desperate. He took a sip of his whisky and tried not to think about it.

He would prefer to think about the lovely Gemma Dean instead, but, eyeing her, Freddie noticed that she seemed a bit less lovely. Dougie was right. She looked drawn. Her dress was ill-fitting, loose in places. He wondered if she'd gone in for the new look—all willowy and fey. It suited some girls—pale, dreary girls who liked to spout poetry and mope—but it didn't suit her. She was a woman with curves and she looked best as her luscious self, round and ripe and ready to burst out of her corset. He pictured himself unlacing that same corset and caressing her warm, heavy breasts. A late-night romp with her would be just the thing to snap him out of his funk.

"Hullo, old girl. How's things?" he said, walking up to her.

"Smashing, Freddie. Just smashing," she said acidly.

She was clutching a glass of champagne. She downed its contents and signaled for another. A waiter refreshed her glass immediately.

"Heard about the election," she said. "Sorry you didn't win."

"So am I."

"Heard about your engagement, too. Guess it never rains but it bloody pours."

"I guess so," he said, feeling vexed. He'd hoped that chatting up Gemma would improve his mood, but so far she was only making it worse.

"Well, it's a bugger," she said, swallowing another mouthful of champagne, "but at least you're free now. And so am I."

Freddie felt the hairs along his neck prickle. He didn't like the direction this conversation was taking. "What do you mean, Gem?"

"You were jilted. So was I."

"Were you? I'm dreadfully sorry to hear it."

She cocked her head. "Are you?"

"You don't doubt me, do you?"

She didn't answer his question. Instead, she asked one of her own. "Remember the last time you came to call on me?"

"I remember every time I've called on you, darling girl."

"Remember what you said?"

"Um . . . something about my campaign?"

"No, something about us marrying. You said you wished you could marry me. But you had to marry India because that's what your parents wanted. Well, now she's broken it off. You're a free man. We can marry. What's to stop us?"

Freddie stalled. "Gem, you know it's not that simple."

"What I know, Freddie, is that you're a liar." Her voice was rising. Heads were turning.

"Gemma, I think you've had enough," Freddie said, steering her to a quiet corner.

"Oh, I've had enough, all right. Of you. And Sid Malone. And every other bleedin' stage-door johnnie."

"Gemma, be *reasonable*," Freddie hissed. "You know how I feel about you. You know I think you're the most gorgeous woman in London, but marriages are made of more than attraction. We come from such different backgrounds. We lead different lives. We've hardly anything in common, really."

Gemma laughed. It was a harsh, ugly sound. "Oh, you're wrong there, mate," she said. "We have more in common than you think. A lot more."

"Do we?"

"For starters, your former fiancée. And mine."

"Gem, old girl, I really would put that drink down. You're not making a tremendous amount of sense."

"Sid Malone is bedding India Selwyn Jones. Is that clear enough for you?"

It was Freddie's turn to laugh. And he did. Loudly. "That's a good one. Really. I don't think I've ever heard anything so absurd in my life."

"I told you she'd come to visit him, didn't I? And about the rubber johnnies."

"Yes . . ."

"You didn't believe me about that at first either. But I was right. And I'm right about this, too," Gemma said. Freddie saw that her eyes didn't look unfocused any more. They were sharp with bitterness and anger.

"No, you're not. You don't know India. She'd never take up with the likes of Malone. Never."

"We followed Sid a few nights ago. Me and Frankie Betts," Gemma said. "He hasn't been around much, and Frankie wanted to see where he's been keeping himself. We saw him take a hackney cab to Brick Lane. Saw it stop just past the caff. Moskowitz's. Where she's staying. We waited. A few minutes later we saw her come out and get into the cab. We kept following them. All the way out of Whitechapel. To a house. They went inside together. We saw the lights come on in a flat on the top floor. They didn't come back out."

Freddie didn't reply. He couldn't. Sid Malone and India—it was unthinkable. Impossible. Not only had India left him, she'd taken up with his greatest enemy—the man who'd robbed the Stronghold, who'd cost him the Home Rule victory, and very likely the election. He'd never been able to recover after his humiliation in the Commons. He'd lost too much credibility.

A red rage boiled up inside him now. A lethal rage. He grabbed Gemma's wrist. "Where's the flat? What's the address?"

Gemma pulled free. "I'm tired of being fucked, Freddie. Fucked and fucked over. You want the information, you can pay for it. Cash up front. Two hundred quid will do nicely."

"Gemma, please . . ."

"You know where I live."

"You bitch!"

"Four hundred," Gemma said. Then she turned on her heel and walked away.

CHAPTER 55

Seamie Finnegan wanted a hot cup of tea like he'd never wanted one be- fore. He wanted dry clothes, a blazing fire, and a nice soft chair.

He'd been standing in the same spot, on the pavement outside Ernest Shackleton's house, for a day and a half, and he was ready to keel over. But he wouldn't. He'd come this far, and he'd stand here another day and a half if that's what it took to get Shackleton to talk to him. He'd stand here for a week.

He'd approached the man after the Royal Geographical Society lecture, but Shackleton had been mobbed and Seamie hadn't been able to get near him. He'd tried again when the crowd died down, but Shackleton had been on his way to dinner at the Explorers' Club.

"Mr. Shackleton, sir, might I have a word?" Seamie had called out, trot- ting behind the man and his entourage.

"What is it, lad?"

"I'd like . . . I'd like to join your expedition, sir."

Shackleton had laughed. So had his companions. "You and all the schoolboys in London!" he said. "We're all full up, lad," he'd added, a bit more kindly. And then he was gone.

"Come on, Seamie," Albie had said. "Come drown your sorrows with a pint. George here says there's a good pub right round the corner."

Seamie didn't answer him; he was still watching Shackleton.

"You want to go after him, don't you?" Willa said.

She had read his mind.

"I wouldn't. If you dog him, you might anger him," Albie said.

"So what?" Willa said. "He'll see that you mean it."

"I'll see you back at the house later," Seamie said, starting off. "Or not."

"Good luck!" Willa called after him.

Seamie followed his quarry to the Explorers' Club. It was nearly mid- night by the time Shackleton came out. As soon as Seamie saw him, he ap- proached him again, but Shackleton cut him off. "I'm not a pheasant," he'd said. "I don't enjoy being stalked."

Still, Seamie did not give up. When Shackleton got into a cab, he did, too, and had his driver follow. He arrived at Shackleton's house as the man was entering it.

"Not you again!" Shackleton said upon spotting him. "What the hell do you want, boy?"

"To join the expedition to Antarctica."

"That's impossible. As I've already told you. Now, if you don't leave, I shall have you removed."

"That is your prerogative, sir," Seamie had replied.

Shackleton had trotted up his steps in a huff. Once inside, he'd pulled the curtains, but Seamie had seen them twitch once or twice. He hadn't had Seamie removed, but he had pointedly ignored him on the several occasions he left or entered his house the next day.

Yet Seamie still refused to budge. He'd stood there from midnight on Tuesday to now—just after nine on Thursday morning. He wondered what would happen to him. He thought he might faint, but didn't know if it would be from lack of water, lack of food, or lack of sleep. And if he did, what would Shackleton do? Step over him? Roll him into the gutter?

As he was pondering these questions, the door to Shackleton's house opened and the man himself stepped out, a white linen napkin in his hand. Lovely, mouth-watering aromas of bacon and buttered toast wafted out after him. Seamie's stomach growled.

"Quite a stunt you've pulled, lad," Shackleton said. "Standing outside my house for thirty hours straight."

"Thirty-three hours and ten minutes, sir."

"I imagine you think me quite impressed."

"I would not presume to know your thoughts, sir. I did not aim to impress, only to demonstrate the depth of my commitment."

"Commitment, eh? At fifty-eight degrees during the day and forty-two at night?"

"It also rained, sir. Last night. From just after midnight to five thirty."

Shackleton stroked his chin thoughtfully. "Did it?"

"Yes, sir."

"The question is, can you do it for forty-eight hours? For seventy-two? For a week? A month? When it's ten degrees during the day and forty below at night? Can you do it in a blizzard when your hands won't work and your toes are turning black? Can you do it then? Think carefully before you answer. Men—better men than you—have died trying."

"I'm not afraid to die, sir. I'm afraid to never live."

Shackleton worked a bit of food from his teeth. "Big words from a boy," he finally said.

"I am seventeen, sir. A year older than you yourself were when you sailed around Cape Horn on the *Hoghton Tower*."

Shackleton was quiet for a few seconds, then he said, "Come inside. My cook's made eggs and rashers." He held up a finger. "I make no promises. I only wish to feed you up a bit before I send you home to your mama."

"My mother is dead, sir. And you may try to send me home, but I won't go. The sea is my home, the wild, uncharted waters of Antarctica, and I will stand right here, in wind and rain, until—"

Shackleton rolled his eyes. "Enough! You'll be on about white whales next. This isn't *Moby-Dick,* you know, all sea dogs and romance. It's a scientific expedition. Can you *do* anything? Have you ever set foot on a boat?"

"I hold the record for the fastest run from Yarmouth to Key Largo in a cutter. I did it alone."

"In a cutter, you say? Bowsprit?"

"No, sir."

"Gaff mainsail?"

"Yes, sir. With a genoa jib set."

"You sailed in that all the way from Nova Scotia to the Keys? *Why?*"

"I wanted a challenge, sir."

"Sounds like you got one. What's your name again, lad?"

"Seamus Finnegan, sir."

Shackleton smiled. "An Irishman, eh? I was born in Ireland myself. Come on, then, Seamus Finnegan, let's get you some tea. I'm still making no promises, but I'd like to hear more about that cutter. Genoa jib, you say?"

Seamie's legs were numb from standing so long. He stumbled on the first step, quickly righted himself, and followed Shackleton inside. Five minutes ago he'd wanted to drop down dead. Now he felt like he could fly. He wanted to whoop, dance a jig. He did neither. He would remain serious and sober. He had a chance, just a slim one, but it was all he needed. He had a crack at Shackleton now, a crack at Antarctica. A crack at his dream.

CHAPTER 56

India woke where she had fallen asleep—in the crook of Sid's arm. He smiled as she stirred and kissed her head.

"You snore. Did you know that?" he said.

"I do not."

"You do. Like an old man."

"Rubbish."

Rain swept against the window. India looked out of it. It had still been twilight when they'd tumbled into bed. It was pitch-black outside now. Inside the room an oil lamp glowed softly from its perch upon the bureau.

"What time is it?" she asked.

"Just gone midnight. I heard the church bell."

She looked at his face. She saw the circles under his eyes and the weariness in them.

"Why are you still awake?" she asked. "Can't you sleep?"

He smiled. "I don't want to. Not when I'm with you."

India propped herself up on one elbow. "But you *never* sleep."

"I do."

"You don't." She frowned at him. "Did you have coffee this evening? Tea? An excess of alcohol?"

"No, no, and no, Dr. Jones. I'm *fine*."

India bit her lip. She didn't believe him. "Something's worrying you, then."

Sid's gaze flickered away from hers and she knew she was right.

"What is it, Sid?"

"Nothing."

He was putting her off. Evading her questions. Lying to her. He always did this. To protect her, he said. It made her furious.

"You can tell me, you know," she said testily. "I won't run back tattling to Ozzie, Cozzie, Rozzie, and the rest of the wide boys."

"I told you it's nothing and it's nothing," he said tightly.

India flung the sheets back and got out of bed. She stalked across the room to the chair where her clothing lay.

"What are you doing?"

"Getting dressed," she said, stepping into her petticoat.

"Where are you going?"

"Home," she replied.

"India, for Christ's sake, why? Why are you doing this?"

"Because you don't love me."

"Of course I do."

She whirled around. "No, you *don't*. You say you love me, Sid, but you don't trust me. That's not love. If you really love someone, you trust her. I told you everything about my life—everything!—in the hospital, when I barely knew you. Just because you asked me to. You promised me you would tell me your story, but you never do. You won't tell me about the past. You won't let me talk about the future. You won't even tell me why you can't *sleep*, for God's sake! Never mind where you came from, or who your parents were, or what you did before . . . before . . ."

"Before I went bad."

"I didn't say that!"

"You didn't have to." He took a deep breath and blew it out again. "India, there are some things you just can't tell people."

"Is that what I am to you? *People?*"

"No," he said stubbornly. He said nothing else.

She pulled her blouse on and buttoned it. A doctor, she was used to dressing quickly in the middle of the night. She sat down on the bed and picked up one of her shoes.

"India, please don't go. Please."

Something in his voice made her put her shoe down and look at him. She saw that he no longer looked angry. He looked helpless and scared.

"Why can't you tell me, Sid? Why can't you tell me who you are?" she asked softly.

He met her gaze and she could see that he was struggling with himself. At length, he said, "I did hard time. Years ago. When I was eighteen."

She nodded, uncertain where he was going, but willing to follow. "Is that where you got the scars on your back?" She had asked him that question before, but he had never given her an answer.

"Yes."

"How?"

"Thirty lashes with a cat o' nine."

"Oh God," India said. She felt all her anger drain away. A terrible sorrow took its place.

"Why, Sid?"

"I threatened a guard."

"Physically?"

"No. I threatened that I would go to the warden."

"Why?"

"To tell him . . . to try to . . ." His words trailed off.

"Thirty lashes could have killed you."

"They nearly did."

"Is that why you can't sleep? Do the scars give you pain?"

"No. Not those scars."

He gazed out the window. She saw that his throat was working. It was as if he were trying to bring the words up from inside himself and couldn't. Suddenly he turned back to her and in an anguished voice said, "I was raped there. In prison."

For a few seconds, India thought she would be sick. "When? Who?" she whispered.

"A guard. Wiggs was his name. Two others held me down. It went on for nearly four months. They always came after dark. I heard their footsteps on the stone floor. Coming closer. Their voices. That's why I don't sleep. I *can't* sleep."

India reached for him, but he shied from her.

"Don't touch me. Don't," he said.

"I'm sorry. I won't. I won't, Sid. It's all right," she said. "You said it went on for four months. What happened then? What stopped it?"

"Denny Quinn stopped it."

"Who?"

"Quinn. Me old guv'nor. He waited for Wiggs to come out of his local one night. He followed him and cut his throat."

India's hands came up to her mouth.

Sid laughed cruelly. "Still love me?" he asked.

Then he leaned back and banged his head against the wall. She'd seen patients in Bedlam do the same thing. Tortured souls trying to crack their heads open to let the bad memories out. She crawled across the bed and got between him and the wall.

"Stop it. Stop it now," she said. "Look at me. Look at me, Sid." He raised his eyes to hers. "I *do* love you. Do you hear me? I love you."

His fists were clenched so hard that the veins stood out on his forearms. His whole body was shaking. His breath was rapid and short. India knew he wanted to punch something, smash something. He'd held the pain in for so long, and now it was coming out and he was terrified. She knew what to do. She would take it from him. All the rage and sorrow. All the poison. Slowly, gently, she reached for his fists. Softly, she smoothed them open.

"Let it out. Let it go," she whispered.

She put her arms around him and held him tightly. He tried to push her away again, but she wouldn't let him. She felt him dig his fingers into her back, felt his body shudder, then heard his sobs, harsh and tearing. His tears were hot against her skin. She held him and rocked him, whispered to him and kissed him and cried for him, but she did not let him go.

When his emotion was finally spent, he raised his head and looked at her. "Jesus Christ, India, what have I done?" he asked, wiping away her tears. "Dragging you into my life. I should have done the right thing that night at the Bark. I should have taken you home. Instead, I'm making you cry for all the horrible things I've done."

"No, not for what you've done. For you."

Sid was silent for a while, then he said, "No one's ever done that. Cried for me."

"No one's ever loved you like I do."

Sid could not look at her, so he looked at his hands.

"Tell me the rest," India said. "Tell me how you got to prison. And what you did when you got out. Tell me where you grew up. What songs your mother sang to you. What your father was like. Tell me."

He had to talk about it. He had to tell her. To trust her. It was his only chance. *Their* only chance.

She rose from the bed and refilled the two glasses on the night table from a half-empty bottle standing next to them. She handed him one. "Here," she said. "This will help." Sid drank deeply. He leaned back against the pillows and closed his eyes. And then he began.

His words came haltingly at first and then in a great gush. He talked for more than two hours, telling her about his life on Montague Street. His family. That his first name had once been Charlie. He told her about his father's death and his mother's. How he'd run away from the sight of his dead mother. How he'd lost touch with his family. India guessed that the memories of them were still very painful for him. He told her how he'd fallen in with Quinn and eventually found himself stuck so deep into the life that there was no way out. He talked until his throat was raw. And when he had finished, he looked at her with weary, hollow eyes and said, "There. That's it. That's everything."

"Thank you," she said.

"I don't know why you're thanking me. It's all as ugly as hell. And telling it doesn't change a damn thing."

"Actually, it does. I know what you need now, Sid. You need to get away from here. Far away. Away from London and your life there. Away from England and all the horrible memories."

"Is that all? Why, let's move to the Riviera, then. I'll book our passages tomorrow."

India ignored his sarcasm. Her brow was furrowed; her gaze inward. "We could go away. We could leave London, the two of us together," she said.

"Oh, aye?" he said. "Am I mistaken, missus, or are you just about to open a clinic in Whitechapel?"

She turned her gray eyes on him. "I would leave it," she said, "for you."

"And close the doors on all those people? The ones you said you wanted to help?"

"The doors will stay open. Harriet and Fenwick and Ella can take over. At least for a little while. Maybe we'll come back one day. When things calm down. When people don't remember you anymore."

"Forget it, luv. The people you're talking about have very long memories."

"No, listen to me—"

"No, India, *you* listen to *me*. It's too late for me, don't you understand that? I'm a lost cause, but you're not. That clinic is your dream. And you've worked bloody hard to see it through. I won't let you walk away from it. You've built something wonderful in this fucking awful city. Something beautiful."

"Sid," she said quietly. "*You* are something beautiful."

He looked away from her, unable to speak, his eyes full of emotion.

India took his hand and squeezed it. "It's *not* too late. We'll start again. As Mr. and Mrs. Baxter. We'll go away. We could go to Scotland. To Ireland. Or to the Continent." And then she suddenly sat up straight and grabbed Sid's arm. "No . . . wait!" She laughed out loud. "My God, it's been right there all along! Why didn't I think of it before? I'll tell you what we're going to do. We're going to begin again!"

India jumped out of bed, ran into the sitting room, then returned to the bedroom with a folder in her hand.

"My cousin called it the end of the world," she said excitedly. "Then he said he was wrong, that it wasn't the end of the world, it was the beginning. He said when he stood there, with only sea and sky before him, he felt like it was the very first day, and he was the very first person, and that there was no ugliness or evil in the world and nothing but beauty all around him."

"India, *what* are you on about?"

She opened the folder and handed him the photographs. "Remember these? This is Point Reyes, California," she said. "It's mine. I own it. That's where we're going."

Sid looked at the photos. She remembered how taken he'd been with them when he'd first seen them. He wanted to believe—in this place, in them, in a new life. She could see how much he wanted that.

"What would we do there?" he asked.

"I'm a doctor. People always need doctors."

"I'm not."

"You can cook. Keep house. Knit socks."

"You've missed your calling. You should write fairy stories. You're bloody good at telling them. You almost make me believe them."

"They're not fairy stories! We'll go there, Sid. You and I. There's an old farmhouse there. We'll fix it up. Live in it. We can start again."

"Aye, luv," he said wistfully.

"We will," she said fiercely. "Do you believe me?"

"India . . ."

She took his face in her two hands. "Say it! Say you believe me!"

Sid opened his eyes, but said nothing.

"There *is* such a thing as redemption, Sid Malone. And forgiveness. Even in this world. Even for you. You can start again, if you choose to. You found a way into the life, you can find a way out. I'll help you."

Looking into his eyes, so deeply green, so full of pain, India willed him to imagine a new life. A new start. A future different from anything he'd ever known.

"Believe me?" she asked again.

"Yes, India," he finally said. "I do."

She kissed him hard, then took off her clothes and slipped beneath him. They made love more passionately than they ever had. And when they were finished, Sid rested his head against her chest. She put her arms around him and told him they would go as soon as she got the clinic open and running. In two weeks' time. Three at the most. They'd take a train to Southampton and then a ship to New York and then another train west— all across America, all the way to California. She would give him one of the photographs to keep with him, to remind him of their future.

"We'll like it there," she said. "I know we will."

Sid didn't answer. She looked down at him. His breathing was deep and steady. And his head was heavy against her chest. His eyes were closed. He was asleep. Finally asleep.

A fresh volley of rain battered against the window. India looked out at the tree branches waving crazily in the wind and the dark skies beyond them. Her eyes were fierce as she watched the storm, daring the thunder and lightning to do their worst. And the black night. And the city and everyone in it.

Sid needed her and she would be there for him. Loving him. Protecting him. No matter what it took, no matter what she had to sacrifice, they would begin again. There *were* beginnings, not only endings. She would show him that. Make him believe it. They would leave the past behind. No one would hurt him ever again. He was hers now. *Hers*. And she would never let him go.

CHAPTER 57

"You *have* to tell her!" Willa Alden shouted at a fitting-room door in Burberry's outfitters in London's Haymarket.

"No" came the muffled reply.

"What are you going to do? Just disappear? Send a postcard from the South Pole?"

The door to the fitting room banged open. Seamie Finnegan clomped out barely recognizable in a pair of baggy trousers, an anorak, and a balaclava—all made from Thomas Burberry's patented waterproof gabardine.

"Oh, *very* stylish," Willa said.

"Burberry isn't stylish, it's durable," Seamie replied, pulling the balaclava off. "And warm."

"I hope so. You're going to freeze your bum off."

"Why, Willa, do I detect a note of jealousy?" Seamie asked.

"There's nothing to be jealous of. You haven't made it to the Pole yet."

"I will."

"We'll see."

"Crikey, Seamie. Can you believe it? Scott, Shackleton, the South Pole—and you'll be there for all of it." That was Albie.

Seamie looked in the mirror. An explorer looked back at him. He couldn't believe it. Not at all. It still seemed like a dream.

Only two weeks ago, he was standing outside Ernest Shackleton's home in the wind and rain, trying to convince the man to take him on the Antarctica expedition. Shackleton had finally taken him inside and fed him breakfast. They'd talked for two hours. He was very curious to hear about Seamie's sailing experience and his winter climbs in the Adirondacks. By the time the maid had cleared the breakfast dishes, he still hadn't said yes, but he hadn't said no, either.

Five days later the lad who was to be the cook's assistant was arrested for public drunkenness. Two days after that Seamie received a letter at 12 Wilmington Crescent, the Aldens' house, inviting him to join the expedition. He'd opened it—in the privacy of his room—and learned that he was to be the cook's assistant. He let out a whoop, then ran straight down the stairs to tell Albert and Willa.

It was the worst dogsbody job possible. He'd be nothing but a scullery maid—peeling potatoes and scrubbing pots—but Shackleton promised him that he'd get off the ship and trek into the interior with the rest of the crew. He would make history, for he was certain Scott and Shackleton would find the Pole—how could men like that fail at anything? It was an opportunity of a lifetime and nothing and no one was going to stop him from going.

"What, exactly, would happen if you told Fiona?" Albert asked now.

"She'd go completely crackers. She doesn't want me to leave school."

"But what's she going to do? You've already made your decision. She's your sister, after all. Surely she'd understand."

"You don't know Fiona. I wouldn't put it past her to show up at the dock and try to drag me off the boat by my ear."

Seamie frowned at his reflection. He wanted to tell Fiona, he knew it was the right thing to do, but he also knew he'd be in for an epic battle. If only he could send a telegram from the boat. Or find some other way to tell her early enough so that she wouldn't worry about his absence, but late enough so that she couldn't stop him.

He felt a tug at the back of his anorak. Willa was pulling it straight, smoothing it across his shoulders.

"You need a smaller size," she said.

Seamie snorted. "Do not."

"You do. It's meant to be worn with *some* room, not too much."

"How do you know?"

"She's in here every week," Albie said. "Hanging her nose over tents and rucksacks."

Seamie watched her as she adjusted his sleeves. Their eyes met in the mirror.

"You *have* to tell her. You know you do. It's cruel not to. You'll feel terrible," she said. Willa was right, but her being right didn't make his task any easier. Looking at her, he suddenly had a brainstorm.

"No, I won't feel terrible. Because I'm not going to tell her," he said. "You are, Wills."

"I'm not!"

"*Please*, Willa. You have to. Fiona likes you. Always has. She'll take the news better coming from you than she would from Albie."

"Forget it, mate. Don't even *think* about me doing it," Albie said.

"I'm going up to Dundee with Shackleton next month. After Christmas. We're going to look at the ship. It's being built especially for the expedition. All you have to do is wait until I'm gone, then go and tell her."

"She'll twig pretty quick that I was in on it," Willa said. "Puts me in a bit of a bad spot."

"I know. I know it does. And I'm sorry. But it's better that way."

"For you."

Seamie winced. "Yeah, I guess so. But for her, too. It would be so much better than her finding out from a letter. Or a telegram."

"Oh, Seamie. You wouldn't tell her by telegram, would you?"

"Only if there was no other way. Please, Wills. Do this for me."

Willa deliberated and Seamie waited, knowing better than to push her. She was her own girl.

"All right, then, I'll do it," she finally said. "On one condition."

"Anything."

"You do the same for me one day. When I go to Everest, you tell my mum."

Seamie smirked. He opened his mouth, ready to tease her, to tell her that was one condition he'd never have to meet, but the look on her face stopped him cold. She was serious. She meant it. Her green eyes held his fast, and looking into them, he had the sudden, unsettling feeling that he was seeing himself—his fearlessness, his adventurous spirit, his own restless, questing soul.

"All right, then," he said. "It's a deal."

Seamie turned back to his reflection. He stood tall, puffed his chest out, and adjusted his trousers. He heard laughter. Willa was still looking at him, her eyes merry and challenging now.

"Better stop preening and start packing, kitchen boy," she said. "If you don't take the South Pole, I will. Just as soon as I finish with Everest."

CHAPTER 58

"Frankie?"

"Aye, Des?"

"There's a bloke here wants to speak with Sid. Says he's the new MP."

"Has he got the prime minister with him?"

"He ain't joking. Says either he sees Sid right now or he's coming back tonight with two dozen rozzers and taking the place apart."

Frankie looked up from his cards to Oz, seated across from him, then to Desi.

"The fucking cheek. I'm sick of this. Who is this tosser? Tell him to come over here so I can kick his arse for him."

Desi motioned for Joe. He approached the table and said, "Are you Frank Betts?"

"What's that to you?"

"My name's Joe Bristow. I want to see Sid Malone."

Frankie turned around in his chair. He looked Joe up and down, noting the work clothes he was wearing—and the prybar he was holding. "Leave your barrow outside, did you?" he asked.

Ozzie snickered.

"I know all about you, Frankie. I know about the Firm. And I know you burned my warehouse down."

"Don't know what you're on about, mate."

"I just want to talk to him. That's all. I want to come to an understanding. Now. Before we butt heads. Before it's too late."

Frankie snorted. "You want to get off on the right foot, is that it?"

"Something like that."

Frankie took a sip of his porter. He didn't offer Joe one.

"If he's not here, then tell him to come see me," Joe said. "Any time. My office is on Commercial Street. Number eight. All I want to do is talk. He has my word on that."

A sickening panic flared inside Frankie. He felt threatened, not by Bristow himself—he was soft, had to be—but by what he represented—the straight world and its sudden pull on Sid.

"Listen, Frankie—"

"I *ain't* listening, mate, so fuck off and peddle your pears," Frankie said, turning back to his card game and his pint.

The next thing he knew the table was gone, smashed to pieces, and his pint with it. Joe stood next to him, prybar raised. "You listening now?" he asked.

Frankie was on his feet in a flash, his heart pounding, fists twitching. He threw a hard right. It caught Joe in the belly, doubling him over. Joe dropped the prybar and Frankie bent to grab it, intending to open Joe's skull with it, when Joe unexpectedly reared up and roundhoused him. Light exploded behind Frankie's eyes; he went down. He groaned in pain, holding his head. It was a street fighter's trick. Bristow had *meant* for him to go for the prybar. The bloke was from East London. He should have remembered that. He opened his eyes. When his vision finally cleared, he saw that Joe was leaning over him.

"That's for Alf Stevens, you piece of shit," he said. Then he straightened and looked around the room, daring all comers. There were none. "Give Sid my message," he said. "Tell him to come." He picked up his prybar and walked out of the pub.

As soon as the door closed behind him a figure walked out of the shadows and into the taproom.

"Frankie, did you burn down Bristow's warehouse?" Sid asked.

"Bloody hell, boss, were you there all along? Thanks for the help."

Sid crossed the room in a few quick strides. He hoisted Frankie off the floor and slammed him into the wall. "I said, *Did you burn down Bristow's warehouse?*"

"Yes! For Christ's sake, let me down!"

But Sid didn't let him down. Instead he hit him, again and again and again, until Frankie was begging him to stop and Des and Ozzie were pulling him off. When he finally released him, Frankie slumped to the floor.

"Why'd you do it?" Sid yelled. "Stevens wasn't one of us. He was an old man, Frankie! He never hurt no one!"

Frankie lifted his battered face. "I done it for *you*. While you were in the hospital. I didn't mean to hurt the geezer. I told him it was time his guv started paying us and he took a swing at me. Knocked a lamp over. I yelled at him to get out, but he wouldn't."

"And now he's dead. And Bristow knows it was you."

Frankie stood. "You're not going, are you? To see him, I mean. Bristow."

"I don't know," Sid said, pacing. "I don't bloody know."

"First the doctor. Now the MP. Next thing, you'll be cozying up to the filth."

Sid turned white. Frankie thought he was going to take another crack at him, but he didn't. "What do you know about the doctor?" he asked, his voice shaking with anger.

"Jesus, guv, I don't give a shit who you're shagging."

Sid took a step toward him, his fingers curling into a fist.

Frankie stood his ground. "Go on, do it. I don't care. Everything's falling apart and you're letting it. The Chinese, the Jews, the Italians—they're all carving up our gaff. Scrapping over the hop dens, the whorehouses, and pubs like a pack of mongrels. And Madden, he don't want just this street or that one, he wants the whole riverside. Are you blind? Can't you see what's happening?"

"I can see, Frankie. I don't care. Madden can have it. All of it."

"*What?*" Frankie said. "But this is *yours*. You built it piece by piece. Fought for it."

Sid reached into his jacket and pulled out a pistol. One of the half dozen they'd kept for themselves from the Stronghold job. He placed it on a table.

"I'm out," he said.

Frankie felt the breath go out of him, the life, the heart. The pain of Sid's punches was nothing compared to the pain of his leaving. "Why, guv?" he asked, in the voice of a bewildered boy.

"I don't want this life, Frankie," he said softly. "I never did."

Sid took a last look around himself. At Desi and Oz. At Lily. At the Bark. The river.

"Des, you're in charge now," he said. "I'll make it right by you. By all of you. Give me a few days."

To Frankie, he said, "Listen to Desi. Learn from him. He knows more about the game than all of us put together." And then he turned to leave.

Watching him go, watching him walk away from them, Frankie's sorrow turned to rage. "Who the hell do you think you are?" he screamed after him. "You can't just leave!"

Sid turned around one last time. His anguished eyes met Frankie's. "I already have," he said. "Take care of yourself, lad." And then he was gone.

CHAPTER 59

Seamie, Albie, and Willa were lying on their backs in the Aldens' garden, staring up at the sky. It was a clear night and the stars were sparkling like diamonds.

"Ask me another, Wills," said Seamie.

"Orion," Willa said. "Right ascension?"

"Five hours."

"Declination?"

"Five degrees."

"Visible between?"

"Latitudes eighty-five and seventy-five. Best seen in January."

"Major stars?"

"Alnilam, Alnitak, Betelgeuse, Mintaka, Saiph, and . . . don't tell me . . . Rigel!"

"And . . ." Willa prompted. "There's one more."

"There isn't. You're trying to throw me."

"There is."

"What is it then?"

"Bellatrix."

"Damn!"

How he hated that. Willa could name the constellations and cite their characteristics all from memory without ever making a mistake. He'd seen her navigate with a sextant on her family's yacht. She was better at it than he was, better than Albie, and almost as good as their father, who was an admiral in the Royal Navy.

"I'll never get them all right," he sighed. "And Shackleton says I have to."

"You will," she said. "Keep swotting. Sounds like you'll have plenty of time for it between here and Greenland."

"Talk about a dogsbody!" Albie said, chuckling.

"Shut up, will you?" Seamie growled.

"First you're a kitchen boy, now you're a kennel boy."

"Don't listen to him, Seamie," Willa said, stifling her own giggles. "Take a sextant with you. The voyage will be the perfect opportunity to practice your navigation."

"When you're not scooping poop!" Albie said, collapsing into laughter along with his sister. Seamie glowered.

The expedition was still months away, but preparations were already in full swing. Clements Markham and Captain Scott had gone to Christiania with Fridtjof Nansen to view the *Fram* and confer on ship design. Shackleton had left for Dundee two days ago to haggle with shipbuilders. Seamie was supposed to have gone with him, but there had been a last-minute change of plan. He was going to Greenland instead. In three weeks' time. To round up a bunch of bloody dogs.

Shackleton had been writing to breeders in Greenland, trying to buy sledge dogs for the expedition, but he'd had no luck. Scott had raised the possibility of Russian dogs, but Shackleton didn't want them. Greenland dogs were the best, he'd said. They were tougher, faster, better able to endure extreme cold. Consequently they were in high demand. Breeder after breeder had told him that he had no dogs left to sell, but Shackleton, never one to take no for an answer, told Edward Wilson, the expedition's junior surgeon and zoologist, to go to the breeders in person—armed with a heap of cash. And he'd told him to take Seamie with him. Wilson would negotiate, and when the dogs were bought Seamie would crate them, feed them, water them, groom them, exercise them, and sing to them.

"Sing to them, sir?" Seamie had said, thinking he'd heard him wrong.

"Yes, sing. They get homesick, just like humans do," Shackleton had replied. "If they look sad, sing to them. It cheers them up. Those dogs are more valuable to the expedition than you are, my boy. I want them happy and well."

After their meeting, Wilson had noticed Seamie's glum expression and told him to consider himself lucky. He could be stuck with Clarke, the second cook, and Blissett, one of the stewards, in a Dundee warehouse, counting boxes of Oxo cubes and tins of sardines.

He felt a poke in his side now and turned his head toward Willa.

"Stop sulking," she said. "It's better than flogging oranges or peddling tea."

She was smiling mischievously. Her color was high. There had been a proper family dinner tonight and she'd had to dress like a girl for it in an ivory silk frock, lace stockings, and heeled shoes. My God, but she's pretty, Seamie thought.

"I suppose it is," he allowed. His eyes lingered on her. He thought she might blush but she didn't, and it was he who finally had to look away. Again.

"I'm hungry again," Albie said. "I'm going to see if there's any hope of a sandwich."

"Bring a plateful, will you, Alb?" Willa said. "And some pickles. And lemon squash."

"Anything else, madam?" Albie said.

"Cake."

He loped off toward the house, leaving Willa and Seamie by themselves. Willa rolled over and propped herself up on her elbows.

"It'll be lonely when you're gone, Seamie. I won't have anyone to talk about climbing with."

"What about Albie?"

"He keeps trying to make me stop. Keeps telling me I'll hurt myself, but really he's just cross because I'm better than him and he hates being shown up by a girl."

Seamie laughed.

"George Mallory—remember him from the RGS?—he wants to go climbing on Mont Blanc in the spring," Willa said. "He's awfully good. I'm going to go with him. At least I hope I am. All depends on whether or not I can talk Albie into coming along. My parents would never let me go otherwise. I might ruin my reputation."

Jealousy, unexpected and unwelcome, shot through Seamie at the idea of Willa and Mallory in the Alps together. "Sounds like fun. I hope you have a good time," he said.

"Do you?" Willa asked, arching an eyebrow.

"Of course, why wouldn't I?"

She shrugged and changed the subject. "I suppose I still have to go and tell Fiona the news? You haven't made up yet?"

"Yes, you do," Seamie said. "And no, we haven't."

He felt heavy-hearted at the mention of Fiona. He would have gone back tomorrow if he could, but he didn't know how. He'd have to apologize, consent to return to Groton, and he wasn't about to do either. He knew his stubborn sister would never apologize, so he was stuck.

"You could go and see her before you go to Greenland, you know," Willa said, as if reading his mind. She often did that. It unnerved him.

"No."

"I'm sure Fiona's cooled off by now."

"*No.*"

Willa sighed. "Just a thought," she said.

She shifted her gaze back to the sky, back to Orion, the great hunter. "Is someone looking up at him in Antarctica now, do you think? Can they see him at Mont Blanc and Kilimanjaro and Everest? How I wish I could be him. I wish I could see what he sees. The whole world! All of its magic and mystery. All of its beauty and power and sorrow and danger."

How the hell does she *do* that? Seamie wondered. How does she put into words exactly what I'm feeling? Still on his back, he looked up at her, at her face, luminous in the moonlight, at the curve of her mouth, at her wide and wondering eyes. And he realized, with a sudden, deep ache, that he was going to miss her. More than he would miss Albie. Even more than he would miss his own family. She was seventeen now. She would be nineteen or twenty when he returned from Antarctica and different. Grown up. She might be engaged. Or married. The thought filled him with a desperate sadness. He wanted to tell her how he felt, but he didn't know how. He was terrible at these things.

"Willa . . ." he began.

She looked down at him. "I know," she said. "I'll miss you, too." And then she kissed him, quick and hard. "Be careful," she said. "Come back."

"Wait for me."

She winced, as if the demand had been unworthy of him. "No."

"Why?"

"If it was the other way round—me going, you staying—would you wait? With all the deserts yet to be mapped, and the mountains yet to be climbed, and the rivers and jungles and forests yet to be discovered. And you just aching to get out there and map them and climb them and make them your own. Feeling that you'd wither and die if you didn't. Well, would you?"

With another girl he would have hemmed and hawed and come out with some sort of fluttery flattering nonsense. Not with Willa. With her, he could tell the truth.

"No," he said. "I wouldn't." He paused, then said, "Does Albie know what you want to do? Do your parents?"

"I talk about exploring all the time, but they think I'm just nattering."

He'd always thought she was, too, but now he wasn't so certain. "Why don't you try to get on an expedition?"

She laughed. "Are you mad? With a boatload of men?"

"Hadn't thought of that."

"Best I could hope for would be to marry a sea captain and make a few voyages with him. No one would ever take me on as a single woman. Can you imagine the scandal? And no one will finance a women's party, either. I could be better than Scott and Nansen combined, and it wouldn't matter. The Royal Geo wouldn't give me a farthing. So I'll have to finance myself."

"How?"

"My mad aunt Edwina. She's my mother's elder sister. She's a spinster and a suffragist. Deadly anti-marriage. She says it's an institution—same as a prison or an insane asylum. She says that young women should have choices, but you can have choices only if you have money. So she's given me some. Five thousand pounds in a trust. I can have it when I turn eighteen. It won't finance an expedition like Scott's, but it should get me around the world a few times."

Seamie was amazed. "You're really going to do it, aren't you? Leave home, leave your family, to go exploring."

She nodded, her gaze hard and determined. "Yes, I am."

He thought of Mrs. Alden and how upset she became every time Willa climbed a hill or went rambling and came home with scrapes and freckles. "It won't be easy, Wills."

"Don't I know it." She was silent for a few seconds, then she kissed him again, and the touch of her lips on his felt bittersweet, for he knew he might never feel them again.

"Meet me there, Seamie," she said.

"Where?"

She raised her face to the night sky and smiled. "I don't know exactly. Somewhere out there. Somewhere in this wide world. Somewhere under Orion."

CHAPTER 60

Frankie Betts knew what had to be done. And he knew he had to do it.

He walked toward Spitalfields Market at a leisurely pace, stopping for a morning pint at a porter's pub, buying a crimson rose for his buttonhole.

He was dressed like a workman today, like Sid usually dressed, in denim trousers, a collarless shirt, a seaman's jacket, and a wool cap. The red rose stood out on his navy jacket. Sid wouldn't have liked that, Frankie knew, but he needed to draw attention today. Just a bit. Just enough so that a man drinking at the pub where he'd stopped, or the flower seller with whom he'd flirted, would recall him.

He crossed Commercial Street, jogging to avoid an oncoming coal wagon. The revolver in his breast pocket banged against his chest as he did. It was Sid's revolver, the one he'd left in the Bark when he'd told him he was leaving.

A haberdasher's window reflected his image back at him as he passed by. He caught sight of it and smiled. At a glance he was the spitting image of Sid. Right down to his hair, which he'd bound into a ponytail under his hat.

The man he was going to see knew what Sid Malone looked like, but Frankie would have wagered a thousand quid that no one else around him did. That was important. He had to leave a witness or two, or his plan wouldn't work. Someone had to be left standing to tell Old Bill what had happened and who was to blame.

Frankie walked into the doorway of 8 Commercial Street, read the directory in the foyer, then skipped up the stairs to room 21. The door was set with a frosted-glass panel. A glazier was scraping a painted name off it— *F.R. Lytton, Member of Parliament.*

"Pardon me, mate," Frankie said, making a to-do of stepping around the man and his tools. A charlady, carrying a bucket of water, followed him in. He winked at her.

Inside the office, another woman was busy filling bookcases and filing cabinets with the contents of several crates and boxes. Her back was to him. The nameplate on her desk said Miss G. Mellors.

"What's the G for, luv?" he asked loudly. "Gorgeous?"

Miss Mellors jumped. She turned around. "May I help you?" she asked frostily.

"I'd like to see Joe Bristow."

"I'm sorry, sir, but Mr. Bristow is unavailable to his constituents right now. His office doesn't open for another hour."

"Give him my name, missus. I think he'll make an exception."

"Sir, I cannot—"

"Give it a go, eh, luv?" Frankie said, cutting her off. "You don't want your guv angry with you when you tell him I've come and gone."

"Very well. What is it?"

"Malone. Sid Malone."

"One moment, Mr. Malone. Have a seat, please."

Frankie sat down, hands on his thighs, and stared at the pattern in the carpet. His breathing was even. His heartbeat steady. Oz would be sweating buckets. Des's hands would be shaking. Ronnie would be shitting himself. But he was calm and cool. Sid always said he didn't have one nerve in his whole body.

He looked up, gauging the distance from the door of Bristow's office to the stairway. He'd have to make a bloody quick exit and hope like hell Old Bill wasn't strolling by as he hit Commercial Street. Once he was on the street, though, he'd be all right. He'd head east, into Whitechapel. There were dozens of places he could hide there, plenty of rabbit holes he could disappear down.

It would work, this plan, he was sure of it. It would bring Sid back from the straight world. Back to the Bark. Back where he belonged.

"Mr. Malone, sir?"

Frankie smiled. "That's me."

"Mr. Bristow will see you now."

"Ta very much."

Miss Mellors ushered Frankie into Joe's office, then closed the door behind him. Joe was seated at his desk in his shirtsleeves. He stood. "Frankie Betts," he said flatly, his hands on his hips. "Trudy said Sid was here. Where is he?"

"He's right here," Frankie said softly, reaching into his jacket.

Joe never had a chance. Frankie aimed the revolver and fired. The gun's kick raised his hand slightly. Worried that he had missed his mark, he fired again. Joe staggered backward into the wall, two bullet holes in his chest, and sank to the floor. Frankie threw the gun down and strode out of the office.

"What's happened? What was that noise?" Miss Mellors shrilled.

Frankie didn't stop to answer. The charlady was mopping near the door, blocking his exit. He grabbed the back of her dress and threw her out of his way. The door was closed. He wrenched it open.

"Oi!" the glazier yelled. "I'm working here!"

Frankie shoved him backward. The old man hit the banister, wind-milled his arms, and fell over it. There was a shout and then a thud and then nothing.

Frankie took the stairs two at a time. He paused in the foyer, wrinkling his nose at the matter leaking from the old man's skull.

"Come on, come on . . ." he muttered, glancing back up at the first floor.

And then he heard it. A woman screaming. Loud enough to shatter glass.

Frankie smiled. And ran.

CHAPTER 61

"India, you can't possibly be serious," Harriet said. "You just got the clinic open and now you want to leave it?"

"I don't *want* to leave, Harriet," India said, pacing the narrow confines of their office. "I don't have a choice. I have to go away. I want you and Ella to take over."

"For how long? A week? A month?"

"Permanently."

Harriet shook her head. "I don't understand this! You worked so bloody hard to make this clinic a reality and now you're going to turn your back on it?"

India thought of Sid. He had done something she feared he never would—he had left the life, left everyone and everything he'd known. For her. He'd come to see her at the Moskowitzes' two days ago and told her that he had to get out of London for good—the quicker, the better. They'd decided they would leave for America in a fortnight's time. Meanwhile he would lay low in East London and she would continue to stay with the Moskowitzes. They'd thought about going to Arden Street, but it was so far from the East End that the journey took hours out of the day, and India needed to spend every spare minute at the clinic now to ensure that it opened by the time she left.

Sid, too, had business to finish in East London. She had seen him this morning. He'd come to the café for breakfast, and they'd had time for a quick word before she had to leave. She hadn't felt well. Her stomach had been troubling her and she hadn't been able to eat a thing. Sid had noticed, he'd said he was worried about her, but she'd told him it was only nerves. He told her he had to go back to the Bark today, to tie up some loose ends. She'd told him she didn't want him to go, that it made her anxious, but he assured her he would be fine. In and out, and then he was done. Forever.

She'd kissed him, then watched him go. His step was lighter as he walked now, his head higher. He looked like a different man. He'd told her that he'd gotten out of prison years ago, but he only now felt free. His words had made her so happy. She couldn't wait until they were on the ship with London behind them and their whole lives ahead of them.

"I mean, really, Indy. It makes no sense at all." Harriet was still railing at her. "What could possibly make you leave the clinic?"

"Not what, Hatch, who," India said quietly.

Harriet gave her a long look. "Well, it's certainly not Freddie. Is it who I think it is? Ella says it's—"

"Don't ask me that."

"It is. Jesus bloody Christ!"

"Harriet, please—" India began, but she was interrupted by the pounding of boot heels in the hallway and the appearance of a breathless young nurse in the doorway.

"Dr. Jones, Dr. Hatcher, come quickly! A man's been shot."

India and Harriet were out of their chairs, and their office, immediately.

"Why has he been brought *here*?" Harriet asked. "We're a women's clinic and we're not even open yet!"

"The officers said they heard there were doctors here. They said the hospital's too far. He's very bad, Dr. Hatcher."

"Where is he?" Harriet asked, striding down the hallway alongside the sister.

"In the surgery. Matron's with him."

"But the surgery's not ready yet!" Harriet cried.

"Looks like it's going to have to be," India said.

The three women flew downstairs, then ran through the foyer and into the surgical ward. Pandemonium greeted them. Two officers were standing inside the doorway, trying to restrain a hysterical woman, whose clothing was covered in blood. Two more were lifting a man onto the operating table.

"Mr. Bristow! Mr. Bristow!" the woman keened. "Oh, help him, please! Somebody help him!" She grabbed Harriet and refused to let her go.

India pushed past them and ran to the operating table. A man was stretched out upon it, unconscious. Ella, already scrubbed and masked, was cutting his shirt off.

"My God, Ella. That's Joe Bristow, the MP."

"He's almost gone, India. For God's sake, hurry," she said.

Joe's bare chest was covered in blood. India could see two bullet wounds through the crimson wash. She ran to the sink to scrub, calling out to Ella for his vital signs. As Ella shouted them, the other nurse, Dwyer, began loading scalpels, clamps, scissors, needles, and suturing thread into the autoclave.

Behind her, India could hear Harriet shouting at the woman. "Calm down! We need quiet here! Quiet!"

She turned to India. "You all right?" she shouted.

India gave her a quick nod.

"Officers, come with me," Harriet yelled. "This way, please." She somehow managed to usher the constables and the wailing woman out of the room, giving India the peace she needed to work.

"India, quick. I need you!" Ella shouted.

Joe Bristow had regained consciousness. He was thrashing his head from side to side. His eyes were open, but unseeing.

"Dwyer! Chloral!" India shouted.

Scrubbed and masked herself now, she raced back to the operating table. Dwyer already had an anesthesia mask over Joe's face. He fought it at first, then his eyes fluttered and he was still. When Dwyer removed the mask, blood—bright and foamy—oozed from his nose and mouth.

"His lungs have been damaged," India said. "How many exit wounds?" she asked Ella.

"None. One bullet's in the spine. I'm sure of it."

India swore. "Is the spinal cord severed?" she asked.

"I can't tell. Reflexes are nil."

India called for a retractor and a scalpel. She would leave the spinal wound for now—it was bleeding, but not gushing—to concentrate on the second bullet hole. It was far more worrying. It was directly at heart level and the damage the bullet had wreaked was horrifying. Two ribs had been shattered, and the shrapnel-like bone shards had torn the flesh apart. The resulting mess made it impossible for India to see the position of the bullet.

She had only seen a handful of gunshot patients during her training, but she knew that bullets usually entered the body at an angle and could be slowed by tissue or deflected by bone. The bullet hadn't entered Joe's heart. If it had, he'd be dead by now. That was the good news. The bad news was that it could be anywhere. A hairbreadth from the delicate pericardium or buried in his liver.

India knew she had to get the second bullet out, and she knew if she wasn't careful, she could push it farther in and do more damage. Working quickly, she cut away as much damaged flesh as she could and picked out the bone shards, but she found she still could not get a good look into the wound. It was too deep, too narrow.

She asked for tweezers and handed her retractors to Ella, telling her to stretch the wound wide open, but she still couldn't locate the bullet.

"I need more light," she said.

"We've got the gas lights on as high as they'll go, Dr. Jones," Dwyer replied.

"Get me a table lamp, then."

Dwyer shot out and returned with a kerosene lamp, its wick blazing.

"Hold it low," India ordered.

Dwyer did so, but still India couldn't see deep enough into the wound.

"Lower!"

"I'm afraid I'll burn you, Dr. Jones."

"Lower!"

Dwyer moved it lower, and India felt the heat on her cheek, smelled the stench of her own singed hair. And then she saw it, or thought she did. A bit of a glint. Not the bloody glisten of tissue or bone, but the hard, dull shine of lead.

"Pull back a little harder. Just a little," she told Ella. Ella, expertly maneuvering the retractors, did so. India took a breath, held it, then inserted the tweezers into the wound. She grasped the bullet, squeezed, and then the tweezers slipped and she lost it. The wound was deep, the tweezers were short, the bullet was slippery with blood. It was nearly impossible to get any purchase.

"Give me a curette," she said.

Dwyer handed her a tool that was long and slender and shaped like a spoon. India eased it into the wound, listening for a click of metal against metal. When she heard it, she pushed the stem of the curette into the wall of the wound, hoping to ease the narrow bowl around and under the bullet.

Joe groaned and thrashed as she did it.

When he was quiet again, she started to slowly, carefully withdraw the curette.

"Come on . . . come on . . ." she whispered.

And then she saw it—the bullet. She'd hooked it. She reached for her tweezers again and this time she could grasp it. She pulled it out and dropped it into a metal pan. A bright gush of blood followed it. Working like lightning, she and Ella packed the wound with sterile gauze, trying to stanch the bleeding. The gauze soaked through immediately. They took it out and started again. And again.

"Shit," a voice said. It was Harriet. She was holding the metal pan and peering at the whitish substance clinging to the bullet. "Lung tissue. Poor sod. He's cooked."

"No, he's *not*. He's got a chance," India said. "It's his lung, not his heart. The ribs deflected it."

Lung tissue was elastic; it healed better than other organ tissue. Patients with lung wounds recovered—sometimes. If the bleeding stopped soon enough. If the infection was slight enough. If the body was strong enough.

India looked at the gauze underneath her fingers. It had soaked through again.

"Bloody hell," she swore. She stared at Joe, frowning, then suddenly stepped back and ripped her gloves off.

"What are you doing?" Harriet asked.

"He's lost too much blood," she said. "I want to transfuse him."

"You can't. It's too risky. Transfusions kill as many patients as they cure. You know that. He could die if we do it."

"He *will* die if we don't."

"We should type him and cross match."

"There's no time, Harriet! We'll use my blood. I'm C."

India knew that what she was doing was dangerous. Blood typing was in its infancy. Three major groups—A, B, and C—had been identified. It was known that mixing type A blood with type B caused fatal reactions, and that type C could be mixed with either. No one knew exactly why and at this moment India didn't care. All she cared about was saving Joe Bristow's life.

"Indy, he needs a lot," Harriet said. "Maybe more than you can give."

"We'll start with a pint," India said. She had already rolled up her sleeve. She'd grabbed a length of rubber tubing and tied it around her upper arm, and was now pulling it tight with her teeth.

"Come on, Hatch, you're good at this," she said, handing Harriet a syringe. "You saved a man at the Royal Free with a transfusion. I saw you."

"And I killed two more," Harriet said, swabbing the inside of India's elbow. She tapped the pale skin there, then sank the needle into a thin blue vein. India clenched her fist and released it, clenched and released. Harriet drew four ounces, called for a second syringe, and drew four more. Then she pressed a gauze pad over the vein.

"Again, Hatch."

"India . . ."

"He needs a lot. You said so yourself."

Harriet drew eight more ounces, yelling over her shoulder for Ella to swab Joe's arm. She put the gauze pad back. India took it, pressing it down. Her head was spinning.

"You all right?" Harriet asked.

"Fine," India said. "Go. Hurry. Don't let it clot."

India leaned against the cool tile wall and closed her eyes. She took a deep breath, and then another, willing her dizziness away.

"Is it all in?" she asked, eyes still closed.

"Just about," Harriet said.

"Ella, what's happening?"

"No change. He's still soaking the dressing."

"Damn it." India opened her eyes. "Come on, Hatch. Again."

"No."

"All he needs is another pint."

"No! For God's sake, India. We're injecting it into him and he's leaking it right back out! He's done for."

"A half pint then. One more go. Either you do it or I'll do it myself."

Harriet grabbed a syringe. "Sit down before you fall down," she snapped.

India sat on the floor. She was glad she had, for by the time Harriet had finished she couldn't have stood if her life depended on it.

"El?" she said weakly.

There was no response, then, "It's slowing. It hasn't stopped yet, but it's slowing."

India smiled. "Well done, Harriet, you vampire, you."

"We're going to need more blood," Ella said.

"I'm C, Matron," Dwyer said.

"Good girl. Swab your arm," Ella ordered.

"Don't talk. Don't move. Just sit still," Harriet said to India. "You!" she barked at a passing nurse. "Go to the pub on the corner. Get a pint of porter and a sandwich for Dr. Jones. Hurry." The young woman ran out. "Dwyer, make a fist," she added, readying her syringe.

India waited on the floor, head against the wall, eyes closed, while Harriet transfused Joe again. Her meal arrived. When she had finished it she stood up and walked back to Joe.

"How's he doing?" she asked Harriet.

"His vitals are holding. Not great, not at all, but they're holding. I'd say he has a fighting chance now. Because of you."

"Because of us."

"I'm going to see to the other wound, dose him with quinine, and then it's time to say our prayers."

"I'll assist."

"Actually, the constables who brought Bristow here are in the porter's office. They want the bullet you recovered. And they want a word with you, too. You up to it?"

India nodded. "How's the woman who came in with him?"

"Still in shock, but better. I gave her brandy. She's having a sit-down."

India and Harriet entered the porter's office. Harriet handed the bullet over and told India to sit down. India noticed that a detective had joined the constables. She recognized him. He was Alvin Donaldson—Freddie's man. The sight of him unsettled her. She knew his presence here had nothing to do with Sid, but she was suddenly fiercely glad that they were leaving London.

Donaldson greeted her, then asked her about Joe's wounds, and if he had said anything intelligible during the operation. India described the injuries and said Joe had been mostly unconscious.

"Will Mr. Bristow make it?" Donaldson asked.

"I don't know. We're doing everything we can for him but his condition is extremely grave."

Donaldson nodded. "It'll be murder or attempted murder," he said to one of the constables, "but either way I've got him. He'll swing for certain this time."

"You know who did this?" India asked.

"Aye, Dr. Jones, we do. Bristow's secretary—Miss Mellors—told us. She was there. She saw him. She was hysterical, as you know, but we managed to get some sense out of her. We got his name. You know him, I believe. You tended to him."

India's blood ran cold. *No,* she silently prayed. *Please God, no.*

"He was your patient a few months back. His name is Sid Malone."

CHAPTER 62

Sid Malone stood at the open window of his bedroom in the Barkentine gazing out at the Thames. It was low tide. A fog lay heavily on the water. Only a few bargemen dared move about in it. Their disembodied voices carried up to him as they called out to one another. For a second he imagined long, twining tendrils of fog wrapping around him, pulling him under, holding him there. He turned away, remembering how India had begged him to stay away from this place.

"Don't go, Sid. Please. I don't want you to," she'd said.

"I'll be fine, luv," he said, shushing her. "I've a bit of business to finish up, that's all. I'll be there and back before you know it."

"Promise?" she asked, her gray eyes huge with worry.

"Promise."

"You won't go back to it, will you? To the life?"

"Not a chance," he said, smiling. "You're stuck with me now, missus. You wanted me, you've got me."

He resumed his packing. A battered leather satchel lay open on his bed. He'd put very little into it. A few pieces of clothing. Some masculine odds and ends. He wanted nothing else, no mementos. He'd come back only to give Desi and the rest of his men their due. The day after he'd beaten Frankie silly for burning down the Morocco and killing Alf Stevens, he'd gone to see a lawyer to put the deeds to the Taj Mahal, the Bark, the Alhambra, and the rest of his properties in Desi's name. Des was a fair man and Sid knew he could trust him to do right by the others. The properties themselves weren't worth so much, but the businesses run from them were. The Firm would make out all right.

Sid folded an old tweed jacket now and placed it in his satchel. He put his pea coat on top of it, then closed it. He took a last look around his room. Once, he could not have imagined a life lived anywhere but in here, on the banks of the stinking gray Thames. He could not have imagined leaving London. And Whitechapel. And his past. But now he could imagine these things. Because of India.

The last night they'd spent together at Arden Street—the night he'd told her about his past—he'd felt something kindle deep within himself. Something bright and warm and perilously fragile. It was a feeling. One he'd lived without for years. One he'd forgotten. But one he still recognized. It was hope.

India had made him believe again. In new beginnings. In forgiveness and redemption. In the possibility of love. She'd healed his heart that night as surely as she'd healed his body months ago. And all he wanted now was to be with her. He didn't know what he'd do once they got to California and he didn't care. He was strong, capable. He'd find honest work. He was done with villainy. He was on the straight and narrow now.

He picked up his bag and headed for the stairs. He would give the deeds to Desi and then there would be only one thing left to do. Just one more thing and he'd be done with Whitechapel, and with his old life, forever.

He had to get his dosh.

It was no secret that he kept money at the Albion Bank. He had legitimate accounts there in which he regularly deposited earnings from his businesses—lending credence to his claim to be a legitimate businessman. What was not known, however, was that he also kept a large safe deposit box there. It was full of cash. He was going to take five hundred pounds for himself—he figured he'd earned that much legitimately over the past few years—to pay for his and India's way to California. The rest—every penny of it—was going to India's clinic. She was giving up her dream for him. The least he could do was make certain the dream survived. He would give the money to Ella. She would know what to do with it.

Sid was glad that he and India were leaving London soon. Word would be spreading that he was off the game. People—people who weren't terribly fond of him—would soon know that he was alone, without his men to protect him. He trotted downstairs now, his satchel clasped tightly. He didn't look forward to this next bit. Desi was angry. They all were. They wanted him to stay. They wanted everything to go on as it always had. Sid understood. It was easier to leave than it was to be left. He was grateful that he could do his leave-taking in private. It was half four and the Bark was closed. Desi stood behind the bar drying glasses.

"That all you're taking?" he asked, eyeing Sid's bag.

"Aye. What's left is yours. These, too," he said, placing a bundle of deeds on the bar.

"Ta, guv. It's decent of you. More than most would have done."

An awkward silence descended. Sid finally broke it.

"Frankie about?"

"No, he isn't. Don't know where he got to. Haven't seen him for days."

Sid nodded. "Well, I'm off, then," he said. "Take care, Des. Keep your eye on Madden and Ko, keep Frankie reined in, and you'll be all right."

Desi nodded. He was about to say something when his words were cut off by a thunderous bashing on the door. "Oi! Go easy!" he shouted, throwing his bar rag down.

"It's me, Ozzie! Open up, Des!"

Des hurried to unlock the door.

"Where's the guv? Is he here?" Ozzie asked, stumbling into the pub. He was carrying a newspaper. Ronnie was right behind him.

"You lost your sight as well as your wits? He's right there! What the hell are you playing at?" Desi said.

Ozzie slammed the door and threw the lock. He tossed the newspaper to Desi. "We haven't much time. Rozzers are only two minutes behind me." He leaned over and put his hands on his knees, trying to catch his breath. "Got to hand it to you, guv, you know how to go out with a bang."

"Oz, for fuck's sake, talk sense, will you?" Desi barked. "What's happened?"

"Ask him," Ozzie wheezed, nodding at Sid.

Desi looked at Sid.

"I don't know what he's talking about," Sid said.

"Read the bloody paper, then!" Ozzie yelled. "It's everywhere! You can't go two yards without hearing some poxy newsboy yellin' his head off about it. The cops are coming down on us like a ton of bricks."

"They've already nicked Pete and Tom," Ronnie said.

Desi unfolded the paper. Sid read over his shoulder. What he saw made his heart stop.

"M.P. Shot," the headline screamed. "Malone on Murder Spree."

He quickly read the lead:

Joseph Bristow, newly elected to Parliament on the Labour ticket, is clinging to life this afternoon after being shot twice in the chest at approximately 10 a.m. in his Commercial Street offices. Several eyewitnesses, including Miss Gertrude Mellors, Mr. Bristow's secretary, have put East London businessman Sid Malone in Bristow's office at the time of the shooting. Gladys Howe of Smithy Street, Hoxton, told the *Clarion* that she saw Malone push Henry Wilkins, a glazier, to his death as he was leaving the scene of the crime. Police have detained several of Mr. Malone's associates and are now hunting for Malone himself. D.I. Alvin Donaldson earnestly entreats anyone having information on Mr. Malone's whereabouts to contact him . . .

No, he said silently, not thinking of himself and the trouble he was in, but of his sister. Not them. Please. Not Fee. Not Joe.

"We're done for," Desi said. "Why'd you do it, Sid? The bloody MP of all people! Did you think no one would notice?"

"I didn't do it!" Sid said.

"Oh, aye? Who did, then?"

"Desmond Shaw! This is Detective Inspector Alvin Donaldson. I have a warrant for your arrest. Open the door."

"Bloody hell!" Desi swore. "On what charges?" he yelled back.

"Harboring a fugitive. Open the door!"

"Keep your knickers on!" Desi yelled. He turned to Sid. "The tunnels," he said. "Go. All of you. I'll hold them off long as I can."

"No. Oz and Ron should stay."

"And get nicked into the bargain? No thanks," Ozzie said.

"They'll keep you overnight, then let you go. They'll have to," Sid argued.

"Keep talking, ladies, and we're all nicked," Desi said tightly.

"We're going with you. There's strength in numbers," Ronnie said, pulling Sid toward the basement stairs. Sid knew that, as much as they hated him right now, they hated the law even more and they'd do everything they could to keep him out of Donaldson's hands.

The three men were down the steps and at the trapdoor in seconds. Sid hoisted it up. Ronnie jumped down and scrabbled for the lantern they kept at the ready. Oz followed. Sid was just pulling the door closed when they heard Donaldson's voice overhead.

"The basement. Quickly," he barked. "There's a bolthole down there."

Feet pounded down the stairs. Sid slammed the door down. He grabbed the large metal ring attached to its underside and hung from it. Ozzie leaped up, caught the ring, and did the same. Together they made more than 350 pounds of dead weight.

"We can't open it, sir," said a voice from above them.

"Get a shovel, wedge it under the edge," Donaldson ordered.

"There isn't one."

"Then smash a bloody keg! We'll use a stave."

"Guv, I can't find the lantern!" Ronnie whispered, panic in his voice.

"Never mind the lantern, find the hook!" Sid hissed.

A thick metal chain hung down from the ring in the door. At its end was an iron grappling hook. There was another ring in the floor. All Ronnie had to do was find it and hook the chain to it. Sid heard him fumbling in the dark, felt his hands against his legs. Finally, he found the chain. There was the sound of metal scraping against metal and then, "She's in. Let's go!"

Sid and Ozzie released the ring and fell to the ground. There was a square of light above their heads as the door came up an inch or so, then slammed back down.

"They've hooked it shut!" one of the officers yelled.

"Find an axe," Donaldson yelled. "We'll chop it open."

Sid found the lantern, pulled a pack of matches from his pocket, and lit it. The light was weak, but it was enough to illuminate a yard or so in front of them, and that was all they needed.

"The Blind Beggar?" Ronnie asked, leading the way.

"No. They'll have men there. I'm sure of it. Head to Sally's. She'll take care of us."

They'd walked fifty or so yards into the tunnel when Ozzie suddenly said, "Guv?"

"What?"

"Why'd you do it?"

"I didn't do it."

"Come on, guv."

"You've been with me for five years now, Oz. Is shooting a man in broad daylight with a room full of witnesses my style?"

"No. But if you didn't, who did? And why did he give your name?"

"I don't know."

"It don't look good."

"No, it doesn't."

"Whoever did it knows Bristow had a beef with you. Maybe it was someone in the Bark. Someone who was there the other day. When he came looking for you and had ructions with Frankie instead. Remember? And when he left, you had a row with Frankie and told him you was out, and then Frankie . . ."

Sid stopped dead. He turned around. "Jesus Christ," he said. *"Frankie."*

C H A P T E R 63

India stopped dead in the middle of Dean Street. She turned around in a circle, panting with exhaustion, hoping to spot a familiar building or sign. Some kind of landmark. They'd come this way when they were running from Devlin, she and Sid. She was sure of it. They'd made a right, hadn't they? Or was it a left?

She started walking again, certain the house she wanted was just up ahead, then stopped again, disoriented. In the time that had elapsed since she'd left the clinic she'd raced to the Bark and the Taj Mahal, desperately trying to find him, but she hadn't.

She closed her eyes, trying to fight down the panic rising in her, trying to clear her head so that she could remember the way. But her mind was jammed with voices. Donaldson's—telling her that Sid had shot Joseph Bristow. Harriet's—pleading with her to hide from him. Ella's—urging her to find him.

"Let me understand this," Harriet had said, following her into her office after Donaldson had left. "You're leaving the clinic to run off with a murderer."

"Don't say that!" India cried, grabbing her jacket and bag. "He didn't do it. I know he didn't."

"When did you last see him, India?" Ella asked.

"This morning, Ella. At your house. He said he was going to Whitechapel. I didn't want him to go. But he said he had to. That he had one last thing to do."

"Good God, India! What more proof do you need?" Harriet shouted.

"None. I don't need any bloody proof. Because I know he didn't do it!" India shouted back.

"Be quiet! Both of you," Ella said. She bit her lip, thinking, then said, "There's one man who can tell us everything we need to know—Joe Bristow."

"If only he would regain consciousness," India said.

"Yes, well, we know what the likelihood of that is, don't we?" Harriet snapped.

"He'll pull through. He will. He's made it this far. And when he does he can tell the police that it wasn't Sid."

"Could be days before that happens. Could be never. Go, India. Find Sid. Before the police do," Ella said.

"Do that, India, and you'll become part of it," Harriet warned. "Help him in any way at all and you're an accessory to a crime."

India had looked at them both, her face a picture of anguish. She told them to take good care of Joe Bristow, that she'd be back in an hour or two, and then she'd run out of the building into Gunthorpe Street, where she'd nearly thrown herself in front of a cab to get it to stop.

"Can I help you, miss?" a friendly voice said now.

India opened her eyes. An elderly man, gray-haired with a black mustache, was leaning on a broom by the curb in front of her.

"I'm looking for someone," she said. "Sally is her name. She's an older woman. She's small, with gray hair."

"That sounds like Raysie's missus. Sally Garrett. She's number four. See it? It's just up there. On your right."

India thanked the man and hurried off. She knocked on the front door of number 4. When no one came, she pushed it open and walked inside. She remembered which was Sally's door; it was all the way at the back of the hall. She knocked but got no answer. She tried again.

"What the hell do you want?" a voice called.

"I want to talk to you," India called back. "I'm a friend of Sid Malone's."

The door was wrenched open. "Keep your bloody voice down!" Sally hissed. She grabbed India's arm and pulled her inside.

"I'm sorry. I didn't mean—" India began.

"Did anyone see you?"

"See me?" India echoed, confused.

"Coming in. Whole of Whitechapel is crawling with rozzers. Were you followed?"

"I . . . I don't think so."

"Did anyone talk to you? Stop you?"

"No . . . wait, yes. A street sweeper. I was lost. He helped me find my way."

"What did he look like?"

"I don't know. Average height. Gray hair . . ."

"Did he have a mustache?"

"Yes."

Sally spat into her fireplace. "Bleedin' Willie Dobbs," she growled. "They'll be here in a few minutes. Bound to be."

"Who will be here?"

"The rozzers. Willie's from the local constabulary. Well, he was. He's retired now. Can't believe he's still using that same mustache. Looks like he tore it off a cat."

"But I don't understand."

Sally frowned. "Not Sid's usual type, you. Not too quick on the uptake. His last one, Gemma Dean, now she was a sharp lass."

She cackled at India's puzzled expression, then rubbed her thumb and fingers together. "Willie's after the reward money, luv. Him and half of Whitechapel. He thinks he's going to get it by watching me. He's seen Sid come and go from here before and he must think he's going to pay me another call. He don't know about the tunnels, though."

"Mrs. Garrett, please . . . what are you talking about? *What* reward money?"

"A thousand quid. For information leading to Sid Malone's arrest. Bloody MP put it up, didn't he? Pillock's gone and got the whole of East London fired up. Promising rewards. Calling for Sid's head. Spouting off in all the newspapers."

"But that can't be," India said. "I've just come from operating on him and he's unconscious. He hasn't spoken at all."

"Not him. The old one. Lytton."

Oh God, not Freddie, India thought. She knew how deeply he hated Sid. He'd obviously seen his chance to go after him and he'd taken it.

"I saw him standing on the steps of the MP's office not two hours ago. He was giving statements to the papers. Telling anyone who'd listen that Sid Malone had done for Joe Bristow, that it was an outrage and not to be borne by decent folk. He was up there making out like he was all broken up over what had happened to Bristow, when only a few weeks ago, he was slagging him off."

"Mrs. Garrett . . ."

"Now, them what are the *real* villains wouldn't turn Sid in for any amount of money, but there are those round here who'd sell their mothers for tuppence. And Willie Dobbs is one. He's in a great deal of trouble, Sid is."

"I know he is, Mrs. Garrett. That's why I'm here. To ask you if you've any idea where he might be."

Sally shrugged. "The usual places, I'd guess. The Bark, the Taj, the Beggar . . ."

"I've been to all of those."

"You went to them places?"

"Yes."

"Well, that was bloody stupid of you," Sally said angrily.

"But why? I want to help him," India said, stung.

"In case you haven't noticed, you don't exactly blend in round here. Woman like you popping into the Bark or the Taj is bound to draw attention. Bound to start tongues wagging. The rozzers aren't entirely daft. They know a villain will surface for two things—his money and his mistress. Nobody knows where Sid keeps his pile, but now, thanks to your antics, they know who his fancy lady is. They don't even need Willie Dobbs, they've prob'ly been following you. You want to help him, dearie? Go back to Mayfair or Knightsbridge or wherever it is you're from and stay the hell away from him."

India looked at the floor. She cleared her throat, then softly said, "I have a letter. I hoped you might be able to give it to him."

"You hoped wrong. If Dobbs does bring the police here, they'll tear me flat apart. They always do."

India reached into her doctor's bag and drew out an envelope. "Please," she said.

Sally snatched it from her and threw it onto the fire. India watched helplessly as it burned.

"You'll put us all in danger now, you daft girl! No letters! Just tell me what it is you want him to know. I'll give him the message."

"Tell him to meet me at the flat on Friday at noon. We'll leave from there."

"That's it?"

"Yes, that's it." Sally might think her foolish, but she was smart enough not to mention the Arden Street address if she didn't have to.

"If I see him I'll tell him," Sally said. "Now it's time for you to be on your way."

She opened the door to let India out, then quickly slammed it shut.

"The police are here," she said. "All thanks to you. Going to give me flat a right going over, I just know it. If they put me in jail, I won't be able to visit Raysie in the hospital, and he lives for me visits. Come on," she said, pulling on her sleeve.

"Where are we going?"

"I'm not going anywhere. You are, though. You're leaving."

"But the door . . ."

"Not that way. Through the tunnels. I'll tell the police Dobbsie's imagining things. That no one came to see me. I'm not getting nicked today. Not over the likes of you."

"The tunnels?" she repeated, paling. "But I don't . . . I can't go down there."

There was a battering on Sally's door.

"Sorry," she said. "You've no choice."

"I can't do this. I don't know my way," India said two minutes later. She was hunched in the tunnel, clutching her doctor's bag, peering back at Sally through the old wardrobe.

A fresh volley of pounding was heard above them.

"You want the Blind Beggar," Sally said. "It's a quarter of a mile. Take two rights, a left, and then the path curves right again. You'll pass smaller tunnels. Steer clear of them."

"What if I get lost?"

"See that you don't."

And with that, the door to the wardrobe slammed shut and India stood alone in the darkness. The smell of earth was so strong she could taste it. She felt as if she'd been buried alive.

Sally had given her a box of matches and a candle. After a few fumbling attempts she got the candle lit, but the guttering flame barely illuminated the ground in front of her. Her chest tightened; it was hard to draw air.

"Breathe," India told herself. "Just breathe." A drop of icy water fell onto the back of her neck, making her shiver. More water trickled down the walls. She realized she was standing in a puddle. "Move. Now," she said. "One step . . . then another."

She forced herself forward, holding her candle in front of her. After she'd gone a few yards, a narrow tunnel snaked off to the left. Two rights and a left, Sally had said. Or was it two lefts and a right? No, two rights, she was sure of it.

After she'd gone a few more yards she saw a turning to the right and took it. Only one more and then a left, bear to the right, and she'd be there. It wasn't as bad as she'd thought it would be. She'd be at the Beggar in no time.

But a few steps into the turn the ceiling suddenly seemed lower and the walls closer together.

Did I take the first right turn? she wondered. Or did I take one of the smaller tunnels Sally warned me about?

Something gleamed whitely a few feet ahead of her. She lowered her candle to it, then gasped. It was a skeleton. The long bones poked through what was left of its rotted clothing. Black beetles crawled over its ribs. India started to shake. She had seen plenty of skeletons, but never one like this. Its wrists were tied together with a frayed rope. Its skull was fractured. Whoever this person was, he had not come down here willingly.

She turned and ran back down the tunnel. Hot wax dripped from the candle onto her hand. The pain made her wince, but she welcomed it. It brought her up short.

Stop it. Stop it right now, she told herself, slowing to a walk. If you don't keep your wits about you, someone will find your bones down here.

She got herself back to the main tunnel, wrapped her skirt hem around the candle's base to shield her hand, and pressed on. It was only a quarter of a mile. That wasn't so much. All she had to do was pay attention and get the turns right. After nearly a quarter of an hour she came to another turning. She held her candle to the ceiling and the walls to make sure it was a proper turning, not a small tunnel, then took it. A few minutes later she sighted the second right. There was only one more turn now. Only one more. She would make it. It couldn't be far.

The ground grew soggier as she walked, and the constant trickling of water grew louder. She knew she was walking under houses, under their cisterns and their middens, and shuddered to think what was in that water.

And then she smelled it—something far worse than cistern water, a stench that was low and gut-tightening: rats. She'd tried not to think about them. She'd tried to tell herself that they might not be there anymore, but they were.

She stopped, not knowing whether to laugh with relief that she was going the right way—or cry with fear. Sid had carried her over them before, but Sid wasn't here now. She would have to walk through them alone.

India heard the trickling water grow louder still. That must be why they like it here, she thought. There's water for them. And then her foot caught on something and she stumbled. She flailed wildly, trying to right herself. The candle flew out of her hand. She landed facedown in something soft and wet. Her arms and chest sank into it. It oozed into her nose and mouth. She sat up, screaming and spitting, trying to wipe it off. It was mud, stinking and thick. She rose up on her knees and reached for the wall, trying to pull herself up on it, but there was no wall.

She sank back to the ground and felt for the candle. Her movements were jerky and random in the darkness. Her hands covered some patches of ground over and over again and skipped others entirely. She realized she would never find the candle this way. It was gone. Buried in the mud. Even if by some miracle she did find it, its wick would be sodden and impossible to light.

Fear frothed up inside her, threatening to boil over into hysteria. She remembered that she had the matches. She had put them in her skirt pocket. She got to her feet and patted her pocket. They were still there. Her skirt was wet with mud, though. Would the matches be too wet to use? She wiped her hands on her jacket, then carefully took the box out of her pocket. Her fingers told her that part of it was wet, but part of it was dry. She slid the cover back ever so slightly, careful to make sure she had the box right side up, then pulled a match out. She struck the match. It sputtered, then flared. India nearly sobbed with relief. She held the match up and saw that part of the wall had collapsed. The trickling water had turned the earth to mud. She walked through the sucking mud, then suddenly turned back, disoriented. She was going the wrong way, she was sure of it. And then the match's flame burned her fingers and she dropped it and stood in darkness again.

She went to light another one, but stopped herself. How many matches did she have left? Twenty? Ten? Two? She opened the box again and felt for them, counting with her fingertip. Five, she had five matches left. How would she find the Beggar's doorway with only five matches?

She leaned against the wall, beaten. She simply did not know what to do next. She couldn't go forward. Without light, she couldn't see where she was going. Without light, she had nothing to keep the rats at bay. They would smell her, and when they did they would swarm her. She couldn't go back, either. It was too far and the police might still be there. She felt tears welling behind her eyes, tears of terror and despair.

An image flashed into her mind—of Sid as a boy. He was alone, keening in the hull of an abandoned boat after his mother's death. Another image followed it. He was a young man now. He was sitting on a metal cot. His hands were clenched into fists. His head was bent. A door clanged open. His head lifted. And then he was on his feet, leaping at the tiny window far above him in the wall. Scrabbling at the uncaring stones, half-mad with the awful knowledge of what was coming and that nothing and no one would stop it. And then a final image. Of him covering a sleeping street child with his coat the night they'd walked the streets of London.

India did weep then—not for herself, but for Sid. For all that he'd suffered. She'd convinced him that he could break away from his past, and he was trying, but someone didn't want him to. Someone wanted to pull him back in. She didn't know who or why, but she knew that she could not let it happen. Even if she had to cross an ocean of rats. She *had* to help him, because no one else would. She tried to wipe the tears from her face, but her sleeve was covered with mud. She laughed bitterly. How could she help Sid when she couldn't even get herself out of this damned tunnel?

"Improvise, Jones. Improvise," a voice said.

Some people heard the voice of God in times of trouble. Or the voice of a beloved mother, long dead. A husband. A friend. Not her. She heard Professor Fenwick.

"You are out for an evening at the theater," he was saying to her and her classmates. "As you stroll down Drury Lane, a runaway carriage mounts the curb. The horses trample a man. His leg is crushed. His femoral artery is severed. You left your doctor's bag at your home. What will save him? Armstrong?"

"Making the proper diagnosis, sir?"

Fenwick had closed his eyes at that; the pain of his students' stupidity was too much to bear.

"Hatcher?" he barked.

"A thorough knowledge of anatomy, sir?"

"Jones?"

"Technical abilities, sir?"

"No, no, no, no, no! When all hell is breaking loose, there is only one thing that will save you—*improvisation*. Turn your gloves into tourniquets. Your bloomers into slings. A bottle of whisky, obtained from a nearby pub, becomes your antiseptic. Jackets and shirts are your dressings. Hardly ideal, but in extremis you have little choice."

India took a deep, calming breath. "Improvise, Jones," she said determinedly. "Improvise."

She thought back to the night she and Sid had come down here. He had been wearing heavy boots and thick trousers. She had neither of those. Her kid shoes and woolen stockings and cotton skirts were no match for sharp teeth. She thought of what she did have: a few matches, a matchbox. She could light the matchbox itself, but it wouldn't blaze for long, and when it went out she'd have nothing left.

"Come on, Jones, what else have you got?"

She had her medical bag. She quickly reviewed its contents. Scalpels and scissors and clamps—all useless. Gauze and needles and suturing thread and chloral. She thought about lighting the gauze, but it was so thin and she didn't have much of it. It would burn out long before she got past the rats.

Chloral, she thought, chloral . . . She tried to move on, to think of other things in her bag, but her mind kept circling back to the anesthetic. It knocked people out. Could it do the same to rats? She scrabbled in the bag for the bottle. It was there. Maybe it would work. Maybe she could knock out enough of them. Maybe they'd run from the smell. Maybe . . .

"Maybe you've lost your mind," she said. "What are you going to do? Make a tiny rat mask? Ask them to line up in an orderly fashion?"

She'd have to open the bottle and splash the liquid around in order to knock the rats out, and she was as enclosed in the tunnels as they were. She might put a few of them under, but she'd certainly knock herself out. Perhaps permanently.

Panic was gnawing at her, fraying the edge of her resolve. The darkness was unnerving. She decided to use one of her precious matches. She needed light, if only for a few seconds. She was still holding the bottle of chloral. Checking to make sure its stopper was in place, she put it back in her bag, then lit the match. The liquid was highly flammable, and . . .

Flammable. A flame. A torch. *I could use the chloral to make a torch,* she thought. *The only thing is, I haven't anything to burn.*

She held the match over her bag, hoping against hope that she'd put extra dressings in it, and forgotten about them, but she hadn't. The match went out. "Bloody hell!" she yelled. It was hopeless. Futile. She'd never get out of here. Someone *would* find her body here. Her bones, actually. The rats would get the rest. They'd eat the leather of her bag, her shoes, everything but her muddy cotton suit.

Her suit . . . *her suit!* She put the chloral down and unbuttoned her jacket. It was muddy and damp, but underneath it her blouse was dry. She stood up and felt under her skirt for her petticoat. It was also damp, but her bloomers were dry. She took her blouse off, stepped out of her bloomers, and wadded them up. She had an idea and it might just work.

She shrugged her jacket back on and knelt on the ground. Feeling her way with her fingers, she pulled out a pad of gauze from her bag and laid it on the ground. Then she took the matchbox from her pocket, took the four remaining matches out of it and laid them on the gauze to keep them dry. Next, she took her scalpel from its case and used it to poke a hole in the top of the matchbox. Then she took her forceps out of the bag, and the chloral, and placed them both on the ground. Satisfied that her preparations were complete, she picked up one match, lit it, and quickly jammed it into the hole in the matchbox.

Working swiftly in its light, she bundled her blouse and bloomers together, grabbed the forceps, and clamped the fabric in its blades. The blades opened on her, the fabric flopped over limply. The match died.

"Damn it!" she cried.

She began again, twisting her blouse tightly. She did the same with her bloomers, then wound them together. The knot of fabric felt small in her hands. She wished it were bigger. A lot bigger. She lit another match and dropped it into a puddle.

She took another deep breath to steady herself, lit another match, and placed it in the box. Then she grabbed a spool of suturing silver—a filament used for closing birth lacerations—clamped the fabric in the forceps, wound the filament tightly around the blades to keep them closed, then secured it around the handle.

The match went out. India laid her jury-rigged torch on her lap. She checked for the chloral one last time, took a deep breath, and lit her last match.

Moving like lightning, she unstoppered the bottle, poured chloral on the fabric, and held it to the fading match. For a long second, nothing happened, then there was a tremendous *whoosh,* and the torch was blazing.

India jumped to her feet. The metal grew hot in her hand. She wrapped her skirt around it, grabbed her bag, and started to run. The tunnel snaked sharply left, the smell intensified, and then she saw them—hundreds of them. For an instant she faltered, then she plunged ahead yelling like an Amazon and holding the torch low to the ground. Frightened by the noise and light, the rats scrambled madly over one another to get away from her. A few ran at her, clawing at her boots, her skirt. She kicked at them and kept going.

And then the tunnel veered sharply left and she was past them. She stopped to catch her breath, to slow the mad banging of her heart. She closed her eyes, willing the sound and smell and sight of the rats away. When she opened them again, she felt calmer—until she glanced at her torch. Most of the fabric had burned away; the flame was dying.

"Bloody hell!" she swore, running again.

Two rights and a left. She'd made the two rights, was that last bend the left? It had to be. She remembered it from the time before, remembered the feeling of being safe in Sid's arms as he carried her past it. Two rights and a left and then the tunnel veers to the right and then you're there, Sally had said.

The tunnel had just started leading to the right when the torch began to gutter. India made another five yards before the flame died. There was no more chloral. No matches. She would have to make the rest of her way in the dark.

Fear started whispering in her ear again, but she refused to listen to it. She was almost there; she knew she was. The Beggar couldn't be far. Another twenty feet. Thirty at the most. She could feel her way. She put her forceps into her bag, placed her hand on the wall, and started to walk again.

It was then that she heard it. A noise up ahead of her. It sounded like a cough . . . like a cough cut short. She stopped dead to listen, but heard nothing. She stood perfectly still for a full minute, then two, but there was no more sound.

Had there ever been? Had she only imagined it? No one but herself would be unfortunate enough—or stupid enough—to be down here without any light.

"Hello? Is anyone there?" she called.

There was no reply. Maybe it's Sid! she thought. Maybe he's hiding out down here.

"Sid? Sid, is that you?"

Still no answer.

The darkness had blinded her eyes, but sharpened the rest of her senses. There *was* someone else down here with her. She could feel him. And it wasn't Sid.

Terror erupted inside of her. She bolted forward, her hand still on the wall, feeling for the door to the Beggar. She had to get to it before whoever was down here got to her. Another yard, two more, then three, and then suddenly there was no wall under her hand, only air and India knew she'd found it—the doorway to the Beggar. She lunged through it, knocking full force into something hard and immobile. The barrel, she thought frantically. She pushed against it, but it didn't budge. She dug her heels into the dirt floor and put her shoulder against it. It moved, ever so slightly, allowing a crack of light through. A terrified cry escaped her. Whoever was down here would see the light. And her in it. She threw her weight against the barrel, sending a bolt of pain through her body. It moved again, and then a bit more. And then she was squeezing past it, pulling her bag behind her. She didn't stop to move the barrel back, but bolted up the cellar stairs.

She did not see a match flare inside the tunnel, only a few feet from the doorway. She did not see its glow illuminate the face of the police constable who used it to light his bull's-eye lantern. She did not see Alvin Donaldson turn to a stunned Freddie Lytton and say, "Looks like Miss Dean was right. Looks like the good doctor *has* taken up with Sid Malone. You heard her call his name, didn't you?"

"Stop her. Why don't you go after her? Arrest her, damn it!" Freddie hissed.

Donaldson shook his head. "No, we'll let her go. She's trying to find Malone. I'd wager they're going to meet somewhere. If we let her go free, she'll draw him to her, draw him out."

"But where? They could be meeting in a thousand different places. Nobody knows where their flat is."

Donaldson smiled. "Gemma Dean knows. Isn't that what you said?"

"Yes, and she wants four hundred pounds before she'll tell me."

"If you want Malone, you'll give it to her."

CHAPTER 64

Fiona stood in front of her armoire, frowning. She was supposed to have afternoon tea with the owner of a building in Edinburgh that she wanted to buy, and she needed to look polished and professional.

"And instead I look like a circus tent," she muttered, looking herself up and down. The navy-and-cream-striped suit did not flatter her. She reached for another suit, one made of red silk faille, and held it up in front of her. It was no better. "Now I look like a tomato," she sighed, putting it back.

It didn't matter what she wore. There was simply no hiding the bump; her swelling belly had ceased to be sweet and cute. It was enormous and heavy, and she felt more like a whale than a woman.

Her hands went to her belly now. The baby would come soon. She wondered if his father would be here to welcome him when he arrived.

Joe's armoire was next to hers. She opened it impulsively, took out one of his suits, and pressed it to her face. It smelled of him—clean and masculine. God, how she missed him. She wanted him to come home. She wanted to be a family again.

"Go and make it up with him," her uncle Roddy had told her. Only this morning. "He loves you."

She almost had. She'd tried. She'd rung Joe's office, his MP's office on Commercial Street, but there was no answer. Then she'd rung Covent Garden, but again there was no answer there either. She'd found it strange— Trudy never let the phone go unanswered—then thought perhaps he'd gone to Westminster and Trudy had accompanied him.

She wanted to make up with him. Desperately. But she knew that for that to happen she would have to let go of Charlie once and for all. Forever. Roddy told her she had lost her brother, and if she didn't accept that she would lose her husband, too. He'd come to visit her earlier in the day, dropping by her Mincing Lane offices unexpectedly.

"Mrs. Bristow? I've a Rodney O'Meara here to see you. No appointment," Minna Calvert, her secretary, had said.

Fiona had immediately brightened. "Send him in!" she said, rushing to the door to greet him.

Roddy was not a blood relation, but he had been her father's closest friend. He had lived with the family and the children had all considered him their uncle. When Fiona's parents had died, Roddy had been both mother and father to herself and Seamie. Later, as a police sergeant, he'd helped her ruin her father's murderer, William Burton. Roddy had left London shortly after learning that Charlie Finnegan had become a criminal because he was devastated by the news and because he never wanted to find himself arresting his old friend's son. Besides Fiona and Joe, only Roddy knew who Sid Malone really was, and he'd agreed with their decision to keep this knowledge from Seamie.

"Hello, Fiona lass!" he'd said, embracing her warmly.

Fiona hugged him back, exclaiming over him. She smiled at his voice, so Irish, so like her father's. It had been months since she'd seen him. He'd grown a little stouter, a little grayer, but he was still her beloved Uncle Roddy.

"What a surprise! Sit down, won't you?" she said, as Minna brought a tea tray. "I didn't know you were coming into London. Why didn't you write to let me know?"

"Didn't know meself till today, lass," Roddy said, settling himself in a chair by Fiona's desk. "A sergeant at the Covent Garden station sent me a telegram this morning. A man named Tom Cunningham killed a woman there two days ago. I've a Tom Cunningham wanted for murder up in me own neck of the woods, so I went to see if he's the same man, and he is. We've got a good case against him. Witnesses in both places. He'll swing for certain and that will be one less villain in the world."

Fiona flinched slightly at that and Roddy's sharp policeman's eyes had caught her discomfort. He was silent for a few seconds, sipping his tea, then he'd put his cup down and said, "Speaking of villains, I paid a quick visit to Montague's while I was in Covent Garden. I saw Joe."

Fiona looked down at her own teacup. "Yes, speaking of villains," she said softly.

"I didn't mean him," Roddy said.

Fiona sighed. "No, I didn't think you did. I guess he told you about Charlie."

"He did."

"And about us."

"Aye."

"Well, I hope you told him off," she said.

Roddy held her gaze. "No, lass, I didn't. In fact, I came here to tell you off."

Fiona felt hurt. "You're not taking *his* side, are you?" she'd said.

"I am."

"But why, Uncle Roddy?"

"Because he's right. It hurts me as much as it does you to know what Charlie's done. What he's become. But there's one thing I know about villains that you don't—once someone goes over to the other side, he doesn't come back."

"But Charlie could. I *know* he could."

"Fiona, lass, you're stubborn as hell and we both know it. I personally t'ink stubbornness is a virtue, but I also t'ink that this time you're taking it too far."

"But I only want to talk to him. To help him."

"I know, lass, but you can't. He doesn't want your help. He's made that plain, hasn't he? So let go. Let go of him."

"I can't, Uncle Roddy. He's my brother. It's hard."

"You've done harder t'ings. Much harder. Charlie's made his choice. He's destroyed his own life and now he's destroying yours."

"He isn't!"

"He *is*. Look at yourself. You look terrible. Miserable. And no wonder. You need your husband. Especially now with a new baby coming. Katie needs her father."

Fiona nodded. Roddy was the only one who understood her feelings for both her brother and her husband.

"I *am* miserable, Uncle Roddy. I miss Joe so much. I want him to come home."

"Then go and make it up with him. He's hurting, too. He loves you, Fee."

"I don't know how," she said helplessly. "I know how to win fights. I don't know how to lose them."

"You're not *losing*, you damned bullheaded woman. Can't you see that? The only way you lose is if you let the darkness that ruined Charlie ruin you, too."

Roddy's right, Fiona thought now. She hung Joe's suit back in his armoire and closed the door. She would ring him again. Right after her meeting. She would see if they could have supper together tonight. Just the two of them.

There was a knock at her door.

"Yes?" she called.

Sarah, the maid, poked her head in. "Beg your pardon, ma'am, but Mr. Foster said to tell you there's a police officer in the foyer who wishes to speak with you."

"My goodness. About what?"

"He wouldn't say, ma'am, but he did tell Mr. Foster that his business is urgent."

Fiona nodded. "Please tell Mr. Foster I'll be down in a few minutes," she said. It's probably about a shop theft or a damaged delivery wagon or some such thing, she thought. Those sorts of unfortunate occurrences were not uncommon in her business or Joe's.

She looked at herself in the mirror one last time. "Circus tent it is," she sighed. She added a string of pearls Joe had given her to the ensemble, then went downstairs to receive her visitor.

She wanted to get the bad news over with quickly. Robbery, accident— whatever it was, she hoped it was not too terribly time-consuming. Her mind was on Joe. She wanted to put their disagreement behind them. She wanted him to know that she cared for him and their family above everything else.

The house was so empty without him. She longed to hear him whistling in his bath, chasing Katie around the dining-room table, or even bellowing at the dogs. She longed to reach for him in the night and feel his strong arms around her.

"Good afternoon, Mrs. Bristow, I'm Detective Inspector Alvin Donaldson," the visitor said, as Fiona entered the drawing room. She realized that she vaguely remembered him. He had been involved in the hunt for William Burton.

"Would you like a cup of tea, Detective Inspector?" Fiona said, ready to ring for Sarah.

"No, thank you," Donaldson replied. He was standing, hat in hand. His eyes flicked nervously to her belly. "Will you sit, ma'am?" he asked, gesturing to her own settee.

"I survived William Burton, as I'm certain you remember. Surely I can withstand the shock of a broken wagon axle or the theft of a few crates of tea. Even in my current condition."

"Please, ma'am," Donaldson said gently.

Fiona sighed. "All right, then. If it will make you happy." She sat down and fixed him with a look of strained patience. "Now then, what's happened?"

Donaldson sat down next to her, cleared his throat, and said, "Mrs. Bristow, have you ever heard the name Sid Malone?"

Fiona felt everything warm and vital inside her turn to stone. Had Donaldson somehow worked out the connection between them? How? And then a darker, far more terrifying thought entered her mind.

"Is he . . . is he all right?" she asked, ashen.

"What?"

"Is he all right?" she repeated, more urgently.

"*Malone?*" Donaldson asked, not seeming to understand her question.

"Yes."

"For the moment he is, as far as I know. But he won't be once we bring him in."

"Bring him in? Why? What's he done?"

Donaldson shook his head. "Mrs. Bristow, you misunderstand me. I am not here to trouble you over the welfare of Sid Malone."

"But he's done something. What is it? Has he burned one of my warehouses? Broken into a wharf?"

"Sid Malone's done something, Mrs. Bristow, but not to your property." He paused, then said, "Mrs. Bristow . . . a few hours ago Sid Malone tried to murder your husband."

Fiona tilted her head as if she hadn't heard him properly. She gave a small laugh. "That's not possible," she said.

"I'm afraid it is. Malone walked into Mr. Bristow's office on Commercial Street and shot him in the chest. Twice. His condition is very poor, ma'am. The doctor who operated got one bullet out, but another's lodged near his spine and can't be removed. He was at a clinic near his office, but he's been moved to the London Hospital and he . . . he's not expected to live. I'm so sorry."

"No. That's not true!" she cried. "It can't be!"

The door to the drawing room opened. Foster entered, looking concerned. "Pardon me, madam, but I heard shouting," he said.

"Mr. Foster!" Fiona cried. She tried to stand, but her legs buckled and she fell to the floor.

"Good God, madam! What is it?" Foster said, rushing to her. Donaldson helped him get her back on the settee, explaining what had happened as he did.

"It's not true," Fiona said again. She shook her head furiously. "It's not true, Mr. Foster. Tell him. Please."

Sarah ran into the room, wiping her hands on her apron.

"Mr. Foster, what's happened?"

Foster couldn't answer her, for Fiona was trying to stand again. "Please, madam, please sit down," he said.

"I have to see Joe," she said wildly, trying to shake him off. "I have to go now. Let go of me!"

"Sarah, have the carriage brought," Foster barked. "Then ring the Alden household. Twelve Wilmington Crescent. Inform Master Seamus that Mr. Bristow has been injured and is in the London Hospital. Hurry."

Sarah didn't move. She stood quaking like a terrified rabbit.

"I said bring the carriage! Now, girl!" Foster shouted. Sarah shot off and he turned back to Fiona. "It's all right, madam," he said. "The carriage is coming. Please, madam, please sit quietly until it arrives. You must remember the baby."

Fiona began to cry. "Why, Mr. Foster? Why did he shoot him?" she moaned.

"Please try to remain calm," Foster pleaded.

But Fiona wouldn't. If Foster couldn't answer her, someone must. "Why, Mr. Donaldson, why?" she persisted, turning to the officer and clutching at his arm.

Foster stole a quick, anxious glance at the door. There was no sign of Sarah. "Best to answer, sir," he said quietly.

"We're not sure, Mrs. Bristow, but from what we can piece together it appears that Mr. Bristow went to the Barkentine, a pub in Limehouse, a few days ago to see Malone. He didn't succeed in finding him, but he did find a lad by the name of Frankie Betts. Mr. Bristow warned that there would be trouble between himself and Malone now that he was MP. He wanted Malone to leave before there was. Words were exchanged. A fight occurred . . ."

Fiona closed her eyes and began to sob.

"What is it, madam?" Foster asked.

"It's my fault, Mr. Foster. It's all my fault," she cried.

"Of course it isn't."

She sank against him, keening. "It is. He did it for me. He tried to help him. To save him. Because of me. Oh God . . . oh, Joe . . . it's all my fault, Mr. Foster. Don't you see? I've killed him. I've killed my Joe."

CHAPTER 65

Freddie Lytton closed his eyes, took a deep breath, and knocked on the door to Gemma Dean's flat. She had the top floor of a two-story building in Stepney.

He hadn't seen her since the party, the one where she'd told him about Sid and India, then refused to give him their address. He'd been stunned by her news, and furious, too. Malone had taken Gemma from him, then the election, now he had India. Freddie had brooded over the news for days. He hadn't left his flat. He hadn't eaten. Barely slept. He just sat in a wing chair, impotent and defeated, hating Sid Malone with every fiber of his being.

And then something had happened. A gift, the most most amazing, astonishing, wondrous gift had fallen right into his lap. Right out of the blue, Malone had walked into Joe Bristow's office and shot him at point-blank range. In a single stroke, both of his rivals had been vanquished. The police were mounting a manhunt for Malone—it was only a matter of time until they caught him—and Bristow, currently at the London Hospital, was not expected to live.

The Liberals' Whip had rung him up to tell him the news. "There'll be a by-election within the month," he'd said.

That was all Freddie needed to hear. His torpor vanished. He was out of his chair, bathed, and dressed in no time. He had not a second to waste. He'd hailed a cab and had gone directly to the hospital.

He arrived there just as Fiona Bristow had. There were reporters everywhere. They mobbed her, pelting her with questions. Freddie ran to her side, put a protective arm around her, and said, "I promise you that the man who did this will be brought to justice. I won't rest until he is."

Fiona had nodded at him, dazed and in shock, before the ward sister escorted her away. The reporters present had caught both the gesture and his every word—just as he'd planned. They all asked for interviews and he gave them—passionately extolling the virtues of his erstwhile opponent, expressing his deep concern for the Bristow family, and then decrying the lawlessness of the East End.

"If one criminal may be so emboldened by the lack of proper law enforcement in East London, what may twenty do?" he asked them. "This heinous piece of villainy is an attack not only on an innocent and upstanding citizen, but on a Member of Parliament, and as such on government itself. Lawlessness of this magnitude can lead to only one thing—anarchy. Malone and his ilk must be stopped, and they must be stopped now!"

He finished his interview by telling the assembled reporters that he was putting up a thousand pounds of his own money as a reward for information leading to the capture of Sid Malone. He didn't have the money, but he hadn't let that stop him.

Before Dickie Lambert even knew that Joe Bristow had been shot, Freddie had commandeered the press and captured the public's interest. He'd gone to his club for supper later that night and read as many of the evening papers as he could get his hands on. Article after article about the Bristow shooting had run—and article after article about him, too. His earlier disgraces—the Stronghold robbery, the Home Rule fiasco—had been forgotten. Most of the reporters, sensing a good story, had painted him as a selfless leader, a knight in shining armor to his fallen adversary's grief-stricken wife and, most important, a prescient politician who understood—perhaps better than the man so recently elected—the threat posed to law and order by the criminal population of East London.

When he'd finished at the hospital, he went to see Alvin Donaldson. He met him as he was coming out of the police station with some officers. Freddie said he needed to talk to him. Donaldson said he had no time to talk; he had to find Malone. Freddie ended up following him to the Blind Beggar and through a series of tunnels under East London. While they were down there, Donaldson confirmed that it was indeed Malone who'd done for Bristow. They had witnesses.

"Then why isn't he in jail?" Freddie had fumed.

"Because we have to catch him first," Donaldson replied. "We almost nabbed him a few hours ago at the Bark, but he got away. He's down here somewhere, I know he is."

They hadn't found him; they'd found India instead. Freddie had told Donaldson about Gemma Dean and her visit to Sid's and India's flat, and Donaldson had told him to get that address. Sid would surface there. He was sure of it.

Freddie pulled a slim buff envelope out of his breast pocket now and weighed it in his palm. It felt right to him; he hoped it would to Gemma. He'd stuffed it himself only an hour ago. He heard footsteps approaching from the other side of the door and quickly slid the envelope back into his pocket. There was the sound of a lock turning and then Gemma was standing in the doorway in a satin dressing gown. She looked worn and unhappy. He smelled gin on her.

"Hello, Gem," he said. "You look lovely. As always." He tried to kiss her cheek, but she turned her face away.

"What do you want, Freddie?"

"A bit of information."

Her eyes sharpened. "Come in, then."

He followed her down the long hallway into her sitting room. There were trunks and suitcases everywhere. Clothes were heaped over chairs. Shoes were in piles on the floor.

"Going on holiday?" Freddie asked.

"I'm off to Paris."

"For how long?"

"Forever. I'm giving up the London halls. Going to the Moulin Rouge. That's where the money is. And speaking of money, did you bring any? That address is going to cost you. The price is still four hundred quid."

Freddie touched his jacket pocket. "It's right here."

"Hand it over."

Freddie shook his head. "Not until you give me the address."

Gemma snorted. "Not a chance. You're always skint. How do I know you even have the money? Until I see it, no address."

Freddie reached into his pocket and drew out an envelope. "Here you are," he said, handing it to Gemma, hoping she didn't look inside it.

She took it, sighing ruefully. "I'm a Judas, me," she said.

"Hardly. Malone's a murderer, Gem."

"Do you really think he shot that MP?"

"I know he did. There were witnesses. You're doing the right thing."

"Maybe, maybe not. Either way, Paris flats don't come cheap."

She opened the envelope. Freddie swore under his breath. He truly wished she hadn't done that. Now things were going to get complicated. He watched her face as her expression changed from confusion to anger.

"You son of a bitch!" she finally cried, turning the envelope upside down. Pieces of newspaper cut to size fluttered out. "What are you playing at?"

"I need that address, Gem."

"Oh, aye? Well, you can go sing for it! Four hundred quid or no deal."

Freddie rose from his chair, crossed the room, and slapped her. Hard.

Gemma's hand came up to her cheek. "Get out!" she screamed. "Get out of here!"

Freddie threw her down on the settee and wrapped his hands around her neck, pressing his thumbs against her throat. "Where is it? Where's the flat?" he said.

She clawed at his hands, tore at his sleeves, trying to break his grip. Her heels scraped against the floorboards. "Please . . ." she gasped.

"The address," he said.

"Let me go!" Gemma kicked at him. Her knee caught him in the groin. The pain was blinding. He staggered backward, bellowing. She broke free and ran for the door. He ran after her, sick with pain, but knowing that if she got out, all was lost. His hands closed on the back of her gown. He pulled her back and hurled her toward the settee. But he missed his mark. She hit a heavy marble-topped table instead. Headfirst.

There was a sharp, dry crack, like a branch breaking. The table went over. Gemma fell to the floor. She moaned once and was still.

Freddie was panting, his hands on his knees, trying not to vomit. "Give me that fucking address!" he spat at her, as the pain began to subside.

But Gemma made no reply.

He walked over to her. "Gemma, I'll beat you bloody, I swear I will," he said, grabbing her. Her head lolled as he pulled her up, then fell forward. Too far forward. Freddie gasped and let her go.

Gemma's neck was broken. She was dead.

As he stood there, looking at her, he realized that he would be in a great deal of trouble unless he could think very fast and very well. He felt no remorse, no horror or sadness over what he'd done. He was well past all that now. He needed two things—he needed Sid and India's address, and he needed to make it look like someone else had killed Gemma Dean.

He thought for a few minutes, coldly and clearly, and then it came to him—an answer. He nodded and set to work.

He knew Gemma kept a diary. He'd seen it. It was slim with a red leather cover. If she had written down the address anywhere, it would be there. He went to her desk and rifled through her papers. He pulled out the drawers and dumped their contents on the floor. He tore the clothes out of her trunks, dug in pockets, but found nothing.

"Where are you?" he whispered, turning around in the room. "Where?"

Then he spotted a carpetbag. It was leaning against an umbrella stand. He turned it over, tumbling its contents out. A wallet, compact, sweets, and cigarettes all fell to the floor, but no diary. Swearing now, he turned the bag inside out and found a pocket. Inside it was the diary. He flipped through the month of November. There were names of people, addresses of restaurants and theaters. He flipped to the inside front cover, and then the back—and then he saw something: *Arden Street. Number 16. Richmond Hill.*

It was scribbled, as if it had been written hastily, or angrily. That's it, he thought. That's the one to try. He pocketed the diary, pleased. He picked up the envelope he'd brought with him, and the fake money, and pocketed those, too. He decided to take Gemma's wallet, because that's what a thief would do, and then he turned the sitting room upside down.

He went into the bedroom next and ransacked it, too, strewing clothing, dumping a mirror, combs, and perfume bottles on the floor. Her jewelry box caught his eye. He turned it over, spilling bits of costume jewelry across the bureau. As he did, her magnificent diamonds fell out and glinted up at him. He picked up the earrings. Then the necklace. He read the inscription: *For Gemma. Break a leg. Love, Sid.* He slipped them into his pocket. They were just the sort of thing a man desperate for money, a man on the run, would take. Especially if that man had given them to her and knew what they were worth.

Freddie was just about to leave the bedroom when he heard it—a long, groaning creak. The kind a loose floorboard makes when someone's stepped on it.

He froze. "Who's there?" he called.

There was no answer. He bent down to the fireplace, picked up a poker, and walked back into the sitting room, slowly and quietly. The sitting room was empty. He made his way down the long hallway to the kitchen. Whoever had made the noise had to be in there now. It was the only room left. He raised the poker, his heart hammering, and rounded the doorway.

A cat was sitting in the middle of the kitchen floor. A white cat with a glittering pink collar. Freddie swore at the animal. He lunged at it, but it was too quick for him. It darted between his legs and shot under the settee.

He let it be and put the poker back. He was nearly finished now, nearly out of the woods, but he knew the last part would be the hardest part. He looked at his hands. They were scratched and bloodied. One of his sleeves was torn. That was good. He would have to do something about his face, though. He went back into the kitchen and found a teapot. He closed his eyes, steeling himself, then smashed the pot into his forehead. He lurched forward at the impact, nearly fell, but righted himself against the sink. When he could see again, he took a bread knife from the cutlery drawer and drew it across his left cheek, from his ear to his jaw. It didn't hurt nearly as much as the teapot had. He waited until he could feel the blood dripping down into his shirt collar, then he walked downstairs and into the street.

Two workmen were walking by. Freddie stumbled toward them. "Help me. Help me, please," he cried.

"Christ, mate, what's happened to you?" one of them said, taking his arm, trying to steady him.

"He . . . he killed her. I saw him. I tried to stop him . . . I couldn't. Call the police. Hurry. He mustn't get away. He mustn't. It's him!"

"It's who, mate, *who*?"

"Malone. Sid Malone."

CHAPTER 66

"You're going to have to get off the game," India said to the emaciated woman sitting on the examination table in the garden shed in the Moskowitzes' backyard.

"I can't, Dr. Jones. You know that."

India peered at the woman's puffy eyes and then examined her chest, tapping the ribs and listening. It was full of liquid. Her breathing was labored.

"How does your water look?"

"Bloody."

"Can you at least stop drinking?"

The woman, Elizabeth Durkin, a prostitute, laughed. "Could you? If you was in my place?"

India sighed. Once she would have lectured the poor woman on the evils of drink and the necessity of vegetables. Now she simply said, "No, Elizabeth, I couldn't."

"What is it? What's wrong with me?"

"Edema, inflammation. I'd have to say Bright's disease."

"In English, Dr. Jones."

"Ginny kidney."

Elizabeth nodded. "What are me prospects?"

"If I could get you into a sanatorium and on bed rest, get the syphilis under control, keep you off the gin and put you on a milk diet, they might be decent."

"And if not?"

"Not so good."

Elizabeth looked up at the slatted wooden ceiling, then said, "You've taken good care of me. The syphilis. The bronchitis. That bout of influenza. I wish you weren't leaving."

"I wish it, too."

"Why are you?"

"There's someone—someone very dear to me—who needs looking after."

"Who'll look after me when you're gone?"

"Dr. Hatcher will. At the new clinic."

"She's not you."

"She's a damn sight funnier. I've seen her make a patient laugh while she was sticking a needle in his bum."

"God knows where I'd be without a laugh now and then," Elizabeth said. She swallowed, then asked, "Is it a hard end, then?"

"Not the hardest, but not the easiest, either. You'll be all right, though. The clinic's almost open. There will be a bed for you there and nurses to look after you. And morphine at the end. You make sure you go when it gets bad."

Elizabeth nodded. Then she reached into her skirt pocket. "I've a shilling to give you today. A ship docked last night. I was the first one there."

India took the woman's hand and curled her fingers over the coin. "You keep that, Liz," she said. "Go in the caff and buy yourself some soup."

Elizabeth hugged her, hard and tight. "Wherever it is you're going, Dr. Jones, the ones there'll be lucky to get you," she said.

And then she was gone. India looked after her, tears smarting. How she would miss Elizabeth Durkin and all the women of Whitechapel. The chattering factory girls. The raucous whores. The new wives. And all the mothers—English, Irish, Russian, Chinese—who somehow kept their children clothed and fed on a pound a week and a prayer. They had taught her so well. More things, and better things, than any textbook ever had.

She heard the bells at Christ Church ring the hour. Ten o'clock. Time to go. The new clinic wasn't even open yet; she and Harriet and Ella were still seeing patients in the Moskowitzes' backyard. And now she would never see it open. She was meeting Sid in a few hours, and they were leaving London—not in a fortnight as planned, but tonight. At least, she *hoped* she was meeting him. She hadn't seen him, or even heard from him, for three days. Since he'd made his last trip to the Bark. Since Joe Bristow had been shot.

Ever since her trip through the tunnels, she'd been sick with worry, hoping against hope that he'd gotten the message she'd left with Sally. They had to get out of London. Immediately. There was no choice. Joe had been transferred to the London Hospital and his condition had not improved. Though he was now under the care of another doctor, she visited him there as often as she could. He was still unconscious, his poor pregnant wife was in shock—India had seen her, she could barely speak—and the papers were howling for Sid Malone's head.

India knew in her heart that Sid had not committed this brutal, senseless act. No one who knew him believed he had. But Freddie did, and the police did, and the press, too. If he was found, he'd be arrested. She knew that he knew that, too, and that he would rather die than go back to prison.

A maelstrom of emotion gripped her now—fear for Sid, and grief at leaving her dream behind. She stepped out of the shed and Harriet Hatcher stepped in, leading a little girl by the hand. The girl's mother trailed after them.

"I *know* Emily likes the dog, Mrs. Burke, but still, you mustn't let her sleep in the dog's bed. That's how she's getting the worms in the first place," Harriet said, rolling her eyes at India as she passed.

India smiled sadly. She looked all around at the yard that had served as her clinic for the past few months, trying to impress every detail of it into her mind. The mangy tom sitting on the fence, and Eddie, the neighbor's ancient, toothless bull terrier, barking at him from the next yard. A dozen chickens in their coop. Aaron, Miriam, and Solly plucking a dozen more. The ancient copper pot, still full of murky water from the morning's wash. And her patients. All the women and children. Harriet's patients now. India had already said good-bye to Harriet. She walked into the kitchen to do what she dreaded most—say good-bye to Ella and her mother. They were working in there. Ella was washing dishes; Mrs. Moskowitz was cooking.

"Crikey, India, is this really good-bye?" Ella asked, wiping her hands on a towel.

"Oh, Ella, I'm afraid so."

"But what'll I do without you? You're my best friend."

"And you're mine," India said, hugging her. "I'll write. As soon as we're settled."

"And you'll come back someday, won't you?"

"I hope so," India said, sniffling.

"What is it? What's wrong?"

"Nothing, I just feel like I'm leaving . . . well, everything! I wonder if I'll ever practice medicine again," she said, her voice quavering.

"Du hok a chainik!"

"My mother just told you that you're talking nonsense," Ella said.

"Are there no sick people in America?" Mrs. Moskowitz asked. "With all that gold in California, there must be plenty of money to pay for doctors."

"You're right, of course," India said, smiling. She kissed her on the cheek. "You were right about something else, too."

"What's that?"

"About love. You were right when you said you don't choose love, it chooses you."

"Don't tell her she's right, India! She'll be impossible!"

Mrs. Moskowitz swatted Ella with her wooden spoon. "Sid Malone is a good man," she said to India. "And he'll become a better one with you at his side."

She kissed India's forehead, then embraced her. She smelled of parsley and garlic and chicken. Of clean laundry and fresh bread. The tears India had been holding back spilled over. She had not felt so sad when she'd left Blackwood. But the crowded noisy flat above the café had been more of a home to her than Blackwood ever had. And the Moskowitzes had been more a family to her than her own family.

"Good-bye, Mrs. Moskowitz," she said. "Thank you for everything."

Mrs. Moskowitz released her and hastily wiped her eyes on her apron. *"Ich bin verklempt.* Go now, *zeeskyte,* before my salty tears ruin the soup. And may God go with you."

"India."

India flinched. She recognized that voice. It was Freddie's. She turned around and gasped. She hardly recognized him. His forehead was horribly bruised and there was a long gash on his cheek.

"Freddie, what happened to you?"

"I need to talk to you. In private."

"I'm sorry, but I was just leaving."

"I'm afraid you can't do that. I'm here with these two constables"—he gestured to the two uniformed men behind him—"on official police business. Their superior, Alvin Donaldson, has allowed me to talk to you, to try to get you to do the sensible thing, the *right* thing."

"What are you talking about?"

Freddie turned to Mrs. Moskowitz. "Might I have a word with Dr. Jones in private?" he said. "Would you please leave us for a few moments?"

"I will not," Mrs. Moskowitz said. "This is my kitchen. I'm cooking. Go sit in the restaurant like everyone else."

"There are people dining in there and I require privacy. You may leave the kitchen voluntarily or these constables will escort you."

Mrs. Moskowitz threw her spoon in the sink. She took her soup pot off the stove, slammed it down on a table, then turned on her heel.

"Gai platz!" she said, pushing open the door to the dining room.

"Mama!" Ella hissed.

"What?"

"You told him to go explode, that's what!"

"He should. No one orders me about in my own kitchen! No one!"

The door slammed shut and India turned to Freddie. "That was very nice, Freddie," she said. "Almost as nice as getting me sacked, but not quite."

"I'm sorry. I had no choice. I need to speak to you."

"First tell me what happened to you."

"A woman was murdered last night. For a bit of cash and some jewelry. I saw it. I tried to stop it and was beaten. Her name was Gemma Dean. She was Sid Malone's former girlfriend, and it was Malone who killed her."

Though her heart was pounding, India's face betrayed nothing.

"And what, exactly, is that to me?"

"Quite a lot, I should think."

"Why have you come here, Freddie?"

"To stop you from running off with him."

Panic gripped her. *How does he know?* she wondered.

"What nonsense," she said, struggling to keep her voice steady. "I barely know Sid Malone and have no plans to run off with him or with anyone else. Now, if you'll excuse me, I have patients to see."

"India, the police *know*."

"About what?" she said lightly.

Freddie didn't reply; he just stood there, watching her face.

He's enjoying this, she thought, and her composure suddenly shattered. "I asked you a question. Answer me, damn it!"

"About your plans to meet Malone. To go away with him."

India's fear turned into full-blown terror. Sid was in terrible danger. But then she remembered that the police couldn't possibly know about the flat. Even if they strong-armed Sally, she couldn't have told them because she didn't know herself. India hadn't told her.

"They don't."

"They do. They know you're leaving today. How? It was easy. One of the officers, a local man, asked a few of your patients if his wife could go to you. They told him you wouldn't be here after today."

"They don't know *where*," India said frantically, "and they don't have an address."

"Actually, they do. Number sixteen Arden Street, Richmond Hill. That's what I was doing at Gemma Dean's. I've taken a personal interest in this case because of Joe Bristow, and I've been doing everything I can to help the police track Malone. I thought if one person might know his where-abouts, it would be Miss Dean. It's common knowledge that they were an item, and that's why I went to her flat. She knew; she'd followed Sid once. She managed to give me the location before she died."

India got to her feet, but Freddie was quicker. He rose, too, and blocked her way to the door.

"Get out of my way," she said.

"India, these constables have orders to keep you here until they receive word that Malone has been captured. If you try to leave, if you try to help him in any way, they will arrest you."

"Is this true?" India asked one of the officers.

"Yes, ma'am, it is," he replied.

India looked at Freddie. "You did this, you bastard," she said.

Freddie's emotion flared, too. "Yes, India, I did. For you, you bloody un-grateful woman. As soon as I learned what was going on, I begged Alvin Donaldson to keep you out of this mess. To keep you out of the newspa-pers and out of jail. Do you know what happens to people who help mur-derers? Do you want to lose your medical license? Do you want to go to prison?"

"He's *not* a murderer. He didn't shoot Joe Bristow and he didn't kill Gemma Dean. I *know* he didn't. You're lying, Freddie. Again."

"Stop being so blind! He *is* a murderer. It's not only me saying it. There are witnesses, for God's sake—Bristow's secretary and the cleaner—who swear it was Sid Malone who shot Joe."

"Why, Freddie? Why are you doing this? Do you hate him so much? Or is it me whom you hate?"

"Hate you? *Hate* you?" He stood close to her so that the officers could not hear him. "I care deeply about you, India. So much that I can't stand by while you destroy your life. You've been down this road before. Haven't you learned your lesson?"

"What are you talking about?"

"Hugh Mullins. He stole from your family and broke your heart, and he was only a thief. Sid Malone is ten times more dangerous. He shot Bristow in cold blood. He turned on Gemma Dean. He would have turned on you, too."

India said nothing. She sat back down at the table and lowered her face into her hands. She was sick to her very soul with fear for Sid. If only she could get out of here. If only she had some way to warn him.

"Would it have been so bad, India?" Freddie said quietly. "The two of us together? We would have had a proper marriage, children, friends, important work, a place in society. Everything."

India raised her head. "Everything? What about love, Freddie?"

"Yes, of course. I was going to say that—"

"No, you weren't."

"Can't you give me another chance, India? We could start again."

India had no capacity left to feel frights or shocks, or Freddie's words would have floored her. Here he was, sending the man she loved to his doom and trying to win her back at the same time.

She looked at him for a long moment, then said, "Go to hell, Freddie."

Freddie colored. He was about to reply, but Ella knocked on the kitchen door and entered, stopping him.

"What is it?" he barked at her.

"I'm sorry to interrupt, but there's a woman just came to the clinic, Dr. Jones. She's eight months gone. Twins. She's begun to bleed. No contractions. Dr. Hatcher's seen her and thinks it might be placenta previa. She wants to send her to the hospital, but she wants your opinion first. I know this is not a good time, but it's a very serious case. Could you take a look at her?"

"Well, Freddie, can I?"

Freddie hesitated. He looked at the constables.

"It's a garden shed, gentlemen. It has a roof, walls, and a floor. I won't be tunneling out."

"I don't see why not," Freddie said. "We'll have to go with you, however. We'll turn our backs during the examination."

"Very well."

India walked out of the restaurant and into the kitchen with one constable ahead of her, and the second one, plus Freddie, behind her. Ella was walking next to her.

"Here are Dr. Hatcher's notes," she said, handing India a lined notebook. India gave her a puzzled look. They rarely took notes in the clinic. They couldn't afford the paper. She looked closer and saw that it was Miriam's lesson book. She opened it. One of the constables held the kitchen door open for her. She walked down the steps into the yard, flipping past page after page of cursive writing exercises. And then she saw them. Two lines. In Ella's handwriting: *Mama earwigged. Get ready to run.*

India had barely digested these words when all hell broke loose.

It began with a horrible sound—the deep, snarling bark of a bull terrier on the rampage.

"Mama!" Miriam screamed. "Help, Mama, help! Eddie got in! He'll kill us all!"

Kill us all? India thought. *Eddie?* He has no teeth!

The next thing she knew, the fearsome-looking dog was tearing around the yard after the orange tom, who had been pitched off its high perch.

"*Gott in Himmel*, do something!" Mrs. Moskowitz shrilled at the constables. "He'll tear the children limb from limb!"

The mothers and children, not knowing that Eddie was noisy but harmless, started to scream and scatter. Chairs and fruit crates went over. Infants were hoisted high. The two officers tried to corner the dog, but Eddie, maddened by the sight of the tom, plowed into one, flattening him, and skirted the other. He raced through the mountain of feathers from the plucked chickens, sending them into the air, careened off the wash pot and into the chicken coop. The wash pot went over and the door to the chicken coop flew open. A dozen terrified hens flew out. The tom leaped on one, and Eddie leaped on the tom. India was blinking at the whirling ball of fur and feathers when she felt Ella's hands on her back.

"The door, Indy! Go!" she shouted.

Panicking, she looked back at the kitchen door. There was no one there.

"Here, India, over here!" a little voice piped. Solly was down at the bottom of the yard, waving at her furiously and holding open a door to a narrow alley that ran along the backs of the houses. India hitched up her skirts and ran. As soon as she was through, Solly slammed the door shut. He grabbed a plank, jammed one end of it against the door, and the other against the alley wall.

"Keep going!" he yelled. "Down there!" He pointed at the east end of the alley. Aaron was waiting there, standing in the back of a wagon.

"Hurry up!" he shouted. India ran to him, stumbling over the cobbles. "Get in," he said, reaching down for her.

She grasped his hand and he pulled her up. Her bag and jacket were already there. The driver tipped his hat to her. She recognized him. She'd delivered his wife of twins.

"Mr. Fein—" she said.

"Lie down behind the potatoes, Dr. Jones. Quickly, please. Before we all go to jail."

Large, fifty-pound burlap sacks were propped up inside the wagon. There was a small space behind them. India wedged herself in it. Aaron pushed her things in after her, then plugged the space with another sack.

"Can you breathe?" he asked her.

"Yes."

"Herschel will take you as far as Covent Garden," Aaron said. "Hire a cab from there. There's still time. You can make it." He jumped out and banged on the side of the wagon.

"Go!"

India heard a whip crack and felt the horses strain forward in their traces. The wagon moved, then picked up speed. She guessed they were heading for the Commercial Road. If they made it, they would soon be lost in the ocean of traffic that flowed around Spitalfields Market. If only Herschel Fein could get her to Covent Garden! She would do as Aaron had said—hire a cab and pay the man to drive hell for leather to Richmond. She heard the bells from Christ Church again. It was eleven now. She had an hour. She needed a miracle.

Sid would come by cab, too. She was certain he wouldn't risk being spotted on public transport. He would come on the Upper Richmond Road, as she would, then turn onto Hill Street. She had to get there before he did. She had to stop him before he turned onto Arden Street. She closed her eyes, urging Herschel Fein on, hoping, praying that she was not too late.

CHAPTER 67

The cab stopped halfway up Richmond Hill, at the mouth of Arden Street. Sid peered down the street, eyes searching, ready to tell the driver to move on at the first hint of anything suspicious. But there were no vans parked outside of Number 16, no carriages. There were no men painting the house or fixing the road. There was nothing out of the ordinary. He paid the driver and got out.

He heard the newsboys. Their cries carried up from the bottom of Richmond Hill.

"Actress murdered! Killer on a rampage! East End villain strikes again!"

He ducked his head and jammed his hands in his pockets. He'd discovered that he'd killed Gemma Dean the same way the rest of London had—from the headlines. Had Frankie done for Gemma, too? Why, for God's sake? The poor girl was innocent. She'd never harmed him or anyone else. And why was *he* getting the blame?

He walked up the street, nerves jangling, muscles tensed for danger, but there was none. A cat strolled across the cobblestones. A woman was pruning her garden. Another was cleaning her stoop. A man oiled the hinges on his front gate.

Sid let out a deep breath—one he felt as if he'd been holding for the last three days. He'd gone to Sally Garrett's flat via the tunnels the night Joe was shot to eat and sleep, and she'd given him India's message. And then she told him how India had left her flat—just as he'd entered it. He knew how terrified India was of the tunnels. He was almost unable to believe that she would do all that she had done—brave the tunnels, leave the clinic, her home, and go all the way to America—for him.

The man oiling his hinges doffed his hat. "Beautiful weather," he said.

Sid nodded back. "Aye, that it is."

He glanced up at their flat, at the big bay window. It was empty. India often stood in it, looking down the street, waiting for him. He let himself into the building, casting a wary glance about the foyer, then quietly walked up the stairs. He hoped she was ready to leave. He wanted to put as much distance as possible between himself and London. He'd be nervous until the ship docked in New York, until they were able to disappear in the crowds and tumult of that city.

He paused at the door to the flat, leaned toward it, and listened. Nothing. He wondered if India had arrived yet. He opened the door and saw that she had. She was standing across the room in the big bay window, looking out of it. For me, he thought, smiling. She must've been just ahead of him, for he hadn't seen her there when he'd looked up just a moment ago.

"You *are* here," he said. "Thank God for that. I was worried. Had a bad feeling."

India made no reply. Had she not heard him?

"India, luv? Is something wrong?" he asked.

She inclined her head slightly, but still said nothing. He walked over to her and put a gentle hand on her back. She turned around.

"Sid Malone, you're under arrest for the murder of Gemma Dean and the attempted murder of Joseph Bristow," she said.

"Jesus!" Sid gasped. It wasn't India. It was a stranger. She must be a policewoman. He backed away, then headed for the doorway. He drew up short when he saw that Alvin Donaldson was standing in it, smiling. Behind him were two uniformed constables.

"Hello, Malone," Donaldson said. "I've waited a long time for this."

"How did you get here? How did you know?" Sid asked.

"Your lady gave us the address."

No, he thought, not India. She would never tell them about Arden Street. She would never betray him. Unless someone got to her, a voice inside him said. And made her believe that you shot Joe Bristow. And killed Gemma Dean.

"I don't believe you. You're lying," he said.

"Believe whatever you like. Just come along quietly."

"Where?"

"To Scotland Yard."

The words came back to him: *under arrest . . . murder.*

"Listen to me," he said quickly. "I didn't shoot Joe Bristow. And I didn't kill Gemma Dean. And while you're here arsing about, the real murderer's on the loose."

"Tell it to the beak. You'll have plenty of time to rehearse your story while you're sitting in a prison cell."

Prison. Sid shook his head, wild-eyed, a bull in a slaughterhouse.

Donaldson held out a pair of handcuffs. "You're done, lad. You can go hard or easy. It's up to you."

Sid looked around; there was no way out but the way he'd come in. Donaldson's soft, he thought. I can take him. But the two blokes behind him were huge.

Donaldson followed his gaze. "I wouldn't," he said, opening his jacket to reveal a holster.

Sid took a step backward. And then another. He was not going back to prison. Not now, not ever. He looked out of the big bay window again, at the beautiful November day, the blue sky, the white clouds scudding in the breeze.

And then he hurled himself through it.

CHAPTER 68

"Bonjour, Madame," India said breathlessly to the woman behind the counter of the French bakery on Richmond Road. "Has Mr. Baxter been in yet today?"

"No, Madame Baxter, he has not," the woman said in accented English. "If I see him, what shall I tell him to buy?"

"Oh . . . um . . . the madeleines!" India said quickly, forcing a smile. "Au revoir, Madame!"

She raced out of the baker's and headed for Hammond's, the florists.

"Where are you, Sid? Where *are* you?" she said aloud.

She'd been dashing in and out of shops on the Richmond Road for the last fifteen minutes, ever since her cab had dropped her there. She looked at her watch. "Only twelve oh six," she said. "He's still on the way. Must be. He's always late getting here." She prayed that he was late today.

He usually got out of his cab on Richmond Road, not at the flat. He liked to amble along the pretty village street, buying a bottle of wine and a dozen white roses before he strolled up Richmond Hill. White roses for his winter rose, he always said. And cakes, always cakes. Because she was too thin. She could see him, his green eyes clouded by concern, trying to coax her to eat one more jam tart, one more biscuit, and her heart twisted inside her.

Why had this happened now? Now, when he was about to renounce his old life and everyone in it? Why couldn't they leave him alone? Let him go?

Her fear threatened to overwhelm her. She refused to give in to it and bravely pressed on, dashing across the street heedless of traffic. At Hammond's the florist's boy said that Mr. Baxter hadn't been in today. The man at the wine shop said the same thing. She checked the newsagent's, the greengrocer's, the bookseller's, the butcher's, her desperation growing with every regretful smile, every shake of the head, every no.

Her only hope was to intercept him here. She knew the police were already at the flat, waiting. She looked at her watch again. It was now 12:35. She spent nearly another half hour standing on the pavement, watching cabs arrive and depart, hoping against hope that she would suddenly see Sid stepping down from one. And then a church bell tolled one o'clock, and she knew it was futile to wait any longer.

With a growing sense of doom, she crossed back over the Richmond Road and began the walk up Richmond Hill as if she were walking to the gallows. Nausea clawed at her. Only one thing enabled her to put one foot in front of the other—the fragile, tiny hope that Sid had not come. That he'd somehow gotten wind of Donaldson's plans. She reminded herself that he was smart and strong, that he'd survived the tough streets of East London. She prayed that the instincts that had kept him alive in a dark world for so long would serve him now.

It was quiet when she reached Arden Street. There were no police wagons, no strange men milling about. She quickened her step, hope surging inside her, and then she saw the broken window, gaping and jagged. It looked as if it were shrieking. She ran the rest of the way, flung open the gate, and dashed up the path. She saw blood on the grass. It was spattered over the dark green leaves of the rose bushes and their faded blooms.

"Oh, God," she cried.

The front door was ajar. She pushed it open and ran to the second floor. The door to the flat was open, too.

"Sid?" she called. "Sid, are you here?"

"Not anymore," a voice said.

India whirled around. Alvin Donaldson was sitting on her settee. A young constable was standing nearby.

"What happened to him? What have you done?"

"I tried to arrest him. I urged him to come quietly, but he didn't. Instead he threw himself through the window."

India sagged. The constable was at her side in an instant.

"Take your hands off me," she said, stumbling to a chair. She did not sit, but held on to the chair back to keep herself upright.

"Where is the body?" she asked. "I want to see him."

"There is no body."

"How can there be no body?"

"He's not dead, Dr. Jones."

India nearly wept with relief. "Where did you take him then? Which jail?"

"He escaped. We expect to find him shortly. He won't last long on his own. He was wounded in the fall and he has a bullet hole in his back as well."

"You shot him," India said brokenly.

"I saw that he was going to run and I shot to wound him, yes."

"How very kind of you. Blood loss and infections kill, too, you know. But I suppose that's irrelevant. Why are you here, Detective Inspector? Why aren't you out hunting him down? Can't you find any bloodhounds? Any bounty hunters?"

"My men are hunting him, Dr. Jones. I stayed behind to search your flat to see if I could find anything that might tell me where he's running to. But now that you're here, I can ask you."

"I don't know. I wouldn't tell you if I did. You must realize that."

Donaldson started to remonstrate with her, but she cut him off. "Why did you have to do this? Why?" she asked, her voice anguished. "He's changed. He wanted to leave the life. He was on the road to redemption."

Donaldson snorted. "Oh, aye? He'll be on it for a while, miss, don't you worry. That's the longest bloody road in the world."

India looked away, her mind racing. She had to find Sid. To help him.

As if reading her mind, Donaldson said, "We'll be watching you, you know."

"I rather thought you'd be arresting me. That's what Mr. Lytton said."

Donaldson shook his head. "By rights I should. But you're more valuable to us out of jail. Malone surfaced today to see you. Maybe he'll do so again."

India closed her eyes. She wouldn't cry. She wouldn't give them the satisfaction. But it hurt her almost beyond bearing to know that Sid had been injured trying to get to her, that he was wounded and she could do nothing for him. She couldn't even look for him now. If she found him, she'd lead the police right to him.

"Dr. Jones, I don't want to argue with you. I want to help you. I know how this happened," Donaldson said, his voice suddenly sympathetic. "I'm no fool. I know what sort of woman you are."

"Do you?" she said, opening her eyes.

"I see your type in East London all the time. In the missions and the soup kitchens. In the orphanages and prisons. Well-bred young ladies look-ing to do some good. Soft-hearted, well-intentioned, and—if I may be frank—dead easy marks for the likes of Malone. He's obviously sold you some story, but you should know that leopards don't change their spots. Sid Malone is one thing and one thing only—a criminal. He's ruthless and dan-gerous. He's done a lot of harm to a lot of people, and now it's time he paid for his sins."

"Are you going to pay for yours?" she asked, her voice hard.

"I beg your pardon?"

"Are you going to pay for *your* sins, Detective Inspector? You're a cor-rupt police officer who accepts money to break up political rallies. You sell opium that you confiscate. You accept bribes from madams."

The young constables' eyes widened.

"That's enough!" Donaldson thundered. "You want to watch your tongue, Dr. Jones. The only reason you're not in jail right now is because of me."

"The only reason I'm not in jail right now is because of Mr. Lytton. Be-cause he paid you not to put me there. Because he still has hopes I'll marry him and doesn't want his future wife's name in a police blotter. If you're going to arrest me, then do so. If not, get out of my flat."

"I won't arrest you, but I'll get Malone, make no mistake. I am going to see that he's tried, convicted, and hanged."

"For two murders he didn't commit? I wouldn't count on it."

"Why is that?"

"Because it costs to bribe magistrates and Mr. Lytton's coffers are low."

Donaldson, glaring, bit back a reply, then left. India watched him go. She would have dropped to her knees in front of him and begged for Sid if she'd thought for an instant it would help, but she knew it would not.

India walked to the broken window—the window where she'd spent so many happy evenings watching for Sid—and carefully pulled jagged pieces of shattered glass out of the panes. When she was finished, she wrapped them in sheets of newspaper and put them by the door.

An image came to her, a picture of Sid alone and bleeding in some dirty alley. She sagged down onto the settee and put her head in her hands and wept. The nausea she'd felt earlier rose again and this time she was sick. As sick as she'd been when she'd lost Mrs. Coburn and baby Harry. She felt now like she did then—weak and despairing, like she was breaking down again. She didn't know what to do. She didn't know where Sid was or if he was even alive. She had sacrificed everything for him—her home, her work, her dreams. She would sacrifice more if she could, but there was nothing left to give.

She stood up. She would go to the landlord's. Then to a glazier's. The flat had been damaged, and it had to be put right. Then she would make her way back to Brick Lane and the Moskowitzes', where she would wait and worry and hope to hear from him. It was all she could do.

CHAPTER 69

"Madam, please! Do allow me. It's a terribly unsafe hour," Foster said, rushing down the hall to the foyer.

But Fiona was already at the door. She'd heard the bell and had come tearing downstairs from her study. She undid the lock now and grasped the doorknob, but her courage suddenly deserted her and all she could do was lean her head against the door, unable to open it.

"Please, madam," Foster said gently.

Fiona looked at him, tears in her eyes, but shook her head. It was news about Joe, she was certain of it. And at half past midnight it was far too late to be good news. Whatever was coming, she had to face it. She twisted the knob and wrenched the door open. She expected to see a police officer or a messenger from the hospital, but the man standing before her was neither. He was sickeningly pale. His clothes were dirty and bloodstained. His left arm hung limply at his side.

"Fiona," he said. "Please . . ."

"No!" she screamed. "No, Charlie! God damn you, no!" She flew at him, pounding her fists against his chest.

The man reeled backward, almost fell down the steps, then righted himself.

Foster was down the steps in an instant. "Mrs. Bristow, please go back inside," he said, pulling Fiona away from her brother. "Leave immediately, sir, or I shall summon the authorities," he said to Sid.

"I didn't do it, Fiona!" Sid cried. "I swear to God. I would never hurt Joe. Never."

Fiona broke free of Foster. "You liar!" she shouted. "There were witnesses!"

"It was Frankie Betts. One of my lads. I think he must've dressed like me. Gave my name. He must've done . . ." Sid's words trailed off.

"Why?" Fiona shouted.

"I don't know. But I didn't do it, Fiona, you have to believe me. Joe will tell you. When he wakes up, he'll tell you."

Fiona shook her head. She was weeping now. "*If* he wakes up."

"He will, Fiona. I know he will. He's tougher than steel, Joe."

"I looked for you, I tried to find you. Why wouldn't you see me?"

"I had to stay away. To keep you away. I wanted to protect you."

"This is my last warning, sir," Foster said menacingly, but Sid cut him off.

"I'm going . . . but please, Fee, please say you believe me. I didn't hurt Joe."

Fiona looked into her brother's eyes. Deep inside. Just as she'd done when they were children and she wanted to know if he was telling the truth. What she saw there told her that he was. She gave a cry and ran to him. He put his good arm around her and pulled her close.

"I'm sorry, Charlie," she sobbed. "I'm so sorry."

"It's all right," he whispered. "I just . . . I wanted you to know. I've got to go now."

"No, you can't. You're coming inside."

"No, Fiona."

"You're hurt. You're coming inside!"

"Madam, are you quite certain?" Foster asked, alarmed.

"Yes," she said, suddenly remembering that her brother was a wanted man, and worried that he might have been seen. "Hurry, Mr. Foster!"

When they were in the foyer, with the door locked behind them, Foster said, "I'll call for a doctor."

"No! No doctors," Sid quickly said.

"But you're bleeding," Fiona said. "You need help."

"I'll be all right. I can't risk anyone else seeing me."

"I think I may be able to help," Foster said. "I was assigned to my ship's surgeon in the navy. If we could go into the kitchen . . ."

"Fiona? What's going on? I heard shouting." It was Seamie. He'd come back from the Aldens' to be with her when he heard about Joe. He was standing at the bottom of the stairs in his pajamas, groggy with sleep.

Fiona looked at Seamie, her heart aching for him, for all that he didn't know, but soon would. "I didn't . . . I didn't want it to be like this, Seamie. I wanted to tell you, but I . . . I couldn't."

"Tell me what?" Seamie said uncertainly. "Fee, who is that?"

"Hello, nipper. Remember me?" Sid said, steadying himself against the foyer wall. He reached out a shaking hand to his brother.

Seamie went white. "Jesus Christ," he said. "It can't be."

"I'm afraid it is," Sid said. His legs buckled and he fell to the floor.

"Charlie!" Fiona shouted, terrified. She ran to him but Foster was ahead of her.

"Master Seamus, kindly take his legs," he said, carefully lifting Sid's torso.

Together they got him downstairs to the kitchen table. Foster laid him out, then took his jacket and shirt off.

"My God, his back," Fiona said, horrified by the scars there. "What happened to him?"

"Cat o' nine tails from the looks of it," Foster said briskly. "The wound's not too deep," he added, pointing to a bullet hole in the fleshy part of Sid's back, just under his left shoulder blade. "Not much damage at all. I'll have the bullet out in short order."

"What about his arm? Is it broken?"

"The arm is fine. His shoulder is dislocated, but I think I can pop it back in."

Foster set Fiona and Seamie to work boiling water and assembling whisky, quinine, and gauze to dress the wound, plus fresh clothing to replace Sid's bloodied things. Sid woke, yelling, when Foster started probing the wound, but the extraction was quick and expert, and he was able to endure it with a shot of whisky. When the wound was dressed, Foster poured him another shot, and then manipulated his shoulder back into place. Fiona could see it hurt him more than the bullet wound. When it was finally over, he dressed himself in one of Joe's old shirts, got off the kitchen table, and sat in a chair, pale and shaking, but better than he'd been.

Foster procured a bottle of Bordeaux, then made a hasty meal of hot soup and sandwiches.

"I'll prepare the larger of the guest rooms, madam," he said when he'd finished. "Might I suggest that Mr. . . . ."

"Finnegan," Fiona said.

"That Mr. Finnegan retires before the maids wake and the cook arrives—at five o'clock. They do tend to talk."

Fiona nodded. She took his meaning. Her brother was a fugitive, and she was endangering not only herself but the entire household, by harboring him.

"Thank you, Mr. Foster. Very, very much," she said. "We will all be very careful."

Foster nodded and departed, leaving Fiona alone with her brothers. Seamie was sitting at the head of the long pine table. Sid was sitting on one side of it. She took a seat across from him. There had been so much commotion—crying and shouting, Sid's collapse, the kitchen-table surgery. Now it was quiet. She could hear the kitchen clock ticking. A slow dripping from a tap.

She looked across the table at her brother. His face was different. Older, haggard. His eyes were wary and hard. But in them she could still see the boy she remembered.

She shook her head, biting her lip to keep fresh tears back, but they came anyway. She reached across the table and covered his large, scarred hand with her own. He was here with her, at last. They were together again, she and Charlie and Seamie, for the first time in twelve years.

"I'm sorry," Charlie said. "For Joe. For this. For everything."

Fiona wiped her eyes. "Eat your soup," she said. "You need nourishment." She looked at her younger brother. He hadn't touched his food either; he looked dazed. "Seamie, luv, eat," she said.

He pushed the bowl away. "I don't want any soup," he said angrily. "Can someone please tell me what the hell is going on?"

Fiona started to, but Sid cut her off. He told Seamie what had really happened to him back in 1889, how he had become Sid Malone, how he had lived his life, why he was now on the run. He glossed over nothing and when he had finished, Seamie, who had been completely silent, turned to their sister and in an unsteady voice, said, "How could you not tell me, Fiona? He's my brother, too."

Fiona tried to explain. "I . . . I thought you would be upset. You were so close, you and Charlie, and I didn't want—"

He didn't let her finish, but jumped to his feet and exploded into a rage. "Christ, Fiona! You are always mollycoddling me!"

"Mind your manners, lad," Sid said.

"Mind my manners? *Mind my manners?* That's rich coming from you. Don't you think it's just slightly rude to crack safes and rob banks?"

"Seamie, that's enough!" Fiona said.

"Were you *ever* going to tell me?" he asked her.

"I wanted to. I was hoping to. I wanted to find Charlie first and persuade him to—"

"To what? Blend tea? Peddle peaches?" Seamie shook his head. "I can't believe this! My brother's not dead, he's alive and well, and the biggest criminal in all of London, and you don't tell me. Anything else you're not telling me, Fee?" He pulled out his chair. "Wait, don't answer. Let me sit down first."

Sid looked at Fiona. "He's angry," he said.

"You're goddamned right I'm angry!"

"What good would telling you have done?" Fiona asked him. "Charlie wanted no part of me. Of us. I didn't want to tell you because I thought knowing those things would hurt you. I only wanted to protect you."

"Well, stop. Stop trying to protect me. I've told you this a hundred times, but you never listen. I'm not a boy, I'm a grown man."

"Then bloody act like one," Charlie said. "Fiona's got a husband in the hospital, a fugitive in her house, and a baby on the way. Last thing she needs is gyp from you."

"All those years," Seamie said. "All those years without you. It would have been nice to have had a brother."

"I'm sorry for that. Sorrier than you'll ever know. But I'm here now."

"Yeah. Gee. Maybe we can go to a ball game," Seamie said bitterly. He picked up the loaf of bread Foster had put out, tore off a piece, and dunked it in his soup.

Charlie took a bite of his sandwich. No one spoke further. Fiona's heart sank.

She had longed for them to be a family again for ages, longed for a reunion. Now she'd gotten one, and it wasn't what she'd imagined. Not at all.

She looked at Charlie, then at Seamie. They were the spitting image of each other. Red-haired, green-eyed. Restless, heedless, impossible to control. Each kept his head down now, eyes on his soup. Seamie looked furious still; Charlie guilt-ridden.

Fiona wished they would talk again, try again. It wasn't an ideal reunion, far from it, but it was better than nothing. Couldn't they see that? She had no idea how long their time together would last. She had no idea what tomorrow would bring. Not for Charlie or for Seamie. Not for Joe or for herself. But for tonight at least, the three of them were sitting in her kitchen. Drinking wine. Eating. Talking. Together again. A family.

Seamie suddenly stopped eating. He cleared his throat. "Charlie?" he said.

"Aye, lad?" Charlie replied.

Fiona took her brothers' hands. She watched them with bated breath, hoping for words of reconciliation and forgiveness, words to bridge the sorrowful gulf of years, words to make them brothers again.

"Pass the salt, Charlie, will you?"

CHAPTER 70

Ella looked at her friend, who was lying on her bed in the attic, and frowned with worry. "Indy, I really think you should eat some breakfast. Couldn't you try a little milk? Some toast?"

"I couldn't. I'm too nauseous. I'm going to be sick any minute."

"But how? You haven't eaten anything."

"Excuse me, Ella."

India rose and ran downstairs to the one and only loo in the Moskowitzes' flat. When she came back to the bedroom, Ella was still there. She walked across the room on unsteady legs, lay back down on her bed, and groaned.

"You're scaring me, Indy."

"It's nerves, Ella, that's all. Nerves always make me heave."

"He'll be all right, you know," Ella said, taking her hand.

"I'm so frightened for him. What if he's suffering, Ella? What if he's sick, with no one to care for him? It's been two days. What if he's dead?" she said, her voice catching.

"Shh! You stop that right now. He's not dead."

"You don't know that."

"I do. He can weather a fall and a bullet, too. He's come through worse. And if he was dead, there'd be a body found and we'd have heard about it. Every newsboy in London would be hollerin' his head off. Sid's all right, Indy. He is."

"Then why haven't I heard from him?"

"He's no fool, is he? He knows you're being watched. The police aren't exactly subtle, are they? One's in here eyeing every customer who comes in. Another's going through the post, poking in every delivery. And two more are hanging about outside."

"Ella, do you think . . . do you think he's had second thoughts?"

"About you? No, you stupid girl. He'll turn up. He'll get a note to you. *Something*. I know he will. You just have to wait, to be patient. Hard as that is."

Ella continued speaking, but India barely heard her. The greasy, roiling surge in her stomach was back. "Oh, God," she moaned.

"*Again?*" Ella said as she ran out of the room. "India, I'm going to send for Harriet."

When she returned to the bedroom for the second time, Ella's eyes narrowed. "You know, you look thinner," she said.

"Yes, well, heaving everything you eat will do that to you."

"How long have you been feeling poorly? How long *exactly*?"

"I don't know. A week, I suppose. Maybe two. I don't need Harriet, Ella. I really don't think it's flu or anything like that. I've no aches and pains. No bronchial symptoms. It's nerves, I'm sure of it."

Ella shook her head. "Crikey, India, it's not *nerves*, you great bloody fool! Call yourself a doctor, do you?"

"What is it, then?"

"Are you having your periods?"

"Yes, of course. I'm due . . . well, let me think . . . I . . ." India paled. "Oh, my God, Ella."

She was pregnant. With Sid Malone's baby. Of course she was. The first few times—at her flat, and then at his—had hardly been planned or prepared for. *Pregnant.* She could barely believe it. A feeling of joy, shocking in its strength and unexpectedness, flooded her.

"Pregnant, Ella! I'm pregnant!" she whispered.

"Now, India, don't get upset."

"I'm not. Even though I think I should be. We'll be a family, Ella. Sid, myself, and the baby. In America. In California. I can't wait to tell him," she said in a gush of emotion. "I'll do it on the ship. As soon as we're safely away from London. Or maybe in New York. Or maybe I'll wait until we get to California. To Wish's land. Maybe that's the right place to tell him something like that." Her smile faded. "Unless he doesn't come," she said, her joy turning to a cold dread. "And then I'll be an unmarried woman with a baby. I'll lose my medical license. What will I do for an income? How will I provide for the baby? The poor thing will be fatherless."

"Enough. Enough now! You're imagining terrible things that will never happen. Sid will come. You'll be together."

"You keep saying that, Ella, but how do you know?"

Ella smiled. "Because my mother said so. *Beshert*, that's what she said. Fated to be together. And if there's one thing I know for certain, it's that my mother is never wrong."

India managed a laugh. She squeezed her friend's hand. And tried to believe her.

CHAPTER 71

In a bedroom at the top of 94 Grosvenor Square, Sid Malone tried yet again to sit up and get out of bed.

He'd had a raging fever for three days, had barely eaten, and now he was as weak as a kitten. The bullet wound in his back had become infected and the fever had swiftly overtaken him. He should have been able to shake it off sooner, but he couldn't. He couldn't rally. He had no fight left in him. Because there was nothing to fight for.

India had betrayed him. She'd given the police the Arden Street address. She'd helped them set a trap for him, knowing he'd be arrested and imprisoned. Knowing what prison had done to him.

A part of him didn't believe it. *Couldn't* believe it. India loved him. She knew who he was, what he was, and yet she'd given up everything—even her clinic—to be with him. Why would she suddenly turn on him?

He knew the answer: because he'd shot Joe Bristow and murdered Gemma Dean.

That's what she would have seen in the papers. That's what the people around her would have told her. And she'd believed them. Of course, she had. How could she do otherwise? He was a criminal, after all. Ruthless. Vicious. Capable of anything.

He remembered the last time they were together. They'd eaten a hurried breakfast at the Moskowitzes' café. He'd told her he had one more thing to do, a bit of unfinished business to take care of. A few hours later, Joe Bristow was in the hospital fighting for his life and witnesses had told the police that he, Sid Malone, had put him there.

She'd probably gone straight to the police, horrified by what he'd done. Or maybe they'd come to her. Maybe they'd found something out about the two of them and had threatened to arrest her. Either way, she'd told them.

He'd thought of trying to get to India—on his own or through Fiona—to tell her that he hadn't committed the crimes he was accused of, but he'd decided against it. It was too risky. The police were likely still watching her. And even if he could talk to her, what good would it do? Whatever she'd felt for him was gone; it had to be. She now believed him capable of murder.

He'd always known he'd be paid back some day for the crimes he'd committed. Now he had been. He had loved, even though doing so had gone against every instinct he possessed, and he had lost that love. And the pain of it was terrible. Worse than the pain any whip or bullet could ever inflict.

He knew he couldn't stay in London. He couldn't stay in England. He would have to start again somewhere far away. He had a few friends, still. Friends along the waterfront. People who had ships and contacts in China, Ceylon, Africa. They would help him . . . if he could get to them.

"I've got to get out of this bloody bed," he said aloud, taking a stiff and shaky walk around the room. "Out of this house."

"Are you nuts?" Seamie said, from a chair near the fireplace. "There's a manhunt on for you. Or did you forget?"

He was sifting through the day's papers, looking for any news on the search for Sid Malone.

Sid sighed, frustrated. If he couldn't get out, he could at least work on himself, build himself back up a bit. He walked around the room again, then he tried to move his left arm. He raised it as high as it would go, stretched it behind him. Beads of sweat broke out on his forehead. A low groan escaped him. It was painful to move it, but he did it anyway. He had to regain the use of it. He was sure he'd broken it in the fall at Arden Street, but Mr. Foster said he'd only dislocated it. The man had also proved himself a dab hand at surgery, taking the bullet out of his back with only a filleting knife and a pair of poultry shears.

"You've a bit of mangled muscle," he'd said as he'd dropped the bullet into a pudding basin. "But no broken bones. Whoever fired at you is either a very good shot or a very poor one."

Sid had been grateful to him, but wary. How did he know the man wouldn't go to the police?

"Do you trust him, Fee?" he'd asked after Foster had left them.

"With my life," she'd said.

The rest of her staff, however, she was not so sure of. She'd closeted him away with stern directions to the servants that a friend of Seamie's who was very ill was staying with them and wasn't to be disturbed. Only Foster was to take him his meals. Sid had now been in the same room for three days, and the confinement was killing him.

"Find anything?" he asked Seamie now.

"Nope," Seamie answered, turning a page.

Sid looked at him and his heart felt so full that he had to look away. Full of love and full of anger, too, for all the things he had missed of his brother's life, all the things he would miss.

"Wait a minute . . . there's something here on the funeral service for Gemma Dean," Seamie said, reading him the details of the service.

Sid felt a deep sorrow at the mention of Gemma's name. He couldn't shake the feeling that her death was his fault. He, Fiona, and Seamie had talked about Joe and Gemma Dean his first night at Fiona's house. He told them how he'd escaped arrest at the Bark, what had happened to him in Richmond, and how he'd hidden in the sewers, only coming out at night, until he could make his way to Grosvenor Square. He knew Fiona's address. He'd kept tabs on her over the years.

"But why would Frankie Betts hurt Joe?" Fiona had asked. "Why would he kill Gemma Dean?"

"Because he's an angry young man," Sid had said.

"At Joe? Over his refusal to pay him money? At Gemma Dean?"

"No. At me. Because I left. This was his way of bringing me back."

"By getting you hanged?" Seamie asked.

"Frankie's not one for thinking through the consequences," Sid said. "I'm sure he thought this would force me underground for a bit, but that I'd eventually come back to the Firm."

As Seamie continued to search the newspapers, Fiona walked in. She'd just returned from the hospital.

"Shouldn't you be resting?" she asked, feeling Sid's forehead. "You're not as warm as last night, that's something, but I wish you'd get back into bed."

Sid did so. "How's Joe today?" he asked.

She shook her head. "No change. He just lies there breathing. He doesn't move, doesn't speak. The nurses are feeding him through a tube. Oats ground to powder and mixed with milk." She paused, then said, "I went to the nursery before I came up here. To put Katie to bed. She asked when her daddy was coming home. I didn't . . . I didn't know what to tell her." Her voice broke.

Sid took his sister's hand. "Shh, Fee. He's healing, that's all. His body's shut down to save strength. He's going to make it."

She looked at him through her tears. "Do you promise?" she asked.

"I promise. Something like it happened to me. I was in the hospital. Somebody was there for me. Pulled me through. You'll do the same for Joe. I know you will."

Fiona nodded. Sid saw that she looked very tired. He moved over in the big bed, and patted the pillow. Fiona took off her boots and rested next to him, curling her feet underneath her. The bed creaked as she settled.

"Watch out, the bed's going to break!" Seamie teased.

"Very funny," Fiona said, scowling.

"How is the baby?" Sid asked.

"Kicking up a storm," she said, then she winced.

"You all right?"

She nodded. "Thumped me good, just then."

"I've been thumped from the outside often enough," he said. "But I can't imagine what it feels like from the inside."

Fiona took his hand and placed it on her belly. He felt nothing for a few seconds, then his hand jumped as the baby gave a hard, sharp kick.

"Blimey!" he said. "He's not half strong. Going to be a rugby player with legs like those."

"Hey, look at this!" Seamie suddenly exclaimed.

"Is it something about Charlie?" Fiona asked.

"No, about me," Seamie said. "Well, sort of. It's about the Antarctica expedition. They've just received a donation of ten thousand pounds from Prince Edward. Listen to this . . ."

Sid smiled as he listened to his brother read, watching his face grow animated, hearing the excitement in his voice. He knew he was due to leave for Greenland in a week's time and he was happy for him. Happy that he had a shot at making his dream come true. He knew Fiona wasn't, however. Seamie had told him about the row they'd had over his decision to leave school. He knew Seamie had been so angry at their sister that he'd left her house and had gone to stay with friends. He'd go to Antarctica, though, whether Fiona liked it or not. Nothing could stop him. Sid could see that.

He had loved getting to know him again in these past few days. And Fiona. This was all he would ever have of them. These precious hours. They were together now, but would soon be separated again. Forever. Fiona would stay here. Seamie would go exploring, but return home between trips. And he himself? He was never coming back.

When Seamie finished reading, Fiona said, "I don't know why you have to go so far away. To such a dangerous place."

"Oh, he was bound to go exploring, Fee," Sid said. "He could never stay still. Don't you remember? He was always wandering off. Eager to see what was round the next bend. Do you remember the time we went to the riverside? The three of us? After Da died. To the Old Stairs by Oliver's to watch the boats. You and I sat on the steps. Seamie played by the water. I told him to stay put, but he wouldn't. Turned my back on him for a second and he was halfway to Limehouse. You won't keep him in one place."

"Or you either," she said.

"I can't stay, Fee. You know that."

"Why not? You don't have to go. When Joe wakes up, he'll tell the police it wasn't you who shot him," Fiona said.

"Aye, he will. But Gemma Dean won't. Because she isn't going to wake up. Ever. I have to leave the country. It's my only chance. I'm not going back to prison."

"But how? How can you leave? You can't step outside the door for fear of being arrested."

Seamie, still combing through the newspapers, said, "Here we go . . . listen to this! 'Murder suspect disappears after shootout.'" He read the rest of the article aloud. The reporter had interviewed Alvin Donaldson, who'd told him he was certain Sid Malone had been wounded in the Richmond ambush that he—Donaldson—had set for him.

"I pulled the trigger myself," Donaldson said. "And I know it found its mark. In addition, Malone was injured from a fall he'd taken during the escape. That, combined with the fact that there is no sanctuary for him in all of London, leads me to believe that he may have died and that it will be only a matter of time before the body is found in some foul lodging house or riverside den. We will not stop hunting for Malone until we do find him. Dead or alive."

"And this . . . this is from Lytton," Seamie continued.

"We hope to take Malone alive, but if we find him dead, then at least Joseph Bristow will know—and in heaven Gemma Dean will know—that justice has been served. Not the justice of England's courts, but the final justice meted out by our Creator."

"Looks like Freddie's already begun his campaign," Fiona said bitterly.

"Do you see what I mean, Fee?" Sid said. "They won't stop until they have me. Or my dead body."

Seamie was quiet for a few seconds, then he said, "Let's give it to them then."

"Give them what?" Fiona said.

"Sid Malone's dead body."

"Steady on, mate," Sid said.

"I'm serious. We could do it. If they got a body, if they thought you were dead, it would make it a lot easier for you to get out of London."

"Fine, Seamie. But how?"

"You have to ask me? You did it back in 'eighty-nine. If it worked then, it'll work now."

"You're saying I should kill someone who looks like me, throw him in the Thames, and hope the body gets found? That's a great idea. Then I'll be wanted for another murder. One I *did* commit."

"No, I'm saying throw someone in who's already dead."

"This is madness!" Fiona said angrily. "What are you doing to do? Rob a grave? And even if you did get a body, the police won't fall for the same trick twice."

"But the last time he did it was twelve years ago," Seamie said. "No one will ever make the connection. The police fish bodies out of the river all the time."

"It's wrong. And it's dangerous," Fiona said.

"But it might just work."

"For God's sake, Seamie, this isn't some *Boys' Own* adventure story!"

"Listen, Fee, just listen, will you? If a body washes up with something of Sid's on it, the police won't have a reason to search anymore. He can leave. Head to the Continent, America, wherever. He'll be free. The only hard part is getting a body."

"Maybe not so hard," Sid said. "A friend . . . a doctor friend . . . told me where they're kept at a medical school. I've seen the place. It'd be a doddle to break in and take one."

"What a wonderful idea, Charlie!" Fiona said. "Then you can add body-snatcher to your list of accomplishments. And maybe you can get Seamie arrested into the bargain."

She was worried, fearful, close to tears. He didn't want to upset her any further.

"You're right, Fee, it's a daft idea," he said. "We won't do any such thing. I'll sit tight here for as long as I need to. Until it's safe."

Fiona expressed her relief. Sid told her she looked tired, and that she should go to bed and get some rest. "For Joe," he said. "And Katie and the baby."

She nodded, kissed both of her brothers, and left.

As soon as the door closed, Seamie turned to him. "When?" he said.

"Tomorrow night."

CHAPTER 72

"Katie has four more teeth and she's talking a blue streak. She misses you terribly and wants you to come home. I told her you would do. Soon. Very, very soon. She sent you this." Fiona paused and pulled a small plush rabbit out of her bag. "It's Walter. Remember him? Your mother gave it to her last Easter. It's her favorite toy. She asked me to bring it to you in case you get lonely." Fiona's voice caught. She squeezed her eyes shut for a few seconds, fighting tears, then placed the rabbit on Joe's pillow. "And she told me to tell you that she loves you very much." She smoothed Joe's hair, straightened his pajama top, and brushed some imaginary dust off the hospital bed. She took his hand in hers, kissed it, and pressed it to her cheek. "Wake up, love. Please wake up," she said.

There was a knock on the door and then a young woman was standing in the room. "Mrs. Bristow?" she said. "I'm sorry to intrude. Am I disturbing you?"

Fiona smiled at her. "No, not at all, Dr. Jones. Come in, won't you?"

"I stop by as often as I can to visit your husband. I was here once while you were. But I don't think . . . well, I don't think you were in any condition then to recognize me."

"I doubt I was."

"How are you doing now? How's the baby?"

"The baby's very well, I think. Very busy doing whatever it is babies do before they're born."

"And you, Mrs. Bristow?"

"Not so well, I'm afraid."

India took a seat in a chair on the other side of Joe's bed. "He's in wonderful hands, you know. Dr. Harris is extraordinary."

"Yes, he is," Fiona said.

India held Joe's wrist and took his pulse. "Has he responded at all?" she asked.

Fiona shook her head. "I try to get him to. I talk to him all the time. I believe he can hear me. Perhaps it's mad, but I feel it."

"It's not mad at all. Many coma patients wake up able to repeat things that were said to them while they were unconscious. Keep talking to him,"

India said. She raised Joe's eyelids and examined his eyes. She gently pinched the flesh of his palms, the soles of his feet.

"How is the clinic progressing, Dr. Jones?" Fiona asked. "I meant to visit it, but it will be a while before I'm able to now."

"It's coming along very well and will be open in another week's time. Dr. Hatcher, as you may know, will head our children's ward. Ella Moskowitz will be our matron. And a teacher of mine from the London School of Medicine for Women, Professor Fenwick, will be our chief administrator."

"And you? What is your role there?"

"I'm afraid I haven't one. Not anymore."

"Why not?" Fiona asked, perplexed.

"I'm leaving London."

"I'm so sorry to hear that. May I ask why?"

India hesitated, then said, "A person, someone dear to me, is in difficulties right now. He needs my help, and so I'm going to be away for a while."

"But you'll be coming back."

"I'm not sure."

"That must be hard for you. I know how committed you were to that clinic."

"It is very hard."

Fiona could see the pain in India's eyes. She tried to lighten the tone a little, to make her smile. "This person . . . he's not your brother by any chance, is he? I have two of them. And they're always in difficulties."

India laughed. "No. I have no brothers. Only a sister."

"Count yourself lucky, then."

As India turned back to Joe, Fiona thought that she might joke about her brothers, but she was actually very worried about one of them. Charlie's fever was down, but he was still weak. She hadn't summoned her family doctor, Dr. Fraser, because it was too risky. If he recognized Charlie, he might go to the police. But Dr. Jones was different. Fiona felt instinctively that she could trust her. Perhaps she would help her. Perhaps she would look at Charlie.

"Dr. Jones, could I ask you something?"

"Yes, anything, Mrs. Bristow. Anything at all."

"Could you . . ."

It was asking too much. Involving her with a fugitive would be dangerous and wrong, and no way to repay the good woman who'd saved her husband's life.

"Could you continue to visit my husband? For as long as you're here? You've brought him this far. Maybe you can pull him out of this."

"Of course I will. I'll do everything I can for him. Listen, why don't you go and get yourself a cup of tea while I'm here? And something to eat? It might be good for you to take a short walk. Good for the baby. I'll talk to Mr. Bristow while you're gone."

"Thank you, Dr. Jones, I will. And thank you for everything you've done for us. For saving my husband's life." She reached for India's hand and held it for a few seconds, then let go, surprised at the sadness she felt. She might see her again at Joe's bedside before she left, but she might not. She thought of how remarkable she was, how good and strong and kind, and she realized she would have liked to have known her better.

On her way out of the hospital, to a small tuck shop she'd seen on the way in, Fiona thought of what she'd almost done, and was relieved she hadn't gone through with it. Charlie would have been furious at her for bringing a stranger to see him. And she could only imagine Dr. Jones's dismay at aiding a man wanted for murder.

As she ordered herself some tea, she commended herself on finally learning restraint, on acting from the head instead of the heart.

"And not before time," she told herself. "But better late than never. For once, Fiona, you've done the right thing."

CHAPTER 73

Sid's sixth sense told him that someone was watching him.

That wasn't good. Now was not the moment to attract attention. He raised his arms, as if stretching, and turned his head slightly, relieved to find that it was only a barmaid and that her eyes were on his empty pint glass, not his face. He signaled for another drink, knowing that's what a working man in a boozer at midday would do. He paid her when she brought it, and thanked her, but she was so busy she barely glanced at him. He pulled his cap low over his brow and continued to gaze out of the pub's window. Just another bloke grabbing a dinnertime pint.

The pub was directly across the street from the Albion Bank. The street was crowded with traffic, the pavements were full of clerks and typists bustling about during their dinner hour. Sid's eyes darted back and forth between the people, looking for Seamie. He'd certainly made him easy to spot, dressing him in a mustard tweed jacket. The lad would stand out like a whore in a nunnery in this sea of black skirts and frock coats.

Sid's eyes darted to the clock over the bank's doors. It was almost twelve thirty. Seamie was due to be on the steps of the bank at exactly half noon and out by a quarter to one. If things went right, Sid would shortly be in the possession of a great deal of money. And if they didn't, he'd probably be in jail.

He hadn't seen Seamie for more than an hour. Where the hell was he?

Sid took a sip of porter to calm his jangling nerves. The last twenty-four hours had been tense. As soon as Fiona left the house for the hospital yesterday morning, Seamie left it, too. He went to the London School of Medicine for Women and walked all around it, noting the placement of doors and windows and trees and the height of its back wall. Then he walked the nearby streets, looking for a carter's establishment or a rag-and-bone man. Lastly he went shopping—buying a bottle of hair dye, work clothes, gloves, a pistol and bullets, rope, canvas, candles and matches, an awl, and a packet of hairpins. He returned home ahead of Fiona and hid his purchases under Sid's bed, and then they'd waited. All day long and into the night. Until Fiona had returned home and they'd all eaten supper together in Sid's room. Until nearly midnight, when the entire household was finally asleep. Then they sneaked out and headed for the London School of Medicine for Women.

Seamie had rented a horse and cart earlier in the day from a rag-and-bone man whose yard was two streets away from the school, paying him double what he'd demanded in order to keep him from asking too many questions. It was waiting for them inside the man's stables, hitched and ready, when they arrived.

The school and its yards were enclosed by walls on three sides. They drove the cart all the way around the back to where Seamie had seen a large oak tree. They climbed the tree and dropped down inside the courtyard. Then they found a basement door with a rickety deadbolt, which Sid had open in no time.

He shuddered now as he recalled what had happened next. Taking care to keep themselves concealed, they'd crept about in the deserted building until they'd found the mortuary. It had been dark in there, close, and chock-a-block with rotting corpses. They'd sorted through them by candlelight to find a red-haired one. Sid thought he'd struck it lucky when the second body he looked at had auburn hair, but when Seamie pointed out that it also had breasts, they'd had to start again. They'd finally found a redheaded man. He was heavier than Sid and his hair was more carroty than auburn, but they couldn't find a closer match, so they took him, bundling him up in a length of canvas, then hoisting him over the wall and into the cart.

It had been a long ride to Limehouse. Seamie had wanted to throw him off Tower Bridge, he smelled so bad, but Sid had insisted on a more private venue—a landing a few yards past the Grapes, a pub he'd been known to frequent.

"Sorry, lad," he'd said as they drew up to the landing. "Here comes the hard part."

He'd tied a kingsman around his nose and mouth and unwrapped the body. Then he took the pistol Seamie had bought for him earlier and fired a bullet into the corpse's left shoulder. It passed through the flesh. The bullet that Donaldson had fired at him hadn't done so, but the rozzers wouldn't know that. Then he took the bloodstained clothes he'd worn to Arden Street, clothes he'd had the foresight to save, and put them on the corpse. Seamie tried to help, but couldn't. He was too busy retching. When Sid had finished dressing the body, he put his wallet, which was monogrammed, into the corpse's trousers and put a gold watch inscribed with his name into its jacket pocket, taking care to button it.

Then he and Seamie heaved the body into the Thames. They'd watched as it bobbed on top of the water, then slowly sank beneath the surface.

"Ta-ra, Sid Malone," he said. "He'll rise again in a day or two. Hopefully not till the fish have had at his face."

They'd made it back to Grosvenor Square just before dawn. Sid got all of three hours' sleep before he was up again, lopping off his ponytail and dyeing his red hair brown. Seamie knocked on his door at ten with a breakfast tray.

"That's a very fetching color on you," he said.

"Very funny. I need to do one more job. You game?"

"Where are we going?" Seamie asked.

"To the Albion Bank."

"No kidding! Are we going to rob it?"

"No, Seamie. Jesus! Would I take a risk like that with you?"

"I suppose not," Seamie'd said with a tinge of disappointment in his voice.

"We're going to make a withdrawal. A very large withdrawal. I need you to go along as a decoy. You game?"

"You bet. What's the plan?"

"Sit down, lad, and I'll tell you."

After they'd talked and eaten and dressed, they left Grosvenor Square a few minutes apart and traveled to the City separately. Sid did not want Seamie with him in the daylight in case someone recognized him and nabbed him.

Where the hell is he? Sid wondered anxiously now, still sitting in the pub. From now on everything would depend on timing.

He knew that his plan might well blow up on him. Alvin Donaldson might have had his bank accounts frozen. He might have seized his safe deposit box. But Sid was gambling that he hadn't. He was good at thinking like a rozzer; it had kept him out of jail on many occasions. He knew that Donaldson was still after him, and he was certain that he'd leave the money right where it was—as bait. He probably thought that Sid was the same as every other villain—in love with the dosh. He didn't know Sid, didn't know he hated the money so much he could barely bring himself to touch it. Donaldson had probably been in to talk to Davies, the bank manager, to warn him that Sid would not leave London without his money, and to be prepared for a visit.

How he hoped he was right.

The plan was for Seamie to pose as him. He would go into the bank and ask for access to Sid Malone's safe deposit box. The clerk would certainly know that Malone was a wanted man and dangerous. He would check the passbook Seamie was carrying to confirm his identity, then lead him to the vaults. Then he'd call the police. Sid doubted he'd be brave enough, or foolish enough, to attempt to collar a murderer by himself. Seamie, meanwhile, was to get the box out, take it to the private viewing room, dump the money into one of the bags he was carrying, and kick the bag under the table. Then he was to get out of the bank as fast as he could, head east on Cornhill Street, toss away his jacket, and do his best to lose anyone following him in the narrow streets that led from the City into Whitechapel. He made Seamie run through the whole plan twice, then warned him that no matter what, he was to leave the passbook and key in the bank. If the police picked him up with those on him, he was done for.

The rest would be up to Sid.

Timing, luck, the stone walls of Albion, and a whole city of gung-ho rozzers stood between him and his money. Between him and redemption.

Sid took another sip of his porter, then he saw it. A flash of red hair. The mustard-colored jacket. Seamie was walking up the steps to the bank right on time. He had a battered Gladstone bag in his right hand. Sid knew there was another bag inside it.

At a quick glance, Seamie looked very much like him. The hair. The clothes. Even the walk. It hadn't come right away, though, the walk. They'd had to work on it. The lad was wiry, his movements quick.

"Walk around the room," Sid had ordered.

Seamie had.

Sid shook his head. "Get off your toes, lad. Walk like the weight is your own."

Seamie tried again, but to no avail. Sid could see that he didn't have an ounce of wide boy in him.

He thought for a few seconds, then said, "Do you have an enemy? A bloke you don't like? Pretend he made a play for your girl. And then you hit him. Laid him out right in front of his mates."

Seamie digested this. Then he walked around the room once more, getting the walk exactly right. Watching him, Sid realized with a deep pang of sadness that there must indeed be a girl. Who she was, he'd never know, for he'd soon be out of his brother's life again. Forever.

He'd forced himself to smile. "Much better," he'd said.

Sid watched now as Seamie disappeared through the bank's front doors. He waited until five minutes had passed, then he put a few coins on the table and left the pub.

He crossed Cornhill Street and climbed the steps to the bank, pulling an envelope out of his pocket as he did, ready to play the part of a working man, awed and befuddled by a grand bank.

But the second he stepped inside he could tell something had gone wrong. The bank's usual security guard, a reedy old geezer who looked like he'd blow over in a breeze, was gone. There were two burly men in his place. The bank manager was talking to them in hushed, agitated tones, pointing toward the back of the bank where the vaults were. He realized, with a sick feeling, that the manager must have put the new guards on in case Sid Malone came calling. Of course he had. Christ, how stupid could he be? He hadn't even thought of that. He'd meant for Seamie to lead the police on a wild goose chase, but he couldn't do that if he didn't make it out of the bank.

"Excuse me, sir," Sid said, walking up to the manager and tugging on his hat brim, "where do I go to open meself an account?"

"Over there," the manager said, gesturing impatiently toward the tellers.

"You see, I've me wages here, and I want to—"

"If you'll just walk that way, sir," one of the guards said.

"Sorry? You'll have to speak up. I've only one good ear."

At that very second Seamie came up the stairs from the vaults and into the foyer.

"Out of the way!" the second guard snapped, pushing Sid behind him.

The guards immediately advanced on Seamie. He saw them and stopped dead.

Keep moving, lad! Sid thought. It's your only chance.

But Seamie didn't.

He's panicking. He doesn't know what to do. He's too green, Sid thought. He took a deep breath, readying himself to take on both bulls. He was ready to fight them to the death if it meant Seamie could get out, but before he could take a step, Seamie's hand went to his jacket pocket. He pulled out a pistol.

Fucking hell! Sid thought. It was the pistol he'd used to put a bullet hole in the corpse. Had he thought his brother had no wide boy in him? He had plenty.

"Think, gentlemen," Seamie said, in an impeccable Cockney accent. "Think real hard. I've nothing to lose. Nothing at all. Can you say the same?"

"Mother of God!" Sid cried. "It's him! It's Sid Malone!" He raised his hands. The manager, the guards, and a few frightened customers did the same.

"Get away from the door. All of you," Seamie ordered.

Sid moved toward the left side of the foyer where the tellers were. He heard whispers coming from behind him. "What the devil's going on?" a man said. He moved to block their view. The others followed him. As they did, Seamie moved closer to the doors.

"Slide the keys to me," he said.

The guard hesitated.

"For God's sake, man, do as he says!" Sid cried. "He's killed two people already!"

The guard unhooked a key ring from his belt and slid it across the floor to Seamie. Seamie put his bag down, never taking his eye off the guards. He picked up the keys and dropped them into his pocket, then picked up his bag again.

"Back up now," he said. "That way. Toward the vaults."

Sid, behind the others now, did as Seamie said. He walked backward quietly and quickly, blessing his brother's quick mind. The guards' eyes, and the manager's, were trained on Seamie. Sid slipped away toward the vaults as Seamie slipped out of the bank's front doors, locking them behind him.

"The key! Get me another key!" Sid heard the manager shout. He ran downstairs and was almost in the viewing room when a woman—a pigeon-breasted, no-nonsense clerk—stopped him.

"Your passbook, please!" she said.

"There's a man robbing the bank," he said breathlessly. "He's threatening to shoot everyone. Run, missus! Hide!"

The terrified woman ran off with a gasp. Sid shot into the viewing room, looked under the table, and saw the battered satchel Seamie had left. He grabbed it and ran back upstairs, heading for the doors, but when he reached the foyer he stopped short and spun around. Alvin Donaldson stood in the doorway, flanked by three constables. The agitated bank manager had gotten the door open. He and the guards were telling him what had happened. Frightened tellers and customers had gathered at the foyer's perimeter and were talking excitedly. Sid fell in among them and edged toward the doors. He could hear Donaldson over the din.

"How the hell did he escape? There were three of you!" he said angrily. "I was right upstairs where I've been for two bloody days! Couldn't one of you have fetched me?"

Sid's heart nearly stopped.

"He threatened to kill us!" the manager said indignantly.

"Are you certain it was Malone? What did he look like?"

"Red hair. Green eyes. Waving a pistol . . ."

"Good Christ," Donaldson said disgustedly. "We could have had him. Fan out," he barked at his men. "Go after him." The constables were out the door and down the steps in no time.

The manager tried to reassure his staff and his customers, telling everyone it was business as usual. He told the guards to get back to their posts. Before they could, Sid ducked behind a pillar, skirted the foyer, and ran out of the door. He trotted down the steps, searching for Seamie, but there was no sign of him. No sign of the three constables, either. More would probably be on the way, however, and he wasn't going to wait around for them. He and Seamie had planned to rendezvous back at Grosvenor Square, and after seeing him in action, he was sure Seamie would make it. The lad had more bottle, more brains, than most of the villains he knew.

He wondered, however, if *he* would make it.

He saw a hackney trolling for customers and flagged it down.

"Where to, sir?" the driver asked as he climbed in.

"King's Cross," he replied. He planned to hole up in a cheap hotel there until after dark. He couldn't let himself back into Fiona's house until after the cook had left and the maids had gone to sleep.

The cab lurched off. Sid put the heavy bag on the seat next to him and looked inside it, at the fat bundles of hundred-pound notes.

Blood money, India had called it.

He was going to wash the blood off now. Even if it cost him his life.

CHAPTER 74

Seamie stopped outside a stationer's shop, ripped his bag open, and pulled out a cap. He slapped it on his head, took off his mustard jacket, and stuffed it inside the bag—ensuring that any constable looking for a red-headed man in a yellow tweed jacket wouldn't look at him twice. He glanced over his shoulder, closed his bag, and kept on walking.

"Head east out of the City as fast as you can," Charlie had told him. "Get to Leadenhall and take it to the High Street. There's a market on to-day. Lose yourself in the crowd. Keep going until you reach the London Hospital. You can pick up a hackney cab there. Take it back home."

"Wait a minute," Seamie had said. "That's Whitechapel. That's your turf. Isn't there a safe house? Somewhere I could hide? Isn't there anyone there who's loyal?"

Charlie had laughed. "Oh, aye. Everyone there is loyal. To himself. There's a price on my head, remember? A thousand quid."

"What about honor among thieves?"

"For Christ's sake, lad, stop reading the penny dreadfuls. There's no such thing. Where's the bloody honor in taking what belongs to someone else?"

Seamie got down Cornhill and crossed Bishopsgate. So far so good, he thought, walking past the small shops and houses that lined the street. Women were washing the steps to their homes or walking toward the market with baskets on their arms. Nobody was paying him the least bit of attention. On the other side of Bishopsgate, he reached Leadenhall. From there he veered onto Aldgate and into the High Street.

He picked up his pace, relieved. He could see the market now, full of strutting costers, thronged with harried shoppers. He had just stepped down off the pavement into the bustle when two uniformed constables came out of nowhere to flank him, moving through the crowd like sharks through water. A third man, in plainclothes, came up behind him.

Seamie felt them before he saw them. There was a sudden tingling up his spine, a tightening in his guts. He glanced back, saw two bobbies' helmets, and tried to run. But he couldn't; the crowd was too dense. He looked about wildly for a place to hide, but all he saw was a butcher's shop.

A fishmonger's. A pub. All dead ends. He was desperate for a side street, an open stretch, but there was nothing.

"Oi! You in the cap! Stop right there!" a voice ordered from behind him. A split-second later he felt a rough hand close on his back.

Seamie took a deep breath and turned around. "What the hell you doin', boy?" he said in a drawling American accent. "Take your goddamned hands off me!"

The officer released Seamie. He looked at his partner, who looked every bit as confused as he did. The man in plainclothes caught up with them. "Well done!" he panted. Then he frowned. "Hold on a mo'. That's not Malone," he said. "What's your name?" he asked Seamie.

"Byron K. LaFountain the Third."

Donaldson's eyes narrowed. "Hand over your bag," he ordered.

"Now wait just a minute—" Seamie said.

"Now!" Donaldson barked.

Seamie did so, grumbling all the while about the lawless people in this lawless country. "Worse than El Paso," he said.

Donaldson ignored him. He was pawing in the bag. He pulled out Seamie's jacket. "This is it," he said. "This is what Malone was wearing— a yellow jacket." He held the bag upside down and shook it violently. "Where's the money?" he shouted.

Seamie blinked at him. He took out his wallet and handed it over. There were ten pounds in it.

Donaldson swore. "Weren't you just in the Albion Bank?" he asked.

"Why, yes sir, I was."

"What were you doing there?"

"I was puttin' up some jewels for my momma," Seamie said. "She didn't trust the hotel safe. She was worried about being robbed, y'see. I told her she was plumb crazy, but now I'm thinking she had the right idea. If this is how the law behaves here, I'd surely hate to see what the criminals do."

Seamie could feel beads of sweat rolling down his back as he spoke. Would Donaldson buy his cornpone charade? Or see right through it? He didn't have long to wonder, for the penny finally dropped.

"Malone's back there," Donaldson said. "At the bank. I bet he was watching. Waiting for us to leave, the canny bastard." He nodded at Seamie. "Grab him. He's part of it."

But Seamie didn't give them the chance.

He ducked the officer's hands, bolted into the crowd, swerved around an old woman hefting a turnip, then ducked under a vegetable cart. The surprised coster gave a shout as he emerged on the other side, but Seamie kept on going, pushing his way through a sea of squawking women milling about on the pavement. He got about ten yards down the pavement when he got stuck by the entrance to a church. A group of worshippers was leaving a midday mass. The priest was with them, bidding them all good-bye. He couldn't move forward, the pavement was blocked. He couldn't go back, so he went up instead. Up the stone steps and into the church. He pelted down the aisle and over the altar. He tried the door to the vestry; it was locked.

"God*damn* it!" he swore.

The constables were running up the aisle now. He had only seconds before they were on him. He spun around in a circle, panic-stricken, desperate for a way out—and then he saw it: a narrow door to the right of the altar. It was slightly ajar. He didn't know where it led. He didn't care. He sprinted across the altar, leaped over a low wooden railing, and stumbled to the door. There was a key in its lock. He tore it out, slammed the door shut behind himself, and fumbled it into the lock, throwing the bolt just as the one of the officers threw himself against the door. It shuddered in its frame, but it held.

There was nothing in the room but a staircase leading up. Seamie took the steps two at a time. He heard the police shouting at him through the door to come out.

"Not a chance, boys," he said, climbing higher and higher. He finally got to the top, pushed open a door above his head, and found himself in the church's belltower. The tower was open on all four sides. The bell hung above his head. Below he could see the teeming high street, the buildings on either side of the church, and the alley which ran along the back of the church. There was no way down, not unless he had wings.

He was trapped. The police would get the door unlocked or kick it down. It would be only a matter of minutes until they nabbed him. He swore, kicking the sides of the belltower. And then he spotted a neatly coiled pile of rope. It was all he needed.

He would use the rope to rappel down the belltower, down the church's slanting roof, and onto the roof of the neighboring building. He'd done it a hundred times before. In the Rockies. The Adirondacks.

No one would see him because no one in this godforsaken place ever looked up. He peered over the side of the tower. The drop was sheer. It was about ten yards to the slanting roof and another twenty to the closest building. The buildings stretched off from the church in both directions. From what he could see, most of them had roof doors. If he could just get to one, he could get back to the street.

It might actually work, he thought. Or I might die.

He bent down, reaching for the rope, then saw that one end of it rose up into the bell.

"Great," he said. If he climbed down that, the bell would start to ring. The police would twig what he was up to in no time. They'd be waiting to catch him when he dropped. He had to silence it.

There was an iron loop on the top of the trapdoor. Seamie grabbed the free end of the rope and pulled the entire length of it through the ring. The rope was long and it took time. When it was through, he made sure there was a little bit of slack in the portion that hung from the bell, then knotted the rope on the ring. By the time he finished he could hear pounding from below. The police were battering at the trapdoor with something heavy. He knew he had only minutes at the most. And no time to knot the rope around himself as he knew he ought to.

He grabbed the rope, climbed over the railing, and righted himself against the side of the tower. No climbing boots. No chalk for his hands. If he managed not to fall and smash himself to pieces, it would be a miracle. He wanted to say a prayer—but he didn't know to whom. Jesus had gone in for fishing, not climbing.

John the Baptist, maybe? No, he was a hiker. Strictly deserts.

Quasimodo? Was he even a saint?

The sound of shouts from below and the crunch of splintering wood convinced him that Quasimodo would do. He crossed himself, took a deep breath, and started his descent.

CHAPTER 75

"Something is strange, Ella."

"I'll say so. Why does Yanki have to practice the 'Kaddish Yatom' in the house? Why can't he go somewhere else to sing? Honestly, Mama, I feel like I'm at a funeral when he does this. Make him stop."

"He's a *chazzan*. You know that. He must practice," Mrs. Moskowitz said absently, staring out of the sitting room window at the street.

"He should go in the back alley, then, and sing to the tomcats," Ella groused.

Yanki had a beautiful voice and normally she loved to hear him singing prayers—but not this one. The "Kaddish Yatom" was a prayer for the dead, and hearing it made her uneasy.

"Mama, what are you doing at the window? Minding everyone else's business? Come away, already! You're making me nervous! You and Yanki both," she said peevishly.

But Mrs. Moskowitz didn't move. "Why are all the police gone?" she said. "They've been outside the café, inside the café, upstairs, downstairs, for days looking for some sign of Sid Malone. And now I can't see one of them!"

"Maybe they followed India. She left half an hour ago. To visit Joe Bristow."

"Usually only one goes after her. It is very, very strange," she said, finally releasing the curtain. "Almost as if they do not wish to catch him anymore."

"I doubt that," Ella said.

"I wonder where he can be."

"God only knows."

No one had heard from Sid for more than a week. Poor India was absolutely beside herself, convinced he was suffering, injured and alone, in some abandoned warehouse or derelict wharf. Ella was suffering, too. For her friend. The whole family was. No one could bear to see India so unhappy, and everyone was chafing from being under constant observation by the police. It was not good for business. Nerves were strained and tempers were fraying.

It was Saturday. The Sabbath. The restaurant was closed and the family was taking a well-deserved rest. Mr. Moskowitz was napping on the settee. Aaron was reading. The younger children were playing a game. As Ella tried to return her attention to a magazine, Yanki's voice rose, grew louder. He was in the dining room, but his voice carried out to the sitting room.

"*Ach!*" Ella shouted. "*Yanki! Genug!*"

Yanki sang louder.

From downstairs the sound of knocking could be heard.

"Another peaceful Sabbath at the Moskowitz residence," Ella sighed.

"Go, Aaron, will you, please? See who it is," Mrs. Moskowitz said.

Aaron trotted downstairs and was back up in the sitting room a few minutes later carrying a large, lumpy parcel wrapped in brown paper. "It was the postman. Here, Ella," he said.

"What is it?" Mrs. Moskowitz asked.

"I don't know," Ella said.

"Did you send away for something?" Miriam asked.

"No."

"Who is it from?" Posy asked.

"It doesn't say."

"Open it already!" Solly said.

Ella did. Under the paper was an old Gladstone bag. She opened that and cried out, "It's money!"

Mr. Moskowitz opened one eye. "This has happened once before, no?"

"No, Papa," Ella breathed. "It hasn't. Not like this. Look at it all!"

She opened the bag wider so that her family could see the bundles of hundred-pound notes. When she did, she spotted a piece of paper that had slipped down between the stacks. She quickly pulled it out and opened it.

"Blimey, El!" Aaron said, picking one up. "These are thick! There must be five thousand pounds in there!"

"No, Aaron," Ella said, her voice shaking. "Five hundred thousand pounds."

Mrs. Moskowitz, who had been standing over her, sat down on the floor with a thump, her hand pressed to her chest.

Alarmed, Mr. Moskowitz got up from the settee, grabbed Ella's magazine, and fanned his wife with it. "Are you all right, Mama?" he asked. "Miriam! The brandy!"

"Five hundred thousand?" she whispered.

Ella nodded. "Yes. It says so right here. There's a note."

Dear Ella,
Here's £ 500,000. Use it for the clinic. Use it to help the people of Whitechapel. The ones who have nothing and no one. Keep them alive. Keep a beautiful dream alive. Help a bad man do a good deed.

There was no date. No signature. There didn't need to be. Ella knew who'd sent it.

"Is that all it says? Where is he? What is he doing?" Mrs. Moskowitz asked, motioning for the note.

Miriam brought brandy and a glass from the sideboard. Solly picked up a stack of notes, wide-eyed. Posy draped herself over Ella's back and clasped her arms around her neck. There was so much noise and commotion that no one noticed India standing in the hallway. In the shadows.

"Was that the 'Kaddish' that Yanki was singing?" she asked softly.

She knew many Hebrew prayers now, from listening to Yanki and Mr. Moskowitz sing them.

"India!" Ella cried. "Thank God you're here!"

"It's a beautiful prayer, isn't it?" India said. "Beautiful and sad. I can't imagine he had any prayers at the end to comfort him. None at all."

"India, never mind the prayer, look at this! *Look!* Five hundred thousand pounds! From Sid. I know it. It must be. Who else could it be?" She held up her hands. "I know what you're thinking, but we're *not* going to send it back. We're just going to thank him."

"We can't thank him, Ella."

"Not yet, not yet. But soon. He will come soon."

"No, he won't. Not soon. Not ever."

"What are you saying? Haven't I told you not to talk that way? Why are you standing out there in the hallway? Come! Come and look at this."

India walked into the sitting room.

Ella gasped at the sight of her. "What is it? What's wrong?"

India's eyes were red with crying and in them Ella saw the deepest despair.

"I didn't know. It's been days and days and I didn't know. Not until I heard them. As I was coming down the hospital steps I heard them shouting it."

"Heard *who*? Heard *what*?"

"The newsboys," India said. "They were shouting it over and over again. They wouldn't stop." She held a copy of the *Clarion* out to Ella.

"Malone Found!" its headline shrieked.

"Where?" Ella asked, reaching for the paper.

"In the Thames. He's dead, Ella. Sid Malone is dead."

CHAPTER 76

India stared at the door to Freddie Lytton's flat. He was at home. She could hear the gramophone playing. She raised her hand, then stood frozen, unable to knock.

She pressed her hands over her eyes. She was quaking inside, sick to her very soul. There was no going back from what she was about to do. She almost left, almost ran down the stairs and into the night, but then she pictured a little child shunned by other children. She heard her—for somehow she knew it was a girl—asking what the word *bastard* meant. She saw her growing up alone, unable to attend the better schools, unable to make friends, unhappy.

It was worth every sacrifice, her child's future. Hers and Sid's. It was all that mattered now. At the thought of Sid she crumpled and had to sit down on the staircase. For three days she had lain in her bed in the Moskowitzes' attic, unable to stop weeping, drowning in a grief that was black and bottomless. She had told herself she would never love again after Hugh, but she had. She had loved Sid Malone and she had lost him, too.

She had wanted to die in those first hours, after she'd heard the newsboys shouting about his death, after reading how his body was pulled from the murky river, so badly decomposed that it had to be identified by a bullet hole and some personal effects. She wept for him, because he never had the chance to know a better life, and for herself, because she would never have the chance to live that life with him.

She refused to eat anything, drink anything, until Ella had come to her on the second day and gently told her that if she did not eat, then the baby did not, either. India realized then that Sid was not completely gone. She still had some small part of him left, a tiny life growing inside her, and she must do everything she could to protect and nurture that life. She had decided then and there to go to Freddie.

"It's the only way," she whispered to herself now. Then she stood up and knocked on his door.

"Just a minute!" Freddie called. The music stopped abruptly. She heard footsteps, the door opened, and he was there, standing in the doorway.

"India," he said acidly.

"May I come in?"

"Oh, you want to come in, do you? A few days ago you couldn't get away from me fast enough. You made a bloody fool of me. A laughingstock. So, no, you can't come in," he said, starting to shut the door.

India blocked it with her foot. "I have a business proposition for you," she said. "It involves money. A great deal of it. Now may I come in?"

Freddie opened the door. He swept a hand before him. When India was inside, he slammed the door.

"What are you doing here? What do you want?"

"I wish to marry you, Freddie."

India noted that even as practised a fraud as Freddie couldn't keep the astonishment off his face.

"*What* did you say?"

"I said I wish to marry you. We can set a date tonight. I have paid a visit to my mother today and convinced her to enlarge upon the terms of the offer she originally made you. In addition, I secured five thousand pounds cash from her." India paused to take an envelope from her purse and place it on the table. She nodded at it. "It's yours tonight if you accept my proposal. Should come in handy, no? You've a by-election to win."

Freddie stared at the envelope. He said nothing.

"Speechless? That's quite unlike you."

"This is a very sudden turn of events. I don't understand—"

India cut him off. "I am pregnant, Freddie. And the father of my child is dead."

Freddie laughed bitterly. "So I'm to raise Sid Malone's bastard, is that it?"

"I do not wish my child to suffer the stigma of illegitimacy. If we marry, you must accept the child as your own and behave toward her at all times as a father. You are incapable of love, I realize that, so I will not ask that for her, merely civility and a modicum of kindness. Those are my terms. Here are my parents.'"

She drew out another envelope. Freddie opened it and learned that he was still to receive Blackwood and the Berkeley Square town house, but the lump sum of £100,000 had been raised to £300,000 and the £20,000 per annum had been doubled.

Freddie digested this, then said, "I have a few terms of my own. Number one: I want heirs."

"I will do my best to give them to you."

"Those heirs—*my* children—will inherit the Selwyn Jones estate."

"I thought you would say that, so I've taken the precaution of asking my parents to establish an independent fund for this child. You will have no control over it. Only I will."

Freddie laughed in disbelief. "They *know* about the baby? You told them?"

"I had no choice. I need you to marry me. I thought a larger dowry would help to persuade you."

"And they agreed?"

"Of course. They would pay a great deal to avoid the scandal of a grandchild born out of wedlock."

"Term number two: You are not to resume your medical work. Not at the clinic, not anywhere. You are to stay away from Whitechapel. From Ella Moskowitz, Harriet Hatcher, all of them. You're to become a proper MP's wife. Quiet, supportive, and firmly in the background."

"Very well."

"Term number three: We marry on the twenty-fourth. Two weeks from now. At Longmarsh."

India's heart lurched. *So soon,* she thought.

"Do I have your word on this, India?"

"You do," she said. "Do I have *yours,* Freddie? Once, a long time ago, you were capable of giving it. Are you still?"

"I give you my word."

She nodded. "I will see you at Longmarsh on the twenty-fourth, then," she said, turning to go. She had to leave. She would go home, to her bed in the Moskowitzes' attic, to her grief, and try to find a way to live with what she'd just done.

Freddie grabbed her arm. "Wait," he said.

She looked at him questioningly.

"All this, India . . . all this because of a bloody *criminal.* I don't understand."

India, doomed and heartbroken, smiled at him. "No, you don't," she said. "You couldn't, Freddie. It's called love."

CHAPTER 77

Fiona's baby kicked. His movements were getting stronger. She had begun to think of the baby as a *he.* It had to be. He had restless legs like her brothers. She rested her hand on her large belly and continued to stare out of her bedroom window.

The gray morning light accentuated the shadows under her eyes, and the worry in them. "Think happy thoughts, Mrs. Bristow," the nurse had told her on her last visit to Dr. Hatcher, more than a month ago. "Happy thoughts are good for the baby."

It had been easier to think happy thoughts then. Her husband had not been lying comatose in a hospital. Charlie hadn't had a price on his head. Seamie had not yet told her about Antarctica.

"Will you know your uncles, little one?" she whispered softly. Her eyes filled with tears. "Will you know your father?" She blinked them away, knowing that if she started to cry now, she wouldn't be able to stop.

Lipton and Twining were dozing at the bottom of her bed. Lipton picked up his head at the sound of her voice. Sarah had brought her tea and toast, but she hadn't been able to touch a bite. She'd dressed herself, but couldn't muster the energy to leave her room. She felt sick with worry.

Seamie had taken Charlie to Gravesend. There were ships there bound for all parts of the globe. Charlie had owned a boatyard, and knew enough about engines to make himself useful belowdecks. He planned to travel east, as far away from England as possible, and leave the ship in some foreign port, finding work of one sort or another.

They had said their good-byes some time after midnight. Fiona had been beyond sad, but she'd tried to hold her emotion in check and not make their parting harder than it had to be.

"You give Joe my regards when he wakes, Fee," Charlie had said.

Fiona had nodded, her eyes downcast.

Charlie had taken her chin in his hand and tilted it up. "Listen to me, he *will* wake up. I know it, Fee. Other blokes might not, but other blokes don't have what he has. They don't have you and Katie and another one on the way. He's got everything in the world to live for, everything to fight for, and I know he'll win that fight."

And then he'd put his arms around her and held her tightly, telling her thank you, telling her he loved her. And then he was gone. And she was watching him go, knowing she would probably never see him again. It was hard and bitter, and she had spent the night tossing and turning, angry that the fates had taken her parents, her sister, and now her brothers, too.

The clock on her bureau chimed the hour. Nine a.m. Where is Seamie? she wondered. Why isn't he back? I never should have let him go. Never should have let them go. They'd sneaked out twice before—once to snatch a body and once to get Charlie's money out of the Albion Bank. The body-snatching trip had gone off without a hitch, they'd said, and she'd seen herself that it had worked, for the news of Sid Malone's demise was all over London, but they'd come very close to being caught on their second outing. Charlie hadn't come back to the house until well after dark that night, and Seamie had come home with a bruised and scraped face. All they would say was that they'd had a bit of bother.

It's still too dangerous for Charlie to be out and about, Fiona thought now, even if he is supposed to be dead. And Seamie . . . what if he'd gotten mixed up in something bad? Anything could have happened to them. They could have been arrested. Hurt. Shot. Killed.

The baby kicked again, violently. "Happy thoughts, Fiona," she said to herself. "Happy bloody thoughts."

There was a knock on her bedroom door. "Fee?" Seamie called, opening it.

The dogs leaped up, yapping and whirling. Relief flooded through her.

"Seamie! Thank God you're all right. I was so worried. Please tell me Charlie made it to the boat," she said.

"He did, Fee. He's fine."

"Where is he?"

"On a ship. Bound for Ceylon."

He sat down across from her. She could see that he was exhausted.

"I'm starving," he said. "You going to eat that toast?"

Fiona buttered a slice and handed it to him. She poured him a cup of tea. "Was it hard saying good-bye?" she asked him.

Seamie shrugged. "I waited with him till dawn. Then he said, 'This is good-bye, lad. Hardly seems fair, does it?' and then he told me he hoped I'd find the North Pole. And I reminded him it was the South Pole I was after. And then he was gone."

"That's all?" Fiona said. "Charlie's leaving and never coming back, and that's all he said? 'Hope you find the North Pole'?"

Seamie shrugged. "It's blokes, Fee," he said.

Fiona nodded, sadness welling up inside her again.

Seamie must have noticed, for he stopped eating for a few seconds and patted her hand. "There's no other way," he said gently. "He *had* to go. He'd be a goner if he stayed."

"I know. I know it's for the best. I just . . . I want you both here with me. I want us to be together. Like a family should be. Is that so much to ask? I'm losing everyone all over again. Charlie, you . . ."

She didn't say *Joe*. She didn't have to. They both knew there was no news. No change. Every day was the same. He was unresponsive. Immobile. Losing weight.

"Aw, Fee," Seamie said, trying to cheer her. "It would never work. You know it wouldn't. What would me and Charlie do here anyway? I'd make a terrible waitress at the Tea Rose. So would he. I'd be dropping the silver and he'd be stealing it."

Fiona tried to smile at the joke, but she couldn't.

"He's out of the life now. He's got a chance," Seamie said. "Isn't that what you wanted for him?"

Fiona looked at him, startled by his perceptiveness. "Yes, Seamie, it is," she said.

"Then let him go, Fee. And let me go, too."

Fiona looked at him. "All right, then, I will. Seems I have no choice, do I?"

Seamie stood. "Come on, let's go for a morning stroll. Over to Hyde Park and back. We'll take Katie with us. You need some sunlight. Some fresh air. Sitting here brooding isn't good for you. Or Joe. Or the baby. Life goes on, Fee. It has to. It's all we've got."

Fiona gave him a puzzled smile. "When did my little brother become smarter than me?" she asked.

Seamie snorted. "About a hundred years ago."

Fiona stood. She and Seamie were about to leave her bedroom when they both heard footsteps pounding down the hallway.

Fiona reached for Seamie, suddenly frightened. "It's something to do with Charlie," she said. "Something's happened to him. I know it."

There was no knock at the door, it was simply flung open. Foster stood there, breathless and flushed from his mad dash.

"Mr. Foster?" Fiona said, surprised by his sudden breach of decorum. She had never seen him act like this, not once in all the years he'd worked for her. "What is it?"

"Oh, madam!" he said with feeling. "He's awake! His eyes are open. He's trying to speak. He's a bit disoriented, at least according to the messenger, but he's *awake!*"

It took a second for Fiona to realize who Foster was talking about. As soon as she did, she was across the room and out the door.

"The carriage, right away!" she shouted.

"On its way," Foster replied. "Sarah's downstairs with your hat and coat."

Fiona was lumbering down the stairs now, as fast as her belly would allow. Seamie had charged ahead of her.

"Please, madam," Foster called after her, "would you kindly give Mr. Bristow my regards?"

"Give them to him yourself, Mr. Foster," she shouted. "There's plenty of room in the carriage."

"That would be highly unusual, madam."

Fiona stopped midway down the staircase. "In case you haven't noticed, so is everything else that goes on in this house."

"Quite true, madam."

"Even so, we're all alive, aren't we, Mr. Foster?" The baby kicked. Lipton and Twining tugged at her skirt. "It's all that really matters. It's all we've got."

"It is indeed, madam."

"Then get Katie, Mr. Foster, and get your coat."

CHAPTER 78

"Sid is it? Sid what?" the chief engineer asked.

"Baxter," Sid replied, caught off guard.

The engineer thrust a shovel into his hands and pointed at a pile of coal. "Welcome to hell, Mr. Baxter."

Sid took the shovel with a smile. A ship's boiler room held no terrors for him. He was already in hell. The night India had come to him at the Barkentine, he had thought that their love was damnation. Now he knew it was. He had known heaven with her, now he knew hell—it was the bleak gray endlessness of the years of his life stretching out one after another, years without her in them.

"Andy McKean," a second boilerman said, by way of introduction. "We'll work the first shift. You'll want to get stripped down. Won't be long now."

Sid had come aboard the *Adelaide* half an hour ago. They'd been waiting for him. Holding the ship was the least the captain could do; Sid had made him rich by buying his smuggled opium. As soon as he was aboard, a tug had nudged them out of dock toward the open water. He'd barely had time to throw his bag in his bunk and get down to the boiler room before the order came down from the bridge—full steam ahead.

"Oi, mate! Let's go!" Andy called.

Sid shrugged out of his jacket and pulled his shirt over his head. Ten minutes later, sweat was pouring off him. He and Andy were no longer men, just cogs in a machine. The monster of a boiler ate every shovelful of coal and roared for more. The fire roasted Sid's skin. The muscles in his bad arm screamed every time he lifted the shovel. The bullet wound in his shoulder sent molten waves of pain through his body. He didn't care. He welcomed the pain, it blocked out everything else—every memory, every promise, every hope.

It blocked out the words he'd seen. Printed on an invitation. An invitation that had been propped up on the mantel of Fiona's study. He'd gone down there during his last night at Grosvenor Square. He hadn't been able to sleep and had been desperate to get out of his room and walk, if only around the house. He'd paced the study, picking up photographs and putting them down again, examining Fiona's books and mementos. And then he'd seen it—elegant black copperplate printed on an ivory card.

> The Earl and Countess of Burnleigh are pleased to announce the marriage of their younger daughter Lady India to Lord Frederick Lytton, second son of Lady Bingham and the late Earl of Bingham. The couple will marry at Longmarsh, the Bingham family seat, in a private ceremony on Saturday, 24 November. They will enjoy a brief honeymoon in the Scottish Highlands then return to London where they will reside at 45 Berkeley Square.

Reading those words, Sid had felt as if someone had reached inside him and torn out his heart. A sense of unreality so strong that it was dizzying gripped it. It can't be, he'd thought. But it was. *Lytton, of all people.* India knew what he was. Knew what he wanted—not her, but her money.

"Why, India, why?" he'd said out loud.

Why would she marry Freddie Lytton after what he'd done to her?

He knew the answer—it was because of him. Because what he'd done to her was worse. Loving her, then betraying that love—as she saw it—by trying to take Joe Bristow's life and taking Gemma Dean's.

In the days that had followed, the anger he'd felt at India had drained away. A terrible grief had taken its place. He couldn't blame her for what she'd done. She was only going back to what she knew—Freddie, an aristocratic marriage, safety, security. If anyone deserved blame, it was him. For allowing himself to believe in love when life had taught him otherwise.

He would never make such a terrible mistake again.

The *Adelaide* was carrying ploughshares and other farm implements to Mombasa in British East Africa, then heading on to the city of Colombo in Ceylon to take on tea. Sid planned to leave the ship in Colombo and find work on a plantation—tea, rubber, he didn't care, as long as he could do an honest day's work for a living wage, hard, physical work that would leave him too tired to think at the end of the day. Too tired to remember. Too tired to grieve.

He had always wanted to go to sea. It would wash him clean, just as he'd once hoped it would. It already had. Sid Malone was dead and gone. He was Sid Baxter now. A lowly boilerman. Invisible. Anonymous. A man with no past, no history. A man with nothing but a future, endless and unwanted.

"Slow down, mate!" Andy yelled. "Pace yourself. This is the devil's own work. You won't last a day at the rate you're going, never mind from here all the way to Colombo."

Sid smiled. "Is that a promise?" he shouted, and shoveled harder.

CHAPTER 79

"India? Are you all right? What's going on in there?" Maud called, rapping imperiously on the loo door.

"Nothing, Maud, I'm fine," India called out.

She wasn't. She was leaning over the tiny toilet in the antechamber of Longmarsh's chapel. She'd been sick in her room twice this morning. And now again here.

"Nerves, that's all," she lied. She wiped her mouth, splashed water on her face, and opened the bathroom door.

Her sister was standing in the room, valise in one hand, a cigarette in the other. She had just returned from Paris. "I arrived this very minute. Lady Bingham said you were in here. India, what the *hell* is going on?"

"I'm marrying Freddie. In about ten minutes' time, in fact."

"That's what Mother told me. Four days ago. When I chanced—*chanced!*—to ring her from the hotel to see if she wanted some silks brought back," Maud said angrily.

"I didn't want you to know. I thought you'd try to stop me. Mother thought so, too."

"Of course I would!" Maud sputtered, throwing her valise down. "Just a few weeks ago you said you never wanted to see Freddie again. You told me all the horrible things he'd done. Why have you changed your mind?"

"Please don't make this more difficult than it already is. I have my reasons. I don't expect you to understand them."

"I would very much like to try."

India looked at her sister. For once she was not mocking.

"All right, then," she said. She sat down on one of the wooden benches in the room and smoothed the skirt of the high-necked ivory suit she was wearing. "I am pregnant," she said. "The baby is not Freddie's. He will acknowledge the child as his own in exchange for my dowry. The world is a very harsh place, and I do not wish my child to suffer for the circumstances of her birth."

"What about the father? Can't you marry him?"

"I was going to. In America, actually. But I can't now. He's dead, you see."

Maud took a deep drag on her cigarette, then exhaled a plume of blue-tinged smoke. "Bloody hell," she said.

"Yes."

"Who was he?"

"I can't tell you that. And trust me, you don't want to know."

"India, this is your *life*. You may be protecting your child's future, but you're destroying your own. Do you understand that?"

"I do."

Maud paced back and forth, shaking her head. "Is Mother here? What about Daddy?"

"They're in the chapel with the Lyttons. They came up from London yesterday. After finalizing the finances with Freddie."

A week ago in London, before the marriage contract had even been signed, Freddie had hired an architect and a decorator to make over the Berkeley Square house.

"A year from now it'll be the most beautiful, glittering home in London," he'd told her. "Be sure to order some new dresses before the wedding. We're having a ball for two hundred as soon as we're back from our honeymoon. Campbell-Bannerman, bigwigs from both parties, everyone who's anyone socially. I'll be damned if I don't get the Tower Hamlets seat back."

India knew that Freddie's ambition had been limited only by a lack of funds. With her father's money behind him, it would be boundless. She thought of all the dinner parties ahead of her. The planning of menus and settings. The tedious introductions and numbing small talk. And never anywhere, in any room, would she ever see Sid's face again, hear his voice, look into his eyes. Fresh grief washed over her. She bent her head so that Maud couldn't see it.

"Mother bought me this suit," she said, plucking at the ruffles on the cuff. "Ghastly, isn't it?"

Maud sat down next to her. She was silent for a few long seconds, then she said, "Do you remember that last time we were all together? Here. With Wish."

"Of course I do."

"I quoted Tennyson to you: '*'Tis better to have loved and lost than to never have loved at all.*'" She laughed mirthlessly. "You said he was a prat."

"I got my comeuppance, didn't I? The love I lost is all the love I'll ever have. But he was right. I'm still glad I had that love, no matter how briefly."

Maud covered India's hand with her own. "It won't be all bad. It can't be. There are compensations, you know," she said. "Distractions."

India laughed bitterly. "What sort of distractions? The kind one finds at Teddy Ko's? No thank you, Maud."

"I was thinking of your clinic, actually."

"There is no more clinic. Not for me. That was one of Freddie's conditions. I'm to be a good MP's wife. Devote myself to his causes."

"Well, then, there are always children," Maud said. "The one on the way and more besides, I'm sure."

"Yes, and there is much else I can do to occupy myself," India said bravely. "Study French for starters. I've always wanted to do that. Never had the time. Italian, too. I can read the great poets. Take up drawing." She closed her eyes. Her face was anguished. "Oh God, Maud," she whispered.

There was a knock on the door and then the vicar poked his head in. "Pardon me, Lady India, but are you ready? Your groom is here."

"I am, Reverend," India said resolutely. She took her sister's hand. "Will you stand with me?" she asked her.

"India, there must be another way. You don't have to do this. Leave. Hurry. I'll deal with Freddie."

India pressed a finger to Maud's lips, shushing her. "I'll sleep tonight knowing that my child will be spared a difficult life. That's all that matters to me now."

Sid was dead, but she had something left of him. He would live on in this child. She would see him in the baby's smile, in her eyes. She would hear him in her laugh.

Charlotte, she would call her, for Sid had once told her that Charlie was his first name. *Charlotte.* Her own child. Not Freddie's, *hers.* She would love the baby as she had loved her father, with her whole heart and soul.

She picked up the bouquet Freddie had selected for her. Crimson roses. He'd handed them to her earlier. "Can hardly expect you to carry white ones, can I?" he'd said. "They're for virgins, not Sid Malone's whore."

India had been shocked by his cruelty, but she'd quickly recovered. "My father's giving you a draft for three hundred thousand pounds today," she'd whispered back. "I rather think that makes you the whore."

His face had darkened then and he'd swiftly left the room. So this is how it will be between us, she'd thought. This was the man she would spend the rest of her life with. The man with whom she would share her bed. Her nerve almost faltered at the thought.

"Come on, Maud," she said. "It's time to go."

They left the anteroom for the foyer. From there they walked into the chapel proper. When they reached the bottom of the aisle, a lone harp began to play.

Freddie was standing at the altar, smiling triumphantly. He was sleekly handsome in a gray morning coat and striped trousers. Bingham stood with him. India took a deep breath, then walked toward him.

The vicar beamed at her, but she barely saw him. He began to speak, but she didn't hear him. She only heard Sid telling her he loved her, telling her their love was a mistake. *It wasn't,* she silently told him now. *It never will be.*

The service was conducted. Prayers were said and vows exchanged. Freddie pushed a ring onto India's finger. She did the same to him. He kissed her chastely and then it was over and they were wed. Lord Frederick and Lady Lytton, man and wife.

Outside the chapel, the sun was setting. Evening was coming down. The Lyttons' tenant farmers had assembled on either side of the chapel steps. They cheered the new couple and threw rice at them. Freddie's mother bustled them along toward the house, where a wedding supper was waiting. Freddie took India's arm. She was glad that everyone was chattering among themselves. It meant she didn't have to say a word to anyone. She looked at Longmarsh as she walked. It was a winter landscape and everything looked gray to her.

As the wedding party rounded a bend that led to the house, they got a surprise. A deer, a huge stag with a majestic set of antlers, stood on the path about twenty yards ahead of them.

"Good God! Where's the gamekeeper when you need him? Call the lazy oaf, Bing! Have him bring the guns," Freddie said.

Freddie released India's arm. He took imaginary aim at the animal and made the sound of a rifle firing. The animal heard it, but did not flinch. He was looking at India.

Run, she told him silently. *Go away from here and never come back.*

The stag blinked. He dipped his magnificent head and was gone.

"Bloody hell," Freddie sighed.

"Another day," Bingham said, clapping him on the back. "You're a married man now, old mole. No more of the sporting life for you."

There was laughter and ribbing. Freddie's sister tousled his hair. Bing told him to hurry up, he was starving, and the party moved off again, but India lagged behind, watching the stag as he ran across a field and leaped over a stone wall.

Tears threatened, but she fought them back. She would not cry. Later perhaps, but not here, not now. She made a vow instead. A real one. Not the meaningless words she'd woodenly mumbled to Freddie, but words that came from her heart. *I love you, Sid,* she said silently. *I always will.*

"Are you coming, darling?"

The voice startled her. It was Freddie, of course. He was waiting for her on the path alone. The others had gone on ahead. She looked at him. His smile, which had been pasted on for the benefit of his family and hers, was gone; his eyes were cold. Longmarsh loomed darkly behind him. She looked one last time for the stag, but he was gone.

And then she nodded and said, "Yes, Freddie. I am."

PART
THREE

London, 1906

Sir David Erskine, sergeant at arms for the House of Commons, looked out across Cromwell Green and frowned. The ceremonies for the State Opening of Parliament had ended. The crowds had dispersed, the king had left, members of both houses had gone about their business. It was a quiet and gloomy February day at Westminster, and that should have made the sergeant at arms happy, but it didn't.

"It's *too* quiet," he said to the deputy sergeant. "I don't like it, Mr. Gosset. Not one bit."

"Could be that he's reformed himself, sir. Could be we'll have an uneventful session this time," his deputy said.

Erskine snorted. "And it could be that pigs will fly. He's up to something. I know he is. We'll hear from him before the day's out, mark my words."

Eyes narrowed, arm crossed over his chest, Erskine looked like an ancient Scots chieftain defending his keep. In a way, he was. As sergeant at arms, he was responsible for maintaining order in the Commons. He had dealt with much during his tenure—everything from lost tourists and loonies to obstreperous backbenchers and bombs—but nothing had quite prepared him for the Honorable Member for Hackney.

"He's a minister now," Gosset said. "The PM put him in charge of labor relations. Perhaps he will conduct himself in a manner befitting his new title."

"I doubt it," Erskine said. "In fact, I think that's one appointment the PM will live to regret. He thinks the man will stop trying to kick down the door to the clubhouse if he lets him in. What he doesn't understand is that the bloody man wants to kick down the clubhouse."

"He seemed perfectly well behaved this morning, sir."

"Aye, *seemed*," Erskine said. "But I was watching him during the king's speech and I saw it. The look. The one he gets when his back's up. That—and the fact that he ducked out as soon as the king left—has me worried."

The State Opening of Parliament had taken place that morning, as it always did when a new government was installed, with much pomp and circumstance. King Edward had arrived amid cheering crowds, proceeded to the Royal Gallery, and had taken his place on the throne in the House of

Lords. Then, as tradition dictated, he sent the Gentleman Usher of the Black Rod to summon the House of Commons. The Commons slammed the door in Black Rod's face, signifying their right to debate without interference from lords or sovereign. Black Rod knocked three times before he was finally admitted, and then the MPs proceeded to the Lords' Chamber, where they heard the king deliver his speech—one in which he set out all that the new government wished to accomplish.

"You think something in the speech set him off?" Gosset asked.

"Knowing him, it might be something that *wasn't* in the speech. No housing for the aged. No schools for orphans. No shelters for stray cats. God only knows. But *I* know that—"

Erskine suddenly stopped speaking. He'd heard it. They both had. The faint whine of an engine.

"Good Christ, here he comes. I knew it, Gosset. I knew it!"

"Where is he, sir?"

"There!" Erskine said, pointing north.

A man in a wheelchair was making his way across Parliament Square. He was moving much faster than a man in a wheelchair normally did because this particular wheelchair had a motor attached to it. It was made by Daimler, and had a top speed of twenty-five miles per hour. Erskine knew that because he'd chased after the damned thing often enough.

The Honorable Member for Hackney advancing on Westminster was bad, but what was behind him was worse—a battalion of women, three hundred strong at least, armed with placards and banners. Trailing the procession were various members of the press. The man sold papers. He was always demonstrating, protesting, making a scene. Erskine reckoned he got more column inches than the prime minister.

He was a hero to many, a fighter, a saint. Erskine knew his story; everyone did. He was an East End lad made good. *Very* good. Determined to give something back to East London, he'd run for Parliament back in 1900 on the Labour ticket, and to the astonishment of the entire country, he'd won. But only a few weeks after his victory a criminal had put a bullet into his spine, paralyzing him. Unable to fulfill the duties of his office, he'd surrendered the seat and a by-election had been held. Freddie Lytton, the former incumbent, had won it.

Many thought he was finished, that he would live out his life as an invalid, but they were wrong. He hadn't let his disability slow him down, much less stop him. By the spring of 1901, he was back in the fray, having won a vacated seat—Hackney—in another by-election. People marveled at his accomplishments, exclaiming how the like had never been done before.

But that's him all over, Erskine thought now, not interested in doing what had been done, only what hadn't.

Gosset squinted at the placards. "*Votes for Women Now!*" he read out loud. "*Fair and Equal Laws for All!*" His eyes scanned the crowd. "Bloody hell, sir. He has Mrs. Pankhurst with him!"

"You've locked the doors?"

"Aye, sir."

"Good man. If he thinks he's getting those harridans inside, he has another think coming." Erskine and Gosset stood their ground, watching as the invading force made its way down St. Margaret's Street to the Strangers' Entrance.

"Do you remember the cabbages, sir?" Gosset asked.

"How could I forget them?" Erskine said.

The Honorable Member, angered by a Tory-backed bill requiring street vendors to pay tax on their barrows, had called the proposal "as rotten as an old cabbage" and had called for costers to demonstrate against it. They had. They'd marched to Westminster and dumped twenty wagonloads of rotten cabbages by the Members' Entrance. The stench had been eye-watering, the mess monumental, and the bill had been killed.

"Remember the howling kiddies?" Gosset asked.

"Oh, aye," Erskine growled.

The Honorable Member had staged *that* stunt when it looked as if his plea for funds for the Whitechapel Free Clinic for Women and Children would be denied. He'd gathered a crowd of angry and voluble East London mothers and their angry and voluble infants and sat them in the Strangers' Gallery. They'd made such a racket that the day's business could not be conducted. The police were called in, the women were removed, and the press had a field day—accusing Mr. Balfour's government of callous indifference to the poor. When the members reassembled, the clinic got its funding.

"And don't forget muck mountain!" Gosset said, chuckling. "I can still see the look on the PM's face when he saw it."

Erskine glared. "Do you find these antics amusing, Mr. Gosset?"

"No, sir. Not one bit," Gosset said, endeavoring to frown.

Muck mountain, indeed, Erskine thought. No one had ever been able to pin that particular bit of knavery on the Honorable Member for Hackney, but it certainly bore his hallmark. After the general election, Mr. Balfour's new government had introduced the Taff Vale Bill, which would hold the trade unions liable for damages employers suffered as a result of strikes. Furious at this gutting of the unions, the Honorable Member had loudly denounced the bill as "a piece of muck that stinks to the heavens." He'd been censured by both the Speaker and the prime minister. News of the bill's passage—and the member's reprimand—appeared in the evening newspapers. Later that same night London carters converged on Parliament Square, dumping load after load of manure in it, until they'd created a mountain of muck. And then they seated an effigy of Mr. Balfour on top of it.

The prime minister had indeed landed himself—and his party—in the muck with Taff Vale, but how deeply he'd put them there hadn't become apparent until a few weeks ago, when the Tories called another general election—and lost. The Liberals not only won, they won by a landslide, and Henry Campbell-Bannerman became prime minister. The Labour Party, too, had seen large gains in the number of seats it controlled and the new prime minister, nothing if not shrewd, had acknowledged the young party's growing influence by appointing several Labour MPs to cabinet positions—including the Honorable Member for Hackney.

As Erskine and Gosset watched, he motored up to the Strangers' Entrance and cut his engine.

"Sergeant Erskine! Deputy Sergeant Gosset! Always a pleasure," he said. His smile was broad and warm, but there was a challenge in his eyes.

"Indeed it is, Mr. Bristow," Erskine said.

"Might we pass? I've a group here wants to speak with their elected representatives. Not elected *by* them, I might add, but *for* them."

"All in good time, sir. But first, I would very much like to say that I wish for the two of us to start off the new session on the right foot."

"I would like nothing more myself, sir."

"Good. Good. Let us understand each other then, Mr. Bristow. This time there will be no rotten cabbages, no shrieking babies, no muck mountains"—he glowered at a petite woman in a long coat and wide-brimmed hat—"and *no* Mrs. Pankhurst!"

Mr. Bristow affected a regretful look while Mrs. Pankhurst began haranguing the sergeant at arms. Erskine listened, grimacing, as Mrs. Pankhurst told him there had been no mention in the king's speech today—none whatsoever—of the government's intention to grant women the right to vote. It was a slap in the face to all British women, she said, a negation of all they had labored for so arduously, an egregious betrayal of their hopes, and she, and the women with her, demanded explanations from their MPs.

"Now, Mrs. Pankhurst, you can't come into the lobby. Not all of you. Not like this," Erskine began.

"Mrs. Pankhurst is completely within her rights to see her MP," Bristow said. "As a British citizen, she can enter the central lobby to speak with him. So can these other women."

"Sir!" a voice shouted from the crowd. "Are you refusing to let the women in?"

Erskine looked for the source of the question. It was a reporter from *The Times*. He had his notebook out, his pen poised. So did a dozen others. Erskine sighed. A military man through and through, he knew defeat when he saw it, and better an honorable surrender than a bloodbath.

He turned back to Bristow. "I cannot let them all in at once," he said. "There are too many."

"How many can you let in?"

"Five."

"Fifty."

"Thirty."

"Done."

As Erskine told Gosset to unlock the doors to the Strangers' Entrance, it began to rain.

"Perhaps we could have some umbrellas brought?" Bristow said. "And some hot tea?"

"Do I look like a parlor maid, Mr. Bristow?" Erskine said.

"I'll arrange it myself. I only wanted your permission to do so. The weather is filthy and the women are delicate."

Erskine snorted. "Oh, aye. As delicate as tigers," he said.

Bristow motored into St. Stephen's Hall, up a ramp placed over the steps especially for his use, then veered off toward the dining rooms in search of tea. As he did, Erskine shouted at his back, "You mind your speed!"

He raised his hand in acknowledgment.

"You flattened three porters last year! And knocked a chunk out of Cromwell's statue!"

When thirty delegates had been selected, Gosset escorted them inside to the central lobby. Erskine surveyed the remaining crowd of wet, bedraggled women, angrily chanting for the vote. At least they had hot tea and a few umbrellas to share. Bristow had done that for them. He was back outside among them now, listening to the grievances of his own constituents—poor women who'd walked all the way to Westminster from Hackney. Erskine wondered how he could hear them over the din.

"It's the first day, Mr. Gosset," he said wearily, when his deputy reappeared. "Parliament's only just reopened and already we're under attack."

Gosset smiled. "Friend of mine served in China during that bother with the Boxers. He said when a Chinese wished you ill, he would tell you, 'May you live in interesting times.'"

"Oh, we've interesting times ahead of us, Mr. Gosset, make no mistake," Erskine said. "With Mr. Bristow on board, we've very interesting times indeed."

CHAPTER 81

"Another one, Maggs?" Sid Baxter said.

"I shouldn't," Maggie Carr said, "but I will."

"That's my girl."

Sid refilled the glasses. Every drop was as precious as gold, and nearly as dear. Whisky, when it could be had, came from Nairobi, a two-day journey by ox cart. Some would have been stingy with the bottle, but not Sid. He poured freely.

Most people, if they were generous, were so because they thought life was short and that one must make the most of it. Sid Baxter was generous because he knew that life was long. It went on and on, even when you had no use for it anymore. It was happiness, not life, that was short, and when it visited—in the form of a fine evening spent talking with a friend—he honored it.

"Won't be sitting on our arses for much longer," Maggie sighed. "Rains aren't far off now. And not before time. I'm sick of eating dirt."

The dry season had turned the red earth of Thika into a fine dust that drifted from the roads and fields into houses and barns, over animals and people, giving everyone and everything a faint terra-cotta hue, but now a breeze rippled through the long grass of the veldt, and out on the horizon, north toward Mount Kenya, lightning flashed and thunder rumbled, ominous and low.

"We'll be planting night and day soon. In about a week's time, I should think." She took a swallow of her drink, looking out over her land. "Seven hundred acres under coffee now. And another two hundred plowed. I wouldn't believe it if I couldn't see it with my own eyes. You're a devil of a worker, Bax."

"Because you're a devil of a boss."

Maggie flapped a hand at him and drained her glass. Margaret Carr was Sid Baxter's employer and his friend. A coffee planter, she was fifty-odd years old and five feet two inches high, but her voice, and her temper, made up for her diminutive stature. A widow—she'd lost her husband several years ago—and childless, she ran her farm single-handedly, relying on hired hands to help with the planting and harvesting.

She sat like a man, her feet up on the railing of Sid's small porch, and swore like one, and worked like one. He'd seen her work from dawn until dusk in her fields, setting plants in the rain, picking the red coffee berries in the blazing sun. She wore a broad white topi on her head when she worked, a man's shirt rolled at the sleeves, and trousers held up with one of Mr. Carr's belts. She never wore skirts, not even the split style favored by the settlers' wives, not even when she went to town.

Sid had met her six years ago, shortly after the supply ship he'd crewed on out of Gravesend, the *Adelaide,* had docked at Mombasa, an ancient Arab trading port on the coast of British East Africa. He'd gone ashore, intending to get back on the ship, which was headed next to Ceylon, but he'd drunk too much, passed out in a brothel, and was robbed blind. By the time he arrived at the dock—holding his trousers up with his hands because his belt had been stolen, too—the *Adelaide* was only a speck on the Indian Ocean.

He'd paced back and forth on the dock, swearing frantically—and uselessly. A woman had been standing nearby, supervising the loading of a ploughshare, four crates of chickens, and six cows. When they were safely in her cart, she approached him.

"You all right?" she asked.

"Do I bloody look all right?" he yelled. He was desperate. The *Adelaide* had made him forget. The work, stoking the boiler, was crucifying. There were storms. He was often seasick. On the ship, it was all he could do to survive. On land, he would have time to think. Time to remember.

"What happened?" she asked.

He explained.

"Ever drive oxen?"

"No."

"Ever plant coffee?"

"No."

"Are you strong?"

"What's that to you, missus?"

"I need help. My husband's dead and my headman's a drunk. I can't pay much, but you'll get plenty to eat, a bed, and your own hut. It's not much, the hut, but the roof's sound and it has a porch."

"You want me to come with you?" Sid asked, astonished.

"I need a new headman and you need work, don't you?"

He thought about this. "I do," he finally said.

"I'm a coffee planter. I've twelve hundred acres at Thika, north of Nairobi. The work's hard, I won't say it isn't, but it's better than starving. Do you want the job or not?"

"Yes."

"Come on, then. Train leaves in half an hour." She led the way to the station, turning around once to ask, "What's your name?"

"Baxter. Sid Baxter."

The engineer on the *Adelaide* had asked him the same question. He didn't dare use Malone, and Baxter—the name he'd used at Arden Street with India—had come out of his mouth before he could stop it. He wished he'd said Smith, Martin, anything but Baxter. He'd wanted to forget India, forget what they'd had. Now he was reminded of her every day of his life.

Maggie had neglected to tell him that she couldn't afford a passenger ticket for him, so he'd had to sit in the baggage compartment on top of the chicken crates. The train's wheels banged and bumped so hard over the un-ballasted tracks that he was black and blue by the time they'd reached Nairobi. Two young men, tall and ebony-skinned, dressed only in short red tunics, met them with an ox cart.

Sid goggled at them until Maggie said, "Two of my workers. Kikuyu. Stunning, aren't they?"

Two days later they arrived at Thika, a handful of huts on a narrow river, tired and footsore. From there it was another ten miles to Maggie's farm. Maggie showed Sid his new home—a wooden shack raised on four posts—then put him to work breaking ground. He'd told her he wanted no wages—not right away—only whisky. She obliged him, giving him a bottle, warning him to make it last.

At night he drank to forget and by day he worked to forget, driving himself to the point of exhaustion. He worked until his clothes were drenched with sweat and his hands bled. Until he vomited with heat sickness. He worked until the sun went down, and then he kept working until he collapsed on his bed and slept without dreaming.

After several weeks of this, Maggie came out of her house one night and walked into her fields. There she watched him, hands on her hips, as he attempted to dig out a tree stump by lamplight. She said nothing at first, just looked at him, her eyes traveling over his burned and blistered skin, his emaciated body.

Then she said, "I've had enough of this. You want to top yourself, do it on someone else's farm, not mine." They'd stood there for a long moment, glowering at each other. And then, in a softer tone, she'd said, "Whatever you've done, or whatever's been done to you, working yourself to death won't undo it. You'll have to live with it. Just like the rest of us."

He'd thrown down his pickax and stalked off to his hut, angry that Maggie had seen inside him. He found other ways to lose himself after that. Other ways to forget. There were quiet times on the farm, times when he wasn't planting and wasn't harvesting and wasn't needed. He started riding out then, going off on safari by himself. He would wander for days, sometimes weeks, traveling as far north as Mount Kenya, west to the Mau Reserve, as far east as the Tana River.

He would take a tent with him, a flask and a rifle, shooting only to eat, for he hated watching an animal die; he'd had his fill of pain. He would cross plains and climb hills, seeing places no white man had seen before, watching lions and elephants and rhinos, following the vast black herds of wildebeest.

He would sleep beneath the stars in good weather, listening to the night noises, half-hoping a lion would take him. During the day he would walk under the endless African sky and talk to India. He would ask her "Why?" and argue with her and accuse her. Sometimes he would rage and shout at her. And once, years after he'd arrived in Africa, he'd taken off his clothing in a storm and lain on the ground, weeping for her, wishing the hard rain would pound the flesh from his bones and dissolve him into the dirt. But it didn't. And so he'd gotten up, muddy and cold, and made his way back to Maggie's farm. By the time he'd arrived, he was sick.

"You finished now?" she'd asked, sponging his brow with a cold cloth and making him swallow quinine. He'd nodded. "Good," she said. "Because whoever she is, she's not worth it."

"But that's the thing of it, Maggs, she is," he'd replied.

He'd stopped trying to kill himself after that, but he hadn't stopped drinking. He spent almost everything he earned on whisky, wine, or whatever could be bought from the merchant Jevanjee in Nairobi. He drank with Maggie and her planter neighbors, and if they weren't available, he drank alone.

"Looking forward to the next few weeks," Maggie said now. "It's a lovely time, isn't it, when the coffee blooms? The white flowers look like snow. And then the beans come, like holly berries against the green leaves. Reminds me of England at Christmas."

"Without the bloody fruitcake," Sid said.

Maggie laughed. She nodded at the newspaper on top of his porch table. She'd put it there earlier in the day. It was one of the London papers, nearly two months out of date, but news traveled slowly to Thika. Its headlines were trumpeting the Liberals' victory in the British general election.

"Did you read it yet?" she asked.

"No," Sid said. He had no use for newspapers. They connected him with the world when all he wanted to do was withdraw from it.

"Well, you should. We've a new government," Maggie said. "And they're transferring the entire African protectorate from the Foreign Office to the Colonial Office. Lord Elgin's been made secretary of state for the colonies. And rumor has it the governor's asked him to send his undersecretary out for a visit."

Sid frowned. He preferred the topic of planting, but all the planters loved talking politics. "It's nothing to do with me," he said. "I stay away from politics. And politicians."

"I try, but they won't stay away from me. If London's thinking of sending a man out here, something's afoot. I guarantee it."

"That's wishful thinking, Maggs. Even if someone does come, what'll he do? Shoot some lions, get his picture in the papers, then go home again and forget all about Africa."

"He can't. Not anymore. Someone's going to have to answer a few questions and soon. More settlers are coming all the time—where will they go? And what of the tribes? The Masai aren't happy about being pushed onto reserves. The Kikuyu aren't either. And the Nandi are furious. They fought a bloody battle against us. They'll do it again. The Land Office is overwhelmed. So are the district commissioners. It's going to turn ugly, Sid. You wait and see."

"What will you do if it does?"

Maggie heaved a long, trailing sigh. "Stay," she said. "I've no choice, have I? My husband brought me here, then died and left me with a farm, four hundred coffee plants, and no bloody money. Twenty years on, and I'm only just starting to show a profit. How about you? What will you do?"

Sid thought of his small, comfortable hut, of his friendship with Maggie, of the rugged, beautiful, indifferent country he'd come to think of as home. He thought of the fragile peace he'd found here. It was all he had.

"As long as you stay, I'll stay," he said.

"You could apply for a land grant yourself."

Sid shook his head. He knew that if he applied for land, he'd get it—six hundred acres in Kenya Province would be leased to him by the British Foreign Office for ninety-nine years at the rate of a halfpenny per acre per year. Some would leap at the chance. He wanted no part of it. He was finished with thieving.

"The British government takes land in Kenya from one set of people and hands it out to another," he said. "Do that back home and it's called robbery. Do it here, and it's called progress."

"Aye, well, call it whatever you like, lad," Maggie said wearily, "but see that we get a good harvest this year. Otherwise you and I and the cook and the *toto* and all the field hands are going to starve."

Maggie talked on, telling him to make sure to get a fence around the north field, reminding him what the gazelles did to the bushes last year. He said he didn't need reminding, thank you, the fence was almost entirely up. He poured another round and they talked on about the milk cow's recent bout of mastitis, the new litter of goats, and a cobra that had been spotted near the henhouse. As dusk came down they could both see the lights of the neighboring Thompson plantation winking in the distance.

"When are you planning to go to Nairobi again?" Maggie asked.

"In a fortnight," Sid said. "Grain's running low. We need more paraffin and a new bit for the horse, and Alice gave me a list of kitchen supplies as long as my arm."

"While you're there," Maggie said, still gazing at the Thompson farm, "why don't you bring back something nice for that lovely Lucy Thompson? I hear she's set her cap for you."

Sid snorted. "She must be a damned desperate woman."

"Oh, rubbish. She's a pretty girl, you know. And the Thompsons have two thousand acres."

Sid sighed. Maggie had tried to matchmake for him before. He decided to nip this particular round in the bud. "It's just not to be, Maggs," he said, affecting a heartbroken look. "There's only one woman for me, but she's broken my heart. She won't have me."

Maggie sat up, her eyes bright with curiosity. "She has? Really?" she said. "Who is she?"

"You, luv. Will you marry me?"

"Oh, you sod, you!" she scolded, but a smile creased her weathered face.

"Come on, Maggs, let's make a go of it. You and me. What do you say?"

"I say, 'No, thank you.' One man was plenty. I'm through with you lot. I like a quiet life, a book at night, a bed to myself."

"I do, too. Try to remember that the next time you start meddling."

Maggie narrowed her eyes. "I wonder sometimes about the woman who made you a bachelor," she said. "It's not a natural state for a man. You're all helpless as kittens without a woman. Every last one of you. If a man's a bachelor, there has to be a reason. One day, Sid, I'm going to find out what it is."

And with that Maggie rose heavily from her chair and bade him good night. Sid watched her go, smiling, knowing that was one thing she would never find out. She liked to play at prying, but she never pushed it too far. He didn't like talking about his past. She didn't like talking about hers, either. Each understood this about the other. It was one of the reasons they got on so well. Maggie knew that he had come from London and had no wife, no children. Sid knew that Maggie and her husband had left Devon for Australia, then left Australia for Africa. Nothing else.

He lived his life now with many unknowables. He didn't know if the seedlings he planted would take, or what kind of yield he would get from them if they did. He didn't know if gazelles or monkeys or blight would destroy the crops, if the sun would wither them, if rain would rot them. He didn't know if the Kikuyu would continue to accept the settlers' encroachment. Or if they would rise up, burn them out, or murder them in their beds. He didn't know if he loved Africa or hated it. If he would die here or leave next year. He didn't know how he got out of bed some mornings with no one to live for, no one to love. He didn't know how he managed to stay alive without any dreams.

There were days in Africa, so many days, when Sid Baxter felt he didn't know a thing about the land, the people, the coffee, or himself—but he did know one thing, one hard, immutable fact: he knew that India Selwyn Jones was gone from his life, and that he would never see her again. Of that much, at least, he was certain.

CHAPTER 82

"It's a blasted money sink," Henry Campbell-Bannerman, the prime minister, said. He was seated behind his desk in his office at number 10 Downing Street.

"On the contrary, it's begun to turn a profit," protested Lord Elgin, the secretary of state for the colonies.

"How much of a profit?"

"We anticipate at least forty thousand pounds for the year."

"Forty thousand? *Forty thousand?* That damned railway cost more than five million! We need to do better than forty thousand. I'm being taken to task for the expenditure in the Commons every single week. That bloody Joe Bristow is hammering away at me, demanding to know why five million have gone to finance a railway in Africa while children here in Britain go hungry. What kind of answer can I give him? He's got me by the throat. Look there"—he gestured to the pile of newspapers on his desk. "His name's on every front page today. In twenty-point type!"

"Well, you can blame yourself for that, Henry," Elgin said. "*You* made him a minister. He's your creature."

"He's his own damned creature, unfortunately," the prime minister shot back. "And he's not the problem. Not the main one, at least. It's the railway. I need you to tell me exactly how we are to make it come good."

"It's very simple," Elgin said. "The railway's fortunes wait upon the settlers' fortunes. Settlers mean crops. Crops mean exports. Exports mean cash—both for those who grow them and for that which transports them. Give me more settlers and I will give you a return, not of forty thousand, but four hundred thousand."

"You need settlers? Go and find some! What's stopping you?" Campbell-Bannerman asked.

Elgin turned to Freddie Lytton, his newly appointed undersecretary. This was a golden opportunity for Freddie. He knew it and seized it.

"It's not that easy, sir," Freddie said, sitting forward in his chair. "It's a daunting task to pack up and move halfway round the world. Certain guarantees need to be made before a man will stake his fortune in Africa. Unfortunately they are not being made, and Britons know it. Stories are trickling back home about the difficulty of securing land. Grants are being made, but not all of them are legitimate. And even when they are, the paperwork is taking years to clear the Land Office. Construction on roads and bridges is proceeding at a snail's pace. And there is constant squabbling among the different layers of authority. The governor is angry with the Colonial Office. The district commissioners complain about the provincial commissioners. And the settlers are angry with everyone."

"And how do you suggest we remedy this?"

"First, we send an envoy from the new government to Africa."

"Let me guess. That envoy would be you."

"Yes, it would," Freddie said. He could see he had Campbell-Bannerman's attention. The old boy was interested. All he had to do now was convince him. "Someone must go to Africa in person and sort this out. I ask you to let me try."

"How will you do it?"

"I'll start by hearing out all factions. I'll meet Lord Delamere and the other men from the Colonists' Association. I'll meet the governor, the PCs, and the DCs. And then I'll do one better—I'll go out to the villages and farms and meet the settlers. When I return to London, I'll have not one side of the story, but all sides. A complete picture. When we know exactly what the problems are, and where, we can begin to address them."

Freddie unfurled a map and spread it on the prime minister's desk. It depicted the result of the European scramble for African land over the past half century—a continent carved up into protectorates and territories by Britain, Belgium, Germany, France, and Italy.

"We do know that a proper survey needs to be completed on the northern frontier," Freddie said, pointing to lands bordering Abyssinia, "so that the region may be properly parceled and leased. Also, the railway must be extended farther into Kenya Province and west to Lake Magadi." His fingers swept over plains and rivers. "Rights must be granted to trading companies and routes secured for them all the way from the Ugandan border to Mombasa. And finally"—he tapped the area to the west of Mount Kilimanjaro—"the relocation of the natives to reserves must be accelerated."

"Such a trip would help address the problems of the existing settlers,"

Campbell-Bannerman said, "but it won't bring new blood to the region, and that—according to your superior—is what is urgently needed."

"I've anticipated that concern, and I believe I have a solution," Freddie said.

"I thought you might."

"I will bring my family with me on the trip."

Campbell-Bannerman raised an eyebrow. "Taking your wife and daughter on holiday will cure the ills of British East Africa, will it?"

"We'll travel through Africa together, and as we go, I'll file stories and photographs with *The Times*. I've friends at the paper who'd be delighted to publish such a series. I'll dispatch reports from Mombasa, Nairobi, the bush, the farms, the highlands—*everywhere*. I'll make the damned place sound like paradise. When John Bull sees how safe it is, even for women and children, when he hears about the acres of fertile land up for grabs, reads about the hunting to be had, there will be a stampede to the docks. I guarantee it."

Campbell-Bannerman digested this. "Be nice to see one of our own on the front pages for a bit, eh, Elgin? Maybe knock Bristow out of the headlines." He turned to Freddie. "But your wife may not wish to go."

Freddie thought, It does not matter what my wife wishes.

He said, "India's adventuresome. Charlotte, too. They'll have the maids hauling out their trunks ten seconds after I tell them about the trip."

He knew that India would do no such thing. She would be furious. She would plead with him to leave Charlotte at home, but he would not. His success in Africa depended upon her presence.

"Are you quite certain it's wise?" Campbell-Bannerman asked. "Most settlers leave their children in England because of the dangers—malaria, dysentery, and all that. To say nothing of lions and leopards."

"All exaggerated, from what I've been told," Freddie said.

The prime minister steepled his fingers. His gaze traveled from Freddie to Elgin. "This has your blessing?" he said.

"Of course."

"Very well, then, Freddie. Go. As soon as possible."

"I will, sir. Thank you for your confidence in me."

Freddie gathered his map and his papers and departed. Elgin had further business with the prime minister, so he stayed.

"Brilliant chap, that Lytton," he heard the prime minister say as he left. "Better watch out, old boy. He'll have your job one day."

"Oh, no. Not my job, Henry," Elgin replied. "*Yours*."

Outside in the hallway, Freddie permitted himself a smile. He couldn't wait to set off. He wished he could leave tonight. The sooner he sorted out Africa, the better. The PM was right, of course. The Uganda railway was a money sink. But it didn't have to be. Anyone with a modicum of vision could see how profitable it might become. The line had an enormous lake at one end and the Indian Ocean at the other—perfect for moving goods from farms and ranches to towns and ports. It traversed endless acres of fertile land, all just waiting to be exploited. There was a limitless amount of money to be made on crops and animals. Then there was tourism and hunting. And as more people came, either to visit or to settle, the building trades would flourish. And then the retail trades.

All it would take was for one man to effect a truce between the warring factions, to get them all working together in pursuit of a common goal. It was a daunting challenge, but Freddie was confident. There would be laurels for the man who turned the money sink into a mint. The Liberals' recent success had done nothing to diminish Freddie's ambition; it had only sharpened it. But one did have to be careful. He well knew that it was social death to be seen as a climber. Ambition was permitted in London—as long as you called it duty. He would make Africa his duty. For king and country. And Africa, in turn, would make him prime minister.

He strode out of number 10 and into the street, where his carriage was waiting. If he succeeded in his goals there—and he *would* succeed—it would make his ascent within the party ranks, already quick by anyone's standards, dizzyingly fast. He'd outpace Elgin, Churchill, Asquith, Grey, and a dozen others. And, most important, he'd outshine that damned Joe Bristow, darling of the press. The man made more of a nuisance of himself in a wheelchair than he'd ever done on his own two feet. He'd been so glad when he'd been shot, thinking he'd be out of the picture for good, but now he wished it had never happened. Plucky cripples always stole the spotlight. Who could compete with Tiny Fucking Tim?

Freddie climbed into his carriage and barked at the driver to take him home to Berkeley Square. He had news to impart. He frowned at the thought. India would be difficult about this. He knew she would. She would be anxious about Charlotte, worried that the girl would catch some horrible tropical disease.

If only, he thought. If only they *both* would.

Nothing would serve him better than his so-called wife and so-called child dropping dead of malaria. Dengue fever. Plague. Whatever. He despised them, wished them gone. And yet he had to pretend otherwise every day of his life. At least in public.

If only India would give him a son. The marriage would at least be tolerable then. The thought of all that he'd worked for—the money, the houses—going to Sid Malone's bastard instead of a member of the Lytton family was unbearable.

They had been married for six years now. Plenty of time for her to have conceived again. And yet she hadn't. A year had gone by after Charlotte's birth, then two. He went to her bed frequently, though he hated to, but nothing ever happened. More than once he'd accused her of preventing a pregnancy. She'd been a doctor; she would certainly know how. He had torn her bedroom apart on more than a few occasions, pulling out drawers, ripping clothing from her armoire, in his hunt for devices. But he'd never found one, and she had vehemently denied his accusations. She had made a deal, she'd said. As long as he kept up his end, she would keep up hers.

He did not believe her. She was taking revenge on him, he was certain of it. She blamed him for Sid Malone's death. For the ambush at Arden Street. This was her way of paying him back.

If only I could start over, he thought now. With India's money, but without India. With a new wife. A new child. A son. *My* son.

The carriage slowed. Freddie looked out of the window and saw he was in Berkeley Square. Number 45, his house, was beautiful, large and grand, a shining symbol of his immense wealth, but when he wasn't hosting dinner parties and garden parties, he spent as much time out of it as possible, wishing to avoid its other occupants. He planned to go in for only a few minutes now—long enough to tell India to prepare for their upcoming trip—and then it would be off to the Reform Club. If he got home late enough, and was sufficiently drunk, he supposed he would go to her bedroom and try yet again to beget a son.

He sighed now, thinking bitterly of the effort *that* took, then told himself to buck up: "You married for money, old chap, and no one ever said you wouldn't have to earn it."

CHAPTER 83

"It's so good to see you, Seamie. I wondered sometimes if I ever would again," Albert Alden said, smiling at his old friend over a pint of bitter.

"It's hard to keep up with people when they're always dashing off to Zurich," Seamie said.

"Try keeping up with people who dash off to the South Pole."

Seamie laughed. He had arrived in Cambridge by train two hours ago. Albie had collected him at the station and they'd made their way back to his rooms at Trinity College, dumped Seamie's bags, then headed out to the Pickerel, an ancient pub and one of Albie's favorites. They hadn't seen each other for nearly six years—since the day Seamie had left to take part in the Discovery Expedition. But as with all true friends, the years fell away quickly and after a bit of catching up it was almost as if they'd never parted.

Albie was a graduate student now, working on his doctoral dissertation in theoretical physics. Seamie had asked him what, exactly, could be theoretical about physics, and Albie's explanation had made his head spin. He'd babbled on about Brownian motion and special relativity and the brilliant young physicist who'd proposed these theories, another Albert—Albert Einstein.

And then it was Seamie's turn to talk. He told Albie about the expedition, and how close they'd come to the Pole—only 480 miles away—before illness and hunger forced them back. He'd returned to London in 1904, and had spent the next two years lecturing in Britain, Europe, and America on the expedition's findings.

After they'd traded news about Seamie's family and Albie's parents, Seamie asked, "And what's Willa doing these days?" His voice was light and casual; his interest was anything but.

"What *isn't* she doing?" Albie said. "Climbing in Scotland and Wales. Mount McKinley. The Alps."

"Really?"

"You're not surprised, are you? You know what she's like. She had some money left to her by a batty old aunt of ours, and she uses it to pay for her trips. I must admit, she's become a damned impressive climber. She set a record on the Matterhorn. Fastest women's ascent. Mont Velon, too. She wants to go to Africa next and take a crack at Kilimanjaro. She wants to climb without quite so much cold weather clobber. Less to haul in and out of the camps, she says."

"Is she there now?"

"No, she's here."

"Is she?" Seamie asked, a bit too excitedly.

"Didn't I tell you? I meant to. She's in town for a fortnight. She came up with some friends from London. The Stephens sisters—Virginia and Vanessa. They've lots of friends here. Their brother Thoby was at Trinity. Bookish girls, a very odd pair, but then so's Wills. Odd, I mean. So they all get on smashingly. Though, to be truthful, she's barely made time for any of us. Too busy hiking with Mallory."

"Mallory? George Mallory?" Seamie asked, trying to ignore an annoying surge of jealousy. "Not the chap we met years ago at the Royal Geo?"

"The very same. He's at Magdalene College now reading history. He's become something of a star in climbing circles. Cuts quite a figure. Gorgeous George, the ladies call him."

"Where are they climbing? I don't recall many mountains in Cambridge."

"St. Botolph's. The Town Hall. Great St. Mary's. . . ."

"*What?*"

"Churches, municipal buildings, colleges . . . they'll scale anything with a toehold. They make bets. First one to the top wins. Wills lost a locket to George and won it back twice. I think she's got his watch now. They call it *buildering*. Instead of bouldering. Funny, isn't it? *Build*ering . . . free-climbing *buildings* instead of free-climbing *boulders*."

"Yes, Alb. I get it," Seamie said. He didn't think it was funny at all. He'd always known Mallory had an eye for Willa.

"They were caught two days ago by a local constable and warned to stop. George, being a reasonable being, did, but Willa won't. Our mother will have fits if she gets herself arrested and it'll all be *my* fault, as always."

"Are they an—" Seamie was about to say *item,* but he never got the chance. The pub door suddenly banged open. He heard laughter, merry and challenging. A woman's laughter. He knew it. He'd heard it in his head in the Antarctic. It had kept him warm in the bitter cold. Kept him sane in the driving snow and screaming winds.

She stepped inside the pub, looking, as always, like Albie's younger brother. She wore an oversized jumper, moleskin trousers, and a pair of climbing boots. She was taller than he remembered. Slimmer, harder, and a hundred times more beautiful.

God, but she's gorgeous, he thought. Her hair was cut impossibly short. On any other woman it would have looked awful. On Willa it was perfect. It showed off her fawn's neck, the strong angles of her face, her luminous moss-green eyes.

Those eyes were trained on her companion now—a tall, strikingly handsome young man. She was joking with him, pushing him playfully. Seamie recognized him; he was George Mallory. Watching them together, he knew he had the answer to his question. They *were* an item. Of course they were. Had he really expected her to wait for him? He'd tried to see her, her and Albie, but they were always somewhere else when he'd called on them and he was always somewhere else when they called on him.

Meet me out there . . . somewhere under Orion, she'd said to him, just before he'd left. Just after she'd kissed him. They had sustained him, those words. For years. He'd believed they'd meant something. He saw now that he was wrong.

Willa turned and looked around the room, her eyes darting and searching until they fell upon her brother.

"Albie! We've been looking everywhere for you!" she exclaimed. "Should have known you'd be in the Pick. We've been for a ramble over the fens. Damp's gone right through me! I feel as moldy as a Stilton. Thank God you've got a table by the fire. Move over, will you? Can I have that sandwich? Who's your friend? My God! *Seamie!* Is that you?"

"Hello, Willa."

She gave him a quick, hard hug. Her lips brushed his cheek. And then, as if remembering herself, she introduced him to George Mallory. They all sat down, talking excitedly. More pints were brought. The fire was stoked. Willa and George, though they'd both read about the Discovery Expedition, wanted to hear about it firsthand. Seamie had to tell them everything. About the long voyage out. The storms and blizzards and the unremitting cold. About the scientific studies they'd made. The trek inland with Scott and Shackleton. About the scurvy and snow-blindness that forced them back. They hadn't made the Pole, but they'd gotten close, exploring three hundred miles farther south than anyone ever had.

"How beastly," Mallory said. "To be that close and have to turn back."

Seamie nodded. "It was," he said. "But we're going again. Scott's trying to put something together. Shackleton, too. I'm signing up with whomever gets the funding first."

Seamie had talked himself weary. He said he was parched and started to rise to get another round, but Mallory made him sit down and went to order it himself. Albie excused himself and headed off to the loo. Seamie and Willa were left by themselves—something Seamie had both longed for and dreaded.

Willa sat back against the wall, crossed her arms over her chest, and looked at him. "So it was cold in the Antarctic, was it?" she asked.

"Very."

"I guess that explains it. I guess the ink froze in your pen. That or the wind blew your stamps overboard."

"Post offices are few and far between at 82° 17′ South," Seamie replied testily.

"How about 51° 30′ North? Any post offices there?" Willa fired back, citing London's coordinates.

"What about you?" he asked. "No time to write in the Alps? Too busy drinking schnapps with Gorgeous George?" he said.

"I don't care for schnapps and I didn't see much of George on our Alps trip. He fell ill. Altitude sickness. I didn't. I set a record."

"There's nothing more important than that, is there?"

"You tell me," Willa said, looking daggers at him.

Seamie leaned in toward her. "Did it mean nothing?" he whispered angrily. "What you said about Orion? That kiss you gave me?"

"Not to you, apparently."

He was about to reply when George returned with a tray.

"Toasted cheese sandwiches are on the way," he said, setting four foaming pints down. Albie was right behind him.

George and Albie caught up on mutual Cambridge friends. When they finished talking, there was an uncomfortable silence. To fill it, Seamie asked Mallory what his next adventure would be.

"I'm going to do some rock climbing in the Lake District over the summer," he said. "And after that I want another crack at the Alps." He turned to Willa. "You should come with me again. Try for the women's record on Mont Blanc."

"No. No more women's records. I don't want the women's record," Willa said. "I want the *climber*'s record. Full stop. You know how important it is to be the first. That's how you get to speak at the Royal Geo. How you get your name out there. How you get funded."

"What about Kilimanjaro?" Albie asked. "Can you get a record there?"

"It's already been climbed," Mallory said. "A German and an Austrian did it in 1889."

"They only climbed the Uhuru Peak," Willa said, correcting him. "It's the highest one, but you can scramble it. It's supposed to be a doddle, really, except for the altitude sickness. The Mawenzi Peak's the tough nut. You need to be a good rock climber to take it. A good ice climber, too. That's the one I want."

"Why haven't you done it, then?" Seamie asked, challengingly.

"Because I can't find anyone to go with me," Willa replied curtly.

"What about you, George?" Seamie asked.

"George isn't interested," Willa said.

"Hire some porters, then," Seamie said.

"The only ones available are local tribesmen and they'll go only as far as the mountain's base. They don't like Kilimanjaro. They say it holds bad spirits."

Seamie was about to tell her the bad spirits would make perfect company for her when the sandwiches Mallory had ordered arrived. They all tucked in, reliving past climbs as they ate.

When they finished, Willa said, "Gosh, all this talk about climbing's got the blood up. Feel like a climb right now, me. Who's game for a bit of buildering? Alb?"

Albie, every inch the academic now in his tweeds and spectacles, blinked at her. "Surely you jest," he said.

"George?"

"No, Willa," Mallory said firmly. "And you shouldn't, either. We were both warned. Do you want to spend the night in jail?"

"They'd have to catch me first." She turned to Seamie. "Well?"

He shrugged. "I don't know. I've never done it."

"Scared?"

"No."

"I'll bet you are. I'll also bet I could beat you to the top of St. Botolph's. It's an easy climb. All pits and ruts."

"I don't need easy."

"Ah, but I think you do. Easy pursuits. Easy conquests."

"What's the wager?"

"What do you want?" she asked him, looking him directly in the eye.

"Nothing," he said, hoping to wound. "Nothing at all."

"There must be something."

"Well, maybe there is."

She raised an eyebrow.

"A new pair of hiking boots."

"Done," she said. Her voice was even, but there was a glint of anger in her eyes.

"And if you win?" he said.

"If I win, you climb Kilimanjaro with me."

Seamie sputtered laughter. "I can't do that. Even if I wanted to. Which I don't. I told you—Shackleton's getting an expedition together. I'm going with him if he does. He wants to leave next year. Preparations have to be made. Lots of them."

Willa leaned back in her chair. "I *am* flattered, Seamie. You must think you're going to lose the wager. It's all right. You can back down. You're among friends here. We won't tease you *too* much."

"All right, then," Seamie said, unwilling to be shown up in front of Gorgeous George. "If you're so eager to buy me new boots, the least I can do is let you."

Willa's eyes sparkled. "Good. Let's go," she said.

They paid their bill and left. Outside, Mallory said his good nights.

"Aren't you even coming to cheer me on?" Willa asked, disappointed.

"I'm heading back to my room. I have reading to do."

"Good night, then, darling George," Willa said. She flung her arms around his neck and kissed his cheek. Seamie looked away. He didn't see George puzzlingly touch the place where her lips had been.

"Yes . . . um . . . well, good night," he said, then he disappeared down the street.

"Alb? Are you coming?" Willa asked.

"And watch my sister and my friend splatter themselves all over the cobblestones? I think not."

Willa rolled her eyes. "See you in the morning."

"I certainly hope so. I'll leave the door to my rooms open, should either of you survive."

After Albie had left, Willa turned to Seamie. "St. Botolph's?" she asked.

"St. Botolph's," he replied.

As they set off, she said, "It's a clear night. Plenty of moonlight. Should be good for climbing. And who knows?" she added archly. "If we're lucky, we might just see Orion."

CHAPTER 84

It was quiet on Tower Bridge. The evening rush was largely over. The sun was nearly gone; dusk was settling over London. A few people were still walking over the bridge, stragglers from the City counting houses hurrying home to warm slippers and hot suppers on this brisk March evening.

But one person—a woman—wasn't walking anywhere. She was standing perfectly still, one hand holding the bridge's railing, another clutching a dozen ivory roses. She wore a black coat and hat—mourning attire—and a veil, too, for she did not want to be recognized. It would have made an incongruous sight—Lady India Lytton, wife of Lord Frederick Lytton, undersecretary for the colonies—standing all alone on Tower Bridge. Explanations would be expected and she did not wish to give any. No one knew it—not the people who passed by her on the bridge, not her family, no one in her entire household—but she came here often, as often as she could, to grieve for Sid Malone.

She felt close to him here, standing on the east side of the bridge, looking toward Whitechapel. She could see him as clearly in her mind's eye as if he were standing right next to her. People said you felt it when someone you love died, you felt him or her gone. She'd never felt him gone. She could still hear his voice, feel his touch. Six years after his death he was more alive to her than all the living people she knew—all save one, Charlotte, her daughter. Hers and Sid's.

Charlotte was India's entire life, her only joy. She was the only color and light in her gray world, her rose in winter. And she came here to tell Sid about her.

"She's beautiful," she said softly now. There was no one nearby, no one to hear her. "Beautiful and kind and smart and good. So good. Not just about manners and lessons and such things, she's good in her heart and soul. Just like you were, though you could never believe that about yourself, could you? She'll be six this year. I see you in her, Sid. Every day I see you in her eyes. They're gray, like mine. But the look in them, the way she regards the world . . . that's all you. Her smile, too." India's eyes suddenly clouded, her voice took on a worried tone. "*When* she smiles, that is. She's such a serious child. So watchful. I wish she laughed more. Played more.

Got into trouble occasionally. She needs . . . well, she needs *you*. Her father. Someone besides me to show her things. Teach her things. A real father who will pretend he's a bear and chase her and catch her and throw her up in the air. Freddie has no time for her. Never did." India paused, then said, "He's not fond or affectionate to her, far from it, but he's always treated her as his own. It's one good thing—the only good thing—he's ever done for me."

India thought, though she did not wish to, of her cold, sterile marriage. Having taken Sid from her wasn't enough for Freddie, he'd also taken medicine from her, forbidding her to practice, to even be involved with her clinic in Whitechapel or with her old friends, Ella and Harriet and Fenwick. Instead she was to be a proper society wife, circumspect, irreproachable, concerned only with the nonstop dinners and parties and social rounds that were so crucial to the success of a young politician.

India had honored her part of the bargain as she'd promised she would. She spent her days planning menus and her evenings making small talk with this lord and that lady, stuffy dignitaries, silly new wives and frightful old ones who talked of nothing but horses and dogs. She did these things week after week, month after month, year after year, until everything real and vital inside her withered. The idealistic, committed young woman who had walked the streets of Whitechapel, lecturing the poor, ministering to the ill, was gone. A pale ghost had taken her place.

It might have been different if she'd had more children, but she'd never conceived again—and not for Freddie's lack of trying. He still came to her bed regularly, determined to produce an heir. He was always quick, but it was still horrible for her. She endured it, though, grasping the bedposts, or twisting her hands in the sheets to keep from crying out. Because she had promised that she would.

He blamed her for their lack of a child—a *real* child, as he put it. He accused her of preventing a pregnancy, or terminating one.

"You're doing it to thwart me," he'd say.

"I'm not doing anything, Freddie. I wouldn't. Ever."

"I think you would. Why wouldn't you?"

"Because it would make me like you. Dishonorable."

She knew that she was not the reason they did not have a child together—after all, she had conceived and given birth to one child. It was Freddie. He was sterile. She was certain of it. But she was also certain that he would never admit it to anyone. Least of all himself. So his night visits continued, and somehow she continued to endure them.

India became aware of a stabbing pain in her right hand. She looked at it. She'd clutched the roses she was holding so tightly, she'd driven thorns into her palm. She could feel the blood now, slick and wet, under her gloves.

She unclenched her hand, pulled a few thorns out of it. Freddie thought them ugly—her hands—and told her so. But Sid had liked to hold them, turning them over in his own, smoothing the fingers flat and kissing the palms. She remembered running her hands over his body, cupping his face, kissing his mouth, and pulling him down to her. He'd told her she had power in her hands. And skill and talent. Magic, even. He'd marveled at how such small, slender hands could have such strength, how they could comfort and heal. They were rough then, always red from being scrubbed. Now they were used only to write out place cards and thank-you notes—not to deliver babies, cut away cancers, or soothe the suffering. Now they were soft and smooth and white. A lady's hands, and useless.

As she continued to stare at them, they blurred suddenly. She blinked her tears back. She mustn't go home with red eyes. Freddie wouldn't notice—even if he was at home this evening and not at his club or out bedding the wife of a close friend. But Charlotte, a sensitive and perceptive child, would. She missed nothing and tended to fret if her mother was quiet or inward.

In the distance, a clock chimed the hour. It was six p.m. and India knew she had to get home. There was much to do. Preparations for a long and arduous trip were underway. She and Freddie were leaving for Africa in a fortnight's time, and they were taking Charlotte with them. India had argued horribly with him when he'd announced this, pleading with him to make the trip alone, or with herself only, for she did not wish to expose Charlotte to fevers and blazing sun and snakes and God knew what else, but he was adamant. "You coddle her too much. She'll be fine," he'd said. India had heard the subtle threat in his voice—and heeded it. She knew what would happen if she didn't.

Once, when Charlotte was four and ill with a fever, Freddie had told India that they were invited to Blenheim for the weekend and that they must go. She said she was not going anywhere, not while her child was ill. Freddie had waited a day, until Charlotte had recovered a bit and was sitting up, then he went into the nursery while India was reading to her. "How's our little patient, then?" he'd asked. "Better, thank you, Daddy," she'd said, glowing with pleasure at his attention. She received so little of it. He'd sat down on the bed, taken the book from India, and asked Charlotte to read it to him. Charlotte said she couldn't. He asked her again and again she said she couldn't, she didn't know how. He'd frowned at her, then he told her he was very disappointed in her and that she must be a very stupid little girl not to be able to read at four. Her tiny face had crumpled and she'd burst into tears.

"Now, are we going to Blenheim?" he asked India, over Charlotte's sobs.

"You are evil, Freddie, not just reprehensible, but evil. How could you—"

He'd cut her off. "I asked if we are going to Blenheim."

"Yes," she'd spat.

"Good," he'd said, smiling. And then he'd walked out of the nursery without another word to either of them.

India was defenseless against him. It ripped her heart out to see the look of confusion and pain on Charlotte's face when her handsome, golden father suddenly turned on her, becoming cutting and cruel. Freddie knew it, and he knew she would do anything in her power to prevent it.

India untied the silk ribbon around the bundle of roses and dropped them one by one into the river, watching as the current caught them and carried them away. All of a sudden, her sorrow at losing Sid, at losing everything that once mattered to her, engulfed her. Unable to hold back her tears any longer, she lowered her head and wept. Below her, the swirling waters beckoned, and for a second she rested her weight against the railing and imagined leaning over, farther and farther. She quickly pulled back, horrified at her weakness. Despair made her think such thoughts and she wouldn't give in to it. She would never harm herself, for Charlotte needed her and loved her and she loved her daughter, fiercely and desperately. She watched the roses float farther and farther downstream, until they were only white specks on the gray water.

"I miss you, Sid," she said in a choked voice. "So much. And I love you. I'll always love you."

She folded back her veil to dab at her eyes. The face revealed was not the face Sid Malone had known. There was no passion in it anymore. The cheeks were pallid, the eyes hollow. India pulled the veil back down and left the river, walking north on the bridge, still straight-backed, but slower now, without purpose, without determination. A gaunt and wasted figure against the dark London night.

CHAPTER 85

Fiona Bristow, pregnant again, lumbered into her study and sat down heavily in an easy chair by the fireplace. Joe sat in the chair opposite, reading the Sunday papers, a blanket tucked around his legs. Katie, her seven-year-old daughter, sat on the floor, carefully drawing a picture of flowers and birds with colored pencils. Five-year-old Charlie glued cotton wool onto a paper rabbit he was making for Easter, and three-year-old Peter stacked colorful wooden blocks into towers. Lipton the terrier slumbered by the fire. Twining nibbled at his tail, but Lipton was too tired to do more than give a sleepy growl.

"Are you hungry, my luvs? I've just sent Sarah for tea and scones," she said.

"Famished," Katie said.

"Starved," Charlie said.

"Mmm," little Peter said, nodding.

"Thanks, Fee," Joe murmured, eyes glued to his paper.

Fiona smiled at him and at their children. They were quiet for once. Peaceful and contented. She folded her hands across her large belly and waited, for she knew it couldn't last. And it didn't.

Peter, suddenly bored with his blocks, grabbed the sticky cotton wool Charlie had glued to his rabbit's backside and slapped it onto Katie's picture.

"Mum! *Mum!*" Charlie cried. "Peter took my cotton wool!"

"Mum, look what he's done! He's ruined my picture!" Katie cried.

"Peter, that was very naughty. Apologize to your sister and brother," Fiona said.

But Peter didn't. He laughed.

"You think it's funny, do you?" Katie asked. She leaned forward and pushed his block tower over. "There! How do you like that?"

Peter didn't like it one bit. He started to wail.

"Katie! He's only little!" Fiona scolded.

"But he ruined my picture!"

"He doesn't know any better. You do."

"But look at it, Mum, just look at it," Katie said, reaching to pick it up.

Before she could, however, Twining, tired of not being able to rouse Lipton, snatched it and ran off.

"Muuuuuuum!" Katie howled, close to tears.

Fiona tried to reach for the dog, but, ungainly at seven months, couldn't get out of her chair. "Joe, luv, could you help me out here?" she asked.

Joe lowered his newspaper. "Oi! Peter! Pack it in!" The newspaper went right back up.

Fiona rolled her eyes. "Thanks, Joe," she said.

A truce was called, bruised feelings soothed, order restored. By the time the tea tray arrived, the children were peaceable once more.

Sarah poured cups of coppery Assam tea for everyone and passed a plate of warm currant scones. Joe barely noticed.

"Must be something fascinating in that paper," Fiona said to him.

He looked up at her and grinned. "There is. Me."

Fiona threw a lump of sugar at him.

"Both *The Times* and the *Gazette* wrote about my call for an inquiry into abuses at the Hackney workhouses. I'm going to get two of them closed down. They're hellholes."

"What did you threaten poor Mr. Campbell-Bannerman with this time? Another march on Westminster?"

"No, something even better. Some*one*, rather. Jacob Riis."

"The photographer? Isn't he in New York?"

Fiona knew the name. Riis was an American social reformer whose ground-breaking book on the plight of New York City's poor, *How the Other Half Lives,* had so outraged the American public that they'd demanded their legislators take steps to improve tenement conditions.

Joe nodded. "I've written to him. Asked him to come and snap away in the East End. Said I'd pay his passage and put him up. I'm waiting for his answer. I've already got the *Clarion* signed up to run his stories and photos. Bloke at the *Daily Mail* says he'd be interested, too."

He went back to his article. Fiona's eyes lingered on him and her heart filled with emotion. Six years ago, she wouldn't have thought she could possibly love him more than she already did. But then the shooting happened and he'd nearly been taken from her, and she found that she could. She found that she loved him more than her own life, and would have given her life for his, had it been possible.

He'd spent weeks in a coma, not moving, not talking, just wasting away. His doctors had all but given up on him when he'd suddenly opened his eyes. His first raspy words were "Where's Fee? Where's Katie?" His next were "Where's that bleeding Frankie Betts?"

A few seconds later he'd realized that he could not feel his legs. She would never forget the look on his face. She'd seen him so frightened, so lost, only once before—the day he told her he was leaving her to marry Millie Peterson.

She'd taken his hand and kissed it. "It's all right, love, it's all right," she'd said.

"It's not, Fee. Not by a long shot. But it will be. I promise."

He remembered everything about the shooting, and he was able to tell Alvin Donaldson and Freddie Lytton that it was Betts, not Sid Malone, who had attacked him. It had taken Donaldson a while to find Betts, but he did. Frankie was arrested, tried, and convicted. He should have been hanged, but he claimed he'd only wanted to frighten Joe, not shoot him. He said the pistol had gone off in his hand accidentally and when he tried to drop it, it had fired again. The judge had sentenced him to life in prison.

Joe had survived his injuries, but his doctors told him he would be bedridden for the rest of his life, an invalid.

"You must understand, Mr. Bristow," one of them had said, "that there are always complications. The legs wither. The muscles atrophy. The blood can't circulate properly. Bedsores are common in paraplegics. They often infect and turn gangrenous. I must prepare you for the possibility that you will lose both of your legs."

Fiona had known Joe her entire life, had known him to be a good man, a brave man, but even she had never truly known what he was made of. Not until she'd watched him defy the fate his doctors had set before him.

Two days after he'd arrived home, he'd had a gymnasium installed in their house. He had parallel bars set up, had his legs braced, and made himself walk between them. The braces bit into his flesh. His arms, weakened by months in a hospital bed, shook with the effort of supporting his body. After a few minutes, they gave out and he fell to the floor. Fiona had run to him then, tears in her eyes, begging him to stop, but he had pushed her away, furious.

"No, *you* stop!" he'd shouted. "Stop worrying. Stop hovering."

"I'm sorry. I didn't mean . . . I . . . I . . . felt for you, that's all."

"I don't want your pity, Fiona. I can take the falls, I can take the pain, but I can't take pity. Not from you."

He kept going, exercising tirelessly, working his fragile body mercilessly day after day. He kept working his legs until the muscle regained its tone. He brought in masseurs to rub his numbed flesh and keep the blood flowing. He accepted that he would never feel his legs again, but he was not prepared to lose them or his life. He became healthy again and strong. He had defied his doctors. Next he would defy the world.

Six months after he'd been shot, Joe announced he was going to run for Parliament again. He'd had to relinquish his Tower Hamlets seat because his injuries had made him incapable of fulfilling his duties, but now he was capable and a new seat had become available. The MP for Hackney had died and a by-election was about to be held.

Westminster thought his announcement was a joke. So did the press and the people in the street—until Joe, in the wheelchair he'd had fitted with a small engine, motored up to pub doors in Hackney, and factory gates, and union halls, and began campaigning with even more passion, more fire, than he had before.

Fiona, Katie, and baby Charlie were all with him the day he'd taken his oath and was sworn in as a Member of Parliament. It was the proudest day of their lives. When they'd walked out of Westminster they were nearly blinded by camera flashes. Joe, the fighter, the East End lad who never quit, had made the people of London fall in love with him from the moment he'd begun his campaign and the love affair had only grown.

And as if having her Joe back, well and happy in his new political role, wasn't enough, Fiona shortly found herself expecting another child. Joe had made it clear when he came home from the hospital that some things might have changed, but it would be business as usual in the bedroom, tumbling into bed with her—literally tumbling—the first chance he got.

"Two of me legs don't work anymore, lass," he'd said, "but me third one still does. I'd have finished Betts's work for him if it didn't."

They'd struggled a bit, but they'd finally found their way. She'd gotten pregnant with Peter a year after Charlie was born. And soon she would have their fourth.

Joe put his paper down now and asked for a scone. She slathered one with thick cream and strawberry jam and handed it to him. She looked at him again as he took it, and at their children, and thought that there was no woman on earth more blessed than she was. Charlie held his cup out to her, asking for more milky tea. His emerald-green eyes caught hers, he smiled his cheeky little boy's smile, and for a moment he looked so much like his namesake—his uncle Charlie—that her heart hurt and she had to look away.

Fiona still blamed herself for what had happened to Joe. She still felt that if she had not searched for her brother, had not meddled in his world,

Frankie Betts would not have come after Joe. She missed Charlie. She hoped he was safe wherever he was. She hoped he was loved. She wished desperately that he could be with them, around the fire, not out in the world alone. She grieved for him sometimes, but she did not speak of him anymore, and she never would. She had come close, so close, to becoming a widow. Katie and Charlie had come so close to growing up without their father. And now here they were, she and Joe, with their children. And that was enough. She knew that for the rest of her life, she would never ask for more than this.

"Uncle Seamie! Uncle Seamie!" Katie suddenly cried. Charlie and Peter joined in.

Fiona turned toward the door and saw her other brother walking into the room.

"How was Cambridge?" Katie asked. "Did you bring us something?"

"Katie, how rude!" Fiona said. "Hello, Seamie, luv."

"Hi, Fee. Hi, Joe," Seamie said. He turned to his niece and nephews and affected a remorseful look. "I'm afraid I was so busy visiting friends that I forgot to go shopping," he said.

Three little faces fell.

"I'm joking!" he quickly said. "Here, presents for all." He dug in his rucksack amid excited squeals and pulled out an uncle's offering of totally unsuitable gifts: a compass for Katie, a clasp-knife for Charlie, and a slab of Kendal mint cake for little Peter. Fiona thanked him, then quickly removed the knife and mint cake from her sons' clutches, quieting their cries of outrage by redirecting their attention to the compass.

"How was your visit?" Joe asked, as Seamie swiped a scone from the tray.

"Fine, but it looks like I won't be able to make Easter dinner next Sunday."

"Oh, dear. Why not?" Fiona asked, disappointed.

"I'm off traveling again."

"Did Shackleton's rich uncle die?" Joe asked. "How did he get the money together for another trip so fast?"

Seamie sat down and shook his head. "I'm afraid I'm not going to the Antarctic. I'm going somewhere else. I made a really stupid bet and lost. And now I'm going to Africa. To climb Kilimanjaro."

"Africa!" said Katie excitedly. "Will you bring us a tiger, Uncle Seamie?"

"A zebra?" asked Charlie.

"An ellyfint?" said Peter.

"All those and more," Seamie said.

"Hurray!" the children cheered.

"For goodness' sake, Seamie, don't tell them that," Fiona scolded. "They'll think you mean it."

"*Africa?*" Joe said over the din. "Cor, lad, you must have had some hand to make a bet like that."

"We weren't playing cards. Wish we had been. I might have stood a better chance. We were climbing."

"With whom?"

"Remember Albie Alden?"

"Of course," Fiona said. "Is that who you're going with?"

"No, not with him. With his mad sister."

Fiona and Joe traded glances.

"Don't even start, you two. It's not like that."

Fiona, unconvinced, raised an eyebrow.

"Willa Alden's not my type. And besides, she's got a bloke."

"Why isn't he going with her?" Fiona asked.

"He can't. He's at university. He has exams."

"What does he say about you going off round the world with his girl?" Joe asked.

"Have you met Willa?"

Joe shook his head. "I don't think so."

"If you had, you'd know that it doesn't matter what George says. Or anyone else, for that matter. She wants to go, and she's going. She would've gone weeks ago, but she didn't have a climbing partner. Now she has. Me." He let out a sigh, then said, "If we do it, we'll set a record on one of Kili's peaks. Make a bit of a name for ourselves. It could turn out to be quite a good trip. For both of us."

"When do you leave?" Fiona asked.

"This Friday."

"That's so soon!"

"I know. I'll barely have time to get my kit together."

"Is it a tall mountain?" Fiona asked.

Seamie laughed. "Quite. The peak we're climbing is over sixteen thousand feet."

"You will be careful, won't you? You'll wear something warm?"

"You bet, Fee," he said. "I'll take my muffler and galoshes and a hot water bottle, too."

Fiona bit her lip. "I'm mothering you again, aren't I? I promised not to. You went all the way to the South Pole and back—"

"Almost all the way."

"And here I am telling you to bundle up. Sorry, luv. I can't seem to help myself."

Seamie smiled. He patted her hand. He was being a good sport. She knew he found her worrying irritating and imagined that she was driving him barmy. She vowed, yet again, to stop.

Fiona had no idea, none whatsoever, that he wasn't irritated with her. Not at all. He was looking at her—as she held a tired Peter in her lap, with Lipton tugging at Joe's blanket and Joe yelling at him and Charlie dripping jam on the floor and Katie sloshing tea—and wishing just for a second that he had what she had. A home. A family. A life. Someone who loved him. Wishing to God that he wasn't about to set off on a trek halfway around the world with a wild and beautiful girl who loved somebody else.

CHAPTER 86

India Lytton took off her eyeglasses and rubbed her temples, trying to massage away a headache. The house was unbearably noisy. They were to depart for Africa in five days' time, and though preparations had been under way for weeks, there was still much to do. She was sitting in her drawing room with Miss Lucinda Billingsley, her secretary, going over the itinerary and packing list for the Kenya trip.

"And on the following Thursday you go to Nairobi," Miss Billingsley said, "to the governor's mansion, where you'll stay for five days, during which time you'll—"

They were interrupted by the sound of the doorbell. Again. A few minutes later the butler appeared in the doorway, clearing his throat.

"Who is it, Edwards?" India asked.

"Lord Frederick's secretary, madam," the butler said.

"Show him to Lord Frederick's study, please," India said.

The doorbell sounded again. A few minutes later India saw Mary, her maid, scurry by laden with bolts of khaki twill. She remembered that Charlotte had gone upstairs for a fitting with Mrs. Pavlic, the dressmaker, at nine o'clock. It was now nearly eleven.

"Mary?" India called after her.

Mary stopped in the doorway. "Yes, Lady Lytton?"

"Where is Charlotte?"

"In her room, madam. Being fitted."

"Two hours is far too long for a child of her age to be kept standing still for a fitting. What is going on? Why hasn't Miss Gibson brought her down yet? They should have left for the park by now."

"Lord Frederick detained Miss Lytton in her room, madam. Along with Miss Gibson."

"*What?* Why?" India said, immediately getting to her feet.

"He said Miss Lytton had not made enough progress in her studies."

"Thank you, Mary. Excuse me, Lucinda. That will be all for now."

"But Lady Lytton, we haven't finished . . ."

India didn't hear what it was they hadn't finished and she didn't care. She was already out of the drawing room and heading for the stairs. She was frightened for her child. The wolf had gotten into the nursery. And it was her fault. All her fault. She should have been paying more attention.

Charlotte's door was ajar and India could hear Freddie's voice, stern and displeased, as she hurried down the hallway.

"Major exports?" he was saying.

And then Charlotte's small voice, nervous and hesitating, "Coffee, sisal, ox hides, wool, copra—"

"Again. In *descending* order of value, please."

There was a pause, then, "Ox hides, coffee, sisal, wool, copra—"

"Copra *before* wool. Haven't I already told you that? And you forgot beeswax."

"I'm sorry, Father, I—"

"See if you can do any better with imports."

"Flour, sugar, tea . . ."

India pushed the door open all the way. Charlotte was standing on a footstool in front of a cheval mirror. Her hands were clenched. Her face was pinched and weary. She raised her eyes to India's and India could see she was struggling to hold back tears. At her feet, Mrs. Pavlic, India's dressmaker, was pinning a hem, not daring to take her gaze off her work. Miss Gibson, Charlotte's governess, was standing nearby, a pained expression on her face.

"What is going on here?" India asked. "You're tiring her. Can't you see that? Is this really necessary?" Her voice, steady and calm, betrayed nothing, but she could have beaten Freddie bloody, and gladly.

"It's her fault," Freddie said. "I set her some lessons. She hasn't learned them."

"I tried, Father," Charlotte said weakly.

"Trying means nothing. Any fool can try. Are you a fool?"

"No, sir," she whispered.

"Then you must succeed. Now, imports."

"Freddie . . ." India began, hatred blazing in her eyes.

Freddie turned his own eyes on her. The look in them cautioned her. *Not in front of the servants,* it said. India knew better than to defy him. He had ways of getting even with her. Many ways.

"Your secretary is here. He's in your study," she said tightly, hoping to draw the beast off.

Freddie rose. "Miss Gibson, I'm disappointed," he said. "I specifically asked you to drill Charlotte on British East African imports and exports and on Kenya's topographical features. I will ask these same questions to-morrow and I expect to see an improvement."

"Yes, Lord Frederick," Miss Gibson replied.

When Freddie was in the hallway, India closed the door to Charlotte's room so that neither she nor the servants would hear her.

"How dare you! She is a *child*! Not a damned trained monkey!" she hissed.

"She is no mere child, India. She is *my* child, is she not? Isn't that what you wanted her to be? She is the undersecretary for the colonies' child. She will be expected to attend official functions in Africa and make conversation with adults. She must impress *them* and she must not embarrass *me*. See to it."

And with that, he left. India watched him walk away. This was the game they played—she and Freddie. He was warning her. Reminding her that she was not to put a foot wrong in Africa. Nor was Charlotte. Neither was to do anything that might reflect badly on him, that might slow his climb to Number 10. Otherwise there would be repercussions. Small cruelties. And large ones.

India knew Charlotte would be upset, so she quickly returned to her. "That will be all for now, Mrs. Pavlic," she said. The dressmaker quickly gathered her things and left.

"Lady Lytton," Miss Gibson said. "She is trying hard. Very hard."

"But are you, Miss Gibson?" India snapped. "Make it a game. Make rhymes. Make acronyms from the words. Do *something*. Find a way. I will not have a repeat of what just happened. Do you understand me?"

Miss Gibson nodded and India dismissed her. She was harsh, but she couldn't help it. She spent so much of her time trying to make sure Freddie had no cause to reproach Charlotte. It was a life lived on tenterhooks, and it took its toll.

As soon as Miss Gibson was gone, Charlotte threw herself onto her bed. "I hate him, Mummy. I hate him," she sobbed.

"Shh, Charlotte," India said, sitting down next to her. "He's your father. You mustn't say such things."

"I shall run away once we're in Africa. See if I don't!"

India stroked her daughter's back. "Oh, I hope not. I couldn't bear it if you did. I would be so sad. What would I do without you?"

Charlotte turned over. "You could come with me, Mummy," she said, sniffling. "British East Africa is very large. I know it is. Father made me memorize the area in square miles. They'd never find us."

India wiped the tears from her daughter's cheeks. Each drop that fell felt like acid eating away at her heart. "Where do you think we should go, my love?" she asked Charlotte, lying down with her.

"Well, we could go to the Sahara, but we'd need camels. We could go into the jungle like Mowgli and Bagheera. Or we could go to the sea. We could sneak off when the boat docks in Africa. It'll be ever so busy, Mummy. No one would see us go. Miss Gibson's been to Mombasa. She says it's very hectic. She says the ocean is blue like turquoise. And that there are parrots and monkeys and the most beautiful flowers you've ever seen."

"And what would we do at sea, the two of us? Tell me a story about us."

"We'd be pirates!" Charlotte said. "We'd wear red skirts and eye patches and pink flowers behind our ears."

"Eye patches *and* flowers?" India exclaimed. "Wouldn't we make a sight?"

"Yes! And we'd wear lots and lots of jewels, too. Great big ruby rings and diamond necklaces that we'd stolen. And we'd have a treasure chest full of gold coins."

"Where would we keep it all?"

"In a huge yellow boat. We'll sail it on the turquoise sea. And it will be so warm and bright on the water and so much nicer than it is here. I love the sea, Mummy, don't you? I should like to live by the sea forever and ever."

Sid had loved the sea, India remembered. He had wanted to live by it, too. Just as his daughter did. To wake up in a house on the coast. With the sun streaming in the windows. He almost had. At Point Reyes. India had never sold that land. She never would. It was their land. Oh, if only Charlotte could have known him. Her *real* father.

"Is my story making you sad, Mummy?" Charlotte suddenly asked, her small face worried.

"Oh, no, darling. Not at all," India said.

"But you looked sad."

"I was thinking, that's all. I was wondering if a yellow boat would be best or if we might prefer a purple one."

"What about yellow *and* purple? A stripy boat!" Charlotte said, smiling. "One with a sunburst on its sails. That would be much nicer than an old skull and crossbones."

India smiled, too, glad to see her daughter happy again. She wondered, as she'd done a million times, if she had done the right thing by her. She had sought to protect Charlotte from the ugliness of a harsh world by marrying Freddie. But had she? Sometimes she did not know. Sometimes she thought there was nothing uglier in all the world than her own husband.

"And then we'll run away to a secret island. Far, far away."

I *should* have run away with you. Long ago. Before you were born, India thought. What have I done to you? Sometimes she thought that living in the meanest slum, just the two of them, without Freddie, would have been better than living here in Berkeley Square with him.

But she also knew that slum children grew sickly, when they grew at all. Slum children were hungry and dirty and worked in factories. Charlotte had her own hardships—namely Freddie—but she would never suffer hunger or poverty. And what her life was now, in Freddie's house, was not what it would always be. One day she would be grown, and would come into money set aside for her by her grandfather. She could leave Berkeley Square, and Freddie, and make her own life, a happy life, with all the advantages money and pedigree and a proper upbringing could afford.

"We'll do that one day, won't we, Mummy? We'll run away to the sea and live there. You and me. In our boat. Or maybe a pretty house on the seashore all decorated with shells. We'll have a lovely life then, won't we?"

India knew that she herself would never have a lovely life. Never. But Charlotte would. She would see to it. She had given up so much to make sure of that. She would give up more. Everything she had, in fact, to ensure her daughter's future happiness.

"Yes, my darling, we will be pirates in a cottage by the sea."

It was a lie, but she had told the child worse. That Freddie was her father. And that he cared for her.

Charlotte snuggled against her mother. "I'm glad we will. Even if it's only a story."

"A very lovely story," India said.

Charlotte lifted her head and looked at her. "Lovely stories come true *sometimes*, don't they, Mummy?"

India smiled at her and nodded and let her think so. It was easier that way. And kinder. So much kinder than telling her the truth.

CHAPTER 87

Nairobi was a swamp.

The rains had turned its red dirt streets to mud so thick and deep that it mired wagon wheels, held oxen fast, and sucked men's boots off their feet. Sid had made the two-day trek from Thika to buy supplies for Maggie. He'd had to leave his wagon at the train depot and walk into town.

He'd been to the blacksmith's to have yokes and tools mended, to the Indian bazaar for salt and spices, the gunsmith's for bullets, and the Norfolk Stores for iodoform, quinine, and whisky. He'd also bought paraffin, candles, four fifty-pound bags of flour, newspapers, bootlaces, soap, and Worcestershire sauce. His final stop had been Elliot's bakery, where he'd bought a fruitcake. Maggie was partial to them.

After he'd tied down all his purchases in the back of the wagon and covered them with a tarpaulin, he headed back into town for his very last stop—the Norfolk Hotel for a drink or two. As he walked, finally free of Maggie's endless shopping list, he allowed himself to look the place over. Nairobi was not a lovely place, but that's why he loved it. It put on no airs, made no pretenses. It took people as it found them and expected the courtesy to be returned.

The town owed its existence to the bosses of the Uganda railway, which ran between Mombasa and Lake Victoria. They'd been laying tracks for three years, east to west, and when they reached mile 327, a flat patch of river-fed land the Masai called Engore Nyarobe—the Place of Cold Water—they decided it would be a good location to quarter workers and ready supplies for the arduous push into the highlands.

As Sid squelched his way through the muddy streets, he saw several bush families who'd come to town for provisions. He could always tell them apart from town families for they walked single file, even in Nairobi's wide streets, as if they were still on a narrow bush path and determined to avoid thorns and ticks. He counted ten new buildings going up on his way to the Norfolk, and saw dozens of carpenters and painters freshening up the façades of the older ones on Station Road and Victoria Street.

Nairobi might have begun as a railway camp, but it had become a boom town. Shabby wooden *dukas* now rubbed elbows with smart new hotels and wide-windowed shops where women bought kid shoes and lawn dresses. The Norfolk had imported a French chef to cook for its guests, and afternoon tea could be had on Duke Street. Balls were given at the governor's house, and race days at the newly built track were festive social occasions. A handful of government buildings constructed from stone lent a note of gravitas to Nairobi and telegraph poles gave it an air of modernity, but one look up and down its streets told even the most casual observer that it was still very much a frontier town. Victoria Street had its brothels, wash houses, and opium dens, and the town was largely populated by speculators, ne'er-do-wells, and eccentrics.

Sid greeted a handful of them as he stepped onto the Norfolk's veranda. Ali Kahn, the town's transport baron, was unloading passengers and trunks from his wagon. They'd shared the ride up from the depot with chickens, goats, and a piano. The Goanese doctor, Rosendo Ribeiro, was sitting in a rattan chair, enjoying a glass of lemon squash. Sid guessed he'd be here, for he'd seen his zebra—the one he rode to see patients—hitched to a post. When he reached the foyer, Sid heard Lord Delamere, a wild and fearless English baron with twenty thousand Kenyan acres, holding forth in the bar. Pioneer Mary, a peddler who strode through the bush like she owned it, a rhino-hide whip at her hip, was in there, too. She could drink Delamere under the table, and often ended her binges by riding off on her mule backward.

"That you, Bax?" Delamere called as Sid walked toward the bar.

Sid tipped his hat. "I'm afraid so," he said.

Jo Roos, Maggie's planter neighbor, was at Delamere's table, along with the Cole brothers, who were also big landowners, and a few other men. Sid had lived in the bush for five years, spending every single day with the Kikuyu, and he now saw his own people much as they did—as either decent whites or sods. Some at Del's table were one or the other. Some were both, depending on the time of day and how much they'd had to drink.

"We've got your neighbor here," Delamere said. "We're holding him for ransom."

Sid looked at Roos, who was nursing a whisky. Jo, a Boer settler who'd come north from Pretoria, was a miserable bastard, always complaining.

"You can keep him," Sid said. "I'm not paying."

Roos scowled, the others laughed.

"Sit down with us, Bax. Have a drink," Delamere said.

Sid sat, feeling a bit out of place, for he knew that Del and the others thought him an odd duck. They didn't understand why he didn't apply for a land grant. They didn't understand why he refused to guide wealthy sports to big game when he could have made a fortune doing so. And most of all, they couldn't understand how he got on so well with the Kikuyu. It was known that he genuinely liked them and that they liked him, too. The men at the Norfolk didn't understand these things, but they welcomed Sid anyway, knowing that one couldn't be too particular about one's company in Nairobi, or one would not have any.

Bottles of whisky and gin were brought and downed as the group talked politics and planting and traded scraps of news and hearsay.

"Hear about the DC for Turkhana?" Roos asked.

Turkhana was a remote posting. Sid knew that its district commissioner was up there by himself.

"Went mad with loneliness. Hanged himself."

"You *would* know that, Jo," Sid said. "How'd you find out?"

"DC for Baringo told me. He was here yesterday. He's the one who found him. Said he'd hang himself, too, if only he could find a tree tall enough to get the job done."

Delamere changed the subject. Isolation and its hard consequences cut a bit too close to the bone for every man at the table. "How's Maggie? How's the farm?" he asked Sid. "Still planting coffee?"

Sid nodded. "We've seven hundred acres under coffee right now," he said. "About to plant two hundred more. And she's thinking of trying some sisal, too. Fifty acres or so. Just to see what it'll do."

"It's good land for coffee, Thika," Delamere said. "High, but not too high."

"You can have the best land in the world. It's not worth a damn unless you find men to work it," Roos said morosely. "The Kikuyu won't work for me. I can't get one bloody man to work in my fields. I offer them money, good money, but they don't take it. Why is that, Bax?"

"Ever see lions on the plains, Jo?"

"Yes."

"Ever watch the sunset at Thika?"

"You insane, man? Of course I have. I live there, don't I?"

"That's why."

"Eh?"

"That's why the Africans won't take our money. What would they do with it? Buy tea sets and jam pots and pictures of the king? Why would they want that rubbish? They have Africa."

Jo looked at him with an uncomprehending scowl.

"I'm afraid your poetry's lost on him, old chap," Delamere said.

"*You* get your coffee harvested, Bax," Jo said stubbornly. "How? How do you do it?"

Sid shook his head. If Jo would only take ten minutes to get to know the tribal people, he'd have his answer. "Deal with the women, not the men," he said.

Jo nodded. "Because the lazy buggers won't work—"

"Because the men won't *farm*," Sid said. "In their villages, farming is women's work. It'd be like you and me hanging out the wash or knitting booties. It's not done. Deal with the women. They're the ones with the business sense."

"They take Maggie's money?"

"No, but they take goats, blankets, and lanterns. Quinine, salve, cloth. And toys for their children. Women'll do anything for their kiddies. That's how they are."

Sid knew that to be true. He'd seen it in the Kikuyu mothers just as he'd seen it in the Whitechapel mothers. In a small, bustling medical clinic set up in the yard of a caff on Brick Lane. He quickly pushed the memory down as he did with all of his memories of India. Then he looked at the clock. It was nearly four p.m. He'd spent two hours drinking and gassing. It was time to make a start. He wanted to be well north of Nairobi by dark.

"Well, gentlemen, it's been a pleasure," he said, "but I've a bit of a walk ahead of me."

"Oh! One thing before you go," Delamere said, "I meant to tell you. I had dinner with the DC for Kenya Province last week and he told me he's looking for a guide."

"For hunters?" Sid asked.

"No, for a surveyor. Last chap who went out was eaten by a python as he crossed the Chinga. Damned snake got his satchel. Swallowed every map he'd made. The new man says he won't take one step out of Nairobi without a guide. No one knows Kenya better than you, Bax, and the pay's good. You should consider it. Give you something to do between planting and harvesting."

"I will. Thanks," Sid said.

As he rose to leave, a pair of painters bustled through the taproom carrying a ladder. Sid recalled all the renovation he'd seen on his walk through town. "What's going on round here?" he asked.

"Don't you know?" Del asked.

"Wouldn't be asking if I did."

"We've a visitor coming from home. The undersecretary for the colonies."

Sid remembered Maggie saying something about that. "Elgin, is it?" he asked.

"No, that's the secretary himself. It's . . . um . . . oh, blast, what *is* his name?" Delamere grabbed a newspaper off an empty chair. "It's in here somewhere," he said, scanning the front page. "It'll be quite the social event."

"It'll be balls and banquets and a lot of bloody promises made, that's what it'll be," Roos said glumly.

"You forgot hunting," Del said. "The bloke'll certainly want to bag a lion. They all do. Ah! Here it is. Lytton."

Sid had been digging in his trouser pocket for a few coins for the barmaid. He stopped and looked at Delamere. "What did you say?" he asked quietly.

"Lytton. Freddie Lytton. Says here that he's bringing a whole battalion of underlings with him. His daughter, too. And his wife, Lady India Lytton. I knew her parents, God rest them, Lord Burnleigh was richer than Midas and a damned good—" Delamere suddenly stopped speaking. He frowned with concern. "I say, Bax, old boy, are you all right? You've gone white as a bloody ghost!"

CHAPTER 88 ❧

"Oh, just look at it, Seamie! Did you ever dream Africa would be like this? All turquoise and red and purple?"

"No, I didn't. I thought it would be sort of brown," Seamie said. "With zebras."

Seamie and Willa stood on deck of the SS *Goorka,* staring like two wide-eyed children at the aspect of Mombasa. Foaming breakers thundered toward its white seawalls, rising sheer and majestic out of the shimmering Indian Ocean. Massive baobab trees ringed the harbor, their trunks thick and stolid-looking next to the airy palms and lush green mango trees. Vivid bougainvillea tumbled down walls and spilled over cliffs. Beyond a tall lighthouse, the heavy battlements of a fort rose into a brilliant blue sky.

"Look over there. It's Fort Jesus, and it's *pink*!" Willa cried. "Just like the book said."

She had brought along a dozen books on East Africa from which she read aloud every night at supper. Last night they'd learned that Portuguese conquerors had taken the city from Arab slavers in the 1500s, building a massive fort to protect it. Two hundred years later it had fallen again, to the Sultan of Oman. In 1840, the wily Sultan of Zanzibar had taken it and had later asked the British to protect it. His crimson flag still flew over the fort, reminding the British that they might currently hold the city, but only on his sufferance.

The *Goorka* had only just slipped through the *mlango*, an opening in the enormous coral reef that protected the harbor, and was now anchoring about forty yards offshore. Boatmen in slender wooden dhows were already rowing out to take passengers ashore.

"I can't believe it! We're here, Seamie! We made it! *Africa!*" Willa said. She grabbed his forearm and squeezed it. It hurt. He didn't care. "What should we do first? See the fort? The village?"

"I think we should send our gear ahead to the hotel and try to find our man from the outfitters."

"Yes, you're right. Good idea. God, but I can't wait to get off this boat!"

"That makes two," Seamie said.

The journey had taken six long weeks on a clanking steamer that had stopped at Malta, Cyprus, and Port Said, poked its way through the Suez Canal, then stopped again at Aden. For Seamie, who'd made a journey to Antarctica on a well-provisioned ship whose crew was determined to reach their destination speedily, the *Goorka* seemed to move at a snail's pace. At every port, fresh water had to be taken on board, as well as livestock, which was put belowdecks to be slaughtered as needed. Willa, impatient for new sights and tired of being confined to the ship for days on end, always insisted on exploring the ports. At Cyprus, and again at Aden, she'd tarried so long that they'd had to run like hell to avoid being left behind.

He looked at her now, as she pulled out her notebook, her beautiful eyes wide with excitement, and his heart ached with longing.

"You've been scribbling in that thing ever since we left Blighty," he said. "What are you doing?"

"Writing it all down. Every bit of it."

"Why?"

"For my paper. The one I intend to give at the Royal Geo when we get back to London. After I've given it, I'm going to make it into a book—a travelogue—and sell thousands of copies so I can finance my next trip. Did that when I climbed McKinley and made a bundle. How shall I describe you, Seamie? Would you rather be an *accomplished explorer* or a *brilliant explorer*?"

Seamie thought, I would rather be your lover, Willa. Neither accomplished nor brilliant, but yours. He said, "How about brilliant *and* accomplished?"

"And let's not forget modest."

He turned away from her and squinted into the sun, worried his emotion might show. This was a mistake, he thought. I should never have come to Africa with her. He should never have taken her up on her dare. Back in Cambridge, he had thought himself in love with her. Now he knew he was.

Every day spent with her was an adventure. Everything they did was exciting. The meal of red grapes and salty cheese they'd eaten with their fingers in Cyprus. The veiled women they'd seen on the balconies of Aden. The merchants and their camels. The spice markets and cloth markets, the voices of the muezzins calling the faithful to prayer. No woman he'd ever met was as curious and fearless—as passionately alive—as Willa. And he had never felt himself to be as alive as when she grabbed his hand and went whooping down piers, pounding down docks, hollering for the crew to hold the boat, they were coming, damn it! They were coming!

What would his life be after this trip? Ruined, that's what. He would never be able to forget her or the time they'd spent together. He'd never be able to fall in love, because loving anyone else would only ever be second best and wrong.

He'd almost told her how he felt a dozen times or more. He'd been close, so close, the words had been on the tip of his tongue, but then he'd remembered that she belonged to someone else. And he would imagine the embarrassment he'd cause her, the pity in her eyes for him as he made his unwanted confession, and he would stop himself.

"We're off, then!" a voice bellowed from behind him, startling him out of his sadness. It was Eamon Edmonds and his wife, Vera. They were a newlywed couple, aiming to plant coffee in the Ngong Hills. Seamie and Willa had become friendly with them, and with other settler couples, during the long journey.

"Oh, Vera, I'll miss you!" Willa said, hugging her tightly.

"I'll miss you, too, Wills. Wave to us from the top of Kili, won't you?"

The two women hugged again. Eamon and Seamie shook hands and then one of the porters was handing Vera over the side of the ship to a ladder, which she used to climb down to a waiting dhow.

Seamie and Willa weren't far behind. They had to lower their rucksacks into the boat first, followed by their climbing gear and tent. They would have to procure everything else they needed—and the porters needed to carry it—in town with the help of Newland & Tarlton, a firm of safari outfitters. They'd estimated they'd need four or five days to arrange it all.

Seamie was glad to get off the boat, glad to be on land again. But more than that, he was eager to start the trek to Kilimanjaro. Eager to distract himself with the planning and provisioning and the hard work of mountaineering. Eager to forget how much he wanted Willa.

They reached the noisy, bustling docks, paid their boatman, then engaged a man with a donkey cart to take their gear to the Mombasa Club. There was a sprawl of narrow pathways leading from the port into the town, but only one thoroughfare that could properly be called a street. It was named after the Portuguese explorer Vasco da Gama. Their contact, Peter Boedeker, had premises there.

"Vasco da Gama Street," Willa said longingly. "Think there'll be a Seamus Finnegan Street one day?" she asked. "Or a Willa Alden Avenue?" She was walking with her head back, the better to take in the minarets and domes of the Arabian town, and the pretty whitewashed houses, their shutters closed against the shimmering heat. She stumbled once and nearly fell, but Seamie caught her.

After a ten-minute walk they arrived at number 46, a white stone building with a small brass plaque advertising the services of Newland & Tarlton, Safari Outfitters.

"Remember, Wills, we're here for a safari. Sightseers, that's what we are."

Willa nodded. They climbed a flight of stairs and found the office on the first floor. The door was open.

"Mr. Boedeker?" Seamie called, walking in. Willa followed him. It was a small room containing a desk, a few chairs, and a filing cabinet. Maps of Africa were hung on the walls.

A man, blond and muscular, was seated at the desk. Seamie thought he might be in his thirties, but his face was so weathered and lined from the sun that he looked more like fifty.

At the sound of Seamie's voice, he looked up. "Mr. Finnegan, Miss Alden. I've been expecting you. Heard the *Goorka* was due in today. Sit down, won't you? How was your trip?"

As Seamie and Willa sat and began to tell him about their sea voyage, Boedeker said a few words in Swahili to a boy seated cross-legged in a corner. The boy dashed out. Before they had finished, he was back again with three tall, slender glasses of hot minty tea, heavily sugared. Boedeker sipped his, then he opened a folder and took out the telegram Willa had sent him before they'd left London.

"Says here you're interested in a safari. West to Kilimanjaro." He gave them each a long look, then said, "What do you want with Kili, then, eh?"

"We want to see it," Seamie said.

Peter nodded thoughtfully. "And you want to see it from this side of the border, correct?"

"Correct," Willa replied.

"You weren't thinking of trying to climb it, by any chance, were you?"

"Climb it?" Willa echoed innocently. "Oh, no."

Boedeker nodded. "Good. Because, as I'm sure you both know, the mountain lies within German East Africa. If you were to cross into GEA at any of the border towns, the Germans would want your documents. They'd inspect your gear and they'd want to know why you're there. If they thought you—an American and a Briton—were there to climb their mountain, they might deny you entry. If you decided to sneak in anyway and got caught, you might be jailed."

Seamie knew Kili belonged to the Germans. Willa did, too. They hoped to get around them by trekking to the mountain under cover of its surrounding jungle. If they made it up, they'd hightail it back to Mombasa and not make their feat public until they were back home. They were taking chances, they knew they were, but they didn't care. They both strongly felt that a mountain—any mountain—belonged not to nations or peoples, but to those who climbed it.

"We just want to get to the border," Seamie said. "Take a few photographs."

"Right, then. I'm going to set you up for a lovely little camping trip to Taveta, just east of the border, so you can have a good old hike through the bush and then take a nice gander at Kili, all right?"

Seamie and Willa nodded. Seamie felt relieved that Boedeker had bought their story and was not going to be troublesome. The three spent some time discussing the quantity and weight of the gear, the food and drink that would be required, and the trip's duration. Both Seamie and Willa had legacies from relatives that funded their trips, but neither legacy was unlimited, and they were both careful with their money. They were both willing to carry gear to economize on the amount of men needed. With that in mind, Boedeker eventually decided that nine porters plus a headman would be sufficient.

"Ten men for two people," Seamie said. "Seems like an army."

"That's nothing," Boedeker said. "Last safari I did, for a party of twenty wealthy Americans—now that was a headache. Fifty crates of champagne, twenty more of whisky, Waterford glasses, Wedgwood china, sterling cutlery, linen for the tables, eight-course dinners . . . I needed a hundred porters on that one. Line stretched out from Nairobi for a mile."

Boedeker told them that he'd have their arrangements made in five days' time at the most. They would provision here, then take the train to Voi—a small town in Kenya Province about sixty miles northwest of Mombasa. They'd be met there by their headman, a Masai tribesman named Tepili. He and the nine porters under his command would get them to Taveta.

Seamie and Willa paid Boedeker and thanked him. He said he would send word to the Mombasa Club as soon as their plans were in place.

They shook hands and Boedeker saw them to the door. As they were about to leave, he said, "Miss Alden, Mr. Finnegan . . . may I give you a few words of advice?"

"Certainly," Seamie said.

Boedeker's genial smile was gone. The look in his eyes was deadly serious as he said, "Beware of the Chagga. Use them if you must, but do not turn your backs on them. When you near the border—and I suggest you cross it well north of Taveta—you'll be in Chagga territory. They're the best guides—no one knows the land around Kili like they do—but they are highly unpredictable. They've killed both Germans and British. Make sure you bring gifts. They are partial to knives and mirrors."

"Cross the border? But we never said—" Willa began.

"I know what you said. I also know who you are. You, Miss Alden, have set records in the Alps and on McKinley."

"How did you know that?"

"I follow the mountaineering news. I'm a bit of a climber myself, you see. I've heard of you, too, Mr. Finnegan. I followed the Discovery Expedition. As did most of the rest of the world, including the Germans. Be very careful. Africa is not the Alps. It is not Antarctica. It is a different creature entirely."

Willa nodded. "Thank you for your advice, Mr. Boedeker. Especially regarding the border."

Boedeker cocked his head. He smiled. "What advice, Miss Alden? I would never give such advice. Newland & Tarlton are not in the business of defying international borders or treaties or encouraging any such irresponsible behavior in our clients. Good day."

"Well, *that* was strange," Willa said when they were back on the street.

"He wanted to help us," Seamie said, "and to warn us. And to tell us that if we get our sorry arses arrested, we're on our own."

"We won't," Willa said confidently. "We'll go in north as he suggested. We were thinking of doing that anyway, weren't we?"

Seamie nodded.

"And we'll take lots of gifts for the Chagga. Maybe we can find some things in town. But I want to go swimming first. Did you see the beaches? Five days, Boedeker said. We've got five whole days to lie on that white sand and swim in that blue water. Heaven!"

Great, Seamie thought. Willa in her swimming costume. That would be just the thing to get his mind off how much he wanted her. He'd been thankful to sit in Boedeker's office. Happy to discuss logistics and obstacles, grateful for a distraction from his aching heart. Now he would have to endure five days together on the beach.

"Seamie?" Willa said. "What's wrong?"

"Nothing," he lied. "I was just thinking. About our gear. We should go to the hotel and make sure it got there. Check in and all that."

"Good idea."

Inside the darkened foyer of the Mombasa Club, a small boy stood in a corner, rhythmically pulling on a rope attached to a ceiling fan made of banana leaves. There were stuffed animal heads on the wall, a worn dhurrie on the floor, and a few chairs scattered about. A small bar graced one side of the room; there was a clerk at a desk on the other side—a tall Somali in a white tunic and red turban.

Seamie and Willa presented themselves. Just as they'd done with Newland & Tarlton, they'd sent a telegram ahead to the hotel, telling the manager they'd be arriving on the *Goorka*.

"We reserved two rooms," Seamie said now.

"So very sorry, sir," the clerk said regretfully. "One."

"But we reserved two rooms. There are two of us," Seamie said stupidly. "Two."

"Very, very sorry, sir. Busy day. English come from London two days ago. Big Bwana and his Msabu. Many peoples with them. Hotel full. You are two men. One room."

"He thinks I'm a man," Willa whispered. "He wants us to share."

"Are there other hotels in town?" Seamie asked.

"All full, sir."

Seamie ran a hand through his hair. He glanced toward the stairs. Two porters were already carrying their things up.

"Hold on—" he started to say.

Willa stopped him. "It's all right. We'll manage. It sounds like some diplomat's come with an entourage. If we don't take this room, we might end up with nothing."

Upstairs, Seamie tipped the porters and looked around the room. It was in the back of the hotel and overlooked a courtyard filled with acacia trees. It had whitewashed walls, a hand basin, and one double bed.

"I'll take the floor," he said quickly.

"Don't be stupid. We'll share the bed. Just don't snore. I'm off to the loo. When I get back, let's go to the beach."

As she left the room, Seamie walked to the window and looked out at the town. Then he turned and stared at the bed. The beach was bad; but the bed was torture. It taunted him. He imagined taking Willa in his arms on it and making love to her. There was nothing he wanted more in the world. Nothing. He lay down on the bed, so he couldn't see it, thinking that might help. But it didn't. He knew that in only a few hours he'd be lying on it next to Willa. Listening to her breathe, aching for her.

He wished they were setting off, wished they were dealing with bumptious porters, hiking in the killing heat, ice-climbing in thin air—*anything*, anything but this.

"Bring on the Chagga," he muttered, then closed his eyes and fell asleep.

CHAPTER 89

"Horses?" Maggie Carr asked. She was sitting at the small table inside Sid's bungalow, watching him pack.

"Two. One for me, one for him," Sid said. "Porters are taking Shanks's pony."

"Porters always do. How many of them?"

"Six."

"Must be traveling light."

"No rifles," Sid said. "No ammunition. No skins and heads to carry back. Only telescopes and compasses. A drafting table, paper, tents, and food."

Maggie nodded.

"I'm off at dawn tomorrow. The bloke wrote that he'd be at Thika township waiting for me. I won't be gone long, Maggs. Two weeks at the outside. Be back way before harvest time. The women know what to do. I've put Wainaina in charge. She's got them hoeing the north field right now—"

Maggie cut him off. "Sid, I don't mind that you're going. Not at all. I'm only worried about *why* you're going."

"I told you why. It's good money."

Maggie shook her head. "I don't believe you. You've that same look in your eye."

"What look's that?"

"The look you had when I first hired you. When you were out in the fields every night, trying to work yourself to death."

Sid flapped a hand at her and changed the subject back to planting. He was leaving to guide a surveyor north to Mount Kenya. He'd told Maggie he wanted the money he'd earn to buy a stove. It was half true. He did want a stove, but he already had the funds set aside for it. The real reason for his departure had come from Lucy Thompson and her mother.

They'd come to call on Maggie a week ago and happened to still be on her veranda when Sid came in from the barn to tell her a jackal had got at the chickens. Maggie had offered him a cup of tea. Mrs. Thompson had asked him if he'd heard the news. He'd gulped his tea and said he hadn't.

The undersecretary and his family had arrived in Mombasa. They were staying there for a week, then they would travel upcountry.

"To *Nairobi!*" Lucy said, all atwitter. There would be a ball for them at the governor's house. It would be the social event of the year.

What Lucy told him next was even worse. "After the ball, the governor's going to take his guests on safari," she said. "To Thika! Can you believe it? They're going to camp where the two rivers meet, then move west to the Aberdare mountains. Mr. Lytton wants to bag a lion, and of course we're lousy with them."

Sid had thought his heart would stop. It had taken him days to recover from the news that Freddie and India were coming to Africa, but he finally had, assuring himself that there was no possible way their paths would cross. Maggie's farm was too remote to allow it. But Lucy's news had changed all that. Sid knew the area where they would set up camp, and he knew that Maggie's farm was a good ten miles north of it. Most likely, the hunting party would never even come close, but he wasn't prepared to take a chance.

Mrs. Thompson, still chattering and looking pointedly at Sid, said that she and Lucy would be making a trip to Nairobi the next day to do a bit of dress shopping. Sid excused himself, ran to his bungalow, and hurriedly scribbled a note to the DC saying he'd heard from Delamere that a guide was needed to take a surveyor around, and that he'd be happy to do it, and could they please leave immediately. Then he'd run back to Maggie's and asked Mrs. Thompson if she would mind delivering the letter.

She had smiled broadly, telling him of course she wouldn't. In fact, she'd be delighted to. Lucy, not Mrs. Thompson, had brought him the man's handwritten reply two days ago, and she had not been smiling.

"It's about a surveyor," she'd said angrily, slapping it down on his table.

"That's right," he said, puzzled by her tone.

"The DC told me. He said you were taking his man to Mount Kenya. To make maps."

"Yes, I am. Is there something wrong with that?"

"I thought it might be about the governor's ball. I thought you'd written for an invitation. For you. For us."

Stupidly, Sid had burst out laughing. *Him* at the governor's ball? He could just see it: "Hello, India. Hello, Freddie. How the hell are you?"

But Lucy had not found it funny. Not one bit. There had been words and tears. She'd stormed out. Maggie had come by a few minutes later. She'd asked him what had happened and he told her.

"Bloody hell, Sid. I told you she was sweet on you."

"I thought you were joking."

"No, I wasn't. That poor girl. What did you say to her?"

"Nothing."

"You must've said something."

"I . . . I laughed."

Maggie looked daggers at him. "You're an arsehole, you know that?"

"I didn't mean to! She caught me by surprise."

"She's a good girl. From a good family. Hard worker and pretty as a picture. She'd make a damned good wife. You could do a lot worse."

"She could do a lot better."

Maggie had gone quiet then and he'd told her about his plans to guide the surveyor and asked if she could spare him.

"You're mad," she said. "Traipsing around the back of beyond with some bloke when a lovely girl wants to go dancing with you."

"Maggie, I'm not going to that ball and that's the end of it. Not with Lucy. Not with anybody. I have my reasons."

"Fine," she'd said angrily. "Go on safari, then. I hope a lion bites your balls off."

That was two days ago. She'd mellowed some since then and had come round to his bungalow to make sure he'd packed his quinine.

As she sat there now, drinking his whisky, she picked up the Mombasa paper that was lying on his table.

"I haven't seen this. Where'd you get it?"

"Jo Roos left it."

"Becoming a man of letters in your old age?" she asked, eyes narrowed.

"What's that?" he said. He was bent away from her, buckling a strap on his rucksack.

"Never known you to read a newspaper. Not one. What's so fascinating about this one?" It was wrinkled and stained and looked as if had been read and reread.

Sid straightened. "Nothing," he said.

Maggie held his gaze. Her expression told him that she didn't believe him.

She looked through it, carefully taking in every headline. Finding nothing, she closed it and pushed it away. But then something on the cover caught her eye—a photo of the visiting undersecretary, Frederick Lytton. He was standing by Fort Jesus with his wife and daughter. The child was squinting at the ground. Lytton was frowning. His wife was looking directly at the camera. Her face looked blurred. Maggie picked the paper up again and looked at it closely. It wasn't the photograph that was blurry, it was the newsprint. It was smudged—as if someone had brushed his fingers over it again and again.

"It's her, isn't it?" she said. "That's why you won't go to the ball. And why you're running out of here like a man with his arse on fire."

"I don't know what you're on about."

"The undersecretary's wife. India Lytton. She's the one who made you a bachelor. I told you I was going to find out who had, and now I have. That's why you're off on this mad safari, isn't it? To avoid her."

"What a load of rubbish."

"Don't lie to me, Sid. You've never lied to me."

"I've never had to," he snapped. They'd lived by an unwritten rule—no prying—and now she was breaking it.

"I'm sorry," she said. "I'm worried about you."

"It's complicated," he said. "There's a lot to it. More than you'd ever want to know. Much more."

Maggie nodded. She looked at the photograph again. "She's beautiful. Even smudged."

"She's more than beautiful, Maggs." He didn't say anything else. He didn't need to. The emotion in his voice—the pain and the longing—said it all.

Maggie pushed her chair back and stood.

"You off home, then?" he asked.

She shook her head. "I'm off to pay a call to the Thompsons," she said. "Someone has to tell poor Lucy she doesn't have a prayer."

CHAPTER 90

"Mummy, do we really have to take our teeth out?" Charlotte Lytton whispered, wide-eyed. "The conductor said all passengers are advised to remove their teeth."

"*False* teeth, darling," India said, smiling.

"But why?"

"No ballast, my dear!" Lord Delamere bellowed. "Bloody idiots laid the tracks right on the ground."

"Hugh! That is *not* language fit for a little girl's ears."

Delamere shrugged. "I forget she's a child," he said. "She's better read, and better spoken, than most of the men I know."

"Be that as it may . . ." Lady Delamere cautioned.

"Right, right, right," Delamere said. He bent down close to Charlotte so that only she could hear him. "They're still idiots, even if I'm not allowed to call them bloody," he whispered. Charlotte giggled. "You'll soon see why. When we hit the plains, and there's no padding on the rails, the wheels will bounce the teeth right out of your head." He grabbed a meringue off a passing waiter's tray. "We'll have to stuff our mouths with plenty of these. As padding. It's the only thing for it," he said, popping the sweet into his mouth, then giving her a pillowy pink grin.

Charlotte dissolved into laughter. India, in conversation with Lady Delamere, stopped talking and laughed along with her. "He's marvelous with her!" she said.

"That's because he's an overgrown child himself," Lady Delamere said.

India rarely heard her daughter laugh like this, and it delighted her. She'd been so worried about bringing Charlotte to Africa, terrified that she would come down with some dreadful disease. Instead, after a week in Mombasa, Charlotte was flourishing. Her cheeks were pink, her gray eyes lively. She had spent her days on Mombasa's white beaches with Mary, India's maid, collecting shells and throwing her lunch to the gulls. She'd met people there she liked, including a young couple who said they were hiking to Kilimanjaro. Even the official events she had to attend as her father's daughter had been exciting for her. She'd marveled at the different faces she saw— English, African, Arabian, Indian—and at the different languages she heard. By her second day in the town she was calling Mary her *ayah,* asking for scones and *chai,* and pestering for *rupees* to spend in the *dukas.*

"Did you know, Mummy," she'd said to India, "that the Swahili word for a white man is *Mzungu.* Only it doesn't translate as *white man,* it translates as *strange* or *startling thing.*" She'd furrowed her little brow, then said, "Do you suppose Father knows this?"

Sitting by the window in Governor James Hayes Sadler's private railway carriage, in a white blouse, khaki split skirt, and lace-up boots, ready to depart for Nairobi with her parents, the Delameres, and various colonial officials, she looked as if she'd been in Africa her entire life. She wore a cluster of bright Masai beads around her neck that Lord Delamere had given her and which she refused to take off.

"Do you like animals, Charlotte?" he asked her now, after swallowing his meringue.

"Yes, sir. Very much."

"You're in for a treat, then. You're about to see hundreds of them. Maybe thousands. When we cross the Athi Plains."

Charlotte gave him a skeptical look.

"You think I'm making it up?"

"Your figures do sound a bit exaggerated, sir."

Delamere roared with laughter. "Tell you what, old girl, you count them, and I'll give you one rupee for every zebra, an anna for every giraffe, and a pice for a lion. Do we have a deal?"

"Oh, yes!" Charlotte said eagerly.

Hayes Sadler joined them. He put his hand on Delamere's shoulder. "Freddie has questions on the Colonists' Association. Thought you could answer them better than I can."

"Certainly will!" Delamere said. "In fact, he's going to get an earful from me on how shabbily London's been treating us." He bade Charlotte goodbye, told her to have her figures ready for him, then followed Hayes Sadler to the compartment ahead of them. Freddie was in it, writing reports and dispatches, all business, as ever.

Suddenly, a whistle blew. The conductor yelled, "All aboard!" Doors were slammed down the length of the train. The engine released a volcanic cloud of steam and the train lurched forward, its iron wheels screeching against the track. Fifteen minutes later they were leaving Mombasa Island and crossing a long bridge to the mainland.

For most of the day, the train ran westward through a green jungle, humid and dense and filled with bright birds, butterflies, and flowers. Here and there it passed plantations where rubber, cotton, or sisal grew; skirted valleys and gorges; and stopped at little substations that were neatly painted and planted with flower boxes and looked as if they belonged in a suburb of London instead of in the wilds of Africa. Charlotte was glued to the window the entire time, taking everything in. She had to be called away for luncheon and again for tea.

By evening, they had left the jungle well behind them and were entering the grasslands. It was there, against the backdrop of a blazing African sunset, that Charlotte saw them—all the animals Delamere had promised her and more.

"Oh, Mummy! Mummy, look!" she cried, upon seeing her first herd of zebra. "There must be fifty of them!"

"More like five hundred, I should think." It was Delamere. He'd dashed out of Freddie's compartment, where he'd spent most of the day, and rushed to sit down next to Charlotte. It was impossible to tell who was more excited.

Charlotte reminded Lord Delamere of his pledge, then gleefully started counting, reaching one hundred in no time.

"My husband has bankrupted us," Lady Delamere exclaimed.

"Tell the damned man to slow the bloody train!" Delamere suddenly shouted. "How can anyone see anything?"

Lady Hayes Sadler blinked. Lady Delamere shook her head. An eager young man in a linen suit, Tom Meade, the assistant district commissioner of Kenya Province, dashed off to have a word with the engineer. And India bit back a smile, more than willing to put up with the odd profanity in order to see her daughter so happy.

"Florence? Florence! Where are my blasted field glasses?"

"Really, Hugh, must you shout so? They're right here!" Lady Delamere said, fumbling them out of her valise.

Delamere grabbed them and handed them to Charlotte. "There!" he shouted. "Ten o'clock! Do you see them, girl?"

Charlotte was silent for a few seconds then, in a hushed voice, she said, "Lord Delamere, are they really giraffes? Truly?"

"Six of them!" he crowed. "Plain as day."

"And look over there . . . a herd of Tommies—Thomson's gazelles . . . and there—those big ugly brutes? Wildebeest. Do you know what the Masai say about them, Charlotte? They say God put them together with what he had left over from all the other animals."

"What about lions, Lord Delamere?" Charlotte said, her eyes scanning the plains. "Do you see any?"

"I don't, but not to worry. If we don't see some here, we'll surely bag ourselves some on safari at Thika. Last time I was up there I shot three."

Charlotte looked stricken. "But I don't want to shoot them," she said.

Lady Delamere gave her husband a look so scorching that he blanched.

"I meant with a *camera,* my dear," he said quickly. "We shan't shoot them with a gun, of course not! In fact, I know the most wonderful guide. He refuses to shoot anything. We'll have him take us to see lions. We'll look him up as soon as we get to Thika. His name is Sid Baxter."

India had been looking out of the window. She slowly turned around. "Did you say Sid Baxter?" she asked, before she could stop herself.

"I did. Do you know him?"

"No, no, of course not," she said, forcing a laugh. The name had to be a coincidence. Sid was dead. "I . . . I heard the name in Mombasa," she lied. "He's very good, I gather."

"The best. He works for a planter up past Thika. He's a bit of a loner, but we shall draw him out. If he can't find Charlotte lions, no one can."

Lord Delamere continued to talk, but India barely heard him. God, but it hurt. *Still.* For an instant, she had been back at Arden Street in their flat. Sid was standing in the doorway, a bunch of white roses in his hand. "Hello, Mrs. Baxter," he said, before gathering her into his arms.

"Mummy? Mummy, are you all right?" Charlotte asked, concern darkening her face.

India quickly smiled at her. "I am, darling. Just feeling a bit tired suddenly."

Charlotte stared at her for a few seconds, as if weighing her words and wondering whether to believe them.

"Why don't you lie down for a bit, India, dear?" Lady Delamere suggested. "We'll keep Charlotte company."

"Will you be all right?" India asked her daughter.

Charlotte nodded, then watched her mother leave the main salon for one of the sleeping compartments. Her mother was lying; she knew she was. She'd seen that look in her eyes before—the sad one she'd seen only seconds ago. It was there when she gazed too long at the vase of white roses she always kept on her desk. And sometimes it was there when she gazed too long at *her.*

"She's fine, Charlotte, darling," said Lady Delamere, patting her hand. "Just weary from all the traveling."

Charlotte realized that her feelings were on her face. She nodded and quickly rearranged her expression into one of pure, unadulterated joy. Though she was not quite six, she had already worked out that grown-ups asked fewer questions of smiling, happy children, and she did not want any questions right now—only answers.

She turned back to the window and looked over the darkening plains, pointing at this animal and that for Lord Delamere's benefit, but she was no longer interested in them. She was too busy wondering who Sid Baxter was and why the mention of his name had made her lovely mother so sad.

CHAPTER 91

The tall, silent boy heated the needle in the flames of the campfire. When it was glowing, he tapped Seamie's foot and spoke to him in Maa.

Tepili, the headman, a Masai who spoke English, translated. "He says do not move," Tepili whispered. "He says be very still now."

"Easy for him to say. He's got the needle," Seamie muttered.

Wordlessly, the boy slid the red hot needle into Seamie's toe, just below the nail, pushing it farther and farther in. He canted it slightly then held his breath and slowly pulled it back out. An egg sac, small and white, popped out of the wound. The boy grinned.

"Jiggers," Tepili said.

"Jiggers," Seamie echoed.

"Very bad. Make you very sick," Tepili said. "No walk, no climb."

"I've heard of them," Willa said, swabbing Seamie's toe with carbolic from a vial. "They're some sort of flea that lays its eggs by the nail. If the egg sac bursts while you're trying to remove it, the beasties get everywhere and wreak havoc. Infection, pain, gangrene, all of that."

"Lovely," Seamie said. "Give me the Antarctic any day of the week. Fifty below and a howling blizzard. Too cold for anything but penguins. Definitely too cold for jiggers, ticks, snakes, scorpions, and giant man-eating spiders."

Willa laughed. "The spider wasn't *that* big," she said.

"It was as big as a bloody dinner plate!"

"What a fibber you are."

"It was!"

"A saucer, maybe," she conceded.

"It jumped on my head!"

"Dropped."

"Jumped!"

It was the first day of their trek, and not a good one for Seamie. A large and horrible spider had attached itself to him as they were passing under some trees, causing him to dance around shouting until he got it off—to the great amusement of Willa, Tepili, and the rest of the porters. He'd also been charged by a gazelle, of all things, cut his hand on a thornbush, been bitten by a tick, and now the jigger. He was looking forward to a good night's sleep on a camp bed with plenty of netting to keep the bugs out.

Willa finished with his toe, and he put his socks and boots back on. Tepili had asked that he and Willa remove their boots after they'd finished supper. They'd thought it strange, but he insisted. He'd inspected Willa's toes and nodded, but when it was Seamie's turn he'd frowned and then the boy had been called. The extraction had been unpleasant, but Seamie was glad the thing had been found. Infections were never good, particularly when one was miles away from a doctor.

"We sleep now," Tepili said. "We walk at dawn." And with that, he was gone.

It was just Willa and Seamie, then, sitting at a camp table by the fire, listening to the sounds of the African night. Willa had her books on the table. She'd brought everything she could find on Kilimanjaro—accounts by Samuel Teleki von Szek, a Hungarian explorer, and the first to attempt Kibo peak, and by the German Hans Meyer, the first to summit it.

"You hate it here, don't you?" she said worriedly. "You're sorry you've come."

Seamie shook his head. "No, Wills, not at all. In fact, I love it. I could do without the bugs, but when we started out from Voi and I could see Kili rising in the distance, its top all white with snow, I was really happy I came. It's beautiful, that mountain. I can't wait to climb it."

Willa brightened. "Africa's extraordinary, isn't it? The golden plains that stretch out forever, the soft hills . . ."

"A lot like Croydon."

"Will you stop? I'm serious."

"I know you are. And I agree, it is extraordinary. I think the most amazing thing of all is the freedom. It's not just a word here, is it? It's a concrete thing. You can see it, same as you see the endless sky, or hear it, like the thundering of zebra. And feel it, like you do the sun on your back. I honestly don't think I've ever felt so free anywhere I've been—not even Antarctica—as I do here."

Willa looked at him closely. "Seamus Finnegan, explorer-poet," she said. "*That's* how I'll describe you in my book."

She bent her head over her books again, jotting notes as she read. He watched her, his eyes lingering on the line of her jaw, the rise of her cheekbones, the curve of her mouth. They'd been on the go for hours, covering just under fifteen miles today before stopping to set up camp. They were dusty and sweaty, and yet she looked as lovely as ever to him.

They'd set out two days ago, taking the train from Mombasa, and disembarking at Voi, a small village due east of the mountain. The journey to Voi had been a long one. The train kept slowing down, adding hours to the trip. Willa had found out why. The diplomat who'd arrived in Mombasa just before they had—Lytton was his name—was on board in a private carriage and his daughter wanted to see the zebras. She was a lovely child; they'd met her on the beach at Mombasa. When they finally arrived at Voi it was already dark and they had to spend the night there in a thatched hut. The next morning they'd started walking west toward the village of Taveta, where they planned to stop and top up their provisions. From there they would veer north, avoiding villages and any overzealous officials who might be policing them.

Seamie was in excellent physical shape and he'd wondered if Willa would be able to keep up with him and with their long-limbed porters. He needn't have worried. She walked tirelessly and without complaint. She never asked to stop and rest, never showed fear—even when they'd startled a fat crocodile on the Voi River. In fact, she was the one who'd pulled that disgusting spider off his head. He kept looking for flaws in her, hoping she would somehow disappoint him and make him fall out of love with her, but she didn't, and his feelings only grew.

He had come to know her so well over the past weeks. He knew her every mood and expression, what she ate for breakfast, how she took her tea. He knew how she smelled—like fresh air and sun-warmed grass. He knew that she liked old men and dogs, and hated crossword puzzles. He'd traveled on a boat with her for six weeks and slept in the same bed at the Mombasa Club for five nights. He would never forget those nights, listening to her breathe as she fell asleep, feeling the warmth of her next to him, aching for her. He'd woken in the mornings to find her arm slung over his chest. Knowing she'd be embarrassed if she woke like that, he'd gently disentangled himself; but not before he kissed her—just once—on her forehead or her cheek.

She looked up at him now, her finger marking a spot in a book. "Fosbrooke here says Teleki got up over seventeen thousand feet on Kibo, but his lips started to bleed badly and fatigue got him and he had to turn back," she said. "The altitude's going to be a bugger."

"We'll just have to go slowly. Drink lots of melted snow. Climb high, sleep low," Seamie said. "We carry loads up, make camp, then we come back down to sleep and recover. We go slow, only netting one thousand feet a day until we're acclimatized. Then, on the last few pitches, we push like hell. Get up to the summit and get down again as quick as we can."

"The good news is that Mawenzi's only supposed to be about seventeen thousand feet. If Teleki didn't start bleeding till seventeen thousand, we ought to be all right. We ought to be able to make it."

"But Teleki was on Kibo. Kibo was no picnic, but Mawenzi looks a hell of a lot trickier. Meyer and Purtscheller reckon sheer faces on all sides. Did you read Meyer on getting up the glacier? He said it took twenty strokes of the ice-axe to cut each step. Twenty strokes for *one* step, while climbing at an angle of three-five degrees and fighting altitude sickness. Our angles are going to be a lot steeper."

"But we've got crampons. Meyer didn't have them."

Seamie thought of the spiked overshoes they'd brought. They were worn strapped over boots, like ice skates, and had metal spikes protruding from them. They were a new invention and largely untried.

"Who knows if they'll work?" he said.

"They will. Also we've a better map than Meyer and Purtscheller had. And a quadrant. Telescope. Jacob's staff. We'll take sightings, add to what we already know, and make an even better map by the time we start off."

Like every good ascensionist, Willa knew that you climbed first with your eyes. During the long sea voyage they had sketched a rough drawing of Mawenzi based on photographs, descriptions, and rough maps made by earlier climbers, but they were both well aware that they could read every word on every page of every book they'd brought, take their own readings and sightings, and it wouldn't matter—when it came to the actual climb, they would still be dealing with an unknown. They would have to find the route for themselves. Find out where the icefalls were, the crevasses, the deadly couloirs and cornices. If they did this successfully, they could well be the first human beings to ever set foot on the Mawenzi summit. If they did not—they could die.

Willa sat back in her chair now and gazed at the fire. "Hadrian climbed Etna in 121 to see the sun rise. Petrarch climbed Mount Ventoux in 1336. Balmat and Paccard took Mont Blanc in 1786 and Whymper got the Matterhorn in 1865. Can you imagine how they felt, Seamie? To be the *first*? To know that their feet were the first to stand on the summit? Their eyes the first to see what no one had ever seen before?"

"I mean to do more than imagine it, Wills."

She grinned at him. "Me, too," she said.

Their eyes met. He thought he saw something in hers, something made of longing and hope. He nearly moved toward her, but then he got scared. What if he was wrong? He looked away awkwardly, said he was dopey with sleep and was going to turn in.

"I won't be far behind you," Willa said hastily. "Take the lantern. I have the fire."

The moment was gone. Seamie stood and bade her good night, angry with himself for not doing something. He tried to work up his nerve again, to at least *say* something, but before he could, they both heard eerie laughter rising out of the night. It made Seamie's blood run cold.

"Listen to that!" Willa said. "Hyenas. Must be your toe. They can smell blood, even a tiny bit, from miles away."

The strange sounds grew louder, closer. Suddenly, a massive, humpback shape lunged out of the darkness. Seamie saw fangs flash as it growled at him. It grabbed his hat—he'd put it on the ground by the tent—and disappeared.

"You bastard!" he shouted, running after the creature. "That's mine!"

The laughter rose higher as he raced after the thief. He stopped. Eyes were on him, all around him, winking ghostly green. He realized he'd run a fair distance from the campfire. He quickly returned to it amid more squeals and barks.

"They're laughing *at* you, not with you," Willa said, trying not to laugh herself.

"They are, are they? Let's see if they laugh at this." He grabbed his rifle and fired a round into the air. There was yipping, the sound of skidding and sliding, claws in the dirt. And then it was quiet again.

"Think Tepili will let us sleep with him?" he asked.

Tepili and the other porters had no use for tents. They'd built themselves a *manyatta,* a small, sturdy enclosure made of thornbush branches, fearsome enough to thwart the boldest hyena.

"I doubt it," Willa said. "He thinks we smell bad."

"How do you know?"

"He told me."

"He didn't."

"He did. He's right, of course. We do."

Seamie sniffed his armpits and winced. "Maybe we'll cross a stream tomorrow. Have a wash."

Willa was squinting at her pages, reviewing what she'd written.

"I'd feel a lot better if you were in the tent, Wills. They might come back."

"All right, then. I'm feeling pretty knackered anyway," she said.

They built up the fire with branches they'd found earlier in the evening, then walked the few feet to their tent. They'd decided to bring only the one. Less to carry that way. It was roomy enough to comfortably accommodate two beds. Privacy was maintained by means of a canvas dividing wall.

"You take the lantern," Seamie said. "I can see well enough to fall into my bed. I've got the rifle in case the hyenas come back. 'Night."

" 'Night, Seamie."

He quickly took off his shoes, socks, and shorts, and climbed under the mosquito netting hanging over the bed. He stared up at it for a minute, then turned his head to the side. The lantern light silhouetted Willa as she undressed. He could see her long legs and the curve of her breasts as she slipped off her shirt. He knew that she slept in a camisole and in the men's drawers she wore under her trousers. He groaned softly. It was too much. He couldn't bear it anymore. He had to tell her how he felt. Even if it changed everything between them. He couldn't go on like this. He could see her bent over on her bed, writing in her notebook. He was just about to call out to her when she spoke first.

"Seamie?"

"What?"

The lantern went out. He heard her tussling around on her bed, trying to get comfortable.

"You still up?"

"Mmm-hmm."

"What makes a good climber? I'm trying to work that out for my book. George says it's skill, but I think fearlessness enters into it. You have to be very sober and careful about your preparations—making sure all your clobber's in tip-top shape, planning your route and so forth—but at some point you have to let go. You can't climb if you're always thinking about falling."

Seamie thought about this, then said, "I think it mostly has to do with arrogance."

"*Arrogance?* Why?"

"Well, when you're climbing, everything's against you. Gravity, wind and weather, altitude, time, geography. You're nothing but a speck on the face of a monolith, one that's been where it is since the dawn of time. But you don't care about any of that. If you did, you wouldn't be there. But you *are* there, daring disaster and death and all of it, a little flea climbing up a mountain. A *mountain.* What is that, if not arrogance?"

More silence, then, "I'd say you're right, but that would mean admitting that *I'm* arrogant," Willa said.

"Mmm. And ambitious. And competitive. And—"

"All right, mate. That'll do," she said, laughing. She was quiet for a bit, then said, "What will you do? After Kilimanjaro, I mean. When we get back home." Her voice was sleepy-sounding now.

"See if Shackleton's already left for Antarctica. If not, talk him into taking me with him. What about you?"

"I think the Alps again. And George and I have talked about Everest. That's all it is, talk. It's too cold and too high, and yet neither of us can stop fantasizing about the climb. He wants it very badly." She yawned, then said, "I don't think he'll ever be happy, not in his entire life, unless he gets it. I asked him why. He said, 'Because it's there.' That's George for you, another poet-explorer. I'm surrounded by them."

"Willa?"

"Mmm?"

"I need to tell you something."

"Mmm?"

There was a long silence as Seamie worked up his nerve. Then he said, "I . . . I love you, Willa. Have for years. I don't expect that you feel the same way about me. I know about you and George. But I had to tell you. I hope this won't bugger things . . . but, well, anyway, there it is. I'm sorry."

There was a long silence. Seamie was in agony waiting for her response. When one didn't come, he was certain it was because she was mortified. Or maybe she was furious.

And then he did hear something—a sound like cloth tearing. He knew that sound: Willa was snoring. She snored like a drunkard and slept like one, too. Once she was out, an earthquake couldn't wake her. He'd discovered that at the Mombasa Club.

Seamie took a deep breath and blew it out again. He was relieved. He'd given in to a momentary bit of madness and he shouldn't have. Luckily, she hadn't heard a word he'd said. Their friendship would go on as it had with no complications. And that was good.

They didn't need complications, not now with fifty miles still to go to get to Kilimanjaro and then a risky climb up Mawenzi.

Willa snored on, shockingly loud. And Seamie smiled. That noise, if nothing else, would surely keep the hyenas away.

CHAPTER 92

"Four children sleeping on wooden pallets the mother scrounged from the docks," Joe said angrily. "If she hadn't got the pallets, they'd be sleeping on the wet floor. Three of the kids are consumptive. *There's* a surprise. Mother chars. Leaves at five a.m., doesn't get back till seven most nights. Father's an invalid, injured at the docks. No compensation."

Joe was talking—almost shouting—from a narrow hallway outside a small, dank basement room in a tumbledown house in Wapping. Water trickled across the floor under the wheels of his chair and into the room where a miserably poor family of six was being photographed. The thin children wore little more than rags. The father lay in a single bed, staring vacantly. The mother's anxious eyes darted between Joe in the hallway and the enormous black camera on a tripod in the middle of her room.

The man behind it, Jacob Riis, adjusted his camera's settings, nodding absently as Joe ranted. His assistant took down everything Joe said in a small black notebook.

Finally Riis walked over to Joe and said quietly, "You are making a great deal of noise, and I need to concentrate."

Joe winced. "Am I? Sorry, Jake. It's just that it makes me so bloody angry."

Jacob patted him on the back. "I know," he sighed. "I know. But your anger doesn't get you your money. Good photos do. And good stories. Read by good people, who then get angry themselves and yell at their MPs. It's *their* anger we need. So quiet down now and let me work."

Joe nodded sheepishly. Since he was of no use here, he decided to go outside. He would find the children and their parents some much-needed food. He pushed himself up the plank ramp they'd laid over the basement steps and out to the street. There were no shops in the immediate vicinity of the house, so he headed north, where he knew there were a few.

As he made his way over the rutted streets, he thought about Jake's words: "your anger doesn't get you your money." Joe knew he was right, but there were times when anger was all he had. Anger made him fight. It had made him bring Riis here, it had made him work to interest newspaper editors in his photos, and it made him keep hammering away at his government's complacency. With any luck it would be anger—not his, but the prime minister's—that would get him the money he wanted. All one hundred thousand pounds of it.

The PM was angry already—not at the condition of the East London poor, unfortunately, but at him. He was furious at Joe's unrelenting criticism of the Uganda railway and the shocking sum that had been spent to build it. He was so angry, in fact, that he'd summoned Joe to his office a month ago, along with select members of the Colonial Office, to see if there was any way they could shut him up.

"It's a quid pro quo we're after," Campbell-Bannerman had said. "You pipe down about the railway and we'll come up with some money for you."

"How much?"

"I think we could see our way clear to twenty thousand pounds."

"That's one-fifth of what I need. It's a bleedin' insult," Joe said, preparing to leave.

"Be reasonable, man! We need that railway."

"To do what?" Joe asked. "Carry a bunch of fat-arsed sportsmen around? Take the quality sightseeing? Deliver land-grabbers to the choicest acreage?"

"That's a damned cynical view," Freddie Lytton had said hotly. "The Uganda line wasn't established to aid speculators, but to further exploration and carry missionaries to the natives."

Joe had laughed out loud. "The government spent five million pounds to transport missionaries, did it? Those Africans don't know how lucky they are. We get prize farmland, new import and export markets, an expanded empire, and they get a god they don't want and some bloody hymn books." He shook his head bitterly. "Well, I guess fair exchange is no robbery. At least they can all sing 'Nunc Dimittis' while they're trying to graze their cattle on the five flippin' acres we've left them."

"You, sir, are out of line," Campbell-Bannerman said coldly.

Joe ignored the censure. "You're planning additional branches on the railway. I've read the engineers' reports. How much are they going to cost? Another million? Two? What are you spending on hospitals in Hackney? On schools in Whitechapel? On soup kitchens in Limehouse? Do you know that right now, as I speak, little children are dying of hunger—bloody *hunger!*—right here in London? No, of course you don't. Because you've never set foot in the East End."

"Your compassion is very touching," Freddie said acidly. "And so unusual in such a wealthy man. It wouldn't have anything to do with courting your voters, would it?"

"No, it wouldn't. And for your information, Freddie, I'm not a wealthy man. I'm a poor man with a lot of money. Big difference. I've never forgotten what it's like to be hungry and cold, and I never will."

"If we give you this money," Campbell-Bannerman asked, "will you call off the dogs?"

"Yes."

"And if we don't?"

"I'll let the whole bloody kennel loose."

"I'd almost say you were blackmailing me."

"For Christ's sake, Henry, I *am* blackmailing you!"

"What, exactly, do you want?"

"I want one hundred thousand pounds to establish five clinics and five schools in my constituency. That's ten thousand a project—to build or renovate, supply, and endow." He threw a thick folder onto the table. "That's how I'm going to do it. It's a comprehensive proposal on suggested sites, builders, and costs."

Campbell-Bannerman had made promising noises, but no promises, and Joe had left Downing Street smoldering. He'd returned to his office, bellowing at Trudy to get Jacob Riis here on the next boat.

So far, Jake had run only three stories—two in the *Clarion,* one in *The Times*—and already the Central Lobby at Westminster was noticeably more crowded, noticeably noisier. The postmaster of the Commons post room had told him he had roughly double the number of incoming sacks of letters. Joe expected to be summoned back to Downing Street any day now.

He had to pass by old St. Patrick's church, with its walled graveyard, to get to the food shops. As he approached it, he saw that a smart black carriage had stopped near the gates. It was unusual to see such an expensive conveyance in this part of town. He rolled closer, then realized with a start that it belonged to him. It was one of two broughams he owned, the one Fiona used. He knew that her parents and sister were buried here and that she tended the graves herself. She must be here now, he thought. He knew where the graves were and headed through the gates down a curving dirt path toward them.

He spotted her amid the headstones. Daffodils and bluebells bloomed all around them. She had raked debris from the grass and was now on her knees, clipping spent leaves. Her movements were awkward and slow because of the baby. He saw her brush dust off her father's headstone, then stretch her hand out to one marked Charlie Finnegan. The real Sid Malone—the lad who had attacked the young Charlie Finnegan, and whom Charlie had killed—was buried there. When Fiona had discovered the truth, she'd refused to change the name, worried that it might provoke unwanted questions. Joe saw her touch the letters of her brother's name, then cover her face with her hands and lower her head. She was weeping.

He sped down the path as fast as he could push the wheels of his chair. The sound of the wheels crunching over the gravel startled Fiona. She looked up.

"Joe?" she said, hastily wiping her eyes. "What are you doing here?"

"Working with Riis. What's wrong, Fee?"

"Nothing. Nothing at all. I just . . ."

"Fiona, I saw you. It's all right, luv, you can tell me."

They were both aware of the damage her pursuit of Sid had done to their marriage. Since the day he'd come out of his coma—and told the police and the press that it was Frankie Betts, not Sid Malone, who had shot him—Fiona had talked about her brother only once, to tell Joe he'd come to their house, and that she and Seamie had helped him get out of the country. She had never mentioned him again after that.

"I try not to think of him too much," she said now. "But it's hard not to when I come here. It's knowing he can't come home that upsets me. Ever. If someone recognized him and went to the police, he'd be arrested. Alvin Donaldson and Freddie Lytton would still like to see him hang for Gemma Dean's murder. I wish he could come back, Joe. I wish I could see him again someday."

Tears came again. Joe wiped them away. It hurt him to know that she had tried so hard for so long to hide her pain from him. And it hurt him to see that she was still suffering. And yet he didn't know what to do to ease her grief. When he'd come out of his coma, and heard that Sid was said to have had shot him, he was able to say that he had not. Gemma Dean, however, had been in no such position.

As soon as Alvin Donaldson learned it was Betts who'd shot Joe, he pulled out all the stops to find him. Eventually he did, in Deptford. Donaldson had interrogated him about Gemma Dean's death as well, but Frankie denied he'd had anything to do with the Dean murder. Suspicion had fallen back on Sid Malone, where it had remained. Joe knew that Fiona was right. Her brother could never come home.

When Fiona's tears had subsided, Joe insisted that she leave St. Patrick's and go home. "The churchyard's no place for you, Fee. Not now. It's not good for you and it's not good for the baby. Go home and sit in the garden and I'll come as soon as Jake finishes."

She finally relented and he accompanied her back up the path and to her carriage. He kissed her good-bye, guilt pricking at his conscience. As the carriage pulled away, he thought of how hard he fought on behalf of total strangers while his own wife cried alone in a graveyard. It wasn't right. He must do something for her. He must try to clear Sid's name. He didn't know how, but he knew it would involve getting to the bottom of Gemma Dean's murder.

He would start tomorrow. With the man who had nearly killed him.

He would pay a visit to Mad Frank Betts.

CHAPTER 93

"Bloody hell," Willa swore.

"Again?"

She nodded, put her pencil down, and trotted off behind a boulder. Seamie, busy taking sightings of Mawenzi's west face from a quadrant, could hear her retching.

"All right?" he shouted.

"All right," came the reply.

A few minutes later she was back, standing at the stove. Snow was melting in a pan on top of it. She swished some of the water around her mouth and spat it.

"What's doing it? Altitude alone?" Seamie asked.

"It's not altitude. It's the Chaggas' angry mountain god. His name is Vomitus and he's mad as hell," she said.

Seamie laughed out loud, bumping the quadrant and wrecking his reading.

At the village of Taveta, where they'd stopped to top up their provisions, they'd found two Chagga tribesmen. It had taken some doing, but Seamie and Willa had persuaded them to guide them through the dense forest that circled the mountain. The Chagga, who had named the mountain Kilema Kyaro, which means That Which Cannot Be Conquered, believed that an angry god lived inside Kili and would punish any who dared climb it. Willa had had to offer them a lantern, a small mirror, a knife, and her gold signet ring before they would agree to guide them. Tepili, who didn't trust the Chagga, had been unhappy and silent throughout the forest trek. Peter Boedeker had cautioned them to be wary of the Chagga, too, but neither

Willa nor Seamie had had any difficulty with them, and thought both Boedeker and Tepili had exaggerated their ferociousness.

"Drink some of that water," Seamie said to her now. "Don't just spit it."

"Ugh."

"Drink. You have to. If you don't, it'll get worse."

"Don't see how it could."

Ever since they'd reached twelve thousand feet, Willa had been plagued by altitude sickness. Their plan had been to climb to the saddle—a long slope of land that stretched between the Kibo and Mawenzi peaks—and set up camp close to Mawenzi. From there they would explore the peak's west face from the ground, using the surveying and navigation tools they'd brought to get a more accurate idea of heights, distance, and hazards before they started climbing.

Their initial difficulty had been staying on course through the dense forest at Kili's base, but their Chagga guides had helped them, bringing them out of the hilly forest and onto the mountain proper without once consulting a compass. Seamie had marveled at the primeval feeling of the forest after days spent trekking on the hot, arid plains. Camphor, fig, and padocarpus trees had shaded them on the climb. Curious colobus monkeys had followed them, swinging along on hanging vines. Hornbills and red-striped turaco birds flew overhead, squawking. And once a leopard dashed snarling from a clutch of giant ferns.

Higher up, the forest had given way to alpine moorland, then cliffs, ridges, and scree, and then to the high-altitude desert of the saddle. The first signs of altitude sickness—pounding headaches—had hit them just past nine thousand feet. Nausea and fatigue followed. Keeping to their plan to climb high and sleep low, they'd taken five days to carry their gear up from the alpine moors over the glacier ice, deposit it at the Mawenzi camp, then climb back down below three thousand feet to sleep. Their Masai porters, unequipped for ice climbing, had stayed behind on the moorland to wait for their final descent. It had been hard work carrying a tent, a stove and fuel, sleeping bags, lanterns, food, clothing, cameras, and tools in rucksacks over the ice. Their ice-axes had been helpful, but the crampons had proved invaluable, performing better than their hobnailed boots. Willa said she'd felt as if she were positively glued to the ice in them.

It had taken Seamie only three days to acclimatize. He still had the odd headache, and his energy level wasn't what it had been on the plains, but he was improving. Willa wasn't. He worried about her, and said so, but she shrugged off his concern. She was suffering, he knew she was, but she made no concessions to her symptoms, keeping up with him in every aspect of their reconnaissance—from trekking and climbing to surveying and photographing.

Willa crumbled a lump of snow into the pot on the stove to replace what she'd drunk, then walked over to Seamie and the small drafting table they'd set up. She looked at the map they were still roughing out, at his jotted readings, then at the mountain face itself. Their reconnaissance was nearly done. By the end of the day, they would have a working map of the west face. She had taken all the photographs she needed for her book. In a day—two at the most—they would start their ascent.

"Still thinking of the couloir?" she asked.

Seamie nodded thoughtfully.

"Could be tricky."

Seamie knew that it *would* be tricky. Couloirs—gullies that were steep and angled—often provided the best access to the summit. Unfortunately, they also acted as chutes for debris. Chunks of ice and rock, loosened by the heat of the sun, could come crashing down them without warning.

"If we're on the couloir early, before the sun's warm, we might be all right. See where that buttress meets the ridge? We climb by that northwest corrie to reach it, bivouac under the ridge for a night, then make a start on the couloir at dawn, clear it, take the summit, and get back down to the ridge. If we need to bivi again, we do. If not, we grab our gear and descend the same way, via the corrie."

Willa was frowning at the snowy face.

"It's not without risk," Seamie added. "We'll have to move bloody fast."

Seamie knew that Willa would understand his meaning—that no quarter would be given to altitude sickness.

She frowned up at the forbidding, snow-covered peak. She was quiet for a few long seconds, then she said, "We'll be the first to summit Mawenzi."

He was struck by the tone of her voice, by the determination in it, the sheer bloody will. It signaled there would be no compromises, no negotiation, only victory or defeat. He'd heard it before—in Shackleton's voice, in Scott's, in his own.

Willa was driven, competitive, ambitious, eager to make a name for herself. It inspired him. And unsettled him. Not because she was a woman. He was used to fierce women—he'd been raised by Fiona, after all—but because he loved her.

One paid a price for winning and sometimes that price was high. The trekking they'd done, even the ice climbing on the glacier, though arduous, was nothing compared to free-climbing a sheer rock face in subfreezing temperatures while straining to pull oxygen into one's lungs in thin air.

He'd have to be able to forget who she was when they were scaling Mawenzi, to forget his feelings for her. He wondered if he'd be able to.

"The route's good," she said suddenly, decisively. "As long as we're off the couloir before the sun's hot, we'll be fine. Let's just hope the angry god isn't too angry that day."

Seamie squinted up at the long icy sweep of the couloir again. He looked at the jagged peaks of the summit and the snow clouds crossing them and said, "Let's hope he's not even miffed."

CHAPTER 94

Charlotte Lytton gazed at the creature at her feet, lying limp and crumpled, blood seeping from its slack lips, flies feasting at its eyes. The porters had placed it there, thinking she would want to see it. She didn't. She didn't understand why anyone would want to do this, to destroy something so beautiful. She raised her head and looked at the man who had shot the lion—her handsome, laughing father. He was being made much of. Lord Delamere slapped him on the back and Sir James Hayes Sadler handed him a glass of champagne. Watching him, she did something she'd done for as long as she could remember. She whispered, "You are *not* my father. You are not. You're a thief. You've stolen my real father and put yourself in his place. Just like in a fairy story."

She could smell the lion's blood now. It made her feel dizzy and sick, but she knew that to faint would make her father angry. So instead, she took his hand and said, "Congratulations, Papa."

He turned to her, smiled briefly, and patted her head, which was what he always did when he wanted to appear loving in public. She knew, however, that he did not love her. It was all right, for she did not love him. She never had. They both pretended. Though she was better at it.

More porters arrived. Some carried zebra between them, others gazelle. The animals were suspended by their hooves on poles, their heads bounced limply, their tongues lolled. Lord Delamere had lied. He said they would not shoot the animals with guns, only cameras. Grown-ups always lied. Charlotte edged away from the dead animals and the laughing men toward her mother and the other women, who were sitting in camp chairs underneath the broad canopy of some acacia trees. She came up behind her mother, pretty in her lawn blouse and khaki skirt, and pressed a cheek to hers.

"There you are, Charlotte, darling," India said, turning to kiss her.

"Papa's back. Lord Delamere and Sir James, too."

"Are they?" Lady Delamere sighed. "And here we were having such a lovely morning."

All the ladies laughed. All but her mother. She stiffened slightly at the sight of her father. It was barely a movement, imperceptible to everyone—everyone except Charlotte. Her mother looked as if she could not breathe when her father was near. It was as if he sucked all the life out of her. He was cruel to her, not with his hands, but with his words. And his silences.

When he was gone, away on the government's business, which he often was, her mother was different. The sadness, almost always there in her eyes, went away. Charlotte often dreamed of them running away, she and her mother. Mostly to the sea, because she loved the sea. But anywhere would do, as long as it was somewhere her father would never find them. She wished they could slip away from their tents at night, ride into the African hills, and never come back. How she loved the grassy plains that stretched out into forever. And the wide blue sky. She loved the Masai warriors, tall and fierce in black feathers and red paint. She loved the Kikuyu villages with their huts and farms and the hardy Somalis who kept their women veiled head to toe.

Perhaps they *could* run away when this awful safari was over. If only for an afternoon.

They had traveled from Mombasa to Nairobi, where her parents were celebrated for a fortnight with balls, dinners, luncheons, and parties. They'd gone to the Delameres' enormous farm after that, where they'd spent another week, then to Lake Victoria, at the end of the Uganda line, and now they were on safari in Thika. When it ended, there would be a holiday in the hills of Mount Kenya. In a house that they'd rented from Lady Something-or-Other. It would be just the three of them and a handful of servants. Her father needed to write articles and reports. He needed peace and quiet to do so. Maybe she and her mother could run away then, while he was busy with his work.

"The great hunters are back!" Lord Delamere boomed, bringing champagne to the ladies.

"Did you catch anything, dear?" his wife asked.

"Scads!" he said. "And Lytton bagged a lion. Big brute of a fellow!"

Charlotte looked over at the growing heap of dead animals. She looked at the lion again, robbed of his grace and majesty, and tears stung her eyes.

She didn't want to see him anymore. She was just leaving the sitting area, ready to go to her tent and fling herself down on her bed, when Delamere stopped her. "All right, old girl?" he asked. He was frowning at her.

She nodded gamely. "Just a bit tired," she said. She knew it was the thing to say when something was wrong but you didn't want to talk about it. She knew because it was what her mother always said.

"Too much sun. Have yourself a kip. Just the thing."

Charlotte nodded. He tousled her hair, disturbing her neat blond braids, and she continued on her way.

"Charlotte?" she heard her mother call, though she pretended she hadn't. Then, "Where's she going, Hugh?"

"She's fine, India. Leave the poor girl be."

"Charlotte, make sure you tell Mary where you're going!" India called.

"For goodness' sake! She's only going to take a nap!" Delamere bellowed.

Charlotte walked toward her tent, the one she shared with her mother's maid, Mary. She looked around for Mary, but when she couldn't find her she went into the tent and lay on her bed. After a few minutes she stood up again. She wasn't that kind of tired, not the kind of tired that made you want to sleep. She was tired deep down inside. It was the kind of tired that made you want to be alone. She had to get away from them all for a bit. Away from her father. Away from the sad, dead lion. She remembered seeing a beautiful, silvery waterfall on their way into camp. She didn't think it was too far away. She would go there and listen to the rushing waters, maybe take off her boots and stockings and dip her toes. She grabbed her doll Jane for company and set off.

Charlotte was a quiet, careful child, not the type to wander too near a camp stove or play with a loaded rifle. People knew that about her, so they did not tend to watch her as closely as they might watch other children. No one made sure she had gone to the tent. India, as Freddie's wife, was obliged to listen with unmitigated interest as Lord Delamere launched yet again into a diatribe on why Parliament must do more to further the settlers' cause. Mary, sitting in the kitchen tent listening to a handsome guide tell her how a water buffalo had given him the jagged scar on his arm, didn't check on her either.

It was not until dinnertime, nearly three hours after Charlotte had left the campsite, that India came running from her tent, wild-eyed, shouting, "Where's Charlotte? Please, has anyone seen my daughter?"

CHAPTER 95

Sid felt the riders before he saw them. He was sitting on the grass by his campfire, finishing his breakfast, when he felt hooves pounding the ground.

They're coming on bloody fast, he thought. Why?

He stood and looked for them, shading his eyes with his hands. He spotted them. Two of them. Coming from the direction of Thika. It wasn't far. He was near enough to have ridden home last night if he'd wanted to, but he'd fancied one more night out under the stars. And, if he was honest, one more night's distance between himself and the Lyttons. He could make one of the riders out now. It was Maggie. There was a man with her. Sid squinted at him. He was young, slim. He knew him. It was Tom Meade, the ADC.

"What the hell does the government want now?" he wondered aloud. "I just took their bloody map maker all around Kenya and back."

Maggie rode up to him breathless and unsmiling. Her horse was lathered. She never rode him that hard. Sid suddenly got a bad feeling. He tried to shake it off.

"Miss me that much, Maggs?" he joked, when she was near enough to hear him.

"Never mind that. We've got trouble," she said. She jumped down and started kicking dirt over his fire.

"What is it? What's up?" he asked, looking from her to Tom.

"Lost girl," Tom said, winded. "Delamere sent me to Maggie's to fetch you. Said you know the area better than anyone. Maggie said you were gone, but due back soon. We looked north, on a hope, really, and saw your smoke."

"Tom, who's lost? Where?" Sid asked, already breaking camp.

"Never mind your things. I'll get them," Maggie said. "Saddle up."

"The undersecretary—Freddie Lytton—his daughter's gone," Tom said. "The Lyttons are on safari with the Delameres and the governor and me and—"

"Her *name*, Tom."

"Charlotte. She wandered off and—"

"How old?"

"About six."

Sid was slipping the bridle over his horse's head. His hands faltered. "Jesus Christ," he said softly. "How long ago?"

"Yesterday afternoon."

Sid turned at that. "For God's sake, Tom! Where are the bloody guides?" he shouted.

"They've been searching ever since her mother discovered she was gone. Can't find a trace of her."

"Where was she last seen?"

"In her tent. But one of the guides tracked her to the river."

"That river's full of crocs. And a python as big as a bloody tree!"

"Not anymore. Guides shot everything."

"Snake, too?"

Tom nodded. "Opened them all up. Nothing."

"She went walkabout then," Sid said. He threw his saddle over his horse's back. *She*. She was India's daughter. He would do anything to spare India what was to come. Anything. Even his own life. But he couldn't. It was too late. He knew it was.

"You'll want to go straight to camp, I imagine. See the undersecretary."

"No, I bloody well won't," Sid said.

"But—"

"I'm going straight to the river. I'm going to hope those bloody fools who call themselves guides have managed to leave a track, a print, something I can use."

"But the Lyttons are out of their minds with worry. Lady Lytton's been sedated. They want to see you."

"There's no time! Don't you understand that? It's lion country, Tom. A little girl all alone out there . . . she's got no chance, has she? None at all."

Tom shrank in his saddle. "What are you saying?"

"That it's a recovery you're sending me on, not a rescue. I'm giving the parents something to bury, that's all. Now get the hell out of my way so I can find what's left before the vultures do."

CHAPTER 96

Sid gazed at the torn, mauled carcasses on the ground and breathed a ragged sigh of relief. He'd heard the flies, smelled the blood. He'd been certain it was her—Charlotte Lytton—but it was only a dead Tommie. He backed away from it warily, knowing that whatever had killed it was probably nearby. He swung back into his saddle and spurred his horse on, riding southwest from Thika, toward the Athi plains.

He'd been searching for the girl for two full days now. After talking to Tom Meade, he'd ridden hard to the Thika river. No one from the Lyttons' party was there anymore. They'd all moved off. He'd cursed them roundly as he looked at the riverbank. Their big, stupid footprints were all over it, obscuring any Charlotte might have left. He asked Tom where they'd gone. Tom said half had ridden west, half east. They would all sweep north and meet at the Tana River.

Sid had kept searching, eyes on the ground, as Tom explained the guides' movements. He walked in a widening arc from the river's south bank, the bank closest to the campsite, hoping to spot something. And then he did. One small, narrow bootprint in the red dirt, its toe pointing east. As he looked at it, he realized that it made sense. It was afternoon when she'd wandered off, Tom had said, and the sun would have been beginning its descent.

Charlotte would probably be fair—like her mother and father—he reasoned, and unused to the African sun. She'd probably been warned against it. She wouldn't walk toward it; she'd turn away from it and walk east.

He'd told Tom he'd be back in three days at the latest. Tom had wanted to come with him, but Sid had refused. He worked best alone.

He'd been rewarded toward the end of the first day with a small white handkerchief embroidered with the initial C. It was caught in some tall grass and crumpled. She must have been crying, he thought. But it wasn't bloodied; that was something. It meant she was alive when she dropped it. Hope flared in him. After spotting it, he shouted her name until he was hoarse, but there was no answer. The trail had gone cold again, but he felt buoyed by the handkerchief. He felt connected to the little girl. He had guessed her moves correctly so far; he knew how she thought. He would keep on trusting his instincts; maybe they would pay off. He'd ridden on into the evening, stopping only when the dark finally forced him to.

Today, twenty-four hours after finding the handkerchief, the hope was gone again and he was angry at himself for having dared to even feel it. He knew better. Everything was against her. Hadn't he said as much to Tom? The lions were only the start. Even if she'd somehow managed to avoid them, there were still the night prowlers—hyenas and jackals. There was the harsh sun. A lack of food and water. There were game pits—large, hidden holes dug by the Kikuyu to trap animals. And there were the *siafu*. It had rained the first night, and the rain always called them out. Sid felt a shiver go up his spine at the thought of them. He'd often seen them—hordes of ravening warrior ants marching in an endless black column. Most creatures knew to get away from them, but those who didn't—or couldn't—were eaten alive. Hens in a henhouse. Puppies. Babies in their cots.

He pushed the thoughts from his mind. He desperately wanted to give India her daughter back. She was the only woman he'd ever loved, and he loved her still. He wanted to help her, to save her from a grief so terrible. The image of her keening over her dead child was unbearable to him. If he couldn't do that, if the lions had gotten her, he would bring back *something*—her boots, perhaps. A ribbon or a piece of jewelry. Something to clutch at, something to hold. But not the remains. For India would insist on looking, he knew she would. People always wanted to look. They thought they could handle it. They had no idea what Africa was capable of.

He rode over a gentle rise on the plains and brought his horse up short. From this vantage point, he raised a pair of field glasses to his eyes and looked for movement in the grass—the raised, blood-stained face of a lion, or a boiling brawl over the kill. He looked for movement in the sky, the lazy wheeling of vultures certain of a meal. But he saw nothing. He was ready to ride on, but something kept him. He held the glasses to his eyes a bit longer, slowly sweeping his gaze along the horizon. Just a minute more, he thought. And then he saw it—a patch of white in an acacia tree. It didn't register at first. His eyes traveled past it, discounting it, then snapped back. There was something wrong about it. It was too large to be a bird. Too bright to be an animal. He tightened the focus. The white was still indistinct, obscured by branches. And then, suddenly, it moved. And below it, something else moved. Something tawny.

Sid fumbled the glasses back into his pack. He spurred his horse. It was her, Charlotte. She was up in that tree and lions were circling below. Hope sparked again. He tried to damp it, telling himself that he didn't know if she was alone in that tree. Or alive. The big cats sometimes defended their kills by dragging them up into low-lying branches.

A hundred yards away he saw them clearly—two lionesses. One reared, put her front feet on the tree, and tensed her haunches, then quickly dropped down again, snarling. Fifty yards away he stopped his horse, grabbed his rifle, and fired into the air. The animals ran. Seconds later he was off his horse and at the tree, looking up into the branches.

A little girl, blond and very dirty, sat about twenty feet off the ground in the crux of two limbs, her head resting against the larger of them. She held stones in her hands. Her skirt pockets bulged with more. Sid was amazed by her resourcefulness. The stones had kept the lions at bay.

"Charlotte? Charlotte Lytton?" Sid called.

The girl picked up her head. She opened her eyes. They were gray eyes, soft as a gull's wing. They were India's eyes. "I'm very sorry, sir," she said hoarsely, "but I am not allowed to speak to strangers."

"I'm not a stranger. My name is Sid Baxter. Your parents sent me to find you."

"What are their names, please?"

"India. India and Freddie . . . *Frederick* . . . Lytton."

Charlotte nodded. She tried to say something, but her eyes fluttered and she slumped forward. The stones fell from her hands and pattered to the ground. She nearly fell, too. Sid was up the tree in a twinkling. He put the girl over his shoulder and got her down. He laid her on the ground, grabbed the canteen from his saddle pack, and trickled water on her face and throat. She woke, clutched at the canteen, and drank deeply.

"Slow down," Sid said, easing her into a sitting position. "Take a little at a time or you'll be sick."

She took another sip, then said, "Please, sir, you forgot Jane."

Sid looked around. "Who the devil is Jane?"

"In the tree," Charlotte said. She tried to point.

Sid looked up at the spot where she'd been sitting. Just above it was a doll wedged into another, smaller crux.

"I'll get her in a minute. I'm more worried about you. How did you get all the way out here?"

"Walked. Sometimes I ran. When I heard things."

"I'll bet you did."

He propped her against the tree trunk, fed her bits of hard cheese that he had in his pack, and gave her more water. He rescued the doll, then he gently patted a cooling salve Maggie had made him for sunburn over

Charlotte's face. Eventually, her eyes became more focused. She leaned forward, able now to sit up on her own. Sid felt an immense admiration for this brave little person.

"You are a very clever little girl, do you know that? I know some grown men who would never have thought to get up a tree, much less take stones up with them."

"My mummy says I must always think for myself. She says all girls must."

"Does she?" Sid asked.

"Do you know my mummy, Mr. Baxter?" Charlotte asked, her eyes large and searching.

"No, I don't," Sid lied.

"I think she knows you. Someone said your name once. On the train. It made her very sad. I don't know why it would. Do you?"

"No idea," Sid said, his voice suddenly husky. He coughed to clear it, then quickly changed the subject. "Do you feel up to riding? For an hour, maybe two? Give us a bit of a head start, it would."

Charlotte nodded.

"We'll get as far as we can tonight, then we'll rest. You can sleep. We'll head out again at dawn. With any luck, I'll have you back at Thika in time for dinner tomorrow."

Charlotte got to her feet. She was a bit wobbly, and Sid was concerned about her, but he was more concerned about the lions. They were the real reason he wanted to get going. He fished in his pack for an extra shirt and tied it around her head for protection against the still-strong sun, then he lifted her into the saddle. He swung up himself, crossed his arms in front of her, and picked up the reins.

She turned and looked at him. "Thank you for finding me, Mr. Baxter. Mummy would have been sad if the lions had eaten me."

"I'm sure she would. And your father, too."

"No, I don't think so."

Sid was sure he'd misheard her. He was about to start off when she said, "I wish you were the Sid Baxter my mummy knew. You seem very nice. I think you would make her smile."

"Shh, now," Sid said. "Don't talk. Lean back against me as we ride and rest as much as you can. You need to save your strength."

They set off at a gentle pace and Charlotte was soon dozing against him. He held the reins in one hand as they rode. His other arm was curled protectively around her. He had ridden in wide, sweeping arcs while searching for her, but now he would make a beeline for Thika. He was certain he could be back in half the time it had taken him to get here.

By the time they stopped for the night and he had gotten Charlotte to sleep in a bed he'd made from plains grass and an old wool blanket, he'd decided that he would leave her at the McGregors' farm, east of Thika village, tomorrow, then get one of the McGregor boys to ride to the Lytton camp to tell them where she was. The McGregors had a nice stone house. Charlotte would be comfortable there. She needed rest and quiet and good wholesome food to recover from her ordeal. Elspeth McGregor had been a nurse back in Edinburgh before she married and emigrated. Sid knew she would take good care of the girl.

He would stay long enough to see her tucked up in bed and then he would ride back to Maggie's. He wanted to be well away by the time Charlotte was reunited with her mother. For despite what the little girl said, Sid doubted very much that seeing him again would make India Lytton smile.

CHAPTER 97

Joe sat in the visitors' room of Wandsworth Prison, waiting. It was a grim place, all cold stone and dark wood. He took a deep breath, trying to steady himself. It was a hard thing to do, facing the man who'd shot him, but there was no other way. He believed that Frankie Betts, not Sid Malone, had murdered Gemma Dean. And he'd come to Wandsworth to try to get him to confess.

Ever since the day he'd seen Fiona weeping in the cemetery, Joe had been determined to find a way to clear her brother's name. He'd decided to make good use of his political connections and had gone straight to the home secretary, Herbert Gladstone, to lobby him personally for permission to reopen the case.

"But why *should* we reopen it?" Gladstone had asked Joe, perusing the file.

"Because it was never really closed," Joe said. "Not properly. The man accused of killing Gemma Dean, Sid Malone, was never actually charged. He died before he could be."

"It says here that there was an eyewitness—Freddie Lytton, no less—who swore he saw Malone finish the poor woman off," Gladstone said.

"Perhaps Lytton only *thought* he saw Malone."

"Doesn't sound very likely. I'm sure he knows what he saw. He's an able-bodied young man, not some doddery old codger."

"Actually, Herbert, it *does* sound likely. The man who shot me, Frankie Betts, tried to pass himself off as Sid Malone when he pulled the trigger and nearly succeeded. He said in court that he dressed up as Sid and pulled out a gun to frighten me. I didn't believe it then and I don't now. But I do believe he might've done the same thing with Gemma Dean. Passed himself off as Sid Malone in order to frame him for the crime."

"But why? Why would he do such a thing? And twice?"

"I don't know, but I mean to find out. If you'll allow me to."

Gladstone, brooding over the top of his spectacles, said, "This sudden interest of yours in the case . . . it wouldn't have anything to do with vengeance, would it? Dissatisfaction over Betts's sentence? Perhaps you're thinking he should've swung for what he did to you, so you'll make sure he does for what he did—*allegedly* did—to Gemma Dean?"

"No, Herbert, it has nothing to do with vengeance and everything to do with justice."

Gladstone had remained skeptical. He hadn't agreed to officially re-open the case, but he'd told Joe to go ahead and see what he could dig up. Then, to aid him in his quest, he'd written to the warden at Wandsworth, explaining Joe's interest in the case and expressing his hope that he and his staff would do everything they could to accommodate him.

Joe hadn't seen Betts since the day, five years ago, that Betts had stepped into his office and shot him—he'd been too weak to attend the trial and sentencing—and it took him a few seconds now to realize that the man whom the guard ushered in and sat down at a table across from him was indeed Frankie Betts. Joe was shocked by his appearance. He seemed to have aged fifty years, not five. He was thin, with the beginnings of an old man's stoop, and his hair had gone gray. His cheeks were sunken, but their color was high. His eyes were bright.

The two men looked at each other for a long time, saying nothing. Frankie was the first to break the silence.

"Come to have a gander, did you? Make sure I wasn't having too good a time? Happy with what you see?"

Joe looked at the man who'd taken his legs from him, and nearly his life, and said, "No, I'm not happy, Frankie. I wish you weren't in here. I wish I wasn't in this chair."

Understanding dawned on Frankie. "Ah, that's it, then. You've come to take a crack at me. Any minute now, the screw'll tie me hands behind me back, me ankles to the chair, and then it's all hear no evil, see no evil."

"I'm not here for revenge, Frankie. I don't need to be. I'm not angry at you."

Frankie laughed in disbelief. "C'mon, guv. You're not even the tiniest bit put out? A little miffed? A tad perturbed?"

"I was, Frankie, but I let it go. I had to or it would have killed me. Sitting in this chair for the rest of my life is a harsh enough sentence. I wasn't going to become a prisoner of my anger, too."

"That's what *he* said," Frankie said bitterly, almost inaudibly. "About the anger. To let it go."

"Who said that?"

Frankie shook his head. "No one. Why did you come? What do you want?"

"Your help."

"My help," Frankie said flatly.

"Yes."

"I'm all ears."

"I'm here about the Gemma Dean case."

Frankie sucked his teeth. He said nothing.

"The police believe Sid Malone killed Gemma Dean. Just like they believed it was Sid Malone who shot me until I woke up and told them different."

Frankie broke Joe's gaze, just for a second. "Aye? So?" he said.

"I think you killed Gemma Dean. Did you?"

Frankie burst into laughter. "No, I fucking well didn't! And even if I had done, do you think I'd tell you? I didn't get the death sentence, remember? I got life. I'd like to keep it that way."

Joe eyed him closely, then said, "Maybe the magistrate didn't give you a death sentence, but Wandsworth did."

Frankie didn't reply.

"It's consumption, isn't it?"

Frankie turned to the guard, who was standing by the wall, arms crossed over his chest. "I want to go back to me cell now," he said.

"Sit down, Betts," the guard said.

"I want to go back. I ain't staying here. You can't make me."

"Warden says you're to answer the MP's questions. Sit down."

Frankie sat. He glared at Joe.

"Help me, Frankie. I'm asking you. You owe me."

Frankie shot forward in his chair. "I'm paying what I owe, mate. Every miserable minute of every miserable day for the rest of my miserable life."

"If you won't help me, help Malone. Help clear his name."

Frankie banged his manacled hands down on the table. "Fuck Sid Malone!" he shouted.

The guard pulled his truncheon from his belt. Joe held a hand up, staying him.

"None of this would have happened if it weren't for Malone," Frankie said angrily. "I wouldn't be here. You wouldn't be in that bleedin' chair. I ain't helpin' him. He's dead. He can go straight to hell for all I care. And that bloody doctor with him."

"Wait a minute. Slow down, mate. What doctor?" Joe asked, confused.

"The doctor! The one with the clinic . . ." He stopped talking. When he spoke again, his voice cracked with grief. "We was the kings, y'see. We had everything, owned the whole of East London. It would have gone on forever, too. Nothing could have stopped us. Nothing but that bloody doctor. Ruined him. Ruined everything." He shook his head, still talking, but not to Joe. "He told me, didn't he? He told me that scars on the outside are nothing compared to the ones they'll put on the inside. He was right. Why didn't I listen?"

Frankie put his head in his hands. Joe waited a bit, giving him time to collect himself, then he pressed him again. "What clinic, Frankie? What doctor?"

Frankie looked at him as if he'd only just walked in off the street. "No one. Nobody. Never mind. I'm finished here." He stood up quickly, knocking his chair over.

Joe swore under his breath. For a moment, he'd nearly had him, he'd been softening, but then he'd pushed too hard and the moment was gone.

"You done with him, sir?" the guard asked.

Joe nodded. "Write to me if you change your mind, Frankie," he said.

"Oh, aye. With love and kisses. On me best scented paper."

"It's a chance," Joe called out, as the guard led him away. "A chance to do some good for once. You won't get many more."

He waited for a reply, but there was none, just the sound of an iron door clanging shut. *He knows who killed Gemma Dean,* Joe thought. *I saw it in his eyes. He knows, but he won't say. It's not fear that's keeping him quiet, either. It's anger. He's furious. At Sid. And at someone else—a doctor. But why? And who is he?*

Joe sat staring at the door, scowling in frustration. He'd been so close. So bloody close. He would have to come back and push at Frankie again until he broke him. But he needed more information first. He needed to find out who the mysterious doctor was.

His frown faded. A look of determination took its place. He knew just the person to help him. She was connected. She knew everyone. Most important, she knew doctors. She would help him; he knew she would because she owed him. He'd gotten her ten thousand pounds of government money and five thousand more in private donations several years ago to put a new children's wing on her clinic.

"Home, sir?" Joe's driver asked, as he came to the visitors' room to fetch him.

"No, Myles," Joe said. "Not yet. I want to go to Gunthorpe Street first. To the Whitechapel Free Clinic for Women and Children."

CHAPTER 98

India and Charlotte Lytton climbed the steps to Sid Baxter's house and peered inside.

"Hello? Mr. Baxter?" India called.

There was no reply.

"Didn't think he'd be in," Maggie Carr said from behind them. She'd met them at the gate as they'd rode up from the McGregor farm. "He told me last night that he was going to ride out to the plains today. Hoped to bag a gazelle for Alice, my cook. I'll tell him you called."

"May I leave him this note, please, Mrs. Carr?" Charlotte asked, holding up an envelope.

"I wrote it to tell him thank you for saving me."

"Of course you may. Why don't you put it on his table?"

Charlotte nodded. She entered the house. India followed, looking all around the small, single room. It was tidy and cozy, yet lonely somehow, as if all the comfortable little touches—the red Masai shawl draped over a chair, the chipped teapot and mugs by the fire, the books stacked on a wooden bench—had been made in expectation of company that never arrived.

"I would like to live here, Mummy," Charlotte suddenly said. "I would like it very much. Do you think Mr. Baxter would let us?"

"I think he would find it awfully crowded, darling," India said.

"I like it here better than camp. Better than Nairobi, too. The governor's house is stuffy. And Lady Hayes Sadler fusses so."

"She does, doesn't she?" India said, smiling conspiratorially.

There was something so wonderfully comforting about Sid Baxter's modest bungalow. So welcoming and familiar. India found herself drawn to the house, and—though she'd never met him—to the man who lived in it.

"I should like to sit at this table and eat a bowl of porridge," Charlotte said. "And then I would like to sleep in that bed. I would have a lovely sleep there. Much better than on a lumpy old camp bed."

India laughed. "You sound just like Goldilocks. Maybe we'd better leave before the bears return."

"Will you join me for a pot of coffee?" Maggie asked.

"Don't you drink tea, Mrs. Carr?" Charlotte asked.

"I certainly do not! Not on the best damn coffee plantation in all of Africa!" she said, grinning.

Charlotte giggled.

"Care for a cup? I'll have Alice fix it for you with a bit of sugar and lots of milk. Plus a biscuit or two."

"Oh, yes, please!" Charlotte said, before India could refuse.

Maggie led them to her house. It was a modest affair, like Sid Baxter's, but much larger. It had a proper sitting room, a kitchen, dining room, two bedrooms, plus an attic. Maggie asked her cook to bring coffee and biscuits, then led her guests to the veranda.

India sat down. She looked out over the fields of glossy green coffee plants. They gave way to the warm, golden plains. Beyond them she could see Mount Kenya towering in the distance, its peak piercing the cloudless sky.

"Mrs. Carr, if I had this view, and this veranda on which to sit and gaze at it, I should never accomplish anything," she said.

Maggie laughed. "If you had seven hundred acres under coffee, you would, my dear. You'd have to."

"Have you no help?"

"I do. The best. That's what Sid does for me. Oversees the farm and workers. Gets my harvest to market. We set a record in London last year. Most money ever paid for British East African coffee. At the moment we have to do our roasting at a neighbor's farm. And pay for the privilege. But soon we'll be roasting right here. I've ordered the machinery. It's supposed to arrive in September. Have to build a barn for it, of course, but we've started. Should be done by summer." Maggie turned to Charlotte. "You tell that father of yours that if he wants to help the planters, he should build a train line from Nairobi up to Thika. Help us get our crop to market faster."

"My father doesn't listen to children, Mrs. Carr. He believes we should be seen, not heard," Charlotte said solemnly.

"Well, isn't he old-fashioned? I get some of my best advice from children. Just the other day little Mattie Thompson told me I should climb trees at sunset. I tried it. He's right. You get the most beautiful view of the evening sky. You tell your father to come and see me, Charlotte. I'll set him straight. On coffee and on children."

"I'm sure he would love to come, Mrs. Carr. Unfortunately, he may not have the time. He works very hard," India said quickly, apologetically.

Maggie Carr nodded, listening to India, but looking, thoughtfully, at Charlotte.

"How old are you, Charlotte?"

"I'm nearly six years old, Mrs. Carr."

Maggie shook her head. "Six is far too young to be sitting on the veranda for long periods of time with grown-ups. There's a new calf in the cattle pen, a dozen new chicks in the henhouse, and we've a tame gazelle named Mocha who walks around the farm as though she owns it. Would you like to see them?"

"Yes, please!" Charlotte said.

"Go into the kitchen and ask for Baaru. He'll take you. Just steer clear of the barn. There's a very bad-tempered ox in there."

"Yes, ma'am. I will."

Maggie smiled as Charlotte clattered off to the kitchen. "Beautiful girl, your daughter," she said.

"Thank you."

"Takes after you."

India blushed, then said, "I can't tell you the agony I suffered when I learned she was gone, Mrs. Carr. I couldn't stop thinking of her all alone out there. With lions and snakes and God knows what else. Apparently I went a bit mad. Had to be sedated to be kept from riding out after her myself. The men all thought it was a bad idea."

India told Maggie about the days spent waiting for news. She remembered going to look in on Charlotte in her tent and not finding her. She remembered turning the entire camp upside down and still not finding her. And she remembered a guide saying footprints had been found leading to the river . . . that they'd checked the river . . . that Charlotte was not there. She remembered collapsing and sobbing and little else, until three days later, when Florence Delamere came rushing to her side to tell her that Charlotte was alive and being looked after at a nearby farm. She'd gotten up from her bed then, still groggy from the sedative, and asked that a horse be brought. Florence had tried to talk her out of riding. Freddie, too. India didn't tell Maggie Carr what had passed between them.

"India, for God's sake be sensible," Freddie had said to her. "You're in no condition to ride. Charlotte is fine. It's better that she stay where she is. They'll bring her to us as soon as she's able to travel."

"Pretend you care, Freddie," she'd replied acidly. "For appearances' sake at least, if not for Charlotte's."

She'd mounted her horse and ridden the nine miles with Tom Meade. She'd run into the McGregors' house, barely greeting them. Mrs. McGregor had taken her to Charlotte immediately and India had sunk to her knees by her daughter's bedside, smiling and crying all at once, scolding her dreadfully for wandering off, then embracing her and covering her in kisses. Freddie, who'd decided to follow after all, sat on the edge of the bed, affecting concern. After India had calmed down a little, she remembered herself; she stood and made the proper introductions. She took Mrs. McGregor's hands in hers and thanked her over and over again.

"I was rather effusive," she said to Maggie now. "I quite flustered the poor woman. She kept trying to take her hands back. Kept telling me it was Sid Baxter I should be thanking, not her. We are so lucky that Tom Meade knew of him and thought to get him."

"You are indeed. No one knows this area like Sid."

India put her coffee cup down. "You know, Mrs. Carr, it's quite an unusual thing, Mr. Baxter's reticence. Most men would not have disappeared after rescuing the undersecretary's daughter. Most would have been front and center, hand out, hoping for some sort of reward. Or busy telling stories to newspapers for money."

"Sid Baxter's not most people," Maggie said.

"So I gather," India said. She dropped her gaze to her coffee cup, then haltingly continued. "Charlotte is my entire life, Mrs. Carr, I cannot imagine what I would have done if I had lost her. I am forever in Mr. Baxter's debt. If there's ever anything I can do for him, anything he needs . . ."

"He was only happy he got to her in time. That's all the reward he wants."

India smiled. "That sounds like something he told you to say. Is he avoiding us?"

It was Maggie's turn to blush. "You have to understand something about Sid—he's a very shy man. Doesn't like people much. Wouldn't be out here in the middle of nowhere if he did."

"I see. Well, I'm disappointed to have missed him. I had very much hoped to thank him in person. But perhaps you would do that for me?"

"I'd be glad to."

India said they must be getting back.

"Are you still on safari?" Maggie asked.

India shook her head. "I've had enough of safaris to last me a lifetime," she said. She explained that she and Charlotte were staying with the Mc-Gregors. Most of the others were staying on at the campsite, enjoying a few more days' shooting. Freddie and Hayes Sadler had traveled back to Nairobi as they had a few days' business there. When that was concluded, he would fetch them from the McGregors' and they would travel together to Mount Kenya for a fortnight's holiday before returning to England.

Maggie and India went to find Charlotte. She was sitting on the steps of Sid Baxter's house with Baaru, a boy of ten. They were feeding Mocha pieces of carrot. India thanked Maggie for her hospitality. She and Charlotte said their good-byes, then Baaru brought them their horses, which had been borrowed from the McGregors. Charlotte's was a pony.

Maggie stood in her yard and waved them off. She watched until they'd ridden all the way down her drive to the road, then she turned and walked past her house through her backyard and into her barn. Hands on her hips, she scowled up at the hayloft and shouted, "You can come down now, you bloody great coward!"

A head appeared over the edge of the loft. "They're gone?" Sid said.

"They are. You're safe."

Sid lowered a wooden ladder to the ground and climbed down it.

"You could have said hello to them. The little girl was sad to have missed you."

Sid said nothing.

Maggie gave him a long, thoughtful look. "Beautiful child, that one, isn't she? Spitting image of her mother. Six years old, she is. Nearly."

Sid still said nothing, just made his way to the barn door.

"Did you see them from the window?"

"No."

"Liar." She shook her head, then said, "I don't know about you anymore, Bax. Running off with the surveyor. Hiding in the barn. Moping and mooning. I just don't understand it. India Lytton's a fine woman, to be sure, but she's not worth all this. No woman is. No man, either. It's time you got over her."

Sid turned and looked at her. "Great idea, Maggs," he said. "Thanks. Care to tell me how?"

CHAPTER 99

"Bloody hell," Seamie swore. He threw his gloves on the ground and shoved his blue, aching hands under his clothing and into his armpits to warm them. "It's an icefall. A bloody great icefall! How on earth could we have missed it?"

"The snow," Willa said, gazing up at the glistening slope. "The light it throws plays with your eyes. Shortens distances. Blurs features. I'll bet we saw it. We just thought it was part of the couloir."

She turned to look at him and he swore again. "What is it?" she said.

He touched his fingers to her lips and held them up so she could see them. They were smeared with blood.

"It's nothing," she said.

"Willa, you're sick. And in case you haven't noticed, there's an icefall ahead of us. It's probably sixty feet high. The angle's seventy degrees. At least. You're in no condition to tackle it. We have to go back."

"I'm fine."

Seamie shook his head. "The sun's too high. We took too long. It's melting the ice. We dodged rockfalls all the way up the couloir."

"We're off the couloir now."

"Willa—"

"Look, Seamie, I'm knackered, I admit it. My head's pounding like a tom-tom. I want to throw up all the time. But I know I've got enough left in me to make the summit. I *know* it. I also know that it's all I've got. If I go down now, I won't get back up."

"That's no way to climb."

"It's going to have to be."

"For Christ's sake, look at the chance you're taking!" Seamie yelled. "You're sick, tired. You're not thinking straight. You're too . . . too . . ."

"Too what?"

"Too damned competitive!"

"Oh, I am, am I?" she said hotly. "Tell me something."

"What?"

"Say I were to go down. Right now. What would you do?"

Seamie hesitated, just for a second, then said, "Go up."

"Of course you would, you bastard."

"Your point?"

"I didn't come this far to let you steal all the glory, Finnegan. I'm summiting Mawenzi with you. I don't care if I have to crawl the rest of the way to do it."

"A good climber would turn back. You know that."

"No, you're wrong. A *weak* climber would turn back. A good climber would reach the summit."

"Summiting's only half the battle. We still have to descend."

"If you were with George Mallory right now instead of me, would you tell him to go down?"

Seamie looked away. He said nothing.

"No, you wouldn't. So why are you telling me?"

"Because—"

Willa cut him off. "Because I'm a woman."

"No, Willa, that's not why."

"Why, then? Tell me."

Seamie looked away. Because I care for you, he thought, and if anything ever happened to you it would kill me.

"I thought so," Willa said angrily. "Do me a favor, Seamie. Don't patronize me. I get that from the rest of the world. I don't need it from you."

Seamie's anger flared. "Go, then," he snapped. "After you."

He knew what he was doing. He was telling her to lead. To pull herself up a seventy-degree slope using only crampons, axes, and brute strength. To cut steps where needed into thick, hard ice. It was hard work under normal circumstances. At nearly sixteen thousand feet, when you were sick and your lungs could not draw enough oxygen, it was crucifying.

"Get out of my way and I bloody well will," she said.

He readied his gear, then watched her attack the icefall. He could hear her breathing. She was laboring to draw quick, deep breaths. She'd learned the technique from Mallory on one of their Alps climbs. It helped get more oxygen into the lungs. Within minutes of her start, Seamie's anger was forgotten. He loved to watch her climb. She was breathtaking, one of the most technically gifted climbers—male or female—he'd ever seen. She seemed not so much to climb a face, but to flow up it, her every movement fluid and sure. She seemed to know by instinct where to place her hands, her feet. Holds he was certain were too small, weren't. Others he was sure would give way, didn't. She lost her footing once, slipping a good ten feet before she arrested her fall with one of her axes—nearly giving him a heart attack in the bargain—but even with the slip, she still made it up the icefall in under an hour.

Looking at her, so strong and graceful, so damned determined to reach the peak, he realized that he'd been wrong the other night, when she asked him what made a great mountain climber. They'd both been wrong. It wasn't skill or fearlessness, strength or arrogance. It was longing. A great unquenchable yearning for that which was always just out of reach. He saw it in her, that longing, that greatness. She would not be denied.

Two minutes later she was hanging over the edge, smiling down at him. "I'm on a col!" she shouted gleefully. "With a lovely huge boulder! I've got a belay! Hold on!"

A few minutes later the rope that had been coiled over her shoulder came flying down to him. He grabbed it, looped it around his waist, and tied it with a bowline. He started up the icefall, distressed to see drops of crimson on it. Her bleeding was worsening. They mustn't mess around. He was very glad of the belay. It was a huge boon. Between the rope and his crampons, he was up the icefall in minutes.

"There it is!" she said, pointing due south of where they stood. "Alden-Finnegan peak!"

"Looks solid," Seamie said excitedly. "And it's Finnegan-Alden peak, by the way."

Willa laughed. "We've some powdery snow to contend with. And a few rocks, but most look well sunk in. We shouldn't have any movement. Let's go."

It was only a short distance to the peak and straightforward. Half an hour later they were only steps away. Seamie was in the lead. Three yards from the top he stopped, looked at Willa, and stepped aside.

"No," she said. "Together."

She took his hand. He pulled her up alongside him and they took the last few steps in unison, each placing a foot on the summit at the same time. They were quiet for a moment, breathlessly taking it all in—Kibo to the west, the ocean to the east, the hills and sweeping plains north and south of them. And then Seamie let out a loud, long, echoing whoop. Willa did, too. And suddenly they were jumping up and down in the snow like children, shouting and laughing, giddy from adrenaline, exhaustion, and too little oxygen. Willa threw her arms around him. He hugged her, pulling her close, burying his face in her neck, and then it happened—without planning to, without meaning to, he kissed her. He tasted her mouth, the blood on her lips. He felt her twine her arms around his neck and then she was kissing him back.

He broke away and looked at her, at her beautiful, weary face. He took her face in his hands and kissed her again and again and then guilt and despair broke through his happiness and overwhelmed him and he pulled away again. "God, I shouldn't have done that. I shouldn't have kissed you. Good Christ, what a cock-up. I'm sorry."

Willa's face, so radiant only seconds ago, clouded. "*Sorry? Why?*"

He looked at her as if he hadn't heard her correctly. "Because of George."

Worry filled her eyes. "I don't understand, Seamie. Is there something between you and George?"

"*Me* and George? No, there damn well isn't! It's *you* and George!"

"You think that George and I . . . that we . . . that we're *lovers?*"

"Aren't you? The way you were with him in the pub in Cambridge . . . you kissed him good night."

"I kissed Albie good night, too."

"Albie's your brother."

"And George is my second brother. If I kissed him, it was just like kissing Albie, believe me. Why didn't you ask me about George? Or ask George about me? He would have told you. He has no time for girls, only mountains. You daft man. Why didn't you say something in Cambridge?"

"Too jealous, I guess."

"I wanted you so. I would have kissed you on top of St. Botolph's."

"Why didn't you?"

"Because I'd already done it in my garden!"

"That was five bloody years ago!"

"It would've been twice that I'd taken the lead. Just how forward is a girl supposed to be? I thought you had someone else. I thought you must."

"No, Wills."

"I wanted you every night of that damned boat ride. Every night at the Mombasa Club. I wanted you to make love to me. When you didn't, I thought it was because of another girl."

"There's no other girl, Wills. Never has been. Not since that night in your back garden. Under Orion."

He kissed her again, long and slow and deeply. Never in his life had he felt like this, so happy, so complete. Insanely excited, yet calm and content. On a mad impulse, he took her hands in his and said, "I love you, Willa."

He thought she might laugh. Blush. Scold him. Tell him he was insane. Instead she simply said, "I love you, too. Always have. Since forever."

She kissed him then and they took one long, last look at the view. And took photographs, two of each of them, with the camera Seamie had lugged up in his pack.

It was nearly one o'clock when they began their descent. The sun was high and bright, but neither Seamie nor Willa, reeling from attaining the summit, and from what had happened between them there, noticed. They didn't notice that the black tops of rocks now peeked out on the short stretch above the col—rocks that had been completely covered earlier. They didn't notice the water trickling in drips off the edge of the col and down the icefall. They didn't notice any of this until they were back in the couloir and they realized the snow was dangerously soft. Until Seamie lost his footing on loose rock and stopped himself sliding a hundred feet only with a hard swing of his ice-axe.

Until ice that had embedded a rock wedged under a boulder on the ridge above them suddenly crumbled in the afternoon heat, releasing both rock and boulder, sending them smashing down the couloir.

Seamie didn't realize any of this until he heard the roar and looked up in time to see the rock-slide bearing down on Willa. Until the boulder clipped her shoulder, knocking her off the couloir. Until she went hurtling past him, screaming, and was gone.

CHAPTER 100

"Will be good harvest, no?" Wainaina, Sid's head field worker, said, pinching off a hard red coffee berry from a lush, healthy bush.

"I think so, but I'm afraid to count my chickens."

Wainaina cocked her head. Her puzzled expression told him that she didn't understand. Sid explained the saying's meaning to her in his poor Kikuyu. She nodded and laughed and told him don't count his chickens, then, but by all means, count his coffee beans. "The bushes should give a ton," she said.

Sid snorted. "More like two, I should think."

Wainaina considered this figure. "Perhaps one and one half," she allowed.

She warned him that with a good harvest would come many demands. The other workers were already counting up the goats they would earn. Some would expect new fences built for their *shambas,* no less than twenty by twenty. Wainaina wanted these things, too, and an iron griddle besides—one just like the Msabu's cook had.

"Tell them they'll get their pens and their goats—and you'll get your griddle—*if* I get my two tons."

Wainaina nodded. Sid nodded, too. He knew this was just the opening salvo in Wainaina's yearly battle to get all she could for herself and her fellow workers. She had to have something to offer the other women, something to motivate them to pick every ripe berry on every bush and leave nothing behind. They would go back and forth, Sid and Wainaina, with Sid demanding ever-increasing quantities of coffee and Wainaina declaring his demands impossible, but making a few more of her own. Another griddle. A length of cloth. Two chickens. A lantern. Sid thought that Jevanjee and the rest of the Nairobi merchants could learn much from her.

The sun had started to sink as they'd begun their discussion. When they finished, Wainaina picked up an old tin pie pan and beat it with a stick, signaling to her workers in fields near and far that it was time to go home.

Sid bid her a good evening and headed for his own house. He was tired. He and Wainaina and the others had spent the day hoeing and weeding, making sure that nothing competed with the precious coffee plants for water and nutrients. They would fuss over them continually now until harvest time, doing everything in their power to ensure a good crop. Sid would be dining alone tonight. Maggie had been invited to supper at the Thompsons'. He had not. Lucy and her mother still weren't speaking to him. Earlier in the day, he'd asked Alice to leave a plate of something cold for him on his own table. He didn't like to eat at Maggie's table when she was not home. As he approached his house, he saw that it was lit up. Dusk was settling. Alice must have left the lantern burning. A nice touch, he thought. Very welcoming. That Alice was a good old girl.

As he got closer, he saw—to his great surprise—that a brown horse was tethered on the far side of his house. It looked like Ellie, Maggie's mare. Had Maggs arrived home early? And if so, why had she tied Ellie here instead of putting her in the barn?

He saw then that the horse wasn't Ellie. Ellie was all brown. This horse had a black muzzle and feet. He tried to place it, then realized that the McGregors had a brown mare with black feet. He'd often seen the missus riding out to the plains on it all by herself on a Sunday. He'd hailed her once and asked her why.

"It's Sunday, Mr. Baxter. I'm going to church."

"*Church?* Where, ma'am?"

She'd made a sweeping gesture, one that encompassed the plains, the sky, and the hills.

"Right in front of you. Have you ever seen one finer?"

That was certainly Mrs. McGregor's mare. Sid hurried now, wondering if something was wrong at their farm. He was tired from the long day and not thinking straight. If he had been, he would have remembered that India Lytton was staying with the McGregors while her daughter got her strength back.

But he didn't remember. Not until he was in his doorway staring at the woman seated at his table. Mrs. McGregor had brown hair. This woman was blond. A few curls had sprung free of her careful twist. This woman was beautiful, too. So damned beautiful. Six years on and she hadn't changed. She was still slender and straight-backed, still lovely. He felt his heart clench in his chest. Six years on, the pain of her betrayal was as fresh as if it had happened yesterday.

Her eyes were closed behind her eyeglasses. She'd been dozing. They opened now. His footsteps had woken her. He was out of the door and down the steps before she'd turned her head. But it was too late; she was already on her feet.

"Mr. Baxter! Is that you?" she called from the doorway "Please don't go! I've waited here for hours for you."

Sid stopped, hands clenched at his side. He did not turn around.

"I'm sorry if I trespassed. Truly I am. I knocked on Mrs. Carr's door first, then yours. I didn't mean to offend you. I only want to speak to you. My daughter and I are leaving soon and she wanted to give you this. Well, you can't see since you won't turn around, so I'll tell you what it is. It's a photograph of her. She wanted to bring it herself, but she couldn't. She's caught a cold, you see. Only a slight one, but I'm worried that she's still delicate after what she went through so I wouldn't let her come. I have left her at the McGregors', tucked up in bed."

Sid made no reply. India advanced to the porch.

"Won't you please forgive me for intruding? It's just that I didn't have anywhere else to wait for you. Couldn't we start again? I'll go first. Hello, Mr. Baxter. How do you do?"

Sid turned around slowly, ever so slowly. He lifted his eyes to hers and quietly said, "Not so well at the moment. And you, Mrs. Baxter?"

CHAPTER 101

For a few seconds, India was senseless. She could not breathe. She could not feel or hear. She could only see. Sid. Her Sid. Dead all these years, now standing in front of her, silent tears on his cheeks.

And then her senses came back, flooding her body with such violent intensity that her legs gave way and crumpled on the porch steps and she had to grab the wooden railing to keep herself from falling to the ground.

Sid stood, hands clenched into fists. He made no move to help her.

"Damn you!" she cried. "Damn you! Damn you!"

He stared at her, saying nothing, then he wiped the tears from his face.

"Freddie said you were dead! The newspapers all said it!"

"I faked my death. I had to. Your husband was going to hang me."

"How could you do it, Sid? How could you let me think you were dead? *Me?*"

He smiled a hard, bitter smile. "How could you let me think you loved me?"

"I *did* love you!"

"Is that why you married Lytton? Because you loved me?"

"I had reasons for doing what I did. Reasons you know nothing about."

"I'm sure you did. Comfort. Money. Safety . . ."

India was on her feet in an instant. She walked the few yards that separated them, raised her hand, and slapped him as hard as she could.

She almost told him then. Almost told him that she married a man she despised and endured his rules, his demands, and his cruelties, all to protect her child. *Their* child. She almost told him. But she didn't. His anger was too much. It frightened her. So did her own. Instead she turned away from him and strode to her horse. She was in the saddle in an instant, reins in hand.

"You can't ride now," Sid said. "It's getting dark. It's not safe. Wait until morning."

"And do what?" she spat. "Spend the night here? With you? I'll take my chances."

She was about to spur the mare on when Sid said, "You've ruined me by coming here, do you know that? Ruined my life all over again. I'd found a measure of peace here. Some small happiness."

India shook her head. She couldn't believe what she was hearing. She couldn't believe any of this. She got down from her horse again and strode back to him.

"I what, Sid? I *what*? I ruined your life? *I* ruined *your* life?" she shouted. "What about my life? I was waiting for you! Not knowing where you were. Not knowing what had happened to you. I found out you were dead on the streets of Whitechapel from newsboys yelling that your body had been found in the Thames. *From newsboys!*"

"It wasn't supposed to happen that way. That fast. The body came up again quickly. Too quickly."

"Oh, well, that's all right, then, isn't it? That explains bloody everything!"

The look in Sid's eyes, the look of fury and pain, softened at her words and he became uncertain, but his voice did not. "Your grief over me didn't stop you from marrying Freddie, though, did it? How long did you mourn me, India? One day? Two?"

"I told you I had my reasons for marrying Freddie," she said.

"Yes, you did. And I told you what they were."

India backed away from him, wounded to her very soul. "Thank God you did it, you bastard. Thank God you spared me a life with you. With a man as heartless and cruel as you are."

She climbed back into her saddle. As she did, Sid said, "Don't come back here, India. Keep away from me. Please."

"Don't worry, Sid. There's no chance of that," India said. She looked down at the reins in her hands, then at him. There were tears on her own cheeks now. "Do you really hate me so much?" she whispered brokenly.

He shook his head. "No, I don't. I don't hate you at all. That's the whole bloody problem, isn't it? I love you, India. Still."

CHAPTER 102

Seamie stopped dead, placed his hands on his knees, and gasped for breath. He looked around himself frantically, hoping to spot a landmark— a familiar boulder, a gnarled tree, anything. His lungs were screaming for air, but he knew he could not rest.

Willa lay on her back in their tent, thousands of feet above him, semi-conscious, her right leg smashed. The falling boulder had knocked her off the couloir. She had fallen a good hundred feet, hitting hard on her right side, then rolling and sliding another twenty before she was able to grasp a jutting rock and stop herself.

The fall had taken only seconds, yet to Seamie it had seemed as if it would never stop. He remembered shouting to her over and over again. And finally she'd shouted back. She was alive, thank God! He came down fast, slipped, and nearly lost his footing. "Slow down, you idiot!" he yelled at himself, knowing that if he fell, too, there would be no one to help her. No one to help either of them. They would die on the mountain.

"Jesus Christ, Willa," he said when he got to her. He didn't ask if she was all right. She wasn't. Her face was covered in blood; there were long gashes on her head and hands. But they were nothing compared to her right leg. It lay twisted at a sickening angle to the rest of her body.

"It's buggered, isn't it?" she said in a ragged voice.

"It's bad," he said.

"How bad?"

He couldn't answer her.

"Seamie, how bad?"

"The bones are through the skin."

She banged her head into the snow. Again and again and again.

"Stop. Stop it, Willa. You can't come apart on me."

"I'll never climb again."

"We're not going to worry about that. Not now. All we're going to worry about now is how to get you off this mountain."

He knew she couldn't do it by herself, and he was afraid to carry her the rest of the way. They still had to get down the rest of the couloir, over an icy ridge, and down the snowy northwest corrie. What if he slipped?

Willa still had the rope coiled over her chest. He knew what to do. He quickly dug a seat in the snow at the base of the couloir. Then he tied one end around her waist, the other around his own. His hands were blue again, the rope was icy and wet, and it took him a long time to tie the bowlines.

"What are you doing?" she'd asked weakly.

"I'm going to lower you down the couloir."

"Then what?"

"I have no idea. I'll work it out when we get there. Let's get you onto your back."

Willa tried to roll over. The broken bones jostled and ground against themselves. She screamed. Seamie almost lost his nerve, but didn't. He couldn't. He had to bully her or they'd never get down.

"Come on, Wills," he said, helping her. "Keep going. Scream if you have to, but keep going. That's a girl."

She did scream, but she got onto her back. He helped her pull her knees up to her chest and hook her hands behind her thighs. He sat in the snow seat he'd dug, braced himself with his feet, and began to let out the rope. The weight of Willa's body took her down the couloir. She screamed again at every rut and bump. The rope ran out before they reached the bottom and he had to shout for her to lower her good leg and dig in with her crampon to keep herself from sliding while he descended to her, then they repeated the whole process. By the time they got to the bottom she was gray with pain.

From there it only got worse. He thought about leaving her tied to the rope, climbing up the ridge by himself, and then pulling her up after him. She weighed about 125 pounds, though, and he knew there was no way he could pull up that much dead weight at this altitude, so he decided to carry her on his back. He made her clasp her hands together around his neck, then he looped the rope around his shoulders and under her bottom, making a crude sling. Every time he moved, he jostled the break again. Gravity pulled on it. Willa was in agony; he knew she was. Several times he felt her teeth on his back as she bit down to keep from crying out. And once he felt her grip release around his neck and he knew she'd blacked out. He'd had to dig in with his feet, grab for her hands, and shout at her until she'd come around again.

The effort of climbing a ridge at fifteen thousand feet carrying extra weight was harrowing. Every step took all his strength. He'd had to pause after each one, trying to breathe, trying to shore up his strength, before he could take the next one. When they reached the top, he'd had to sit down for some time before he had the strength to lower her again, this time to the top of the corrie. From there the slopes eased and the snow and ice began to give way to rock. Relieved, he hurried his pace, desperate to get Willa to camp. It was a mistake. He slid in some scree, stumbled, and fell. Willa, still on his back, fell with him, banging down on her broken leg. The pain was so bad, she'd blacked out again. He got up, cursing himself, and half-walked, half-staggered his way back to camp.

It was nearly evening by the time he got Willa into their tent. He laid her down on a bed, got a fire started, and got busy cleaning her wounds. She had a deep gouge on her brow. Another on her palm. The rest were scrapes. He washed them with melted snow, then poured whisky from a flask they'd packed into the cuts. It stung, he knew it did.

"How about the leg?" she said, in a voice worn thin by pain.

"I'm getting to it," Seamie replied. He took a clasp knife from his pocket and cut her trouser leg open. He knew she was watching his face, so he worked to keep it blank. He had to work hard for he had never seen jagged bone ends sticking out of a person before. He didn't know what to do. He thought about trying to set the bones, but it was impossible. He would never be able to set the edges together properly; she needed a surgeon for that. He thought about trying to splint them, but he knew that merely touching the leg would cause her unbearable pain. He finally decided to douse the fracture with whisky.

"This is going to hurt," he said.

She nodded, then went rigid as he poured the alcohol into the wound.

When she could speak again, she said, "Is it hopeless?"

"I don't know. Perhaps if we could get to a doctor, get it set, you'd have a chance at it healing."

Willa laughed bitterly. "Mombasa's one hundred and fifty miles away. Nairobi's about the same. I can take my pick, I suppose, since I'll never make it to either."

"Yes, you will."

"How, Seamie? It's impossible. I can't walk and you can't carry me. Not all the way to Mombasa."

"I'm going to go down to the base camp. Get the porters," Seamie said. He'd been formulating this plan all the way down the mountain.

"They won't come. They're afraid."

"They *will* come. I'll offer them all our gear. Compasses, field glasses, tents, the whole lot. They'll take it. I know they will. They can get a fortune for it. And in return I'll get them to fashion a stretcher. We'll put you on it and take turns carrying. When one gets tired, another can relieve him."

"And you'll walk all the way to Mombasa like that?"

"No, we'll walk to Voi. If we can just make Voi, we can get on the train there and ride the rest of the way to Mombasa."

He quickly set about making her a plate of hard cheese and tinned sardines, then filled her canteen with water from the stove and set it by her bed together with a lantern. When he finished, he covered her with both their sleeping bags.

"I'll be back tomorrow," he said, slinging his own canteen across his chest.

"Seamie, if something happens . . ."

"Nothing is going to happen, Willa. Nothing."

"But if it does . . . I just . . . I . . . well, I love you."

He'd seen the fear in her eyes, though she'd done her best to hide it. He'd knelt beside her, taking her hands in his. "I love you, too. We'll have the rest of our lives to talk about this, I promise you. Do you believe me?"

"Yes."

"Good. Rest now. You're going to need all your strength for what's to come."

She nodded. He kissed her and left. It was already seven o'clock and he was desperate to put as much ground behind him as possible before nightfall. He half walked, half ran down the mountain. The moon was almost full and shone brightly, illuminating his way. He had no pack to weigh him down, no snow or ice to slow his steps. His trip to Antarctica had made a navigator out of him, and he managed to stay on a south-southwest track by the stars alone, stopping only a few times to check his compass.

Shortly after three o'clock in the morning, after he'd been walking for more than eight hours, he was nearing the place where he thought the base camp should be. He knew it would be quiet because of the hour, but he expected to see the light of a fire, to smell its smoke. He thought he might be greeted by one or two of the porters who'd heard him coming. Tepili and his men slept lightly, always attuned to the sounds of the night.

And then he *did* smell something—something so strong, so foul, that it doubled him over and made him retch. It was the smell of death, of human bodies rotting. Seamie grabbed a handkerchief from his pocket and pressed it over his face. He stumbled on toward the camp, dreading what he would find.

He saw the tent; it was shredded. A trunk was opened and up-ended. Boxes and crates were smashed. The entire site had been ransacked.

"Tepili?" he called out. "Tepili, are you there?"

There was no reply, only a low, menacing growl. He looked to his right; a leopard was standing over what was left of a body, baring his teeth. Bones and fangs glinted whitely in the moonlight.

"Get out of here!" Seamie shouted. He picked up a rock and threw it at him. The animal ran. Seamie stumbled through the camp. He found another body and another. They had arrows in them. Leopards didn't shoot arrows. The Chagga did, though—poison-tipped ones.

Boedeker had told him the Chagga could be hostile. Tepili had, too. Their chieftain, Rindi, was not fond of outsiders, Tepili had said. He'd tolerated the Germans and British at times, fought with them at others. His son Sina was the same. And it wasn't only whites who angered the Chagga; they clashed with the Masai, even with members of other Chagga villages.

Seamie had thought Tepili a bit of an old woman, seeing trouble where there was none, but now he saw that he was right.

It had all been too easy, he thought now. The Chagga had agreed to guide them, brought them here, and left them. It must have been their plan all along to go back to their village, assemble more of their tribesmen, and then attack. First the Masai porters. And then himself and Willa, too. He remembered that the guides had asked when they were coming back and he had told them. His blood froze at the thought.

He had to get out of here. Now. Whoever had done this might still be close by. Christ, why had he yelled for Tepili? Why had he made so much bloody noise? He had to get off the hills and back up the mountain and he had to do it before daybreak.

Exhausted, hungry, afraid for his life, Seamie wanted nothing more than to sit down and rest, if only for a few minutes, but he couldn't. It was too dangerous. For him and for Willa. If the Chagga found him here and killed him they would kill her, too. She couldn't hope to survive on Kilimanjaro alone.

He started back the way he'd come, walking as quietly—and as quickly—as he could. And then something occurred to him—something that scared him more than what he'd just seen, more than the Chagga—he would have to get Willa off the mountain by himself. There were no more porters. No more Tepili. There was no one to help him now. He was all alone.

CHAPTER 103

Joe rapped on a frosted glass door on the ground floor of the Whitechapel Free Clinic for Women and Children.

"Come in, already!" a woman's voice called.

Joe poked his head around the door. "Sister Moskowitz?" he said.

A heavily pregnant woman was sitting at a desk. She raised her head and smiled at him. "Wrong on both counts. It's Rosen, not Moskowitz. I'm a married woman now. And it's Doctor, not Sister. I finished my degree last spring. *And* you're to call me Ella. Always. Anyone who gets the government to give my clinic ten thousand quid is on a first-name basis with me for life."

"Married? And a doctor?! Congratulations on both counts!" Joe said, smiling. "Who's the lucky bloke?"

"His name is David Rosen. He's a doctor, too. Works at the Royal Free Hospital. I met him there during my clinical training."

"Am I right in thinking that there might be an addition to the Rosen household soon? Perhaps I'm being too forward."

Ella laughed. "You're on the maternity wing, Joe, and I'm the head obstetrician. We talk about these things here. Come in, come in! Does your chair fit through the door? Good! Will you have some rugelach?"

Ella fed him pastries and had a nurse bring him a cup of tea. He knew better than to refuse either. This is how it worked with Ella and her family. Whether he was sitting with her and discussing infant mortality in the East End, visiting her mother and father at their café to talk about economic opportunities for immigrants, or meeting her brother Yanki, a rabbi now and head of East London's largest synagogue, to talk funding for the Jewish Orphans' Home, it was always the same—first you ate, then you talked.

"So," Ella said, after she and Joe had polished off a dozen rugelach between them. "What can I do for you? Another bill to go before the Commons? You need statistics? Case histories?"

"No statistics today, Ella. But history of a sort. I'm trying to get the home secretary to reopen a murder case."

"Whose?"

"Gemma Dean's. An actress. She was killed a few days after I was shot."

"I remember the name, but I didn't know Miss Dean personally. How can I help you?"

"You're going to think this is a barmy question, but here goes. Do you remember Sid Malone? Big-time East London wide boy?"

"Of course I do. Him and his lads ate at the caff all the time. Oz, Ronnie, Des—the lot. He was a good bloke, was Sid. Not everyone would say so, but I do."

"Malone was accused of shooting me. He didn't do it, of course. Frankie Betts did. Sid was also accused of murdering Gemma Dean. I don't believe he did that, either. I thought Frankie might have done it, so I went to see him. Asked him point-blank if he did and he said no. I believe him. Then I asked him if he knew who did do it. He said no to that, too, but I don't believe him. He knows, but he's not saying. I'm not sure why."

"What does all of this have to do with me?" Ella asked.

"Frankie got very shirty with me while I was asking him about Sid. Furious, in fact. Started raving about a doctor. And how he'd ruined everything, this doctor. Said he worked in Whitechapel. At a clinic. Well, there's only one clinic in Whitechapel—this one. You were involved in it from the start, so I thought you might know if Sid was ever connected to it, and if so, who this mystery doctor is."

Ella looked away. His questions had clearly made her uncomfortable.

"I promise you, Ella, I'm not looking to land anybody in the shit. Was Sid involved?"

"Very much so," Ella finally said. "The reason we're still here and have been able to take over the buildings on either side of us is due to him. He gave us half a million quid. Right before he died."

Joe whistled at the amount. "What about the doctor?" he said. "Can you tell me his name?"

"*Her* name."

"How's that?"

"The doctor was a she not a he. Dr. Jones. India Selwyn Jones."

Joe thought he recalled the name. "Jones? Not the one who saved Fiona at the Labour rally? The one who married Freddie Lytton?"

"The very same."

"How are she and Sid connected?"

Ella looked at him, saying nothing, taking his measure. "This goes nowhere, right?" she finally said.

"Right."

"Sid and India were lovers. She was going to give up everything to be with him. They were going to leave the country together. They almost did, but all hell broke loose. Sid was accused of shooting you. And of killing Gemma Dean. He had to hide. India was terrified for him. Scared that he'd be caught and hanged."

"But she didn't leave with him . . ." Joe said.

"No, she didn't. Sid died and she married Freddie Lytton."

"Why?"

Ella shook her head. "That's something I can't tell you."

"Ella, I have to know. I want to clear Sid's name. It's not right that he was blamed for a murder he didn't commit."

"It doesn't matter what he's blamed for anymore, does it? Sid's dead. But other people are still alive. And they could be hurt if certain things were revealed. Badly hurt."

Joe decided that if he wanted more information he would have to volunteer some of his own.

"Ella, Sid's not dead."

"What?"

"He faked his death so he could get out of London. Start again some-where else."

Ella sat back in her chair, blinking at him. *"Gott in Himmel,"* she whis-pered. "How do you know this?"

"Because I know Sid. He's my wife's brother."

"You're joking!"

"No, I'm not."

"How could he have done that to India? How could he let her think he was dead? She was devastated when she heard his body had been found in the Thames."

"Maybe he thought she'd be better off without him."

"She wasn't. *Isn't,*" Ella said. She shook her head, obviously stunned. "Blimey, that's some bit of news, Joe. I really have to hand it to you."

"Now you see why I want to clear Sid's name. As long as he's wanted for the Dean killing, he can never see Fiona again. Or any of his family. He can never come home."

"Good," Ella said quietly. "He shouldn't."

Joe gave her a puzzled look. "Why, Ella?"

Ella looked away from him. "It's complicated, Joe. Very bloody compli-cated."

"You have to tell me what you know. You have to trust me."

"If I do, you must swear to tell no one."

"But—"

"No one. Not even your wife. Especially your wife. Swear it, otherwise I won't tell you."

"All right, then," Joe said unwillingly. "I swear."

"India was pregnant. With Sid Malone's child. When she learned that he was dead, she went to Freddie Lytton and asked him to marry her and to raise the child as his own. He agreed. For a price." Ella explained India's and Freddie's history to Joe, then said, "She would never have married Lyt-ton if she thought Malone was alive. *Never.* She loved Sid deeply and she despised Freddie. But she felt she had no choice. She did not want her child to be illegitimate."

"Sid never knew?"

"India never had the chance to tell him."

It was Joe's turn to feel stunned. His mind was swirling with all that Ella had told him. "That means . . ." he started to say.

"That means Freddie Lytton's daughter is really Sid Malone's," Ella said bluntly. "And that you and your wife have a niece."

"My God, Ella. I *have* to tell Fiona. I have to. She's my wife. I can't keep this from her. And Sid . . . if he ever does come home, he has a right to know, too. He's the child's real father."

"You can't, Joe. *Think,* for God's sake! What if Sid does come back? And what if you and Fiona tell him? What if he goes to see India? Demands to see the child? It could destroy the girl's life. And India's, too. Freddie Lytton, as we all know, is not a very nice bloke."

Joe knew Fiona would want to know about this. To withhold information like this from her felt like a betrayal, but he'd sworn to Ella that he wouldn't tell her. He didn't know what to do.

"Maybe Freddie would be reasonable, Ella. Maybe he would—"

"What? Invite Sid in for tea and scones? Let him visit the girl on weekends? Make sure everyone lives happily ever after? Keep dreaming, lad. The only way that I can see Fiona finding out, or anyone finding out, is if India chooses to tell her. And that's just not going to happen, is it?"

Joe took a deep breath and blew it out again. "You've put me in an awful position, Ella," he said.

"You put yourself there. I didn't want to tell you, remember? I did only because I know you're an honorable man. A man who'll keep his word to me. Was it worth it? Do you have your answers now?"

"Far from it," Joe said. "Only more questions. Mainly, how does Frankie Betts fit into all of this?"

"I have no idea," Ella said. "But I'll tell you one thing. I never believed one word of his bollocks about not meaning to shoot you and the gun going off by accident. I saw those bullet wounds. He meant it."

"I think he meant it, too. I could see him having it in for me after I fought with him in the Bark. But one thing I've never understood is why he would dress up as Sid to come after me and tell my secretary that he was Sid?"

They both sat in silence for a bit, mulling this over, then Ella said, "You know, in a strange way, I think that might also have had something to do with love."

"Don't tell me Frankie was in love with Dr. Jones, too?"

"No, not Dr. Jones, *Sid.* He loved him as a friend, as a brother, and then Sid betrayed him by walking away. By leaving to be with India. By going straight."

"But if Frankie loved Sid, wouldn't he want to help me clear his name?"

"You're thinking like the good man you are, not the vindictive little shit Frankie Betts is. Try to see it like he did. He's angry at Sid, he wants to hurt him. How do you hurt a man who wants to go straight? You vilify him.

Make him out to be a murderer. Shoot one person, murder another, see that he gets the blame for both. Force him back into the fold. It didn't work, though. Sid died. Or so we thought. But Frankie still found a way to make the best of it. He couldn't have Sid alive and a villain, so he'll have him dead and a villain. It's not much, but it's all he's got."

Joe shook his head. "Dr. Rosen, you're a wonder. Where'd you learn to think like a villain?"

Ella grinned. "Same place you did . . . Whitechapel."

Joe affected an insulted expression. "I beg your pardon?"

"I've been reading those articles by Jacob Riis. Scorchers, every one."

"It's responsible photojournalism in the service of social reform."

"Is that what you call it?"

"I do."

"Some might call it blackmail."

"Might they?"

"What are you after?"

"One hundred thousand. For schools and clinics in Hackney."

"Good. Keep up the pressure."

Joe thanked Ella for her time and her information, then rolled his chair out of her office.

Ella walked with him.

"What's your next step, then?" she asked, as they reached the front door.

"I think it's back to Wandsworth. To go one more round with Frankie."

Ella's eyes searched his. "You still don't think he killed Gemma Dean, do you?"

"Everything you said makes sense, but I saw Frankie's eyes when I asked him if he'd done it. Either he's a bloody good actor or I'm a very poor judge of who's lying and who's not. So that begs the question: if he didn't do it, then who did?"

CHAPTER 104

Freddie shaded his eyes from the blazing sun and gazed out over the African veldt. Joshua, Ash McGregor's roan stallion, tossed his head and whinnied, eager to gallop.

"In a moment, old chap, in a moment," Freddie said.

The tall grass waved lazily in the breeze, a vast golden ocean, but Freddie barely saw it. He was imagining the beautiful plains plowed under, turned into farms for coffee and sisal, or pasture for cattle and sheep.

The weeks he had spent in Africa, talking to everyone from government officials to planters and ranchers, guides and missionaries, had convinced him of one thing—with more settlers and a proper infrastructure, British East Africa could become an engine of unparalleled economic growth, growth that would benefit not only the colony itself, but all of Britain. Crops and animals on the plains, rubber and quinine plantations in the jungle, tourism everywhere—the possibilities, and the tax revenue, were endless. And those same settlers selling their goods back to mother England would be buying goods from her as well—farm implements made from Sheffield steel, cloth woven in Lancashire mills, china from the Staffordshire potteries.

As Freddie saw it, the problem wasn't that the British government had put too much money into Africa, but that they hadn't put enough in. Whatever was invested would be returned a hundredfold. He knew that his task, once he returned home, was to convince his peers in the Commons, Lord Elgin, and the PM himself, of Africa's potential.

He intended to ask the government to enlarge the Uganda railway, to add routes north and south off the main line. He would also ask for old roads to be improved and new ones to be laid. For dams and water lines to be built. For telegraph lines to be extended. And to accomplish all this, he would ask for funds. Four million to start.

He knew he would have to make a damned good case in the Commons for money like that, especially when feeling against further expenditure on the railway was high, but he'd already begun. He was writing glowing articles on BEA, its bounty and its beauty, for *The Times*, and sending back detailed reports, packed with figures, tables, and photographs, to Elgin. By the time he returned home, he hoped to have swayed both the public and their elected representatives to his cause. With the pump thus primed, he would go before the Commons and make his case. And then it would be *his* name that was regularly seen in the headlines, not Joe Bristow's.

How he would relish that, turning the tables on Bristow. As far as he was concerned, Joe and his tedious demands for clinics and schools in East London could go to hell. Educating the working class was nothing but a waste of good servants. England's future lay with her colonies, not in her slums.

Joshua snorted and stamped. Freddie patted the animal's neck. He'd returned from safari several days ago and had been closeted inside Ash McGregor's study ever since, writing articles, reports, and speeches, and was now glad of an afternoon's ride. He needed a bit of air. Needed to clear his head. And he needed to find out what the hell was going on with India.

Something was, he was certain of it. She was not herself. Normally she had the stamina of a dray horse. She had to—being a political wife took an ungodly amount of energy. But suddenly it seemed that all her energy had deserted her. She looked pale and agitated. Her eyes were red-rimmed, as if she'd been weeping.

Freddie had wished to speak to her when he'd first arrived at the McGregors', but he hadn't been able to because she wasn't there. She'd gone out riding, Elspeth McGregor told him, as she had almost every morning, and tended to stay out for hours. He'd asked Mrs. McGregor to send her into the study when she returned.

He'd been reading various documents—among them a dispatch from Nairobi—when he heard a knock on the study door. It was India.

"Elspeth told me you wanted to see me," she'd said, walking into the room.

"Mmm," he said. "I've news. We have to . . ." He had looked up at her and he'd stopped speaking, surprised by her appearance. Her eyes were dull; there were dark shadows under them. Her face was shockingly pale.

"Are you ill?" he'd asked.

"No."

"You don't look well."

"I am perfectly fine."

He'd frowned. "Can't you put some rouge on?"

"Surely you haven't called me in here to discuss my toilette."

"No, I haven't. I wanted to tell you that you have to pack. You and Charlotte are going to Nairobi with me in a week."

"Nairobi? Why? I thought we were going to Mount Kenya for a fortnight."

"We are. But we're going to Nairobi first. That idiot Meade completely forgot that the Colonists' Association is throwing a dinner for me. Can't say no. They'd be frightfully offended."

"I will go, but Charlotte stays here. She's still under the weather."

"I'm sure she's fine. You mollycoddle her. Even Delamere says so."

"She's *not* going."

Freddie had returned his gaze to his papers. He raised his eyes once more to hers, irritated by the unusual note of defiance in her voice. "She will. It won't look good if she doesn't."

"It won't look good if she ends up in the hospital. If you drag an ailing child on a two-day journey into that dust-ridden cow town simply for a planters' dinner and she becomes seriously ill as a result, you will look to the world like the heartless man that you are."

Freddie considered this. "All right," he finally said. "You and I *are* going, however."

"Very well," India said. She headed for the doorway.

"Where are you going? Do you not need to pack?"

"Mary will see to the packing. I'm going out for a ride. I need air. It's stifling in here."

"Where are you going?"

"I don't know. Perhaps toward the mountain."

Freddie watched her go. Her clothes looked downright baggy on her. Had she not been eating? He tapped the end of his pen against his teeth and thought, There is something wrong. Very wrong. I wonder what it could be.

India had always been a terrible liar. Utterly incapable of speaking untruths. Oh, she'd mastered the white lies. She'd learned how to compliment an ugly dress, smile at beastly children, pretend to be fascinated by crashing bores—she'd had to; he'd never have survived in politics otherwise—but she'd never learned how to hide her heart. Not even from him.

She was hiding something now, though. He was certain of it. He would find out what. People would do almost anything to keep their secrets hidden. She certainly had. She'd gone as far as marrying him to keep the world from finding out that Charlotte was Sid Malone's bastard.

He'd stood and looked out one of the study's windows. A few minutes later he'd seen India on a brown mare, galloping away. He hardly considered himself a navigator, but he knew the rudiments and he knew that the mountain lay north and that she was riding west.

There was a knock behind him. He turned. Elspeth McGregor had stepped into the room.

"Would you like some tea, Lord Frederick?" she'd asked. "Or coffee, perhaps?"

Freddie had smiled his golden smile. "You've caught me idling, Mrs. McGregor," he'd said charmingly. She'd laughed, flushing slightly. "The view's dashed distracting," he'd said. "Can't keep my eyes off it."

"It is something to see," Mrs. McGregor had agreed.

"I'm very curious about this lovely place. I know the mountain's to the north and Nairobi's south, but what's to the east of us?"

"Ukamba Province," Mrs. McGregor had replied. "And the northern hills of the Luitbold range."

"I see. And to the west?"

"Well, there's Roos's place directly west of us. He's a coffee planter, but not a terribly good one I'm afraid. Past him, there's Maggie Carr's farm. She *is* a good planter. She has Sid Baxter working for her. He's the one who saved Charlotte. Lady India's been out there to visit. More than once. To tell him thank you."

"Has she?"

"Oh, yes. Loves the ride, she says. Who wouldn't? The landscape is so beautiful, and it gets even more dramatic the farther west you go. Beyond Maggie's place is the forest preserve, you see, for the Kikuyu, and beyond that's Lake Naivasha."

"Sounds glorious! You've been ever so helpful, Mrs. McGregor. Truly. We shall have to make a trip to the lake, Lady India and I, if time permits. There is simply too much to see in Africa and too little time in which to see it." He'd smiled again.

"Coffee then, Lord Frederick?"

"That would be lovely. Thank you."

"Cream and sugar?"

"No, thank you. I take it black and bitter. Like my heart."

"Oh, Lord Frederick!" Mrs. McGregor had said, giggling and flapping a hand at him. As soon as she'd closed the door behind herself, Freddie's fake smile had dropped away.

Baxter. Sid Baxter . . . Why did the name sound familiar? he'd wondered. He was sure he'd never known a Sid Baxter in all his life. And yet it had nagged at him, just as it had done when he'd first heard it on safari. *Baxter*. He'd told himself that he was being foolish, that there was nothing in it. He'd sat down to work again, forgetting about Sid Baxter, but he hadn't been able to put India's strange, unhealthy appearance from his mind for days.

And then, just this morning, days after as he'd watched India—still pale, still thin—barely touch her breakfast, it hit him. She was expecting a baby. That explained her appearance, her lethargy, her lack of appetite. She was pregnant . . . and she was riding hard every morning to try to undo the pregnancy. She had probably lied to Elspeth McGregor about visiting the Carr farm. She was probably out galloping on the plains hoping to jostle things loose. She must have left whatever it was she usually relied upon to end pregnancies in London. She wouldn't have risked packing it in case someone discovered it while unpacking her trunks—Mary perhaps, or a maid in the governor's household.

As he'd watched India pick at her food earlier, Freddie decided that he would take a ride west himself. He'd let India go alone, as she did every morning, and after she had returned, he would ride out himself. He was riding west now, just as he'd seen India do. He would visit Margaret Carr. Pay her a friendly social call. She was a planter, wasn't she? And he was here to cement relations between the settlers of British East Africa and the British government. He had every reason for making her acquaintance. He would ask to see her holding, flatter her with questions about coffee and how it was planted, grown, harvested—all of that. If Sid Baxter was around, he would thank him for finding Charlotte, and then he would casually ask both Baxter and Mrs. Carr about India's visits. And God help her if she had not made any.

Freddie touched his heels to Joshua's flanks now. The restless animal needed little encouragement, and horse and rider were soon streaking across the plains. They arrived at the Carr plantation less than an hour later and cantered up the drive to the bungalow. Freddie dismounted and handed the reins to a Kikuyu boy who came out to meet him.

"See that he's walked and watered," he told the boy. "Where's Mrs. Carr?"

The boy, small and wide-eyed, didn't answer.

"Christ, why can't these bloody people speak English?" Freddie muttered. "Where's Mrs. Carr?" he repeated loudly. "Where's the Msabu?"

The boy pointed past the bungalow.

Freddie looked where he was pointing and saw coffee fields in the distance. He thought he saw movement in one of the fields about a half mile away. Reaching into his saddlebag, he pulled out a pair of field glasses and held them to his eyes. Kikuyu women, dressed in red, moved slowly through the green coffee bushes. A flash of white among the red caught his attention. He focused on it and realized he was looking at a woman in a white shirt. She was small and broad and shouting to someone across the field.

That's Margaret Carr, he thought. He shifted his head to the left slightly and saw the person she was calling to. It was a white man. He was bent over a coffee plant. His face was mostly hidden under the brim of a bush hat. Baxter, he thought.

Freddie had just decided to walk out to them when Baxter straightened. He turned toward Mrs. Carr, took off his hat to fan himself, and shouted something back at her. As he did, Freddie caught a full view of his face.

"Good God," he whispered. "It can't be. You're dead."

He lowered the glasses and squeezed his eyes shut.

"It's the heat," he said. "It's muddled my mind."

After a few seconds he raised the field glasses again. Baxter was still facing him, still hatless. And Freddie was quite certain now that the image he was seeing was not caused by the heat.

Baxter. Sid Baxter. The name had seemed familiar to him because it *was* familiar. It was the name Sid Malone had used at Arden Street. Alvin Donaldson had told him so.

Fury, white hot and blinding, rose in him. Now he knew why India looked so upset and why she rode out from the McGregors' every bloody morning. It wasn't to undo a pregnancy as he'd thought; she had discovered that Sid Baxter was really Sid Malone. And she was carrying on with him again, damn her.

At the thought of that, of India with Sid, Freddie's rage was suddenly doused by fear. Freddie knew that she'd married him only because she thought Sid was dead. But he wasn't. He was alive and very well, from the looks of things. She'd chosen Sid over him once . . . what if she did it again? The scandal of a divorce—not to mention the loss of the Selwyn Jones fortune—would ruin him. If India left him, he would never become prime minister.

Freddie took a deep breath. He must not give in to his emotion. Not yet. Nobody could know that he'd been here or what he'd seen. He didn't want to give India time to warn Malone or give Malone time to run. Everything must proceed just as it had been. India must continue with her morning rides, suspecting nothing, for Freddie needed a bit of time himself. Time to send a messenger to Nairobi. Time to send a telegram to Scotland Yard. By the time he and India arrived in Nairobi themselves, for the colonists' dinner, the Yard would have wired back. Only a few days.

"You! Boy!" he shouted at the child who was now leading his horse away. The boy turned.

"Bring him back. Quickly! Give me the reins," he said, striding over to him.

He mounted and was off down Maggie Carr's drive again in seconds. There was nothing to indicate he'd ever been at the farm except a bit of red dust in the air, kicked up by Joshua's hooves. It would settle and the halfwit boy would probably forget to tell anyone he'd been there. Even if he did tell them, he wouldn't be able to give them a name.

He rode back to the McGregors' farm hard, urging Joshua on with his crop. A million questions swirled in his head. He had no answers to them. Not yet. But there would be plenty of time for answers later. When Malone was in jail.

Sid Malone had obviously faked his death once. Freddie was determined to see that he didn't get the chance to do it again. Malone would die. In England. On the gallows. He would see to it. And this time, it would be for real.

CHAPTER 105

Seamie felt Willa's head, hot and heavy on his back. She was out. Again. She had mumbled deliriously for the last hour and now she was unconscious. She was in trouble; he knew she was.

He stopped, wiped the stinging sweat out of his eyes, and squinted at the horizon. A hill, and beyond it more hills, no doubt. Above them, the merciless sun. And behind them, Kilimanjaro.

He pressed the heels of his hands to his eyes. "Where's the bloody station?" he shouted. "Where are the bloody tracks?"

There was no answer.

He spotted a copse of acacia trees about a hundred yards east and walked toward them. Once there, he gently lowered Willa into the shady grass.

"Come on, Wills," he said, propping her up and patting her face. "Wakey, wakey."

She mumbled a protest.

"You have to drink something. Come on, now. Wake up."

He unscrewed the cap on the canteen and lifted it to her lips.

She grimaced and turned her head away.

"Please, Wills, please. For me."

She opened her eyes. They were dull and unfocused.

"There's a good girl. Come on, just a sip."

He got a thin trickle of water down her throat before she gagged.

"No more . . ." she rasped. She sank back into the grass and he saw that her ankle was now as thick as her thigh.

"I'm going to take a look at that leg," he said. When he'd peeled away the last layer of the makeshift dressing, he had to stifle a curse.

Willa heard him. "What is it?" she asked weakly.

"Close your eyes," he said. "Rest for a minute." He tore strips off his shirt and quickly rewrapped the leg. He didn't want her to see it. It was horribly infected. The skin was hot and shiny. Red streaks snaked across it like lines on a map. The bone edges, still protruding, had blackened and the puncture was leaking pus.

"Oh, God. I can smell it," Willa said, suddenly lucid.

"That's me, Wills," Seamie said, trying for a smile.

"Seamie . . . please. Leave me here. Leave the rifle."

"Don't talk like that."

"I can't go on."

"I can."

"If you don't leave me we're both going to die," she said angrily. "You know that, don't you? I'm done for, but you still have a chance if you'd just take it!"

"Be quiet. Climb on. We're going now."

"I can't."

He pulled her up by her arms and manhandled her onto his back. He banged her leg, causing her to shriek with pain. She swore at him, hit him, and then wept, but he ignored her. He didn't care. All he cared about was putting one foot in front of the other. He was nearly spent. He'd been walking for five days now. He had to find the train and soon.

He'd made it back to the Mawenzi camp after a harrowing trek through the forest in the dark, expecting to feel a Chagga arrow in his back at every step. Willa had been so glad to see him.

"Are we going now?" she'd asked. "Is Tepili here? And the others?"

He'd sat down beside her and explained what had happened.

"Oh, God," she'd said, her eyes bright with tears. "All of them, Seamie? They're *all* dead?"

"I think—I hope—that some of them got away. I saw only five or six bodies. Maybe they ran and the Chagga gave chase. Maybe that's why no one came after me."

After Willa had wept for Tepili and the others, the gravity of her own situation began to sink in. "So that means there's no food for us . . . no one to take our gear . . . no one to get me down the mountain," she'd said.

"Right on all counts but the last one," Seamie replied. "I'm carrying you down."

"*What?* How?"

"On my back."

"Are you mad?"

"I can do it. I've carried heavy packs. In deep snow. At twenty below. I can carry you."

"But what about the photographic plates . . . our maps . . ."

He shook his head. The plates had survived their descent because he'd been carrying them, but they were too heavy to carry any farther. He'd worked it all out on the way back to her. He could carry her, the bare essentials, nothing else.

"No. I'm not leaving the plates behind," she said. "Without them we've no proof we reached the summit."

"The hell with the summit."

"Seamie, we've worked too hard—"

He angrily cut her off. "Your bones are sticking out of your skin and all you're worried about are the bloody photographs? Do you understand that you will die if we don't get you to a doctor?"

"One plate," she said. "Please. Just one. I'll leave my boots here. And my belt. To cut the weight."

They'd argued bitterly until finally it was decided that they'd bring one plate, Willa's notebook, a canteen of water, a compass, money, and the rifle. They would pack the other photographic plates in her pack, their books in his, then wrap it all up—together with their valuable instruments—in the canvas tent and shelter it all in the overhang of a nearby boulder in the hope of returning and collecting it.

Seamie had filled the canteen then. He'd stuffed what little dried meat and cheese they had left into the pockets of his jacket. He stashed their gear, then used a length of climbing rope to fashion a sling that would allow him to take Willa's weight on his back. He could see that she was already weak. She wouldn't be able to hang on by herself the entire way. Then he'd had to do what he was dreading most—deal with her leg.

"We have to do something," he'd said. "We can't leave it as it is, just hanging. It'll bounce with every step. Catch in the undergrowth when we reach the forest."

Willa hadn't hesitated. "Pull it straight and splint it," she said.

"It's going to hurt."

"I've no choice."

He gave her a bit of rope to bite on, braced her knee, and pulled her damaged leg. She arched her body; her fingers clawed at the dirt. The leg straightened some, but the jagged bones still protruded. He didn't know what else to do, so he wrapped the wound with a length of cloth he'd torn from his shirt, then splinted it with covers he'd ripped off one of their books.

"Are you ready?" he asked.

Willa, still panting from the pain, said, "Are you?"

He nodded, got her up and into the sling, and they were off. He climbed down as far south as he dared to get them below the peaks and into easier terrain, then he headed northeast. His plan was to get to Tsavo—a station on the Uganda line—and take the train from there to Mombasa.

Tsavo was about eighty miles from their camp. Seamie knew he could have made twenty miles a day on flat, easy terrain. But the trek ahead of him was neither flat nor easy and he was carrying Willa.

Maybe if we're lucky, he'd thought, we'll come across a village where we can hire men to help us. If we're really lucky, we'll stumble across a plantation with oxen and wagons. But they weren't lucky. They'd found no villages, seen no people. It had rained two days straight, drenching them. Their food had run out. They'd found a stream on the third day and filled the canteen, but it was low again and Willa, half-delirious with fever, needed to drink.

As he plodded on now, his back aching, his legs like pillars of lead, he wondered if he'd miscalculated the distance. Had he turned too far south when they'd gotten off the mountain? If so, they'd miss the railway completely and it would be another seventy miles—at least—to the coast. They'd never make it.

"We can't be far," he said out loud, to comfort himself as well as Willa. "We just can't be. I'm not the world's best navigator, but I can't have taken us too wildly wrong. And even if I've gone too far north and we miss Tsavo, we'll hit *something*. Bound to. Kenani station, maybe, or Mtoto Andei. We're going to get there, Wills. You're going to be all right."

There was barely a response from Willa, just a few mumbled words. He was about to start up yet another hill when he heard a long, loud whistle. Way off in the distance.

"Willa!" he shouted. "Did you hear that? It's the train! The tracks must be just beyond that hill."

If he could get to them, he could try to flag the train down. Get the engineer to stop it. And if he couldn't, they'd have to spend another night walking, trying to find the nearest station, but Willa didn't have another night.

"Wills?" he called out.

There was no answer.

"Willa, wake up."

"No more, Seamie, please . . ." she whispered.

"I'm going to put you down now," he said, lowering her into the grass. He put the rifle near her, in case of animals, and the canteen. "There's a train coming. I hear it. The tracks have to be close. I'm going to make a run for them." Her head was lolling; her eyes were fluttering closed. He dug his fingers cruelly into her shoulders and shouted at her. "Willa, wake up! You've got to stay awake."

And then he ran. As soon as he was over the hill, he saw them—the tracks. They were about a quarter of a mile away. He saw the train next. It was small and black in the distance, trailing a plume of smoke. It was heading west, not toward Mombasa, but Nairobi, and it was moving fast.

Seamie tore down the hill. He stumbled at the bottom, righted himself, and then ran faster and harder than he'd ever run in his life. The long plains grass whirled around his legs and snarled his steps. He ploughed through it, heedless, stumbling again and again. The tracks were coming closer. Only a hundred yards, then twenty, and then he was on them.

The train was coming on fast. It was only a mile away at the most. He stood on the tracks, jumping and waving, shouting at it to stop. He took off what was left of his shirt and waved it over his head. But the train kept coming.

"Stop, you bastard!" he screamed at it. "Stop!"

But it didn't, it barrelled toward him, whistle shrieking. He jumped clear of the tracks at the last possible second.

"No! Goddamn you! No!" he cried, watching as it sped past him.

It was leaving and taking Willa's last chance with it.

But then he realized it was slowing, ever so slightly. He heard the brakes screeching. He saw faces, some puzzled, some worried, looking at him from the windows.

It's stopping, he thought. It's stopping! Oh, thank God!

He started running again, desperate to catch up to the engine, but a conductor hailed him from one of the passenger cars.

"Please!" Seamie cried, when he reached him. "You've got to help us. My friend's badly injured. She's just over the hill. We have to get on. I have to get her to a doctor. Please . . ."

The train stopped dead. Giant whuffs of steam came out from under it. The conductor hopped down. "Hold on, son, I can barely hear you. What's happened?"

Seamie explained. He said he'd been trying to get to Mombasa and asked if there was a doctor at Nairobi. The conductor said there was. He said he'd hold the train and asked Seamie if he needed help fetching his friend. Seamie said he did and the conductor shouted for the stoker.

Weak with relief, Seamie turned to point to where he'd left Willa, and that was when he heard it—sharp and unmistakable—the sound of a single gunshot.

CHAPTER 106

"It was the McGregors' stallion that was here around lunchtime, I'm sure of it. Joshua, he's called." Maggie shaded her eyes with her hand. "Reckon it was that lovely Mrs. Lytton. Saw her out yesterday, too, but she was riding the mare then."

Sid knew Maggie wanted a reaction from him. He didn't give her one; he just kept hoeing. The sun was low over the horizon. Wainaina and the other Kikuyu women had gone home an hour ago, but he was still at it. He'd gone out into the fields at daybreak and hadn't stopped, not even in the blistering noon sun. He welcomed the pain in his hands and arms and back. It blocked out the pain in his heart.

"I know she came by, Sid. I know she spoke to you," Maggie said, fingering a clutch of coffee berries. "Baaru told me. Were you ever going to tell me?"

"No."

"What happened?"

"Nothing."

"Nothing? How'd you get that mark on your face, then?"

Sid drove his hoe into the ground viciously, irritated by Maggie's meddling. She'd come out to the north field to look at the plants, she'd said. He doubted that. She'd come out to the north field to needle him.

"We had words, all right? She belted me," he finally said, hoping the admission would satisfy her.

"Did she? Well, I imagine you deserved it. Probably were horrible to her." She paused, then said, "My eyes aren't as good as they used to be, but I could swear whoever was riding Joshua earlier was wearing trousers. Can't be Mrs. McGregor. She always wears a skirt. Mr. McGregor barely rides at all. Too tall to be one of the boys. There's no one else there. Must be that Mrs. Lytton wears breeches when no one's looking." She sighed. "Poor woman. Always alone. Just like you."

"I like my own company," Sid said.

Maggie moved off down a row of bushes—sampling berries, checking leaves, pinching off shoots here and there. She wasn't finished with him, he knew that. He could feel her eyes on him. She had more to say and when she worked her way back to where he was, she said it.

"You coming in for supper? Alice is roasting a haunch of that gazelle you bagged."

"I'm going to keep hoeing for a bit."

"Are you?"

"Aye."

"It's angry work, hoeing."

"Bloody hell. Here we go."

"Tell me, Sid. Who are you angry at? Mrs. Lytton? Or yourself?"

"I'm not angry at anyone, Maggie," Sid said, working to keep his voice even. "I'm just trying to keep the plants healthy. So we get a good harvest. You *do* want a good harvest?"

"You've been at it since five this morning. It's seven now. That's fourteen hours. You had no dinner. I checked. Your clothes are soaked with sweat and your hands are torn to bits."

"My hands are fine. I've a few blisters is all."

"Still doing penance, eh?" Maggie asked. "Still looking for forgiveness?"

Maggie's words hit home. "For Christ's sake, leave me alone!" he snapped. "I don't need to be forgiven. I'm only getting what I deserve. No more. No less."

But Maggie had no intention of leaving him alone. "Who are you to say what any of us deserves?" she snapped right back. "Are your sins so much worse than everyone else's? Your soul beyond redemption? What sets you so far apart from the rest of us?"

"You don't know what I've done. You don't know what I was."

"No, I don't. I know what I've done, though. And what I was."

"Rob banks, did you, Maggs? Steal from people? Break heads?" he asked acidly.

"No."

"Didn't think so."

"I killed a man. My husband."

Sid stopped hoeing. He straightened. He'd worked for Maggie for six years, yet he could count on one hand the number of times she'd mentioned her husband.

"Sam, his name was," she said. "Samuel Edward Carr. We had two children. A boy of four named Andrew. And a two-year-old girl, Mary. We were in Australia before we came here. And in Devon before that. I loved it there. Would have stayed forever, but Sam was restless. He wanted land. Open spaces. So we sold our place, packed up the kiddies, and set out. Bought five hundred acres of ranch land in New South Wales. Planned to raise sheep . . ."

Her voice trailed off. Her eyes were far away, seeing things he couldn't see, things from long ago. "What happened?" he asked quietly.

"The dusk was coming on one night. Just like it is now. Our house wasn't built all the way yet. We were still living in a tent. We'd finished our supper. I collected the dishes and went to wash them in the stream. Usually I took the children with me, but Andy had twisted his ankle and I didn't want him hobbling after me. I asked Sam to keep an eye on them while I was gone. We had an open fire by the tent, you see, and I didn't want the children near it. I shouldn't have done that. I should never have done that. Sam wasn't used to minding small children. He had no idea how easily distracted they are.

"Just after I left, our dog started barking. We had a few sheep in a pen and some hens in a makeshift henhouse. Sam was always worried about the dingoes—they'd carried off a lamb and some hens—so he went to check on the animals. He told Andy to watch his sister. I'd just finished the washing up when I heard the screaming. I dropped everything and ran. It was almost dark then and I saw my children. Their clothes were in flames. They were running. Trying to escape it. They didn't know not to. Sam got to Mary. I got Andy. We rolled them into the dirt to put the flames out."

Maggie stopped talking suddenly and it was a good long minute before she could continue. Sid couldn't imagine what was going through her head—the memories, the images.

"Mary kept screaming," she finally said. "Right to the end. Andy took longer. He hung on for almost a day. He didn't scream. Just moaned. He told us he'd tried to keep her from the fire, but she'd gotten too close and her dress had caught. He'd tried to put it out, but his own clothes caught. I couldn't hold him as he died. Couldn't even touch him. His skin was gone. He kept saying, 'I'm sorry, Mummy. I'm sorry . . .'"

"What happened then?"

"We buried them. Sam wanted to stay. We couldn't, though. I burned the house to the ground. Wanted to throw myself into the fire, but Sam caught me and held me down. He sold the animals and our land. Didn't get much. He brought me here. It was the only place we could go, really. He'd heard the government was looking for settlers. That they were leasing land cheap. Five years later he was dead. Because of me. Because I couldn't forgive him. I blamed him for our children's deaths. I couldn't let go of my rage. My grief. We lived together and yet we were totally apart. There was no warmth. No kindness. He used to look at me across the table, you know. Or out in the fields. His eyes always asking me . . . pleading. There was so much pain in those eyes. It killed him, finally. He was a good man. He deserved forgiveness, but I couldn't give it to him. It would have meant forgiving myself, you see."

Maggie stopped talking. She seemed to him to have aged a hundred years in the last few minutes. He saw that it had cost her dearly to tell him these things. Finally, she said, "It's getting on. I'm going to head back to the house."

The dusk had settled now. It would be dark soon. She always insisted on being in the house before dark. Now he knew why.

"I'll have Alice keep your plate warm," she said. Never had her voice sounded so old, so weary.

"Maggie, I . . ." he began, searching for something, anything, to say to her.

She laid a gentle hand on his arm. "You want to be forgiven, Sid?" she asked softly. "Then learn to forgive."

CHAPTER 107

India stared at the plains of Thika for the last time. They were leaving tomorrow, she and Freddie and Charlotte. She wouldn't be seeing this place again. She had ridden out here every morning for the past few days. She wanted to impress the place upon her memory—the way the grass moved in the breeze, the scudding clouds, the distant hills. She wanted to be able to remember it, because it was where Sid Malone lived.

Seeing him again had devastated her. She was not able to eat. She barely slept. She felt disoriented, unreal, as if she were moving in a dream. The world, once solid under her feet, was solid no longer. Despair engulfed her. For herself, and what she had lost so unnecessarily. For Charlotte, because her real father was alive, but she would never know him. And for Sid, because he would never know his beautiful daughter.

She moved woodenly through her days, wondering at the cruelty of the gods. How could they take Sid from her once, only to do it again? How could Charlotte grow up under the cold eye of a man who despised her instead of in the arms of a father who loved her? How could she, India, live, day after day, year after year, with a vision of what might have been and the unbearable knowledge of what was?

She was seated on the McGregors' mare, still gazing toward the Carr farm, when she saw a horse and rider leave the farm. She figured it was

Maggie on her way to a neighbor's. But the rider turned out of the drive and headed toward her, getting closer and closer, never veering, and India realized, with a cold dread, that it was Sid. Why was he coming to her? Did he know it was her? Or did he think she was someone else?

Panic-stricken, not wanting to face his anger a second time, she touched her heels to her horse, turning the animal toward the McGregors'.

"India!" he bellowed from behind her. "India, wait!"

She wanted to stop, wanted to answer him, but she was afraid. Instead, she dug her heels in harder, spurring her horse to a gallop. But Sid's horse was faster and in only a few seconds he was alongside her.

"Stop!" he shouted.

"No!" she shouted back.

"Please, India!"

Finally, she did.

"I thought it was you," Sid said, as the horses slowed to a walk. "Well . . . Maggie said it was. She said you ride out here every day."

"I did. I do," she said quickly. "I mean . . . I won't anymore. We're leaving soon and I—"

"Look," he said, cutting her off. "I'm sorry about the other night. I was awful to you. I shouldn't have shouted at you and I shouldn't have . . . oh, sod it . . . it's no good, this. Why did you come to Maggie's, India? *Why?*"

"I didn't mean to!" she cried. "I'm sorry. How did I know Sid Baxter was you? You can't blame me for that. I had no idea."

"Sid Baxter? Didn't the name ring *any* bloody bells?" he yelled.

"Yes, it did. But I didn't think it could possibly be you, because you're supposed to be dead!"

"I haven't slept since I saw you. I can't eat."

"I'm very sorry, but you must stop shouting at me. I shall leave if you don't."

"Sorry," he said, in a softer voice. "Don't go. Stay. Please." He dug frantically in his saddlebag. "Would you like some dinner? I brought sandwiches. Alice made them. And cake. And a bit of port. It's all she had."

India looked at him warily.

"I won't shout anymore. I promise. Look, there are some flame trees there. We could sit under them."

"All right."

They rode to the trees and tied their horses.

"That's a nice spot, right there," Sid said, pointing to a patch of grass half in the sun, half in the shade. But neither of them sat. Sid stood with the saddlebag in his hands. India stood, arms crossed over her chest, cupping her elbows.

"You're here, then. In Africa," he finally said.

"Yes, Sid. Yes, I am."

"Freddie's sorting things out, is he? Between the government and the settlers?"

"He's trying."

"Think he'll succeed?"

"I'm certain of it. He always does. One way or another."

"Foreign secretary, is it?"

"Undersecretary for the colonies."

"He's done well for himself."

"Yes, he has."

"How's Charlotte feeling?"

"Better, thank you."

"She's an amazing girl. Smart as a whip. I've never met a child like her."

India closed her eyes for a few seconds, squeezing back tears. Here she was, standing next to Sid. Sid, whom she'd loved more than any other man in her entire life. Sid, whom she'd thought was dead. Here she was, standing next to the father of her child, making small talk with him when all she wanted was to run to him and kiss him, tell him all about Charlotte, and tell him she loved him.

"India, is something wrong?"

"No, nothing," she said quickly.

She opened her eyes again and raised them to the horizon to avoid looking at Sid. She affected a look of calm detachment, determined not to lose control. As Sid continued to talk, another voice spoke to her—one from the depths of her memory.

"You *what*? You *feel*, Jones?" this voice said. "You are not in my classroom to feel . . ."

Professor Fenwick. She hadn't thought about him in years. How like him to pop in at a time like this to lecture her. He was right, though—it was better not to feel. Feelings carried too high a price. Hugh Mullins had taught her. Whitechapel had taught her. But Sid Malone had been the best teacher of all.

"Well, anyway, I just wanted you to know that I'm sorry about the other night. I really am. I'm just happy to know that you're happy, India," he said.

As he spoke those words, a choking anger filled her. She tried desperately to tamp it down, but she couldn't. It twisted and roiled inside her.

Why had he always been able to do that? To make her so angry? At Teddy Ko's. Again at the London Hospital. In the Barkentine. At her flat. In the dark streets of Whitechapel. They had never talked in those days without fighting. Even now, when he was trying hard to apologize, he made her angry.

"You deserve happiness," he continued. "More than anyone."

In an instant the anger ignited into rage. It was too much, this. To hear from the man she loved that he was happy she was happy being married to a man she hated. It was unbearable.

"Is that what you think?" she asked, Fenwick's warning now forgotten. "That I'm *happy* to be married to Freddie?"

"Well, aren't you?"

"No, you bloody fool. I'm not."

Sid winced. "Steady on. I was trying to be nice to you," he said.

"But you're not nice. You're stupid and heartless."

"What's wrong, then? Why aren't you happy? You should be," Sid said, his voice sharp again. "You got what you wanted, didn't you? A nice respectable man for a husband instead of a criminal. What's the matter? Aren't all the houses and horses and parties and balls enough?"

"No, they are not. Good day, Sid," India said, turning on her heel. She had to leave. Now. Before she did lose control.

"Not so fast." Sid's hand closed on her arm. He spun her around to face him again. "Why the hell did you marry him?" he asked.

"I had my reasons," she spat, trying to shake him off, but he wouldn't let go.

"Yes, Joe Bristow and Gemma Dean, right? You thought I did for them. That's why you changed your mind."

"What are you saying?"

"Just tell me one thing. Did the police come to you, or did you go to them?"

"What police? What are you talking about?"

"Arden Street. You told them about Arden Street. You helped them set a trap for me."

"No," she said. "That's not true. They found out—"

"Bloody right they did. You told them!"

"Is *that* what you think? That I betrayed you to Freddie? I would've given up everything for you—medicine, the clinic, my home. I *did* give up everything!" she shouted. "I gave up my life for you." She was weeping now. Unable to break his grasp, she buried her face in his chest.

"Then how did they find out? Donaldson told me my lady had told him."

"He meant Gemma Dean, not me. She told Freddie. Before she died. At least, that's what he's always said." She looked up at him. "Why didn't you come for me? I waited and waited. Before Arden Street and after. I was out of my mind with worry waiting for you."

"I thought you'd betrayed me. I thought you wanted nothing to do with me," he said, looking as if someone had reached inside him and ripped his soul out. "All these years . . ." he said softly.

"All these years I thought you were dead. And all these years you hated me."

"I never hated you," he said. "I wish I could have. It would have made my life so much easier." His voice broke.

India heard it. The sound of his pain was agony to her. She couldn't bear it. She wanted to stop it. Instinctively, she took his face in her hands and kissed him.

"Let go of me, India," he said. "I didn't know . . . I thought . . ."

"You thought I'd run to Freddie. Changed my mind about you. You thought I did what I did because I didn't love you enough. Oh, Sid. You never thought you were good enough. Never thought you deserved to love and to be loved."

"I can't do this, India. I can't be near you like this and then just walk away again."

"Then don't walk away. Please don't walk away," she whispered. "Love me, Sid. If only for now. If only for an hour. Please still love me."

She kissed him again. The smell and taste and feel of him felt to her like rains in a desert. Her soul, dry and parched, nearly dead, came to life again. She sobbed, then laughed, then held him tightly, burying her face in his neck. And then he was kissing her, and his arms were tight around her.

"I never stopped loving you," she whispered to him. "Never, Sid. Not for one day."

He pulled her down with him into the grass and made love to her. It was hard and fast, angry and bruising. When he finished, he lay on his back, hands over his eyes. She took them away and kissed his tears, and then his mouth. She unbuttoned his shirt and kissed his throat, and his chest, taking her time, wanting to remember it all—the feel of his skin, the warmth of the sun on her bare back. His body was harder and thinner than she remembered, his face and arms were bronzed by the sun. Her lips brushed the place over his heart, where the skin was so pale and fragile-looking. She kissed him there and then she made love to him, tenderly and slowly, wanting it to last forever.

When it was over, she lay with her head on his chest and he held her close, just as they'd done in Arden Street. They talked. He told her about escaping from London and coming to Africa and finding himself stranded in Mombasa. He told her about Maggie Carr and how she'd saved him and all about his life here. She told him about the day she'd learned he was dead and the tearing grief she'd felt. About going to London Bridge to throw flowers into the Thames. She told him about her home in London and the dead and meaningless life she lived there. She told him how she missed medicine and Whitechapel and, most of all, him. And she told him about the happiness Charlotte brought her and how much she loved her.

When she finished, he looked at her and said, "Come back to me, India."

She touched a finger to his lips. "Shh. Don't. It's not possible. He'll never let me go. Never."

"He loves you, then. Loves Charlotte . . ."

India laughed mirthlessly. "He loves neither of us. It's my father's fortune he loves. It's a staggering amount of money, but it comes to him only through me. My father set things up that way to make sure he never divorced me."

"Can't you divorce him?"

"He's told me that if I ever try, he will take Charlotte. I don't doubt for a second that he would. He has friends in high places. I could never do it. Never abandon her to him. It would be like handing a lamb to a wolf."

"I'll come to London, then. I'll see you. Somehow . . ."

"No," she said sharply. "If Freddie ever found out you're alive, if he even suspected it, he'd come after you."

"Why? I didn't shoot Joe Bristow. Frankie Betts did and he's been sent to prison for it. It was in all the papers. Even in Mombasa."

"He'll try to hang you for Gemma Dean's murder," India said.

"But I didn't kill her!"

"Do you think that matters to him? He'd see you as a threat to his marriage and his money. He's a ruthless man, Sid. A hateful man. You've no idea how hateful."

Sid's eyes searched hers. "Is he cruel to you, India?"

She looked away.

"And Charlotte?"

"He mostly ignores her. Unless a photographer's lurking."

"But she's his daughter."

India looked away. She almost told him then. Almost said, "No, she isn't. She's your daughter." She wanted to. Desperately. She wanted him to know that he had made her; that they both had. But she didn't because it would have been unspeakably cruel to tell him Charlotte was his and then take her away from him forever.

Instead she said, "I have to get back. I'll be missed. There's packing to do. We're leaving for Nairobi tomorrow morning." She picked up her camisole and blouse and put them on. She buttoned her riding skirt and stood.

"And then you leave for London," Sid said flatly, standing now, too.

"We've a family holiday at Mount Kenya to endure first. Then we leave."

"I just got you back and now I'm about to lose you all over again."

"And I you."

India felt she should be weeping now, but she didn't. Neither of them did. The pain was too deep for tears.

"I'll wake up and think I dreamed this," he said. "Tomorrow. When I have nothing again."

"We'll have this," she said. "This day. This memory. This love. No one can take that from us. I know you're alive, Sid. That's so much more than I had."

"If only I'd got to you. In London. If only I could have found a way . . ."

"Don't. Please."

"I love you, India."

"And I love you."

They held each other then, not wanting to let go, each knowing it was for the last time. And then, when she could bear it no longer, India broke his embrace. She took his hand in hers, held it to her cheek, and said, "No matter where I am in this world, no matter what I'm doing, I'm thinking of you and loving you. Always, Sid. Always and forever."

She kissed him one last time, mounted her horse, and rode away toward the McGregors'. Freddie's there, she reminded herself. She must show no tears, no emotion, no weakness. She would blame the color in her cheeks, and her loose curls, on a long ride. He must never, ever suspect what had just happened. Charlotte's happiness depended on it. And Sid Malone's life.

She sat up tall in the saddle, rode hard and fast, and did not once look back.

CHAPTER 108

"This is hopeless. Totally hopeless," Dr. Rosendo Ribeiro, Nairobi's one and only doctor, said. "It's the worst fracture I've ever seen. How did she do it?"

Seamie explained what had happened on Kilimanjaro and how he'd gotten Willa to Nairobi. It took everything he had to get the words out. He was dangerously exhausted. It was evening now. He'd arrived at Nairobi station only minutes ago, after enduring an endless train ride. He'd asked the first man he saw where the hospital was and the man had pointed to a rickety bungalow only yards from the station. He'd run to the building with Willa unconscious in his arms. The hospital was really only a doctor's surgery, little better than a field hospital, with its dirt floors, sagging beds, rusty sink, and flies.

"She broke the leg five days ago?" Dr. Ribeiro repeated. "I'm amazed she's not dead. It's got to go."

"What's got to go?" Seamie asked, confused. "She can't go," he said now. "She needs to stay. She needs help."

"Not *her*. The leg. The leg has to go. We'll take it below the knee. We'll try to cut as close to the fracture as we can, but it all depends on how far the gangrene's spread."

"No!" It was Willa. She was conscious now and struggling to sit up on the bed where Seamie had placed her. "I heard you. You're not taking my leg."

"Miss Alden, if we do not amputate, you will die," Ribeiro said. A young man hurried by. "Mr. Pinto, I need you. Scrub up!" he barked at him. "The gangrene's spreading," he said to Willa, "and your bones can't be set. They're too damaged. Surgery's your only chance."

Willa turned to Seamie. "Don't let him. Please don't let him," she begged.

Seamie bent down to her and stroked the hair off her forehead. There was blood in it. She'd tried to shoot herself—to kill herself—when he'd left her to run for the train, but she was so weak she'd lost her grip. The bullet had missed her forehead and grazed her temple. It was the pain that drove her to it, he'd told himself. She hadn't been in her right mind.

"Willa, you're too sick," he said to her now. "Your body can't take any-more. You're going to die if you don't have the operation."

"I'll die if you cut my leg off!" she cried. "I'll die if I can't climb!"

"It's delirium talking. She's not in her right mind, Mr. Finnegan. But you are and I need a decision from you," the doctor said. "Now."

Seamie pressed the heels of his hands to his eyes. He didn't know what to do. If he let them amputate, he would be betraying her wishes, but if he didn't, she would die.

"Mr. Finnegan?"

"Do it," he said.

"No!" Willa screamed. "Please, Seamie, please!"

"It'll be all right, Wills," he said, his voice cracking. "It'll be all right."

"Mr. Finnegan, if you'd stand aside, please," the doctor said. He mo-tioned for his assistant. "Pinto, chloral."

The man advanced on Willa with a mask. She fought him off, knocking the mask to the floor. Dr. Ribeiro pinned her arms. "Hurry, please, Mr. Pinto."

"No!" she screamed, thrashing her head from side to side. "No!"

The assistant hooked one arm around Willa's head, immobilizing her, then he pressed the mask over her face. Her eyes, fearful and pleading, sought Seamie's. He had to look away.

"There, Miss Alden, that's a good girl," Dr. Ribeiro said soothingly. "Take a deep breath. Good. Now another . . ."

After a few seconds Pinto said, "She's out."

"Good. Let's be quick, please. Swab from the knee to the break. Then get me a bone saw, scalpels, clamps, a cautery iron, sutures, and needles."

"Good God, what a mess," Pinto said, cutting Willa's blood-stained clothing away. "The muscle's putrid and the—"

"Thank you, Mr. Pinto," Dr. Ribeiro said. He turned back to Seamie. "Mr. Finnegan, unless you've a very strong stomach I'd advise you to leave now. There's a good hotel in town. The Norfolk. It's not far. We'll take care of Miss Alden."

Seamie didn't want to leave Willa.

"Go, Mr. Finnegan. Now, please," Dr. Ribeiro said.

"Is there . . . is there anything I can do for her?" Seamie asked.

"Yes," the doctor said. "Pray."

CHAPTER 109

Tom Meade poked his head into Freddie Lytton's borrowed office in Nairobi's Government House. He was heavily laden with folders and documents.

"Good morning, sir," he said.

"Mmm. Morning," Freddie replied absently. He was busy writing up his account of bagging a lion at Thika for the readers of *The Times*. He would leave out the part about Charlotte going missing. It made the place look dangerous and him look careless.

"Your schedule, sir," Tom said, placing a typed agenda on Freddie's desk.

Freddie glanced at it.

"You should never have come back to Nairobi," Tom said. "Everyone's clamoring for you now that you're here again. You've a ten o'clock ribbon-cutting at the racetrack. New stables, I believe. An eleven o'clock with the surveyor for Seyidie Province—seems there's a bit of a bother with the Germans over a boundary dispute in the Vanga District—a noon luncheon with the Merchants' Association, and a two o'clock with the DC for the Northern Frontier. I've scheduled nothing after that as you've the dinner at the governor's residence tonight to prepare for." Tom then started placing the folders he was carrying on Freddie's desk one by one. "For your remarks tonight. Here's the population summary for the whole of BEA by district, farm classification by size and by type of crop . . ."

"Is there anything from London?" Freddie asked impatiently.

"Yes. A telegram from Scotland Yard, I believe." Tom reached into yet another folder and drew a telegram from it.

"Good man. Thank you," Freddie said, eagerly reaching for it.

He'd sent a telegram to Alvin Donaldson, now a superintendent at the Yard, four days ago, asking him to find the coroner's report on Sid Malone's body and advise whether or not the identification was irrefutable. Donaldson had replied to say that it was not. The body fished out of the Thames back in 1900 had been so badly decomposed that no facial features had remained, only a few patches of red hair. It had had a few personal effects on it—effects identified as having belonged to Malone—and those were what had been used to identify it. It was just as Freddie had thought. Sid Malone had faked his own death. He hadn't needed Donaldson to tell him that; he'd only wanted him to provide confirmation. He'd discovered for himself that Malone was alive and well in Thika.

If Freddie had been concerned about what was going on with India when he'd ridden out to the Carr farm, he'd become downright fearful of her intentions by the time he'd returned. This was no stray fancy on her part; this was Malone. She'd left him for Sid once; she'd do it again—he was certain of it.

He remembered now how she'd looked the evening before they'd left on the long journey to Nairobi—upset, flushed, and tousled. She'd been with Malone; he was certain of it—the devious little bitch. Perhaps she was already putting her plans into place, figuring out how to escape. He could not permit that to happen. *Would* not. He'd worked so hard to get where he wanted to go, and nothing—and no one—was going to stop him.

"Is there anything the matter, sir?"

Freddie, tense and anxious, lost in his thoughts, had completely forgotten about the ADC, who was still in his office, awaiting further instructions.

He looked at him now and gravely said, "Yes, Tom, I'm afraid there is. We've a very dangerous man in our midst. A fugitive. He's wanted in London for murder. I need to speak to the governor this morning. I want this man found immediately and taken alive. I will accompany the police and personally oversee the arrest."

"A murderer? *Here?* Who is he?"

"He went by the name of Malone in London. He goes by another name now. Baxter. Sid Baxter."

"Sid Baxter? I don't believe it, sir."

Freddie smiled. "I don't care what you believe, Tom."

Meade's eyes hardened. "There are protocols," he said coldly. "Even in Nairobi. The governor is not the only one who will need to be notified. May I ask what you intend to do?"

"I plan to arrest him, of course. And then I plan to hang him."

CHAPTER 110

Can you smell despair? Joe wondered. Can you see it? Touch it?

He had always believed it to be an intangible thing, a state of mind. Until he'd come to Wandsworth. Here it was real. It stalked the corridors, echoing in the hollow *pok pok* of the guards' steps. It dripped down the gray granite walls, festering in their cracks, filling the room with its moldering stink. It seeped into flesh and bone, as chilling as the damp, creeping cold of a grave.

"Wandsworth was a model prison in its day," the warden said cheerily, as he accompanied Joe from his office to the visitors' room. "It was built in the panopticon style in 1851 with cell blocks radiating from a central control station from which the guards can see everything that's going on. Designed to be a new type of humane prison. *Panopticon*," he repeated, relishing the word.

"Really? Humane, you say?"

"In relative terms, of course."

"It's not relative, humanity. One's either humane or one isn't."

The warden smiled. "Everything's relative, Mr. Bristow. Ever been to Reading?"

"No."

"It antedates Wandsworth by a few years. It was operated on the separate and silent system. Single cells with solid doors so that prisoners couldn't see one another. Walls so thick you'd never hear another human voice. The convicts were made to wear masks whenever they were out of their cells—long pieces of fabric with holes cut out for their eyes. Meals were taken in the cells. The inmates lived alone, deprived of contact with others. No words of comfort. No friend to pat you on the back, no cell mate to whisper comfort when you cried out at night. It was all thought to be reforming and rehabilitating, but prisoners went mad there, Mr. Bristow. So much for humanity. And speaking of mad, how'd you fare with our friend Betts last time?"

"Not too well, I'm afraid."

The warden sighed. "Maybe you'll have better luck this time. I hope so, for there may not be a next time. He's not long for this world. TB, you know."

"I thought so," Joe said, remembering Frankie's sunken eyes, the high color in his cheeks.

"Well, I'll leave you to it, then," the warden said. "Do remember to keep the table between you. The guard's there, of course, but prisoners can become violent."

Joe laughed. "He can't possibly do me more harm than he's already done," he said.

The warden left and Joe wheeled himself over to one of the long tables. He had come to try yet again to get answers from Frankie Betts. Keeping what he'd discovered about Sid, and about Sid's child, from Fiona was killing him. She was his wife and she had a right to know these things, yet he couldn't betray Ella. Or Dr. Jones. Or the child. His hands were tied, and he didn't know what to do to get them untied, but he felt instinctively that any chance he might have of making things come right lay with Frankie Betts.

After a few minutes the heavy iron door that led to the cell blocks opened and Frankie walked out.

"Jesus bloody Christ," he said. "Not you again."

He looked terrible. So bad, in fact, that Joe almost felt sorry for him. Almost. "Hello, Frankie," he said. "I'm happy to see you, too."

"I want to go back to me cell," Frankie said to the guard.

"Sit down, Betts," the man said.

"I did some investigating, Frankie," Joe began.

"Well, ain't you a regular Sherlock Holmes."

"Found out about the doctor. The one you mentioned last time. Dr. Jones. I can see how she must've rankled you. She took Sid away, didn't she?"

"Never heard of her. Don't know what you're talking about. You should leave. You're wasting your time."

"You were angry, weren't you? You didn't want Sid to go away with the doctor. You wanted him back in the fold. That's why you shot me. To land Sid in the shit. Make him go underground. Make him a villain again."

"You should write mystery stories, you."

"People I talked to think you killed Gemma Dean, Frankie. They say you had to. You botched my shooting, so you needed to kill someone else. As a way of keeping Sid on the run."

"Doesn't matter what people say. Gemma's dead as a doornail. And so's Sid."

Joe leaned in close. "Here's a bit of news for you . . . Sid's not dead. He's alive. The body in the river? Not his. He faked it. So he could get out of London."

"You're lying," Frankie said. But in his eyes Joe saw a flicker of doubt.

"I'm not." Joe sat back again. He regarded Frankie for a few seconds, then said, "Sid didn't kill Gemma. I know he didn't because I have his word on it. You didn't, either. I've no idea how I know that, but I do. So who did kill her, Frankie. Who?"

Joe got a cough for a reply. A deep, wet, racking cough that left Frankie wiping blood from his lips.

"You're dying, Frankie," Joe said softly. "Don't take Sid with you. Let him live. Let him come home."

Frankie, sick and gray and broken, looked at the floor. Joe could see he was struggling—with his disease, with his conscience, with himself.

"Please, Frankie," he said. "It's me asking. *Me*. The man you put in a wheelchair for the rest of his life. Do you have any idea who killed Gemma Dean?"

Frankie raised his eyes and said, "Oh, aye, guv. I've an idea, all right. I saw him. I was there."

CHAPTER 111

Sid knew.

He knew before the ox cart stopped at the end of Maggie's drive. Before the horses were tied. Before the men from Nairobi stepped onto her porch. He knew when he saw the dust rising in the distance, swirling up from the red dirt road, that it was over. That they were coming for him. Somehow, somewhere deep inside himself, he'd always known it would end this way.

He was shoeing Maggie's mare when Baaru shouted at him that strangers were coming.

He straightened, gazing toward the road. He finished his work, gave the horse to Baaru to lead back into the barn, and went into his house to wash. He put the few pieces of clothing he had into his battered leather satchel, and his books, for he knew how slowly the days passed in jail.

I should've gone away, he thought. Far away. I should've headed into the bush and stayed there. Why didn't I?

He knew why. He'd wanted to see India. To be near her. What did it matter if they jailed him now? If they hanged him? What did he have to live for? For a moment he felt a deep and wild sadness at losing the life he'd made for himself here, but then he asked himself, What life? Life is what he would have had with India. This was no life. This was just an existence.

When he finished packing his things, he went to Maggie's house. He went in the back door and walked through Alice's kitchen and into the sitting room. There were half a dozen men in there. And Maggie.

"If you don't take us to him, we'll have to get him ourselves," a man said. It was Ewart Grogan, one of Nairobi's judges.

"I'm not taking you anywhere until you tell me what this is about," Maggie replied. "Who in blazes do you think you are walking in here, ordering me about, telling me you need to see my foreman, but not telling me why?"

"It's all right, Maggs. I'm here," Sid said.

"Do you know why we're here, Sid?" Grogan asked.

"I've a fair idea."

Grogan nodded. "Take him," he said.

An officer advanced on Sid, pulling a pair of handcuffs off his belt. "Sid Malone," he said, "you are under arrest. I'm charging you with the murder of Gemma Dean."

"*Murder?*" Maggie squawked. "What are you doing? His name's Baxter, not Malone. You fools have the wrong man. Let go of him!"

"I can't do that, ma'am," the officer said, cuffing Sid.

"Will someone please tell me what's happening?" she yelled, as the officer led Sid out of her house and down the porch steps. There was a popping sound and then a blinding flash of light. "What the devil was that?" she shouted, looking around wildly. There was a camera on her front lawn. A man stood behind it, his head hidden under a black cloth.

"You son of a bitch!" she shouted. She ran to him and kicked him in the backside as hard as she could. He lost his balance and fell over. The camera fell with him. "Get off my land! Now!"

"Mrs. Carr! Please calm down!"

Maggie spun around. "Tom Meade! Is that you skulking? What the hell is this about?"

Tom was standing in her front garden. "I'm sorry, Maggie. We have to take him," he said. "Governor's orders."

"Take him? Take him *where?*"

"To Nairobi. To jail."

"They're arresting me, Maggs," Sid said. "They think I murdered a woman. Years ago. In London. Her name was Gemma Dean."

"You didn't, did you?"

"No."

"You've nothing to worry about, then. I'll follow you in two days. Soon as I can get Roos or the Thompson boys to take over here. I'll get you a solicitor, Sid. I'll have you out of there in no time." She turned to Grogan. "And I'll have *your* head! The cheek! Trespassing on my land, marching into my house, making off with my foreman . . ."

As Maggie continued to harangue Grogan and Meade and everyone with them, Sid saw a tall, blond man standing on the path, at a distance from the house. Though he'd steeled himself, his blood still ran cold as the man approached him.

"Mr. Malone," the man said. "It's been a long time."

"Not long enough, Freddie."

Maggie, red-faced and sweating, grabbed Sid's arm. "Don't you worry, lad. I'll have you out in no time. You'll be home before the harvest."

Sid looked into Freddie's cruel, triumphant eyes, then quietly said, "No, Maggie. I don't think I will."

CHAPTER 112

"Why did you do it, Freddie? Why?" India cried, striding into her husband's bedroom.

Freddie, knotting his tie in front of a tall cheval mirror, turned to her and said, "Do *what,* my dear?"

"You know bloody well what!"

"Do keep your voice down. We are guests in the governor's house."

"And the governor's wife just told me about Sid Baxter's arrest. Over tea and toast. That's where you were for the past few days, isn't it? You rode out to Thika so you could arrest him yourself?"

India had almost cried out with shock at the news, almost wept with fear for Sid. It had taken every ounce of control she possessed to finish her breakfast and take her leave of Lady Hayes Sadler.

"Let him go, Freddie," she said now.

"You overestimate my authority."

"You don't have to do this."

"India, my conscience—"

"Your *what*?"

"Will simply not permit me to turn a blind eye to the law, to allow a murdering villain to walk free."

"You are the villain, Freddie. Not Sid."

"I did not murder Gemma Dean."

"Neither did he."

"A magistrate will decide that."

"A magistrate bought and paid for by you."

Freddie looked at his tie. The knot was lopsided. "Blast," he said and began again.

"How did you find out? Did you follow me?" India asked him.

"I rode to the Carr farm to make the acquaintance of Margaret Carr. I saw him there. I had no choice but to order his arrest. I would be negligent in my duties as undersecretary had I not."

"He will hang. You know that, don't you? If you persist in this, he will be convicted and executed."

"I certainly hope so."

India caught her breath. "*Why,* Freddie? Why must you be so cruel?"

"One must protect one's belongings."

"What do you want? The money? The houses? I'll give them to you. Sign them over to you. I'll give you everything," she said, desperation in her voice. "Just let him go. Please."

"It's not as easy as that, I'm afraid. Your wily father made the terms of the trust rather iron-clad. And it's not *just* the money, you know. I've my reputation to consider. I'll never become prime minister if my wife runs off with her bit of rough."

India took a deep breath, steeling herself for the offensive. She had never dared to do what she was about to do, she had been too afraid of the consequences, but she had to act now or Sid would die. "If Sid Malone is given a fair trial, Freddie, I give you my word that I will never see him again. I will remain to all appearances your loyal wife. If he is hanged, I will divorce you. And do everything I can to destroy your reputation."

Freddie laughed. "Not if you care about Charlotte, you won't."

India had anticipated that threat and prepared for it.

"I will, Freddie," she said. "Even though I care greatly about Charlotte. You forget that I have my own funds. I can afford to hire my own solicitors. The best in London. I *will* get my divorce, make no mistake, I'll take Charlotte with me, and I'll ruin you into the bargain. You'll never be prime minister. Never."

Freddie frowned thoughtfully at his reflection. "I daresay that you'd get your divorce and cause a scandal, too, but if you so much as attempt it, I promise you, you will never see Charlotte again. I have many friends. In the Inns of Court. In the Home Office. Why, even in Number Ten. I'll call upon them all to have you ruled an unfit mother."

"You're bluffing," India said, certain now that he was desperate, confident that she had the upper hand. "You have to prove me morally lacking and you can't. Because I'm not. I've not put one foot wrong in all the years of our marriage and you have nothing that says otherwise."

"Not during our marriage, no, but certainly before it. How about the contraceptives you underhandedly dispensed as a new doctor? I'm sure Edwin Gifford would be only too happy to testify about that. And the time you spent with Malone, a known criminal. Your landlady in Arden Street can tell the court how you pretended to be man and wife. And then there's your mad dash from the Moskowitzes' to warn him of the trap the police had set, so we can add aiding and abetting a fugitive to the list. Hardly the sort of activities a mother of high moral standards engages in. Don't you agree? No? Well, it doesn't matter if you do or you don't. The magistrate will."

Freddie had finished with his tie and was standing close to her now—so close that she could smell the scent of the soap he used, the starch in his shirt. She forced herself to look at him.

As their eyes met, he said, "Divorce me, and you will never see her again. Never. Not the odd weekend. Not Christmas. Not even her birthday. I'll send her to live at Blackwood with only a governess for company—a governess that I select and instruct. A bitter, severe old woman. I'll tell her that you abandoned her because you no longer love her. I'll break her heart, India, and I'll blame it all on you. It's your choice to make—your lover or your child."

India closed her eyes. What a fool she was to think she could beat him. There was no choice. There never had been.

A sharp knock was heard at the door.

"Enter," Freddie barked.

It was the maid. "Pardon me, Lady India," she said. "I'm terribly sorry to disturb you, but will you be needing your formal gowns for your fortnight at Mount Kenya or may I pack them for the return trip to London?"

Slowly, quietly, her heart tearing in two, India said, "Send them to London, Mary. Pack my tea gowns and riding habit."

"Yes, ma'am," Mary said, closing the door behind her.

"Quite sensible of you, old girl. Now, if you'll excuse me, I have work to do. And you have packing. Just think . . . a family holiday. A fortnight together. What a jolly good time we'll have. I'm so looking forward to it."

CHAPTER 113

Seamie stood on the porch of Dr. Ribeiro's surgery, peering in through a window. The sun wasn't up yet, but a paraffin lamp was burning inside, illuminating the small room. He could see a man sitting on a chair by a bed, reading. That was the doctor. Willa was lying in the bed under a sheet, motionless.

Seamie rapped on the window softly. In a few seconds the door opened and the doctor stepped out. "Mr. Finnegan, is it?" he asked wearily.

Seamie nodded. He could see from his bleary eyes and rumpled clothing that the man hadn't slept. He'd been keeping vigil over Willa.

"I thought you'd be here early, but not this early. It's not even five o'clock yet. Couldn't you find the Norfolk?"

"I found it. Took a room. Had a wash. Tried to sleep, but I couldn't. I had to come back," Seamie said. "Is she all right?" he asked, looking at Willa again.

"She will be," Dr. Ribeiro said. "She's a fighter. She lost a bit of blood during the operation, of course, and she's weak, but her fever's come down a little. Now that the gangrene's gone, she'll make a good recovery. I'm sure of it." He frowned, then added, "Of course, it's very hard on a woman—an operation like that. They put a great deal of stock in shapely legs and dainty ankles."

"Willa didn't," Seamie said. "She put stock in strong legs. She climbed mountains."

"Well, she won't be doing any more of that, and it's a good thing, too. What was she thinking? The top of a mountain is no place for a woman."

"It was a place for her," he said quietly.

"Was it? Look where it got her," the doctor replied briskly, obviously unused to being corrected.

"I brought her these," Seamie said, holding up a bag containing some new clothes, and the latest newspapers. "I bought them yesterday. Can I leave them by her bed?"

"You may. Just be careful not to wake her. She needs her sleep. Sleep is the great healer." He bustled off to the back of the room. Seamie heard water running, smelled paraffin and coffee.

He walked to Willa's bedside as quietly as he could. As he was placing the bag down, he saw that she was awake. Her eyes were open; she was staring at the ceiling. She looked so pale to him, so lifeless and small.

"Wills?" he whispered, touching the back of his hand to her cheek. "How are you feeling?"

She didn't turn to him; she didn't look at him. "My leg's gone," she said in a dull, lifeless voice.

"I know it is," he said, forcing himself to look. He saw the bulge of her thigh under the sheet, her knee, and then nothing.

"How could you let him do it?"

"I had no choice. You would have died."

"I wish I had."

"Don't say that. You don't mean it. You're in shock."

"How will I climb?"

"I don't know, Willa," Seamie said, his voice faltering. "I don't know."

She closed her eyes. Tears leaked from under her dark lashes.

"Please don't cry. It'll be all right. You'll see." He didn't know what to do. He wanted to take her into his arms, to kiss her pale cheek, but he was afraid to. Afraid of her anger, of her despair. Afraid that she was right. That the doctor had taken more than her leg. That he'd somehow cut away her spirit, too.

"I brought you some things. New clothes, the papers . . ."

"I'm tired," she said, not opening her eyes.

Seamie nodded, feeling wounded by her words, by the accusation in them. He wanted to hear her say that she still loved him. He wanted to tell her that he loved her. Instead he said, "All right, then. I'll come back later."

He took the clothes out of the bag and put them on a chair at the foot of her bed. He put the newspaper on a small table by her head. A headline about a local man's arrest shrieked up at him. He barely noticed.

As he was making his way toward the door he noticed the doctor motioning to him from the back of the room. He joined him.

"She was awake? Talking?" Dr. Ribeiro asked.

"Barely," he said. "She blames me for what happened. She's angry."

"They all are at first. It's hard to lose a limb. Acceptance comes slowly, but it does come. Give her time."

Seamie nodded, rubbing a hand over his face.

"Mr. Finnegan, have you eaten anything recently?"

"I don't know," he said. He didn't. It was so hard to remember. The last few days had passed by in a blur of fear and desperation. "I think the conductor gave me something on the train. A sandwich."

"Listen to me, if you don't take care of yourself, you'll wind up in here, too. Go back to the Norfolk, have a proper breakfast, and then sleep. Let Miss Alden sleep. And the next time the two of you talk, things will be better. You'll see."

Seamie thanked him and headed for the Norfolk. On the way, he told himself that the doctor was right. He and Willa were both spent. He would visit her again tonight when they were both a bit recovered. Things would be different then. They each needed time to adjust.

Nairobi was not a large town and Seamie was back at the Norfolk in fifteen minutes. It was a pretty hotel—built of stone, with a shingled roof and a long veranda.

"The dining room's not open yet, sir. It doesn't open until seven," the clerk at the front desk told him when he inquired about breakfast. "However, the bar's open. If you'd like to sit there, I can have some toast and coffee brought."

Seamie made his way to the bar. Other men were already seated in the room. Three or four looked like planters. There was a priest, two military men, and a traveling salesman. He found an empty table and sat down. A waitress came almost immediately with a steaming pot of Kenyan coffee. Seamie poured himself a cup and savored it. The waitress came back with hot toast, fresh butter, and a pot of strawberry preserves. After days of dried goat meat and muddy water, coffee and toast seemed like the greatest of luxuries to him.

He decided that after he ate he would have a long hot bath and a kip. And when he woke things would look brighter. He was sure of it. Willa was still in shock. As she recovered, she would begin to think more clearly and see that he'd done the only thing he could do. He hadn't forgotten what had happened on the mountain. Nothing could make him forget. Not the accident. Not the five hellish days that followed. He'd told Willa that he loved her. And she'd said that she loved him, too. That was all that mattered. They were strong and they had each other and they would get through this.

He ate another piece of toast, sipped the bracing black coffee. He was beginning to feel like a human being again. Now all he needed was a newspaper. And maybe a cigarette. There was no sign of any tobacco for sale at the bar, but he did spot a paper folded up on a table near one of the planters.

"Excuse me, is that yours?" he asked the man, pointing to it. "Do you mind if I take a look at it?"

"Not at all," the man said, handing it to him. He turned back to his friends. "You see that headline?" he asked them, his voice loud with amazement. "Baxter's been arrested."

"Sid Baxter? Bloke who works up at the Carr farm?"

"The very same. Turns out he's wanted in London for murder. Killed some actress there a few years back. Got out of London on a supply ship. Changed his name."

Seamie froze. He put his cup down and unfolded the paper.

"No," he told himself. "It's not him. It can't be. World's not that small. It's just a coincidence, that's all."

But it was him. There was a photograph. Black and white, grainy. And with a long jagged line running through it, as if the plate had been cracked. It showed a man coming down the steps of someone's porch, his hands cuffed. His head was slightly bent, but Seamie knew him all the same.

It was Sid Malone. His brother.

CHAPTER 114

Sid sat on the dirt floor of his jail cell, his back against the wall, his head in his hands. A bowl of *suferia,* a slop made of boiled beans, sat untouched beside him. A mattress, filthy and bug-ridden, lay on the floor. A battered tin chamberpot stood in one corner.

Sid's eyes were closed, but he was not asleep. He hadn't slept all night. Images from his past, hellish memories of his time in prison, replayed behind his eyes, torturing him. He heard the footsteps again, coming to his cell at night. Felt the desperation, the fear. He heard the guards' laughter, heard Wiggs telling him he'd be back one day.

This was his life now—this despair, this suffocating fear, this desperate loneliness—and he knew it would be until the day he stood on the gallows and a guard put a noose around his neck. Wiggs was dead, but there were more like him. Plenty more. And they were waiting for him.

Sid heard footsteps again. They were coming down the hallway outside his cell. He flinched at the sound.

"Jesus Christ, it *is* you! You know something? This is getting pretty bloody old."

He looked up. A face looked back at him through the bars. He thought he knew it, but it seemed so haggard, so hollow.

"It can't be," he finally said. "It bloody can't be. *Seamie?*"

Seamie nodded. "In the flesh," he said. "What's left of it."

Sid was on his feet in no time. Seamie reached a hand through the bars to him; he took it.

"How the hell did you get here?" Seamie asked.

"Might ask you the same thing."

"It's a long story."

"You've got a captive audience."

Seamie laughed wearily.

"Sit down," Sid said, pointing to a chair behind his brother.

Seamie pulled it over to the bars and sat. He leaned over, elbows on his knees, hands clasped in front of him, and grinned at his brother. "Can't believe this," he said.

"Nor me. You look terrible. Bloody awful," Sid said, forgetting his own misery. "What happened to you?"

"I climbed Kilimanjaro," he said. "On a bet."

Sid listened in amazement as Seamie recounted the whole adventure for him, all the way from a dare made in a pub in Cambridge to the trek off the mountain to Willa's operation. He gave a low whistle when Seamie finished.

"Is she going to be all right?" he asked.

"The doctor says she will. I don't know. She looked awful just now."

"She's bound to, though. She must've been in terrible pain. And then the infection and the operation . . ."

Seamie shook his head. "It's more than that," he said. "She looked gutted. As if they'd taken a lot more than her leg. Climbing's everything to her and now she'll never climb again. She blames me. I know she does."

"Who is she to you?"

Seamie stared down at his clasped hands. "No one special. Just the love of my life."

Sid's heart ached for him. "She'll be all right, lad. You'll see."

Seamie nodded, but didn't look convinced. "Well, anyway, that's my sad story," he said, trying to buck up. "Tell me yours."

Sid told him everything. For the first time, he told him about India. He told him about coming to Africa and meeting Maggie and achieving some small measure of peace. He told him how grateful he'd been for that peace and how it had been smashed forever only days ago when he'd come face-to-face with India again. And then her husband.

"The paper says he's having you returned to London to face charges in the Dean case."

"He means to hang me. I know he does."

"Why?"

"Because I'm a threat."

"To his marriage?"

"To his millions."

"Luckily, he's not the one who'll make that decision. There has to be a trial. With a judge and jury. They'll see there's no case and set you free. They'll have to."

"You don't know Lytton. When it comes to villainy, he makes me look like a bleedin' amateur. He'll get his verdict. By buying the judge or intimidating him." The despair he'd felt, momentarily chased away by the shock of seeing his brother, came flooding back. "I'm a dead man, Seamie."

"Look, you can't—" Seamie began.

His words were drowned out by the sound of angry voices coming down the hallway.

"You must wait here!" a man said. Sid recognized it; it was the guard's. "Nairobi law states that a prisoner is allowed only one visitor at a time."

"Get out of my way, George! I've traveled two bloody days to get here. I've been forced to leave my farm in the hands of a drunken ninny. My women won't work. And seven hundred acres of coffee are going to hell while I'm standing here. All because that damned Hayes Sadler arrested my foreman. So you can take your Nairobi law and stuff it up your arse. Let me through!"

Sid recognized *that* voice, too.

"Hello, Maggs," he said, as she strode into view. "You got past George, I see."

"Self-important fool," she growled. "You'd think he had Jack the Ripper in here. Crikey! Who's this? He's the spitting image of you!"

Seamie stood.

"Meet my brother, Seamus Finnegan. Seamie, may I present my employer, Mrs. Margaret Carr."

"How did you get here?" Maggie asked him.

"It's a long story, ma'am," Seamie said.

"You can tell me later, then. We've other things to discuss now." She sat down heavily on the empty chair. "I've been to see Tom Meade, the weasel. I shamed him into telling me what's going on. They're going to hold you for three more days then put you on a train to Mombasa. Then it's a packet ship to London and Wandsworth."

Sid closed his eyes at the mention of the prison. He felt sick to his very soul.

"Sid? Sid! Are you listening to me? Pay attention. We have to make a plan. We have to talk about this."

He opened his eyes. "Talk about what?"

Maggie lowered her voice. "Your escape."

"I'm not escaping. They can take me to London. I don't care anymore. I've got little enough to live for."

"Don't talk that way. Don't even think that way. You have to get out of here. Go on the lam. To Ceylon. China. Somewhere Lytton'll never find you."

"How, Maggie? How?"

"We'll think of a way. This isn't Newgate, you know. It's a two-bit ram-shackle chicken coop of a jail. People have broken out before. You can, too."

Sid shook his head. Despondency had overtaken him once more. He had lost the will to fight.

"Come on, Charlie. Mrs. Carr's right. You have to try," Seamie said.

"*Charlie?*" Maggie echoed, her eyes widening.

"It's his real name. The one our parents gave him," Seamie explained.

"Charlie." Maggie sat back in the chair. She was quiet for a few seconds, then she said, "I knew it. I bloody knew it. The first time I set eyes on her."

"Knew what?" Sid asked.

"When did you leave London?"

"Nineteen hundred. Why?"

"Timing's right. She's nearly six years old. She would've appeared a bit early, mind you, but many of them do. Women always put it down to a fright or a fall."

"Maggie, what are you on about?"

"I wanted to say something, Sid. I did. Back when Mrs. Lytton first came to see me. I wanted to, but I didn't think it was my place. And who could blame me? You're not the easiest man to talk to about things like this. Can't stand anyone's nose in your business. Even if it is for your own good."

"Maggie . . ."

"Couldn't *you* see it? It's all there. The shape of the face. The eyes. The smile. Did the possibility never even occur to you?"

"See *what*?"

Maggie leaned back in the chair. She crossed her arms over her chest. "Think about this, Sid. Think real hard. India Lytton named her daughter Charlotte. *Charlotte.*"

"So?"

Maggie rolled her eyes. "She didn't name her Fredericka, did she?"

It took a few seconds for her meaning to sink in.

Sid stood. He walked the bars, wrapped his hands around them. "Maggie, you don't think . . ."

"Oh, but I do."

Seamie looked utterly confused. "Would someone like to tell me what's going on?" he said.

Sid looked at him, with light in his eyes. And pain. And wonder. And joy.

"I have a daughter, Seamie," he said. "Her name is Charlotte."

CHAPTER 115

Seamie returned to the Norfolk at noon in a state of profound exhaustion. He had soldiered on bravely for days—driving his weary body beyond the limits of its endurance in order to get Willa to safety. And now, instead of a well-earned rest, he was faced with an entirely new problem—the brother he never expected to see again, the brother he loved, was in jail awaiting trial for murder.

He went to his room and lay down on his bed, meaning only to close his eyes and rest for a half hour before getting up again to check on Willa. Instead he fell into a deep sleep and didn't wake up again until eight the following morning.

"Bloody hell," he groaned as he opened his eyes. He looked out of the window, at the bright sky and then at his watch. He stood up, washed, then raced downstairs. He was supposed to have met Maggie Carr for dinner. She was seated in the lobby when he got downstairs. She stood when she saw him.

"I'm sorry," he said. "I slept like a dead man."

"I'm not surprised, lad. I knocked on your door last night, but got no answer," she said. "I decided I'd let you sleep. You're no good to anyone half dead. Are you better now? Feel up to some breakfast?"

Seamie explained that he had to get to the hospital. He was supposed to have checked on Willa last night and hadn't. He was worried about her. He was worried about his brother, too.

"Stop worrying," Maggie said. "We'll work something out. You got the girl off the mountain, didn't you? You can get Sid out of Nairobi jail. Go check on her. Meet me back here at noon. We'll talk then."

Seamie ran all the way. When he got to the surgery he was astonished to see Willa, pale and thin and drawn, hobbling between her bed and the window on a pair of crutches. He rushed to her side, terrified she would fall.

"It's a bit soon for those, don't you think?" he said. "You've only just come through an operation. Whose idea was this? Is the doctor pushing you to do it?"

"It's all right, Seamie. No one's pushing me. I asked for them to be brought."

Dr. Ribeiro appeared at the foot of Willa's bed. "I think that's enough for now, Miss Alden. You mustn't overdo it," he said.

Willa nodded. She sat down on the bed and surrendered the crutches. The doctor gave her water to drink, then helped her lie down, propping pillows behind her back. Seamie noticed that she gritted her teeth when she moved her right leg. When the doctor left to attend to a new patient, he asked her again if she wasn't doing too much too soon.

"I only did it for a few minutes. Just to try it out," she said. "I have to. I have to get used to them, you know."

"How are you feeling?"

She mustered a smile. "Better. Though I tire easily."

She's calmer, he thought. Not despairing, like yesterday. Not hysterical, like the day before. That's good.

Calm was not a word Seamie would normally have used to describe Willa and if he hadn't been so tired himself and so worried about his brother, he might have looked a bit more closely into her eyes and seen the anger there simmering just below the surface. He might have listened a bit more closely to her voice and heard the frayed note in it. He might have realized that this sudden calmness was nothing but a front. But he did not.

Willa asked him how he was doing and if he'd gotten some rest. She asked about Nairobi and his hotel. And then something happened between them that had never happened before—their conversation ran dry.

After a moment of awkward silence, Willa said, "I apologize. I'm a terrible bore, aren't I? I'm tired again. Want to sleep all the time."

"No, I'm sorry," Seamie said. "I'm keeping you from resting. I'll go."

He poured her another glass of water, then said, "Willa, I may not be able to come to visit you tomorrow. Or the next day."

"Is something wrong? Are you all right?" she asked.

"I'm fine, but I've a friend who's in a bit of trouble."

"Here in Nairobi? I didn't know you had friends here. Who is it?"

"Um . . . he's . . . no one you know. He's an old school chum. I may need to accompany him on a bit of a hasty trip. Up country. Just for a day or two. I'd be back by the end of the week. If I even go at all. Will you be all right if I do?"

She smiled. "I'll be fine," she said. "Do you have the rest of my things? My wallet and money and such? I'd like to have some cash at hand in case I need something while you're gone."

"That's a good idea. If I don't get back here tonight, I'll send someone from the hotel over."

"Seamie," she said, suddenly catching his hand in hers.

He turned around.

"Seamie . . . I love you."

"I love you, too, Willa. So much." He took her in his arms and held her tightly. How he had longed to hear those words.

"And I'm sorry."

He released her. "For what?"

"For everything."

Her eyes were welling. He didn't want her to cry.

"Shh, Willa, it's all right."

"It's not."

"It will be. Rest now."

She nodded and lay down. He checked the cuts on her head and hands, to make sure they were healing properly. She told him to stop fussing, so he pulled the sheet up over her shoulders, kissed her forehead, and left.

He saw Dr. Ribeiro on his way out, and stopped him to ask him if he was certain it was good for Willa to be on crutches so soon.

"It's a good sign, Mr. Finnegan," the doctor said. "It means she's accepting what has happened to her. Most amputees won't even talk about crutches for weeks, never mind trying them out only days after they've lost a leg. Miss Alden seems determined to deal with her new circumstances. She's a strong woman. A brave woman. I would encourage her if I were you."

Seamie left feeling encouraged himself. They had survived a terrible ordeal, the two of them, and Willa was mending, body and soul. She loved him still. She'd told him so. Just knowing that made him feel strong and sure again.

He knew he would need that strength in the next few days. Willa was out of the woods, but his brother was in dire trouble. Sid needed him, needed his help. He believed what Sid said about Freddie Lytton—that he'd stop at nothing to hang him. And he knew that Sid had to escape. Now. While he was still in Nairobi. He would have armed guards on the train ride to Mombasa and there would be no hope of escaping once he was on board the ship to London. Or from an English prison. They had to get him out, and they had to do it now, but how? Nairobi prison might not be Newgate, but it still had a warden, and a jailer, and armed askaris standing guard. Whatever they tried would be risky and dangerous.

He hurried out of the surgery, down its shaky wooden steps, and out into the dusty Nairobi streets, eager to meet Maggie and hear what she had to say. If the two of them didn't end up in jail themselves by the end of the week, it would be a miracle.

Seamie did not look back as he walked away from the hospital. He was too intent on what lay ahead of him. He did not see Willa standing in the window, propped up on her crutches again, her hand pressed to the glass, her face wet with tears.

CHAPTER 116

"This is preposterous! Outrageous!" Herbert Gladstone sputtered, throwing a document down on his desk.

"Betts swears it's true," Joe Bristow replied. He was seated across from the home secretary.

"Then why has he waited for six years to say anything?"

"He didn't think anyone would believe him."

"He's damned right nobody will believe him. Nobody. I'd advise you to drop this, Joe. Immediately. You'll only end up making a laughingstock of yourself, of me, and of my office."

"I can't do that."

"Why not?"

"Because I believe him. And I want you to officially reopen the Gemma Dean case."

"Think about what you're asking. You want to accuse a government minister, a man who's never been in any sort of trouble with the law, who, in fact, has a sterling record of service to king and country, of murder. *Murder*. On the word of a convicted criminal! It's absurd! It's utter madness!"

"It's also the bloody truth!" Joe said hotly. "I got you a sworn signed statement from Betts. And I want you to reopen that case. Sid Malone did not kill Gemma Dean, and I want to clear his name. I know how it looks, Herbert. But how it looks is not how it is."

Gladstone gave Joe a long look. "No, not at all," he said at length. "How it looks to me, at least, is like a political assassination. A radical Labour MP trying to do his Liberal rival in."

"Blimey, Herbert," Joe said, disgusted. "You know me better than that. If I wanted to go after Lytton politically, I'd do it in the Commons. As I've already done. Many times. I'm not after any kind of political victory. I'm after justice."

Gladstone continued to eye Joe, weighing his sincerity. Then he picked up the document he'd thrown on his desk minutes ago—Betts's sworn statement—and began to read it again.

Joe watched him, remembering how stunned he himself had felt when Frankie Betts told him it was Freddie Lytton who'd murdered the actress. And that he knew it was Lytton because he'd seen him do it.

"I was there," he'd told Joe, the last time Joe had gone to visit him in prison. "I went over to Gemma's place a few days after I shot you. I'd brought her a present. A white kitten with a pink collar. She was feeling low, you see, over Sid. She liked cats and I thought it would cheer her up. And butter her up. I was hoping to get information out of her. I thought she might've heard from Sid. Might know where he was hiding. Might even be hiding him herself. When I got there I heard voices coming from inside the flat. Angry voices. A man's and a woman's. At first I thought it was Sid and that he and Gem were having a row. But the voice was too plummy to be his."

"Where were you?" Joe asked.

"In the hallway."

"If you weren't in the flat, how did you see the killing?"

"Picked the lock. Walked in. Then walked down the hallway to have myself a gander. That was the hard part—getting down the hallway. It was long, and I had to keep that damned mog quiet. Stuffed it under my coat. Almost smothered it. I saw them both. Plain as day. Lytton walloped her, then he choked her. She kicked him in the balls and broke away. Then she tried to get to the hallway. And out the door, I imagine."

"Why didn't you stop him, Frankie? Why didn't you help her?" Joe had asked.

"I didn't know he was going to kill her. Didn't think for a second that he had it in him. If I had known, I would've stopped him. I thought he was only roughing her up a bit. They were talking about Sid, you see. He was trying to get an address out of her. The place where Sid went to meet the doctor. I knew about that place. Arden Street. He wasn't there. I'd looked for him. But I wanted to listen in case Gemma knew about another hiding place. I thought she might've been holding out on me. I thought Lytton might get it out of her."

"What happened next?"

"Gem never even made it to the hallway. Lytton grabbed her and dragged her back into the sitting room. He wanted to throw her on the settee, I think, but he missed and she hit a table instead. A marble table. She hit it hard. Broke her neck."

"What did Lytton do then?"

"He went quiet for a bit. Then he started destroying the place. Breaking things. Turning things over. Making a right bloody mess. He must've had it in his head by then that he was going to blame Gem's death on Sid. Make it look like a robbery and all. I saw him stuff her diary and wallet into his pocket. Then he went into her bedroom. Wrecked that, too. I was behind him, out in the hallway, watching. I saw him steal her jewelry. The earrings and necklace Sid gave her. Worth a fortune, those. Word got out. Everyone was waiting for them to reappear."

"Who's 'everyone'?"

"Every wide boy in London. Every rozzer, too."

"I don't understand."

"Lytton put it about that Sid killed Gemma. That he'd seen him do it. The police investigating the murder found that Gem's diamonds were missing, and naturally reckoned that Sid had taken them because he was on the run and needed money. No respectable jeweler would touch them, of course. No tuppenny-ha'penny pawnbroker could afford to. They were worth thousands. Tens of thousands. So everyone knew he'd have to approach a fence if he wanted to move them. Joey Griz was the biggest and the best, and the rozzers were watching him night and day. They were watching a lot of lesser lights, too. But Sid never showed. Because he didn't have the goods. Freddie Lytton did."

Frankie went on to explain how Lytton had almost caught him. Frankie had stepped on a creaky floorboard. Freddie'd heard him and picked up a poker and Frankie had had to hightail it. There wasn't time to get back down the long hallway to the door, so he'd ducked into the kitchen instead. He hid in the broom cupboard, jostling a bucket as he did, making more noise. He thought he'd be found out for sure, and then he'd remembered the cat inside his coat. He tossed it out of the cupboard into the kitchen, half dead. He hadn't had time to close the cupboard door all the way and he saw what happened next. The cat just sat in the middle of the kitchen floor for a few seconds, looking dazed, before it came to its senses and ran off. Lytton, who saw the animal, must have assumed it had made the noise. Frankie watched from inside the broom cupboard as Freddie smashed a teapot into his face. Then he left the flat, with Frankie not far behind him, and raised the alarm, telling two men who came to his aid that Sid Malone had killed Gemma Dean.

Joe had been astonished by Frankie's story. He knew Lytton was an underhanded politician, but he'd never thought him capable of murder.

"Why didn't you come forward?" he'd asked Frankie. "You could have helped Sid."

"I didn't want to help him. Back then, it suited me just fine if he was wanted for Gemma's murder. It would bring him back to the Bark. Back to the life," he said. "And besides, who'd believe me? Who's going to believe me now, guv? Looking at you, I'm not even sure you do."

But Joe did believe him. Frankie had nothing to gain by telling his story. And much to lose. When Lytton heard his accusations, he'd undoubtedly pull some strings to have Frankie moved to a worse prison, if not put into solitary.

Frankie had told him all of this a week ago. Joe had been spending tense and hectic days ever since trying to arrange lawyers and police officers, apprising the warden of what was going on, and scheduling one final visit to Frankie. He'd worried the whole time that it would all be for nothing, that Frankie would change his mind at the last minute and refuse to give a statement.

But Frankie hadn't changed his mind. He had made a condition, though—he wouldn't speak to Alvin Donaldson. "You've got to get me another copper," he said. "If someone's getting a promotion out of this, it isn't going to be him."

Afterward, when the others had left, Joe had asked the warden for a few minutes alone with Frankie.

"Thank you," he said to him. "It's a good thing you've done."

"Will you get Lytton for this?"

"I'll try, but it's going to be bloody hard."

"The diamonds, mate. Find the diamonds and you'll find your man."

"Easier said than done," Joe replied.

Frankie nodded. He looked at the floor, then back at Joe. "Two nights ago they gave me last rites. I'm a Catholic, me. Or was. Once upon a time. It was bad, I don't mind telling you. Coughing blood all over everything. I pulled through, though. By sheer bloody-mindedness. I wanted a little more time. So I could do this. Will you tell him? Sid, I mean. Will you tell him I did this?"

"Maybe you can tell him yourself one day."

Frankie smiled. "Ah, guv, we both know that's not going to happen."

"Do you want me to tell him?"

"Aye."

"I will then."

Frankie nodded. He looked at Joe's legs, at the chair he was sitting in, and pain filled his eyes. "As much as I can, I want to set things straight . . . as much as I can . . ."

He was a dying man asking for forgiveness. Should he give it? Frankie had tried to kill him. He'd taken his legs from him. He would never run with his children. Never dance with his wife. Never stand by his daughter's side when she married. And yet it wasn't himself he pitied. It was Frankie. He'd never known what it was to live. To love and be loved. To have a family. Pride. Respect. And now he never would.

"I know, Frankie," Joe said. "I know you do. You have."

"Thank you," Frankie whispered. And then he was gone, shuffling back to his cell under the watchful eye of the guard.

Herbert Gladstone sat back in his chair now, shaking his head. "What do you want me to do, Joe?" he asked. "I've just read the statement again. Top to bottom. Just to make sure I didn't miss anything. There's nothing there. Nothing I can work with. Just one man's word against another's. And the man in question happens to be serving life in prison."

"You can question Lytton. Send some detectives to his home."

"Not for some weeks. He's still in Africa. And what if I did? Say I do send some detectives to ask him whether or not he murdered Gemma Dean, what do you think will happen? Do you really think he'll say he did it? Even if he did do it. Which I don't believe for one second."

Joe was about to argue with the man when his secretary rapped on the door and came into his office.

"Beg your pardon, sir, but this just arrived," he said, handing his boss a telegram.

Gladstone shook his head as he read it. His face darkened. "It never rains but it pours."

"Is something wrong?" Joe asked.

"I've just received word that your Mr. Malone has been arrested."

"*What?* Where?"

"In Nairobi. He's in jail there. He's going to be brought to Mombasa and shipped out to London."

"Lytton's there, too, isn't he?" Joe said.

"Yes, he is. He's the one who ordered the arrest."

"Of course he did," Joe said. "If he can get Malone convicted for Gemma Dean and hanged, no one can ever point the finger at him."

"You're trumping things up now," Gladstone said testily. "Freddie Lytton has no reason for wanting Sid Malone dead. He knows Malone was accused of the murder, and I'm sure he wants only a fair trial and justice for Miss Dean. As do we all."

Joe felt desperate. Freddie did indeed have a reason for wanting Sid dead, but Joe couldn't tell Gladstone that. He couldn't tell him the truth about Sid's connection to Freddie and to India. But he knew that connection imperiled Sid's life. Much more than a false charge for the Dean murder did. Freddie's wife loved Sid. His child belonged to Sid. Freddie had reasons, all right. Far too many of them.

"Please, Herbert," Joe said now, "this case needs to be reopened. Freddie Lytton is not above the law. No one is. He needs to be questioned."

Gladstone cut him off. "No. Not until you get me something better than this," he said, tapping Betts's statement. "I need more than the word of a convict to do what you're asking me to do."

"If you won't reopen the case for me, can you at least do me this favor? Can you keep Malone's arrest quiet?"

Gladstone gave him a long look. "As a favor to you, Joe, I will keep my office from giving it to the papers, but I cannot control what comes from Africa. If Lytton alerts his associates in the press, they will certainly run the story. And I imagine he *will* tell them. He enjoys appearing in the headlines even more than you do."

Joe ignored the dig. "How long do you think I have?" he asked.

Gladstone shrugged. "A day. Two or three at most."

Joe nodded. "I'll be back," he said.

"I don't doubt it," Gladstone said wearily.

Inside his carriage, on his way home, Joe gave in to an uncharacteristic feeling of hopelessness. He had exactly what he'd set out to get—the true identity of Gemma Dean's killer—and yet he had nothing, because he couldn't prove it.

And if that wasn't bad enough, the man whose name he was working so hard to clear had just been arrested and faced a trial for murder.

God, just wait until Fiona finds out about that, he thought. She'll be beside herself. And her with a baby due in only a few weeks' time. He prayed that Gladstone would keep his word and keep the news out of the papers.

And then there was the little issue of Sid's child. A daughter he might or might not know he had. A niece Fiona knew nothing about, for he, Joe, had still not found a way to tell her without breaking his promise to Ella.

He thought about Frankie's statement and how he could always simply go to the papers with Betts's confession himself. It might save Sid. And it might well destroy Freddie Lytton. And either way, the child—an innocent little girl—would be right in the middle of it all.

It seemed as if there were obstacles wherever he looked. He had no idea how to proceed. He was well and truly stuck. As he was riding along, brooding, Frankie's words came back to him. *The diamonds, mate. Find the diamonds and you'll find your man.*

"Great idea," he muttered. "I'll just wire Freddie in Nairobi and ask him where he stashed them."

But the more he thought about it, the more he wondered if there might not be something there, some small possibility. Frankie said the fences had been expecting Sid, but Sid had not shown up because he hadn't had the jewels. What if Freddie had? What if he'd sold them?

It was a long shot, he knew it was. And yet anything, no matter how slight, was better than nothing. He leaned forward and rapped on the window at the front of the cab. It slid open.

"Yes, sir?" his driver said.

"Slight change of plan, Myles. Take me to Limehouse, please. Narrow Street. Pub called the Barkentine."

"Are you quite certain, sir?"

"I am."

"Very well, sir." The window slid shut.

He would ask a few questions, talk to a few people. See if Desi Shaw was still around and the fence, Joe Grizzard. Now. Tonight.

Before time ran out.

For Sid. For the child. For all of them.

CHAPTER 117

India sat on the veranda of the house where she was staying, gazing at the snow-capped peaks of Mount Kenya, so white against the turquoise sky. The house, a sprawling bungalow built of fieldstone, had a paved terrace, tall windows, dormers, a shingled roof and dozens of rose bushes climbing and tumbling all about it. It would have looked equally at home nestled in the Cotswolds as it did in Kenya.

Lady Elizabeth Wilton, its owner, had written in a letter that it was located in the most beautiful place in all of Africa, and that no one who had visited it had ever disagreed. India, however, saw none of its beauty, felt nothing of its magic.

She had barely been able to function since Sid's arrest. She was hollow-eyed, listless, nearly ill with worry. Just thinking of him in a jail cell tortured her, for she knew what prison had done to him, she knew the despair he would be feeling. Thinking beyond that—to London, to his trial and inevitable sentencing—made her weep.

She had to do something to help him, but what? She had money of her own, more than enough to hire good lawyers for his defense, but she would have to contact them on the sly. Freddie could not find out. There was no telegraph office, no post office, for ten miles. Fort Henry was the closest village, but if she sent a servant there with letters, Freddie would know.

She would have to wait until she got back to London before she could make her move. But what if she was too late? Freddie had told her nothing about his immediate plans for Sid, but she'd been able to get some information out of Tom Meade and had learned that he was going to be taken from Nairobi to Mombasa on the railway, then put on a packet boat bound for London. She and Freddie wouldn't leave for London themselves until a fortnight later, and she knew Freddie had done this on purpose. He wanted Sid tried and hanged before she reached London. She would have to slip away from him somehow and contact her London lawyers. When they returned to Nairobi. Or when they were in Mombasa, awaiting their ship.

Could the fates be so cruel? she wondered for the millionth time. Had she really been allowed to discover that Sid was alive, only to see him hanged? India knew the answer to her questions: the fates were indifferent; it was Freddie who was cruel.

"More tea, Msabu?"

India turned to Lady Wilton's butler. They had rented the house from her and the servants, too. The butler was a tall, graceful man dressed in a white tunic and trousers. "No, thank you, Joseph," she said.

"And for the Missy?" Joseph asked, nodding at Charlotte's empty cup and her empty chair.

India realized, with a start, that her daughter was gone. When had she slipped away? And how had she not noticed?

"No, I don't think she'll be wanting more. Have you seen her?"

"She was in the kitchen with the cook. Helping her make a cake. But I think now she is hunting for nightingales."

"She's not underfoot, is she?"

Joseph smiled. "No, Msabu. She is not that kind of child."

"If you see her, will you send her to me, please?"

India felt terrible. She was so wrapped up in her private pain, she hadn't even noticed her child's absence. Charlotte had obviously become bored and had slipped away. As soon as she came back, India would make it up to her. They would go for a walk or take a picnic into the hills. She must put a brave face on things for Charlotte's sake. She mustn't be so inward, so distant; she was all the girl had.

India thought, with a brief flush of pleasure, how happy Charlotte was here. In fact, she was flourishing. She'd made a full recovery. Her color was good again and her spirits high. She was free here to ride and explore the whole day long, without her father demanding her quiet, decorous presence at this ceremony or on that tour.

Mercifully, they'd both seen very little of Freddie. He'd gone riding today. He wanted to see the mountain, he'd said, and wouldn't be back until after supper—hours from now. She was glad of his absences. He was always either out riding or shut up in Lady Wilton's study, writing his endless reports.

He tended to rise late here, take lunch, and then disappear into the hills, or into his work, laboring far into the night, not stopping until two or three o'clock the next morning. She always knew when he finished. Awake in her bed, she would hear the haunting strains of the "Raindrop Prelude" echoing through the house and smell the scent of tobacco. He liked to smoke when he finished his work. And he liked to listen to his music box. He never went anywhere without it. At home it resided in his study, under the portrait of his ancestor, Richard Lytton, the Red Earl. When he traveled, he insisted on bringing it with him and insisted on packing it himself. No one else could touch it. Not even Charlotte, who, for some strange reason, also loved the sad melody. She had taken it down once when she was quite small to listen to it. Freddie had found her sitting on the floor with it, and had punished her severely. She was never to touch it, he said. Never. No one was.

As India was thinking of the music box, she suddenly heard a crash from inside the house, and then a few notes of the melody, strangely off key.

She was just rising from her chair, about to go and see what had happened, when Charlotte appeared, white-faced.

"There you are, darling," India said. "I was wondering where you'd got to."

"Mummy," she said quietly. "Mummy, come quick."

"Why? What is it?"

"I've broken Father's music box."

"Charlotte, no!" India said. "How?"

"I was playing in the study. With Jane. We were under the desk, pretending it was a fort. We pretended that the Masai were attacking. I got up to run out of the study and knocked the table where the music box was resting. It fell to the floor."

"Charlotte, you should never have gone in there!"

"I know, Mummy. I'm sorry," she said, panic in her eyes.

"How bad is it? Maybe we can fix it. Is it smashed? Are there springs sticking out?"

"No, Mummy. No springs. Just jewelry."

"Jewelry?" India repeated, puzzled. She followed an anxious Charlotte into the study. The box was on the floor, open and upside down. One of its feet had come off. A small drawer was sticking out of it, spilling what indeed looked like jewelry across the carpet. India knelt down. She carefully picked it up. "It has a hidden drawer," she said. "It must've popped out when it hit the floor."

Something glinted against the dark colors of the carpet. India picked it up. She stared at it, not comprehending. It was her dragonfly comb; the one that had belonged to her mother. The one that Hugh Mullins had taken and pawned. She turned it over. It had her mother's initials, ISJ—the same as her own—engraved on the back.

But it can't be, India thought, her hand going to the back of her head, because that comb was in her hair. Her father had gotten it back from the police. Its mate had never been found. Hugh had been accused of stealing them both and had gone to jail for refusing to return the second one.

"It's just like yours, Mummy," Charlotte said. "The one in your hair."

India pulled her comb out and held it next to the one from the music box. Two perfectly matched dragonflies. Commissioned from Louis Comfort Tiffany by her father as a gift for her mother. The only two of their kind. She suddenly found it difficult to breathe.

"Mummy?" Charlotte said. "Mummy, are you all right?"

"Charlotte, darling, fetch that for Mummy, please," she said, pointing to a sparkling diamond earring a few feet away. Charlotte did so. India turned it over in her hand. It was long, a chandelier style, made of flawless, brilliant white diamonds. It had a small medallion near the bottom. Worked in tiny diamonds in the medallion were the initials GD. India did not recognize the piece; the initials meant nothing to her. She reached across the carpet for the necklace. It, too, had the same medallion, but larger and in the center of the piece. She turned the necklace over. There was an inscription on the back:

For Gemma. Break a leg. Love, Sid.

India's hand came to her mouth. *Break a leg* . . . That's what one said to performers to wish them luck before a show. Gemma. *Gemma Dean.* The woman with whose murder Sid had just been charged. She had been an actress—and Sid Malone's lover. This necklace, these earrings . . . they were hers. Sid had given them to her. They'd gone missing after her death. She remembered hearing about that. What were they doing here, in Freddie's music box?

India's stomach suddenly knotted with fear.

"Charlotte . . ." she said, pointing to the last piece of jewelry, a heavy gold ring. A man's ring. Charlotte picked it up and placed it in India's hand. The fear she'd felt was replaced by grief now. The ring had a crest on it. She recognized the crest, for she had seen it many, many times. On her cousin's hand. It was Wish's ring.

"No. God, no . . . ," she moaned. She closed her eyes, still clutching the ring, and doubled over. Her head sank to the floor. "Hugh, Wish, Gemma Dean. . . . It couldn't be . . . he couldn't have . . ."

"Mummy!" Charlotte cried, alarmed. "Mummy, what is it?"

Charlotte's voice seemed to come to her from far away. It sounded muffled and distant. And then she heard another voice. A man's voice. Only yards away.

"Joseph!" it bellowed. "Where's the blasted boy? Call him to my office! I need help with my boots."

India's head snapped up. It was Freddie. He'd returned from his ride early. She could hear his footsteps. On the porch. In the foyer. And heading toward the study.

CHAPTER 118

India grabbed Charlotte's arm so tightly that the little girl winced.

"Charlotte, say nothing about this to anyone," she hissed. "Nothing! Go to your room. No, not that way! Use the veranda door. Wait for me there."

"But Mummy—"

"Do as I say! Go!"

Charlotte ran.

The footsteps were getting closer. She scooped up the jewels and dumped them into the drawer. She picked up the music box with trembling hands and slid the drawer back into place. She tried to push it closed, but it stuck.

"Come on . . . come on!" she whispered.

The footsteps stopped outside the door.

"Ah, there you are," she heard her husband say.

She pulled the drawer out and felt inside with her finger. A tiny spring had come loose. She yanked it out and pushed the drawer in once more. It clicked shut. She set the music box back on the table. It tilted to one side. Freddie would notice it immediately. *The foot,* she thought. *Where's the bloody foot?*

". . . not the black ones. Do you understand me? The brown brogues."

She crawled around on the carpet, feeling for it. Something small and hard bit into her knee. It was the foot. She snatched it up and carefully placed it under the box. There was no time to glue it. She prayed that Freddie did not want to listen to it now. She was about to dash out of the study to the veranda when she heard the doorknob turn. It was too late; she would never make it in time. He would see her and demand to know what she was doing in there. She looked wildly about the room, desperate for a place to hide. There was nothing, nowhere.

And then, at the very last second, she spotted a tiny porcelain hand poking out from under the massive mahogany desk and dived for it.

She was on her knees under his desk when he opened the door. He was confronted by the sight of her backside.

"What the devil are you doing?" he barked.

"Looking for Jane."

"*Who?*"

"Charlotte's doll. Ah! Here she is," India said. She backed out from under the desk, clutching Jane, and stood up. Her face was flushed, her breath short—not from her exertions under the desk, but it would look that way to Freddie.

"Why is Charlotte's doll in here? Charlotte is not supposed to be in here," he said.

"She was playing under your desk. Pretending it was her fort."

"She's *not* to be in here. See that it doesn't happen again."

"I'm sorry. I will."

The *toto* came in bearing a pair of Freddie's shoes. Joseph was on his heels with a tea tray.

"*Not* the black wingtips!" Freddie bellowed. "The brown bloody brogues! How many times do I have to tell you?"

The boy, confused, turned to go.

"Look, just bring what you've got. I don't have all damned day. Put them down and help me with my boots."

India, grateful for once for Freddie's foul mood, hurried out of the study and down the hallway to her bedroom. Once there, she locked the door and sat down on her bed, clutching Jane tightly.

"It's not true," she moaned. "It can't be true."

Voices, urgent and frightened, whispered inside her head. Hugh's and Wish's.

She heard Hugh telling her, tears in his eyes, that he'd taken only one comb, that he'd never touched the second one. Never even seen it.

She saw her lovely, laughing cousin, just before he'd died, telling her about the donations he'd secured for her clinic, his voice full of pride and excitement.

She remembered a picture she'd seen of Gemma Dean in a magazine, bright and beautiful, wearing her dazzling diamonds.

"Why?" she said aloud. "Why would he do it?"

A voice, a low, cold voice deep down inside her, answered her question.

"For you," it said. "For your money. Everything he's done, he's done to get your money. He killed them because they were in his way. And if he finds out that you know, he'll kill you, too."

CHAPTER 119

"Good morning, George," Maggie Carr said as she walked by him on her way to the cells. She stopped suddenly, held her hand to her mouth, and coughed until she was red in the face. Seamie put a comforting hand on her back.

"You all right, Maggie?" George Gallagher, the prison guard, asked.

"No, I'm bloody well not. I started coughing yesterday and it's only getting worse." She coughed again and dug in her skirt pocket for a tin of cachous.

"Nairobi throat," George said. "Comes from all the dust. Never mind those lozenges, they don't do a thing. Drink hot water with honey and lemon. That's what my wife gives me. Works like a charm."

Maggie said she would and George returned to his newspaper. He knew better now than to argue about the one-visitor-at-a-time rule.

Maggie coughed again and Seamie gave her a look. She was not to overdo it. They walked out of the guardroom and down the corridor to Sid's cell. He stood up when he saw them, hands grasping the bars.

"Morning, lad," Maggie said. "We've come to sit with you for a bit. How are you feeling today?"

"I'm fine," Sid said. "Have you . . ."

Maggie held a finger to her lips. "Oh, yes. I've news of the harvest. Roos sent a letter with the Thompson boy, telling me the plants are all fine."

Sid stood tensely as Maggie talked on and Seamie fished in his jacket pocket.

Sid no longer looked despondent; he looked like a trapped and frantic animal. Everything had changed for him two days ago when Maggie had told him that Charlotte Lytton was his daughter. He hadn't believed it at first, but then he'd told them that he had to get out, one way or another. That he couldn't go back to London. He'd do anything, take any risk, but he wasn't going to be hanged. Not now. Not before he'd had a chance to ask India face-to-face if Charlotte truly was his.

Seamie had assured him that they'd think of something. "Just give us a little time," he'd said.

"I don't have any time," he'd replied. "They're putting me on the train in a few days."

Seamie glanced over his shoulder now. The corridor was empty. He pulled a piece of paper from his pocket and handed it to Sid. *Keep talking while you read this,* was written at the top. He knew that George could hear them. And that he'd become suspicious now if they all suddenly went silent.

Sid made mechanical comments to Maggie's news about the farm while he read the paper he'd been handed. Seamie knew what it said; he'd written it out in his room last night after he and Maggie had finalized their plans.

We're breaking you out. We trade clothes. I go in the cell. You walk out with Maggie. She'll explain outside. Pick the lock.

Sid looked at him when he finished reading. He mouthed two words, "With what?"

Seamie held up a finger. He was talking now. He was babbling on about an imaginary firm of solicitors in London whom he'd engaged to take Sid's case. As he spoke, he quietly took off his boot and pulled out a butter knife, a fish fork, and a corkscrew, and handed them through the bars. It was the best he could do on short notice. He didn't dare risk buying screwdrivers and awls in the local hardware store. The shopkeeper might remember.

Sid examined the implements, then put the corkscrew down. He threaded his hands through the bars and got to work. Progress was slow and fumbling. He was working backward, his wrists bent at a painful angle in order to get leverage. Maggie and Seamie babbled on, desperate to cover the sounds of scraping metal. The lock was massive and the tumblers heavy. Five minutes elapsed, then ten. Sid's brow was slick with sweat. Seamie was running out of things to talk about. And then they heard it, a metal thunk. It echoed loudly down the dank hallway. He and Maggie exchanged panicked glances.

"Oh, *blast!*" she exclaimed, waving Sid back from the door. "I've dropped my cachous! Fetch them for me, Seamie, lad. Will you?"

Seamie heard George rise from his chair. He motioned for the tin. Maggie dug in her pocket and gave it to him. He opened it, frantically scattering lozenges across the floor. When George came around the corner, Seamie was on his knees, tin in hand, picking up the lozenges.

"Everything all right?" George asked, casting his eye over Sid, who was at the back of his cell, sitting in his customary spot on the floor.

"I've lost my cachous," Maggie said petulantly.

Seamie made as if to hand the tin back to her.

"I don't want them now," she said, aggrieved. "Not after they've been on the floor." She took the tin from him and handed it to George. "Will you toss them in the rubbish bin for me, George, please?" she asked.

"No loss, Maggie. I told you, it's honey and lemon you're wanting, not these."

He returned to his desk and Seamie felt his heart start beating again. Still talking, he gingerly opened the door, stepped into the cell, and exchanged his clean shirt and jacket for Sid's dirty ones. Then he handed Sid the corkscrew and fish knife. He held on to the butter knife. Sid slipped the implements into his boot.

When they were both dressed again, Sid hugged him hard. Seamie took his cap off and placed it on Sid's head, and then Sid was gone, closing the cell door behind him. They said their good-byes loudly, then Seamie watched as Maggie and Sid disappeared down the corridor. Sid had his clothes on; they looked almost exactly alike. Seamie prayed that would be enough.

He wedged himself into the front corner of the cell. He could just see the guard's room from there, if he stood on his tiptoes.

"We'll be off, then, George," he heard Maggie say.

"Bye, now," George said, not bothering to look up from his paper. "Don't forget the honey and lemon."

Seamie walked to the back of the cell and stood under the window, holding his breath, listening for shouts, the sound of running feet, gunshots—but he heard nothing. Just the sounds of a typical Nairobi morning—horses and carts, builders pounding away, the odd shouted greeting. He exhaled. Relief washed over him. They'd done it. Now all Maggie had to do was get Sid out of town. Quickly.

He walked back across the cell, picked up the chamber pot, turned it upside down, and hit himself in the face with it. When he could see straight again, he sat down on the floor and, using his butter knife, started prying the handle off the pot. It was only riveted on and it didn't take him long before he had it off. He turned the mattress over, made a small hole in the ticking, then buried the knife and handle inside it. Then he flipped it back over. He thought about Willa as he worked, hoping that she was all right. It would be hours before George came to bring Sid lunch and discovered he was gone. Once the alarm was raised, they would hold him here. They'd question him, ask him how it had all happened, try to shake his story. It might be a day, maybe two, before he was able to get back to her. He silently told her that he loved her and promised her that he would be with her soon.

Then he closed his eyes and did his best to look unconscious.

CHAPTER 120

India lay in bed. The house was silent. The clock in the sitting room had just struck three. She waited a few more minutes, blinking in the darkness, then threw back the covers and rose, fully dressed. She found her boots where she'd left them and hurriedly put them on. She pulled a small bundle from under her bed. It contained bread and cheese, a canteen of water, and a good deal of money. It was all she was bringing. They needed to travel like the wind, she and Charlotte. Extra weight would slow them.

Carefully, quietly, she made her way to her bedroom door. She turned the knob slowly, telling herself to be patient. Holding her breath, she opened the door, slipped out into the hallway, then closed it behind her. Charlotte's room was across the hall. Freddie's was down at the end.

She had lain awake in the dark since eleven o'clock, willing him to go to bed. He'd finally done so just after one. She'd heard him retire and then she'd made herself wait for two hours to elapse, until she was certain he was deeply asleep. It had been agony, the waiting, but she knew she must not be hasty. If Freddie was not fully asleep, if he heard her, she was done for. She had made her plan yesterday—after she'd found the jewelry—and she knew she would get one chance and one chance only.

She crossed the hallway now. Halfway there, a board creaked under her foot. She waited, every muscle tensed, ready to dash back into her room should Freddie's door open. Five minutes passed, ten. She pressed on.

"Mummy?" a little voice said, as she slipped inside Charlotte's room.

"Shh, my darling," she whispered. She knelt down by her bed and said, "Charlotte, you need to do exactly as Mummy tells you now. I want you to get up and get dressed. Put your riding things on. Be as quiet as a mouse and don't light the lamp. Do you hear me?"

"Yes, Mummy."

"We're going traveling, you and I. I'm going to saddle the horses now. I want you to meet me on the porch in ten minutes. Walk down the hall in your stocking feet. Unlock the front door and leave it unlocked. Put your boots on outside. Do not make a sound, Charlotte. Not one sound. Can you do that for me?"

Charlotte nodded, her eyes large and worried in the darkness.

"Good girl. I'll meet you on the veranda. Hurry."

India left her room and headed for the kitchen. She went out the back door and ran to the barns. There she risked lighting a small lantern and saddled two horses, a mare and a pony. She talked softly to them, patting them and reassuring them so that they would not kick. They were lively animals, high-spirited and fleet, but she knew Charlotte could handle the pony. She was a fearless rider. She'd taught her herself.

When she had them saddled, she poured oats into two feed bags and attached them to the horses' heads. If they were eating, they would not whinny. She led them out of the barn, toward the house. As she drew near she could see that Charlotte was on the veranda, dressed and ready.

"Mummy, may I take Jane?" she asked softly.

India nodded. She motioned for her to mount. When she was in her saddle, India gave her the mare's reins to hold, and the bundle of food and water. There was only one thing left to do now—she had to get the music box. Without it she had no proof of what Freddie had done.

Steeling her nerve, India went back into the house. "Carefully, now," she told herself as she opened the door. She walked into the hall and glanced up the staircase. No one was there. The house was still. All she could hear was the ticking of the clock. She made her way to the study, slowly placing one foot in front of the other. Her heart was pounding. If Freddie woke up . . . if he found her now . . .

She forced herself not to think about it. She thought about Sid instead. The music box—and what was inside of it—would save him; she knew it would. She and Charlotte would ride as hard and as fast as they could to Thika, rest for a few hours overnight, then continue on to Nairobi. Once they got there she would go to Sir James Hayes Sadler and show him the jewelry. She would tell him how she found it, how she thought Freddie had gotten it, and demand that he be arrested and Sid freed. And if she failed to convince him, she would travel to London on the same boat with Sid. She would hire the best barristers in London. No matter what it took, she would see that Sid was spared and that Freddie paid for what he'd done.

As she reached the study, India prayed she was not too late. She prayed that the governor had not already sent Sid back to London. Moving quickly, she opened the door and made her way across the room in the dark. A movement caught her eye. She stopped short, stifling a cry of fear . . . but it was only the curtains fluttering in the night breeze. The study, like the rest of the first floor, had French doors which led outside. The maid must have left them open.

She rushed to the small ebony table where Freddie kept the music box. She misjudged the distance in the dark, however, and banged into the table, barking her shin. Her hands fluttered over the top, feeling for the box.

It wasn't there.

She felt for it again, worried she'd somehow missed it, but no, it wasn't there. It was gone. Could she have forgotten where she put it? Frantic now, she stumbled to the fireplace, feeling along the mantel. But it wasn't there either.

A small cry of desperation escaped her. She had to go. Now. But she couldn't leave without the music box.

"Where are you?" she whispered in the darkness. "Where the hell are you?"

She heard a noise from behind. Gasping, she spun around. A match flared. In its glow she saw Freddie's face. He was sitting at his desk, smiling. The music box was in front of him.

"Hello, darling," he said. "Looking for something?"

CHAPTER 121

Freddie held the flaming match to the wick of a lamp. It caught. He trimmed it, then replaced the chimney.

"Did you think I wouldn't find out?" he asked.

India made no reply. Her mind was racing. She had to get to Charlotte. Get to the horses. Freddie knew. The music box was lost now.

"I knew something was wrong when I went to play it tonight. The foot fell off and the drawer was broken. You saw them, didn't you? You saw my treasures."

India took a step backward, then another. If she could get to the door ahead of him, she might have a chance.

"Where are you going?" He came out from behind the desk. "I asked you a question."

India knew she must show no fear. On the contrary, she must make him afraid.

"I'm going to Nairobi," she said. "With Charlotte. I'm going to tell them what you've done. I'm going to set Sid Malone free."

"That's quite a daring plan," he said, slowly walking toward her. "It might've even worked, that plan. *If* you'd had the music box. Or rather, what's inside it. But you don't, do you?"

The servants, India thought. They didn't live in the house, but in outbuildings. Get to the door, she told herself. Get down the hall and to the porch. Then scream like hell. Freddie must have read her mind, for he was suddenly on the other side of the room, at the door, locking it.

"You won't be going after the servants, I'm afraid," he said. "And you won't be going to Nairobi. The only place you're going is back to bed. And when you wake in the morning, this little episode will be forgotten. Never to be mentioned again."

India's anger got the better of her. "It *will* be mentioned again," she said, when she should have said nothing. "To the police. And the magistrate. To the governor. You found those combs, didn't you? You found them, offered one to Hugh, and kept one. What a perfect plan! When he pawns the first one, everyone assumes he has the second. He goes to jail for refusing to return it. Even though he can't return it. Because he doesn't have it. You do."

"Very clever, old girl. You've grown devious over the years." He moved closer to her, but she moved away.

"And you've grown vicious. When did it happen, Freddie? When did it start? You didn't used to be this way. We used to walk in the woods, you and I. When we were children. At Blackwood. When did you change?"

Freddie looked at her, suddenly stricken, then dropped his eyes. Hope flared inside India. She thought she might have him. Might have wounded him. She continued, hoping to cow him, to break him.

"You killed Wish, didn't you? You killed him and took his ring off his hand and then told us he'd pawned it. How close were you to him when you shot him, Freddie? Did he see you pull the trigger? Did he beg you not to do it?"

"Please, India . . . don't," he said. He took a halting step toward her, then another, and then he stopped. His hands came up to his face. He pressed his palms over his eyes.

India pressed her advantage. She moved closer to him, leaned in, and said, "He was your *friend,* Freddie. Your oldest, dearest friend. *Was.* Until he started meddling where he shouldn't have. It was the clinic, wasn't it? You killed him right after he talked about getting donations for me. He was a threat. The clinic was a threat. It might've kept me from marrying you. And poor Gemma Dean. She wasn't a threat, was she? Just a bloody good way to frame Sid Malone."

"Oh, God," he said, his voice breaking.

"You killed three innocent people. You took everything from me. Everything I ever loved. You're a murderer. *You're* the criminal, not Sid."

Freddie's head snapped up. His hand shot out and closed around her neck. He pushed her backward, slamming her into the wall, and held her there, squeezing.

It had all been an act. A way to gain her trust. To get close to her. How could she have been so stupid?

"Let me go!" she rasped.

"You want to go, India? You want to leave? Fine. You'll go. But not to Nairobi. Not you and not Charlotte."

"You wouldn't! You wouldn't hurt her, a little girl."

Freddie laughed. "I'm tired of raising your cuckoo, India. I want heirs. Proper children. *My* children. From a proper wife. I'll have them, too. Just as soon as I get rid of you and your bastard."

"Let Mummy go!" a voice said from behind them.

It was Charlotte. She was standing behind Freddie's desk, holding Jane . . . and the music box.

She must have come in through the veranda doors, India thought. She must have heard us.

"Charlotte, put that down," Freddie said.

Charlotte shook her head. She took a step backward, toward the doors.

"Put it down. Now," Freddie ordered. "Or I will beat you black and blue."

Charlotte turned and darted out through the doors into the night.

"Charlotte!" Freddie bellowed, starting after her.

India lunged at him; she caught his arm and pulled him back. He whipped around and punched her viciously in the face. White lights went off inside her head, blinding her. Her lips were slick with blood.

She ducked her head down, trying to avoid his blows, dug her nails into his flesh, and screamed, "Run, Charlotte! Run!"

CHAPTER 122 🌿

Tom Meade ran down the long corridor and up the staircase that led from his office to the governor's, leaving a score of bewildered clerks and functionaries in his trail. No one ran in Government House. Ever. For any reason.

He charged past the governor's secretary and barged into the man's office, red-faced and panting.

Sir James Hayes Sadler was seated at a large round table with a dozen other men. He turned around, looked at Tom, and said, "Have you lost your mind?"

"No, sir."

"You've interrupted a very important meeting."

Tom looked around the room. His immediate superior, the district commissioner for Kenya Province, was there, as well as other DCs, Lord Delamere, and leading members of the Colonists' Association. "I realize that, sir," he said. "And I'm very sorry, but I have a telegram—"

"Can't it wait?"

"I'm afraid it cannot. It's from the home secretary's office."

Hayes Sadler blinked at him. "Are you quite certain?"

"Here, sir," Tom said, handing it over.

Hayes Sadler read the message. "I'll be damned," he said. "I can hardly believe this." He looked at Tom. "You're *positive* this came from Gladstone's office?"

"I am. I didn't believe it myself. I replied, asking for confirmation. It's genuine."

"What is it, James? What's happened?" Delamere asked.

Hayes Sadler sat back in his chair. He took off his glasses. "It appears that the home secretary wishes to speak with Lytton—to question him, actually—about his possible role in the murder of Gemma Dean. He wants him to return to London as soon as possible."

Cries of disbelief were heard.

"Believe me, I'm as shocked as you are," Hayes Sadler said. "Apparently an accusation against Lytton has been made back in London and a rogue MP is championing the man who made it—a convict—threatening to go to the papers with a sworn statement. Gladstone's trying to defuse him and spare Lytton the embarrassment of having this nonsense appear in the papers. I'm to get word about this to him as quickly as possible."

The table erupted into a tumultuous discussion. Most believed Lytton entirely incapable of such a deed. There's nothing in it, they said. It's utter rubbish. But a few wondered why, if there was nothing to it, had the home secretary involved himself?

When the hubbub died down, Hayes Sadler said, "We'll have to send someone to fetch Lytton back from Mount Kenya. Tom, you go. See Grogan before you leave. Ask him if he can spare two men to go with you. For form's sake. I'm sure there's been a mistake. Perhaps Lytton can get it sorted with a few telegrams. A pity we have to trouble him on his holiday. Oh, and Tom, inform Sid Baxter of what's happened, will you? This is all damned perplexing, I must say."

"Um . . . yes . . . well, you see, sir, that's the other thing I came to tell you," Tom said, wincing. "As regards Sid Baxter . . . we're going to have some difficulty informing him of anything. You see, he's not at the jail—"

"What do you mean, he's not at the jail? He hasn't left for Mombasa yet. I know that for a fact. I signed the papers myself."

"Yes, well, I'm afraid he *has* already left . . . but not on the train. And not for Mombasa. You see, sir, it appears Sid Baxter has escaped."

CHAPTER 123

Charlotte, her cheek swollen where Freddie had slapped her, her mouth cruelly gagged, turned around, trying to catch a glimpse of her mother, trying to make sure she was all right. Her tiny face, her fearful eyes, were like a knife to India's heart. She was so brave. Freddie had brutalized her. He had bound her hands and stuffed a rag into her mouth. He had given her no food or water and had made her ride hatless in the blazing sun. She was terrified, in pain, and yet she was worried for her mother.

India smiled at her as best she could—her own face was horribly swollen from Freddie's fists. She ached to comfort her child, to put her arms around her, but it was impossible. Freddie had beaten her senseless. He had caught Charlotte and taken the music box from her. When India came to, she saw Charlotte seated on the stallion Freddie always rode. She herself was seated on the mare she'd saddled earlier. The animal was tethered to Freddie's horse, as was Charlotte's pony, but India would have followed even if it had not been and Freddie knew it. He knew she would never let Charlotte out of her sight.

"Sit up," Freddie had said to Charlotte before they'd set off. "Hold on to the pommel. If you fall, I'll leave you on the ground." And then he'd spurred his mount and they were cantering down the drive in the predawn darkness.

It was now approaching noon. India had tried to pay attention to where they were going. She knew they'd ridden west of Mount Kenya, but that was all she knew. She'd never come out this far before. She looked at Freddie, at what he was wearing, at what he'd brought with him, for clues. But he had only a saddlebag and a canteen and they told her nothing.

India would have killed Freddie if she could have, for hurting Charlotte. She told herself he meant to teach them both a lesson. To scare them into silence. She could not bear to think about the alternative—that he was going to murder them. He wouldn't, she told herself. He couldn't. There would be too many questions. A search party. He'd never get away with it.

They rode on. India was parched; she knew Charlotte would be, too. Finally, when the sun was nearly overhead, they stopped by a river. India thought for sure that Freddie would allow them to get down, to take a drink. He didn't. Instead he jumped down himself, drew the music box from his saddlebag, and threw it into the water. India watched it sink and her heart sank with it. Her evidence was gone. The only proof she had of what he'd done. Then he bent down by the riverbank, cupped his hands, and took several long drinks. When his thirst was slaked, he climbed back onto his horse and dug his heels into the animal's sides. India screamed at him through her gag as her mare lurched forward. Charlotte needed water. Couldn't he see that?

A voice inside her, the same voice that had spoken to her when she'd first found the jewelry, said, *Of course he can see it. He doesn't care.*

India started to weep then. She couldn't pretend any longer. He had taken them out here to do away with them. She prayed now that he would be quick and that he would kill Charlotte first. They rode for another half hour. Then Freddie stopped again. He got down and lifted Charlotte down. He took a pistol from his saddlebag and stuck it into his waistband. India saw it. Her eyes grew wide with fear. He walked over to her and pulled her down off the mare.

India's wrists were still bound, but she could use her fingers. She clawed at the gag, pulling it out of her mouth. "Freddie, please. I beg you . . ." she said.

"Start walking. That way," he said, pointing straight ahead at an acacia tree. Charlotte did so. India did not.

"You can't do this. Please! Not to an innocent child."

"Go!" he shouted, pointing the gun at India's head. Charlotte, frightened, broke into a run. India turned and ran after her. As she did, she was horrified to see the girl vanish. Right into thin air. One second she was there, the next she was not.

"Charlotte? *Charlotte!*" she screamed, still running. She saw it at the very last second—a black, yawning pit opening at her feet—and only barely managed to stop short of the edge. She knelt down. She could see her daughter at the bottom, struggling to her feet.

"Charlotte! Are you all right?"

India never heard Charlotte's answer. She felt a rough hand on her back and then she was tumbling into the pit herself. She twisted as she fell, trying to avoid Charlotte, and landed on her right side, knocking the wind out of herself. She writhed on her back, trying to draw air into her lungs. She heard Charlotte crying. Smelled soil and blood. When she could finally breathe again, she stood up and clawed at the pit's earthen sides.

"It's no use," Freddie said. He was kneeling at the pit's edge, looking down at them. "It's twelve feet deep. You'll never get out. It's a Kikuyu game pit. I'd heard about them. Never seen one until two days ago when I nearly fell into it. Damned handy things. The natives use them to catch food. And marauding lions. They dig them deep then cover them over again with grass. The animals never suspect a thing until it's too late."

"Freddie, don't do this," India pleaded.

"It's already done."

"You'll never get away with it."

"Oh, but I will. I'll ride back to the house in a day or so. Sunburned, parched. Half out of my mind with fear and grief. I'll tell the servants we rode out at dawn to see lions. I'll say that we stopped to eat. You and I became drowsy and napped. Charlotte wandered off. Everyone will believe me. She's done it before. We split up to look for her and lost sight of each other. I kept hunting for you both for days. Finally decided to come back and get help. I'll get a search party together and we'll head off in a totally different direction. You'll never be found, of course. It'll be assumed that lions got you."

India tore her gaze away from Freddie and looked at Charlotte. She was white with terror. "Leave me here, Freddie, but take Charlotte. Please take her back. She's done nothing. You cannot be this cruel. Not even you."

Freddie shook his head. "She's far more valuable to me dead than alive. She's about to make me a very wealthy man."

India realized what he meant—with herself dead, and Charlotte, too, the Selwyn Jones fortune would automatically go to Freddie. She knew now that there was no help for them. None at all. They would die here. Slowly and brutally.

Freddie stood. He was leaving.

"No!" India screamed raggedly. "You can't leave us to die like this. Give me the pistol. For God's sake, have mercy on us!"

Freddie smiled regretfully. "Can't do that, old girl. Should someone ever find you, they'll find the pistol, too. Don't want them to put two and two together, do I?"

And then he was gone. And there was nobody. Nothing. Only the blue sky above them and the merciless African sun.

CHAPTER 124

By the time Sid had reached the Wiltons' house, he'd ridden for nearly two days, stopping only when total darkness made it impossible to continue. A ride this far upcountry usually took three if not four days, but he'd driven his horse hard, wanting to put as much distance as possible between himself and Nairobi.

He remembered walking down the corridor to the guardroom—certain George would see that he wasn't Seamie and raise the alarm. But George, absorbed by the racing sheet, hadn't even raised his head. He and Maggie had sailed out of the guardroom, through the foyer, and down the steps to the street. The stern *askari*s posted in front of the prison, their eyes trained straight ahead, took no notice of them.

Maggie had hurried him across the street to the Norfolk. But instead of going inside, she led him around the back to where Ellie, her horse, was stabled. She pulled him inside one of the barns, then made him crouch down in Ellie's stall.

She pulled out some rope that had been buried in the hay on the floor. "Here," she said, handing it to him. "Quickly, tie my hands and feet."

"Why?"

"So I can tell whoever finds me that you overpowered me and took my horse. Otherwise it'll be me sitting in a jail cell."

"Good idea," Sid said, looping the rope around her ankles.

"Your brother's."

"What's going to happen to him?"

"He'll tell them the same thing. With a variation or two. You pulled the handle off the chamber pot, sharpened it on the stone floor, then picked the lock. You got out and held the handle to my throat, hit Seamie, threw him into the cell, and forced me to accompany you out of the building."

"All without attracting George's attention?" Sid said, starting on Maggie's wrists. "That's very impressive of me."

"The story has its flaws, but it's all we've got," she said. She nodded at her horse. "Ellie's saddled and ready to go. There are two canteens in the saddlebags, enough food to last you three days, and twenty quid. My rifle is buried in the hay, just to the left of the door. Yes . . . right there. You've got to go now, Sid. Before George twigs. Get out of Kenya as fast as you can. Head south for the German border."

"I can't do that, Maggs," he'd said, slinging the rifle over his shoulder. "I have to go north. To Mount Kenya. I have to see her. See *them*. I have to know."

"Lytton'll have you arrested again. You know that, don't you?"

"It's a chance I have to take."

She shook her head. "You damned stupid man," she sighed. "Be careful, won't you?"

He kissed her cheek. "Thank you, Maggs. For everything."

She waved his words away with her bound hands. "Don't forget the gag," she said. "Use my handkerchief. It's in my pocket."

He had ridden out of Nairobi on the backstreets and only fifteen minutes later he was streaking north toward the plains. He'd reached Thika by nightfall and quickly skirted around it, not stopping to camp until he was well past it, for his face was too well known there.

When he arrived at the Wiltons' house, he was prepared to find himself in danger. He was prepared for vicious rows and threats, for the possibility that Freddie might try to have the servants overpower him or even shoot him.

He was not, however, prepared for what he did find—nothing. No India, no Freddie, no Charlotte, just half a dozen worried servants clamoring around him, anxious for news of the family.

The most senior of them, a man named Joseph, told him he'd found a note on the kitchen table early that morning. It had been written by the Bwana and it said that they would ride out early because the missy wished to see lions. They would picnic in the hills and return home in time for tea. But they hadn't. The Bwana liked his tea at four sharp, Joseph said. It was half past seven now and there was no sign of him. It was most irregular. Something had happened, he was certain. He felt it.

Sid felt it, too. His sixth sense, the one he'd relied on during his London days to tell him when a job felt right and when it didn't, was talking to him again. It was shouting at him.

"Which way did they head?" he'd asked Joseph, his eyes already scanning the horizon.

"The note says they went to the hills. That means north. But the cook was up early—her baby would not sleep—and she saw them from her house. She saw them leave and says they rode west, toward the plains. She says the child was riding with her father. On his horse."

"Why?" Sid asked, thinking it strange. "Didn't she have her own horse?"

Joseph shrugged. "I do not know. The pony is gone, but she was not on it. Had I seen them I would have stopped them. Where they've gone is no place for a woman and child. The lions in the hills are bad. But on the plains they are thick as ticks on a dog."

"What time did they leave?"

Joseph turned to the cook and spoke to her in Swahili. "She says half past three."

Sid swore. It was now nearly eight in the evening. The trail was nearly sixteen hours old.

"Can you get me a fresh horse?" he said. "I'm going to start after them," he said.

"No, Bwana. Not at this hour. It is too dangerous. Go in the morning."

"I'll be fine. They may not be."

Joseph had a horse brought. He also had two canteens filled and some food prepared. Sid put the provisions in his saddlebag and thanked him. And then he was off, riding hard down the drive, his keen eyes fastening on a trail of flattened grass he saw up ahead. It veered in a westerly direction, just as the cook had said.

"What have you done, Freddie?" he said aloud. "What the hell have you done?"

CHAPTER 125

India held Charlotte tightly against her. Between them, they had managed to untie themselves. She could feel her little body trembling. Above them, three lionesses circled the edge of the pit. One dipped a paw into the void, overbalanced, and skittered backward. Another growled constantly, angry at being so close to prey yet unable to get at it. A third, the most fearsome, crouched still as a statue, bright eyes glinting, a silver thread of saliva suspended from her lips.

"Will they jump down, Mummy?" Charlotte whispered.

"No, darling. They're too afraid. They know they can't get out again if they do."

India hoped to God she was right. She had no idea what lions could or couldn't do. What if they did jump down? She and Charlotte would be defenseless against them. She knew it would be a horrible death, and yet she'd started to think it would be a merciful one. They'd been in the pit for nine hours now. Hunger and thirst had set in.

India had been a doctor once. In what seemed like another lifetime to her now. She knew what death from starvation looked like. The body lost fat and muscle tissue as it began to consume itself. The skin became pale and dry. Lethargy set in, followed by swelling of the limbs, and then heart failure. She knew, too, that it wouldn't be starvation that killed them, but dehydration. As a student, she'd read about cases where victims had lasted five, even six, days without water, but a period of three days was more typical. Two in hot weather.

It was a hard death, dehydration. The mouth and lips dried out. The tongue swelled and cracked. The eyes became sunken, the cheekbones sharp beneath the skin. The urine dried up and the bladder burned. The heart raced. Breathing became rapid. Victims suffered pounding headaches, nausea, grogginess, and delirium. But worst of all was the thirst. It tortured people, drove them mad.

India wanted only one thing now—the strength to outlast Charlotte. She wanted Charlotte to die first, so that she did not have to witness her mother die and then spend her final hours alone. India wanted to live long enough to comfort her at the end, to hold her in her arms as she died.

And she would die. India accepted that now.

During their first few hours in the pit she had wanted to rage and scream at the sky, to crawl insanely at the walls of their deep grave. She had tried everything she could think of to get out. She'd stood Charlotte on her shoulders, hoping that she could reach the edge and pull herself out, but they fell several feet short. She tried to stretch herself horizontally across the pit and climb up and out, but it was too wide. When the realization had sunk in that they could not get out, that they had no food and no water, that there was no one—no human being—for miles and miles, she had nearly come apart. It had taken everything she had, every ounce of courage and self-control, not to.

One of the lionesses roared again. India scrabbled at the bottom of the pit until she had a clumpy handful of red dirt. She threw it at her. It missed and the animal snarled. "Go away," India shouted at it. She threw more dirt. Handful after handful, not bothering to squeeze it into clumps anymore. "Go away," she sobbed. She threw until she was panting. Until Charlotte wrapped her arms around her waist and buried her head in her skirts and said, "Stop, Mummy, stop. They're gone."

She sat back down then, leaned her back against the wall, and pulled Charlotte to her.

"It will be all right, Mummy," Charlotte said.

"Will it, my love?" India murmured, kissing the top of her head.

"Yes, Mummy. Look." She plunged her small hands into her skirt pockets and pulled out a treasure trove of diamonds, gemstones, and gold.

"It's the jewelry," she said, spreading the pieces out over her skirts.

"My goodness. How did you get it?"

"I took it from the box while I was in Father's study," Charlotte said, turning the dragonfly comb over in her hands. "Before you noticed me. I took it so we can give it to the police in Nairobi. Just like you said. Once we get out of here we'll give it to them and tell them what a bad man he is." Charlotte went quiet for a bit, then said, "He'll come, Mummy."

"Who will?" India asked tiredly.

"Mr. Baxter. He'll come for us. He found me when no one else could. He'll find me again. He will."

"Yes, darling, he will," India lied, knowing that the end might be easier for her if she had something, some small shred of hope, to hold on to.

She thought of Sid now. He would be on his way to London. She took comfort in knowing that she'd never told him the truth about Charlotte. At least he'd never have to know it was his child who'd died on the plains of Kenya. If he even lived long enough to hear about it.

India was just closing her eyes when she heard a low growl. It was one of the lionesses. She was back. India could see her head silhouetted against the night sky. Her fangs gleamed whitely in the moonlight.

"Go!" Charlotte shouted at the animal, just as India had moments ago. "Go away!"

She stood up, still clutching the dragonfly comb, and threw it at her. By some miracle, she hit her. The teeth must have dug into a sensitive place on the animal's face, for she snarled and ran away.

"Good shot, darling," India said, trying her best to smile.

Charlotte sat down again, nestling back into her. It was cold in the ground. And damp.

India closed her eyes for a few seconds, intending only to rest. Instead she fell into an exhausted sleep. She didn't see Charlotte staring up at the distant stars. She didn't hear her whispering fiercely to the night.

"He'll come, Mummy, you'll see. He will," she said. "He'll come."

CHAPTER 126

Seamie had wanted flowers, but there was no florist in Nairobi. He'd thought about chocolates, but he couldn't find those, either. Nairobi's Victoria Street was not London's Bond Street. Far from it. He'd finally been able to find a shop that provisioned safaris, and there he bought a new clasp knife and a canteen. He left the shop pleased with his choices. He knew that Willa would like them better than flowers and sweets.

He was walking down Victoria Street with his gifts now, on his way to the surgery. He was going to see if Dr. Ribeiro would let him take Willa to the Norfolk for lunch. He knew her; knew she'd be bored out of her mind in the hospital. He would see if he could hire a donkey cart and show her something of the town. Take her mind off herself and what had happened to her. He was looking forward to a leisurely meal himself. He desperately needed to rest, to go slow for a bit, to recover from the shocks of the last week.

It had been several days since he'd last visited Willa. And for a while it had looked like it might be a damn sight longer. Everyone—from George the prison guard, to Ewart Grogan the judge, to the governor himself—had been highly suspicious of his and Maggie's story. They'd been accused of helping Sid to escape, and had been jailed for a night themselves. Seamie's resemblance to Sid Baxter was noticed, and he was grilled about it. He insisted that he was no relation to Sid, produced his papers to confirm his name was Finnegan, and told them he and Sid had been friends in London. He said he'd read of Sid's arrest in the papers and had been distressed to hear of a friend's troubles. He went to visit him, to try to help him keep his spirits up, and treachery was what he'd received for his troubles.

The police had tried to shake his story—and Maggie's—but they'd both stuck to their statements. With no proof to confirm their suspicions, the officers who'd questioned them were finally forced to release them. That had been late yesterday evening. He'd wanted to see Willa then, but the surgery was closed and he hadn't been able to scare up the doctor. Instead he'd gone with Maggie to the Norfolk—not to the dining room, but straight to the bar. He'd never in his life been so in need of a whisky. The need had grown even stronger when Maggie told him where Sid had gone.

"He'll get himself thrown right back in the nick," Seamie had said.

"If he does, he can bloody well get himself out," Maggie had replied. "I'm too old for any more prison breaks."

They'd emptied a bottle between them, then stumbled off to their rooms, utterly exhausted. He'd said good-bye to Maggie over breakfast that morning. She had to get back to her farm, she said. She had her coffee to worry about. She invited him to come and visit her at Thika. He said he would. He thought that Willa would like her. Perhaps, when she was a bit stronger, they could make the trip out to Thika.

He bounded up the surgery's steps now. When he opened the door he got a surprise: Willa's bed was empty. He walked over to it, confused. The small table next to it was bare. Every time he had come to see her it had been covered with books, newspapers, a packet of biscuits, a water glass. Her boots were gone, so was the clothing he'd bought her. Had she been moved somewhere else?

"Mr. Finnegan?"

He turned around. It was Dr. Ribeiro.

"Miss Alden's checked herself out," he said. "Over my strenuous objections, I might add."

"Checked out? Where is she? Is she at the Norfolk?" he asked. How could he have missed her?

"I don't believe so. She had my assistant help her to the station."

"But that can't be," he said. "I don't understand."

"Perhaps this will explain," the doctor said, handing him an envelope. "She left this for you. If you'll excuse me, I need to attend to another patient."

Seamie sat down on Willa's empty bed, placed his parcel next to him, and opened the envelope. There was a single sheet of paper inside. It had yesterday's date on it.

Dearest Seamie,

By the time you get this, I will be gone. I'm taking a train to Mombasa today and getting on the first ship out. I'm sorry to say good-bye this way, but I don't know what else to do. I can't see you again. It hurts too much.

    You saved my life and nearly lost your own into the bargain, and I know I should be grateful to you, but I'm not. I'm angry and heart-broken. I wake up every morning in despair and go to sleep the same way. I don't know what to do. Where to go. How to live. I don't know how to make it through the next ten minutes, never mind the rest of my life. There are no more hills to climb for me, no more mountains, no more dreams. It would have been better for me to have died on Kilimanjaro than to live like this.

I'm leaving Africa. I don't know where I'll go. Somewhere where I can work out how to live a leftover life.

I love you, Seamie, and I hate you. I'm torn apart. Please don't try to find me. Forget me. Forget what happened between us on Mawenzi. Find someone else and be happy.

> I'm sorry.
> Willa

Seamie put the letter down. He wanted to run after her. To take the train to Mombasa and find her. Maybe it wasn't too late. Maybe she was still there. Maybe he could find her. Talk to her.

But then lines from her letter came back to him—*I can't see you again. It hurts too much . . . I love you . . . and I hate you . . .* and he knew that she could never look at him again without anger, without sorrow. He would be a living, breathing reminder, every minute of every day, of what she'd had and what she'd lost. He didn't want to be that. Not to her.

He felt a gentle hand on his shoulder. "Mr. Finnegan, are you all right?" It was the doctor again.

"Fine," he said quietly. "Thank you." He handed him his parcel. "Maybe one of your patients can use these."

Then he walked out of the hospital into the sunny streets of Nairobi, his heart shattered. All around him, horses and carts trundled to and fro. Men shouted. Children played. Women hurried in and out of shops.

Seamie didn't see them, didn't hear them. He saw only Willa. He saw her as she had looked, exhausted and triumphant, on top of Mawenzi. He felt her lips on his. Heard her tell him that she loved him.

"I'm sorry, too, Wills," he said silently to her. "Sorrier than you'll ever know. But what could I have done? Tell me, what? Was I supposed to stand there and watch you die? I love you, for God's sake. I love you."

CHAPTER 127

It was night on the African plains, the darkness hung heavily, and yet Freddie Lytton felt that his future had never looked brighter. It was as bright as the stars twinkling in the sky. As bright as the bold orange flames of his campfire.

He lifted a flask to his lips, closed his eyes, and drank. He was dizzy with exhaustion, a little bit drunk on whisky. He'd ridden too far for one day. Stayed out in the sun too long. His skin was red, even blistering in some places. He'd let himself burn on purpose. He thought it would help his story. Make him look so crazed with fear for his family that he'd completely forgotten about his own welfare.

He pressed a finger to the livid skin on his forearm and winced. Well, it would all be worth it soon enough. Already he was free. Free of India. Free of her bastard. Soon he would be rich as well. Wealthy beyond his wildest dreams. Everything India's father and mother had left to her—the houses, the money, even Charlotte's money—would come directly to him now. It had taken him years to achieve this, but he'd finally succeeded.

When he returned to London—after the inquest, the funerals, the whole bloody charade was behind him—he would be free to remarry. To choose any woman he liked. He would wait, of course, until the prescribed period of mourning had elapsed. And then he would marry a beauty, a sparkling social butterfly with an unimpeachable pedigree. Someone who would look lovely on his arm as they came and went from dinners and parties. And he would father sons with her. Heirs. *His* heirs. Nothing would stop him now. Nothing. His new wealth, a new wife, and the laurels he would soon earn from his masterful handling of the African question, would take him where he'd always longed to be—Downing Street.

"At last," he said aloud, his voice ragged from both his exertions and the whisky. "At last."

As if in response to his voice, another voice called from out of the night. It wasn't speaking, though, this voice. It was keening.

Freddie's head snapped up. He sat still and rigid, certain, for just a second, that it was India or Charlotte he was hearing. Still screaming. Still sobbing. Just as they'd done when he'd rode away from them. Leaving them in the pit. Leaving them to die.

But he knew that was absurd. It was just a trick played upon him by a weary mind. He was miles away from the game pit now and what he'd heard was only the high, shrill cry of a hyena. He'd heard the animals before, on safari with Delamere and Hayes Sadler. He'd been told they were afraid of man, afraid of his fire. They would skulk and skitter around a campsite, never fully showing themselves, loping off—ugly and misshapen—at a loud noise, a quick movement.

"Unearthly sort of racket, isn't it?" Delamere had said. "They sound like the dead to me. Come back to haunt us. I hate them."

Freddie did, too.

As he looked into the darkness, a pair of shining green eyes stared back at him. They were joined by another pair, and then two more. He heard the horses whinny and kick at the ground. They were tied nearby. He clapped his hands at the hyenas. Two of the animals shot off. Two remained.

"Go!" he shouted at them.

But they didn't budge. One blinked its green eyes. The other let loose an awful, yipping laugh.

"Filthy little sods," he muttered.

For a split second he imagined that the eyes looking at him were India's eyes. Charlotte's eyes.

"Go to hell! All of you!" he shouted at the darkness. He heard scrabbling, yipping, and then the night was quiet again.

He passed a shaky hand over his face. "Get a grip, old man," he said. "You've been out in the bush too long."

He tried to steer his mind away from the day's events. He tried to imagine himself back home in London. At the Reform Club. Westminster. Ascot. But all he could see was India. Not as she looked when he'd left her to die, but as a child. At Blackwood. When she'd seen the bruises on his body and cried for them. She was still the only one who had ever done that—cried for him. She'd been kind to him once. She'd loved him once. And he had killed her. And her child.

He'd murdered a child. An innocent child.

Hugh Mullins had gotten in his way. Wish, too. Gemma Dean had thwarted him. And India, the bitch, had been ready to go to the police with his music box. She deserved what she'd gotten. They all did. But Charlotte didn't.

An image of the girl came to him now. She was at the bottom of the game pit. Dead. Vultures were in there with her, picking her bones clean. Her gray eyes—India's eyes—were black and unseeing.

"Stop it! Stop it!" he shouted, jumping to his feet.

Yips, snorts, and guttural laughs came back at him. He didn't hear them. He was too busy telling himself that what was done, was done. They were dead by now. It was over. He would never do it again. He would never have to. He took another sip of whisky, lifting the flask with shaking hands.

As he lowered it again, the face of his ancestor came to him. Richard Lytton. *Wouldst be king?* the Red Earl asked him. *Rip out thine own heart.*

"I thought I had," he whispered. "Long ago. Years ago. I thought it was gone. All gone. Nothing left."

He heard laughter again. The earl's? The hyena's? His own? He didn't know. He took a deep breath, trying to calm himself. This lunacy, this attack of nerves, had to stop. He told himself that he was tired, that was all. And he realized that he was hungry. He hadn't eaten for hours. He decided that he would have a meal. Get some sleep. These were only night terrors. Things would look fine again in the morning.

Earlier in the evening he'd gathered branches that had fallen from some nearby flame trees. He fed a few to the fire now, building it up. Its light heartened him. He sat down again, dug in his saddlebag—it was near him on the ground—and fished out a hunk of hard cheese, a square of ginger-bread, and a handful of dried figs. As he was cutting off a bite of cheese with a clasp knife, the blade slipped and sliced into his finger.

"Blast!" he said, sucking on the wound.

The pain sobered him slightly. He would have to dress the wound. He knew better than to ignore it. Leave a sliced finger unattended in a place like Africa, and the next thing you knew some damned bush doctor was cutting off your arm.

He dug into his saddlebag again, with his good hand, until he found what he was after, a small bottle of carbolic. He poured it over his finger. As he did, the hyenas started up again, barking and laughing.

He suddenly remembered something else that Delamere had told him about hyenas—that they could smell blood from a distance. A glance assured him that his rifle was within easy reach. Just in case. He finished with the carbolic, capped the bottle, and bound his finger with a clean handkerchief.

The noise from the bush grew louder. More manic.

Uneasy now, Freddie put the carbolic back into his saddlebag. He was just reaching for his rifle when something came hurtling out of the darkness at him. It smashed into him, snarling and snapping, and knocked him onto his back. Freddie could smell the low stink of the creature, feel its wet, rotten breath on his face as he fended it off, hammering at it with his fists, kicking at it.

He felt his boot connect with something hard—the animal's flank, he thought. He heard shrieks and yowls and then it was gone. He rolled onto his side, panting and shaking. He lunged for his rifle, but it was too late. The pack was on him. He curled into a ball, trying to protect his vitals, but it was no use. He felt teeth sink into his back, his shoulder. He screamed and lashed out with his legs. He felt more teeth. In his ankle. His thigh. Fangs flashed before his eyes and a pair of jaws closed on his throat.

His blood splashed onto the golden grass; it pattered down onto the dark red earth. Nature, in its way, was merciful. The slashing teeth did their work quickly. But Freddie was still alive, still conscious, when a large hyena, a female, unable to frighten her pack mates away from his throat and his belly, howled with frustration and tore into his chest, cracking through bone with her powerful jaws, shredding flesh with her long, lethal claws.

He could only writhe and scream silently, for his throat was gone now, as the great beast raised her bloody head above the fray, then plunged again. And again. Until she had feasted. Until she was sated.

Until she had ripped out his heart.

CHAPTER 128 🥀

Sid kicked out the last remaining embers of his campfire over the riverbank into the water. He'd already tucked his bedroll behind his saddle and wolfed down a hasty breakfast. It was not quite light yet, but he wanted to get going. He had to find India and Charlotte. Two full days had elapsed since they'd left the Wiltons' house. Dawn was about to break on the third.

He'd tracked them to this river last night, and then the trail had gone cold. Perhaps it had rained here since they'd come through. Or perhaps the winds had blown strongly. Whatever the reason, he could no longer see the swath the three riders had cut through the grass, could no longer find any tracks.

Yet he would not give up. They had followed a westerly direction so far, barely veering. He would gamble that they'd held the route. As he rode away from the river he took visual notes of the landscape, remembering a large boulder, a cluster of trees, the way the river curved, making a map in his head in case he came back this way.

He spent the entire morning searching fruitlessly, tacking across the plains as a sailor might across becalmed seas, desperate to catch sight of a hoofprint, broken brush, anything. Just before noon, he spotted something. He crested a hill and saw movement in the grass. His stomach clenched with fear. He knew what it was before he'd even raised his field glasses— vultures, at least twenty of them, their black feathers rusty with red dust. They were pecking and squabbling. Feasting in the sun.

He spurred his horse on and then he prayed. Like he hadn't since he was a boy. He prayed for the strength to endure whatever it was he would find.

He heard the flies first. Their buzzing grew louder the closer he got to the kill. Then the smell hit him—blood and organs, baking flesh. The vultures squawked and brawled as he drew near, angered by his presence. He spotted their prize—it was a black pony. He saw the bite marks across its neck. Smaller than a lion's. Hyenas, he thought, and fear turned his heart to dust.

"Charlotte!" he cried.

He jumped down from his horse and thrashed his way through the bloodied grass, knowing what he would see next—her small, fragile body, bloodied and broken. She wouldn't have stood a chance against them.

But it wasn't Charlotte's body he found. It was Freddie's. The vultures hadn't quite finished with his face. One of his eyes stared blindly at the sky.

Sid cupped his hands around his mouth. "India!" he shouted, spinning around in a circle. "Charlotte!" He got no reply. He did it again and again. Still nothing.

He got back on his horse and rode out from the kill in widening circles, his eyes scanning the grass for bodies, blood, anything.

Where were they? Bodies didn't just disappear. Hyenas tore them to pieces. They dragged them, shook them. There were always traces— flattened grass, smears of blood, scraps of clothing. How could there be *nothing*?

"Where are they, Lytton?" he yelled, an edge of hysteria in his voice. "You bastard! You fucking bastard! Where the hell are they?"

He finally found a second horse, dead, about twenty yards away from the pony, and then he saw a third—alive and standing in some tall brush, on top of another hill, about a hundred yards away. It took him the better part of an hour to cajole the frightened animal to him, but he finally did, with soft words and oats, tying its reins to the saddle of his own horse. He rode in circles again and again, but he found nothing.

"Where are you?" he shouted, his desperation growing.

And then he saw it, grass broken and flattened by riders. He was back on his horse in seconds, following the trail. He rode for hours and hours, calling out as he rode, looking for more signs, but just before noon the trail ended, and still he had nothing. No trace of them.

Looking around, he saw a hill about half a mile away. He rode to the top of it, then took out his field glasses to see if he could spot any movement. Any animals. The white of a woman's blouse. Charlotte's blond hair. *Anything*. He took his time, careful to inspect every inch of the landscape.

He kept looking, kept hoping against hope, but he saw only hills, brush, and grass. He had nearly completed a full sweep of the area when something glinted at him. He squinted against the brightness. A watering hole, he thought. The sun was directly overhead; its rays must be reflecting off it. He looked away, but something pulled his eyes back to the glinting. It was about a mile due east of where he was.

"If that's a watering hole, it's the smallest one in all of Africa," he said to himself. There was no mud around it. No ruts and gouges in the earth from claws and hooves. But there was something near it . . . it looked like a shadow on the grass. A large, circular shadow. The only thing was, there was nothing nearby to cast that shadow.

"It's a game pit," he said. "They've fallen into a game pit."

Seconds later he was racing down the hill toward it. He lashed his horse mercilessly, shouted at it to go faster.

"Please, please let them be all right," he begged.

He pulled up on the reins a few yards from the pit, jumping off the horse before it had stopped, stumbling to the edge.

"India!" he shouted. "Charlotte! Are you in there?"

He saw two bodies at the bottom of the pit, a woman's and a girl's. The woman was lying motionless. The little girl was sitting up, cradling the woman's head in her lap.

"India . . . oh, God, no. Charlotte! Charlotte, can you hear me?"

The little girl lifted her dirty, tear-streaked face. "Mr. Baxter," she said weakly, blinking in the sun. Then she turned and gently touched her mother's cheek. "Mummy, wake up. It's Mr. Baxter. He's come for us. I knew he would. Mummy, please wake up."

м

CHAPTER 129 🦋

India had died.

She knew she had. The thirst had driven her mad, and then it had killed her. She had fought to hang on for Charlotte's sake, but she'd lost the battle.

Wish was with her now. He silently pressed her hand between his. It was hard for him to talk with half of his face gone. Hugh was here, too. He put the pair of dragonfly combs into her hands and folded her fingers closed over them. He'd told her he loved her, but others did, too, and she must stay with them.

"Open your eyes, India," he said.

She'd tried, but it was so hard. Her lids were so heavy. Her body was so tired. She could feel her heart, struggling to beat. Her lungs, straining to draw air and push it out again.

"India, please, please open your eyes."

A different voice now. Not Hugh's. She tried again to do what the voice wanted. And this time she succeeded. She didn't know where she was, but she could see flames. She saw their orange glow, felt their heat. I'm in hell, she thought. No, I can't be. I've been there already. Hell is the pit where I died. With Charlotte.

Charlotte.

India felt her blood surge through her veins at the thought of her child. *Where is she? Where is my daughter?* She swallowed and tried to speak, but her tongue felt thick, her throat rusty.

"Charlotte . . ." she rasped, struggling to sit up. A searing pain shot through her skull, blurring her vision. She sank down again, overcome by dizziness and nausea. "Charlotte, answer me," she whispered. "Please answer me."

She felt a hand on her brow, heard a voice. "Shh, India. Charlotte's fine," a voice said. "She's here. She's asleep."

India suddenly knew the voice. "Sid . . . is that you?" She could barely see him. Her eyes wouldn't work properly.

"Yes, it's me," he said. She felt his hands on her. He gently raised her up and held a canteen to her lips. She drank, then asked for more.

"Let that settle."

"You're dead, then. They hanged you," she said, her voice like sandpaper. "I . . . I tried to stop them. I tried . . ."

"India . . ."

"Is this heaven, this place? It must be if you and Charlotte are here."

"India, listen to me. You've had a terrible time of it. You were unconscious when I found you. I nearly lost you on the way here. Please don't die on me, India. Please, please don't die."

"Where is here?"

"A campsite. By a river."

A river. The river they'd passed by with Freddie. Fear jolted through her. "Go, Sid! Run! Freddie . . . he'll kill you. He's killed people. . . ."

"India, lie down."

"But Freddie . . ."

Sid pressed a spoon to her lips. A bitter-tasting fluid trickled down her throat.

"No!" she cried, fighting it. "No laudanum! We have to run."

"India, lie still! You have to rest now. I'm going to take you back to the house. You need a doctor."

India tried to get up again, but the drug made her dizzy. She lay back and wept.

"I used to be a doctor," she said, her voice breaking. "I used to have a child. She was your child, Sid. I've lost her now. I've lost you. I've lost everything . . . everything."

"Nothing's lost, India. Nothing. You'll be a doctor again if you want. You'll begin again. We'll begin again, all three of us. Where the world begins again."

India didn't understand. She was so tired. The man speaking sounded so far away; his words made no sense. Nothing did. It was a dream. All of it. Only a dream. She closed her eyes and fell into a deep and deathlike sleep.

CHAPTER 130

India smelled roses. Their warm, spicy scent delighted her.

Roses? How can that be? she wondered. The last things she had smelled were dirt and blood, fear and despair.

She opened her eyes. A vase of flawless ivory blooms stood on her night table.

"Do you like them, Mummy?" a little voice piped up.

It was Charlotte. She was sitting on the edge of a chair by the window, grinning.

"I picked them for you. They've only just bloomed. Joseph says that Lady Wilton calls them her winter roses. Because of the color. Oh, Mummy, I'm ever so glad you're awake!"

And then she was out of her chair, and across the room, and her arms were around India's neck.

"Darling Charlotte," India said. "You're alive, you're all right." She held her tightly; her tears—of joy and gratitude—fell on Charlotte's neck. "I'm sorry. I'm so, so sorry."

"It's all right, Mummy. We're fine and that's all that matters," Charlotte said.

After a few minutes India released her. Charlotte helped her sit up and she realized she was back in her bedroom at the Wiltons' house. "How did we get here?" she asked.

"Mr. Baxter brought us."

Sid. Sid had come for them. It was his arms she'd felt around her. His voice she'd heard. It hadn't been a dream.

"He found us, Mummy, just as I said he would. He pulled me out with a rope. He had to get in the pit himself to get you out. He made a harness, and he and I got the horses to pull you up. He took care of us and brought us back here."

Sid had come *here*? India's happiness turned to terror. Freddie would kill him. She flung back the bed covers and put her feet on the floor. Nausea gripped her.

"Charlotte," she said, "where's Mr. Baxter now? Where's your father?"

"Mr. Baxter had to go. I wanted him to stay but he said he couldn't. He left two days ago. The hyenas got Father. I heard the grown-ups talking about it."

India blinked at her. "What?" she whispered. "My God. Charlotte, is he . . . is he dead?"

"I hope so. I never want him to come back. Never."

There was a knock on the door.

Mary entered the bedroom. "I thought I heard your voice! Oh, it's good to see you awake, ma'am! But you must get back into bed!" She hurried to India's side, eased her legs up off the floor, and pulled the bedclothes back over her. "We were all so worried about you. How are you feeling? Can I get you a pot of tea? Something to eat?"

"Mary, is my husband dead?"

"Oh, Charlotte!" Mary said, dismayed. "I said you weren't to tell your mother such things. Not yet. She's too frail."

"Is he?" India repeated, sharply this time.

"Yes, ma'am, he is. Mr. Baxter told us. He told Joseph where he'd found him and Joseph sent two men to bring his remains back. They left yesterday. I'm so very sorry, ma'am."

India lay back against her pillows. Mary, the servants, and the rest of the world would expect her to feel sorrow, but she felt only relief.

"Where is Mr. Baxter?"

"He has left."

"Did he leave anything for me? A note?" India asked.

"No, ma'am."

"Nothing? Nothing at all?"

"He told me he was riding east. That was all he would say, I'm afraid. I asked him to stay. I knew you would want to thank him in person, but he refused. There's someone else here to see you, however. A Mrs. Margaret Carr. She has a young man with her. His name is Seamus Finnegan. I told her that you can't possibly receive them now. You're far too weak. Not fit to be seen in your present condition."

"Oh, never mind about that," a woman's voice boomed. "It's only me who's seeing her."

"Mrs. Carr! You cannot come in here! I asked you to please be seated in the drawing room," Mary protested.

"And I told *you* I've no time for dilly-dallying. Get your missus a wrapper, will you? Hello, Mrs. Lytton. I'm sorry to barge in like this, but it's about Sid. There's a lot to tell you and we need to tell it before Tom Meade arrives and he's only about half an hour behind me. You decent, then? Good. Seamie! Come in! Hurry, lad!"

Seamie stepped into the room. India gasped, then recovered herself. "I'm sorry. I thought for a second that you were someone else."

"Sid Baxter?"

She nodded.

"I'm his brother, Seamus Finnegan. I'm very pleased to meet you. And pleased to see you again, Miss Lytton," he said, smiling at Charlotte. "We met on the beach at Mombasa. Do you remember?"

Charlotte nodded and smiled.

"His brother. Sid's brother," India repeated wonderingly. Remembering herself, she said, "Mary, please bring something for our guests."

"May I bring you tea, Mrs. Carr?" Mary said tightly.

"I'll want something stronger than tea," Maggie said. "I've been riding nonstop for the last ten hours. I can barely feel my backside."

"Brandy and port, please, Mary," India said. "And sandwiches."

Mary left and Maggie and Seamie seated themselves, Maggie on the bed and Seamie in Charlotte's abandoned chair.

"What the devil happened to you, Mrs. Lytton? You look bloody awful. I tried to get Madam there to tell me," she said, hooking her thumb in the direction Mary had taken, "and you'd think from the look I got that I'd asked what size drawers you wear."

Charlotte giggled. Maggie winked at her. India was happy to hear her daughter laugh. She was worried that after everything she'd seen and heard, everything that had happened to her, she might never laugh again.

India told Maggie and Seamie about the music box and what was inside it. She told them what Freddie had done to them, and why, and that he was now thought to be dead.

"The bloody bastard!" Maggie spat. "Hyenas are too good for him! He should've lived to go to London! He should've had to answer the charges!"

"Charges?" India echoed. "What charges? I don't understand."

"The Home Office telegraphed Nairobi. They wanted to question your husband in connection with the Gemma Dean case," Maggie said.

"How do you know that?" India asked.

"I'm not supposed to. But Delamere's a good friend of mine, and he told me that he was in a meeting with the governor when a telegram came through from the home secretary. Apparently a man in London accused Freddie of committing the murder. His name is Frankie Betts. He said he saw it all. Saw Lytton kill the girl. Saw him take her jewelry. Gave a sworn statement. That's why Meade's coming. To get Lytton. And that's why we've come. To tell Sid. We hoped we could catch him, but we're too late."

"If only we still had the jewelry," India said. "It would've helped to confirm Freddie's guilt, dead or alive."

"We do have it, Mummy," Charlotte said.

"But it was in the music box, darling. Don't you remember? And that's at the bottom of a river somewhere."

"No, it isn't. I have it. I stuffed it inside Jane's bloomers. Don't you remember? I threw a piece at the lioness who was growling at us. Mr. Baxter told me that's what saved us. He said he saw it sparkling in the sun."

She ran out of the room, leaving India, Maggie, and Seamie to exchange puzzled glances. In a few minutes she was back, her hands full of jewels. She laid them on India's bed.

"Charlotte, you are a remarkable girl," Seamie said. Maggie tousled her hair. India beamed at her. And Charlotte flushed at the praise.

India looked at the jewels. They were proof. Proof of Freddie's treachery. They were also reminders of the lives he'd stolen. Someone had died for every piece of jewelry she held—Hugh, Wish, Gemma Dean. The sorrow she felt thinking about it was almost unbearable.

"Maggie, there's something I don't understand," she finally said. "Sid saved us, but how did he get to us? He was in jail. And why would he leave again so quickly? Charlotte told me he left yesterday."

Maggie and Seamie exchanged glances. "He escaped," Maggie said.

"How?" India asked.

"Charlotte, my girl, do you think you might be able to find old Mary and see how she's coming with those sandwiches? Tell her not to bother the cook too much. Just a bit of cheese and pickle on some bread will do."

Charlotte nodded and skipped out of the room.

Maggie turned back to India and said, "The *how* of it is that he overpowered Seamie and made him change places with him. Then he forced me to walk him outside the prison. He tied me up in the Norfolk's barn and took my horse." She gave India a long look. "At least that's what we told the police."

"I understand," India said. "And they'll never hear differently from me. But why did he come here? If Freddie had seen him, he would have tried to kill him. And if he was prepared to risk Freddie's wrath, why did he leave when he knew Freddie was dead?"

Seamie sat forward in his chair. "He came here because he thought Charlotte might be his. He wanted to know for sure. He planned to ride out here and ask you."

India nodded. "She is his," she said quietly.

"Sid's daughter," Seamie said, smiling. "And my niece. No wonder she's remarkable."

India laughed. She liked this young man immensely. He was brave like his brother. And good, she could see that. He had Sid's eyes, too. They were as green, as lively, and in their depths—as sad.

"Yes, his daughter. If he knew that, if he even thought it, why would he rescue us and then disappear? He didn't even tell us where he was going. Or if he'd ever be back. Why didn't he stay with me to ask me about Charlotte? Why didn't he stay with her?"

India thought she might know the answer to her many questions, but she couldn't bear to admit it.

"He was afraid of the law catching up with him," Maggie said. "When he escaped, he didn't know about Frankie Betts's statement. Didn't know that Freddie was going to be questioned."

"Perhaps," India said. She looked at her hands, then sadly said, "But I think the real reason is that he's angry with me. For not telling him about Charlotte. For keeping the truth from him for all these years. I almost did tell him. A few weeks ago. But I knew we were going back to London, and that he might never see her again. I thought it would be cruel. So I didn't tell him. And now he's so furious that he doesn't want to see either of us ever again."

Maggie and Seamie exchanged worried glances.

"I'm sure that's not it," Maggie said.

"I'm sure it is," India said. "It must be. Nothing else could explain his leaving without so much as a note telling me why. Or where he's going."

There was a noise from outside India's bedroom door. A small, scraping sound.

"Charlotte?" India called.

There was no reply.

"My God. I hope that wasn't her. I hope she didn't hear—"

India didn't get to finish her sentence for Mary came bustling into the room wringing her hands.

"Mary, is Charlotte hiding there?"

"Where?"

"Outside my room?"

"No, ma'am."

"How about those sandwiches?" Maggie said. "Where are they hiding?"

Mary glared at Maggie, then she said, "Lady India, I'm terribly sorry about the delay with the tea but the kitchen's in an uproar. The men are back. They've . . . they've found Lord Frederick's remains. And the ADC's arrived from Nairobi with his men. I've told him you're unwell, but he insists on speaking to you. And to Lord Frederick. He doesn't know, you see, and I don't know what to do," Mary said, near tears now. "I didn't know if I should tell him what's happened."

"Tell Joseph to see that our guests are fed, Mary. Tell him to make up enough beds for everyone as well. Tell Tom I'll be with him shortly, then please come back and draw my bath."

"Are you certain that's wise, Lady India? You're still weak."

"It's probably not wise, but I've no choice. While I'm with Tom, you may start packing our things."

"Will you leave now?" Maggie asked when Mary had bustled off again.

"As soon as I can. I'll speak to Tom Meade and tell him what happened. I'll give him the jewelry and tell him what I know about it. I'll have to make arrangements for Freddie's remains. I'm sure there will be an inquest in Nairobi. When it's over, Charlotte and I will return to London."

Maggie nodded. "We must let you dress," she said.

Seamie was silent. He and Maggie were nearly out of the door when he turned around and said, "Lady Lytton . . . India . . . stay. Wait for him."

"He's not coming back here, Seamie. I know it. I feel it. I've lost him. Again."

"He *will* come."

India shook her head sadly. "I had the chance to tell him. I didn't take it. I don't think I will get another."

CHAPTER 131 🌺

Joe lowered his weary head into his hands and let out a long, defeated sigh. He was in his carriage on the way home from the home secretary's office. He'd just been to see Gladstone again, desperate for news on his quest to reopen the Dean case, only to find out that there wasn't any.

The home secretary had summoned Freddie Lytton home, but had received no response. It seemed that no one could find the man.

Joe had made it known to Gladstone—after getting nowhere with Desi Shaw and Joe Grizzard—that if the Home Office continued to do nothing about Frankie Betts's accusations, he would take Betts's statement to the papers himself.

"What if you're wrong, Herbert?" he'd asked him. "What if you're wrong and I'm right, and you do nothing when you had the chance to do something?

What if I do end up finding out where that jewelry got to? What if I get a second witness, a second statement? And you never so much as questioned the accused? It'll look like a double standard. One set of laws for privileged cabinet ministers, another set for everyone else."

Gladstone had drummed his fingers on the desk, then said, "All right, I'll do this much. I'll telegraph Nairobi. Tell the governor there what's occurred. Tell Lytton to return to London. See what he has to say about it when he arrives. You'll have to give me some time though, Joe. He's out in the middle of East Africa; I think there's only one telegraph machine in the whole place and no telephones. It might take a few days to find him."

Joe had said that was reasonable. He promised to sit tight and do nothing. But that was a week ago. He'd been so disappointed today to find that Gladstone had had no meaningful news from Nairobi. Only a telegram from the governor saying they were still trying to locate Lytton. That there appeared to be some problem up at Mount Kenya, where Lytton was holidaying. He would be in touch as soon as he knew more.

He raised his head now and looked out of the carriage window. He was empty-handed. He had so hoped to do this for Fiona. To give her the gift of her brother. Safe, sound, and back in her life. He'd tried—pursuing every avenue he could think of—but he'd failed. Desi Shaw told him that he'd never heard a word about anyone trying to move Gemma Dean's jewelry. And Joe Grizzard had said the same thing. Wherever he went, whatever avenue he tried, he encountered nothing but dead ends. He was no closer now to clearing Sid Malone's name than he had been when he'd first sat down across from Frankie Betts. The carriage stopped outside 94 Grosvenor Square. It had been built especially for him, and allowed him to get in and out easily in his wheelchair. He lowered the folding ramp—he liked to do these things himself and not have people fuss over him—and carefully rolled down it. Then he rolled himself up the ramp in front of his mansion. He reached up to ring the bell, but before he could do so, the door was yanked open. He expected Foster to be standing on the other side, but it was Fiona.

"Thank God you're home!" she cried. She was clutching two sheets of paper in her hands. Her face was streaked with tears. She was talking so fast, Joe could barely understand her.

He heard the words *Charlie, Seamie, Africa, jail, amputation, Kilimanjaro,* and *rhinoceros* in quick succession.

Rhinoceros, he thought stupidly. *That can't be good.*

As he rolled himself into the foyer, he saw that Katie and Charlie were sitting on the stairs, their faces peeking through the spindles. Anna, the nurse, sat with them, holding little Peter in her arms.

"Calm down, Fiona," Joe said, mindful of the fact that she was in the ninth month of her pregnancy and due any day. "Take a breath. Now, what's wrong?"

Fiona tried again to tell him, but fresh tears overtook her and she couldn't.

At that moment Foster breezed into the hall, a tea tray in his hands. "Cook's made a lovely jam sponge, sir. And a dish of custard sauce to go with it," he said.

Joe wondered if the entire household had gone mad. "Mr. Foster, I'm hardly interested in puddings right now!"

Foster inclined his head toward the stairs. "The children, sir."

"Of course. I'm sorry. Katie, Charlie, would you like a nice dish of pudding?"

"Mummy's crying," Katie said.

"A cinoseros bit Uncle Seamie's leg off," Charlie added.

"It's *rhinoceros,* and I'm sure nothing of the sort happened. Go downstairs with Anna. You can have some pudding with Cook. She'll tell you a story."

"But . . ."

"*Go.* Mummy and I will come down later. You be sure to save us some pudding, all right?"

"I'll put this in the drawing room for you, sir," Foster said, disappearing with the tray.

The children followed Anna to the kitchen as Joe led Fiona to the drawing room. Foster had already poured the tea. He left, quietly pulling the doors closed behind him. Joe made Fiona sit down. He moved close to her. Their knees were touching.

"Fee, luv, you've got to calm down," he told her. "This is no good for the baby. Whatever's happened, we'll sort it out. Now tell me, what *has* happened?"

Fiona handed him the papers she was holding. "It's all there," she said, her voice catching. "It's all in the telegram."

"This is a telegram? It's two bloody pages long! Who's it from?"

"Seamie."

Joe started to read.

Dear Joe and Fiona, the telegram began, *Despite what you may soon read or hear, I am well.*

Bloody hell, Joe thought.

Seamie continued by apologizing for not contacting them sooner, but a rhinoceros had knocked a telegraph pole down a few miles outside Nairobi and it had taken a week to fix it. He hoped that they had not yet heard any news out of Nairobi. Joe then learned all about the climb to the top of Mawenzi, the accident, the cross-country trek, and the operation.

"Blimey," he said. "That poor lass. It's a miracle she's alive."

"We have to go to the Aldens," Fiona said. "Seamie wants us to. He wants us to tell them what's happened to Willa."

"We can do that, Fee. We'll do it this evening. Willa will make it. Seamie's all right. There's no reason to be so upset."

Fiona wiped her eyes on her sleeve. "Keep reading," she said.

Joe did. And saw why she was crying. Sid Malone had been found working on a coffee plantation in British East Africa, Seamie explained, and had been arrested by Freddie Lytton. The governor had planned to send him back to London to answer charges for the murder of Gemma Dean.

"It's all right, Fee," Joe said, putting the telegram down. "It's going to be all right."

"*All right?* How can you say that, Joe? It's far from all right. Freddie Lytton is behind this. Lytton! He wanted to hang my brother years ago. He would've too, if Seamie hadn't got him out of London."

"What does the rest say?" Joe asked. He'd read only to the bottom of the first page.

"I don't know," Fiona said, still distraught. "The telegram arrived only a few minutes before you did. I hadn't read past the part about Charlie's arrest."

Joe kept reading.

"Bloody hell!" he whispered.

"What?" Fiona said nervously.

"It appears that Freddie Lytton won't be hanging anyone."

"Why not?"

"Because he's dead. He was mauled to death by wild animals."

"Oh, my God, Joe. Oh, the poor man. What about his wife? India . . . is she all right? They have a child. Please don't tell me anything happened to her."

"Blimey!"

"What, Joe?"

"Lytton tried to kill them."

"Who?"

"His wife and daughter."

"You must be joking."

"Sid stopped him. He saved India Lytton and the girl."

"But how? He's in jail."

"No, he isn't. He broke out. He saved them and then he disappeared. He's a fugitive. According to Seamie, no one has any idea where he's heading."

Fiona pressed her hands to her cheeks.

"Seamie says he's fine and he's coming back to London. Along with India and Charlotte Lytton. On the next ship that leaves Mombasa."

"I can't believe this, Joe," Fiona said, lowering her hands. "We have to do something. We have to find him. We have to help him. He's all alone."

Seamie concluded his telegram by saying there was more to the story—including a coffee planter, a music box, and some diamonds—and he'd fill them in when he saw them in person.

Some diamonds, Joe thought. Gemma Dean's diamonds? He'd wager the answer was yes. For the first time in many weeks, hope flickered inside him.

If his instincts were right, and they usually were, India Lytton had somehow found Gemma Dean's diamonds, and the discovery had almost cost her her life. And Sid Malone had somehow learned that Charlotte Lytton was his daughter. Joe didn't know how, but he'd find out. As soon as Seamie came home.

Fiona was still talking, still frantic to find Sid. Joe leaned forward in his wheelchair and took his wife's hands in his.

"Fiona, I've something to tell you," he said.

"What is it?"

"Several weeks ago, before any of this happened, I started working to try to get the Dean case reopened."

Fiona looked at him, a puzzled expression on her face. "You did?" she said. "Why didn't you tell me before now?"

"I didn't want to say anything until I knew I really had something. I didn't want to get your hopes up for nothing. I've been working on it for weeks. I've discovered that there was an eyewitness to Gemma Dean's murder. Frankie Betts."

"You went to see Betts?" Fiona said. "My God, Joe."

"I had a feeling he knew something. I was right. He's given a statement saying he was there when Gemma Dean was murdered. He's sworn that your brother didn't do it."

"Who did?"

"Freddie Lytton."

Fiona gasped.

"Fee, there's more to it than you know. More to it than maybe even I know from the sound of this telegram."

"Tell me, Joe."

"I can't, luv. At least, not yet."

She pulled away from him, wounded. "Why?" she asked.

"Fiona, six years ago I asked you not to search for Sid. Not to get involved with him. Not to bring him into our lives. Remember?"

Fiona nodded. She couldn't look at him now and he knew why. She felt that her search for Sid had resulted in the shooting that had paralyzed him.

"Look at me, Fee," he said, tilting her chin up.

She did and he saw the pain in her eyes. So much pain. For him. For her brother. For everything that had happened to two men whom she loved so dearly.

"I'm asking you again, Fee. I'm asking you not to get involved. Just for now. Wait for me, Fee. And trust me."

"But Joe . . ."

"Just for now. Give me a bit of time. That's all I'm asking. A few weeks at most to put this right. I *will* put it right. I promise you that. But you have to trust me. Do you, Fee? Do you trust me?"

He knew that there was no reason for her to trust him. Not on this. He'd always made his views on Sid Malone perfectly clear. He wanted nothing to do with him. And he didn't want her to have anything to do with him either. Once those views had nearly cost him his marriage. Nearly cost him his life. He knew what he was asking of her. He was asking her to do the impossible. To not try to help the brother she loved. To let him do it instead. He squeezed her hands again. "Fee, you've got to give me an answer. Do you trust me?"

She looked at him, and he saw the answer in her eyes before she spoke it.

"Of course I do, Joe," she said. "With all my heart."

CHAPTER 132

Nearly five weeks after Seamie's telegram arrived at 94 Grosvenor Square, Seamie himself arrived.

Fiona and Joe were sitting in the conservatory of their home, on a bright Sunday morning in June, when he did. Fiona had her feet tucked up under her and a pot of tea on a table beside her. She knew she should be doing something productive—reading sales reports, reviewing advertisements, going through applications to her charitable fund—but she couldn't manage anything more demanding than the morning papers. She was still feeling tired. She had given birth to their fourth child—a girl—two weeks ago. She and Joe had named her Rose, after Joe's mother.

Rose was a lovely baby, healthy and strong, and both Fiona and Joe were deliriously happy about the newest addition to their family. The birth and subsequent recovery had taken all Fiona's energies, and had taken her mind off the recent events in Africa. But now, a fortnight after Rose's birth, with the papers in front of her, and their continued reports on the gruesome death of Freddie Lytton, they were fresh in her mind again.

Horrifying details about Lytton's death—and his life—had come to light. Fiona had learned not only that he'd probably killed Gemma Dean, but that he was implicated in the deaths of other people, too—a young groom named Hugh Mullins. And his wife's cousin, Aloysius Selwyn Jones. And it was his wife who had implicated him.

India Lytton had found evidence of his wrongdoing in the form of jewelry hidden inside a music box, the papers said. She had tried to bring the jewelry to the Nairobi police, but had been found out by her husband before she could. He'd abducted her and their daughter, and had tried to kill them.

They would have died in a game pit had it not been for Sid Malone. Malone, a London gang leader once accused of murdering Miss Dean, had faked his own death in London and escaped to Africa, where he'd found work on a coffee plantation. While visiting Kenya Province, Lytton had recognized him and had him arrested. But Malone had escaped from the Nairobi jail, pursued the Lyttons—for what reason, no one seemed to know—and saved the lives of Mrs. Lytton and her daughter. After he'd brought them to safety, he'd vanished.

There were so many unanswered questions. No one knew why Freddie Lytton might have killed Gemma Dean. No one knew why Sid Malone had saved Mrs. Lytton. And no answers were likely to be forthcoming to the reading public either, as Mrs. Lytton had rebuffed all reporters, and Malone's former employer, Mrs. Margaret Carr, had actually shot at them from the porch of her bungalow. It was a mystery, much of it, and would remain so.

But Fiona didn't like mysteries. She wanted answers. To many things. But most of all she wanted to know where her brother was. If he was in trouble. If he needed her help. And if he was ever coming home to them.

Fiona suspected that Joe knew some of the answers. But for some reason he wouldn't, or couldn't, tell her. Not yet. She wanted to talk to him about it. To pepper him with questions. But she didn't. He had asked her to trust him. And she'd told him that she would. Now she had to be patient. It was the hardest thing for her—patience. It was nearly impossible. She knew how to think, to do, to fight. She didn't know how to sit still and wait.

As she was pouring herself another cup of tea, and asking Joe if he wanted one, the doorbell rang. They both heard it echoing through the house.

"Who can that be? On a Sunday?" Fiona asked.

Joe looked toward the doorway, a tense, expectant look on his face.

"I think I know," he said quietly. "I think we're about to have some company."

"Yes, I gathered as much, Joe. Did you know people were coming? Why didn't you tell me? Here I am in a raggedy old tea gown," she said, getting to her feet.

"You look fine, luv. As beautiful as ever. Sit down, will you?"

"Sit down? But I need to change."

"Sit, Fee. You should sit."

She did, but unwillingly. "Could you at least tell me who it is?" she said, wondering at Joe's odd behavior.

"Seamie."

"Seamie! He's back? That's wonderful! But he's not company, luv, he's family."

"He has some company with him, I think. I hope."

"Joe, you're behaving very oddly. Will you please tell me what's going on?"

"Remember Seamie's telegram?"

"Yes, I do. I've been thinking of little else for the past few weeks. Though I know I'm not supposed to."

"After we received it, I sent Seamie a telegram of my own. I asked him to come directly home after his ship docked. And to bring the Lyttons with him."

"The Lyttons?" Fiona said, puzzled. "Why? Surely India Lytton has better things to do after a long sea voyage than visit people she barely knows."

"I can't tell you that. She has to."

"It's something to do with Charlie, isn't it?"

"Yes."

Fiona's blood froze. "Joe, what is it?"

"Fiona, I asked you to trust me. Now trust me."

The visitors were ushered in. Fiona hugged her brother tightly and made much of him. Katie and Charlie ran in from the garden, where they'd been playing, squealing with delight at the sight of their uncle, bombarding him with questions about Africa and what he'd brought them.

Fiona shushed them, and then greeted a tired-looking India Lytton and her daughter.

"It's a pleasure to see you again, Lady India," she said. "And to meet your daughter. I only wish the circumstances were different."

"You're very kind to have us, Mrs. Bristow," India said.

Fiona could hear the strain in the woman's voice, see the deep fatigue in her face. Charlotte, a beautiful little girl, quiet and shy, looked tired, too. Why on earth are they here? she wondered.

Katie and Charlie were so interested in the new child in their midst that they stopped badgering their uncle for gifts and asked Charlotte if she'd like to play with them in the garden.

"We're playing pirates," Katie said. "Want to be our prisoner?"

Charlotte's eyes widened. Fiona winced. Only a few weeks ago she had been a prisoner. For real. In a game pit. Why, oh why, couldn't her children play something sensible and normal—like house?

"Oh, don't worry," Katie said. "We won't make you walk the plank or anything. We just need someone to ransom for a chest of gold doubloons."

Charlotte thought about this. She nodded.

"Good!" Katie said. "Come on, Charlotte, this way!" She grabbed Charlotte's hand and pulled her after her as she raced out of the conservatory into the garden. Charlie followed them.

"I'm sorry," Fiona said. "It was an unfortunate choice of words."

"Please don't worry about it," India Lytton said. "It's just what she needs now. Other children. Games. A bit of fun."

India watched her daughter through the conservatory windows. A smile came to her weary face as Charlotte ran and shouted with her new friends. Fiona couldn't imagine what the two of them had been through.

"It's such a beautiful day," she said. "Let's all go into the garden. Get a bit of air."

Anna, the nurse, was already out there. She was sitting on a blanket in the shade of a lilac tree, holding baby Rose. Little Peter was sitting next to her, playing with toy soldiers. India immediately went over to admire the new baby. She asked Fiona how her labor had gone, nodding as Fiona told her the details, then she gave Rose her finger and smiled approvingly at the baby's strong grip.

"Will you go back to medicine, Lady India?" Fiona asked, watching her.

"I don't know, Mrs. Bristow."

"It's Fiona, please."

India smiled. "Fiona, then," she said. "And you must call me India. I miss medicine terribly. But I haven't been able to think that far ahead.

There was the inquest in Nairobi, you see. So many questions from the police there. And the reporters. There were swarms of them. They never left us alone."

"I'm sorry. It must have been so awful for you."

"There's more ahead of me, I'm afraid. My parents are dead, but I have to see my sister. She's been terribly worried. And there is Freddie's family. I've brought his remains home. They'll be interred at Longmarsh. And then there are questions to be answered here. From the police, from lawyers. There's Freddie's will to deal with. And estate agents, too. I want to sell our Berkeley Square house and everything in it. And an estate in Wales, too. I don't even know where to begin."

"I'll send my solicitor over to you tomorrow. And my estate agent. They're both wonderful. They'll help you," Fiona said. She liked India Lytton tremendously. She had liked her the first time she met her, years ago at a Labour rally, and she would have done anything to help her.

"Thank you very much, Fiona. I do appreciate it. I'm afraid it's all become rather too much . . ." Her voice trailed off.

"I understand. Sit down, won't you? You must be so weary after your journey. Come and have a cup of good strong tea."

Fiona seated her guests around a white cast-iron table shaded by lilac trees. Linen and plates were soon brought, followed by a fresh pot of tea and a pitcher of lemon squash. Sandwiches appeared next, along with a heaping bowl of red strawberries, currant scones, cream and jam, and then cakes.

The children were called to the table when the food was brought, so the adults kept the conversation light. Fiona, Joe, India, and Seamie talked mainly about their voyage home, what they'd seen en route, and the weather. When Katie, Charlie, and Charlotte had eaten a few sandwiches and a cake or two, they asked if they might be excused, eager to get back to their game.

Fiona looked at them as they flew off and smiled. "They get on so well together," she said. "They've only just met, but it looks as though they've known one another forever." She wondered, as she said these words, exactly when the conversation would turn more serious. Seamie had much to tell them, she was certain. And Joe had undoubtedly brought India Lytton here for a reason. She wondered how long she would have to wait to find out what that reason was.

Not long at all, as it turned out, for as soon as the children were out of earshot India turned to her.

"Fiona . . ." she said.

"Yes?"

"I need to tell you something. It may come as a bit of a shock to you. I'm sorry for that, but you should know that Charlotte is your niece."

Fiona stared at her, not comprehending. "How can that be?" she finally asked.

"She is Sid's daughter. His and mine. Sid and I were lovers years ago. We had hoped to be together, but things didn't exactly work out as we'd planned."

Fiona felt blindsided. She turned to Joe, reaching for his hand. He took it and held it.

"Does he know?" she asked India. "Does my brother know?"

Seamie answered that question. "He does, Fee. It's what made him break out of jail. He'd given up. He had no fight left in him at all until Maggie Carr told him she was sure Charlotte was his daughter."

"How do you know that, Seamie?"

"I . . . um . . . well, I sort of helped him do it."

"That figures," Joe said.

"Does Charlotte know?" Fiona asked.

India shook her head. "She doesn't. She just thinks Sid Baxter is an awfully nice man. And that Freddie is—was—her father. I will tell her one day, but not now. She's been through a lot recently. Too much."

Fiona turned to Joe again. "Did you know?"

"Yes, Fee. I've known for weeks."

"So I'm the only one who didn't know. Why didn't you tell me?" she asked, feeling betrayed.

"I couldn't," Joe said. "I'd given my word that I wouldn't."

"I don't understand."

Joe explained how he'd gone to talk with Ella Moskowitz—Ella Rosen now—and what she'd told him.

"She didn't want to tell me," he said, "but I pressed her, and she finally told me about Sid and India and their child, but she swore me to secrecy. She was worried about what would happen if Sid found out Charlotte was his. I wanted to tell you, Fee, it was killing me that I couldn't, but I couldn't break my word to Ella. So I had to find a way to tell you without telling you myself."

Fiona sat back in her chair. Her head was spinning.

"Are you all right, luv?" Joe asked.

She nodded. "I will be, I think. Blimey, will somebody pour me another cup of tea?" she said, trying to take in all that she'd just learned.

There were many questions after that. Fiona wanted to know everything. How India and her brother had met. How they had lost each other and found each other again. Why she had married Freddie Lytton. India, saying she was tired of living lies, held back nothing. She also told them what Sid had told her about his life in Kenya. Seamie was then able to tell them how Sid had escaped, and that he'd been determined to get to India, regardless of the risks involved, to find out for certain if Charlotte was his.

After India told them how Sid had found them and brought them back to Lady Wilton's bungalow, Fiona asked the question that was in all of their minds: "Where is he now?"

"I don't know," India said. "He brought us back to the house, then left. Without a good-bye. Without anything." Her eyes filled with tears as she said, "I think he's very angry with me. For not telling him. I had the chance when we met again. At Mrs. Carr's farm. And I didn't take it. I didn't want to hurt him, you see. But I don't think he understood that. I think he doesn't want anything to do with me now. Anything to do with us."

Fiona's heart went out to India Lytton. She was suffering terribly.

"I can't accept that, India," Seamie said. "I was there when Maggie Carr told him Charlotte was his. I saw his face. He was on fire to get to you. To get to Charlotte. Why would he take the risks he did to see you, then stalk off in a huff? It makes no sense."

"Seamie's right," Fiona said.

"Then why did he leave?" India asked.

"He was afraid of being caught," Joe said. "That's the only explanation. When he escaped from the Nairobi jail, word hadn't got out yet about Betts's statement. He had no idea that Freddie Lytton was going to be questioned. As far as he knew, he was still going to hang for Gemma Dean's murder."

"But why didn't he leave me any word about where he'd gone?" India said. "There was nothing. Not even a note."

"Are you certain?" Fiona asked.

"I'm positive. He left me nothing. Nothing at all."

"Perhaps he didn't have time. Maybe something spooked him," Joe said.

"Yes, maybe that was it," India said, but Fiona could tell from her expression that she didn't believe it.

The adults sat together talking for another half hour or so and then India, looking exhausted, said that she would have to be going. Fiona asked Foster to bring a carriage for them. She called the children to her and told

Katie and Charlie that they would have to say good-bye to their new friend. But only for now.

"I'm so pleased to have met you, Charlotte," she said, kneeling down to take her niece's hand in hers. "I think you're a very special little girl."

Charlotte blushed. She put her arms around Fiona's neck and hugged her. And Fiona hugged her back tightly and then kissed her cheek, before reluctantly letting her go.

Please, Charlie, she thought, watching her and her mother get into the carriage, please come back to them. They need you so.

When the Lyttons had left, Fiona closed the door. Anna whisked the children away to the nursery for a nap, and it was just the three of them— herself, Joe, and Seamie.

"I'm off for a kip, too," Seamie said. "And a bath. I'm knackered. I'll be back down in an hour or two."

"Take your time, Seamie, luv. It's good to have you home."

"It's good to be home," he replied. He started up the staircase then stopped. "Fee?" he said.

"Yes?"

"Did you go to see the Aldens? Did you tell them about Willa?"

"Of course. We went right after we got your telegram."

"How did they take the news?"

"It was very hard on them. On Mrs. Alden especially. Luckily Albie was there to be with them."

"Have they heard anything from her?"

"When we first visited them, they hadn't. But Albie's been by since to tell us they've had a postcard from Ceylon. And another from Goa. She said she was going to work her way north. To Darjeeling—"

"And then Tibet," Seamie said.

"Yes. How did you know?"

"Everest. She wants to see Everest."

His voice was heavy, his eyes sad. Fiona could see that he was hurting over his friend's terrible accident and wanted to say something comforting to him, but he was already up the stairs, leaving herself and Joe alone.

"More tea for you?" Joe said.

"No, something a bit stronger, I think."

They returned to the conservatory and sat down again. Joe said he was tired of his wheelchair and wanted something softer, so Fiona helped him ease himself onto the settee, then sat down next to him.

Foster brought them a bottle of vintage port and two glasses. When he left, Fiona looked at her husband, her heart full of love for him. She took his hand in hers and kissed it. He had confronted the man who'd tried to kill him, Frankie Betts. He'd badgered the home secretary to see that justice was done. He'd even brought herself and India Lytton together— so that he could make sure she learned the truth about Sid, and about Charlotte.

"You did all of this, Joe. So much," she said softly. "For Sid. Even though you don't like what he was. What he did."

"I did it for you, Fee. I wanted to give your brother back to you. Back to you and Seamie. I wanted you to stop grieving for him."

Tears came to her eyes. Tears she'd held back all morning. "Oh, Joe. I was so wrong, all those years ago," she said. "I should never have looked for him. Never should have tried to see him. If I hadn't, none of these things would have happened. You wouldn't have been shot, you wouldn't be in a wheelchair . . ."

"Ssh, Fiona, don't. I'm the one who was wrong. For trying to make you stop. Stop hoping. Stop loving. Stop believing."

He took her in his arms and held her and they sat that way, close and silent, for some time. Until Fiona said, "Do you think he'll ever come back to us?"

"I do."

"But it's been more than five weeks, luv," she said worriedly. "Five weeks at least with no word. I didn't want to say anything in front of India. But I know she feels it, too. How can she not? He was all alone when he left her. All alone in Africa, and we all know what can happen there. We know what nearly happened to Charlotte when she wandered off from the campsite. And what did happen to Freddie."

"He'll be all right, Fiona. I know he will. Look what he's come through already. He'll come through this, too. He'll find his way back to them, Fee. He will." He took her face in his hands and kissed her. "Don't give up on him, luv. Not you. Not now. Not after all these years. All the heartbreak. All the pain. He needs you now like never before. Needs you pulling for him. You helped him once before. Help him now."

"How, Joe?" she asked through her tears. "How?"

"That's easy, my love. Just do what you've done all along. Believe in him, Fee. *Believe*."

CHAPTER 133

India sat in the drawing room of 45 Berkeley Square, sipping a glass of brandy. It was late, after midnight, but she'd lit no lamp. Moonlight poured in through the tall windows, washing the room in silver. She was alone. All the servants had gone to bed.

She was weary after her long sea voyage, wrung out after visiting the Bristows, yet she could not sleep, so she'd stayed up gazing at the moon. It was full tonight and magnificent in its pale beauty. She wondered if it was shining down on Africa now. And on Sid, wherever he was.

The Bristows had been her last chance. When Seamie told her in Nairobi that Joe wanted to see her, and that Fiona was his sister—and Sid's—her heart had leaped. She felt certain that he would have contacted them. They were his family. He would at least let them know he was all right. But he hadn't. Perhaps he'd known somehow that she would contact them. And he didn't want them telling her where he was. Or anything else about him. It was hard, so hard, to know that he wanted nothing to do with her now.

A clock chimed the hour from somewhere in the house. Some damned antique that had belonged to her mother. She would sell it. She would sell everything. She would leave this place soon, she and Charlotte. It held too many bad memories, too many memories of Freddie.

She would return his personal effects to Bingham. And the ghastly portrait of Richard Lytton, the Red Earl. It belonged to Longmarsh. It had never belonged here.

"I never did, either, come to think of it," she murmured.

She would put the house on the market by the end of the week. Consign its contents to an auction house. They would live with Maud—she and Charlotte—until they found a new home. She didn't know where they would go, or what she would do, but she would work it out. Slowly. One step at a time. By herself.

"Mummy?"

India turned around. Charlotte was standing in the doorway in her nightgown and wrapper.

"What is it, my darling? Why are you up so late?"

"May I ask you something?"

"Of course."

"When we were on the train to Nairobi, Lord Delamere said Mr. Baxter's name and it made you sad. I know it did. I saw your face. Did you know Mr. Baxter before you went to Africa? Did you know him in London?"

"My goodness, Charlotte, what a question."

"You have to answer, Mummy. You have to. It's very important."

"If I answer, will you go back to bed?"

"Yes. Did you?"

"I did."

"A long time ago?"

"Yes, a long time ago."

"Is he my father?"

"Charlotte!"

"*Is* he? I heard Father say that I wasn't his. In the study. I heard him call me a bastard. Just before he took us to the plains and put us in the pit. I didn't know what the word meant so I asked Mary, but she scolded me for even saying it. So then I asked a boy on board the ship and he told me. I'm glad I wasn't my father's child. I never felt like I was his. Is Mr. Baxter my father? My real father? You *have* to tell me, Mummy."

"Yes, Charlotte, he is."

"Did you love him once?"

"You are asking me some very grown-up questions."

"I have had to be very grown-up over the last few weeks."

India nodded. "Yes, you have. Fair enough, then. Yes, I loved him. Very much."

"Do you still?"

"Yes."

"Is he good?"

"He is."

"Does he make you sad?"

"Charlotte, why on earth do you want to know these things?"

"Answer, Mummy! Does he?"

India thought for a moment, then said, "He doesn't, no. He makes me very happy. It's not being able to be with him that makes me sad."

"Mr. Finnegan, he's Mr. Baxter's brother, isn't he? That's what he said at Lady Wilton's house."

"Yes, he is."

"And he's also Mrs. Bristow's brother. So that makes him my uncle and

Mrs. Bristow my aunt. And Katie and Charlie and Peter and baby Rose are my cousins."

"Yes."

Charlotte absorbed this, then said, "I think they are all very nice people and I like them very much."

"I agree with you. I like them, too."

Charlotte looked out the window at the moon, her brow crinkled in thought. Then she said, "I have something I'm supposed to give to you. From Mr. Baxter. I didn't want to for the longest time. Not until now."

She reached inside her dressing gown pocket and pulled out an envelope.

India gasped. "Charlotte, how long have you had this?" she asked.

"Mr. Baxter gave it to me just before he left Lady Wilton's house."

"Oh, Charlotte! Why didn't you give it to me then?"

"Because I thought he made you sad and I don't want you to be sad anymore." She kissed her cheek. "Good night, Mummy. I hope whatever the note says makes you happy."

"Don't you want to know what it says?" India asked.

"You can tell me in the morning. I'm awfully tired. It's very hard work being a grown-up."

India opened the envelope. It contained a single sheet of paper with handwriting on it—Sid's handwriting. And a photograph that was folded in half and yellowed at the edges. India unfolded it and caught her breath. She recognized it. She'd given it to him. A long time ago. It was a picture of the land Wish had willed to her. Point Reyes. On the coast of California. The image was creased, it had faded a bit, but it was still beautiful. She opened the note with trembling hands.

My dearest India,
By the time you read this, I hope I will be miles away. I know the police will find me if I stay. I'm afraid I might've been seen riding out to the Wiltons' place. If I was, all of Nairobi will know by now. The Kikuyu are unholy gossips and word travels faster by bush telegraph than you can imagine.

I wanted to stay with you. I wanted to see you well again. I wanted to begin to know the beautiful, brave creature that is our daughter. But I'm afraid that if I don't go now, I'll lose the chance forever.

Although I told everyone at the Wiltons' house that I would head east, I am making my way west across Africa. With any luck, I'll make it to Gabon and Port Gentil, where I hope to find a ship. I haven't much money and will probably need to take work where I can find it. I think it will probably take me the better part of a year to get where I want to go. It will not be an easy journey and I know I won't come through it unscathed, but come through it I will. For more than anything in this whole world, or the next, I want to see you and Charlotte again. I want to live with you both and love you both and make up for all the sad, hard, hopeless years, the years without you in them.

You taught me what love is, India. What faith is. You made me believe in those things. I still do. I always will.

Believe in me now. Believe in us. The three of us.

Meet me where the sky touches the sea.

Wait for me where the world begins.

EPILOGUE

1907

Juan Ramos, stationmaster at Point Reyes, crossed his arms and checked his wristwatch: 5:12 p.m. They'd be here any second now. He craned his neck, the better to see up the Mesa Road. He had a clear view. The streets, bustling during the day, were empty now. The farm wagons, laden with cans of milk and tubs of butter, and the fish carts, stacked high with crates of salmon, trout, oysters, and crab—all bound for San Francisco—had returned home hours ago.

As his minute hand clicked to 5:13, he spotted them—two straight-backed figures in a trap—the English doctor and her daughter.

Juan Ramos knew the lady doctor. All the locals did. She'd opened a clinic on the Mesa Road, and she never turned anyone away. Those who could pay, did. Those who could not brought her butter and cheese, fish, tortillas, eggs, and fiery pepper sauce.

She'd come here a year ago, and had taken over a huge parcel of prime ranchland that bordered Limantour Beach. It was seven miles out of town on a winding, hilly road. Another Englishman, a speculator, had bought it back in 1900. There had been talk of a lavish resort then, of rich people coming up from San Francisco by the trainload, of renovations made to the station, of new businesses needed to service the wealthy, but it had all turned out to be just that—talk.

Rumor had it the speculator had gone bankrupt and that the doctor had bought the land from him. Some said she had money of her own and would build a great mansion, but so far she'd been content to live in the old clapboard farmhouse that stood on the property and leave things much as she'd found them.

On weekdays the doctor attended to her patients, and her daughter attended the local school. On Saturdays and Sundays they did not come into town during the day—not even for church—but were usually seen, skirts hiked up and knotted, walking along the beach, picnicking on the spit, or exploring Drakes Estuary in a rowboat. Yet, no matter what day of the week it was, no matter what the weather or the season, Juan knew that come evening they would always be here, the two of them, waiting at the station.

The doctor drove past him now, guided the horse to its usual spot, and alighted. Her daughter did the same. They didn't bother to hitch the animal. He stood placidly, used to this nightly ritual.

"Evening, Dr. Baxter, Miss Charlotte," Juan said.

"Good evening, Mr. Ramos," the doctor and her daughter replied.

The little girl walked into the station but the doctor stopped to talk. "How are your mother's hands?" she asked.

"Much better," Juan said. "The arthritis barely troubles her now. She said the pills you gave her are working miracles."

The doctor smiled. "Good, I'm happy to hear it. You must make sure she keeps on with them, Mr. Ramos."

Juan assured her that he would, then watched her as she walked from the foyer to the platform, as she did every evening, to meet the 5:15 from San Francisco.

Day after day they waited, but the person they waited for never appeared. The doctor and her daughter would linger until the very last passenger had disembarked, until the conductor had blown his whistle and slammed the carriage doors, until the train had pulled out of the station.

He'd asked her once for whom she was waiting. "Mr. Baxter," she'd replied. "My husband."

Juan believed her at first. He thought that she had come out here ahead of her husband. To set up the house for him. He believed Mr. Baxter would come because the doctor so clearly believed he would.

But then days had passed. And weeks. And months. A year. And still Mr. Baxter did not come. The women of the town began to talk. Some said he would not come for he'd been killed in a war. Others said he'd deserted her. A few were certain he'd been killed prospecting.

Juan began to feel sorry for the doctor. He wondered if perhaps she was not quite right in her mind. It was hard for him to see the hope in her eyes, and her daughter's, as the train pulled in. Harder still to see their disappointment when no one called out their names and no one came rushing to embrace them.

"Perhaps tomorrow," the doctor would say, as she and her daughter walked by him on their way home.

"Yes, perhaps tomorrow," Juan would reply.

He found it difficult to keep believing in Mr. Baxter, but he found it more difficult to stop believing in him. To do so would have been to admit that the hard and simple things of life—love, hope, faith—were foolish and counted for nothing.

The 5:15 steamed in now, and for a few moments, Juan forgot the doctor and her daughter as he waved at the engineer, barked at the porter to look lively, and took the nightly mail bag from the conductor.

He did not, at first, notice the thin, haggard man who got off the train after everyone else. The man was handsome, but gaunt. He walked with the help of a cane. There were lines in his tanned face. They made him look older than he was.

He did not see the doctor go pale. He turned only when she cried out. And then he saw them both—mother and child—run to the man and throw their arms around him.

He saw the man close his eyes and bury his face in the doctor's neck, saw him bend down to the girl and kiss her. But he didn't hear the doctor ask him what happened, where he'd been, how he got here. Or hear him tell her that it was a damned long story. He didn't hear the doctor say that she had plenty of time to listen to it—the rest of her life, in fact.

Juan did see the conductor handing down Mr. Baxter's bag. A porter moved to take it, but he ordered him away.

"Please, sir," he said to Mr. Baxter. "Allow me."

The doctor introduced them and then Juan followed them out to the trap. Charlotte scrambled into the back. The doctor climbed into the driver's seat. Mr. Baxter climbed in beside her, slowly.

Juan put his bag in the back, then waved them off. He was still standing on the pavement as they pulled away and he could hear Mr. Baxter say, "This is just like the fairy stories you used to tell me. A long time ago. In Arden Street."

And the doctor reply, "It's even better, my love. You won't believe how beautiful your new home is. It's the sea and the sky. Fresh salt air. The morning sun streaming in through its windows. It's everything you ever dreamed of, everything you wanted."

"The story ends happily, then?"

The doctor leaned over and kissed him. And then she kissed her daughter. Not caring who saw her. Not caring who heard.

"It does, Mr. Baxter," she said. "It has."

ACKNOWLEDGMENTS

I would like to warmly thank Catherine Goodstein, MD, for generously sharing her insights on why one chooses to become a doctor, and her recollections of her own medical school days—both of which were invaluable to me. Dr. Goodstein's compassion, intelligence, and strength are all attributes I bestowed upon the character of India Selwyn Jones. India was also inspired by two pioneers of western medicine: Elizabeth Blackwell, the first woman to earn a medical degree in the United States, and Elizabeth Garrett Anderson, the first woman to gain medical qualification in Britain. In 1840, when Dr. Blackwell earned her degree, and in 1870, when Dr. Garrett Anderson earned hers, a large portion of society felt that a woman who wished to practice medicine was at best unnatural, at worst indecent. Condemned by the medical establishment, politicians, and the press, these two brave women fought tirelessly for the right to become doctors. After they won that right, they paved the way for future generations by founding medical colleges for women. Dr. Blackwell also opened the New York Infirmary for Indigent Women and Children, which employed female doctors and nurses.

I am indebted to the librarians and archivists at the Wellcome Library, the Royal College of Physicians Library, the Royal Free Hospital Archives Centre, and the House of Commons Library—all in London—for their knowledge, expertise, and patience. London's wonderful Science Museum provided a wealth of information on medicine and medical implements of the early twentieth century, as did Harold Speert, MD, in his books on the history of obstetrics and gynecology. Memoirs by Elspeth Huxley, Winston Churchill, and Isak Dinesen, Errol Trzebinski's *The Kenya Pioneers*, and Lord Cranworth's *Profit and Sport in British East Africa* provided me with information on colonial East Africa. Barbara W. Tuchman's *Proud Tower* was invaluable to understanding the political landscape of pre-war Europe. Thanks also to Alex Dundas for answering many questions on mountaineering, past and present, with passion and precision.

I am grateful to my agent, Simon Lipskar, and my editors—Leslie Wells in New York and Susan Watt in London—for their enthusiasm, guidance, smarts, and talent. And most of all, I am thankful to my wonderful family for always encouraging me and always believing in me.

JENNIFER DONNELLY is the author of the award-winning young adult novel *A Northern Light*, as well as *The Tea Rose*, her first novel.